THE SWORD OF LIGHT

THE COMPLETE TRILOGY

AARON HODGES

Written By Aaron Hodges
Cover Art By Christian Bentulan

The Sword of Light Trilogy
Book 1: Stormwielder
Book 2: Firestorm
Book 3: Soul Blade

The Praegressus Project
Book 1: Rebirth
Book 2: Renegades
Book 3: Retaliation
Book 4: Rebellion
Book 5: Retribution

First Edition

The National Library of New Zealand
ISBN-13: 978-0473387815

Aaron Hodges was born in 1989 in the small town of Whakatane, New Zealand. He studied for five years at the University of Auckland, completing a Bachelor's of Science in Biology and Geography, and a Masters of Environmental Engineering. After working as an environmental consultant for two years, he grew tired of office work and decided to quit his job and explore the world. During his travels he picked up an old draft of a novel he once wrote in High School – titled The Sword of Light – and began to rewrite the story. Six months later he published his first novel, Stormwielder. And the rest, as they say, is history.

FOLLOW AARON HODGES:

And receive a free short story…

Newsletter:

www.aaronhodges.co.nz/newsletter-signup/

Facebook:

www.facebook.com/Aaron-Hodges-669480156486208/

Bookbub:

www.bookbub.com/authors/aaron-hodges

For the ones who believed.
Who encouraged and supported me.
You are my inspiration.

THE THREE NATIONS

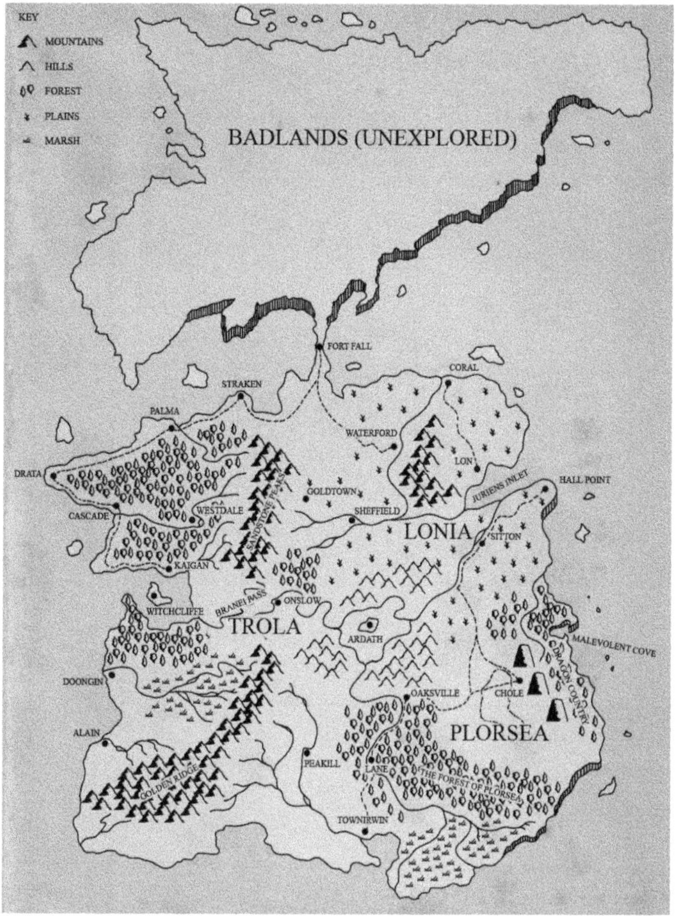

BOOK ONE: STORMWIELDER

PROLOGUE

Alastair sat alone in the darkness, staring into the flickering fire. Holding out his arms, he let its heat wash through his rain sodden cloak. The autumn storm had caught him in the open, drenching him to the skin before he could guide his horse to the shelter of the nearby trees.

A rumble of distant thunder echoed through the trees, and shivering, Alastair shifted closer to the flames. He stifled a groan as his old joints cracked with the movement.

Adding a fresh stick to the blaze, Alastair watched the greedy tongues of flame lick up its length. Wind rustled in the dark branches overhead and the fire flickered, its feeble light casting long shadows across the tiny clearing.

A head appeared in the nearby trees, its long face stretching out towards him. Alastair's heart clenched and he reached for his sword, before he realised it was only his horse. Snickering, his mount shook its head and retreated into the shadows.

Shivering, Alastair released his sword hilt and cursed himself for a fool. He knew all too well the dangers of the night, the creatures that stalked the shadows of the Three Nations. Once he had been one to stand against such things. Now though…

He shook his head, forcing away the morbid thoughts. He was still a warrior; his name was feared by the beasts of the dark.

But he could not dismiss the whispers of his own doubt. It had been decades since he'd last fought the good fight, and the long years between had stripped him of his strength. The old man shivering at autumn shadows was a spectre, a ghost of the Alastair that had once battled the demons of winter.

And now the demons had returned.

"If only," he whispered to the cold night. The words carried with them the weight of regret, the sorrow of wasted decades.

If only he had known.

If only he had prepared himself.

Instead, the great Alastair had settled down and put the dark days behind him. And in his absence, the dark things had come creeping back. Now their shadow stretched across the Three Nations, threatening to shatter the fragile peace he had worked his whole life to create.

It was only when Antonia came to him that he had realised his folly. Her reappearance shattered the peaceful world he'd built for himself, and dragged him back to a life he'd thought long buried.

"Find them," she'd ordered, and he had obeyed.

Yet things never were simple when *she* was involved. For two years now he had searched, seeking out the family he had helped to hide so long ago. But the trail was ancient, and his quarry had long since perfected the skills he'd taught them.

He had tracked them as far as Peakill before the line vanished. For all he knew, they were all gone. He prayed to Ansonia it was not so.

The wind died away and the chirp of crickets rose above the whisper of the trees. The fire popped as a log collapsed, scattering sparks across the ground. He watched them slowly dwindle to nothing and then looked up at the dark canopy. Through the branches, he glimpsed the brilliance of the full moon.

Alastair gritted his teeth. She would come tonight. His hands shook as a sick dread rose in his throat. The world would feel the consequences of his failure.

"Not yet, there is still time," the soft whisper of a girl's voice came from the shadows.

Antonia walked from the trees. A veil of mist clung to her small frame, obscuring her features. But her violet eyes shone through the darkness, the firelight pale by comparison. Those eyes held such power, such resolve, that Alastair shrank before them. The scent of roses filled the grove, cleansing the smoky air as she strode towards him.

"It doesn't matter. They're gone, and I'm not strong enough to continue. Find someone else to fight this battle, I'm done!" He lowered his gaze, unable to meet her eyes.

"There *is* no one else. You were there at the beginning – now you must see things through to the end," her voice shook with anger. "Look at me, and tell me you would abandon everything we have worked for!"

Alastair glanced up. "I abandoned my *family* for your cause," he ground out the words. "I have sacrificed *everything* for you, what more do you want? It's over, they're gone."

He stared at Antonia, expecting anger, scorn, disappointment. She smiled. "It's not over, Alastair. There is still hope. Elynbrigge has found them."

The breath caught in Alastair's throat as he stared at the Goddess. "Where?" he choked.

Antonia laughed, the sound like raindrops dancing on water. "The trail was old, but they are alive and well in

Chole. You will find them there. He will watch over them until you arrive."

Alastair jumped to his feet, scattering firewood into the flames. The blaze roared, leaping to devour the fresh meal. He ignored it. The fire be damned, *they were alive!*

"Wait," Antonia's tone gave him pause. "First, you must go to Oaksville. There is someone there who needs you. When you find him, take him with you. Be quick; Archon won't be far behind."

"Who is in Oaksville?" The town was close, but the detour would cost precious time.

"*Eric.*"

Before he could question her further, she was gone.

For a long time Alastair stood staring at the space where she had stood. Her words trickled through his thoughts, banishing his guilt, his anguish. In their place, a fragile spark of hope lit the darkness.

He didn't sleep that night. Instead, he mounted his horse and rode through the darkness, into the dawn. As the sun rose into the sky and drifted towards noon, he topped the rise over Oaksville and looked down on the town.

Below, Oaksville lay nestled in the crook of a valley. Sickly pillars of smoke curled up from behind its walls, obscuring the rooftops.

Alastair kicked Elcano into a gallop.

CHAPTER 1

A pillar of smoke rose from the burning house. Flames roared and heat scorched his eyes, but he could not look away. The blaze lit the night, chasing the stars from the sky.

Amidst the fire, the silhouette of a boy appeared. He stumbled from the wreckage, clothes falling to ash around him. Sparks of lightning leapt from his fingertips, leaving scorch marks on the tiled street. Soot covered his slim face, marred only by a trail of tears running down his cheeks. The wind caught his mop of dark brown hair, revealing the deep blue glow of his eyes.

He wore an expression of absolute terror.

"Help me!"

Eric screamed as he tore himself from the dream. Gasping, he fumbled for his knife, fear rising to swamp his thoughts. The blade slid clear of his belt, and then tumbled through his hands. Diving forward, he caught it by the hilt and rolled to his feet.

A wall of vegetation rose around him, sealing him in. The dark fingers of branches clawed at his clothing as he spun, scanning the clearing. But there was no one there.

He was alone.

His shoulders slumped as the last traces of the dream fell from him. He sucked in a breath, his heart still thudding hard in his chest. Returning the blade to his belt, he cast another glance around at his surroundings.

The clearing was unchanged from the night before. The trees still stood in a silent ring, their leaves speckled with the red and gold of early autumn. Where the canopy thinned overhead he could make out touches of the blue sky, but below the dark of night still clung to the undergrowth.

Eric shivered as goosebumps prickled his skin. Rubbing his arms, he wished for the thousandth time he possessed more than a holey blanket and worn leather jacket to fend off the cold.

Reaching down, he stuffed the blanket into his bag with the rest of his measly possessions – dried meat, a waterskin, and a holey change of clothes. He wore the steel bracelet his parents had given to him as a child around his wrist. The familiar dream clung to him as he moved, the boy's face lurking in the shadows. He knew that face. It was his own.

He shivered again and flung his bag over his shoulder with a little too much force. Pushing aside the dream, he pulled on his travel worn boots and brushed the leaves from his hair, determined to forget the bad omen. Just a little way through the forest was the Gods' Road, and about a mile along its rutted surface was the town of Oaksville. There he planned to make a fresh start for himself. And he wasn't about to let a bad dream stop him.

Straightening, he squared his shoulders and started off through the trees. Excitement quickened his pace – this was it. Today he would end his self-imposed exile. In the two years since his fifteenth birthday, he had wandered alone through the forests and plains of Plorsea. In all that time, he had kept his own company, speaking only occasionally to strangers he encountered on the road.

The isolation had very nearly driven him insane.

He paused at the edge of the Gods' Road and crouched down in the shadows. Looking left and right, he waited, checking for signs of movement. Even in daylight, the wilderness was not safe for a lone traveller. Just the day before he had been forced to hide as a troupe of Baronian raiders rode past.

Once such a sight would have been rare anywhere in the Three Nations. But lately the nomadic bandits had grown bold, pushing closer and closer to major establishments such as Oaksville. The king had sent soldiers to dispatch them, but so far all efforts to apprehend the Baronians had been unsuccessful.

A minute passed, and satisfied he was alone, Eric straightened and turned west along the Gods' Road. Before long, the trees either side of the path began to thin, giving way to the grassy steeps of a valley.

Squinting into the rising sun, Eric strained for his first glimpse of the town. A layer of fog clung to the slopes, but it was quickly fading in the rising sun. Buildings began to take shape – wooden houses with tall smoking chimneys, the three-pronged spire of a temple, a crumbling castle amidst the slate roofs, the old stone walls ringing the town.

Eric's spirit soared at the sight. Then the first gust of wind reached him on the hilltop, carrying with it the clang of hammers and clip-clop of hooves. His nose wrinkled at the tang of smoke. The image of a burning house flickered into his mind.

He paused mid-stride, and a voice whispered in his mind.

Go back!

Ice trickled down Eric's back. His knees shook, and his

heart pounded like a runaway wagon on a cobbled street. He gripped his fists tight against his side as his vision swam.

What if I'm not ready?

Turning his head, Eric looked back up the hill. The long grass rippled in the wind, the trees beyond shadowing its movement. He felt a sudden yearning to return to them, to escape the rush of civilisation waiting below. But in his heart, he knew the forest had nothing left to offer him. It could not give him friendship, or the comfort of human touch.

You're ready – nothing has happened in months.

Eric drew in a lungful of air and faced the town. Taking another step, his chest constricted as the terror returned. But this time, his nerve held, and step-by-step, he made his way down the valley.

He looked up as the outer wall loomed, its great stone blocks casting the path into shadow. Ahead, a gaping hole in the stonework swallowed the road whole. A guard stood to either side of the gates, dressed in the chainmail and crimson tunics of the Plorsean reserve. Each held a steel-tipped spear loosely at their sides. The one on the right spared Eric a glance as he passed by, then returned his eyes to the road.

Eric passed between the open gates and into the darkness of the tunnel. Moss covered the giant slabs of rock, while iron grates peered down from the ceiling, once used to pour burning oil on invaders who breached the outer gates. These walls dated back to darker times, before peace had come to the Three Nations.

Taking a breath, Eric continued on, until he stepped from the tunnel and back into sunlight.

He hesitated as he found himself on the edge of a bustling marketplace. The gateway opened onto a tiny square where people were rushing to and fro, ducking between the vendors and patrons that packed the tiny space. Bearded men thrust silver fish into the faces of passers-by. Others waved loaves of the bread in the air as they cried out their prices. Coal braziers burned in the corners, filling the air with the scent of smoke and roasting meat.

Eric staggered back as the buzz of a hundred voices assaulted his ears. Dust swept up from the cobbles, catching in his throat, and coughing he turned to retreat back to the haven of the tunnel. As he moved, his feet tripped on the uneven ground, and he crashed down on the stones. His ears rang as his head struck.

Groaning, he looked up, his vision spinning.

A face appeared overhead. "Careful there, mate." The man offered a hand. Eric recognised the western twang of a Trolan accent.

His arm shaking, Eric took the man's hand. He staggered as the stranger hauled him to his feet, and felt a steadying arm on his shoulder.

"Looked like a nasty fall," the Trolan offered. "You okay?"

The man wore a dark brown cloak and towered over Eric's five feet and seven inches. A matted beard and moustache covered his chin, while a broad smile detracted somewhat from the twisted lump that served him for a nose. His brown eyes looked down at Eric from beneath bushy eyebrows. Silver streaked his black hair.

Eric nodded. "Don't know what happened," he stuttered. "I was just… overwhelmed."

"Country boy then?" The man unleashed a booming laugh. "Remember my first time in a town like this. They stole every penny I had. Not the pickpockets, mind you, those crooked merchants! Bought a dagger that snapped the first time I dropped it. Prey on the weak, these townsmen. Don't you worry, mate, us country folk look after our own. The name's Pyrros Gray, what can I do for you?"

Eric grinned. The man reminded him of the warm manner of people in his village. "My names Eric. Is there some place quiet I could sit, just for a while? My head is spinning."

"Pleasure, Eric. I know a place – a tavern not far from here. Usually pretty quiet at this hour. Follow old Pyrros, we'll have you there in no time."

Without waiting for a reply, Pyrros set off through the crowd. Eric quickly chased after him, suddenly afraid to be left alone in the press of bodies. His legs were unsteady beneath him and his head throbbed with every step, but gritting his teeth he pressed on after the Trolan.

Halfway through the throng of bodies, a woman stepped between them and thrust a wet trout in his face. "Cheapest in town!" she yelled over the crowd.

Shaking his head, Eric side-stepped the merchant. She shouted after him, but he ignored her, his eyes scanning the crowd for Pyrros.

"There you are, Eric! Thought I'd lost you!"

Eric spun, and his shoulders sagged with relief as he found Pyrros beside him.

Pyrros laughed as they started off again. "So what brought you to Oaksville, mate?"

Eric shrugged. "I wanted a fresh start."

"Well, we'll see what we can do bout that. Come on, almost there."

Together they slipped into a narrow alleyway that twisted away from the marketplace. Tall brick walls hemmed them in on either side, casting the alley in shadow. The drone of the markets died off as they rounded the first corner. Rotting wood and discarded garbage lay heaped in piles, but someone had worn a trail between the mess.

Eric wrinkled his nose as they passed a pile of decomposing fish heads. Stepping around it, he hesitated. "Are you sure this is the way?"

Pyrros turned and grinned. "It's a short cut. Away from the crowds, you know."

A chill breeze blew through the alley and the hairs on the back of Eric's neck stood on end. He looked up and saw Pyrros grinning back at him. But now his face no longer seemed so friendly.

Slowly, Eric drew to a stop. Laughing, Pyrros turned back and placed his hands on his hips.

"What's the matter, Eric?"

Eric shook his head as he retreated a step. Inwardly he cursed his stupidity, in allowing himself to be lead away from the crowd. His skull gave another sharp throb. Gritting his teeth, he struggled to concentrate.

"I think I prefer the crowd to the garbage, thanks." Eric swallowed as Pyrros's eyes hardened.

Quickly he turned away, preparing to flee. But two men now stood in the alley behind him, blocking his path. One held a wooden baton loosely in his hand, the other a heavy club. Both stood at least a foot taller than Eric. They were dressed in the plain clothes of villagers, but their smiles suggested darker intentions. They spread out across the alleyway, blocking Eric's escape.

"Don't bother running, mate," there was menace in Pyrros's voice now. "Make this easier on yourself."

Eric half-turned, keeping the other men in sight. "What do you want?"

Pyrros shrugged. "Trades hard with the Baronians ruling the wilderness. Not much work for an honest merchant." He took a step towards Eric as he spoke, his boots crunching in the filth of the alleyway. "Gotta change with the times."

Eric retreated, but that only narrowed the distance with the other men. "I don't have any money."

Pyrros laughed. "Don't want your money, mate." He

looked Eric up and down. "Young lad like you should fetch a good price in the Trolan mines."

Ice wrapped around Eric's heart. "You're a *slaver.*"

He shot the man a look of pure disgust. Slavery had been forbidden in the Three Nations for centuries. Those who still practiced the trade were considered the scum of the land – and faced execution if they were caught.

"Eric, how could you accuse old Pyrros of such a thing?" Pyrros placed a hand on his chest in mock hurt. "I just keep my eyes open, is all. Help spot the ones no one will miss. Marked you the second you walked through the gates. Looked like a lost little foal, standing there in the square."

Eric clenched his fists. "My parents are coming later. They'll look for me–"

A burst of laughter cut him off. The men behind him were creeping closer. Eric shrank back from them, his eyes flickering back and forth as he weighed up his options. His heart raced and blood pounded painfully in his head.

This cannot be happening!

Scratching his beard, Pyrros casually took another step. "These Baronians will introduce you to that new life you were looking for, mate. Give it up."

Eric's shoulders slumped, and bowing his head, he stepped towards Pyrros. The man grinned and reached for him, but at the last second Eric spun and leapt at the man with the club. As he moved he drew the knife from his belt, but the man was already ready for him. Grinning, the thug lifted his weapon.

Shifting on his heel, Eric twisted again and dove for the gap between the Baronians.

He almost made it.

The breath exploded between Eric's teeth as the club caught him in the chest and hurled him backwards. The dagger slipped from his fingers as his strength fled. Choking, he slumped to his knees, before another blow sent him tumbling backwards.

Fury flared in his chest as the Baronians entered his vision, broad grins darkening their faces. Overhead, thunder clapped, and raindrops began to fall.

Footsteps came from nearby. Pyrros appeared, a frown on his rugged face. "You disappoint me, Eric. I took you for a quick learner."

Lifting his boot, Pyrros slammed it into Eric's side. Agony tore through Eric's chest as he rolled onto his side, eyes watering as he gasped for air. But another blow caught him in the stomach and hurled him back.

Groaning, Eric gritted his teeth, the embers of his fury taking light, burning suddenly in the darkness of his mind.

"Stupid boy." Now the rain was bucketing down, filling the alleyway, soaking through the clothes of his attackers. Pyrros' boot lashed out again, smashing into his ribs and head.

Eric curled into a ball as the assault continued. He shrieked with the pain of each blow, fear and rage battling within.

Then red flashed across his vision, and something snapped inside of him. A terrible light exploded through his mind, slipping from the deepest recesses of his consciousness. Its power swept through him, washing away all thought, all sensation. He no longer felt the blows of his attackers, or the rain, or the dirt beneath his fingers. All that remained was an all-consuming hate, a need to lash out.

A tormented scream echoed through the alleyway as the last barrier in his mind shattered.

Eric opened his eyes. Blue light lit the stone walls around him, freezing the men in its glare. He watched the rage in Pyrros's eyes turn to terror, saw the Baronians glance up, smelt the burning as it came.

Heard the boom as the lightning struck.

The men vanished into the blue light, their screams cut short by the roar of thunder. There was no chance to escape. One second the three were standing there, the next the lightning had consumed them.

But it did not stop there.

With a deafening crack, the sky tore asunder, unleashing the lightning hidden behind the black clouds.

Screams rose over the thunder, as destruction poured down on the defenceless village. Splinters of wood and stone filled the air as the blue fire tore whole buildings apart.

Eric struggled to his feet. His anger had vanished, his hatred spent. He stumbled towards the marketplace, mouth agape, horror clutching at his soul.

No, no, no, this cannot be happening – not again!

He watched as the lightning rained down, burning a deadly trail through the marketplace. Booths exploded before its wrath, staining the air with smoke and debris. Dozens had already fallen, their clothes blackened and crumbling, their bodies broken. Gusts of wind swirled through the square, picking up rubble and tearing roofs from buildings. The rain streamed down, but even that could not wash away the stench of the burning.

Eric stumbled amidst the chaos, powerless to save his hapless victims. Falling to his knees, he watched the destruction through the haze of his tears. Lightning struck his frail body, but he felt nothing. Bolts of energy danced along his skin, raising goosebumps wherever they touched. Yet he remained unharmed.

Why?

When the thunder finally died away, a devastating silence spread over the square. Eric's gaze swept the wreckage, taking in the burnt beams and canvas. Not a stall was left standing, and the flames were already beginning to spread. Bodies lay scattered amidst the ruin, half-buried by the rubble.

This is my doing.

Movement came from his right. He looked across as a man struggled to his feet. Their eyes met, and the man's eyes widened with horror. Looking down, Eric saw that lightning still played across his chest and arms. He closed his eyes, unable to face the guilt, the accusations.

Noise came from elsewhere now, as more survivors rose to view the shattered remains of their lives – and see the boy with lightning dancing on his skin.

Eric stared back, his heart heavy. He had to say something, to explain, but he could not find the words. His body ached and his muscles burned but he struggled to his feet. He swayed as blood rushed to his head. Then, determined, he opened his mouth to speak.

"*Demon!*"

Eric froze as a man drew a dagger from his belt and started towards him. Others quickly rose to join the man, tearing makeshift clubs from the rubble as they went. Their faces hardened to grim masks, and the angry buzz of voices filled the square.

Fear caught in Eric's throat as he stumbled backwards. He searched again for the words of explanation, to tell them about his curse, that it had not been his fault.

Because in his heart, he knew it would be a lie.

He had prayed the curse had lifted, that he might finally be free. But deep down, he had known the truth, the danger he posed to everyone around him.

A weight settled on his shoulders as he realised he could run no longer. This was all his doing; he needed to accept responsibility, to finally put an end to the darkness inside of him.

The villagers hesitated as they neared him, fear giving

them pause. Burns marked their skin and clothing, but flames burned in their eyes, fuelled by the horrors they had witnessed.

Trembling, Eric stared at the makeshift blades and cudgels. His heart raced and he clenched his fists, struggling to ignore the hollow in the pit of his stomach. His ribs ached where the clubs had struck him earlier, and the bruises were already beginning to swell on his arms and legs. He shuddered at the thought of the pain still to come.

Cautiously, the survivors edged closer, numbers fuelling their courage.

Eric backed away, his courage fading with each step. The villagers increased their pace, sensing his fear. He stumbled backwards over the rubble, unable to tear his eyes from the crowd, and crashed to the ground. The shock lifted the spell.

Scrabbling to his feet, Eric ran for his life.

CHAPTER 2

Eric sprinted down the burning streets. The roar of angry voices chased after him, driving him through the downpour. Dodging past the wreckage of shattered homes, he squinted through the rain, seeking out a path. Wind whipped across his face, slicing through his waterlogged jacket and sending icy drips down his spine.

His eyes watered as clouds of acrid smoke drifted across his path. Lifeless bodies lay amidst the pooling water, thick droplets of rain splattering around them.

Eric ran on. Soot clung to him, mixing with the rain, turning his skin black. He passed a hand through his filthy hair, struggling to think, to find a way through the chaos. His legs trembled, and he sucked in great, shuddering mouthfuls of air. He was at the end of his endurance.

The glow of approaching torches flickered in the lengthening shadows. The day was dying, and Eric could only pray the darkness would come soon. He drove himself on, the freezing wind buffeting him, his footsteps splattering in the flooded streets. Water filled his boots and his leggings squelched with every stride.

A shout came from behind him, followed by the *clang* of a crossbow. Eric ducked as a steel bolt struck the wall a few feet to his right. Glancing back, he saw a crowd racing down the street and ducked into an alley before the bowman could fire again.

Why?

The thought chased itself around his head. He scrambled through the alley, scarcely able to see in the shadows. A jagged piece of steel tore his arm, but he ran on.

He burst from the alleyway back into the open streets. The sun had finally set, leaving only the dying flames to light his way. They cast the world into a realm of shadows.

Curses came from behind him, and Eric glanced back in time to see the first of his hunters emerge into the street. They held flaming torches high above their heads, casting back the shadows, exposing their gaunt faces to the light.

Weaving through the rubble-strewn street, Eric listened for the tell-tale whistle of arrows. Water flicked up in his wake, shining in the fire's light. An arrow shrieked past his shoulder, raising goosebumps as it went.

He glanced back without breaking stride, and saw a man with a crossbow hurriedly winding his weapon. The *clack* of its springs echoed down the street, before the smoke closed in, hiding them from view.

Turning, he ran on through a world twisted by his destruction.

THE DARKNESS WAS FINALLY COMPLETE, the last flames snuffed out by the blanket of night. The rain had ceased and the clouds parted to reveal the star-studded sky. The moon had yet to show its face, yet to cast its pale glow on the devastation below.

Eric huddled among the ruins of an old building, listening carefully for footsteps in the street outside. A chill breeze drifted through the hole in the wall, sending a violent shiver through his rain-drenched body. His teeth chattered, but he clenched them tight, terrified they might give him away.

Finally he allowed himself to breathe, satisfied for the moment he was safe. He sat back on his haunches, and his hand brushed against something soft and yielding. Glancing down, he saw the glassy eyes of a dead man staring back at him. Terrible burns blackened the man's face and clothing, and where the flames had not reached, his skin was a pallid grey.

Stomach wrenching, Eric threw himself back from the body. His gut heaved, and bending in two, he emptied the pitiful contents of his stomach onto the cracked floor.

When there was nothing left to throw up, Eric sat back on his haunches and held his face in his hands. His throat burned and anxiety gnawed at his chest. Silently he returned to his spy hole and peered outside to check if anyone had noticed the commotion.

Through the cracks in the walls, he watched the full moon rise slowly into the sky. Its cool light offered no warmth, yet the sight still gave him comfort.

Eric froze as the soft crunch of a footstep on gravel carried to him from the street outside. Another followed, barely audible over the thudding of his heart.

Swallowing hard, he tried to dislodge the lump in his throat. He peered out into the street and saw the silhouette of a man moving through the shadows.

A brown cloak billowed out in the wind, revealing the gold embossed hilt of a short sword strapped to the man's waist. Moving faster, he emerged from the shadows, seeming to make straight for Eric's hiding place. Silver lines of thread embroidered his clothing, weaving intangible patterns down his arms and legs. A grey hood obscured his face, but Eric could feel his eyes as they searched the wreckage.

Crouched in his hiding place, Eric hardly dared to breathe. Muscles tensed, he told himself he was safe, hidden by the shadows. But still the man came closer.

"Come out," the man whispered, his voice old and rasping. "I'm not here to hurt you."

Pulling back his hood, the man revealed his long grey hair and a clean-shaven chin. His lips curled into a frown as his piercing green eyes searched the shadows where Eric hid.

Staring into those eyes, Eric found himself trapped in the heat of the man's glare. Time seemed to slow, and for a moment Eric felt as though his mind must be an open book, as though those eyes could see straight to his very soul. Shame welled within him, the crushing weight of his guilt threatening to overwhelm him.

Then the old man blinked, and Eric shuddered as the spell broke. He sank to his knees, staring at the muddy ground as the crunch of footsteps drew to a stop beside him. Exhaustion curled its way through his limbs, and he closed his eyes in listless surrender.

But nothing happened. A long silence stretched out, before he finally looked back up. "What are you waiting for?" he spoke through gritted teeth. "Just do it."

The emerald eyes stared down at him, but the old man made no move to draw his sword. Anger flickered in Eric's chest as he straightened, giving him strength.

"What do you want?" he growled.

The old man blinked again. "To help you."

Eric stared up at the old man, struggling to find the words to respond.

"To help me?" he said at last. He threw out his arms, gesturing at the wreckage. "Why would you want to help me? Can't you see what I've done, what I create? Only a demon would want to help someone like me."

The man's eyes hardened. "I am no demon, boy. I am just a man. But I am the only chance you have of controlling that power inside you."

Slowly, Eric pulled himself to his feet, until he stood in front of the man. "Who are you?" he whispered.

"My name is Alastair. And I suggest you come with me, now, before the others find us."

Alastair.

The name had a familiar ring – where had he heard it before? Regardless, he was not prepared to trust again so easily – not after what had happened in the marketplace.

He stood his ground as the man started to turn away. "Why should I trust you, Alastair?"

Alastair glanced back, a frown tugging at his lips. Then he shrugged. "You probably shouldn't," reaching down, he drew his sword from its sheath and flicked it into the air. Catching it by the blade, he offered it hilt-first to Eric. "You hold onto this for now, if it makes you feel safer. You can give it back once I've earned your trust."

Eric stared at the blade for a second, before reaching out to accept the old man's offer. Alastair nodded as the sword left his hand, and then stepped from the crumbled building back out into the street. Eric quickly followed, doing his best to avoid the debris strewn across the cobbles.

Ahead, Alastair slipped off the road and into an alleyway. Eric followed close on his heels, the sword clutched close to his body. He had never used one before, and the weapon felt awkward in his hands.

The old man moved on, drawing Eric deeper into the gloom. Silently he cursed his naivety, allowing himself to be led into another alley, and he gripped the blade tighter.

But Alastair did not look back, and glancing around, Eric

realised with a shiver the buildings to either side of them had collapsed. The heavy stone walls had remained intact, but now they leaned out into the alley, forming an unstable roof above their heads. Moonlight flooded through cracks in the stone, lighting the way ahead.

Eric swallowed at the thought of all that stone and wood perched preciously above him. But the time for doubt had long since passed. Silently he followed the silver streaks of Alastair's cloak through the gloom, taking reassurance from the man's seeming indifference to the danger looming above them.

As they neared the end of the alleyway, Alastair came to a sudden stop ahead of him. Eric froze, holding his breath as he listened for signs of movement.

A shuffling sound came from the shadows as a dark figure stepped into a column of moonlight. Brown eyes flickered with recognition as they fell on Eric.

"*You,*" a voice hissed.

CHAPTER 3

Gabriel crouched in the shadows, his head bowed, and waited for the end to come. Grief wrapped around his heart, its thorny tendrils tearing at his soul, its agony far worse than the dull ache of his battered body.

As the night's chill seeped through his rain-soaked clothes, he could feel his life fading away. But he welcomed the spectre of death with open arms. At least in death he would be free of the pain, would be reunited with those he had lost.

How did this happen?

Just this morning he had been happy, celebrating his engagement to the girl of his dreams. He had been sitting around the table with his parents, enjoying a simple breakfast of oats and fruit, grinning at the glow in his fiancée's eyes. His father had been teasing him about Margaret staying the night, but they were to be married, and nothing could dent his joy.

How wrong he had been.

Before beginning work with his father in the family

forge, Gabriel had headed down the road with the horseshoes they had completed for a client the night before. But only a block from home, everything had changed.

There had been no warning, just a flash of light and a clap of thunder. Then death had come raining from the sky. There was no defence, nowhere to run or hide. Lightning danced through the streets, consuming all it touched, indiscriminate in its victims.

When it finally passed, Gabriel had found himself standing alone amidst the ruin. As others began to pull themselves from the rubble, he had turned and stumbled towards his house, his dread growing with every step.

It had taken him a long second to find his home amidst the ruins of his street. The two-storey villa was gone – all that remained were the broken walls and scattered roofing tiles. Flames flickered amidst the ruin, already beginning to grow.

Plunging into the ruins, Gabriel screamed for his fiancée, for his father and mother, desperate for a response.

He had found them in the back of the house, where they must have gathered to wait out the storm. Tears streamed down Gabriel's cheeks as he collapsed to his knees and reached for the beam that had impaled his father's body. His mother lay next to him, her neck bent at an awful angle. Their empty eyes stared up at him, frozen in terror.

Then a moan had carried to his ears, and Gabriel moved further into the room, searching desperately for the source.

He had found Margaret close to his parents, buried under heavy bricks, her loving face the only part of her left exposed. Her eyes flickered open as Gabriel crouched beside her.

"Gabriel," a trickle of blood ran from her mouth as she spoke.

"I'm here, Margaret, it's okay. You're going to be okay," he whispered.

But his words were a lie. Kneeling beside her, Gabriel could not ignore the horror of her injuries. The collapsing wall had crushed her chest. It would not be long.

He stroked her hair, whispering soft comforts as her eyes flickered closed. Her breathing grew shallow, each inhalation harsh and gurgling, and then with a long sigh, she was gone.

Heart breaking, Gabriel had buried his head in his arms, and sobbed for the love he'd lost. When he finally stood, he did not pause to look around, but strode from the ruin, desperate to escape, to flee the ruins of his life.

Outside, he had encountered the other survivors, and learnt of the boy who danced with lightning, of the demon who had brought this curse down on Oaksville. Filled with rage, with a need to lash out, Gabriel had joined the mob in their hunt.

Yet while the gates were sealed, their prey had vanished. Exhaustion quickly quenched his anger, and without it, grief returned to drown him. As night approached, despair had taken hold, and with the last of his strength, Gabriel had dragged himself into an alleyway. He could see the cracks riddling the stone walls, knew it would not be long before they crumbled. Closing his eyes, he had settled in to wait.

But now he could hear the scrape of boots as someone approached through the darkness. Lifting his head, he stared into the shadows. His breath stilled as two figures stepped into view.

An old man came first, his greying hair shining silver in the moonlight. But it was the boy who followed him that drew Gabriel's attention. A mop of dark brown hair hung across his face, but beneath he could see the bright blue glow of his eyes.

The same eyes the townsfolk had whispered of.

The eyes of the demon.

Mud and ash covered the boy's clothes, and he held a

short sword gripped tightly in one hand. Holes in his tunic revealed his pale flesh beneath. Cuts and grazes marked his skin, but there were no burns, no blisters.

Taking a breath, Gabriel summoned the last of his strength and stood. "*You!*"

CHAPTER 4

Eric retreated as the stranger advanced on him. Alastair stepped between them, but he was dwarfed by the young man. Rage blazed in his brown eyes and his shoulders heaved as he stared down at Alastair. Lines of exhaustion criss-crossed his face.

But Alastair did not back down. "Step aside, boy."

The stranger shook his head. "They're all gone, all *dead* because of him," he ground out the words. "*Why?* What did they ever do to you?"

When Eric didn't respond, the stranger took another step. Eric shrank before his unwavering gaze, the terror in his chest swelling with every breath. He licked his cracked lips, his mouth as dry as sand.

Alastair threw out an arm to block the man's path. "Stop," he ordered.

The stranger blinked, his eyes flickering to Alastair. "You protect him?" he gaped.

Alastair stared him down. "What is your name?" he ignored the question.

"Gabriel," the young man swallowed as his eyes met Alastair's. Suddenly he looked uncertain, but taking a breath, he steadied. "I won't let him escape. Out of my way, old man."

Gathering himself, Gabriel tried to push past Alastair, but the old man shifted to block him.

"Last chance, old man," Gabriel growled, grimacing. "I won't ask again."

But still Alastair did not move. Gabriel swore and clenched his fists, then without warning, he launched himself at the old man. Eric gripped the sword tighter, preparing to leap to Alastair's aid.

But Alastair was faster. Turning on his heel, he sidestepped Gabriel's headlong rush. The boy gave a yelp as Alastair's hands shot out to catch him by the coat. Using the momentum of Gabriel's charge, the old man twisted again, and sent his would-be-attacker headfirst into the brick wall.

There was a harsh crunch as Gabriel struck, followed by silence as he collapsed on the ground.

Eric's mouth fell open as he stared at the unconscious man. Looking up at Alastair, he struggled to hide his shock.

How did he move so fast?

"Come, Eric," Alastair said as he stepped past Gabriel. "There's not much time before day break."

Still staring at the comatose Gabriel, Eric nodded and moved after the old man.

A few seconds later they emerged into an empty street. Glancing up, Eric found the town walls towering over them, a silent shadow against the night sky. Beyond, the moon had finally taken its place amongst the stars.

Alastair took the lead again, crossing the street and picking his way through the rubble of an old building, until they reached the foot of the town walls.

Eric shivered as he stared at the giant stone blocks. They stretched some thirty feet above them, their surface worn smooth by the passage of time. The ramparts of this wall had overlooked Oaksville for centuries, dating all the way back to the Great War. In all that time, they had stood strong against the dangers without.

That is, until today.

A knotted rope trailed down from high above, flapping in the night's breeze. Alastair took the rope in one hand and held it out to Eric.

"The gates were barred when I reached the city, I was forced to improvise my entrance. You go first, but wait at the top for me. There is another rope on the other side of the ramparts. If you hear a guard, whistle, but most of them are busy elsewhere."

Eric shivered as he took the rope, the strength fleeing his legs. His heart raced as the sickly taste of fear choked him.

He was terrified of heights.

But he was out of options. Hands shaking, he slipped Alastair's short sword into his belt and gripped the rope in both hands.

You can do this, he repeated the words to himself like a mantra.

A cold sweat beaded his brow as he started to climb. Going hand over hand, he made his slow way up, planting the toes of his boots in the shallow cracks he found between the stones.

For the first few steps, the going was relatively easy. But as he drew higher, the stones became worn, the cracks between them finer, and his old boots struggled to maintain their grip.

When he was twenty feet up, they finally slipped on the slick surface. Eric screamed and grasped desperately at the rope as his body slammed sidelong into the wall. The coarse fibres cut into his hands, but somehow, he held on.

By the time his feet found a new purchase, his arms were

trembling with the exertion. Chest heaving, he scrambled up the last ten feet and swung himself over the crenulations. In those final moments, he didn't care whether a guard waited for him, only that he escape the yawning chasm beneath him.

Gasping for breath, Eric slumped against the crenulations and waited for Alastair. He could hardly believe he'd made it. Moments later he heard the thud of boots on stone, and looked up as Alastair leapt down beside him.

The old man grinned when he saw Eric slouched against the ramparts. "I'll go down first. You look like you could use a breather."

With that he crossed to the other side, reached between the crenulations, pulled up a rope, and vanished over the side.

Pulling himself back to his feet, Eric turned to gaze back over the town. Oaksville stretched out below, its dim remnants cast in grey by the moonlight. Flames still burned in places, but the rain had tamed the worst of it. The distant screams of the desperate and dying rose from the wreckage, and a cloud of smoke hung low over the town.

With misty eyes, Eric turned away. This was far worse than he had ever imagined. Oaksville would never recover from such a blow. He had been its doom. Thinking of the hundreds of shattered lives, he swore to himself he would find a way to make things right.

Beside him, the rope went slack. Taking a long breath, he picked it up and leaned back over the side. Heart pounding in his chest, he summoned the last of his courage, and started down.

His arms shook as he clung to the rope, his strength fading quickly now. He needed to reach the ground, and fast.

Almost halfway down, a sudden gust of wind knocked

him sideways, sending him crashing into the wall. Tasting the metallic tang of blood, he spat it out.

Without thinking, Eric glanced down and saw the rope trailing away beneath him to the ground far below. His vision swam, and ice swelled in his chest. Suddenly he could not breathe, could not move, his whole body paralysed with terror.

The gale appeared from nowhere. Its breath ripped at his wet clothing, kissed with the icy chill of the far north. The temperature plummeted and Eric's teeth started to chatter. Shivering, he clung to the rope, his only lifeline amidst the storm.

Eric stared at the wall, struggling to beat back his fear. As he watched, the rain-soaked stones started to glisten, the freezing wind turning the water to ice.

"No…" Eric whispered.

He closed his eyes, his breath coming in raged gasps. He could sense the strength in his fingers fading, sucked away by the cold and his exhaustion. His boots slid from the wall, unable to find purchase on the slick ice, leaving only his tenuous hold on the rope keeping him aloft.

His fingers went numb as the wind howled again, drawing the last heat from his trembling body. His eyes watered, the tears freezing on his cheeks as he fought to hold on.

But it was impossible. Bit by bit the feeling in his fingers faded away, until as if by a will of their own, they released his last hold on life.

And Eric fell away into darkness.

Gabriel lay in the mud, his will broken, his last hope of avenging his family wasted. Despair wrapped its cold fingers around his heart. Sprawled in the filth of the alleyway, he couldn't even summon the will to sit up.

Gabriel.

He closed his eyes as the voice whispered in his mind, pervasive, insistent. It had drawn him from the darkness of oblivion, returning him to the agony of life.

But all he wanted now was the sweet relief of death.

Not yet.

Gabriel shivered as the voice came again. Overhead, a low groan came from the bricks. Opening his eyes, he looked up at the broken walls, at the cracks threading across their surface. He lay motionless, breath held, waiting for it all to come crashing down.

Coward.

There was an accusation to the voice now, and anger flickered in his chest.

"I am not a coward," he growled to the empty alleyway.

Prove it.

Gabriel closed his eyes, trying to push away the whispers. But now he saw again the boy and his protector, the old man who had felled him so easily. His hand trailed up to his forehead, feeling the sticky wetness of the gash where he had struck the wall.

Rage and hate swelled in his chest, pushing aside the despair. How could he rest in peace now, knowing he had allowed the boy to escape? Knowing his family's killer walked free?

Get up.

Placing his hands beneath him, Gabriel staggered to his feet. A groan came from the bricks above him, and stones rattled down. Dust stained the air, filling his lungs. Turning, he strode down the alleyway, and out into open air.

As he stepped onto the street, a roar came from behind

him, followed by a whoosh of air as the bricks came tumbling down.

But Gabriel no longer cared. There was only one thought in his mind now, one all-consuming desire.

Kill the demon.

CHAPTER 5

"Come closer, let me see your face." The voice snaked its way through the cracks in Eric's consciousness.

Something within him shrank from it, fighting against the darkness creeping through his mind.

"Do not be afraid. You have a gift. Let me show it to you…"

Cracks spread through his mind, his defences crumbling before the darkness. The silhouette of a face began to form.

"Ahhh," the voice let out a long sigh. "I can almost see you now, my child. Almost…" the voice was eager, touched by greed.

Alarms sound through Eric's mind and his instincts screamed for him to flee. With a wrench, he tore himself free.

An ungodly wail echoed through the darkness. Then light flashed through the shadows, and the dream ended.

"No!" Eric screamed.

Gasping for air, he sat bolt upright and looked around. The forest stretched out around him, and for a second he struggled to remember how he'd come to be there. Then it all came rushing back – Oaksville, the Baronians, the storm, *the fall.*

Eric quickly patted himself down, unable to understand

how he'd survived. There had still been some twenty feet of open space below him when he'd released the rope.

He jumped as a dry, rasping chuckle carried across the leaflitter. Looking around, he found the old man seated on a log behind him. He held his short sword in one hand and was slowly sliding a whetstone down its blade. The whisper of stone against steel carried across the clearing.

"Awake at last," he said.

Taking slow, measured movements, Eric pulled himself up and turned to look at the old man. He frowned, struggling to recall his name. The cold ashes of a fire lay between them, and through the treetops Eric could just make out the rising sun.

"Alastair," he said at last, his eyes drawn inexorably to the sword. "Where am I? What happened?"

The laughter came again. "You fell," he smiled. "Luckily, I caught you."

Eric shook his head, his frown deepening. "Caught me? That must have been twenty feet…"

"Guess I'm stronger than I look." At that, he slapped his knees and stood. "How are you feeling? I must have carried you at least a mile last night. I'd rather not repeat the experience."

Eric shivered, remembering his bone-numbing weariness from the night before. Placing his hands against the damp ground, he pushed himself to his feet, stumbling slightly as he straightened.

"I'm alright," he said hesitantly, swaying on his feet. His eyes narrowed. "Why did you help me, Alastair?"

The old man only waved a hand. Sheathing his sword, he picked up a few items off the ground and then looked back at Eric. "Because you needed help. Now, we'd better get moving. It won't be long before the townsfolk realise you've slipped through their noose. At least a few are bound to come after you."

Eric clenched his fists at that, fresh guilt welling in his throat. "Maybe I should let them catch me," he whispered. Biting back tears, he looked across at Alastair. "After what I did, I deserve it."

Alastair stilled. "Maybe," he mused, his face hard. "But what happened was an accident, and martyring yourself won't bring those people back. It won't rebuild their houses or restore their livelihoods."

"Then what do you propose I do?" Eric replied bitterly. "Destruction follows me wherever I go."

"That's what you need to change." Alastair's eyes found him across the clearing. "Maybe I can help you with that."

Eric's words caught in his throat. He stared at the old man. "What do you mean?" he managed finally.

Alastair only smiled. Waving a hand, he turned towards the trees. "Later. For now, we need to get well clear of Oaksville. Come."

At that the old man started off into the trees without looking back. After a moment's hesitation, Eric shook his head and moved after him. If he'd carried Eric half the night, it didn't seem likely the old man would betray him now.

They moved quickly through the forest, the old man setting a pace that even Eric struggled to keep up with. He found himself wondering at the man's age – his wrinkled face looked at least seventy years old, but he moved with the agility of a far younger man. And he'd managed to overpower Gabriel in the alleyway, despite the other man having an extra foot on Alastair.

The trees pressed in around them as they moved, the earth turning to mud beneath their feet. The scent of fresh rain hung heavy on the air, and the first calls of the morning chorus carried through the forest, lifting the last traces of sleep from Eric's mind. He caught a flash of red in the canopy, and looked up to see a gang of Parakeets hopping through the trees.

Settling into the rhythm of the trek, he allowed his mind to wander. He turned Alastair's words over in his head, pondering their meaning. How could the old man help him? He could not begin to imagine controlling the power inside him. When it rose, it came like a flood, sweeping away all thought of resistance. There was no standing against it.

They were moving downhill now, and Eric struggled to keep his feet on the muddy ground. He grasped at seedlings and low hanging branches as he moved, careful to control his descent, even as Alastair pulled ahead. Eric tried to pick up the pace, but suddenly his feet slipped out from beneath him. Landing flat on his back, he slid the rest of the way down the slope, finally coming to rest in a muddy heap at the bottom.

Groaning, he picked himself up and tried to wipe the dirt from his clothes. He turned as laughter came through the trees. Alastair stood nearby, his arms folded and a wry grin twisting his lips.

"That was graceful," he remarked.

Eric spat dirt from his mouth and shook his head. "Where are we going?"

"The Gods' road, if it's safe," Alastair replied as he started off again. "But we don't have to walk much farther. I left my horses… ah, here we are."

Alastair drew to a sudden stop and gave a short, sharp whistle. Movement came from the trees as two horses stepped from the shadows. The leader stood over sixteen hands tall with a glistening coat of midnight black. A silver streak marked its brow, and a worn leather saddle was slung loosely over its back. Muscles rippled along its powerful frame as it wandered over to Alastair and nuzzled at his shoulder.

The second horse was smaller, with a chestnut coat and blue eyes that stared at Eric with a strange intelligence. It wore a thin leather saddle and carried four saddlebags. Wandering across to Eric, it gave a loud snort and shook its head.

"His name is Briar," Alastair called across to Eric. "And this beauty is Elcano."

Reaching down, Alastair quickly tightened the straps of Elcano's saddle before moving across to the other horse. "I didn't think I'd be gone so long," he spoke as he readied the horses. "In fact, from what I'd seen I thought my visit would be quick. You're quite the elusive quarry, Eric."

Eric frowned. "Why were you looking for me?" he tried to keep the frustration from his voice, but the old man's stubborn silence was already growing old.

Beside him, Alastair gave Briar a pat on the stomach and straightened. "A friend sent me. I wasn't sure why, until I saw what had happened," he sighed. "I'm sorry I didn't arrive in time. And I promise you, all your questions will be answered soon. But right now, we need to move. The higher the sun gets, the more likely they are to come looking for you. Do you know how to ride?"

Swallowing, Eric shook his head. Lips pursed, he eyed Briar. The horse may have been small beside Elcano, but his bulk still dwarfed Eric. Trying not to look intimidated, Eric reached out and ran his hand along the horse's mane.

"I've ridden one once or twice," he offered.

Alastair's lips twitched. "Very well. A quick lesson will have to suffice. Come here, stand on Briar's side."

Silently, Eric listened to Alastair's instructions. He watched as the old man placed his foot in the stirrup and demonstrated how to swing himself into the saddle, before dismounting again. Nodding, he waved for Eric to copy him.

Briar shifted on his hooves as Eric reached out and placed his hand on the saddle horn. Turning its head, the horse looked back at him and nickered. Eric forced a smile and gave Briar a reassuring pat.

"Place the toes of your left boot into the stirrup, hold onto the saddle horn, and then try swinging yourself up," Alastair offered from beside him.

Nodding, Eric did as he was told. Pushing himself off the ground, he tried to swing his other leg over the saddle. Halfway through the manoeuvre he lost his balance, but as he started to fall backwards Alastair gave him a quick shove. He tumbled forward, inhaling a mouthful of horsehair in the process, before settling into the saddle.

Eyes watering, he straightened and looked down at Alastair. "I think I'll stay up here. I'd rather not try that again just now."

"Agreed," Alastair chuckled. He moved across to Elcano and swung himself into the saddle in one fluid movement.

Eric shifted uncomfortably, trying to find his balance as Alastair continued his instruction. "Now, hold the reins in one hand, like this," he demonstrated. "Pull them gently in the direction you want Briar to go – not too hard mind you, or you'll hurt his mouth. A gentle push with your heels will get him started, although he's pretty good at just following Elcano. Pull back on the reins if you want him to stop. Ready?"

"Ahhh," Eric held the reins in his hand, still trying to put the directions together in his head. "What was the first part again?"

"Just try not to fall off." Alastair grinned.

He gave another whistle, and Elcano turned and started off into the trees. Before Eric could attempt to follow Alastair's directions, Briar moved off after the other horse, and suddenly it was all he could do just to hold on.

Gripping the reins in one hand and the saddle horn with the other, he ducked as a low branch swept past. The thud of the horse's hooves carried up through the saddle with each step, rattling his spine, and using the stirrups he tried to lift himself from the saddle. The thudding eased, but his legs quickly began to tire.

Ahead, Alastair was drawing away, and remembering the old man's instructions, Eric gave Briar a short kick. The horse snorted and shook his head, but he picked up the pace.

A few minutes later Alastair slowed as the trees opened up around them. Briar moved up alongside the old man as they turned onto the Gods' road. Eric glanced around as sunlight filtered through the thin canopy overhead, wary of being seen, but the road was empty.

"Is this a good idea?" he asked, his teeth rattling as they picked up the pace.

"It's the only way. The forest is too dense around Oaksville, and it doesn't open out until you reach the desert. It would take days to get anywhere," Alastair answered.

"But surely they'll send patrols out along the road?" Eric argued.

"As soon as they realise you've escaped," Alastair nodded. "But I'm hoping we'll be quick enough to stay ahead of them."

He flashed a grin and then kicked Elcano into a gallop. Feeling the horse shift beneath him, Eric had a second to grab at the saddle horn, before Briar leapt after Elcano. He gasped as he found himself lifting into the air, and he clenched his thighs around the saddle, desperate to hang on.

Eric's heart raced as his feet pressed into the stirrups, holding him in place, and sucking in a breath he looked ahead. Briar had closed the distance Alastair had opened between them, and now they were right on the other horse's tail.

Slowly, Eric found himself settling into the rhythm of Briar's stride. Fire burned in his legs as he crouched in the saddle, but he pressed it down, concentrating on Alastair's back. The pounding of hooves drowned out the sounds of the forest, and sunlight flashed through the trees, lighting the way ahead.

As they raced down the Gods' road, Eric's mind strayed, wondering again at the mystery of the old man. Though he knew nothing of Alastair, something about him seemed to inspire trust. Or maybe Eric was just desperate for what he offered – a way to control the curse inside him.

Glancing ahead, Eric watched as the Gods' road slowly curved away from them. The trees to either side of the path obscured their view beyond the bend, but by now they were far from Oaksville, and any hunters were bound to be behind them. Eric felt the weight lifting from his chest with each thud of Briar's hooves, his fear falling away. Guilt still wrapped around his heart, but clear of the town, he found his will to live returning. Alastair was right – his death would achieve nothing. But alive, Eric could at least try to right his wrongs.

As they raced around the bend, Eric caught a glimpse of movement in the woods to either side of them. Frowning, he glanced back and saw black-garbed figures stepping from the trees. Looking ahead, he opened his mouth to shout a warning to Alastair. But the words died on his lips as he saw Alastair pulling hard on Elcano's reins.

Ahead, a trail of wagons blocked the road. Black-garbed men and women moved between the wagons, each carrying some variety of sword, axe or club. Most of the men sported thick leather armour stained the same black as their clothes. Thick beards covered their faces, and several bowmen sat on the wagons. Sunlight glinted off their steel-tipped arrows as they pointed them at Alastair and Eric.

"*Baronians*," he heard Alastair curse as Briar drew to a stop beside the old man.

Ice spread through Eric's chest as the men he'd spotted in the trees moved to surround them. Baronians were the scum of the Three Nations. They considered themselves above the laws of the lands, beyond the power of kings or councils. Nationless vagrants, the Baronian tribes wandered between the nations, wreaking havoc wherever they went. Normally they would never come so close to a settlement as large as Oaksville. But seeing them now, Eric had a terrifying suspicion about what had brought them so close.

Amongst the black-garbed ranks, a giant of a man made his way towards them. Thick leather armour covered his massive chest and he wore his hair pulled back in the Baronian fashion of a ponytail. A two-handed greatsword was strapped to his back, and his beard was matted with filth. His black eyes stared at them as he drew to a stop in front of the horses.

"Well, well, well, what do we have here?"

CHAPTER 6

Gabriel had not taken long to sift through the remains of his family home. The flames had finally died with the evening rain, but what they had left behind was barely recognisable. In the ruins of the forge, he found a few gold coins that were his family's life savings, along with a short sword an old soldier had once given his father as payment. He took both, carefully tying the sword and its sheath to his belt.

During his search, he had studiously avoided the room in which his family lay. But as he was leaving, a glimmer amidst the rubble caught his eye. Reaching down, he'd lifted the silver necklace from the ashes. It was the necklace he had given his fiancée as an anniversary gift. At the end of the silver chain, a tiny blue sapphire glinted in the light. He had saved all year to afford it. He could still remember the light in her eyes as he placed it around her neck.

He wore it around his own neck now, a silent reminder of all he had lost. Wandering down the dark streets, Gabriel slowly made his way towards the city gates. Lost souls stumbled past him, their eyes empty, their faces black with soot.

Watching them, an idea came to Gabriel, and he slowed. His eyes were drawn to a man wearing the uniform of the city guard.

The man did not look up as Gabriel approached. In the dull gloom, he could have been a statue. He sat alone on a crumbling wall, his head held in his hands.

"What are you doing?" Gabriel asked bluntly.

The guard took a long time to move. When he did, he looked up at Gabriel, blinking slowly in the moonlight. "What?"

Reaching down, Gabriel gripped the man by the shoulders and shook him. "I said, *what are you doing?*" Gabriel growled. "Why are you sitting here like a coward, letting the demon escape?"

Light flickered in the man's eyes and with a giant hand he pushed Gabriel away. He staggered to his feet, towering over Gabriel. "A coward, am I?" his hand shot out and caught Gabriel by the shirt. "Come here, little man, let's see how brave you are?"

Though Gabriel was anything but little, he had no desire to go toe to toe with the guard, and he quickly tore himself free. He raised his hands in a sign of peace. "How about we both prove our bravery, and go after the demon?"

The guard stilled at that. He glanced away, his shoulders slumping. "Long gone by now," he muttered. "And what is a mortal man to do against something like that, anyway? The Gods know we almost had him, but he slipped through our fingers."

"He had help," Gabriel whispered. He stepped in close to the man and placed a hand on his arm. "But they can't have gotten far. I saw them not long ago, near the eastern wall. If they're heading east, they won't get far through the forest. They'll have to return to the Gods' road eventually."

The man shrugged. "Maybe. But like I said, what can we

do? Only the Goddess could stand against that darkness. And she isn't exactly easy to reach these days."

"The Goddess be damned!" Gabriel cursed. "If she cared, she would have stopped the demon before it came here. No, it's up to us to stop it, before it claims more lives. We may not have its power, but I have a sword, and last I heard, a demon still dies when you stab it."

The guard frowned at Gabriel. "You're just one man."

"Join me and there will be two," Gabriel replied.

The silence stretched out, their eyes locked in a silent battle. But Gabriel did not look away, and finally the man nodded. "You're a tough little bugger. But you're right, someone's got to stop that demon." He held out his hand. "The name's Tom."

After that, their numbers slowly swelled, until come morning, two-dozen men had joined Gabriel at the eastern gates. They had gathered up stray horses and weapons as they wandered the town, and now Gabriel felt confident about their chances. He still wore the short sword strapped to his waist, but many of the men around him were armed with crossbows. If they could track down their quarry, Gabriel was confident things would end differently this time.

Word came at dawn confirming Gabriel's suspicions. Tracks had been found at the base of the eastern wall, leading off into the forest. Unable to wait any longer, Gabriel and the other men set off through the eastern gate. The clatter of hooves on cobbles was deafening in the tunnel, but ahead the bright light of the world beyond beckoned.

Sitting comfortably in the saddle, Gabriel kicked his horse into the lead as they emerged from the gate. While they had never been rich, the forge had provided his family with enough for a modest existence – including a horse and wagon. In his free time Gabriel had often taken the gelding off into the forest with Margaret, to wander at their leisure.

Now though, Gabriel's mind was focused on the chase. His thoughts were far ahead of him, picturing the twists and turns of the Gods' road. If they'd climbed the wall, it meant the boy and old man were on foot. They should have no trouble getting ahead of them – after that, it was only a matter of closing the noose around them.

The breeze picked up as he kicked his horse into a gallop. The others followed suit, and they raced up the hill from the town. He did not look back as they entered the trees – he had no wish to see the smoking ruin of his home. The trees loomed around them as they pushed on, their branches stretching overhead to blot out the sky.

Amidst the woods, the stench of the burning town faded away, replaced by the richness of the earth and trees. The fury of their passage sent leaves whirling around them and birds flew shrieking into the trees at their approach. Within a few minutes, Gabriel's horse began to snort, unused to the hard pace. But as it slowed he dug in his heels, determined to outpace their quarry.

Faster.

The thought slivered through his mind, driving him onwards. A need rose within him, a longing to see the demon pay, to watch its face as he plunged his sword into its black heart. His chest ached as red flashed across his vision. He could almost smell the blood, taste the thrill of revenge.

Ahead the Gods' road bent way to the right, concealing what lay beyond. Crouching in the saddle, Gabriel pressed his mount harder, feeling the beast shuddering beneath him. They would have to slow down soon, regardless of his own desires. Their horses were work beasts, not trained for such a hard pace, but he would press them for as long as he could.

As they raced around the bend, Gabriel heard a shout from one of the other men. He glanced across in time to see an arrow sprout from Tom's chest. His mouth fell open as

Tom slumped in the saddle and tumbled from his horse. Tugging at the reins, Gabriel tried to slow his mount, but it was far too late for that.

Black-garbed men streamed from the trees around them, while ahead the road straightened, revealing the massed ranks of black-garbed men and wagons. Before Gabriel and his men could recover, the men roared, and charged.

~

ERIC SAT FROZEN in his saddle as the massive Baronian drew to a stop in front of the wagons. Hands on his hips, the man stared up at them, his black eyes glinting in the low light. Swallowing, Eric reached unconsciously for his knife, before remembering he had lost it in Oaksville. Briar shifted beneath him, his ears lying flat against his skull. Beside him, Alastair sat straight in the saddle, calmly returning the Baronian's glare.

"Well, well, well, what do we have here?" the Baronian repeated.

"Out of the way, Baronian," Alastair growled. Elcano stamped his hoof to reinforce the old man's words. "In the name of the Goddess."

"Oh, the Goddess is it?" The Baronian threw back his head and howled with laughter. The others joined in, and the forest rang with their mirth.

Eric glanced at Alastair, his skin tingling at the thought of all the arrows pointed at his exposed body. One slip of a finger, one over eager bandit, and it would all be over. He hoped Alastair knew what he was doing.

When the Baronians eventually fell silent, their leader took another step towards Alastair. "Well, I'll admit, that's a new one," a broad grin split his face. "Doesn't matter though.

I'll tell you the same thing I tell all the others: to pass you'll have to pay the toll."

"And what is the toll?" Eric croaked.

"All that you have." The big man's tone brooked no argument.

Alastair met the Baronian's ultimatum with silence. Sweat dripped down Eric's back as he stared at the old man, willing him to speak. His guts roiled at the thought of giving over his measly possessions. He had lost his bag at some point during his flight through Oaksville, but he still wore the steel bracelet around his wrist. It was all he had left of his parents.

"What's your name?" Alastair asked suddenly.

"Thaster." The Baronian grinned, apparently unconcerned by Alastair's change of tact. "Now, if you don't mind, we have business elsewhere. You've come from Oaksville, have you?"

Eric shivered as greed flickered across Thaster's face. It was clear what the man's intentions were, why the Baronians had ventured so close to Oaksville. The pillars of smoke staining the sky behind them made it clear something had happened to the town. Looking around at the men of Thaster's tribe, Eric prayed there would be enough fighters left in Oaksville to repel the raiders.

He didn't like their chances though.

"Where we've come from is none of your business, Baronian," Alastair was speaking again, "Now, out of my way. I have no intention of providing any more funds for your misdeeds."

Steel rasped on leather as Alastair slowly drew his sword from its sheath. Eric gaped, his heart lurching in his chest. For a moment, Thaster stared at the old man in obvious disbelief. But his hesitation only lasted a second. Reaching up, he drew his greatsword.

"Very well, old man," Thaster grinned and glanced back at his men. "Take care of..."

Thaster's voice trailed off as the distant pounding of horse hooves reached them. Thaster frowned, shifting to stare down the road towards Oaksville. A few of the black-garbed bandits faded into the trees, and several of the bowmen shifted their aim, waiting for the horsemen to appear.

"Bring friends, did you?" Thaster growled. "Pity they're too late. Hunter, Laurel, put an arrow in their hearts."

Eric flinched and closed his eyes as bowstrings twanged. There was no time to move, to throw himself to the side. Helpless, he waited for the sharp steel to tear through his flesh. But it did not come. A heavy silence fell over the road, broken only by the thunder of approaching horses.

Opening his eyes, Eric looked around. Alastair still sat comfortably in his saddle, his hand outstretched towards Thaster. Hovering in the air between them were two steel tipped arrows.

As Eric gaped, Alastair flicked his wrist, and the arrows went spinning off into the trees.

"Out of the way," Alastair growled. As he spoke, an invisible force seemed to strike the crowd of Baronians, sending them all stumbling backwards a step.

Thaster's face had paled to white in a space of a second, but he straightened now. A scowl twisted his lips as he looked around and saw his men shrinking from the old man. "Cowards!" he screamed. "Fire! Kill him!"

But suddenly the pounding hooves were right on top of them, and twisting in the saddle Eric watched as two-dozen horsemen barrelled around the corner of the Gods' road. A twinge of panic twisted in his chest as he saw the man in the lead – the same man that had accosted them in the alleyway. His eyes were dark with hate as he kicked at his foam-flecked horse, urging the poor beast on.

Then arrows flashed through the air, and several horses went down in a tangle of thrashing limbs and hooves. The man from the alleyway looked up and dragged on his reins, turning his horse a fraction, and the arrows went shrieking past him. Drawing a short sword from his belt, he drove his horse at the nearest Baronian.

As Eric turned back towards the wagons, a horse crashed sidelong into Briar, driving him from the centre of the road. Crying out, Eric tugged at the reins struggling to control his mount. He ducked as an arrow hissed past his head, then swung to face the other horseman.

"Come on!" Alastair yelled as Elcano slammed into Briar again, sending them staggering towards the trees.

Alastair's brow was furrowed and his jaw clenched tight, his hands raised above his head. But Elcano seemed to be obeying some unspoken instruction. He leapt at the bandits to their left, scattering them from his path, and then raced into the woods. Before Eric could so much as dig in his heels, Briar sprang after him.

Eric crouched low in the saddle as a wall of greenery loomed. Then he was amidst the trees, clinging to the saddle with everything he had, desperately trying to follow Elcano's path through the trees. Ahead, Alastair sat slumped in the saddle now, his head bent, but still he did not slow.

Branches flashed at Eric's face as they tore through the shrubbery, threatening to hurl him from the saddle. His ears throbbed with the erratic beat of his heart, and his breath came in ragged gasps. He still could not believe what he had just seen. The man from the alleyway – Gabriel he remembered his name now – had followed them, had chased them all the way from Oaksville.

And, impossibly, Alastair had stopped two arrows mid-flight.

But there was no time to consider either now, and

keeping low in the saddle, he tried to avoid the branches flashing for his face. He had no hope of controlling the horse now, but ahead he saw Alastair finally pulling back on Elcano's reins.

With a low whinny, the horse drew to a stop, and to Eric's relief, Briar did the same. Still gasping for air, Eric slid from the saddle. His legs crumpled as they touched the ground, their strength exhausted. A swarm of insects rose up to meet him, biting mercilessly at his skin, but in that moment he didn't care. He grasped at the damp ground, drawing reassurance from its firmness, and looked up at Alastair.

A distant scream carried through the trees, and Eric turned to stare back in the direction of the road. There was no sign of movement, and slowly the far-off sounds of clanging metal faded away. Facing Alastair again, his anger flickered into life. What had the old man been playing at on the road, baiting the Baronians like that?

"What the *hell*–" the words died in his throat as he saw the arrow embedded in Alastair's shoulder.

Alastair swayed in the saddle, his face pale, his brow creased. With painstaking slowness, he lifted his leg and swung himself down from Elcano. He staggered away from the horse and slumped against a tree, then slowly slid to the ground.

"Are you okay?" Eric breathed. He climbed to his feet and took a hesitant step towards Alastair.

The old man shook his head. Closing his eyes, he reached up and took a hold of the arrow. In one smooth movement, he tore it from his shoulder and hurled it into the trees. Eric stared as blood began to ooze from the ragged wound it had left.

"What… what happened back there?" Eric stammered.

Grimacing, Alastair opened his eyes and glanced at him.

"Magic," he muttered. "Except the Baronians must have had a Magicker of their own, one with power over the Light. Something interfered with my power, there at the end."

"The Light?" Eric frowned. He hadn't understood half of what the old man had said. "You're a Magicker?"

The old man forced a smile. "Ay, Eric," Alastair replied. "And so are you."

GABRIEL GASPED as he struck the ground. The force of the impact drove the air from his lungs, flooding his chest with pain, but instinctively he rolled to the side, carrying him clear of his thrashing horse. It kicked and screamed on the ground beside him, a black-shafted arrow embedded in its broad chest. Other horses stampeded around him as his men attempted to defend themselves against the hoard of Baronians.

He scrambled in the mud for his sword as another horse screamed and went down. His fingers clenched around the hilt, and then he was back on his feet, swinging to meet the first of the black-garbed bandits. The rain of arrows had ceased as the men in the trees raced to join the battle, but they had already done their job. Half his men were down, the others either unhorsed or surrounded.

Swearing, Gabriel swung at the nearest Baronian, but the man leapt from his blade's path and started to laugh. Gabriel gritted his teeth and went after him, painfully aware of his inexperience in combat. He had never been in a real sword-fight before. His only experience came from playing with his father's blade when the forge was quiet. Still, work as a blacksmith had made him strong, and he had no intention of dying easily.

Fight.

The thought swept through his mind, lighting a fire in his chest. A surge of adrenaline added strength to his weary limbs, and with a growl he swung again at the Baronian. This time the Baronian was not quick enough to retreat, and raising his axe he caught the tip of Gabriel's sword on his blade. Clenching his fist, Gabriel drove forward, freeing the blade and sending it deep into the man's chest.

The axe slid from the Baronian's fingers as he staggered backwards. For a second he clutched at his chest, trying to stem the bleeding, before he toppled face first to the ground. Elation swept through Gabriel, washing away the fear. Grinning, he stepped over the body and searched for his next opponent.

Kill.

Blood pounded in his head, and his vision flickered red. He snarled as another Baronian charged him, his battle axe swinging for Gabriel's face. Ducking the decapitating blow, he rushed forward and punched out with his short sword.

The axeman twisted at the last moment, then his fist flashed out to catch Gabriel in the cheek. The blow caught Gabriel off-balance and he tumbled backwards. His vision spun as he struck the ground and rolled. He heard the *thunk* of an axe striking dirt. Before the man could try again he kicked out, and felt a satisfying thud as he knocked the axeman's feet out from beneath him.

Ignoring the pain in his face, Gabriel gathered himself and dove on his attacker. His sword had been lost when he fell, but he slammed a fist into the man's face before he could raise his hands to defend himself. The power behind the blow slammed the Baronian's head back into the hard-packed earth. Then he surged back against Gabriel, struggling to throw off the blacksmith. But in close quarters, he was no match for Gabriel's muscular bulk.

Grinning, Gabriel reached out and wrapped his fingers

around his foe's throat. Panic flashed across the man's coal-speckled eyes, and his arms flailed, trying to break Gabriel's steely grip. Veins bulged on his forehead as he wheezed, frantically trying to draw breath.

Watching the light fade from the man's eyes, Gabriel felt a thrill of exhilaration. He found himself joying in his newfound strength, in this power to give or take life. As the man sagged in his grip, Gabriel began to laugh. Finally releasing the man, he straightened and looked around.

The dead and the dying covered the road, and nearby the last of the townsfolk were fighting back to back. Beyond them, more Baronian's stood amidst their dozen wagons, their attention fixed on two fleeing horsemen. Gabriel caught a glimpse of grey hair and a flash of youthful blue eyes, before the horses vanished into the trees.

His gut clenched with rage. There was no mistaking them – it was the old man and boy from the alleyway.

So close!

Gabriel's hands shook as he picked up his sword and stumbled to his feet. His clash with the Baronians had carried him clear of the conflict that had engulfed his comrades, but now he stood on the opposite side of the road to where his quarry had vanished. And somehow they had found horses, while he now found himself on foot.

Cursing, Gabriel gripped his sword tighter and stepped towards the press of bodies. He would fight his way through, or die trying.

A blinding light flashed across his vision, and he staggered backwards, pain lancing through his forehead. When he looked again at the road, it seemed a dark figure hovered over him, a ghost or demon from the other side. The figure leaned towards him, stretching out a pale hand.

Go back!

Then it was gone. Gabriel stood for a second longer, his

whole body trembling with terror. Sucking in a breath, he tried to find the rage, the hatred that had driven him so far. But there was only fear now, only an empty, unmanly cowardice.

He stumbled backwards, retreating from the sound of clashing swords and screaming men. As he reached the trees, he saw the last of his comrades stumble backwards, a sword embedded in his chest. Their eyes caught across the distance as the man sagged to his knees. His mouth opened in a silent cry, and then he was gone.

Gabriel choked and looked away. Guilt twisted in his stomach as he fled into the trees. He waited for the screams to follow him, for the shouts as the Baronians gave chase. Gasping for breath, he leapt over a half-rotten tree trunk and staggered on.

Only after a few minutes did Gabriel realise no one was following him. He stumbled to a stop and turned back towards the road, listening for the sound of pursuit.

But there was nothing. An eerie quiet hung over the woods. The trees were still; not even a breath of wind stirred the branches overhead. The buzz of insects and the chirping of birds had been silenced. Beneath the thick canopy, the world was cast in shadows. They seemed to press in around Gabriel as he turned, suddenly unsure of which direction he'd come from.

Gabriel…

The hackles on Gabriel's neck stood on end. He shivered, looking around again. The voice had almost sounded real this time. But he was alone amidst the trees, and shaking his head, Gabriel started off again.

Gabriel…

He stilled as the voice came again. Then panic rose in his chest, and he started to run. The whispers chased after him, seeming to come from all around, wrapping him in terror.

His rage fled before it, his thirst for revenge drowning in it, until all that remained was the fear.

When he finally stumbled into the clearing, he was at the end of his strength. Falling to his knees, he bent his head, gasping for air. The whispers came from all around him now. His heart pounded hard against his chest, but Gabriel could run no further. Gathering the last of his courage, he stumbled to his feet.

The clearing he'd found himself in was small, barely more than a patch of barren ground amidst the trees. A dark pool of water had gathered in its centre. Ripples trailed across its surface as light raindrops fell through the gap in the canopy. Beside it sat an old stone alter, its surface covered by moss and lichen.

The patter of rain on leaves gathered strength, and a fine mist rose from the pool. It collected amidst the trees, concealing the earth, cutting Gabriel off from the world. Amid its silvery tendrils, the darkness began to coalesce. A figure took form, its black presence filling the clearing. The forest seemed to retreat before it, the ancient trees withering before its black power. Silhouettes danced about the spectre, forming a cloak of living death.

Gabriel stood transfixed as the voice whispered through the clearing, taunting him, drawing him in.

Gabriel… it said. *Welcome, my child…*

A tremor went through Gabriel as the spell broke. He staggered, and then reached for his sword. But as he drew the silver steel into the light, he knew it was hopeless, that mortal weapons were nothing to this creature. Even so, he gripped it tight, and stepped towards the darkness.

Stop.

The force behind the voice was enough to send Gabriel to his knees. He stared up at the evil presence, his hope withering, a vast emptiness opening inside of him. The sword slipped from his fingers.

"What do you want?" he croaked.

To help you.

Gabriel shivered. Closing his eyes, he shook his head. "It's not real. It's not there," he muttered, willing himself to wake, to pull himself from the nightmare.

Look at me!

Gabriel reeled back as the voice became a roar. Around the clearing, ancient tree trunks groaned, and the very ground seemed to shake before the creature's power. He opened his eyes and looked up, his gaze catching in the pitch-black of the creature's eyes.

"What are you?" Somehow he found the courage to speak. "What do you want with me?"

To help you on your quest.

"Why?" the words leapt unbidden from his tongue. "Surely the demon boy is your kin?"

Laughter echoed through the mist, sending a shiver down to Gabriel's very soul. The creature shook its black head.

My reasons matter not, the creature's words snaked their way through Gabriel's mind. *Do you not want revenge, my child?*

Gabriel shivered. Gritting his teeth, he fought to resist the temptation that rose within him. "Why would I need your help, demon?"

The laughter came again, a soft, crackling sound that clawed at his ears. He tried to block it out, but it slipped past his defences, carrying with it the sick sense of corruption. Dark tendrils wrapped around his soul, calling for him to join in, to give way to his hatred.

Look around you, the voice said at last. *Your friends are dead. Your town is in ruins. And here you sit, freezing in the rain, as your quarry slips away.*

Gabriel stared up at the dark face, willing himself to spurn its words, to turn away from its darkness.

"What are you offering?" he found himself asking.

I will grant you immunity to their magic, and the means to track them.

Uncertainty gripped him. What the demon offered would guarantee his success. Without their magic, the old man and the demon were only mortal. Today he had proven he was a match for mortal men. If the demon spoke the truth, they would not escape justice again.

He looked at the demon, the creature of shadows and darkness. What would it possibly gain from their deaths? And what price would it ask in return?

Their deaths...

The words echoed in his mind. Suddenly his choice was clear. Whatever it asked, his life no longer mattered. And if he accepted its offer, he would rid the world of at least one evil. If he declined, both would continue unchecked. The decision was simple.

"I accept," he whispered.

And darkness descended around him.

CHAPTER 7

Eric stared across the empty fire pit, shivering as an autumn breeze blew through the trees. The sun had set an hour ago, drawing the last of the heat from the forest. He had gathered the wood for a fire before realising it the foolishness of the idea. It would draw their hunters like moths to the flame. But now he was seriously reconsidering his conclusion. Surely the trees would shield the light…

Angrily, he shook his head and glanced again at the sleeping Magicker. The old man had said little since his pronouncement after the chase. Instead, he had set about making a poultice for his wound from herbs he pulled out of the saddlebags. Afterwards he had muttered something about the townsfolk being distracted by the Baronians, propped himself up against a tree, and then promptly fallen asleep.

That had left Eric to spend the last several hours agonising over the meanings of his words.

Magicker.

He shook his head and shifted himself into a more comfortable position. It couldn't be true. It wasn't as though he had never considered the possibility of magic, but Magickers were noble born. For commoners, magic was the cheap tricks of the circus. Real magic was unheard of, reserved for the rich and powerful.

Closing his eyes, Eric concentrated on the ache of his body, trying to distract himself from the barrage of questions whirling through his mind. The day's ride had left him hurting in places he had never dreamed of. Even his knees were sore – though Gods only knew how that had happened.

He looked at Alastair again, watching the old man's chest rise and fall. He seemed to have regained some of the colour in his face now, though Eric still found himself wondering whether he would ever wake. He had no experience with wounds, but the jagged tear left by the arrow did not look good.

"Good evening, Eric."

Eric jumped as Alastair's eyes flickered open, and he almost fell off the log he was sitting on. Groaning, the Magicker straightened and looked around. He raised an eyebrow when he saw the empty fire pit.

"You've been busy," he gave a pained smile. "How long was I asleep?"

"The whole day. Anyone ever tell you that you snore?"

Alastair chuckled softly. Staggering to his feet, he slowly stretched his arms, wincing as he moved his injured shoulders. "Every morning, when my wife was still alive."

"You were married?" Eric asked, and then cursed himself for getting distracted. He had more pressing questions to ask.

"A long time ago now," as Alastair spoke, he reached up and lifted his bandage to inspect his wound. "But that's not what you're really interested in, is it?"

Eric shook his head. "You said you were a Magicker. You said I was one too. But that's impossible."

"And why would that be impossible?" Alastair replied softly.

"Because only nobles have magic…"

Eric clenched his fists as he waited for a reply, barely daring to breath. He didn't want to face what it meant if Alastair was speaking the truth, if he really had magic. Until now, the dark power inside him had been a curse, some uncontrollable force that lashed out with a will of its own. But magic… magic was controllable, malleable to its users demands.

If he truly had magic, that meant he could have controlled it, could have stopped the destruction that had engulfed Oaksville.

"No. It's true, most of those with magic are from powerful families. But the gift does not recognise royalty, or wealth, only blood. It is passed down from generation to generation."

"But my parents… they didn't have magic," Eric grasped at the fact like a lifeline.

"Magic can lie dormant for generations before reasserting itself," Alastair fell silent for a moment. "Such cases usually have horrifying implications."

Eric closed his eyes and looked away. *No, it's not possible!*

His arms began to shake and a numbness spread through his body. "I thought it was a curse," he whispered.

"No, Eric. The power comes from within you. What happened in Oaksville was wild magic, an unleashing of your power in response to your emotion, to your fear or anger."

Eric slid from the log, his knees sinking into the damp earth. A low gurgling sob built in his chest. His fingers dug into the soft dirt, grasping for something solid to cling too. His eyes never left Alastair's.

"Could I have stopped it? Could I have saved them?"

It's all your fault, the words whispered through his mind.

A strong hand clasped him by the shoulder. "You could not have saved them, Eric. Once released, you stood no chance of containing that power. Without training, without preparation, you never stood a chance."

"But it was still me."

"It wasn't your fault, Eric," Alastair's emerald eyes bored into Eric. "Magic is a wondrous thing, but it has a mind of its own. It does what it wants, when it can. And it will do all it can to preserve itself, to protect its host from outside threats."

"You make it sound like its alive?"

"In a way, it is," Alastair replied.

Eric shivered, turning the words over in his mind. "It's still a part of me though," he paused. "I need to learn how to control it."

Alastair laughed softly, his face soft. "I said I would help you, Eric. I meant it. I will be your teacher."

Relief flooded Eric's chest. He sat back against the log and closed his eyes, letting out a long sigh. For the first time in years, he felt a touch of hope. When he opened his eyes again, Alastair was standing over the fire pit. He held a piece of flint in one hand and a knife in the others. Sparks leapt from the flint as he struck it with the knife.

"Are you sure it's safe to light a fire?"

Alastair nodded. "The Baronians and townsfolk will be preoccupied with each other tonight. And I'm not a young man any more. My bones ache in this cold."

Eric shivered as he recalled the charging horsemen, and the face of the man from the alleyway. "He was with them, you know?"

"Who?" Alastair looked up at the tremor in Eric's voice.

"Gabriel," Eric closed his eyes, recalling the hate and anger in the man's eyes. "The man from the alleyway. He was with the horsemen, the hunters from Oaksville. Yet another death caused by my actions."

"You cannot blame yourself for the decisions of others," Alastair said softly.

Eric only nodded. He watched in silence as Alastair lit the fire and settled down on the log opposite him. Finally he shook himself from his melancholy.

"Why couldn't you just light it with your magic?"

A smile tugged at Alastair's lips. "Do you recall what I said about the Light earlier, Eric?"

Frowning, Eric tried to recall the old man's words, but none of it had made sense to him. He shook his head.

Alastair laughed. "Perhaps I should start from the beginning. Magic is a complex, chaotic force, but it is still a force of nature. It has rules, Elements that divide it. The Light is one of those."

"What do you mean by Elements?"

"The Three Elements are the Light, the Earth, and the Sky. All natural magic falls within the bounds of one of these Elements. Most Magickers control just a small part of the whole. For instance, my power manipulates the forces of attraction between objects. That comes from the Light. But I cannot control fire, or light itself, which are other aspects of that Element."

"And my magic?"

"Yours is different," Alastair paused. "From what I have seen, you control all facets of the Sky. Such an ability is rare, and while the Sky is the weakest element, it makes you a formidable Magicker."

"The storm I created didn't seem weak," Eric replied bitterly.

"No, but you should also understand, your magic did not create that storm. Only the Gods can bring about something, from nothing."

Eric tilted his head in confusion. "What do you mean?"

"Your magic did not create, but drew the storm from elsewhere. It manipulated distant weather patterns, until they converged on Oaksville, forming a destructive maelstrom of lightning and wind. But it was not *created*."

Running a hand through his hair, Eric struggled to process the new information. But his mind was sluggish, exhausted from the day's events and distracted by the constant ache of his body.

On the other log, Alastair smiled. "I think perhaps that is enough for now. A night's rest will be good for you. As I said, magic comes from within you. When you use it, it draws on your life force. You will need rest to recover the strength it took. I will keep watch. We'll leave before first light. Hopefully the Gods road will be clear now."

Eric nodded, struggling to contain a yawn. He still had questions, but his eyes were drooping and he could no longer deny his exhaustion. It would be useless to continue their discussion now. Grabbing a blanket he had taken from Briar's saddlebags, he curled up in front of the fire and closed his eyes.

As his consciousness slowly drifted away, images appeared in the darkness of his thoughts, some as clear as day, others little more than blurs. Then, as it often did, his mind turned to his parents, and his fifteenth birthday.

"Eric, catch!" The nectarine tumbled towards him.

Reaching up, Eric plucked the fruit from the air and sank his teeth into the soft flesh. His friend sat in the branches above him, munching on a second nectarine. Juice ran down his youthful face. Behind him, an autumn sunset lit the sky blood red.

"So how does it feel to be old, Eric?" Mathew asked.

Eric shrugged. "No difference, really. But my father's already talking about getting me in the fields."

Mathew laughed. "That's too bad. Maybe you should just forget about this birthday thing. Growing up sounds like hard work."

Eric grinned back. "I don't think it works that way."

"Eric!" A woman's voice carried up the hill. "Come help set the tables!"

"It begins," Mathew mocked.

Shaking his head, Eric waved his friend goodbye and started down the hill. His mother's call came again, and he began to run, taking care not to slip on the muddy ground. Below, the little town spread out beneath him, the wooden houses with their thatched roofs ringing the hill.

He was puffing by the time he reached his back door and pulled it open. Leaning down, he took care to scrape the mud from his boots before entering. His mother could be terrifying when she was angry, and birthday or no, trekking mud through the house was bound to bring her wrath down on him.

"There's the birthday boy – or should I say man!" His father greeted him with a booming laugh.

Moving across the room, he scooped Eric up into a bear hug. His strong arms crushed the air from Eric's lungs before releasing him. He stared up into his father's dark amber eyes, and smiled.

His mother's voice echoed up the corridor, and his father laughed again. "Sounds like it's dinner time. We'd better not keep your mother waiting," his father said.

"Better late than never I guess," his mother greeted as they moved into the dining room.

Her hazel eyes found Eric from across the room. Despite her grey hair, his mother had lost none of her vitality. She moved around like a woman half her age. A smile tugged at her lips as she put her hands on her hips.

Eric bowed his head, struggling to conceal his own grin. "Sorry mum, I came as soon as I heard you!"

His mother shook her head, laughing softly. "Oh don't worry; it's your day after all. Come here!"

They embraced before the three of them sat down at the small table. The rich aroma of roast lamb filled the room, its source sitting centrepiece on the table, surrounded by potatoes and broccoli and an assortment of other vegetables. It was a feast unlike Eric had ever seen.

The evening flashed by in a rush, filled with talk of Eric's childhood and his dreams for the future. As the night grew long, Eric resisted his exhaustion for as long as he could, before finally bidding his parents goodnight.

But in his sleep, darkness wrapped around his dreams. He watched as armies of demons marched across the valley of his hometown. The villagers fled before them, but the hordes overran them, slaughtering all who crossed their path. His village burned, the fires spreading until the whole valley was aflame.

Screaming, Eric wrenched himself from the dream. But awakening in his home, he found the nightmare had followed him. His room was burning. Flames clung to the walls and lightning danced across the ceiling, leaving scorch marks in its wake.

He screamed again and threw off his blanks. Lightning caught the covers as he ran for the door, chasing after him. He fled the bedroom, the heat swamping him. The house was already ablaze, and smoke filled the corridor. Holding his breath, he sprinted for his parents' bedroom.

A blast of heat forced him back as he yanked their door open. His eyes burned but he pushed forward and stared inside. Through the smoke he made out the burning bed and its occupants. Nothing living remained in that room.

Choking on his grief, Eric stumbled back, tears boiling from his face. Turning, he fled from the nightmare.

When he burst through the front door, a crowd had already gathered outside. He staggered towards them before the strength went from his legs, and he collapsed to his knees. Swaying, he opened his mouth and croaked out a desperate plea.

The crowd stared back, unmoving. No one spoke, no one approached to help. Their eyes were transfixed, their mouths wide open. Some sported burns, and ash covered their faces, as though they had tried and failed to enter the inferno.

Whispers spread through the watchers as Eric reached out to them in silent entreat. They drew back as one, fear touching their faces.

It was then he noticed the lightning. Sparks crawled along his skin, jumping between the raised hairs on his arms. Yet he felt nothing.

Eric fell backwards, scrambling to brush it from him. Lightning burst from his skin and struck the ground. Thunder cracked and the crowd screamed.

"Help me," somehow Eric's burnt throat managed to croak the words.

The crowd stared back. Still no one spoke.

Then he saw Mathew amidst the crowd. "Help me, Mathew!"

Mathew's face was a mask of terror, but still he took a shaking step forward. He had always been brave, always been the one to leap from the high cliffs into the river, when Eric had been too frightened.

Eric reached out a hand to his friend. "Help me, Matthew," he repeated.

Mathew ignored him. Instead, he drew his dagger. Eric had seen it many times. It had been a birthday gift from his own parents last year. It was a good blade, although nothing expensive. Now it glowed red in the light of the flames.

"Leave, Eric. Leave now, or I swear by Antonia I'll plunge this blade through your heart."

~

GABRIEL GROANED as the darkness retreated, returning him to the world. Sitting up, he sucked in a breath. His chest ached and his head throbbed, as though a thousand needles were piercing his skull. Yet at the same time, he felt rejuvenated, filled with a strange new energy. Already the pain was fading.

Closing his eyes, he searched his body, looking for a change. Nothing seemed different, but even so, he could feel *something* had been altered.

He looked around for the demon, but the clearing was empty now, the trees silent. Pulling himself to his feet, he walked across and picked up his sword from the damp earth.

As he straightened, movement came from the woods. He watched as a wolf emerged from the trees. Eyes as bright as the moon watched him. It bared its yellowed teeth, its jet-black hair black fur bristling as a low growl rattled deep in its throat.

Gabriel raised his sword as the beast took a step towards him. He pointed the tip at its chest, silently cursing the demon and its useless gifts.

A sudden laughter whispered through his mind as the wolf halted.

Greetings, Gabriel. I am here to track the two you seek.

CHAPTER 8

By the time the sun rose the next day, Eric and Alastair were a long way from Oaksville. Alastair had woken Eric in the dark, dragging him still half-asleep through the woods. They had led the horses until the trees opened up and they found themselves back on the Gods' road. There they had mounted up and ridden east at an easy trot.

Now Eric could not help but glance over his shoulder to check for signs of pursuit. He still half-expected another pack of horsemen to come for him, with Gabriel at their lead. But the road was silent, and the trees overhead hid any sign of the distant city.

While Alastair was confident the people of Oaksville would be too preoccupied defending their city to come after him again, Eric was not so sure. He had seen the rage in Gabriel's eyes on the road. If he had somehow survived the battle with the Baronians, nothing in the Three Nations would stop him from coming after them.

For now though, it seemed he was safe – from the hunters at least. He wasn't so sure the same could be said about his safety around Briar. The horse bounced along beneath him, seeming to take an almost human pleasure from Eric's every muffled wince and groan. And every so often the gelding would drift sideways towards the trees, forcing Eric to duck as the branches flashed for his face. By noon, his whole body had been beaten black and blue, and it came as a relief when Alastair called a break.

Unfortunately, it only lasted long enough for them to devour a few scraps of dried beef, and Eric climbed back into the saddle with no small amount of trepidation. As he settled his feet into the stirrups, Briar looked back at him and gave a low whiny.

Beside him, Alastair chuckled as he mounted Elcano. "I think he likes you."

"How can you tell?" Eric raised an eyebrow.

"He hasn't walked you into any *big* trees yet."

"I thought you said he had a good temperament!" Eric exclaimed.

"Oh he's fine." Alastair gave Elcano a kick and they started off again. "He's just a bit of a character."

Eric snorted as he followed the old Magicker. "If you say so."

As silence fell between them, Eric found his thoughts drifting to their discussion from the night before, and something occurred to him. "Tell me more about the Elements," he asked. "The Earth, the Light, and the Sky. The Three Gods control those same three powers, right?"

"Correct. Each of the Three Gods is a master of one of the Elements. In fact, they're the living embodiment of those forces. That's why, unlike us, they have the power to create."

"And what exactly does each Element control?" Noticing Briar beginning to pull ahead, Eric gave a short tug on the reins, bringing the gelding back under control.

"Well, as I said last night, the Light is the manipulation

of raw energies in the natural world. It allows a Magicker to control fire, or light, or even another's magic. For myself, I am able to manipulate the forces of attraction between objects. In terms of raw power, the Light is the most powerful of the Elements."

"Then there is the Earth – which controls the physical embodiments of the natural world. Animals, plants, even the earth itself. Human's too, in terms of healing physical wounds."

"And finally there is the Sky – your Element. It is a wild and unwieldy force, Eric. The most uncanny and chaotic of the three Elements."

Eric nodded slowly to himself as Alastair spoke, piecing the information together. Above, a breeze rattled the tree branches, and copper leaves rained down around them.

"What about dark magic?" he asked at last. For so long he had blamed his curse on that mythical force. He wanted to know how it differed.

"Dark magic is the antithesis of all that true magic comes from. It is a perversion of the natural world. To wield it, a Magicker must ignore the Elements and give themselves over to their magic," the old man took a breath. "Magic is a perilous force, and given freewill, it incites only ruin. Allow it free rein for too long, and you become a puppet to the very power you seek to control."

Eric shivered. The more he heard of the perilous force, the less it seemed the blessing Alastair claimed. They fell silent then, continuing through the trees at a hard pace. As the day progressed, they took several more breaks, even walking themselves for a time to allow their mounts a rest.

Slowly the trees to either side of the road shrank, their trunks growing twisted and their leaves turning a sickly brown colour. Eric sneezed as dust rose from the road to catch in his nostrils, and the air grew hot as the afternoon sun set in.

"We're close to the edge of the desert now," Alastair commented eventually. "It rarely rains here. The trees that survive have deep roots that can reach the water far beneath the surface."

"Why are we heading this way?" Eric asked as he wiped sweat from his brow.

"The hunters didn't really leave us much choice," Alastair replied. "But fortunately, I already had plans to head for Chole."

"The Dying City?" Why?" In Eric's wanderings, he had always stayed well clear of the desert, and the city in its centre.

"There is someone there I've been looking for."

"Who?" Eric paused, thinking, then continued. "Is this someone like me?"

"Not quite," Alastair chuckled. "But I cannot say who, only that I'm running out of time. We'll have to travel through the desert itself to make it to Chole in time."

"What?" Eric squeaked. He coughed, trying to regain his voice. "You can't be serious?"

Dark tales were told about the desert around Chole. It had been created a hundred years ago, at the height of Archon's war, when the Three Nations banded together to repel an invasion from the north. Archon, a Dark Magicker of incredible power, had driven his forces deep into the heart of Plorsea, to the gates of Chole itself, before a great spell had been cast by the Gods to drive him back.

But in the aftermath of the battle, the once green lands around the city had been turned to dust. And the dark creatures Archon had once commanded had come to call it home. Now few dared to venture into its depth, and fewer still returned.

"There is an old road that crosses the desert, from the time before Archon's war," Alastair was speaking again. "Don't worry, I've past that way many times before. Most of the tales are exaggerated."

"But your shoulder…" Eric began.

"Relax, Eric," Alastair shrugged his injured shoulder. "I am a fast healer. By tomorrow it shouldn't be causing me so much pain. And even if it did not, it would not affect my magic."

Eric fell silent, not entirely reassured. He shifted tack. "What about the city? I could lose control of my magic again."

"We have a few days yet before we reach Chole. Don't worry, Eric. I cannot make you a master overnight, but I can at least help you gain some control over your power before we arrive."

Nodding, Eric turned his attention back to the road. He had run out of arguments, though the unknown quantity of the Chole desert still made him shiver.

They reached the end of the treeline as the sun dipped towards the horizon, lighting the sky afire. The forest ended abruptly either side of them, giving way to cracked brown earth. The desert stretched away into the distance, where three volcanic peaks rose from the skyline. The plains were devoid of movement, of life. Only the petrified corpses of the old forest remained, their ancient carcasses littering the baked earth.

The road veered away to the left, tracking the outskirts of the desert, but a thin track continued into the arid land.

Alastair spurred his horse onto the path, and glanced back to check Eric was following. "Keep your eyes open. We're in a different world now. The tales might be exaggerated, but this land is by no means safe. Dark creatures hide in these crevasses."

Eric nodded and suppressed a shiver. It did not take much imagination to fear a place like this. Suddenly he found himself thinking the hunters might be preferable to whatever nightmares stalked the desert plains. He prayed to the Gods Alastair knew what he was doing.

He stared up at the three volcanoes stabbing up into the red sky. The one in the middle was known as Mount Chole, but the others remained nameless. They had erupted from the earth at the apex of Archon's war, as the spell was created to cast him from the Three Nations. The Magickers of the time had saved the city from the lava flows, but their magic could not stop the shadow the peaks created. Their presence drove back the humid coastal storms, plunging the land around Chole into drought.

A century later, the once great city had become known as the Dying City. Eric just hoped he would not be the final nail in its coffin.

Eric sat in the darkness, staring into the crackling flames of the campfire. Alastair sat close by, his arms stretched out towards the fire, eager to fend off the chill that had come with nightfall. Above, a thousand stars crowded the night's sky, and the moon had just appeared on the horizon.

Shifting on the log, Eric took stock of his body's aches. The day's ride had taken its toll, leaving bruises on top of bruises, but he was pleased with the progress he had made. Already he felt more comfortable in the saddle, slowly settling into the rhythm of the horse beneath him.

Beyond the light of the fire, the darkness was absolute. Staring into the pitch-black, Eric couldn't help but shiver, imagining unseen eyes were looking back at him. His neck tingled, and he glanced at Alastair, wondering how the old man could seem so relaxed.

Feeling a need for a distraction, Eric forced himself to speak. "Do you think Gabriel's still out there?"

"If he was with the horsemen like you say, I do not think so. The Baronians would have slaughtered them all before continuing to Oaksville. But the man was driven, pushed past the brink of sanity. He may have found a way to survive."

Eric took a moment to reply. "I think he's still alive. I think it would take more than a few bandits to stop him," he paused. "He terrifies me."

Alastair nodded. "A man with nothing left to lose is a man without restraint. But there is more to your fear than that, isn't there?"

Eric jumped as the fire popped. His heart was still racing as he settled back on his log. "I have no defence against him," he replied eventually. "Whatever he's become, it was my actions that created him."

"And you think that makes your responsible for him?"

"I guess," Eric shrugged.

There was a long pause before Alastair replied. "There is nothing you can do to change the past, Eric. All you can do now is try to make a difference for those who remain, to balance the scale against what happened in Oaksville…"

Alastair's voice trailed off as he turned suddenly to look out into the darkness. Eric frowned, opening his mouth to reply, but Alastair waved a hand and scrambled to his feet. Clenching his jaw shut, Eric followed the old Magicker, his muscles screaming their protest.

"Quickly, get your back to the fire *Now!*" Alastair hissed.

Eric spun to face the darkness as Alastair unsheathed his blade. The flames had robbed him of his night vision, but as he stared into the black, shapes slowly took form. His ears twitched as a rattle of stones came from away to their left, followed by the crunch of footsteps from the right.

He shook his head, squinting in the direction of the sounds, struggling to pierce the black. Had it just been his imagination? His eyes flickered back and forth, but all he could see were the shadows of long dead trees and the dim outlines of their horses.

Then one of the shadows moved, and a roar erupted from the silence. Eric shook with fear as he staggered back. He gagged as the stench of rotting meat drifted through the air. Then Alastair stepped in front of him, sword raised, and shouted a challenge to the darkness. Despite his wound, he looked strong and steady. The firelight flickered on his coat, catching the silver lines weaved into the fabric.

The roar came again, and fingers trembling, Eric bent down and picked up a burning brand. With his other hand, he drew the knife Alastair had given him as they made camp earlier that night, and stepped up next to the old Magicker.

A cold wind swept through the campsite, and Eric fought to calm himself.

Was that me?

With a final roar, the beast charged from the darkness. One moment there was nothing, the next the dark creature was racing forward, jaws wide to devour them. It stood ten feet tall on its hind legs, all corded muscles and sleek black scales. Scars crisscrossed its chest, glinting in the firelight, and a muscular tail stretched out behind it. Long claws reached for them, and rows of razor sharp teeth filled its massive mouth.

Its blood-red eyes locked on Alastair. The horses screamed as it leapt towards the old man. But Alastair stood strong, refusing to retreat from the beast. He raised a hand, and Eric's ears popped as an invisible force caught the beast mid-air and hurled it sideways. Alastair rushed after it, sword in hand, the other still moving as he worked his magic.

The creature crashed into an outcrop of rock, but regained its feet before Alastair could get close enough to strike. With a bound of its powerful hindlegs, it leapt over Alastair's head. The old man spun to face it, but before he could raise his blade to defend himself, the tail whipped out and caught him in the chest. Alastair cried out as the blow sent him tumbling backwards across the ground.

Eric gaped as his mentor disappeared into the shadows. Arms trembling, he clenched the burning brand tighter and raised his knife. He crouched low as the creature turned towards him, and before it could charge, hurled the flaming branch at its eyes.

The creature reared back as the branch struck, sending sparks scattering through the night. A high-pitched scream rent the air, so shrill it sent Eric to his knees. Dropping his knife, he clamped his hands to his ears, as a pain like shards of glass drove deep into his skull.

When the sound ceased, he threw himself at the fire and gathered up another stick. He turned, slipping in his haste, and braced himself for the worst. But a few feet away, Alastair had re-joined the fight. The beast and Magicker circled one another warily, their gazes locked in a deadly battle of cat and mouse. Alastair's face was grazed and he was limping, but still he refused to back down.

Beside him, the creature still looked whole. Their efforts had done nothing to pierce its scaly armour, and Eric shuddered as he stared at the yellowed teeth, imagining them rending and tearing at his flesh.

Alastair's sword shimmered in the orange firelight as he attacked, the blade lancing out to tear through the creature's forearm. The monster roared, its claws slicing at Alastair, but the old man danced back and they cut only thin air. His movements were steady despite his injuries. Only the tightness to his face gave away his pain.

Snarling, the creature threw itself at Alastair. A rock the size of a man's head flew through the darkness, smashing the monster's jaw and knocking it to the ground. Alastair lowered his arm and leapt forward, driving his sword down at the beast's skull.

But the creature raised its arm, and the sword plunged through its forearm. Before Alastair could pull away, its claws swept out, tearing through Alastair's hamstring. The metallic tang of blood filled the air as Alastair shrieked. Somehow he kept hold of his sword, tearing it from the creature as he fell backwards. Thick black blood ran from the creature's arm, but it didn't hesitate now. Leaping forward, it towered over Alastair, jaws wide to tear his head from his shoulders.

Letting out a shriek that was half rage, half despair, Eric threw himself forward, desperate to do something to sway the course of the battle. The creature's head turned and watched him come. As he came within range it spun, lashing out with its tail to knock him from his feet. Before Eric could rise, the tail crashed down on his chest, pinning him to the ground

Stars flickered across Eric's vision as it pressed down, crushing the air from his lungs. Suddenly he found himself unable to breath. Darkness swirled as it turned back to Alastair.

"*No!*" Eric hissed.

He felt the familiar power stir within him. For once he did not resist – it was their only hope now. He surrendered to it, let its power boil through him. Strength flooded his aching body and swept from him in a rush.

Above, the wind howled with a violent voice. Gales formed overhead, driving down towards them. They rushed around the campsite, picking up dust and stones. The firelight flickered, threatening to die. With a final, desperate shriek, Eric willed them towards the monster.

The winds gave a collective roar, and obeyed. They struck the creature, hurling it from Alastair and pinning it to the ground. In an instant, the old man was on his feet. Teeth bared, he stumbled forward, sword gripped tight in his hand. Blood soaked his leggings and he almost lost his footing, but before the creature could recover, Alastair lifted his blade and drove it deep into the creature's chest.

The creature gave another blood-curdling scream and lurched to its feet. Its claws lashed out, catching Alastair in the chest and hurling him from his feet. Then it turned and reeled towards Eric, the sword still stabbing from its chest.

Eric scrambled backwards, eyes wide, mouth gaping. He could not believe it. How could the beast suffer such a blow, and still live?

The beast gave a horrible, gurgling cry as it took another step towards him. Then it fell, slowly toppling forward to crash to the ground. A cloud of dust billowed out around it, blinding Eric. When it finally cleared, the creature lay still, its dead eyes staring up at him in silent hate.

Gabriel stood at the edge of the desert, staring out into the darkness. Night had fallen an hour ago, and they could go no further. Impatience gnawed at his stomach. He did not want to stop, not when his quarry was so close.

I will not let them escape. Not again!

We must wait, another voice spoke in the sanctity of his mind.

"Why, beast?" Gabriel turned to the wolf at his side. "Can't your master protect us from the desert creatures?"

A low growl rattled up from the wolf's throat. *My master*

is occupied elsewhere. His magic will not protect you from tooth or claw. The beasts that lurk here will kill you, if they find you. The woods are safer, for now. One less night spent wandering the cursed desert.

Gabriel gritted his teeth. "Very well," he snapped, storming back into the trees.

He could see the wolf shadowing him as he searched for a place to camp. He had already grown to hate it, hate its constant reminder of the deal he had struck. Regret was never far from his thoughts.

What was I thinking?

You needed help. You found it, the wolf supplied.

"Stay out of my head!" Gabriel snapped back.

The creature lifted its shaggy head and howled. The noise cut through the night, raising goosebumps on Gabriel's neck. The distant hooting of an owl fell suddenly silent.

Glaring at the wolf, Gabriel reached down and drew his sword. Steel scraped on leather as he pulled it clear and pointed it at the beast.

The howling ceased. The black beast lowered its head and growled. Baring its teeth, it took a step towards him.

Gabriel tried to suppress a shudder as he took a step back. "Just keep quiet, mutt," he snapped, and sheathed his sword.

Closing his eyes, Gabriel put his hands on his head. How had his life come to this? Everything had crumbled so quickly, he was struggling to come to terms with it. He tried to picture his parents, his fiancée. Their images floated through his mind, and his chest constricted with emotion. But their faces were blurred and indistinct, and as he watched, flames burst within his mind, consuming his family once more.

Rage rose in Gabriel's throat as he opened his eyes. He smashed his fist into a nearby tree, and clung to the pain that shot through his knuckles. Pain was the only thing that felt real now, the only reminder that he still lived. Everything else had been taken from him. Even his memory was fading.

All he had left was his hatred, his burning need to see the boy and the old man punished.

Perhaps then he would finally find peace.

CHAPTER 9

Silence settled over the night like a blanket. The fire had burned low, leaving only the dim glow of embers to light the camp. The metallic tang of blood was heavy on the air, mingling with the reek of rotten meat and smoke. A thousand stars stared down from above, indifferent witnesses to the slaughter.

"*No, no, no*," Eric whispered as he fell to his knees beside Alastair.

Sharp stones sliced through his leggings, but he hardly felt them. Stretching out a trembling hand, he pressed his finger to Alastair's neck, searching for a pulse. The old man's eyes were closed, and he did not respond to Eric's touch.

"Please…"

Tears stung Eric's eyes as he grabbed the Magicker by the shoulders and shook him. An iron fist clenched around his heart, robbing him of breath. And still the old man did not move.

"Come on, Alastair!" he shrieked, not caring what dark creatures might hear him. "You can't do this, you can't die!"

Hot tears ran down Eric's cheeks and dripped onto Alastair. It did not take a doctor to see the man's wounds were mortal. His right leg was a tangled mess; muscles torn from bone, his tendons hanging by a thread. The other leg was twisted at an awful angle, with a shard of bone protruding from his shin. The final blow had shattered his ribs, leaving a deep indentation in his chest.

A shudder racked Eric's body as he sat back on his haunches, defeated. He thought he'd felt the faintest flicker of a pulse, but even if the old man lived, he would not last long. And even if he did, they were stranded here, miles from help.

"Please wake up," he begged to the night.

"Don't cry, Eric," a voice whispered from the darkness.

Eric gave a strangled cry and leapt to his feet. Spinning to face the voice, he scrambled for his dagger, only to realise he had lost it yet again. Clenching his fists, he scanned the darkness, searching for the speaker. His body shook with pain and exhaustion, but he was determined not to die without a fight.

"Who's there?" he hissed.

"Do not be afraid, Eric," the voice was soft, feminine.

"Who are you?" Eric growled. "How do you know my name?"

Stones rattled as a young girl stepped into the light. Her features were faint, as though viewed through a veil of mist. Of her face, only her violet eyes were visible. Their brilliant glow lit the night, casting back the shadows. An elegant sky-blue dress wrapped around her slight figure, decorated by images of vines and flowers that appeared to shift before Eric's eyes. The scent of lilies filled the air, casting away the stench of the beast. Her bare feet carried her across the stones, hardly seeming to touch the ground.

"I am Antonia," she said simply.

Eric's stomach clenched as he gaped at her, unable to

form a response. It wasn't possible. Antonia was the Goddess of Plorsea, Master of the Earth. This girl couldn't be older than twelve years old.

"Ho... how?" he managed finally.

"How did I come to be here?" The girl took another step towards him. "How can I be Antonia? How, how, how... You humans always have so many questions," the girl's voice was rich with mirth.

Eric swallowed hard. He tried to speak again, but could not find his voice.

The girl was only a few steps away now. "We can 'how' all night, Eric. But first, I must save the old man."

She swept past without waiting for a reply, her movements smooth and graceful. A faint glow seeped from her skin, mingling with the violet of her eyes to cast back the shadows. Suddenly the terror had gone from the night, as though the young girl's presence had banished the evil of the desert.

Eric stared as Antonia crouched beside Alastair. His heart pounded like a galloping horse and he could not tear his eyes away as the girl stretched out her arm and placed a hand on Alastair's chest.

"Would you stop *staring*?" Antonia spoke without turning.

Eric opened his mouth and then closed it, but no sound emerged.

Snorting, Antonia glanced back at him. "Honestly, you look as though you've seen a– *oh!*" her eyes widened and she placed a hand over her mouth. "Oh damnit, I'm sorry, Eric. I forget sometimes."

She snapped her fingers, and the mist that concealed her features faded away. The radiance of her skin and eyes softened, bringing her features into focus. Curly brown hair hung across her face and cascaded down her back, while a tiny button nose sat between her violet eyes. Light freckles dotted her dimpled cheeks and a strand of hair was caught behind her left ear.

As their eyes met, Eric was struck by their depth. They were not the eyes of a girl that watched him, but those of some ancient presence, an eternal being of immeasurable knowledge. Staring into those eyes, Eric felt he might lose himself…

Then the Goddess blinked, and a wry grin twisted her lips. "I'm not sure that helped." She laughed. "Am I not what you expected?"

To his surprise, Eric found himself grinning back at her. The vice around his chest relaxed and he found his voice again. "Not exactly," he paused, his eyes flickering to Alastair. "Can you really help him?"

"Watch and see." Turning away, Antonia placed her hands on Alastair's chest again.

A slight frown creased Antonia's forehead as she closed her eyes. A shadow passed across her face, and she hunched her shoulders, her tiny fingers digging into the torn cloth of Alastair's shirt. Blue veins stood out against her creamy skin.

From nowhere, a faint green light appeared to bath the two of them. It swirled around Alastair, seeping into his skin and swirling into his wounds. Within seconds, the muscles of Alastair's leg began to knit themselves back to the bone. The angry red tears closed on his arms and chest, while the colour slowly returned to his face. His chest rose as his lips opened to take a breath.

Eric could only stand in watch in disbelief as all sign of Alastair's injuries faded away, until only his torn clothes remained as a reminder of the battle.

Finally, Antonia gave a little gasp and sat back on her haunches. Sweat trickled down her forehead, and for a second her aura of invincibility vanished. Her hands shook as she staggered to her feet.

"He'll sleep for the night," she said as she straightened and looked at Eric. "That gives us time to talk, Eric."

Eric's head shot up as she spoke his name. His fear came rushing back, and he stumbled as the girl's violet eyes settled on him. Antonia was the Goddess of Plorsea; was she here to punish him for Oaksville?

But Antonia only smiled, the wariness falling from her face. "I am not a vengeful soul, Eric. I can sense your remorse. It weighs on you like an anchor. I know you desire redemption."

"What do you mean?" Eric looked up at her last words.

Antonia laughed. "Such a serious soul. We can discuss that later. For now, why don't you ask a few of those questions burning a hole in your chest?"

Eric sighed and shook his head. Then he smiled, and asked the first thing question that came to him. "Why do you look so young?"

Antonia giggled. "Blunt too, I see. Most take hours to gather the courage to ask that."

"And do you usually answer them?" Eric was slowly relaxing, emboldened by Antonia's easy manner.

"Of course. People deserve to know the truth of those who rule them. Even their Gods." She paused, her voice taking on a serious tone. "Five hundred years ago, the three of us were only spirits – the eternal embodiments of magic, but powerless. Priests worshipped us in their rituals, but we were unable to respond, to touch the physical realm."

"During that time, there were only two nations – Lonia and Trola. A great war had been waged between them for decades, bringing death and destruction to the citizens of both lands. Their Magickers cast terrible spells, and entire armies were lost in the chaos. It seemed only a matter of time before the two nations wiped one another from existence."

"So the priests of both nations came together, and embarked on a great gambit to summon the spirits of magic to physical form. Knowing us to be creatures of balance, they prayed we would bring peace. Joining their powers, they worked a great magic – one unlike any that had come before, or has been seen since. The spell brought us into the physical world, and allowed us to assume the bodies we still wear today. It was then I chose this body."

"And it worked?"

"In a way." Antonia smiled. "Darius, the oldest, remained in Trola while Jurrien went east to Lonia. Together they returned the surviving armies to their homelands. I gathered the refugees, those disillusioned with their own nations, with nowhere left to call home, and led them into the wastelands left behind by the war. Together we created Plorsea from the ruins, to be a buffer between the hatred of Lonia and Trola. The people loved us, for we were gentle and kind, where their rulers had been hard, and driven by selfish desires. And the new kings and queens we lifted up to rule them were loved as well."

"But our coming also sowed the seeds for the creation of Archon. In that, we failed, for our presence ultimately led to a new conflict that almost destroyed all the good we had created."

A fresh breeze carried the stench of the beast to where they sat. Eric wrinkled his nose, his stomach roiling. Antonia frowned, and standing she moved across to the corpse.

"The two of you did well to slay it. Few survive an encounter with these creatures."

"What are they? How can they survive in this place?"

"They are called Raptors. And not by my will, I assure you," she raised her arm.

Light spilt from Antonia's hand to bathe the beast. Tendrils shot from the ground to wrap around its broken body. They twisted and grew, tightening as they moved. Leaves sprouted along their length and the Raptor's body shook. Fresh vines erupted from its flesh, weaving together to cover the black scales. A minute later, an azalea stood where the beast had lain. Pink flowers slowly opened, filling the air with their rich scent.

"That's better," Antonia nodded to herself.

Eric sat down, hard. He remembered Alastair's words, about how the magic of the Gods differed from mortal's. Antonia had created the azalea bush from nothing. He stared at her, seeing now what his ancestors must have seen all that time ago, to follow her into the wastelands that had become Plorsea.

But he could also see the strain on her face. Her skin had paled and she was panting softly.

"Are you okay?" he asked.

"I'm fine," Antonia straightened "It's just difficult to work my magic in this place. The curse that lies over this desert is one I cannot break alone. The earth itself has been tainted by Archon's darkness. It fights my magic. Within a few days the bush will die, like everything else good in this desert."

"So you cannot bring back the rain, restore the forest?"

"Jurrien and I tried, once. But it was beyond our strength. It is Archon's last mockery – that *my* nation be cursed with this place of death," the Goddess's voice was laced with bitterness.

Eric breathed in the sweet scent of the flowers, drawing strength from the plant's beauty amidst the darkness of the desert. He thought back to the war a century before, when Archon's forces had marched across the land, bringing slaughter wherever they went. While the Great Wars had been all but forgotten, Archon's war was still fresh in his nation's memory. Just the mention of Archon's name was enough to cast a cloud over a room.

"Who is Alastair?" Eric asked at last. "Who is he searching for?"

Antonia stilled, her violet eyes hardening. She stared into the fire, and for a moment, Eric did not think she would answer him.

"Alastair is an old friend of mine," she said at last. "His purpose is a great secret, one few know of. Can you be trusted with such a secret, Eric?"

Now it was Eric's turn to fall silent. He stared at the Goddess, wondering at her words, and the secret behind Alastair's rush to reach Chole. Then he swallowed his hesitation. He owed the Magicker his life. Whatever happened, Eric would not betray him.

He looked the Goddess in the eye as he replied. "I swear by… er, Antonia, that you can trust me."

"Good," Antonia smiled, but this time the gesture did not reach her eyes. "I'll hold you too it."

She sat down beside him. "I'd better start at the beginning, although you will know parts of the story. Two hundred years ago, my brother, Darius, vanished. He abandoned Trola and the Three Nations, and no soul has heard from him since. He did not even tell Jurrien or myself where he went. He simply disappeared."

Eric frowned. "I always thought the Gods at least knew where Darius had gone. But what does this have to do with Alastair?"

Antonia grimaced. "I said I'd start from the beginning, Eric. Try not to interrupt. Now, when Darius left, he at least had the foresight to leave behind a sword infused with his power over the Light."

"Yes, the Sword of Light –"

"Eric… Is this my tale, or yours?" Antonia's eyes glittered dangerously.

Eric nodded and quickly shut his mouth.

"Unfortunately, the sword was useless. Worse than useless, in fact. It was fatal to any Magicker who touched it – or so it seemed. Even Jurrien and myself were repelled when we tried to wield it. For a time, we allowed Magickers from across the Three Nations to test the Sword. It burned them all to ash. Eventually the price was too much, and we had to stop."

"So for the next hundred years, Trola was Godless. And without the Light to aid us, Darius and I were stretched thin. The land weakened and dark things crept from the holes we had banished them too. The hearts of the people grew hard. Even Plorsea and Lonia suffered, for our power is infinitely weaker without the union of the Three."

"Then, a hundred years ago, the dark things vanished. No one could explain it, but the people began to speak of Darius's return. Only Jurrien and myself knew better; we would have sensed if our brother was near."

"It was not long before the dark things returned. Ghouls and Raptors and countless unnamed beasts flooded down from the Northern Wastelands, marching beneath the banner of Archon."

"Archon's war," Eric breathed.

He looked up when Antonia did not continue. Fire burned in the Goddess's eyes, but despite her fury, Eric found himself grinning. It seemed even the Gods had a limit to their patience.

Eric managed to look contrite. "Sorry, won't happen again."

Antonia smirked, a sly twist to her lips that spoke of drastic consequences if he disturbed her again.

"Okay, where was I? Archon. He was Trolan once, one

who protested our appearance and rule. He wielded a powerful magic, but it was not enough for him, not enough to touch us. So he gave himself to its dark side, and used it to slaughter the master of the priests who had summoned us. For that, we banished him to the Northern Wastelands."

"It wasn't until he reappeared leading his dark army that we realised our error. His power over the dark magic had made him immortal, and he had spent centuries mastering it. I have never seen a more potent human, nor one with so little humanity remaining to them. His power could not be matched."

"Even by you?" That had always confused Eric. How could Archon have wreaked such havoc when two Gods still opposed him?

Antonia sighed. "With Jurrien at my side, we stood against Archon's magic. We attacked him with every ounce of power we could summon. The darkness consumed it all, and threw it back in our faces."

"The dark magic tore through us, ripping through our defences and piercing our very spirit. For a second, I thought it would consume me. It was only a last, desperate attack from Jurrien that saved us. My sense returned then, and I threw up a wall of vegetation between Archon and ourselves. Before he could burn through, we fled."

Antonia's little body shook and tears gathered in her eyes. Eric hesitated, and then reached out and took the Goddess's hand in his. It seemed a futile gesture, considering who and what she was, but it was all he could offer.

Shifting closer, Antonia leaned her head against his shoulder. "You're a sweet soul, Eric," she hugged him before continuing her tale. "With our magic defeated, the only choice left was open battle. Archon was powerful, but his army still had to cross the Gap. So we mustered fighters from every town and city in the Three Nations, and for the first time in four hundred years, the people marched to war."

Eric was silent now. He had heard this part of the tale before, but the way Antonia told it was personal. She had been there, witnessed and mourned each death. Archon's threat had been real to her – not some story passed down through the generations.

"Archon's army came like hell itself unleashed – demons and beasts and men. A thousand Raptors like the one you fought tonight, and many creatures more terrible. The men who fought alongside them were the scum of society, those we had been banished to the north in punishment for their crimes."

"Against them stood the men and women of the Three Nations. Flames seared holes in our ranks and the earth opened to swallow men whole. The claws and swords of the enemy seemed endless. Yet for every brave soul that fell, another would step forward to take their place. And damn it, we were winning."

"Then Archon joined the battle. He soared overhead on wings of darkness, morphed beyond recognition, blackening the heavens with his magic. Clouds gathered around him and the air throbbed with his power. Jurrien released his magic, trying one last time to tear the monster from the sky. It was only seconds before he collapsed, overwhelmed by Archon's power."

"Then the sky opened up, and it was not rain or lightning that fell, but *fire*. Flames swept across the Gap and thousands fell like leaves before a forest fire, consumed by Archon's dark firestorm. Brave souls, all."

"I watched in horror, powerless to save them. My heart broke as I felt each life end, each soul erased from existence."

Tears spilt from Antonia's eyes and ran down her freckled cheeks. Eric hugged her again, unable to find the words to comfort her. All those people. Their bravery and strength had meant nothing against Archon's magic. They had never stood a chance.

Antonia sniffed and in a half-choked voice, continued. "We fled with the shattered remnants of our army. I used what magic I could to stall the dark host, but we lost many more as we retreated. Jurrien's defiance had cost him dearly, and I alone was left to stand against Archon's might."

"Only one king survived the catastrophe at The Gap. His name was Thomas, the king of Trola. He led the retreat, gathering the broken armies of the Three Nations and leading them to the relative safety of the south. At his side was his champion and bodyguard – Alastair."

Eric blinked. It took a full second for him to process what he had just heard. He broke away from Antonia, and stared at her, mouth agape. "That's not possible… that would make Alastair… That would make him over a hundred years old!"

Antonia nodded. "Alastair has enjoyed an unusually long life. One in a thousand Magickers will age far slower than a normal human."

Seeing Eric was still lost for words, Antonia smiled. "Thomas and Alastair made it as far as Chole, but there they were ensnared and forced to make their last stand. The enemy had spread out across the land, wreaking havoc as they went, until we were completely encircled.

Eric's skin tingled as he remembered what came next. "Isn't this where you give–"

"*Eric!*" Antonia shrieked.

He winced, glancing across at her meekly. "Sorry?"

Antonia shook her head. The sly grin returned and there was a sparkle in her eyes as she looked at him.

"You really are impossible. I think it's time I tried this a different way."

At that, Antonia leaned across and placed her hands on either side of his head. Her grip was light but slowly she began to apply pressure. Eric stared into her eyes as they took on a look of intense concentration.

"This won't hurt – much," Antonia said.

Then pain tore through Eric's skull, and everything went black.

CHAPTER 10

These are Alastair's memories... Enjoy, *Antonia's voice whispered through the darkness.*

Then light flashed, and Eric's vision returned. But he no longer sat by the campfire, was no longer even himself...

Alastair stared out over the forest of campfires that encircled the city, watching for the first hint of the coming attack. The specks of light stretched away to the north as far as the eye could see, a dark reflection of the star-studded sky above. Thick smoke hung in the air and his mouth tasted of ash. Plorsea was burning, and Chole was all that remained to stand against the flames.

The city's walls stretched away to either side of him, manned by the men and woman of the Three Nations. They stood in silence, staring out at the enemy, their fear concealed by masks of courage. It made Alastair's chest swell to look at them. These were ordinary citizens – farmers and merchants, fishermen and foresters – yet they had all answered the call. Each of them would stand to the last against Archon's evil, helpless as their sacrifice might prove.

Taking a deep breath, Alastair retreated from the crenulations. The wall was sixty feet high and just over fifteen feet wide. No siege engine would break them, but the forests surrounding Chole would provide plenty of wood for scaling-ladders.

Stretching his arms, Alastair shifted through a series of movements, preparing his muscles for the coming fight. Chainmail rattled beneath his cloak, but its weight did not bother him. He had spent so long in the armour, it was almost a part of him now. He closed his eyes, allowing fear and thought to drift away, until there was only the movement of his body, only the pattern of blocks and steps and blows he had committed to memory so long ago.

Around him, he could sense the men and woman staring, but he paid them no attention. His movements grew faster, fending off a host of imaginary soldiers. Opening his eyes, he leapt, and his sword sliced the air. The blade hissed as it struck his ghostly foes, and he stepped up his tempo again, until his sword was nothing but a blur.

When he finished, a slight sheen of sweat marked his forehead, but the warmth spreading through his limbs told him he was ready. His mind was clear, his worries fallen away, replaced by the cool determination to survive, to triumph.

"Are we ready, Alastair?" the king's shout carried through the gathered soldiers.

Turning, Alastair watched as King Thomas made his way along the wall, greeting men and woman as he went. Soldiers straightened as he passed them, his presence adding steel to their courage. That was the effect Thomas had on people. He fought alongside his people, and they fought all the harder because of it.

Alastair smiled as the king drew to a stop beside him. "We'll show them a thing or two, old friend."

Thomas returned the grin and gripped Alastair's shoulder

in silent agreement. His chainmail gleamed in the light of the enemy fires, and he wore an open-faced helmet over his short auburn hair. His hazel eyes stared out over the battlefield, and a stubborn frown replaced the smile.

"Do not lose hope, Thomas," Alastair said softly. "She will find a way."

The king nodded as horns sounded from the enemy ranks. Below, figures shifted in the darkness as the enemy moved forward. In the darkness, it was difficult to see what they faced, but the glint of metal suggested human warriors would mount the first attack.

The enemy horns sounded again and the thump of ten thousand marching feet echoed from the walls. The men below surged forward, their battle cries breaking over the defenders like a wave. Sword hands quivered as several men backed away from the parapets.

Then Thomas stepped up to the edge of the wall and raised his swords. "Archers, ready!" his voice carried down the battlements, absent of fear.

His cry galvanised the men and they stepped back to retake their positions. Archers slid to the front as below the enemy charged across the open ground.

"*Fire!*" Thomas shouted as the enemy came within range.

A volley of arrows rose from the wall, their steel tips shrieking as they tore the air. They rose high into the sky before gravity took hold, and then fell in a deadly rain into the ranks below. The enemy charge faltered as screams rose from the killing ground. The front ranks of men withered, but those behind pressed on, trampling their dead and injured beneath iron-shod feet.

A second volley tore through the enemy, and a third, but fewer fell now, and Alastair saw the following ranks were better armoured than those who had led the charge. He glimpsed scaling ladders amidst their ranks, and gripped his sword hilt tighter.

An arrow shot past his head as the enemy archers came within range. Alastair ducked back, but nearby another defender was too slow to react. An arrow caught him in the throat, and he staggered backwards, disappearing over the edge of the wall without so much as a cry.

The thud of wood on stone drew Alastair's attention back to the enemy. He looked across as another massive ladder rose through the night to crash against the parapets. Defenders raced to push the ladders away, but the weight of enemy climbers had already pinned them to the wall.

Drawing his sword, Thomas leapt forward as the first of the enemy reached the battlements. Alastair followed close behind, sword held low, ready to defend the king's back. Thomas's blade caught the first attacker in the face, and he fell away with a scream. But another quickly took his place, axe already swinging as he leapt up the ladder. Alastair thrust out his blade to block the blow, and then stabbed out at the man's stomach.

The clash of steel on steel and the cries of the dying spread across the wall. Men and women, fears forgotten, launched themselves at the attackers, driving them back, sending them screaming to the ground far below. Yet their resistance came at a cost, and already the bodies of fallen defenders dotted the battlements.

Another man sprang to the ramparts. He came up fast, a second hot on his heels, and leapt at Thomas. The king ducked a blow from the axe and thrust out with his sword, catching the man in the chest. Alastair turned aside an attack from the second man, and then slashed his sword across his throat.

After that, Alastair lost track of the number of enemies that fell to his blade. Time slid by, marked only by the endless waves of attackers, and the screams of the dying. At one point, a lunatic with a mace had exploded over the parapet, his weapon already in motion. The blow smashed Thomas from his feet, but Alastair had cut him down before he could gain a foothold. When Thomas had staggered upright, he'd sported a fresh gash across his forehead, and his helmet had vanished. Even so, the king had thrown himself back into battle like a man possessed.

When the enemy horns finally sounded, a ragged cheer went up along the wall. Thomas raised his sword and shouted his defiance at the fleeing enemy, while Alastair allowed himself a smile. They had earned their respite, however brief it might be.

A few minutes later, Thomas sat down heavily beside him. He had found his helmet, but the dent left by the mace made it unwearable.

"Not much use now," he shrugged as he tossed it over the side. "Saved my life though. Thought the bastard had me for second."

Alastair shook his head. The king might be an inspirational fighter, but Alastair feared his recklessness would be the end of him. It was a wonder he had survived so long, where his equals in Lonia and Plorsea had fallen.

"Where is she, Alastair?" Thomas whispered suddenly. "She should be here."

"I don't know, Thomas," Alastair breathed. "Helping, I hope."

"I'm right where I need to be," they jumped as Antonia's youthful voice came from nearby.

Turning, Alastair found the girl sitting on the parapet beside them. His shoulders sagged as he took in the state of the young Goddess. Her leaf-green dress was scorched black, the silky material melted and bubbling, as though drawn straight from the fire. Her hands were scratched and bleeding and lines of exhaustion stretched across her face. Dark shadows hung beneath her eyes, and even their violet glow seemed to have dampened.

Alastair stepped forward and wrapped the girl in his arms. He had known her all her life, but never had he seen her in such a state. She looked defeated, broken.

"Can you save our people?" Thomas asked as Alastair drew back.

"No," Antonia's voice cracked as she shook her head. "Archon has cast his dark magic across his soldiers. It muffles my magic. I cannot force a passage through, not for a whole city."

Thomas's shoulders slumped, but to his credit, he displayed no other emotion. Alastair gritted his teeth, trying to keep his own despair from his face. They could not afford to show weakness in front of their people.

"I'm so sorry," Antonia whispered.

Anger flickered in Alastair's chest. "Damn your sorries, Antonia. Where is your brother? Where is Darius?"

Antonia's face darkened and a dangerous glint appeared in her eyes. Her tiny fists clenched and a faint light seeped between her fingers.

"Leave my brother out of this, Alastair," Antonia spoke with deliberate slowness.

Thomas stepped between them and attempted a smile. "Stop this, the two of you. It solves nothing," his voice was soft, but commanding.

Alastair sucked in a breath and allowed himself to relax. "You're right," he turned to Antonia. "You should leave, Antonia. You at least can survive to continue the fight. Gather a new army. Perhaps we can weaken his forces enough for you to stand a chance."

Antonia shook her head. "There is no hope there, Alastair. Mortal powers will not stop him. He toys with us, even now. There is only one hope. The Sword of Light."

A frown twisted Alastair's lips. "The Sword is in Kalgan, a thousand miles from here. And even were we able to reach it, there is no one to wield it."

The violet eyes of the Goddess caught Alastair's. "You know there is a way from Chole to Kalgan, Alastair, an ancient passage between the two cities."

An icy hand clenched around Alastair's gut. "You cannot be serious?"

"There is no other choice."

"Then there is no choice at all. The curse is too strong. Far better Magickers than me have tried to break through. None returned. The Way is certain death."

"No," Antonia growled. Her hand swept out, encompassing the endless armies of Archon. "*That* is certain death. Archon and his army will destroy everything we have created, and remake the world in his twisted image. The Way is our *only* chance."

"And you? What will you do, Antonia?"

"Jurrien and I will wait for you in Kalgan. I cannot take you on the paths we will walk, nor can I follow you through that ancient magic. So for now, we must part."

A tremble ran through Alastair's body. He clasped his hands together, struggling to find an alternative to Antonia's plan. But she was right. The Sword was their only hope, the only chance they had of victory. Both himself and Thomas were powerful Magickers. If either of them could do what no one in a hundred years had managed, and unlock the blade, they might stand a chance of turning back Archon's dark magic.

"I'll see you in Kalgan," Antonia whispered. Stepping forward, she hugged Alastair tight. "Thomas has the better chance, protect him with your life," her voice tingled in his ear.

Then she was stepping away, already fading from sight. For a moment, the scent of flowers hung heavy in the air. Then that too faded away, leaving only the stench of smoke and death.

"Let's go, Thomas," he said, turning to the king.

Thomas nodded. "One moment."

He waved one of his officers over, and after a quick conversation, returned to Alastair's side. "Let's go. They'll hold the wall for as long as they can. Let's not let them down."

Alastair nodded and led the king from the wall. They raced down the stone steps, their swords slapping at their sides. At the bottom, Alastair turned right, moving into the narrow alleyway between the buildings and the wall. Long grass grew from the soft earth, giving way beneath their boots. Alastair scanned the granite blocks as they moved, searching for the signs that marked The Way.

It had been years since he'd contemplated the ancient gateway. Few knew of its existence, but it was an old magic that formed a link between the cities of Kalgan and Chole, the capitals of the ancient nations of Lonia and Trola. After the coming of the Gods, the southern lands had become Plorsea, and Lonia's capital had been shifted to the coast.

A war horn sounded from above, followed by the muffled cries of the enemy charge. Alastair picked up the pace as bowstrings twanged. Time was running short.

Finally, Alastair drew to a stop and faced the wall. Here thick vines covered the stony surface, their white blossoms glowing in the light of the moon. They swayed gently in the breeze, moving like snakes across the ancient granite.

"Why have we stopped?" Thomas hissed beside him.

"We're here," Alastair replied. "These vines conceal the

path we must take. Only magic can make them reveal the path."

Thomas smiled. "Then allow me."

Stepping forward, he placed his hand on one of the vines. His face did not change as he stared at the thorny tendrils, but slowly his breathing softened. A ripple went through the vines, and a faint green glow lit the alleyway. Slowly they curled back on themselves, slivering outwards, obeying the silent call of Thomas's earth magic.

Beneath was not the solid stone of the city walls, but an empty abyss, stretching away into oblivion. A strange light bathed their faces, and Alastair felt the dark pull of its power on his soul.

"Beware, Thomas," Alastair said softly. "The magic was corrupted by Archon's coming. Keep your soul closed, or it will destroy you."

"Where does it lead?" the king asked.

"We'll find out soon enough," Alastair's voice was bleak. It was likely whatever waited on the other side would be the last thing either of them saw.

But there was no time for second thoughts now. Sucking in a breath, Alastair stepped into the abyss.

CHAPTER 11

As Alastair crossed the threshold, a twisted rainbow streaked across his vision. The world spun, and suddenly he was falling. A sharp screech drilled into his eardrums and he tasted blood.

Gritting his teeth, he endured.

A second later, thunder clapped, and he struck the ground with a bone jarring thump.

Groaning, Alastair struggled to keep himself from throwing up. Slowly his senses returned and he opened his eyes to look around for Thomas. His vision blurred, but after several moments, the world clicked back into focus. He stared, open mouthed, unable to comprehend the sight that greeted him.

The ground around him was littered with the bones of long-dead men and women. Empty eye sockets stared at him from human skulls, toothy grins frozen on their stark white faces. Thomas crouched nearby, his face pale and eyes wide as he took in the nightmare they'd fallen into.

A blood-red sky stretched overhead, its infinite expanse unmarked by clouds or sun or stars. Sheer cliffs rose around them, their bleached white stone surrounding them in every direction bar one. A path led down the hill, threading its way between the piles of bones.

"What is this place?" Thomas's voice shook.

"The Way," Alastair said, standing. "We had better move quickly. Time passes differently here, and we have none to waste."

Thomas nodded, brushing off the dust of the dead. His hands trembled as he picked himself up.

"Follow me," Alastair started off down the path, his boots crunching on the shards of broken bones. "Stay alert, who knows what lurks in this realm."

"What happened here, Alastair?" Thomas's voice was steady now.

Alastair sighed. "The Way was once a wholesome place. It served as a neutral ground for negotiations between Lonia and Trola. Only a few souls are able to enter at one time, so there was no way one nation could ambush the embassy of another."

"But how did it become… *this?*"

"A curse. For a long time, no one understood who or what had caused it. We know now it was Archon. Dark magic has corrupted everything in this land, sucking the life from it. Your magic is useless here, only the raw energy of the Light can pierce the darkness of the curse."

Thomas loosened his sword. "Then we will rely on your powers – and our steel."

Alastair nodded. "Something waits out here. No one has passed this way in four hundred years and lived to talk about it."

Thomas fell silent. They plodded on, their progress witnessed only by the glares of empty skulls.

~

ALASTAIR DREW TO A STOP, his weary legs groaning with the pain of the long march. Without the sun or stars to aid him, he had lost all track of time. But looking out across the canyon, he knew they had finally reached the end of their journey.

A granite arch stood guard at the end of the canyon. Flowers were etched across the stone, entwining one over another in an endless pattern. Fog drifted in the air behind the arch, concealing what lay beyond. It could only be the exit.

His heart would have soared, if not for the creature barring their path. It stood beneath the archway, the living embodiment of Archon's curse. Empty eye sockets glared at them from the naked skull, held aloft by a crooked spine. A grin stretched across its yellowed jaw, brandishing its broken teeth. Bones rattled as a skeletal arm reached down and drew a rusty scimitar.

Alastair felt the cliffs closing in on him. A weight settled on his shoulders as he watched the creature step towards them. This was the monster that had slaughtered all those who had come before them. Now it sought their lives, and Alastair doubted there was anything he could do to stop it.

"Stay behind me, Thomas," Alastair whispered from the corner of his mouth.

He started forward again, his eyes never leaving the undead skeleton. As he walked, he drew his short sword. Power swelled inside him as he gathered his magic. On the wall he had held it back, knowing it would be needed later.

Now that time had come, though he was no longer sure it would make a difference.

"Out of my way, damned spawn of hell," Alastair boomed.

His voice echoed back and forth off the crumbling stone,

slowly dying away, until it seemed some old man had spoken the words.

A dry, rasping cackle came from the undead creature, and it raised its blade in mock salute.

Alastair grimaced, and then turned his mind inwards. His magic leapt in response, an old associate, eager to give its aid. Power surged through his veins, feeding fresh strength to his weary limbs, focusing his mind. Raising his fist, Alastair allowed his thoughts to spread beyond himself, to the world all around him.

With a collective groan, stony boulders rose from the floor of the narrow canyon. Pressure throbbed in Alastair's mind as he threw out his arm. As one, the boulders shot forward, accelerating towards their dark foe.

The skull's grin widened. It too raised a hand, but Alastair's projectiles hurtled onwards. Twenty feet, then ten, then five. Grinning, Alastair gave one final push.

An earth-shattering *crack* tore the air as the boulders disintegrated. Slivers of burning rock flew across the canyon, burying themselves in the cliffs, and the stench of burning rock rent the air.

Alastair staggered back, the aftershock of his failed magic tearing through his mind. As he started to fall, strong arms reached out and caught him. Through the agony, he heard the creature's mocking laughter. Footsteps crunched on gravel as it started towards them.

Cursing, Alastair straightened and pushed Thomas back. He gripped his sword and regathered his scattered magic. Screaming his anger, he swept out an arm, and magic surged away from him.

The skeleton rose ponderously from the ground, its bony limbs swinging wildly at empty air. Alastair gave a violent gesture, and sent it hurtling into the canyon wall. Dust exploded outwards as it struck

But when the dust cleared, the skeleton had already regained its feet. With slow, deliberate steps, it continued towards them.

Alastair hardened his grip on his sword. His attacks had not even phased it.

"We cannot win this fight, Thomas. I do not have the power. But I can distract it while you make a break for the gateway."

Thomas shook his head, but Alastair cut off his response. "It's our only chance. One of us must reach Kalgan – and Antonia thinks it must be you."

Thomas fell silent at that, and Alastair prayed the stubborn king would do as he was told. Squaring his shoulders, he strode towards the approaching creature, sword held loosely in one hand, magic crackling in the other.

The skeleton drew to a stop when only a few steps remained between them. "Yield, and your deaths will be quick," its voice grated like nails on a chalkboard.

Alastair answered with steel.

Steel shrieked as their blades met, sparks flying in the dusty air. Alastair jumped back as the scimitar reversed its cut, but its tip still tore through his cloak, narrowly missing his flesh. He swore and slashed out again. The rusty blade spun to block and their blades met with a boom of steel and magic.

The creature pressed forward, but Alastair dove to the side and its blade whistled over his head. Stones ground through his cloak as he rolled and came back to his feet. His foe turned to follow him, and Thomas darted past.

Alastair allowed himself a smile, and almost lost an arm for it. Time faded away, as threw everything he had into the frantic battle with the creature. His sword became a blur, each movement sheer instinct, each attack pure desperation.

Yet still it was not enough. Each swing of the creature's bony arm brought the rusted scimitar closer to his flesh.

When an attack finally slipped past his guard, Alastair had no chance to retreat. The rusted blade flashed out, its blunted tip tearing through clothe and chainmail, and lancing deep into his side. He shrieked as red-hot agony tore through his body.

Grinning, the creature twisted the blade. The strength fled Alastair as the steel tore deeper, and the sword slipped from his fingers. He collapsed to his knees as the skeleton jerked back its bloodied sword. Cackling, it lifted the blade over Alastair's head.

The rattle of gravel was all that gave Thomas away. Hissing, the skeleton spun, catching Thomas's desperate attack on the curve of its scimitar. Then it was on the attack, its blade flashing for Thomas in a narrow ark. The king retreated, his sword twisting out to deflect the blow. But with a sharp crack, the blade shattered, and he staggered backwards, still holding the now useless weapon out in front of him.

Growling, the skeleton raised its scimitar.

"*No!*" Alastair screamed.

The magic rushed from him in a flood. It struck the skeleton like a fist of iron and flung it backwards into the cliff-face. It disappeared into a cloud of dust and falling rock.

Thomas rushed to Alastair's side and hauled him to his feet. With his spare hand, he swept up Alastair's sword, and then the two of them staggered toward the archway. The distance seemed to grow with every step. Exhausted and in agony, it was all Alastair could do to stay conscious.

"Leave me, you fool," he croaked.

He could feel the king's strength fading, but Thomas staggered on, ignoring his pleas. Glancing back, Alastair saw the skeleton step from the dust cloud. Dark rage twisted its yellowed jaw.

"For that, your deaths will last for eternity," the ground shook with the creature's anger. Above, cracks spread along the cliff-face and stones rattled down to the canyon floor.

For every step they took, the skeleton took three. The click of its bony joints echoed down the canyon as it closed on them. Alastair begged again for Thomas to leave him, but the king pressed on, his lips drawn tight. The archway grew slowly closer.

Then, with a deafening roar, the cliff-face the creature had struck broke free. They looked back in time to see an avalanche of stone come crashing down on the skeleton, burying it beneath a mountain of rubble.

Thomas and Alastair watched as the landslide continued towards them. Turning, they stumbled for the exit, passing through the arch as the first tumbling rocks reached them. Mist rose up to greet them, and at its touch, the world turned to blazing white.

Safe, the word echoed through Alastair's mind.

As the white faded, the citadel of Kalgan took shape around them. Alastair stared at the great grass lawns of the inner keep, not quite able to believe they had made it. The night sky stretched overhead, studded by stars, clear of the choking smoke that surrounded Chole. The seamless granite walls of the keep rose around them, and somewhere in the darkness an owl hooted. A cool breeze pressed against Alastair's cheek, carrying with it the salty tang of the ocean.

A crystal case stood in the centre of the lawns. Within, throbbing with a soft white glow, was the Sword of Light. It stood tip down, its three-foot blade silver in the moonlight. Its hilt provided a two-handed grip and was bound by hard leather. A great diamond decorated the pommel, shining like a miniature sun.

"*You made it!*" a girl's shriek pierced the night.

Antonia came sprinting across the lawn towards them.

Alastair winced, bracing himself as he watched her hurtle towards them, angling himself to protect his wound. But at the last second, she skidded to a stop. The smile fell from her face, concern replacing joy.

"Are you okay?"

Alastair grunted, fighting to stay conscious. His legs buckled, but Thomas kept him upright.

"He's been stabbed," the king answered for him.

Antonia nodded. Moving forward, she laid a hand on Alastair's wound. Warmth flooded his side. He watched Antonia's youthful face as she closed her eyes. Pinpricks danced across his wound, but he kept his eyes carefully averted. The sight of his own flesh knitting itself back together tended to make him retch.

When Antonia removed her hand, Alastair finally allowed himself to look down. His flesh was whole, his pain gone, and with a sigh he took his arm from Thomas's shoulder.

"Thank you, Antonia," he looked at The Sword of Light. "What now?"

"Now..." the Goddess hesitated.

"Now Thomas must take up The Sword," a new voice carried across the grass, weary, but laced with power. "If Darius meant anyone to use it, it would be the kings of Trola. I know your father tried, Thomas, but age had stripped him of his strength. I believe you are strong enough to succeed, where he failed."

They turned as Jurrien strode across the lawns. The Storm God had seen better days. Exhaustion lined his face, and his skin was a sickly yellow. But determination shone from his icy blue eyes as he joined them, and there was a spring in his step that had been missing since the battle of the Gap.

He drew up beside Antonia. "You must do it now,

Thomas. You have been gone for over an hour. Chole won't last much longer."

Thomas nodded. His jaw clenched and his eyes locked on the Sword of Light. He knew the risks. If Jurrien was wrong, the Sword would burn him to dust. But Thomas did not hesitate. Clenching Alastair's sword to his side, he approached the case. A powerful spell had been cast on the crystal to protect the Sword, but Alastair's blade was infused with spells of its own, and lifting the blade above his head, Thomas brought it down on the case. Light flashed, followed by the soft tinkling of a thousand crystals falling.

Dropping Alastair's weapon, Thomas stretched out a hand and wrapped his fingers around the hilt of the Sword of Light. His hands shook as he lifted it from the case and turned to face them.

Then his body jerked and his mouth fell open. His wide eyes stared across at them, unseeing, as light flashed from the blade.

Heart racing, Alastair made to step towards the king, but Jurrien's hand on his shoulder held him back. They stared as another tremor went through Thomas. A silent battle was taking place within the king, and there was nothing any of them could do to help.

Suddenly Thomas's body went limp and his eyes fluttered closed. For a moment nothing happened, then the Sword flashed again, and Thomas straightened.

The tension fled Alastair as the king smiled. Antonia grinned, already moving to the king's side. Reaching out, she grasped his wrist.

"Well done, Thomas. Your ancestor, Artemis, would be proud," she straightened, turning back to Jurrien. "Are you ready, brother?"

Jurrien nodded. "I'll manage. Let's get this over with."

"What do you need me to do?" Thomas asked.

"We need you to link the power of the Sword with ours," Antonia answered. "We'll do the rest."

"How?"

"Spread out," Antonia and Jurrien stepped back, creating a triangle between the three of them. Alastair backed away.

"Call on the Sword's magic the same way you do your own, Thomas. When you feel it respond, focus it into the centre of the triangle. Like this." Closing her eyes, Antonia held out her arm towards the centre of their triangle.

Alastair shivered as green light flowed from her arm. It swirled around the boundaries of the triangle, the embodiment of the Earth itself. As he stared into its depths, Alastair glimpsed long rolling hills and ancient forests stretching towards the sky.

Jurrien went next. He did not bother to raise his arm: blue light seeped from his entire body, the power of the Sky leaping out to meet the Earth. A low growl echoed across the citadel as the powers came together, and the image of a stormy sky flashed through Alastair's mind.

Then Thomas raised the Sword. A frown marked his forehead as he closed his eyes. The glow of the Sword of Light flickered and brightened. Thomas opened his eyes as white light crackled from the blade and poured into the centre of the triangle, joining the whirling tide of God magic.

The conflagration flickered, the colours changing from blue to green to white, and then all at once. The energy bubbled, leaping and pushing against some invisible barrier, seeking escape. It stretched higher, towering over them, a column of pure, unimaginable power.

"Now!" yelled Antonia.

The column burst and the flickering light shot upwards. A thousand feet above, the magic shattered, and a million colours flooded outwards across the night's sky.

In that instant, Alastair glimpsed a shadow from the

corner of his eyes, sliding across the grass towards the trio. He turned, seeking the source, but they were alone on the lawns, and he dismissed it as some trick of the light.

Staring up at the sky, his heart soared, the weight lifting from his shoulders. This was the end of Archon. With the God's power over the three Elements restored, they were invincible. It was time to stop jumping at shadows.

At that, Eric watched the image fade, slowly giving way to black, and he fell away into sleep.

CHAPTER 12

The next morning, Eric woke to a long, wet tongue dragging across his face. Screaming in disgust, he rolled away. When he opened his eyes, he found the long snouts and friendly eyes of the horses staring down at him. They shook their heads and snorted, the sound almost like laughter, and then ambled off.

"Good morning, Eric," Alastair called. "How was your night?"

Eric sat bolt upright and looked around. Alastair stood nearby, poking a stick into a freshly lit fire where a rack of sausages hung over the flames. The sun was still low on the horizon, colouring the sky a bright orange, but Eric could already feel the heat of the desert touching his face.

"Where did she go?" he asked as he stumbled to his feet.

Other than himself and Alastair, the campsite was empty. The only sign the Goddess had ever been there was the Azalea bush. It stood out in stark contrast to the barren desert around them, a reminder of Antonia's power.

"Our unexpected visitor?" Alastair smiled. "She doesn't tend to hang around long."

Eric stared at Alastair, then in two steps closed the distance between them and pulled the old man into an embrace. His eyes stung, but he did not cry; there had been enough tears the night before. He was surprised at the strength of his relief. While he had only known Alastair a couple of days, his fate was inescapably bound to the old man now. Alastair had lifted him from the depths of his despair, offered him hope and purpose.

"Glad to see you too, Eric," Alastair laughed.

Eric smiled as he released him. "You didn't mention you were on a first name basis with the Goddess of Plorsea."

"Yes, well, we have a complicated past," he turned away to retrieve the sausages from the fire, and then handed one to Eric.

Eric took the offered sausage carefully between his fingers, wincing at the heat, but his stomach was growling and he carefully took a bite.

"I know," he muttered after he swallowed. "She showed me Archon's war. I knew you were old, but who knew you were so *ancient*?"

Alastair scowled. "Old, and a great deal wiser than you, boy. How much did she show you?"

"She showed me your journey through the Way, and how Thomas and the Gods cast the spell to banish Archon."

"I see. And did you see what happened afterwards?"

Eric shook his head.

"Typical Antonia, always leaving out the finer details. It was the clash between Archon and the God magic that created *those*," he pointed at the trio of volcanoes marring the horizon. "The collision of magic tore the crust of the earth itself, releasing the pent-up forces beneath. The three cursed peaks were the result."

Eric shivered. "I see."

"Do you see the lesson there, though?" Alastair probed.

Frowning, Eric fell silent, and Alastair continued. "Even pure magic, cast with good intentions, can have disastrous results. Nature is infinitely complex, and magic is only a small part of that complexity. The smallest act can set in motion a chain of events that not even the wisest of Magickers could predict."

"So the *Gods* created this desert?"

"That was a part of it. The peaks create a rain shadow over Chole, cutting it off from the moisture laden air from the oceans. But the severity of the desert was Archon's last curse. The God magic was enough to banish him and shatter his armies, but without Darius' total mastery of the Light, it could not destroy all trace of the dark Magicker. His evil lingers here, a final curse over the land and everything in it."

"What happened to the king, after he used the Sword?"

"Thomas returned to Trola and lived a good life. Then he died," Alastair said softly.

Eric's neck tingled at the way Alastair spoke the words. There was something in the old Magicker's tone that suggested there was more to the story.

"How did he die?"

Alastair sighed. He turned to stare out at the horizon. "He was a good man, Eric. And a good king. He dedicated his life to healing the damage left by Archon's war. He travelled often, working to strengthen the unity between the Three Nations. He even visited the wildlands of each nation – including Dragon Country. It was there that he met his end."

"How?" Eric breathed.

"Thomas's Earth magic allowed him to befriend most living creatures. He was there negotiating a pact with the Gold Dragons, an alliance ensuring their support if the Three Nations were ever threatened again."

"And they killed him?"

"No," Alastair whispered. "No, Thomas and his people met the dragon tribe in Malevolent cove. The treaty was signed, and the dragons departed in peace. It was then… it was then that something went wrong."

"You weren't there?" Eric asked.

"No," Alastair bowed his head. "Fool that I was, I left Thomas in the care of younger Magickers, and started a new life for myself in Lonia. I travelled to Malevolent cove afterwards, once word of what had happened reached me. But by then it was far too late."

"What happened?"

"An ambush, I think. The king's party were found dead – some slain by a sword, others without a mark on them. But Thomas was not with them. I searched for weeks for my friend, but I never found so much as a trace."

Eric swallowed. "And the Sword of Light?"

"It had remained in Kalgan, and passed to his oldest child, and his grandchild after that, and so on until today."

There was a sense of finality in Alastair's words as the old man stood. Moving around the camp, he started to pack the last of their belongings into Briar's saddlebags, leaving Eric to ponder his words.

"We'd better get moving," Alastair said at last. Without waiting for a reply, he swung himself up into Elcano's saddle. "We still have one more night in this desert left to survive, let's not make it two."

Eric sighed and quickly scrambled onto Briar's back. He was getting better at it now, but he could still sense Alastair's amusement. Straightening, he looked across at Alastair. "You still haven't said who you're looking for."

"Antonia did not tell you?"

"No," Eric looked Alastair straight in the eye. "Who is it, Alastair?"

A smile tugged at the old man's lips. "A family," he said. "That's all you need to know for now."

At that, he gave Elcano a kick, and with a shrill whiney, the horse took off into the desert, leaving a dust cloud in his wake. Coughing, Eric pointed Briar after the old man and covered his mouth with the collar of his cloak. Ahead, Alastair checked his speed, allowing them to catch up, before turning and continuing at a slower pace.

GABRIEL JOGGED across the barren plain, his long legs carrying him easily across the dry earth. He held his sword in one hand and his waterskin in the other as he ran. The waterskin was already half empty, but the wolf promised it could find more.

The burning sun dominated the horizon, and the distant peaks cast their long shadows across the plain. As he ran he scanned the desert around him, though he knew his quarry was still at least half a day ahead. The wolf loped effortlessly alongside him, tongue panting in the scorching air. It was never far from his side now.

They had headed off an hour before sunrise, Gabriel's impatience finally winning out over caution. The night had been long, his dreams haunted by monsters that chased him through the darkness. Faces came and went, most unknown to him. He was glad to finally wake, and cast them back into the darkness.

They came across the campsite around midday, but Gabriel could make little sense of what they found. Three sets of footsteps were evident on the dusty ground, though the third set could only have come from a child. Stranger still, there were hints of a fight – long claw marks in the gravel, a congealing pool of blood, and shattered boulders.

Most confusing of all, an azalea bush stood in the centre of the campsite, its pink blossoms shining in the hot sun. Their sweet scent filled the air, and for a second something fluttered in Gabriel's chest. The hate that clenched his heart melted away, and he felt the pain of all he had lost seep through.

They have already left, hours ago. We must move on, the wolf's growl cut through Gabriel's pain, and the hate came rushing back.

Nodding, Gabriel set off again. The crumbling path threaded its way through the desert, between dusty boulders and petrified trees, often splitting in two or disappearing altogether. If not for the wolf, he would have lost his way within an hour. As it was, he was left to follow helplessly in its wake.

Yes, they came this way, the wolf whispered as they moved. *Not far now, not far.*

As the day drew on, Gabriel found even his newfound energy fading beneath the heat of the sun. He slowed, his sword growing heavy, his throat parched. By mid-afternoon his legs were burning, and each step had become an agony. Still he pushed on.

As his thoughts drifted, an image flickered through his mind, and for a moment he found himself in a tiny room, standing before a great furnace, his arms up to their elbows in thick leather gloves. He clutched a pair of steel tongs in his hands, a horseshoe glowing in their iron grip. A man larger than life stood beside him, his giant grin hidden beneath a woolly beard. The roar of the furnace filled his ears, and his chest swelled.

Then the image faded, and Gabriel groaned as he found himself on his knees. He closed his eyes again, searching for the image, the memory, but it was gone.

At his side, the wolf growled. *They are escaping.*

Gabriel swore, remembering his prey. He leapt to his feet, his exhaustion forgotten. He still remembered one thing. He could see their faces with crystal clarity.

Kill the ones who hurt you!

~

INKEN LAY on the hard desert ground, her body a mess of agony. Sharp rocks stabbed through her thin clothing, digging into her skin, and the pounding in her head was growing worse. Her mouth was parched and her thoughts jumbled and confused. A groan rattled up from deep in her chest at the thought of water, but her waterskin was long gone, and she could no longer muster the strength to stand.

The shortcut across the desert had been ill-advised to say the least. Yet it had been her only chance to reach Oaksville before the other hunters. If only she had left three nights ago, when the messenger pigeon had first flown into Chole. Within hours the city's underground was abuzz with the news – that a massive bounty had been offered for the head of a demon boy said to have burned Oaksville to the ground.

Inken, like most, had scoffed at the news at first. The letters had to be a hoax; the idea of such an attack on Oaksville was ridiculous. But over the next few days, more birds had followed, confirming the city's plight. Oaksville had been attacked – first by magic, then by Baronian raiders.

By the time Inken decided to try her hand at the commission, half the bounty hunters in Chole were already well ahead of her. But she knew they would not dare to take the desert path. The short cut would shave at least a day off the journey, allowing her to overtake the other hunters. She had scoffed at the superstitious fear that blinded the others, confident her longsword and bow were enough to fend off any trouble.

How arrogant she had been. The childhood tales should have warned her. The people of Chole made no secret of the dangers lurking outside the city walls – but Inken had dismissed them as legend, as fears long since rendered void by the ending of Archon's war.

It had not taken long for the truth behind the tales to reveal itself. If not for her horse, she would have been finished in those first few minutes. Before she had even realised her danger, the gelding had reared up on its hind legs and bolted, leaving Inken clinging desperately to the saddle horn.

It was only then she had seen the beast. It exploded from the earth beside the trail, its short yellow fur blending perfectly with the scorched ground. Powerful muscles propelled it after them on all fours, its claws digging deep into the hard ground. Even on four legs, it stood as tall as her horse, with jaws large enough to crush her skull.

The chase seemed to last hours. Only an inch separated the two beasts, and all Inken could do was close her eyes and hang on.

She wasn't sure when the beast had finally given up, only that when she finally looked back again, it had vanished.

But her horse galloped on, its eyes wild and mouth foaming in its frenzy to escape the creature. She tugged desperately at the reins, eager to slow their pace in the treacherous terrain. But the gelding plunged onward, oblivious to everything but its terror.

Then the horse was falling, tripping over the uneven ground, and Inken was flying from the saddle. The earth rushed up to meet her, and all she could do was raise her arms to protect herself. She struck with a jarring thud, following by a searing pain as something went *crack.* Her momentum sent her tumbling over the jagged rocks, her head and chest and legs slamming into unseen rocks, before she finally came to a rest in a broken pile of flesh and bone.

The horse screamed again, struggling to rise behind her. Inken struggled to sit up, but pain swept through her, and she collapsed back to the ground. She glimpsed the terrified animal from the corner of her eye. Its front leg was bent at a sickening angle.

Darkness swept across Inken's vision then, and she had gladly given way to the respite of unconsciousness.

When she woke again, the horse's screaming had ceased. Looking across, she saw its still body lying next to her, its glassy eyes staring into nothing.

Inken had closed her eyes then, willing strength into her shattered body. Summoning her courage, she struggled to her feet. Agony lanced through her right leg and she knew it was broken. The rest of her was a mess of red and blue. Her arms looked as though someone had flayed the skin from her body. Her nose throbbed, and bracing herself, she reached up to twist it back into place. The cartilage gave a sickening crack, but the relief was immediate.

Somehow, she had started hobbling back towards the road. For hours she had walked, unarmed and without food or water. Her weapons and saddlebags had been dislodged during the chase. With every agonised step she expected the beast to reappear and finish her, but the desert remained empty. Somehow, she had survived.

But now she was finished. An hour ago she had fallen, and she no longer had the strength to get back up. The pain was unbearable, and her energy had long since melted away in the sun's heat.

Fool, she cursed herself. *How could you have been so arrogant?*

Lying helpless in the baking sun, Inken waited for death.

It didn't seem right for it to end like this. She was still only nineteen, yet to reach her twentieth birthday. But of course, life was never fair. She knew that better than most. Fair would have been two loving parents, rather than a mother who abandoned her to an abusive father. The old drunk would be laughing now – he had always said she would amount to nothing.

She blinked as a sound came from her left. Opening her eyes, she looked around, expecting to see the yellowed eyes of the feline come to finish her. Instead, she saw two horsemen trotting past, not five yards away.

"Help!" Inken tried to shout, but her throat was so dry the word came out as a whisper.

"Help me!" She tried again, louder this time. "Please!"

"ALASTAIR, why did my magic only... awaken... when I turned fifteen?" The question had plagued Eric for a long time.

"So late?" Alastair asked from the back of Elcano.

Eric nodded.

"Most develop earlier, but that is in families with a long lineage of magic." As they rode his eyes scanned the ground ahead, seeking out signs of predators. "Magic always awakens on the anniversary of our births, but which birthday that is depends on the individual and the environment they've been exposed too. The more magic you are in contact with in childhood, the faster your own will develop."

"Okay," Eric fell silent again, his thoughts lost in the past, and what might have been.

They continued across the desert at a fast trot, their horse's hooves eating up the rocky miles one after the other. Behind them, the sun dropped towards the distant horizon, casting long shadows across the plains. Eventually Alastair slowed their pace to a walk, taking care on the rough terrain.

"The spring isn't far now," Alastair reassured him.

Before Eric could reply, he heard a rattle of stones from away to their left. He pulled up on Briar's reins and turned towards the sound, a frown deepening his brow. Dropping his hand to the hilt of his dagger, he scanned the ground, searching for movement.

"Help me," the call was so soft, Eric thought he might have imagined it, until it came again. "Help!"

The hairs on the back of his neck prickled as he searched for the source. The voice had been distinctly human, and female, but who would be mad enough to venture this far into the desert? Other than themselves, of course.

Eric was about to give up when one of the rocks seemed to move. The next instant he realised he'd been staring straight at her. The dull brown jacket and leggings she wore blended in with the dirt and baked stone, so that she seemed a part of the desert itself.

"Alastair!" he cried as he nudged Briar off the trail.

The young woman's hazel eyes followed him as he approached. Eric shuddered as he drew close enough to take in her injuries. Her scarlet hair was matted with dirt and blood, and a dried trail of blood ran from her scalp. Tears in her jacket revealed bloody wounds and purple bruises, while her leg lay twisted at an awful angle. The relentless sun had burned her skin bright red. Her eyes were swollen, and ringed by dark shadows.

As Eric drew up beside her she struggled to sit up. Her courage shocked him – he could not imagine the will-power it would take to overcome her injuries. But it was not enough, and with a low whimper she slid back to the ground. Her eyes closed as Eric reached her. Her body began to shake.

Alastair dismounted behind him and the two crouched

beside her. Pulling out his waterskin, Alastair cradled her head in his hands and held the skin to her lips. Tipping it gently, he allowed a small amount to trickle into her mouth.

After a few swallows the girl started to cough, and Alastair withdrew the skin. "Don't speak, girl. Save your strength."

Eric pulled a blanket from his saddle and covered her, hoping it would help protect her from the sun. He wondered what had happened to her, and how she had come so far into the desert without food or water, and only the knife strapped at her side for protection.

Alastair gave her another gulp of water and then replaced the cap on his waterskin. "That's enough for now. Anymore and you'll be sick."

"Thank you," somehow she managed a smile, her parched lips cracking with the movement. "I'm Inken." Her eyes closed again.

"Eric, help me with her. We will have to be very careful, who knows what injuries she has. I'll ride with her on my horse. We need to get her to the spring. She needs water and broth to replace the salt she's lost in the sun."

"Will she make it?"

"I don't know. Her best chance is if we get her to the spring. It's not far." They knelt on either side of her and draped her arms over their shoulders. "Careful, this arm is broken. You'll need to take most of her weight."

"What do you think happened to her?"

"We'll have to ask her that when she wakes. Now help me get her on Elcano."

Eric carefully took her weight on his shoulder. For a small woman she was heavy, her arms and legs thickly muscled. He wondered again who she was, and what she had been doing out in the desert alone.

Together they managed to get her slung over Elcano's saddle. Alastair climbed up behind her, and Eric helped to arrange her so she would not fall. Then he mounted Briar, and they set off again, keeping their pace slow and steady. Behind them, the sun slowly set, staining the horizon red.

CHAPTER 13

Eric poked restlessly at the fire with a stray piece of wood. Dust and sand had worked its way into every seam of his clothing, and however he sat he could not get comfortable on the rocky ground. His aching backside was relieved to be free of Briar's bouncing saddle, but now he found himself on edge. Staring out into the darkness, he could only imagine what dread beasts might be staring back.

At least they'd found the spring. Water trickled down a nearby rock face and slowly gathered in a bowl of loose soil at its base. They had almost emptied the pool filling their waterskins, and now Briar and Elcano stood nearby, waiting patiently for their turn to drink.

A rocky escarpment hemmed them in on three sides, hiding their fire from prying eyes. An eerie silence hung over the campsite, and the pop of the fire echoed loudly in the darkness.

The girl, Inken, lay nearby, shivering by the fire. They had covered her with blankets and managed to give her more water, but she still had not stirred. Her hair blazed red in the firelight, its glow strangely mesmerising. The hard lines in her young face had softened with sleep, and her chest rose and fell in a gentle rhythm.

They had cleaned the sand from the worst of her wounds and bound her broken arm and leg to branches they had scavenged from the long dead trees scattered through the desert. There was little more they could do for her now, not until they reached Chole and found a healer.

Alastair sat stirring the pot of stew he had just taken from the fire. Earlier he had added the last of their food to the mix, little more than a sprinkling of vegetables and salted pork. If Inken woke, she would need the sustenance, and even Eric was beginning to weaken from lack of food.

Placing the pot back over the fire, Alastair looked across at Eric. "Still needs some more time. I'm going to check to see if our fire is properly hidden. I don't want any more surprises."

Eric shivered. "Okay, I'll keep an eye on her. Be careful."

He watched Alastair disappear into the night and then returned his gaze to the young woman.

What were you doing out here?

While Inken was a few inches taller than him, she could not have been much older than his own seventeen years. The skin of her hands was rough and lines marked her brow, suggesting a hard life, but even so, he could not begin to imagine what might have driven her out here.

Still, with luck she would recover from this. The temples of the Earth were renowned for their healers, although whether the temple in Chole still survived was another matter. With the city fallen into disrepute, he would not have blamed the priests for leaving.

Eric added their last stick to the fire. Alastair had hacked the branches from one of the fallen trees when they'd first arrived at the spring. The heat and dust of the desert had turned the ancient logs the colour of rock, but beneath they were still wood, desiccated by time into the perfect firewood.

"Who are you?"

Eric jumped, sending sparks skittering from the fire. A giggle came from the pile of blankets, rich and good-natured, but quickly trailing off into a groan. "Oh, I shouldn't have done that!"

Standing, Eric walked around the fire to sit beside Inken. In the flickering light, he saw that one of the gashes on her face had split and was bleeding again. He offered her the waterskin and then gently pressed a damp cloth to her face to stem the bleeding.

Inken accept the skin and took a long gulp. She didn't flinch as Eric wiped the blood from her cheek, but her eyes never left his face. When she finished drinking, she replaced the cap on the skin and handed it back. "Water never tasted so good."

Eric smiled. Taking the skin, he took a seat across from her. Inken's eyes were sharp now, and Eric could almost see the questions ticking through her mind.

"Thank you, kind stranger." Her big hazel eyes stared across at him. "Sorry for my lack of manners just then. May I ask who you are?"

Despite his misgivings, Eric found himself grinning. "My name is Eric and my old friend is Alastair. We're travelling to Chole. You're lucky we saw you as we passed. What were you doing out here?"

Inken offered him her good hand, and Eric took it gently. "Thank you, Eric, I owe you my life. I made the foolish mistake of trying to reach Oaksville by the desert trail. I was lucky my mare outran the beast that ambushed us, but she didn't make it. When she fell, it nearly killed us both."

Eric stilled at the mention of Oaksville. His heart began to pound and he scarcely heard the rest of her story. He swallowed, trying to find a way to break the news to her, already seeing the grief and tears that would fill her eyes.

"I'm sorry, Inken," he croaked at last. "I don't know how to say this, but we came from Oaksville. There wasn't much left."

Inken nodded and her face tightened. "Argh, everything hurts," she shook her head. "I know what happened to Oaksville. The town's Magistrate sent a pigeon. He offered a lot of gold for the head of the demon who did it. I was hoping to claim it."

Eric's blood ran cold. The muscles of his neck tightened as he stared at the girl. Suddenly he saw Inken in a whole new light. The lines of her face seemed to harden, and a dark glint appeared in her eyes. The muscular curves of her body lost their sensuality, becoming those of a warrior, a hunter.

His eyes flickered to the dagger at her side. Her fingers lingered near its hilt. Suddenly he wished they'd disarmed her while she lay unconscious. An icy hand seized his heart.

What if she finds out who I am?

He realised he was staring and gave himself a mental shake. "You're a brave woman, to hunt a demon."

Inken chuckled. "I'm no longer sure if I was brave, or stupid. Trying to tackle the desert alone was bad enough. I had given up hope when you appeared. And I don't have a chance in hell of claiming the reward now."

"Perhaps it's for the best. What would you have done against a demon anyway?"

Inken absently flicked a strand of hair from her face. "Demon, Magicker, or mortal, an arrow from the shadows will kill most things."

Eric gulped, his voice deserting him.

Before the silence could stretch too long, Alastair reappeared. He strode across the rocky ground, his footsteps little more than a whisper, and sat down opposite them. A pile of firewood tumbled to the ground beside him.

"Hello," Inken greeted. "You must be Alastair."

Alastair smiled. "I am, and you are Inken."

She nodded. "So why are the two of you travelling to Chole?"

When Alastair did not reply, Eric answered for him. "Alastair has someone to meet," he said shortly. "I'm just along for the ride."

Inken nodded, her hazel eyes studying him with a strange intensity. Eric tried to keep the fear from his face. Despite her injuries, he did not like the idea of the woman hunting him. She had the look of someone who was good at her job.

Shifting back to his seat on the rocky ground, he leaned back and closed his eyes. The world seemed to rock beneath him, as though he were still in Briar's saddle, and he quickly opened his eyes again. Beside the fire, Alastair stirred the pot of stew and then added more wood to the flames. Eric licked his lips as the rich aroma of broiled meat drifted across to him.

His eyes slid past Alastair to where Inken lay in her pile of blankets. Her eyes were closed again, though he doubted she was asleep. Her brow was drawn tight and her eyelids flickered. Despite her quest to kill him, or perhaps because of it, Eric felt a strange connection between himself and the enigmatic woman. Her very presence made his heart race, though whether from fear or something else, he could not tell.

"It's ready," Alastair announced.

Eric sat up and took the wooden bowl Alastair offered him.

"Give it to Inken," he said.

Eric nodded reluctantly and moved across to the injured

woman. Her eyes snapped opened as he approached, but she smiled when she saw him. "Ahhh, my hero returns. And with *food*."

Eric found his smile as he offered the bowl.

Inken reached out to take it, and then hesitated. Her cheeks flushed red. "I'm not sure I can hold it," she opened her hands to show the raw flesh of her palms. "Do you… do you think you could help me?" her blushed deepened. This was a girl used to taking care of herself.

Eric's face grew hot. Just sitting near the young woman was making him nervous. His thoughts scattered around his head and he managed to stutter something incomprehensible.

"Please, Eric?"

Eric looked down at Inken, lying helpless beneath her blankets, begging for his help. Her broken arm lay limp at her side, and the muscles of her neck twitched with the strain of sitting. The tears on her hands were so deep he thought he could see the glint of bone.

Casting aside his doubts, he nodded. "Okay."

Sitting beside her, he offered her a spoonful of broth. Heat washed across his face as the spoon disappeared into her mouth. She closed her eyes and chewed, her brow creased with pain, as though even the simple task of eating took a great effort. But a few seconds later she swallowed, and he offered her another mouthful.

Suddenly Eric found himself smiling. The whole scene was surreal – here he was, sitting by a warm fire, spoon-feeding a woman hired to kill him.

In the orange glow of the fire, Inken's burns were almost invisible. He found himself studying her as she ate, searching her eyes for a hint of the killer within. Yet all he could see was her injured beauty, her reluctant vulnerability. He could not connect the girl before him with the image of a ruthless bounty hunter.

When Inken finished the stew, Eric stood and returned to his own seat. Alastair offered him another bowl and Eric gladly gulped it down. His stomach rumbled as he ate, eager for the sustenance.

"We have time for one more lesson before we reach Chole, Eric. I think we had better make good use of it."

"Ssh," Eric glimpsed at Inken, but her eyes had closed.

Alastair waved a hand. "Don't worry about her. I heard you speaking as I returned. I slipped a pinch of sleeping herb into her bowl. She'll sleep through the night."

Eric sucked in a breath, trying to calm his frayed nerves. "What do we do with her?"

"Nothing. I don't think she has made the connection between you and Oaksville. So long as we're careful, there shouldn't be any danger. Now finish that stew. We have some real magic to learn."

Eric swallowed the last morsel and placed the bowl beside him. The meat had been tough and the vegetables tasteless, but even so, he could feel the energy returning to his arms and legs. He followed Alastair as he walked from the firelight out into the night. His eyes scanned the darkness as they moved over the uneven gravel, searching for any hint of the desert beasts.

"Okay." Alastair stopped suddenly and faced him. "As you know, magic in its fundamental state is controlled by emotion. Fear, anger, love, hate; if the emotion is strong enough, your magic will respond. To *harness* its power and bend it to your will, you must discover the link between the magic and your emotions. We achieve this through meditation."

"Meditation?"

"Meditation is a technique apprentices learn at a young

age, so they can develop control over their mind and body. Eventually, it allows Magickers to find their magic, and summon it at will," he paused, his eyes losing their focus. Around them pieces of gravel lifted into the air. "In other words, meditation will allow *you* to manipulate the weather, rather than your emotions."

"Right now, I'd be happy just to stop myself losing control," Eric sighed.

Alastair smiled. "We will start with that. There are certain dangers to consider before we go further, but in time, you will be capable of far more. Now, let us begin. Sit down and cross your legs." Alastair obeyed his own command as he spoke.

Eric quickly copied the old man, wincing as the gravel dug into his backside.

"Now, close your eyes and try to clear the thoughts from your mind. Take a deep breath, and exhale slowly, until all the air has been emptied from your chest."

Closing his eyes, Eric took a deep breath. His lungs swelled, and then contracted as he slowly exhaled. He repeated the exercise, smiling at how easy it was. Idly, he wondered whether the old Magicker was playing a joke on him.

"You're thinking, Eric," Alastair's voice cut through his thoughts.

"What?" Eric's eyes snapped open.

"Your eyelids were flickering. Think of *nothing,* Eric. It's okay, most take a long time to master the practice. Try again."

Eric nodded, shaken by Alastair's interruption.

Alastair stopped him again after another minute. "You're still thinking too much."

Eric sighed. His mind kept flickering from one thought to the next, unable to turn off. So much had happened in the last few days, and whenever he pushed one thing away, another rose to take its place.

"It can help to repeat a word each time you exhale," Alastair offered.

"Like what?"

"Well, when I was an apprentice, we were told to breath out 'ing'," Alastair said.

"I don't think that's even a word, Alastair."

The old man scowled. "Just try it. By focusing on something benign, you will find it easier to let your thoughts to fall away."

Eric grimaced. "Okay, I'll give it a go."

He closed his eyes again and breathed out, whispering 'ing' as he did so.

In, out. In, out. In, out.

His heart slowed and some of the tension fell from his shoulders. The word *ing* vibrated through his consciousness, drawing his thoughts like moths to the light. Everything else drifted away, until he seemed adrift on a sea of black.

I'm doing it, he exulted.

The thought shattered his concentration. Opening his eyes, he grinned at Alastair. "I think I had it for a second there."

Alastair laughed and stood. "Good, keep practising then," he stretched his arms. "Call me if you need a hand, I won't be far. I'm going to go keep watch."

The old man disappeared. Eric sat back and began again. Watching the old man move away, he had been reassured. Alastair looked stronger than ever, his injuries healed and forgotten. He looked more than a match for the creatures of the night now.

Gradually he sank back into the calm centre of his mind, away from the distractions of the physical world. It came faster this time, as though it were a skill he had once known, and now remembered. Even the slow thumping of his heart faded away, leaving him alone, cut off from sensation, from all sense of time. He drifted, separate from himself, a ghost within his own mind.

After a time, a memory surfaced. It was here, amidst this emptiness, that he would find his magic. As though waiting for the thought, a blue light appeared in the distance. He floated towards it, slowly at first, but growing faster, until he became a blazing arrow. The speck grew, becoming a lake of brilliant blue, stretching out beneath him, immense and overwhelming.

The glow washed over him, its warmth intoxicating. Thin threads of light rose from the lake and swept towards him. Tentative tendrils stroked his consciousness, and slowly wrapped around him. Power surged through Eric as they connected, filling him with strength. A need curled through his consciousness, a desire for more. He dropped slowly towards the lake, the threads weaving all around him, tiny hooks burying themselves in his being. The light rose to meet him, shifting as it came, becoming the jaws of a great wolf.

Fear touched Eric as the jaws widened, but it was too late to flee. The magic was all around him, binding him tight, and before he could move the jaws snapped shut. The blue light flooded him, pouring through his consciousness. Drowning, Eric tried to wake, but the tendrils held him tight, drawing him deeper and deeper into the darkness of his mind.

Freed of its prison, the wolf blazed brighter. It grew, even as Eric shrank. He could feel it merging with him, its power eating away his resistance until they became one.

Back at the campsite, Eric opened his eyes, but it was no longer the boy who stared out. The force within grinned, feeling the strength flowing through his veins and muscles, the power crackling at his fingertips. Eric's body tensed, and then lifted slowly to his feet.

The power looked around. Invisible tendrils of magic stretched out, searching, seeking power. Far away, over the rainforests to the west, they found it.

The storm clouds had been building through the day, feeding off the moisture laden air. Energy crackled across the sky, water and air and dust smashing to create friction, igniting the lightning within.

The threads of magic tore great chunks from the storm, drawing it across the miles to where Eric's body waited. It arrived with a boom of thunder and flash of white, as lightning struck Eric's outstretched arm. Roaring, it gathered around him. Thunder boomed again and again, as fresh bolts of electricity fell tumbling from the sky.

Eric lifted his fists in exaltation, as deep within his mind, a voice screamed. But the magic, the *power*, was everything now. Exhilarating, intoxicating, indestructible.

"Eric, stop!" a voice shouted over the thunder.

Eric pointed an arm at the speaker. No enemy would stop him now. Blue energy crawled along his arm and leapt from his fingertips. Lightning shrieked through the night, and he watched a shadowy figure dive from its path. Light flashed as it struck the cliffs, turning the stone to molten rock.

"Eric, listen to me. I am Alastair, your teacher!"

Alastair.

The name rang through his mind, but he shook his head. He needed no teacher now. Another bolt chased the figure through the darkness. The stench of burning rock filled the air, and Eric breathed it in, revelling in his power. But still the man escaped him.

"Die!" he shrieked, his voice metallic. Lightning flashed

from him in all directions, burning white tracks across his vision.

"Eric, you must stop. The magic will destroy you. Remember Oaksville!"

Oaksville.

Eric paused as the word reverberated through his mind, cutting a track right to his soul. Some small, forgotten part of him grabbed for it like a lifeline in a stormy sea. Sanity clawed its way back from the deepest recesses of his mind. Horror struck him like a physical blow and he stumbled.

Oaksville, Oaksville, Oaksville.

The word chimed in his mind, drawing him back. But with a roar, the magic rose again, burning away thought and reason. Eric gritted his teeth, determined to force it down, guilt warring with fear. He would not let it consume him, not this time.

The lightning around him flickered, but he could not release it, not with Alastair and Inken nearby. Its heat radiated across his skin, and sucking in a breath, he pressed it down. It danced across his arms, flickering, alive, but to his astonishment, it obeyed. Bit by bit, the electricity faded away, drawn down into the darkness in his chest.

Closing his eyes, Eric forced the lightning deeper, taking his magic with it. The lake appeared again, angry now, raging against him. But Eric had found his courage, and gritting his teeth, he hurled the lightning down into the lake. It struck the surface and disappeared.

In an instant, the lake calmed, its surface turning glassy smooth.

Opening his eyes back at the campsite, Eric felt the strength go from his legs, and he crumpled to the ground. Footsteps crunched on gravel as someone approached, but Eric suddenly found himself unable to move. He stared up at the night's sky, unable to even close his eyes.

Alastair's face appeared overhead. "Too close," the old Magicker shook his head. "I'm sorry, Eric. That was my fault. I have never seen anyone go so far, so fast. Most do not discover the dark side of their magic for years. But tonight you met the beast that lives within you, and survived. Next time, it will be easier. Rest now."

And reaching down, Alastair closed Eric's eyes with a gentle hand.

CHAPTER 14

Inken squinted into the noonday sun, gritting her teeth as the heat seared her burnt skin. Sweat ran down her back and the air was suffocating, but at least they were almost there.

A granite bridge stretched away from them. The old stone structure spanned almost half a mile and was wide enough for five horses to ride abreast. But the days of such traffic through Chole were long gone, and there was no one in sight. The wind whistled between the stone railings as they started across.

The bridge stretched across a crater almost two hundred feet deep – all that remained of what had once been Lake Chole. Inken glanced at Eric and Alastair as they started across. Alastair still looked fresh, almost excited in fact, though he'd walked all morning across the unforgiving desert. Eric lay slumped in the saddle of the other horse, his face pale, his eyes sunken. His condition confused her – he had seemed fine the night before – but she had more pressing concerns.

That morning she had woken with a throbbing headache

and her vision spinning. Her thoughts had been sluggish and confused, but she knew enough to realise she'd been drugged. It had taken almost an hour for the symptoms to wear off.

Then there were the strange things she'd seen around the campsite as they'd ridden out. The air reeked of smoke, and not just regular wood smoke. Scorch marks had dotted the cliffs, and in places the stone had warped, as though melted by some great heat. It did not take much to guess *something* had happened during the night. And she would put good gold on it having something to do with Eric's sickness.

Yet despite her suspicions, she could not bring herself to think ill of the young man. He had been nothing but kind to her the night before. He had seen her, saved her, when he could easily have left her there to die.

Shaking her head, Inken tried to dismiss the thoughts whispering through her mind – the thought that the signs around their campsite were all too similar too the description given of Oaksville.

"The bridge is a reminder of our folly," she said suddenly, determined to distract herself.

Eric stirred, twisting in the saddle to look at her. "What do you mean?"

"The original bridge was destroyed when Archon laid siege to Chole. Afterwards, it took years for Chole to recover. Almost a decade passed before construction on a new bridge started. By then the rains had retreated behind the volcanoes and the lake had already begun to shrink."

"And they still built it?"

Inken nodded. "The change was so gradual that people convinced themselves it would be temporary. So they built the bridge. And here it now stands, spanning barren rock, a testament to their ignorance."

The silence resumed and Inken looked away. She found herself missing the easy conversation of the night before.

Sitting beside the fire with the young man, she had felt strangely comfortable. Despite her embarrassment at her weakness, and needing Eric's help to eat, Inken had found herself strangely relaxed around the young man.

But now a tension hung between them. *Something* had changed.

"What will you do in Chole, Eric?" she tried again.

Eric was staring over the rails at the sheer drop down to the crater floor. He shivered and looked back at her. "I'm not sure. I guess we'll take you to the temple first. Hopefully they still have a healer. Then I think we'll look for some food. I'm starving."

Inken's stomach growled in agreement. She could feel her injured strength shrinking with hunger. She prayed to Antonia that they would find a healer at the temple. Alastair had done his best to patch her up, but without a healer it would take months to recover. And even then, she would be left with deep scars all over her body. The thought made her tremble. She had never thought herself vain, but even so…

"What about you, Inken?" Eric ventured. "What will you do?"

What will *I do?* She asked herself, then glanced at Eric. *Claim the bounty?*

Aloud, she said. "Once I'm healed, there's a few friends I'll visit, to see about getting some new equipment. They'll have a good laugh hearing about my folly. At least it'll make for a good story."

Eric chuckled. "I'm sure they will be happy to see you."

"Perhaps," Inken said. "How long will you stay in Chole?"

Eric glanced at Alastair. "I'm not sure..."

Inken nodded. She'd quickly realised it was the old man who made the decisions between the two.

Perhaps Eric is just a pawn, she thought. *Or maybe they're just two weary travellers,* she argued with herself.

"What are the people here like, Inken?" Eric asked.

"The desert has made us hard," she smiled. "But most are friendly enough to outsiders. The city would quickly perish without them. The only resources we have are a few gold and sulphur deposits – everything else we buy from the trade caravans that come through every month."

The city walls loomed overhead as they reached the end of the bridge. The wind had worn the great blocks of stones smooth and cracks riddled the mortar holding them in place. The ramparts above the gate were empty, but a single guard stood on the path ahead, hiding from the sun in the shadow of the tunnel.

The guard stepped forward as they approached, a spear gripped lightly in one hand. Behind him, the tunnel into the city stood open, the wooden gates long gone. No one had bothered to replace them when they'd fallen. Timber was expensive here, and the desert protected Chole now.

The steel rings of the guard's chainmail rattled as he barred their path. "Stop. What is your business in Chole?" he spoke loudly, but in a disinterested voice.

Inken grimaced. As much as the city tried, that was the way of things in Chole. As the population shrank, order was slowly dying, as more and more turned to crime to survive. Meanwhile, the city guard dwindled, and those who remained were less than scrupulous.

"My name is Alastair and this is Eric. We found this woman in the desert. She's been badly injured, so we're taking her to Antonia's temple to be healed."

The guard glanced at Inken. Thank fully she didn't recognise him. It would be bad enough telling the tale of her folly herself, without word travelling ahead of her.

One look at her face was enough to convince the guard.

He waved them through without another glance. Inken sighed as they entered the shadows, the absence of the sun's heat offering instant relief for her burnt face.

Beyond the wall, the tunnel opened out into narrow streets. Buildings hemmed them in on all sides, all in a state of crumbling disrepair. The neighbourhoods closest to the walls tended to be the poorest, and here the houses were little better than flea-ridden hovels. Open sewers ran along the roadway, deep enough to swallow unwary pedestrians. Garbage littered the streets, and a pack of dogs looked up as they approached, before retreating down the street. The rats ignored them.

The streets remained quiet as they rode deeper into the impoverished city. Those citizens they glimpsed moved quickly about their business, ignoring the strangers. Others sat in hopeless silence, leaning against the grimy walls, their hands stretched out in entreat. As they passed a homeless man who had lost both of his arms, Inken caught a glimpse of tears in Eric's eyes. His gaze lingered on the desperate man as they rode past, but he did not speak.

His reaction only added to her confusion.

They moved on, slowly leaving the poorest districts behind. Fountains appeared, although Inken had never seen them alive with water. They stood as another silent reminder of Chole's past. The gravel road turned to bricks, but even here the passage of time and people had worn deep grooves into the streets. The piles of garbage shrank, but unfortunately the stench remained.

Inken watched Alastair closely as he led them confidently through the maze of streets. It was clear he'd been here before – probably many times. Chole's streets were a rabbit warren at best, and few other than locals could find their way here. Landmarks were rare – one dead garden looked much like all the others.

The city seemed empty and they made good time. When they finally turned up the street towards the temple of the Earth, Inken's breath quickened. Here at last was a building that had resisted the erosion of time. Marble columns as thick as the giant redwoods to the west towered over them, while above three spires stretched into the sky. Stone steps led up to an outdoor patio, where green-robed priests stood in quiet meditation. A quiet chanting drifted down to them.

At the bottom of the stairs, a lonely priest stood and waved to them. As Inken dismounted, men appeared to take their horses, while the priest nodded towards the steps.

Inken's heart sank. There were only two-dozen steps to the top, but she knew even that was beyond her strength. Again she was forced to swallow her pride and ask for help. Even with the support of Alastair's shoulder, she was gasping by the time they reached the top. But her heart warmed a little when she saw Eric following them up, supported by a hand from one of the priests.

They made their way through the meditating priests, drawing the eyes of a few curious watchers. Inken quickly averted her face, aware of their stares. She was tense with anticipation, waiting for some hint of whether a healer was present. If there was no healer, she would have to make do with a doctor, but she knew which option she preferred.

Another priest waited for them in the doorway to the inner temple. His robes were green edged with gold, with white bands adorning the sleeves and collar. A purple diamond patch on his right breast marked him as a doctor. He offered a friendly smile as they approached, wrinkles appearing around his amber eyes. His hair was jet-black streaked with grey.

Concern replaced his smile as he took in her injuries. "Welcome, travellers. My name is Michael. Please, come this way," he spoke in a calm voice, but Inken could see the concern in his eyes.

They followed him through the doorway. Inside was dark, the only light coming from a scattering of candles, and the air was thick with incense. A worn green carpet covered the floor, and at the end of the room was a simple wooden alter. Citizens and priests knelt on their knees around the room, offering their silent prayers to the Goddess Antonia. In the far corner a young man played a piano, the gentle music welcoming them into the sanctuary.

Michael led them to a small door behind the alter and through into a corridor. Doors lined the hallway on the left, while on the right windows opened out onto a central courtyard. Inken shrugged off Alastair's hand and hobbled across. Mouth wide, she peered through the glass panes, unable to believe the sight that greeted her.

A garden filled the courtyard in the centre of the building, alive with the green of the earth. Plants grew from soft, moist soil, defying the fierce heat of the sun. They thrived between the brick walls, trees and vines thrusting from the earth, ignorant to the desert outside.

Inken felt a new respect for the priests blossom in her chest. To grow anything in Chole was considered a miracle, but they had achieved far more than that.

Behind her, Michael coughed, drawing her attention away from the courtyard. He waved her on, and they continued down the corridor. Snatching glances through the windows as they walked, Inken found herself wishing she had visited the place earlier. She had never paid much attention to the Gods and their temples, but perhaps she needed to reconsider that path. Her heart fell as Michael opened a door and led them out of sight of the gardens.

Inside, they found themselves in a simple room without any adornment. A man sat alone on the tiled floor, watching them with pure white eyes. Skin hung in folds from his face and long locks of grey hair tumbled down his back. A narrow scar stretched across his face and his arms were thin and frail. He wore a robe similar to Michael's, except where a pink diamond had replaced the purple.

Inken sighed in relief, recognising the mark of a healer.

"Welcome, Alastair. It has been a long time," the healer's voice rasped like gravel.

Alastair grinned. "So it has, Elynbrigge. *She* has been keeping me busy, but it is good to see you again, old friend."

"Ay, it is. But I hear your search has been unsuccessful."

Alastair nodded. "And I hear yours has borne fruit."

Elynbrigge smiled. "Ay, it has."

Inken looked from one old man to the other, half a dozen questions jostling for her attention. Beside her, Michael was clearly just as confused, and he took a moment to regain his composure.

Clearing his throat, he said. "Elynbrigge has only been here a few weeks, but he is a great healer. You are very lucky, young lady. Our temple does not usually host healers of Elynbrigge's talent."

"And it won't for much longer either, I am afraid," Elynbrigge added.

Michael nodded, his eyes touched by sadness. Inken could understand his disappointment. The priests here were clearly dedicated to preserving Antonia's temple. It would be a sting to their pride to lack anyone with healing magic, when it was such a large part of the Earth temple's duties.

"Alastair, I am afraid I must keep you waiting a while longer," Elynbrigge continued. "First, I must attend to this young lady you have brought me. I can feel her pain from here. Please, sit down, my dear."

With Michael's help, Inken lowered herself to the ground in front of the ancient man. Her broken leg made even this a struggle, and she was forced to sit with her good leg bent beneath her, and the broken one stretched out straight along the ground. She used her good arm to hold herself up, and cradled the other close to her body.

Elynbrigge laughed. "Michael, her discomfort is screaming in my ears. Please, my dear, you may lie down. The others can clear out if there is not enough room."

Inken sighed with relief as she stretched out on the cool tiles. "Thank you. My name is Inken, by the way," she added.

"A pleasure to meet you, Inken," Elynbrigge replied. "Now, to business. Your injuries are quite severe, but they are within my ability to heal. It will be painful, however, and time consuming. You will need to be brave, and patient."

"It's okay, I can take it," Inken glanced at Eric and Alastair. "Thank you for saving me, Eric, Alastair. I owe you both my life. If you ever need my help, you only need to ask."

She closed her eyes then, wondering where the words had come from. She wasn't even sure who they were, or what they intended to do in Chole. Yet even as tendrils of doubt spread through her mind, Inken realised she had meant the words. Whoever Eric and Alastair were, they *had* saved her life, and one way or another, she would repay that debt.

"It was our pleasure, Inken. Perhaps we will see each other again. But for now, we will leave you to your healing," Alastair turned to Elynbrigge. "We will talk soon, old friend. I will return after we have made ourselves comfortable."

Elynbrigge nodded back. Alastair waved goodbye and left the room, Eric following in his wake. But the young man hesitated in the doorway.

"I hope we do meet again, Inken," he said, turning back. He flashed a smile. "In better circumstances, I hope. Take care!"

Then he was gone and Inken felt suddenly, unexpectedly alone.

"Brace yourself, Inken. We begin."

Eric stared up at the pale ceiling, relishing in the sensation of a bed beneath him. He couldn't remember the last time he'd slept in a real bed. It wasn't a very soft one, but compared to hay, hammocks and the rocky ground, it felt like heaven.

He closed his eyes, wanting the release of sleep but knowing it would not come. A restlessness had come over him since leaving the temple, one he could not shake.

Through the window, he watched the sun setting over the Dying City. There was no mystery about where that nickname had come from. Their second storey room looked out over empty streets. The few merchants he'd seen during the day had already packed away their wares, surrendering the city to the unscrupulous night. A handful of guards still patrolled, but Eric suspected they would do little to control the city's denizens once darkness fell.

He prayed the inn would be a safe haven for them at least. It stood proud amidst the abandoned buildings, the only such establishment for blocks. The tavern downstairs was well lit and decorated with old wooden chairs and tables, giving it a homey feel. The innkeeper had unlocked the door cautiously when they'd first knocked, but welcomed them with a smile when he recognised Alastair. He offered them their pick of the rooms, and Alastair had quickly taken the one at the end of the upstairs hallway.

The room contained two single beds and a small table and chairs. A wide double window stood in the far wall, and a long dead fireplace in the other. The room smelt of dust and old cloth, but the thick wooden door at least ensured little noise permeated through from downstairs. Their saddlebags were draped over the foot of the beds, and they had left their mounts with the inn's stable hand.

Eric thoughts drifted, turning slowly to Inken. He hadn't been able to shake her from his head since they'd left the temple. Images flashed through his mind: the way the moonlight had reflected off her soft curves, her gentle smile as she looked at him, the cool glint of the killer in her eyes. He pictured her slipping through the night, bringing the soft kiss of death to her foes.

He groaned, running his hands through his hair, and tried to push the images away. Inken no longer mattered – despite its poverty, Chole was huge, and there was no way she would find them in its twisted maze of streets and alleyways. And she still didn't know who he was – or at least, he hoped not.

The noise from downstairs was growing louder, as a few patrons slowly filed in from the streets. Earlier they had taken their fill at the bar, devouring several bowls of the thick stew and a loaf of bread the innkeeper offered them. Afterwards, Eric had been shocked to see how many silver coins Alastair handed the man. Apparently, food and board did not come cheap in Chole.

Somewhere outside the room a door banged, and the floorboards creaked as someone moved down the corridor. A second later the door opened and Alastair moved inside, closing the door gently behind him. He had gone to check on the horses after their meal.

"How are you feeling, Eric?" he asked as he moved across and sat on the other bed.

Gathering his strength, Eric sat up. "Feeling better," he paused. "But I think I've waited long enough. What the hell happened last night?"

Alastair stared back at him. "You tell me."

Eric shivered, thinking again of desert, and the madness

that had come over him. "It was as though my magic was alive, like it was some whole other consciousness. Its power was… irresistible."

Alastair nodded. "What you achieved last night usually takes months. I seriously underestimated you," he paused. "Perhaps the way you have tapped into your power in the past helped you reach it. Either way, it is a dangerous thing, a Magicker's first conscious contact with their magic. I am sorry, I should have warned you."

Swallowing, Eric remembered the icy grip around his consciousness, the awful helplessness he'd felt as something *else* took control of his body.

"What makes it so dangerous?" he whispered.

"Magic is not an inert force. It lives to break free of the prison your mind traps it in, to take control of its host. Last night you touched it, unprepared and unprotected, and it struck. Without the right preparation, you never stood a chance."

"I could have killed you."

Alastair nodded. "That was my fault."

Eric looked up at the old man. "How do I control something like that?" he fought to keep the fear from his voice.

"You master your fear. That is its only weapon against you. If you do not fear it, your magic cannot harm you."

Eric stared. He had never experienced such terror before. It was as though his fear had turned to pure energy, to a force in itself, one that swept away his will to resist. How could he conquer such a beast?

"Eric," Alastair interrupted his thoughts. "Do you know what you did there, at the end?"

He shook his head.

"You drew the lightning into yourself."

Eric shrugged. "I didn't know what else to do. If I had released it, it might have killed you."

"An interesting tactic. Very few Magickers dare to draw aspects of their element into themselves. Outside forces tend to be chaotic and unwieldy, it's a miracle you managed it. But it may come in useful in the future. You should be able to draw that lightning back to the surface, should you ever need it."

Eric allowed himself a smile, though he doubted he would ever need the lightning again. The room fell into a comfortable silence, and he allowed his eyes to close. As sleep tugged at his mind, a final thought came to him.

"Alastair, what would have happened, if I hadn't come back?" he asked.

"Your magic would have exhausted your life force, and burnt your mind dry. Your magic was consuming massive amounts of energy – that's why you could barely move afterwards. A few more minutes, and you would have died. Or at least, your soul would have. Your body would have lived on, controlled by your magic. That is how demons are created, Eric."

Eric drew in a deep, shuddering breath. His heart hammered hard in his chest and it felt as though an iron fist had wrapped around his stomach.

"Good night, Eric," Alastair murmured from the other bed.

But it was a long time before Eric slept.

CHAPTER 15

The heat in the room was sweltering. Cursing, Eric sat up and threw off his sheets. From beneath the curtains, he spied the tell-tale glow of daylight, and cursed again. Through fuzzy eyes, he saw Alastair's bed was empty. Groaning, he pulled himself from the bed and stumbled across to the window. Sunlight flooded the room as he threw back the curtains.

Outside, the sun was high in the sky, almost noon. Eric was not surprised. He'd lain awake for half the night, willing himself to sleep, but when it had finally come, blue flames and demons had stalked his dreams. Alastair must have decided to leave him to sleep.

At least he felt better than the morning before. His arms still ached and his legs threatened to cramp, but the pain was already receding, and stretching his arms, he pulled on a fresh shirt. His stomach grumbled. Looking around the room, his eyes settled on a handful of silver coins on his bedside table. Presuming they'd been left for him, he swept them up and headed out the door. It took an effort to reach the stairs, and by the bottom his legs were shaking, but he made it safely through the big wooden doors and into the tavern below.

Lunch was still an hour away, but the room was already filled with the aroma of roasting meat and Eric quickly made his way to the bar. Seating himself on a barstool, he waved to the innkeeper. The man smiled when he saw him, showing his yellowed teeth.

"You're looking better today," he observed. "Sleep must agree with you."

Eric smiled back. "A little. I'll feel even better after some food though," he slid the coins onto the counter as he spoke.

The innkeeper laughed. "No doubt. I'll see what I can rustle up," he took two of the coins and handed the others back, before disappearing into the kitchens.

Eric slumped against the counter as he waited. Through the barred windows he could see the street outside, baked dry by the harsh sun. The reflection off the pale bricks was so bright it hurt his eyes and the air shimmered with the heat. Despite the cool shade of the bar, a trickle of sweat ran down Eric's back, and his clothes stuck to his skin.

A few minutes later a waitress appeared and placed a plate in front of him with a smile. Eric thanked her and picked up his fork and knife, his mouth already watering. He shovelled a forkful of mashed potatoes into his mouth, and then started on the roast beef. Gravy spilt on his chin as he wolfed it down, but he hardly noticed until there was nothing but crumbs left on his plate.

Eric licked his lips and sat back on the stool. His mind drifted, and he was surprised to find himself smiling. Oaksville lingered in his thoughts, but despite the chaos of the past few days, he felt at peace. Alastair might be quiet company, but his presence was far better than the exile Eric had suffered for so long. Then there was the enigmatic Inken, and the confusion he felt whenever he thought of her.

His life was changing so quickly, he could scarcely believe it. In less than a week, he had gone from a fugitive to an apprentice Magicker. He had met a man over a hundred years old, a bounty hunter hired to kill him, and the Goddess Antonia herself.

But where was Alastair now? He glanced around the tavern, but there was still no sign of the old man. A few patrons had filed in while he ate, and were now waiting patiently for food and drink. The doors creaked as another man pushed inside, and rising from his stool, Eric decided it was time to head back upstairs.

Back in his room, he quickly found himself bored, with nothing to do but wait for Alastair's return. Outside a trickle of human traffic flowed through the sweltering streets, and within the room the air grew stifling. Eric fanned himself with his hand, wondering how the locals coped with such temperatures. Why did they stay, knowing their city was doomed?

Goosebumps prickled Eric's neck as his thoughts returned to his magic. He could feel the terror in his chest, swelling at the memory of the night in the desert, rising to choke him. Eric tried to push it away, but it persisted.

Alastair had promised his magic would be a gift, but the old man had lied. Every day Eric's magic offered a new threat to his life. What would have happened if he had not regained control? Remembering the ruins of Oaksville, he tasted bile in his throat. The faces of the dead flashed through his mind, and he fought back tears. Antonia had spoken of redemption, but how could he make up for what had happened, when he could not even master his magic?

He shivered as a thought occurred to him. Biting his lip, he turned the notion over in his mind, wondering whether it was possible. He could not change the past, but he might still change the future. Without magic, he could spend an eternity righting wrongs, and never account for the evil he had cast over Oaksville. But with the power his magic offered…

If only he could overcome his fear.

A memory leapt unbidden from the depths of his mind. Long ago, he had been swimming in the river near his house, when a strong current had dragged him under. It took all his energy to pull himself back to the surface. Even then, the undercurrent had threatened to drag him back down, and with water filling his mouth he had lunged for the bank. His hand had caught in an overhanging root and with the last of his strength he'd pulled himself onto the bank.

When he'd finally made it home, he had found his father and sobbed the story to him.

"I was so scared, Dad. I'll never go swimming again," he had finished.

"Why, Eric? You have always loved the water. Why let one bad experience ruin that? Next time, you'll be more careful."

Eric remembered his terror then, sapping away his courage. "I can't Dad, I'm afraid."

His father had crouched beside him then and taken him by the shoulders. "There is no shame in fear, Eric. Fear is natural. We are all afraid at times. But you must not run from fear. If you do, it becomes a beast that will devour you. Real men take their fear, and learn from it. Do not feed the beast, Eric. Instead, you must make it your own," he stood. "Come."

"Where are we going?"

"To the river."

Eric smiled at the memory. He had swum again that day, and many times since. The fear had still been there, lurking in his mind, but over time it had lessened. He could hear his father now, telling him to face his fear, not to run from it.

And he knew what he had to do. Today would be his first step towards redemption.

Closing his eyes, Eric lay back on the bed and began to meditate. This time it took a long time for the chaos of his thoughts to clear, but he persisted, determined to put the last few days behind him. One by one, his worries fell away, and the darkness of his inner consciousness rose all around him.

He flinched as the first tendrils of his magic reached through the darkness to touch him. Its whispers seeped through his mind, sinking deep into the recesses of his consciousness. Terror rose in his throat, and a voice screamed for him to flee, but he crushed it down. Blue light flooded his mind as the great lake took form, banishing the darkness. Yet here it was not the dark he feared, but the light.

Eric gritted his teeth and summoned his courage. He had come too far for second thoughts. If he ran now, he might never stop. Bracing, he gathered himself, and then reached out to touch the light.

For a moment, nothing happened. Then the pool of light shimmered and changed, drawing in upon itself. Great legs clawed their way into existence, and teeth snapped at the darkness. Lightning rippled outwards from the beast as it stepped towards him.

All Eric could do was stand frozen in place as the monstrous image approached. It towered over him, filling his mind. Throwing back its shaggy head, the wolf howled. The sound tore through Eric, shattering his courage and sending him to his knees.

You must not run from fear, Eric, his father's words rose from long ago.

Eric clung to them, to the image of his father standing beside the river, waving him on. Suddenly he was back on his feet, staring at the wolf through the darkness, his chest swollen with a red-hot heat. As he stared at the beast, he felt his fear slip away, like water between his fingers.

Growling, the wolf took another step towards him. Yet as it approached, it seemed to shrink. His soul soared, and summoning his nerve, he moved towards it. Its growl turned to a whimper as it continued to wither, until it was no more than a puppy at his feet.

Eric smiled as he watched it darted at him, but he could see through the illusion now, to the magic at its heart.

His magic – the magic he needed to restore Chole.

Reaching down, he grabbed at the wolf pup. As his fingers met the glow at its core, a surge of power swept through him, lighting his soul aflame. But now it was *his* to command – he was the master now. All he had to do now was use it.

The blue flames swelled within him, gathering force, and Eric thought back to when his magic had taken control, how it had reached *beyond* him to summon the storm. Could he do the same?

Focusing his mind, Eric thought of the sky beyond the window, imagining himself aloft in its great blue expanse. The darkness blurred and spun, and then the weight of his body fell away. Opening his eyes, he found himself soaring upwards, the rooftops of Chole falling away beneath him. Tendrils of magic branched out from him, searching out the powers of the Sky.

Gazing through the eyes of his inner mind, Eric found himself free of all physical sensation – pain, hunger, exhaustion, all had vanished, leaving only the pure essence of his being.

Then a tingling ran through him, and he turned towards the east, sensing the gathering strength of the distant storm. Pulling his magic close, he willed himself towards it. His consciousness jerked, and then he was soaring from the city, out over the towering volcanic peaks. Arid air blew around him, and he felt the death lingering in its touch, drawing the life from the land.

It was time to put an end to that.

Moving faster than thought, Eric left behind the deathly peaks. Below the land turned from arid rock to thriving forests. As he moved beyond the deserts touch, the sickness shrivelled and died, replaced by the warmth of life.

Then the land too gave way, replaced by the dark waters of the ocean. A storm raged around him now, the howling winds driving great waves to batter the rocky coast. Trees on the windswept land bent beneath the hurricanes onslaught, and the air was filled with torn branches and flying leaves. Precious rain poured down on salty seas.

Again, Eric drew on his memories of the night in the desert. The magic had formed hooks and lines to gather the power of the storm. He would do the same.

The black clouds around him glowed blue in the light of his magic. Willing hooks to form, he flung them deep into the storm, and directed the lines of his power to wrap their way around the clouds. Wisps of the storm slipped from his grasp and raced away, but Eric kept on, determined to succeed.

Finally, he summoned the power at his core, and started to pull. With a boom of thunder, the storm began to move. Lightning flashed and the wind howled louder as it struck the land and picked up speed. Leaving behind the ocean that had born it, it raced across the forests of Eastern Plorsea, following Eric's silent command.

But as the jagged peaks loomed, the storm stalled, and Eric felt an invisible barrier pushing back against him. Gritting his teeth, he drew on more magic and pressed harder. Energy crackled as he poured his strength into the bonds holding the storm, willing it onwards.

A sharp screech echoed from the mountains, and sparks leapt across the sky. Lightning flashed again, and with a dull boom, the storm shot forwards, wheeling onwards towards Chole. Eric sensed something crumbling, as though a barrier had been shattered, but his strength was fading, and he felt the distant pull of his body drawing him back.

For a second he lingered, watching the storm as it continued towards Chole.

Then with a sudden rush, the weight of his body returned. Opening his eyes, he made to sit up, before tendrils of agony wrapped around him. With a groan, he lay back on the bed, embracing the pain.

He had faced the beast, and survived. Nothing was beyond him now.

Sleep beckoned, and he welcomed it with open arms.

"Thank the Gods!"

Eric jerked awake as a voice shouted out, quickly followed by a door slamming. Blinking sleep from his eyes, he looked around and saw Alastair stalking towards him. The old man towered over the bed, his face dark with rage. Reaching down, he grasped Eric by the shirt and hauled him from the bed.

"*What did you do?*" Alastair yelled.

Eric gaped, fighting for breath as the collar of his shirt bit into his neck. His mind was sluggish with sleep, and he struggled to understand what Alastair was saying. "Wh… what?"

"What? You damn well know what! You summoned your magic!"

A strange calm settled over Eric as he looked up at the

old Magicker. He had no idea how Alastair had found out, but he did not regret what he'd done.

"I had to do it, Alastair," he said softly. "Or the fear would have overwhelmed me. But how did you know?"

Alastair shook his head, his expression grim. Gently, he set Eric back on the bed. "Every Magicker in the city would have sensed what you did. All magic is entwined, Eric, and such a massive expenditure of power sent shockwaves across the city. When I felt it… I thought the worst had happened."

Eric stared up at the old man, seeing the dark rings beneath his eyes, the hard set of his jaw. Alastair was exhausted, worn down by the last few days, and Eric had only added to his anxiety.

"Sorry," he said at last.

Silence fell between them then, and Eric heard then the pattering of raindrops from the roof. Looking across at the window, he saw water running down the glass. He grinned as a weight fell from his chest.

"You took a terrible risk, Eric," Alastair spoke softly. "You have no idea the destruction you could have caused…"

Eric turned to meet Alastair's gaze. "I know, Alastair. I've lived with the fear of what I might do for years."

"Then why did you do it?"

"Because I had too. What happened in the desert, it unmanned me. I was terrified of what lurked inside me. If I had let that fear fester, it would have destroyed me," he took a breath. "And I knew I could make a difference here, could do something good for a change."

Alastair closed his eyes and let out a long sigh. Eric waited for him to argue, but the old man only shook his head, and smiled. Reaching out, he placed a hand on Eric's shoulder. "You did well, Eric. The people of Chole will celebrate this day for years to come. I only hope it lasts. Jurrien tried to do the same thing a century ago, and failed. But perhaps Archon's curse has weakened with time."

"I felt something, when the storm crossed the mountains. Like something shattering."

Standing, Alastair moved to the window and looked out into the street. "I'm glad you succeeded, Eric. I'm glad you mastered your fear. But this is just the beginning. Your magic is a fickle beast, and it will never stop trying to take control. Please, *please,* refrain from using it without me," he paused. "How are you feeling now?"

Eric slowly pushed himself into a sitting position. His arms ached with the movement, and he could feel a cramp beginning in his calf. "Not the best."

"You probably emptied your pool of magic, maybe even used some of your own lifeforce. You need to be careful with what you attempt – even magic has its limits, Eric."

Nodding, Eric put a tentative foot on the ground and stood. He winced as agony shot up his leg. Stumbling forward, he clutched at the desk for support. Closing his eyes, he sucked in a breath and then looked at Alastair. "I might need a bit more sleep."

Alastair chuckled. "You need to restore your strength," he glanced out the window at the gathering darkness. "We should probably shift to a new inn, after the beacon you just sent out to the other Magickers in the city."

Eric groaned and Alastair laughed again. "But you're in no condition to go anywhere. We'll have to risk it. If anyone wished us ill-will, they would probably have arrived before me. I was on the other side of the city when I sensed you."

"What were you doing?" Eric asked without thinking, his curiosity getting the better of him.

"Speaking with Elynbrigge."

Eric's heart clenched. "He told you where to find the family you're searching for?"

"Yes," Alastair smiled. "I will go to them tomorrow."

"Then take me with you," Eric insisted.

Alastair frowned. "Why?"

"Because I want to help," Eric said carefully. "You've done so much for me, Alastair. I want to help make it up to you."

Alastair fell silent, and Eric waited, his breath held, expecting the old man to refuse. But finally Alastair nodded. "Okay. But you will need to obey me without question. I do not expect trouble, but if anything happens, I need to know you will do as I say."

Eric nodded as Alastair's emerald eyes fixed on him. "I will, Alastair."

"Excellent, then let's get something to eat. You will need your strength tomorrow."

A low growl came from Eric's stomach, and he nodded grimly. Grinning, Alastair took the lead, moving out into the corridor and down the stairs to the inn below. Eric stumbled after him, using the walls and railings on the stairs as support. His whole body throbbed with each beat of his heart, as though he had spent the afternoon in a meat grinder, rather than lying on his bed. Halfway down he almost gave up, but then the rich scent of meat wafted up to him, and somehow he found the strength to make it the rest of the way.

A boisterous clamour of sound washed over them as they entered the inn. Eric stumbled to a sudden stop in the doorway, unable to believe what he was seeing.

In the far corner of the room, a band was playing. Two guitars, a cello and a set of drums filled the room with vibrant, joyous music. Someone had pushed the tables up against the walls, making way for the city's revellers. People packed the room, dancing and hugging and laughing as water dripped from their soaking clothes. Pints of beer and glasses of wine were raised high as people spun to and fro in rapturous ecstasy.

Alastair took the lead, threading his way through the crowd to where a few empty tables remained near the far wall. Eric sighed with relief as he slid onto the bench, and watched as Alastair disappeared back into the throng. He prayed the old man had gone for food. Sitting back, he stared at the chaotic dance floor, struggling to comprehend the scene. The reserved people of Chole had been transformed by the rain. Eric couldn't help but grin at the sight.

It took a quarter of an hour for Alastair to return, a plate of steaming food held in each hand. He placed them on the table and disappeared again, returning a few minutes later with two flagons of ale. The music was too loud for conversation, so together they dug into the food. Eric wolfed down the roast pork and potatoes, only pausing every few bites to wash the food down with ale.

When his plate was empty, Eric sat back and belched. "Thanks, Alastair, I needed that," he shouted over the din.

Alastair chuckled as he wiped gravy from his beard. "My pleasure."

Before Eric could respond, the door to the street swung open with a bang. Rain spilled into the room, whipped about by the swirling wind. People laughed as they stumbled back from the door, allowing two men to move inside. Lightning flashed as the door swung shut behind them, catching on the steel hilts of the swords they wore on their belts. Their eyes swept the crowd, and settled on the table Eric and Alastair were sitting at. They moved across the room with purpose, parting the crowd before them.

Alastair rose as the two approached. The two drew to a stop in front of them, their expressions unreadable, though neither made to draw their swords.

"Was it you, Alastair?" the older of the two asked.

He wore the purple robe of a war Magicker. Beneath his collar, Eric glimpsed the faint gleam of chainmail. His bald head shone in the light of the torches, and a wiry moustache hung beneath his long nose. He regarded Alastair with a cool stare, seemingly unaware of Eric's presence.

Alastair ignored the question. "Who are you?"

The man who had spoken turned out his hands. "Forgive me. My name is Balistor. I am a Magicker of the Plorsean army. We have met once before, though I doubt you would remember."

"And you?" Alastair addressed the other man.

Straightening his shoulders, the man offered Alastair a salute. He was not a large man, but his arms were finely muscled, and he moved with the subtle confidence of a warrior. He too wore chainmail, its links clearly visible beneath his scarlet tunic. The faintest trace of stubble marked his chin, but otherwise he was well-kept, his brown hair cropped short.

"Sergeant Caelin, at your service. It's an honour to meet you, sir." He offered his hand to Alastair.

Eric was impressed. Sergeant was a remarkable rank for someone who looked not much older than twenty. Though what had brought two men of the Plorsean army to the little inn still confused him.

Caelin's tawny green eyes flickered to Eric and he held out his hand. "And who are you?"

Eric stood hesitantly. "I'm Eric, Alastair's apprentice."

"It's nice to meet you," Caelin replied.

"So, was it you, Alastair?" Balistor interrupted their exchange.

"The rain, you mean?" Alastair smiled. "No, that was Eric."

Now both men turned to stare at Eric, and he suddenly found himself wishing he had never left the room. Dropping his eyes, he studied the tabletop, doing his best to ignore the shock in their eyes.

"Was there something you needed, gentlemen?" Alastair said after a moment.

"Quite the opposite," Balistor smiled. "We are here to help you."

"What makes you think I need your help?" Alastair said blankly.

"King Fraser sent us," Caelin spoke over Balistor. "He told me who you are searching for, said Antonia came to him in a dream. I was sent to offer my aid, along with Balistor here. When Balistor sensed the magic earlier, we guessed it might be you…" Caelin trailed off as he noticed the look on Alastair's face.

"That little Goddess needs to learn when to keep her meddling to herself," he cursed, then shook his head. "So, why do I need the two of you?"

Eric glanced between Alastair and the two soldiers. What was so important about this family, that the king of Plorsea had decided to get involved?

Caelin bowed his head. "All I can offer is my sword, Alastair. I have served the king for many years, and put my life on the line for this nation. I will do the same for you."

Balistor snorted. "Which of course counts for little when you're surrounded by Magickers. King Fraser chose me for my magic, Alastair. I am a master of fire," he spoke with a pride bordering on arrogance.

Eric watched the two closely, wondering at their story. Why would King Fraser only send two men to help Alastair, if his quest was so important?

Alastair questioned the men for some time, somehow making himself heard over the music and the crowd. Eventually Eric slumped back in his seat and laid his head on the table, too exhausted to pay further attention. He had heard their story – it was up to Alastair to judge the truth behind it. After all, he was the one with all the answers.

Finally Alastair seemed to accept their story. He sent them away to restock their supplies and together Eric and Alastair returned to their room. Eric fell onto his bed before the door had even closed, his eyes already drooping. Sleep weighed heavy on his mind, but he rolled onto his side and flashed one last glance through the window.

Outside, the rain continued to pour down on the Dying City.

GABRIEL STARED at the ancient walls. Rain bucketed down around him, running over his face, washing the tears from his eyes. Holding out his hands, he watched the water wash the blood from his fingers.

Shivering, he looked down at the body. The guard lay sprawled at his feet, Gabriel's dagger embedded in his throat. Blood still pumped from the wound, staining the ground red, but slowing already. Glassy eyes stared up at him, unblinking. A final tremor went through the man, and then he lay still.

Gabriel could not tear his eyes away from the man's face. Just a few seconds ago, he had been a living and breathing person. Now he was a corpse, his soul fled, his life extinguished.

What have I done?

He was in your way, the wolf growled.

Gabriel shivered. *In my way? He was only doing his job.*

He looked at his hands again. The blood was gone, but the guilt could not be washed away so easily.

He was a murderer.

What have I become?

What you must. Now come, before we are seen, the wolf padded ahead, disappearing into the tunnel through the wall.

Straightening, Gabriel followed the beast, the guard forgotten. His purpose came crashing back, the image of an old man flickering across his thoughts.

They must die. They must suffer for... for...

He paused midstride. "What did they do to me?" he whispered into the night.

It doesn't matter. The old man must die.

Gabriel nodded. His wolf was right.

The old man must die.

CHAPTER 16

Eric shivered as the rain poured down around him. Water gushed from the rooftops in an endless torrent as they moved through the streets of Chole. He was thankful for the cloak Alastair had given him, though even the thick oilskin was not enough to keep the damp from seeping through.

Alastair took the lead, threading his way through the crowds of revellers dancing in the streets. The arrival of morning had not deterred them. Soaked to the skin, they continued to dance into the new day.

Eric smiled as he watched them, taking pleasure in their ecstasy. Ahead, Alastair strode confidently through the flooded streets. At each corner he would glance back, checking Eric was keeping up, before moving on. Eric did his best to keep up with the pace the old man set, though his legs ached like he'd just run ten miles.

It took half an hour in the rain soaked streets to reach their destination. From outside, the house looked like any other. Thin cracks spread through the white-washed walls, and water ran from the tiled roof down into the long-dead garden. Its walls pressed up against the neighbouring buildings, leaving no passage through to the rear, while a thick steel door barred the front.

Alastair stopped at the door and banged on the knocker to announce their presence. Then they waited, huddling beneath the tiny eaves to escape the rain. After a minute, Alastair knocked again, but it was clear from the silence inside that no one was home.

Frowning, Alastair leaned across to peer through the barred window.

"Maybe they're out?" Eric ventured.

Alastair shook his head and continued to stare through the glass. Eric shifted on his feet, glancing back at the street, feeling suddenly exposed out in the open.

Then Alastair took a step back from the door and raised his arm. Eric's ears popped as he felt something sweep past, and then a shrill shriek came from the metal door. He spun to face it, and watched as the steel buckled and flew backwards off its hinges. Eric stared as Alastair strode forward through the hole it had left, his sword now in hand.

He shook himself awake as Alastair disappeared inside and glanced around, but no one seemed to have noticed the disturbance. Then he quickly moved after his mentor. Stepping over the twisted remains of the door, he peered into the dark corridor, his heart beating in his ears.

A crash came from farther inside, and he stilled, listening for Alastair's voice. After a moment he pressed on, his hands balled into fists.

He sensed movement from the door at the end of the corridor, and moved towards it. Another crash came, and slowly he drew the dagger from his belt, unsure what waited in the room beyond. Taking a breath, he stepped around the corner…

And froze in the doorway. His eyes swept the room,

taking in the table flipped on its side, the broken porcelain plates and half-eaten food scattered across the floor. Books had been torn from their shelves and then discarded, while high on a windowsill, a single cactus in a pot remained untouched. A large mat covered the floor, woven with an intricate scene Eric could not quite make out through the blood covering it.

Eric's stomach churned as his gaze settled on the man and woman sprawled across the matt. They lay face down, their faces hidden, their life blood congealing in a pool around them. Their clothes had been slashed and torn, revealing deep cuts to their back and arms.

Retching, Eric turned away. He struggled to keep down his breakfast, but lost the fight. Tears stung his eyes as he sucked in a breath.

Footsteps echoed on the wooden floor, and Eric spun back, raising his knife with a scream. But it was only Alastair. He moved into the room from another door and stood over the bodies, his face grim. He still held his sword in one hand, but the blade shook as he sucked in a breath.

"What… what is this, Alastair?" Eric croaked.

Sheathing his sword, Alastair crouched beside the couple. "This is the family I was meant to protect," his voice shook.

"Who did this?" Eric managed to whisper.

He could hardly breathe. He had seen death before, but never like this. As he glanced at the bodies again, he saw now that several of their fingers were missing. Whoever had done this had not given the couple an easy death.

Alastair cursed as he stood. He looked around the room, his emerald eyes shining with rage. But whatever he was searching for, he did not find it, and finally his shoulders slumped as he looked back at Eric.

"Archon's hunters. Vile, scheming men willing to sell

their souls for the power he can grant them," he spoke through clenched teeth.

Eric could only stare at Alastair. His mouth opened and closed, but he could not find the words, and no sound came out. A shadow seemed to have fallen across the room, a darkness that stole away all light, all hope.

Archon.

Finally Eric managed to shake his head. "No," he gasped. "That's not possible. He's gone, banished by the Gods. I saw it myself, in Antonia's vision."

Alastair turned to face him. "Banished, but not destroyed. The Sword of Light had the power, but Thomas did not have the knowledge to wield it. And now Archon's strength has returned."

Eric could feel a shriek building in his chest, fed by a terror he had never felt before.

Archon.

Even now, a century after the dark Magicker's conquest, the name was feared.

"How?" he kept his gaze averted from the bodies, as he struggled to regain his composure.

Alastair moved across the room and glanced out the window, before returning to the centre of the room. "I told you the Sword of Light had passed to Thomas's children, and on down the royal line, until today."

Eric nodded, his lips pursed tight as he listened to the old Magicker.

"But I did not tell you the rest of the story," Alastair closed his eyes, and a shadow passed across his face. The lines on his brow deepened, and when he looked at Eric again, he could see the sorrow behind them. "Thomas was cursed that day in Kalgan, when he and the Gods cast Archon from the Three Nations. The curse was subtle – a failsafe that did not attack him directly, but worked slowly overtime. By the time we realised what had happened, it was too late."

"You said Thomas lived to be an old man," Eric pressed.

"He did," pain flashed behind Alastair's eyes. "It was not his life the curse affected, but his magic, and the magic of his descendants. Down through the decades, their magic has weakened, corroded by Archon's darkness. With it, their control over the Sword has slipped. And now the magic of the Trolan King has failed. There is no one left to wield the Sword of Light."

Goosebumps stood up along Eric's arms as he stared at Alastair. "That means…"

Alastair nodded. "The last traces of the spell the Gods cast has dissolved. There is nothing left to stand between the Three Nations and Archon."

Ice trickled down Eric's neck. His throat constricted as he saw again the massed armies of Archon outside the walls of Chole, saw the fear in the eyes of Antonia as she spoke of his coming. Slowly he shook his head.

"What… how…" his eyes were slowly drawn to the murdered couple. "Who were they?" he whispered.

The silence stretched out for so long Eric began to think Alastair wouldn't answer. He was about to ask again when the old man straightened suddenly and shook his head. "Thomas had a sister. Her name was Aria. When we discovered the corruption in the magic of Thomas's children, we sent Aria into hiding, in case the day came when the Trolan kings lost their magic completely. The woman is her descendent."

Eric swallowed. "What does this mean then?"

Alastair's eyes did not leave the young couple as he replied. "They have a daughter."

~

Gabriel stood in the road and watched the house. People walked around him, giving a wide berth to the beast at his side, but he ignored their stares. He had only one thought now, one purpose. The rain did not bother him, nor the mud or the cold wind. All he cared about now was revenge.

"They went in there?" he asked.

Yes, the voice whispered in his mind, indistinguishable from his own thoughts.

"Are they still there?"

No, the wolf lifted its rain-soaked muzzle. *But there is something inside you must see.*

Nodding, Gabriel crossed the street and approached the house. As he drew closer, he realised some great force had caved in the door. Rain swept through the jagged hole where it had stood, soaking wooden floor boards inside. Cautiously, he stepped across the threshold and moved deeper into the house.

It didn't take him long to find what he needed to see. They lay in a pool of their own blood, faces pressed to the ground, their bodies marked by gruesome wounds. His chest contracted as an image flickered through his mind – of a house in ruins, and three pairs of eyes staring blankly up at him, dead amidst the rubble.

There is something else, the wolf moved around the room, its nose pressed to the ground. *Someone else.*

Growling, the wolf sank its fangs into the woven matt and dragged it sideways. The bodies came with it, leaving a bloody smear on the wooden floorboards beneath. Straightening, Gabriel walked across to the space that had been revealed. The blood had soaked through the matt and congealed in the gaps between the wood, making the trapdoor easy to recognise. Bending over it, Gabriel used his knife to pry it loose. The hinges groaned as it opened, revealing a ladder leading down into the darkness.

"Stay here," he said to the wolf.

Levering himself into the hole, Gabriel descended into the black. Six rungs down, his feet found solid ground, but in the darkness he could not see anything but the thin lines of light cast by the gaps in the floorboards.

As he straightened, a shriek erupted from the shadows. Gabriel hardly had time to spin around before a body slammed into him. Something caught him in the face, and he staggered backwards. He scrambled for purchase, but unseen objects littered the ground, and suddenly he found himself falling.

Before he could regain his feet, the creature landed on his chest. Howling like a banshee, it lashed out at him, catching him in the chest and face. Nails clawed at his skin, aiming for his eyes. Raising his arms, he struggled to fend off the attack. He gathered his strength and rolled to the side, sending his assailant toppling.

"*Die!*" the girl screamed as she leapt at him again.

Lunging forward, she sank her teeth into his shoulder. Still on the ground, Gabriel howled and swung at her face. The blow caught her in the cheek and sent her rolling into the darkness. A second later she came at him again, her screams echoing in the narrow space.

"*Die, die, die!*"

This time he was halfway to his feet when her shoulder collided with his stomach. The breath exploded between his teeth, but he managed to keep his feet.

"Stop," he choked. "It wasn't me. Please, let me help you!"

To his shock, the girl suddenly went still. Then a sob tore through the darkness, and she slid to the ground and buried her face in her arms. The light caught on the golden locks of her hair.

"Go on. Just kill me," she whispered.

Gabriel crouched down and wrapped his arms around the girl. She stiffened at his touch, but he did not let go. For a long time, they sat that way in the darkness, the silence stretching out between them. Breathing in the musty scent of her hair, Gabriel felt memories stir within him. The face of another woman rose in his mind.

My fiancée, tears sprang to his eyes as memories rose from the darkness of his mind. *I couldn't save her.*

Then he was weeping too, the hot tears spilling down his face in an endless torrent. In his arms, the girl looked up at him, her blue eyes shining in the light from the trapdoor. Slowly her sobs slowed, and taking a long breath, Gabriel regained his composure.

Seeing the shock in her eyes, Gabriel shrugged and gave a sad smile. "Come on. Let's get out of here."

The girl nodded, silent now, and followed him up the ladder. At the top, Gabriel climbed out and helped her over the lip of the trapdoor. In the daylight, he finally got a proper look at his unknown assailant.

Tears still brimmed in her sapphire eyes, but reaching up, she quickly wiped them away. The sunlight played across her hair, setting the blond curls aglow, while a single copper lock hung down across her face. Wrinkling her nose, she blew it from her eyes and then reached up to tuck it behind one ear. Her head came up to his shoulders, but despite her diminutive figure, she still had the curves and figure of a grown woman. Gabriel guessed she would be around sixteen or seventeen.

Before either of them could speak, a growl echoed across the room. Remembering the wolf, Gabriel spun to face the beast. It stalked across the floorboards, teeth bared, the hair along its neck bristling.

Gabriel held out a hand. "Easy, it's okay."

She must die!

Gabriel drew his sword. The wolf was right. The girl had to die.

He turned to face her – and found himself drawn into her sapphire eyes. They had widened as he drew his sword, but there were no more tears, no fear. Instead, she clenched her fists and drew herself up, ready to fight.

What am I doing?

Staring at the girl, he felt something crack within him, and his sanity came rushing back. Slowly, Gabriel lowered his blade. How could he even think about attacking her?

The wolf, he realised.

He turned again, and pointed his sword at the beast. The demon in the forest had tricked him, stolen away his memories, his soul. And for… what? Gabriel could no longer even remember.

"No more, demon spawn. Our deal is done," he growled.

So be it, the wolf whispered in his mind. *Then you shall die!*

Before Gabriel could react, the wolf leapt. It crashed into his chest, flinging him from his feet. Its teeth snapped at his face, but as he fell its momentum carried it past before it could catch him. The girl flung herself out of the way as it hurtled at her. Claws screeched on the floor, digging long grooves in the wood as it turned back towards him.

Gabriel hauled himself to his feet and faced the wolf again. From the corner of his eye, he saw the girl grab a chair and hold it out before her, ready for the next attack. The wolf howled, the sound echoing loudly in the little room, and began to circle. Its bright yellow eyes watched him, seeking a way past. He kept his sword low, pointed at its throat. He would not be knocked down so easily a second time.

Gathering himself, Gabriel lunged forward with his blade. The beast dodged back, but its claws slipped on the hard floor, slowing its retreat. Wrenching the tip of his sword around, Gabriel swung again, and brought it down on the wolf's skull.

The blade bit deep, scraping against bone. He gagged as a rotten stench filled the room. Yelping, the wolf retreated further. This time Gabriel let it go. If he followed, he would give it enough space to slip around him and attack the girl. Black blood dripped from his sword.

He crouched low as the wolf rushed him again, and stretched his sword out before him like a lance. At the last moment, he lunged forward, and the wolf ran straight onto the blade. Its momentum drove the tip deep into its chest, and howling, it staggered, wrenching the blade from his grip. Then the beast's weight crashed into him, throwing him to the ground.

Straightening, the wolf growled and staggered towards him. Before he could find his feet, it leapt. Air exploded from Gabriel's chest as it crashed down on him. Bloody saliva dripped from its maw as it leaned closer. The sword was still embedded in its chest, close to where its heart should be, but not close enough it seemed.

Goodbye, Gabriel.

As its jaws opened to tear out its throat, a chair came out of nowhere to smash the wolf from Gabriel. Before it could regain its feet, the girl leapt over him, and swung the chair again. A wild scream tore from her lips as it struck, crashing down on the beast's back. Again and again she swung, smashing at its head and chest. One blow caught the sword and drove it deeper. Finally, the beast's strength gave out, and it slumped to the ground unmoving.

Even then, the girl did not cease. Her face stricken with anger and grief, she smashed the chair into the broken body, until her weapon had been reduced to nothing more than a wooden club.

Pulling himself to his feet, Gabriel moved to the girl's

side and caught her arm as she raised it for another blow. She went still then, and a great shudder went through her.

"They're gone," she sobbed.

Her eyes were fixed on the man and woman lying dead on the rug, and Gabriel felt a wave of sympathy sweep through him. Taking her in his arms, he hugged her tight. "I know. I'll look after you."

She shuddered then, and her sobs cut off. Her chest swelled as she took a breath and pulled away.

"We should go," her voice was steady. "There are people out there, looking for me," she closed her eyes. "I wish I knew why."

Gabriel nodded. Reaching down, he pulled his sword from the wolf and wiped the blood away on the its fur. Silently, he made a vow to himself. Never again would he allow his sword to be used for evil.

He moved towards the door and paused. Turning back, he asked. "What is your name?"

"Enala," she said.

"I'm Gabriel."

Together they walked out the front door, and disappeared into the rain swept streets.

CHAPTER 17

For three days they searched for her. Three endless days in the wind and rain, questioning the family's acquaintances, scouring the streets, seeking any sign of the missing girl. Elynbrigge had given them a name – Enala – and a description of a young girl with blonde hair, marked by a single lock of fiery copper.

Yet there was not a whisper of her, not a single trace or rumour.

To make matters worse, wherever they went, Eric now found himself constantly looking over his shoulder. After what had happened to Enala's parents, he could not shake the feeling of being watched. Archon's servants could be anywhere, and judging by the way they had tortured the couple, they knew of the missing daughter.

In the race to find Enala, Alastair had been forced to bring Balistor and Caelin into the fold. Though Eric didn't know whether he trusted them or not, it seemed they had little choice now. The odds of finding the girl in the massive city grew less each day, and they needed the man power.

Now Eric was sitting at the table in their room. He held

his hands out to the fire, where a few lumps of coal burned, and cursed his wet clothes. Three days ago the rain had been a blessing, but in the search for Enala it only added to their misery. While the city celebrated around them, his spirits grew lower each day.

Archon was coming, and the Gods were helpless before his power. Only Enala could wield the Sword of Light, and add its magic to theirs. The fate of the Three Nations hung by the fragile thread of her life.

Alastair sat across from him, his face lined, his eyes downcast. A shadow hung over him, growing deeper with each passing day, with every false lead.

Outside the sun was setting on a third day of constant rain. Balistor and Caelin were still out searching the streets and pursuing leads. Alastair and Eric would head out again after dark, but for now, they were at the end of their strength.

"Where is she?" Alastair whispered to himself.

Eric shook his head. He could not begin to guess what the girl must be feeling, where she would go now. She obviously knew her parents were dead – they had watched the house for over a day before giving up on that avenue. But where would she go from there?

His heart sank as he thought of her alone in the Dying City. At night, denizens still ruled the streets, and he feared something might already have happened to the young girl.

I know you desire redemption, he shivered as he remembered Antonia's words back in the desert.

Now he finally knew what she'd meant. It had not been Chole she'd wanted him to save, but all the Three Nations. This was his quest, to help Alastair, to protect this girl. Then, maybe, he might finally put the ghosts of Oaksville to rest.

But only if he wasn't too late, only if Enala still lived.

He jumped as the door to their room suddenly burst open. Lightning flashed outside, casting the room in its blue glow. By its light, he saw Caelin standing in the doorway. His chest panting, he stepped inside and swung the door shut behind him. Thunder boomed, but over its roar, Eric made out his words.

"I think I've found her."

~

INKEN SIGHED as she sank onto the barstool and took a long sip of her ale. The cold drink was exactly what she needed after the day she'd had, though it did nothing to calm her worries.

Around her, the tavern was buzzing, alive with the laughter of her fellow bounty hunters. Sitting back on the stool, she took a moment to appreciate the sight, still not quite able to believe the transformation the rain had brought. Inken had never thought she'd see the day when the battle-hardened veterans of the Federation danced together like children. And yet here they were, still celebrating after three days of endless rain.

Her friend Kaiden sat beside her, one giant hand around a jug of ale, the other clutching a greasy haunch of lamb. Words tumbled from his mouth in a torrent, but Inken hardly heard him. Her thoughts were elsewhere; silently counting the years it would take to pay off her new debt.

She had spent the last few days attempting to restock her supplies after her disastrous trip through the desert. But despite the rain, equipment in Chole remained expensive, and she had been forced to take on debt from several lenders just to garner the funds for a mount and new weapons.

Maybe it wouldn't have been so bad, if not for the horse. The gelding had cost half her debt, and was a decent enough animal, but its colour left a lot to be desired. Limited by her funds, she had been forced to take what she could – but a white horse was about as conspicuous as you could get. Even the thickest criminal would soon hear about a warrior woman riding into town on a white horse.

The rest of her equipment was at least satisfactory. She now wore a light, well-balanced sabre that would give her extra reach in the saddle, and the oak recurve bow she had leant against the bar had obviously been carved with great care.

Inken looked up as a man brushed passed her, but he did not stop to apologise. She caught a wisp of smoke as he moved on across the tavern, but with his hood pulled up, she could not see his face. Even so, her curiosity was peeked, and she watched as he walked across to one of the larger tables.

The men at the table continued their conversation for several seconds before they finally noticed the newcomer and looked up. One muttered something Inken did not hear, but the hooded man only shook his head. Then, without warning, he leapt onto the table top.

Cursing, the men jumped back as mugs of ale tumbled into their laps. Across the tavern, the room fell silent as the other hunters turned to stare. Inken gaped as the hooded man spun to face the room, ignoring the enraged men around him.

"Bounty hunters!" he boomed. "I have a message for you! Some days ago, a bounty was offered – a lifetime's gold for the death of a demon. Some of your companions rode out to claim it."

A low murmuring spread around the room, as several men started to their feet. The men the hooded man had knocked from the table slowly drew daggers from their belts, but the newcomer paid them no attention.

"They failed!" the room stilled at the man's announcement. "And now the demon is here, in this proud city."

Silence stretched through the room as the hunters exchanged glances. Inken's heart began to race.

No, it can't be...

"Oaksville's Magistrate has been slain, but I am here to make good on his offer," as he spoke, the hooded man reached into his cloak and drew out a clothe bag. He tossed it to the ground, and the room stared as golden coins spilled across the floor. "There's a bag like that for every hunter who comes with me now. We will bring this demon and its accomplices to justice. Who's with me?"

Around Inken, the room erupted into cheers. But she did not move from her stool. Her heart sank as the man jumped down from the table and moved through the room, drawing the hunters with him. Her eyes were fixed on the gold coins, already disappearing into greedy hands.

The reward would more than cover her debt – would even provide enough for a new horse. And if the hunt was for a demon, why should she hesitate?

What if it's Eric? A voice whispered in the back of her mind.

Shivering, Inken looked up as Kaiden paused in front of her.

"You coming?" he grinned at her, open greed in his eyes.

Inken saw again the golden coins spilling across the ground. Taking a long breath, she nodded. This was an opportunity she couldn't afford to miss.

THE MAN in the black cloak strode down the street without looking back. He knew the fools would follow – they always did when gold was involved. They were blinded by their greed, their so-called ideals vanishing when wealth was at hand.

His anger flared then, as he remembered the defiance of Aria's ancestors. They had taken their secret to the grave, refusing to give up their daughter under even mortal agony. Instead they had forced him to watch Alastair and Elynbrigge, in the hope the old men might find the girl for him, as they had done with the family.

But after three days, his patience was at an end. It was clear the old Magickers were as clueless to the girl's location as everyone else. Their usefulness had come to an end – it was time to remove them from the game. He grinned at the thought. His master would be pleased to see the end of his wily old foes. It would be a heavy blow against the cursed Goddess.

Striding down the muddy streets, he cursed the rain. Somehow, the boy had shattered his master's curse, and restored life to the city. In the end, it would not matter, but he was glad his trap would also bring an end to the young Magicker. Though it was a waste to destroy one with such power, it was far better than seeing it join the other side.

In the darkness ahead, the lights of the inn loomed through the pouring rain. Reaching out with his mind, he searched for the aftertaste of magic. It clung to the boy like mud, but now it was gone, the inn empty of power.

Leaving the hunters outside, he strode inside to investigate. The innkeeper had not seen where they had gone, but one of the waitresses mentioned seeing them heading east from the inn.

Outside again, he gathered the hunters around him. Leaving most to take up stations around the inn, he gave them a description of Alastair and his group, and left them with instructions to kill on sight. Looking at the grizzled faces of the hunters, he knew they would obey his instructions without question. They knew they faced a demon, they knew such a creature would slaughter them all if they gave it a chance.

It wasn't true, of course, but the lie served his purpose well.

Taking the remaining men, he started down the streets leading east. A few blocks from the inn, he paused again at a crossroads, and nodded slowly to himself. If Alastair and the others returned the way they had come, they would inevitably arrive at the crossroads. Stationing the remaining hunters in the shadows, he left them there with the same orders as the others.

Then he moved off into the night, satisfied his trap would succeed with or without his presence. He hoped to return in time to see Alastair finally meet his end, but in the meantime there was one more thing he had left to do, one last chess piece to eliminate.

Sucking in a breath, Eric took another step up the worn staircase. The stone was slick beneath his feet, and he moved with measured care, doing his best not to glance at the open space away to his left. Above he heard the footsteps of the others moving confidently upwards, but he did not dare look anywhere but his feet. Silently he prayed they were close to the top of the wall.

The wind howled around him, threatening to pluck him from the treacherous staircase, and reaching out a hand he clutched at the stones to his right. Smooth as they were, they offered little purchase, but he still drew a small measure of reassurance from them. Shivering, he moved on, silently cursing himself for leaving his cloak behind.

Above, the crunch of footsteps ceased, and after a moment's hesitation, Eric drew to a stop. His gaze still locked to the steps, he blinked rain from his eyes, and waited for his companions to resume their climb.

Laughter carried down to him. "What are you doing, Eric?" Caelin called.

"Why have we stopped?" Eric shouted back.

"We've reached the top, Eric," Alastair's voice was rich with humour. "You're just a few steps away."

Eric's cheeks grew hot, and cursing under his breath he moved up the last few steps and scowled at the two men. Then he walked past them, out onto the battlements. The path along the top of the wall was lined on either side by tall crenulations, which offered at least some shelter from the wind. The wall stretched away through the swirling rain, lit only by the occasional torch.

Caelin took the lead again, moving off along the parapet. Eric and Alastair followed close on his heels, eager to reach the end of their quest. Somewhere up here was a man who might have seen Enala. They had already been to the eastern gate where they had expected to find him, only to learn he had been switched to a patrol atop the wall.

Overhead, lightning flashed, and Eric wondered what the guard had done to deserve the switch in duties. Thunder rolled across the wall, so loud Eric almost had to cover his ears. For three days now the storm had raged, and looking out across the city, Eric found himself wondering how much more it could take.

On the other side of the wall, Mount Chole loomed above them, its slopes stretching almost to the wall itself. He remembered Alastair mentioning how the Magickers of the city had halted the lava's advance, and staring out into the darkness, he could almost imagine the molten rock crawling towards the city.

Ahead, a figure loomed through the gloom. He wore a heavy trench coat over his chainmail and a hood pulled tight around his head, though Eric doubted either did much against the rain. As they drew to a stop beside him, lightning lit the mountainside beyond, and for a moment it seemed to Eric the slope was moving. Then the darkness resumed and he turned his attention back to the guard.

Caelin stepped up to the guard, but Eric could not make out the words that passed between them. Then Caelin nodded and returned to speak with Alastair.

"This is the man," he shouted over the storm's fury. "He'll say that much, but he's refusing to tell me about the girl."

Alastair scowled and elbowed his way past Caelin. Striding up to the guard, he slipped his hand inside his cloak. The guard flinched back and reached for his sword, but Alastair only drew a small cloth bag from his cloak. He tossed it to the guard, who barely managed to catch it before it tumbled over the side.

"Wha–?" the guard stuttered.

"That's what you want, isn't it?" Alastair moved a step closer, until he stood nose to nose with the guard.

Despite Alastair's obvious age, the guard shrank beneath the old man's gaze. His mouth opened and closed, before he quickly snatched a glance inside the bag.

"The girl," Alastair growled.

"What, yes, of course, my memory is coming back," he nodded and tucked the pouch inside the pocket of his coat. "There was a girl. She left by the eastern gate a few hours ago. Pretty little thing. Was on gate duty then. Shoulda kept my mouth shut, might still be down there in the dry."

Alastair nodded impatiently. "Yes, yes, but the girl, what did she look like? Did she follow the road?"

"Can't tell you much I'm afraid," the man glanced out at the mountains. "The rains great and all, but it makes keeping watch a right chore. Her hair was hidden beneath her hood, but from what I glimpsed it was blonde. Small face, small nose, small girl. Oh, and crystal blue eyes. Only glimpsed them when she glanced back, at the end. They followed the road round the base of the mountains and up towards the north, far as I could see."

"They?" Alastair interrupted.

"Yeah. There was a guy with her. Didn't get a good look at him either. He had a sword, couldn't have been much older than her, but that was all I noticed. Strange business, two young folks venturing out in this," he nodded at Caelin. "We were discussing it, the boys and me, when your buddy there heard us."

Alastair nodded slowly to himself, and with a wave, moved away from the guard. A few steps along the ramparts, he glanced back. "Thank you. I'd appreciate if you didn't mention the girl to anyone else."

The guard grinned and patted his chest. The clink of coins carried to Eric over the pounding rain. "Don't think I need to, sir!"

Turning back to Eric and Caelin, he shook his head. "It might be her. She matches the description Elynbrigge gave me, but he said nothing about a boy. Still, it's the only lead we have. Eric and I will go after them. Caelin, find Balistor and head back to the inn. Bring the horses and try to catch up. We'll leave signs for you to follow if they leave the road… Eric, are you listening?"

Eric shook his head. He moved past Alastair to the edge of the crenulations, and stared out into the darkness beyond the wall. Over the rumbling of thunder, he heard an answering roar, like an echo of the sky's fury. His eyes strained to pierce the darkness, searching for the source.

Then lightning flashed, casting its glow across the mountainside, revealing the stark rock in its eerie light. And mud – mud rushing down the slope towards them, a wall of earth tumbling down the side of Mount Chole.

"*Landslide!*" he screamed.

Alastair and Caelin turned to stare as another jagged bolt of lightning flashed across the sky. A second later the darkness returned, but by then they had all seen it. The guard screamed as he raced past, and beneath their feet, the wall began to shake.

"*Gods,*" Caelin cursed. "It'll bury half the city."

No, no, no! Not again!

Staring into the darkness, Eric sank to his knees, his hands tearing at his hair. He felt no fear, only a deep despair, as he resigned himself to death. At least here, finally, he too would be a victim of his own folly. There was no escaping the oncoming flood of stone and mud.

Then Alastair stepped up to the ramparts, his hands raised above his head. The wind whipped around him, trying to cast him from the wall, but he stood against the storm's fury, his eyes fixed on the tide of death rumbling towards them.

"What are you doing?" Eric shouted over the roar of falling earth.

"What I must," Alastair faced the mountain.

Eric's head pounded and his ears squealed as Alastair gathered his magic. Red burned across his vision, and for a moment he was blind. The wall beneath them shook harder, until it seemed the stones themselves would come unstuck, and the whole structure would come crumbling down. On hands and knees, Eric crawled to the edge of the ramparts and looked out at the oncoming nightmare.

The landslide came on, but now the earth before the wall was rising into the air. Boulders and stones and mud and water alike disobeyed the laws of gravity, while around them the air shimmered with magic.

On the wall, Alastair's arms began to shake. His neck stretched taught, the tendons strained to breaking point. His lips drew back in an awful scowl and he clenched his teeth, as though he held the weight of the city on his shoulders. Soon his whole body was shaking, but still more debris rose to join the conflagration before the wall.

Eric groaned as one of Alastair's legs gave way, and the old man sank to one knee. The lines on the Magicker's face deepened. It could only be a matter of time now. No man could take such strain.

Then Alastair threw down his hands, and Eric felt another surge of energy. Suddenly the host of debris before the wall was no longer stationary, but racing upwards, a second landslide to match the first.

A deafening boom shook the wall as the two mammoths of earth met. Mud sprayed forty feet above the mountain plains, and a high-pitched screech rent the air. Boulders the size of houses shattered with the force of the collision, and on the wall Eric and Caelin ducked for cover as stone rained down on them. Out on the plain, mud swirled, and began to settle.

On the ramparts, Alastair crumpled without a sound. Covering his head, Eric crawled to where he lay, and used his body to shield the old man from the hail of rock. Alastair's face was deathly pale and he did not respond as Eric shook him. Desperately he felt his wrist for a pulse, and let out a long sigh as he found the faintest beat.

"Is he alive?" Caelin called.

"Barely," Eric responded.

CHAPTER 18

Elynbrigge opened his eyes as a cool breeze blew through the open window. Every breath was an effort now, each exhalation a struggle that left him gasping. The blood flowed sluggishly through his veins, and his chest ached with each laboured beat of his heart. It would not be long now before death came for him, but before then, there was one last thing he needed to do.

Gathering his strength, he called out. "Michael! Michael, I need you."

It only took a few seconds for the priest to appear. The young man frowned when he saw Elynbrigge and quickly knelt beside him.

"Elynbrigge, are you okay?"

Elynbrigge wheezed as he nodded. "Yes, yes, as good as I will ever be."

With Michael's help, he managed to sit up. Though his own eyes had long since given in to the advance of time, he saw the young man clearly with his inner eye. The doctor's soul shone with strength, with the courage he had hidden beneath years of prayer and study. Elynbrigge drew reassurance from the sight, though guilt still ate at his soul, knowing the sacrifice he was about to ask of the young man.

"I am old, Michael, that is all," he continued. "But my health is not your concern now. There are others who need your help."

Michael frowned as he rocked back on his haunches. "Why do they need me? Surely your magic would serve them better – I'm only a doctor."

"You sell yourself short, Michael," Elynbrigge smiled. "I am too weak to help them now. And these people will not be coming here. You must go to them."

He described the path Michael would need to take to the inn where Alastair was staying, and silently prayed the old Magicker had the strength to make it back. The unleashing of power he had sensed had unmistakably been Alastair's, but rarely had Elynbrigge sensed such an expenditure of power. It would be a miracle if his old friend survived. It was true, Michael could do little to help the company, but he was all they had now.

"Why do these people need me? Who are they?" Michael questioned.

Elynbrigge smiled. "They are the ones who brought the injured woman. My old friend needs aid, and you are all they have left," he paused before continuing. "If you go to them, you must leave with them."

"Why?" he heard the confusion behind Michael's voice. "My place is here, with the temple."

"If you return here, Michael, their enemies will come for you. They will take you and torture you until you break. And they will burn this temple to the ground."

As Elynbrigge finished, Michael stood and began to pace the room. Elynbrigge could sense the man's anger, could see it in the sudden red of his soul. He had been given an impossible choice. To follow his calling and aid those in need, he would need to sacrifice everything he knew, everyone he loved.

But time was trickling away, and Elynbrigge could sense death approaching. Michael needed a final push, though Elynbrigge was loath to give it. Closing his eyes, he let out a long breath, and made his decision.

"These people are servants of Antonia," Elynbrigge whispered. "If you help them, Michael, you will be serving the Goddess herself. You may even meet her."

Michael exhaled sharply. "Antonia herself?"

Elynbrigge almost wished he could take back the words, but he only nodded, his soul sick with guilt. He could feel the joy flooding through the young doctor. The choice was gone – who would turn down the chance to meet their God?

"I would give my life to serve the Goddess," Michael said.

It may come to that, Elynbrigge thought, while out-loud he said. "Then go to them – there is no time to waste. Good luck, my friend. May Antonia watch over you."

Michael fled the room, leaving the old priest to gather his thoughts. Silently, he sent up a prayer for Michael's soul. If he survived this quest, he would be a priest no longer. Win or lose, the darkness would change him forever. He was strong though, possessing an inner strength that would rise to the challenge. Elynbrigge prayed it would be enough.

It was not long before his second visitor arrived. Elynbrigge straightened as the hooded man stepped into the room, though he could not help but flinch as he glimpsed the man's soul. It flickered with the angry red of rage, tainted purple with a dark hate.

"Elynbrigge, it is a pleasure to finally meet you," the voice was soft and mocking. "I've heard much about you, though I am afraid you do not live up to the legend. Age does not become you."

"Time claims us all."

The man laughed. "It will not come for me, nor my master. The darkness defies its passage. When Archon comes, I will live forever."

"And yet you do not live at all," Elynbrigge's voice was touched with sadness. "What is left of the man you once were? Where is your soul? What is immortality, without joy?"

"It is *immortality*. I would not expect *you* to understand," his voice was touched with hate. "But I thank you for your information. Without you, we would never have found the family."

Elynbrigge's heart twisted at the man's words, but he did not back down. "The girl still lives. She will be the end of you all."

A cold laughter echoed through the room. "The girl has fled. Not even Alastair can find her now," the man paused. "And it is time we removed you both from the board."

Despite himself, Elynbrigge felt the cold touch of fear at the man's words.

"There is no need to kill me," he whispered. "I am an old man, my days of power long past. I will play no part in this fight. My only desire now is to spend my final days healing the sick. Will you not give me that?"

His visitor cackled. "You and Alastair alone remain from the days of Archon's war. For that alone, you must die. The last shackles of the past fall tonight, and neither you nor Alastair will be here to see the dawn of our new age."

"Alastair will not die so easily," but Elynbrigge knew his words rang false. At this moment, his old friend had nothing left to give. "And I would rather die than see your new age."

"Death, I can grant you," the man raised his hands.

~

ALASTAIR'S BREATHING was growing weaker with each breath. He hung over Caelin's shoulders, his head bouncing loosely with every step. He seemed little more than a pile of bones and skin now, as though the magic had drained away his substance, leaving only a husk in its place.

Eric followed close behind the sergeant as they moved through the silent streets. The rain had begun to clear, but its heavy scent still lingered in the air. Above, the first slivers of the moon pierced the clouds, casting thin rays of light across the city. Lanterns burned on the street corners, lighting their way.

The young soldier led them through the twisting streets, his pace even despite Alastair's weight on his shoulder. Eric's breath came in ragged gasps as he struggled to keep up, and his eyes scanned the shadows. The memory of the murdered couple still weighed heavily on his mind. Archon's servants could be anywhere, and without Alastair they were vulnerable. But nothing moved in the shadows, and they continued on through the streets unobstructed.

When Caelin finally paused to catch his breath, Eric took a chance to look around. They stood at a crossroads, its four corners lit by flickering lantern light. After a moment, Eric realised he recognised the buildings around them, and let out a long breath of relief. They were only a few blocks from the inn now.

Smiling, he turned towards Caelin, when a faint rustling came from behind him. He spun, and glimpsed the gleam of steel as a blade hurtled from the shadows. He dove to the side, but too slowly, and gasped as the dagger plunged into his side. The breath exploded from his lungs as he struck the ground, and white light danced across his vision.

Caelin dropped Alastair and leapt over Eric, his sword already sliding from its sheath. A dagger appeared in his other hand as the soldier faced the shadows.

On the ground, Eric muffled a groan. Glancing down, he saw the dagger's hilt protruding from his side. Hot blood ran down his leg as he tried to move, and he quickly lay still. Looking up, he watched as three men emerged into the light. Their dark clothing clung to the shadows at their back. Big, muscular men, they hefted their greatswords and closed on Caelin, spreading out as they approached. They moved quickly, eager to encircle their prey. Once surrounded, Caelin would have no way of defending himself against all three of them. The fight would be over before it began.

But Caelin was no fool. Before they could spring their trap, he sprang at the man on his left. His sword snaked out, and his opponent only managed a clumsy jab to turn the blow aside. He staggered backwards, his eyes widening as Caelin attacked again. Steel rung on steel as their swords met, before Caelin drove his dagger deep into the man's stomach.

Tearing back his dagger, Caelin retreated a step and brought his sword to the ready. The wounded man staggered after him a few steps, and then pitched face-first to the ground. Groaning, he clawed at the hole in his stomach as a dark puddle formed around him.

Caelin faced the remaining thugs and grinned, raising an arm to beckon them forward. They exchanged a glance, and then drew closer together, wary now. Caelin stood fixed in place, his sword raised high in his right hand, his bloody dagger low in his left.

The night rang with the clash of steel as the men charged. They were no novices, and their swords buzzed like wasps, the tips stabbing out like stingers seeking flesh. But for every blow, Caelin's blades were there to turn them aside, and for a while the young soldier seemed untouchable.

Then Caelin grunted, and staggered backwards. A trail of blood ran from a cut across his forehead, dripping into his eyes. Boldened, his foes chased after him, swords poised to strike. The first man drew ahead, crossing the other's path as he thrust his blade at Caelin's throat.

At the last moment, Caelin straightened, his sword swinging around to block the blow. But the man came on, intent on the kill. He raised his greatsword high above his head, and swung it down at Caelin's head.

Sparks flew as the blades met, and Caelin was forced back a step. The thug swung again, and Caelin retreated further, his breath coming in ragged gasps now. The second attacker struggled to join the fight, but Caelin was retreating too fast, drawing the first man with him.

Suddenly the two-handed attacker froze mid-swing, his sword still raised above his head. Then he slowly toppled backwards, and Eric gaped as he saw Caelin's dagger buried in the man's throat.

Caelin strode over the corpse, his face grim. The last man backed away, his face pale, and dropped his blade in surrender. Caelin continued towards him, until the man turned and fled down the street.

His shoulders slumped then, and with measured care he returned his sword to its sheath. Turning to look at Eric, he forced a smile. "Are you telling me I have to carry you *both* now?"

Eric would have laughed, if it weren't for the pain. Gritting his teeth, he reached down to grasp the hilt of the dagger.

"Leave it," Caelin said. "You'll do more damage if you pull it out. And you'd probably bleed to death before we got two blocks. Best leave it for a professional."

"What do we do?"

"We get to the inn. When we're safe, I'll send for someone. Then we go after the girl."

~

THE HOODED MAN watched silently from the shadows, cursing the incompetence of the bounty hunters. Still, he was not surprised. They were a probe, a test of their strength before he revealed himself. Now two were wounded, the third exhausted. Creeping closer, he prepared himself, already imagining the ecstasy he would feel as he drove his blade through Alastair's damned heart.

"Then we go after the girl," the soldier said.

He froze. What did he mean? Had they finally found the girl, after all this time? Had Enala emerged from hiding? If so, it would not take long to track her down himself. But it would be faster still to hear the information from them, as he had the family. His master had been enraged to hear she had escaped him the first time. If she slipped through his fingers a second time… it did not bear thinking of.

Sliding back into the shadows, he slunk down a nearby alley. If he beat them back to the inn, he could delay the ambush. He needed time to listen for what they knew about the girl. He would have them wait an hour before launching their assault.

Then he would wipe the board clean.

ERIC GROANED as Caelin kicked his way through the inn's wooden door. A wave of warm air spilled over him, and every face in the dining room turned to stare. Caelin stumbled inside, Eric slung over one shoulder, Alastair the other. Eric could feel the sergeant trembling beneath their weight, overwhelmed by the cold and exhaustion.

"Are you okay?" a voice called from the back of the crowded room.

"A doctor," Caelin croaked, sinking to the floor.

"Here!" a man responded as someone threaded their way through the crowd.

Eric looked up at the voice. "That's *Michael*, the priest from the temple. What is he doing here?"

"Elynbrigge sent me," Michael said softly as he crouched beside Caelin. "What's happened?"

"Explanations can wait," Caelin snapped. "Please, take the old man, for God's sake. Before I drop him."

Michael bent and took Alastair over his shoulder. The old Magicker remained unconscious and Michael staggered beneath his weight. He was not a heavily built man, and Eric doubted the doctor would make it far beneath Alastair's weight.

"I'll take him," Balistor appeared from the crowd.

"Where have you been?" Caelin grunted. Michael handed over Alastair's limp body to the Magicker.

"Looking for the girl," Balistor grunted as he took the old man's weight. "What the hell happened to you three? No one was here when I returned."

Eric watched through a haze as they moved through the inn. His heart pounded in his chest as he saw people staring. It was not safe. Word of their entrance would spread quickly, and their enemies would not be far behind. They needed to leave the city and go after Enala, if she had not been buried by the mudslide. He tried to speak, but each footstep sent a fresh wave of agony through his side.

People moved aside as they pushed their way through the crowd and moved up the stairs. Eric focused on the heavy thud of Caelin's boots, the sound anchoring him to consciousness. At the top of the staircase, Balistor led the way to their room and unlocked the door with Alastair's key. Caelin and Michael followed him inside.

A wave of relief swept through Eric as Caelin laid him on his bed. He sank onto the soft cushion, his mind swimming, and for a moment he felt as though he were floating. Then his vision began to whirl, and he closed his eyes, willing it to stop.

"What happened?" Balistor asked grimly.

"We were attacked," Caelin said. "Ambushed on our way back to the inn. I stopped them, just."

Glass chinked and Eric cracked open his eyes. Balistor had laid Alastair on the other bed. Michael sat beside the old man, busy rummaging in his shoulder bag. His hand emerged holding a vial of bright green liquid. He placed the vial to the old man's lips and gently tipped a few drips into his mouth.

"This is a restorative potion," the doctor announced to the room. "It's the strongest I have, but his heart is barely beating. I don't think it will be enough.

"No," Eric croaked, trying to sit up.

Caelin placed a firm hand on his chest, pushing him back down. "Stay calm, Eric. Save your strength," he turned to the doctor. "Is there anything else you can do?"

Michael shook his head. "I'm only a doctor. A Magicker or Healer might find a way to save him, but he's too far gone for my skills," his eyes settled on Eric. "But the young man I might be able to help."

Eric shrank back against the bed as Michael moved to his side. The doctor's eyes were grim as he studied the dagger protruding form Eric's side. The look on his face sent a chill down Eric's spine.

Am I going to die? He dared not voice the question.

Eric shrieked as the doctor reached down and prodded the flesh around his wound. He flinched away from the doctor's touch, and his hand flashed out to catch Michael by the tunic. Baring his teeth, a low growl came from his throat as he stared into the doctor's amber eyes.

But Michael only tisked and calmly brushed away Eric's

hands. He dived into his bag again, coming up with a bottle of clear liquid. He removed the cap, and the harsh tang of alcohol spread through the room.

"Hold him down. This is going to hurt," Michael said.

Eric tensed as Caelin and Balistor took a hold of his arms. He struggled to stay calm as Michael prepared a swab. He knew the alcohol would burn away any infection in the wound, but just the thought of the pain it would cause brought tears to his eyes.

Taking the alcohol soaked swab, Michael leaned over Eric and grasped the dagger's handle. Slowly, he began to draw the blade from Eric's side.

Eric arched his back as his mouth opened, but he could not even find the breath to scream. Fire burned through his side, stealing away his breath, and waves of shock rippled through him. The world spun and he fought against his comrades' strength, desperate to free himself from their iron grasp. A string of curses tumbled from his mouth.

When the darkness finally rose up to claim him, Eric embraced it with open arms.

THE BOOM of a distant explosion tore Eric from the darkness. He sat up as a scream echoed through the room, and saw Michael standing at the open door, staring out into the corridor. Alastair still lay in the opposite bed, but Caelin and Balistor had vanished.

Without thinking, Eric's hand went to his side. His fingers found the jagged edges of his wound, held together by neat rows of stitches. Pain rippled through him as he took a breath, but his head at least seemed clearer now.

Michael looked back and blinked when he saw Eric awake. Quickly he moved back to the bed.

"I washed it out as well as I could, under the circumstances. After I stitched you up I gave you a little concoction for the pain. You were lucky though; the blade didn't hit anything vital. I'll put a poultice on it later," he paused. "If there is a later."

"What do you mean?"

"Something's happening downstairs. Your friends have gone to investigate."

At that moment, Caelin strode back into the room. "We have to go," he winced as a scream came from somewhere below. "Now."

Moving to the window, Caelin levered it open and peered outside. Eric shivered as the cold night air swept through the room.

"There are men downstairs – hunters. They're looking for us. Balistor is holding them at the stairs. You three are going out the window."

"I don't think that's a good idea," Michael ventured.

"What about you, Caelin?" Eric demanded.

"We'll follow you. Pick up Alastair, doctor," Caelin ordered.

Michael hesitated until Caelin stepped towards him, and then raised his hands in surrender. Looping his bag over one shoulder, he reached down and picked up Alastair in both arms. Straining beneath his weight, he moved to the window. The broad frame allowed him to step up onto the sill without difficulty, but there he paused, glancing back at them.

"You don't expect me to jump, do you?" Michael asked.

Without answering, Caelin gave the doctor a kick in the back, and Michael and Alastair vanished through the opening.

Smiling, Caelin looked back at Eric. "Alastair chose your room well. There's a big bale of hay beneath the window.

They'll be fine. Now, it's your turn. Careful with the landing, you're probably going to burst a few stitches."

"Wait!" Eric struggled as Caelin lifted him from the bed.

Caelin didn't bother replying. Stepping across to the window, he tossed Eric out.

Panic flooded Eric as he suddenly found himself falling. His limbs flailed in every direction, scrambling for a hold that wasn't there. The stitches in his side pulled tight, and below, the haystack rushed up to meet him. Closing his eyes, Eric stretched out his arms to break his fall, fear gripping his stomach.

Something stirred in Eric's chest, and suddenly he was no longer falling. He opened his eyes, and gasped as he found himself hovering several feet above the haystack. Wind swirled around his body, pushing him upwards, holding him aloft in a maelstrom of air.

Staring in bewilderment, Eric's terror fell away. The winds went with it, and he dropped unceremoniously the last few feet into the damp hay.

A shout came from overhead, and Eric looked up in time to see Caelin tumbling through the air. He disappeared into the haystack beside Eric.

Balistor appeared next. He stood in the window, fire leaping from his hands to catch on the wooden frame. Then the Magicker went stiff, his eyes widening in shock. His hands slid from the windowsill and he toppled forward through the window. The fire in his hands died, and Eric gaped as he saw an arrow protruding from his back.

Then Michael was hauling Eric up, dragging him from the haystack. Caelin followed a step behind them, carrying Balistor over his shoulder.

He'll have carried all of us by the end of the night, Eric almost laughed at the thought.

They gathered in the alleyway, their breath steaming in

the icy air as they looked up at the window they'd fled through. The fire had engulfed it and the room beyond, preventing their pursuers from following them through. But it would not take them long to circle around, and looking at their ragged group, Eric realised there was no way the two men left standing could carry the rest of them to safety. Looking around, he spotted the rear door to the stables nearby, and his heart lifted with sudden hope.

Then the unmistakable whisper of steel on leather came from the shadows. Men began to emerge into the firelight – five, ten, a dozen. Each held their weapons at the ready, the cold steel glinting in the light of the flames above. They quickly spread out to encircle the five companions.

Eric swallowed. Backs to the wall, surrounded by enemies, there was no escape.

Caelin stepped forward, his sword sliding from its scabbard.

"Come on then," he growled. "Who dies first?"

CHAPTER 19

Inken cursed as the wet roofing tiles slipped beneath her feet, and quickly took a step back. But she was too late, and she swore again as a tile broke free and tumbled down into the street below. The crash echoed through the empty alleyway. She winced, imagining the angry glares of the hunters below. Shaking her head in a silent apology, she sat back at a safer angle and eyed the inn's dark windows.

It was a good trap – she had to give the hooded man that. A dozen men were set to storm the front of the building in just under an hour. They had been all set to go when their mysterious benefactor returned with new orders to delay their attack. He had been just in time – only a few minutes later, word had been passed along to Inken that the group had returned.

In case the men who went in front failed to bring down the demon, a dozen men had also been left in the alleyway out back to seal off all avenues of escape. Inken had volunteered to scale one of the buildings overlooking the alley, her intuition telling her their prey was wily enough to elude a frontal assault. The hooded man had offered extra gold for each kill, and she fully intended to collect it.

A shout erupted from the inn and Inken calmly reached down and strung her bow. Nocking an arrow, she scanned the windows for movement. It would not be long now.

Before she could react, two people hurtled from a second storey window. Gaping, Inken straightened and peered down into alleyway, expecting to see them crumpled on the bricks below. But a smile tugged at her lips as she saw them scrambling from a haystack, and she shook her head, impressed by their ingenuity.

As she took aim, another body flew from the window, but to her surprise this one did not reach the haystack. She froze, staring at the dark-cloaked figure hovering in the air, gusts of straw swirling around him.

"Magic," Inken whispered.

Silently she shook herself free of her shock, and drew back on her bowstring. Her target was completely exposed, without so much as a shred of shelter to protect him. Drawing in a deep breath, Inken squinted down the length of her arrow, preparing to loose as she exhaled. Then the figure rotated in the air, and Inken caught a glimpse of his face, of his unkept black hair and shocking blue eyes.

Eric!

Her jaw dropped and suddenly her heart was racing. She hesitated, her arm beginning to tremble with the force of her bowstring, but she could not release. Then whatever forces that were holding Eric aloft vanished, and he disappeared into the haystack. Easing back on her bowstring, Inken struggled for breath, frozen with indecision.

Footsteps clattered in the alleyway as the bounty hunters emerged from their hiding places. Two more bodies tumbled from the window, bringing Eric's party to five. The hunters would be on them in moments.

Worry touched Inken's heart as she noticed a green-robed man carrying Eric from the haystack.

Has he been injured?

She frowned at the thought, struggling to push her compassion to the back of her mind. She had a job to do, a bounty to collect. She had to put an end to these men, before others claimed her reward.

She nocked her arrow again. The hunters below were spreading out to surround their quarry, backing Eric's group up against the alley wall. Inken took aim as a man stepped from the group and drew his sword. He faced the hunters without fear, his eyes calm.

A shiver ran through Inken's body as she watched them. She drew in a breath to steady her aim, but her heart still raced.

Can I do it? she asked herself.

Then she exhaled, and loosed her arrow.

THE LARGEST OF the hunters raised his sword and grinned. Michael stepped back, his arms shaking, until his back was pressed against the stone wall. Eric struggled to summon his magic, but it slipped from the grasp of his sluggish mind.

Between them and the hunters, Caelin stood strong as the hulking man raised his sword and charged.

Before he could take two steps, a black-feathered arrow sprouted from the man's head. He halted midstride, his sword slipping from limp fingers. Slumping to his knees, he crumpled to the ground.

The other hunters froze, their eyes lifting to scan the roofs for the hidden archer. A couple shrank back a step, but one threw caution to the wind and leapt at them with a snarl. A second arrow took him in the shoulder, spinning him to the ground. More quickly followed, and chaos spread through the hunters as black-feathered missiles rained down on them.

Roaring, Caelin charged into their midst. He screamed his fury as his sword cut a ragged hole through their ranks. In seconds, the last vestiges of the hunters' courage dissolved, and then they were fleeing down the alleyway, leaving half their number dead behind them.

Caelin dared not follow them. Looking up, he scanned the rooftops for their hidden ally, though in the dim light it was an impossible task. Breath held, they waited beneath the burning window.

Moments later, the echo of horse hooves echoed down the alleyway from the opposite direction to which the hunters had fled. Caelin spun, sword raised.

"Put that away," Inken ordered as she rode up. "And get your horses. You're going to need them."

Eric gaped as he stared up at her. She sat astride a silver horse, aglow in the light of the fire in the inn. The curls of her scarlet hair tumbled down her sun-kissed face, where the marks of the desert had vanished, revealing the smooth curves of her cheekbones. She wore a tight-fitting leather jerkin and pants that hugged her body tight. A sabre hung from her belt and a bow had been strapped to her saddle.

She grinned as their eyes met. "Good to see you again, Eric. I couldn't help but notice you were in a bit of trouble."

Michael's grip around Eric slipped, forcing him to take some of his own weight, and he stifled a groan. Inken dismounted and moved to his side, her brow creased.

"You're a welcome sight," Eric attempted a grin. "But I've had better days."

Inken nodded quickly and flashed him a wink before turning to Caelin. "The horses, quickly. They won't take long to regroup."

As she spoke, a roar came from behind them, and Eric turned to see fire tearing through the roof of the inn. A crash came from deep inside the building and a blast of hot air swept from the lower windows. Guilt touched his chest, knowing they had caused the inn's demise. There was sadness too – the little room upstairs had been the closest he'd had to a home in a long time.

Caelin and Inken ran into the stables, leaving Eric leaning on Michael. Together they watched the alleyway for hint of movement, though they were helpless to defend themselves should the hunters return. But for once, luck went their way, and a few moments later their comrades returned leading the horses.

Eric's heart lifted as he saw Elcano and Briar emerge from the stables, followed by three horses he guessed were Balistor's, Caelin's and Michael's. With Michael's help, he climbed up into Briar's saddle, before the doctor went on to help tie Alastair and Balistor to their own saddles. Both remained unconscious, and staring at Alastair's hollowed face, Eric's could not suppress the sinking feeling in his stomach.

But there was no time to contemplate his mentor's fate. Inken mounted her shining white horse and took the lead. She waved them on along the alleyway, the echo of horse hooves on stone loud in the narrow corridor.

They emerged from the maze of alleyways several blocks from the inn, and quickly picked up the pace. Eric winced as the thud of Briar's stride sent pain lancing from his side, but he kept his eyes fixed on Inken, waiting for some sign, some reason for her rescue. He was still struggling to come to grasps with her appearance. She was a bounty hunter, after all. Those had been her comrades back there, maybe even her friends. What could have driven her to stand against them?

Caelin rode up beside her, his eyes fixed straight ahead. "We need to take the north gate. The east is blocked."

Inken nodded. "We'd better move quickly. There's a hefty price on your head – half the bounty hunters in the city are out looking for you. They won't be far behind."

"I'll take the rear then." So saying, Caelin tugged on his reins, allowing the others to overtake him.

"What happened to you?" Inken asked as they drew level.

Eric shivered, trying to clear his thoughts. Whatever Michael had given him had left him lethargic, and he found his mind drifting, distracted by the sight of Inken. "Long story…" he hesitated. "But I was stabbed. I'll tell you the rest when we're clear of the city."

"You have magic," Inken pressed. "I saw it. Does that mean..."

Eric closed his eyes. She didn't need to finish the question – it was obvious what she was asking.

Did you destroy Oaksville?

"Yes," he forced out the words through grated teeth. "Yes, it was me, before Alastair found me, and saved me from my magic. He's a Magicker as well. After Oaksville… after Oaksville he made me his apprentice. He is teaching me to control my power, so… so no one else dies."

Taking a breath, he risked a glance at Inken. Silent tears trailed down her cheeks, sparkling in the moonlight. Her expression was unreadable, and Eric quickly looked away.

"Did you bring the rain?" Eric jumped as Inken spoke again.

He hesitated, remembering the thundering landslide that had almost buried half of Chole, and then nodded.

"Thank you," Inken's voice was barely a whisper.

Silence fell between them, and a few minutes later they slowed their horses as the northern gates appeared ahead.

"Are you up for a race?" Inken asked as she turned to him.

Eric forced a smile, but a shudder ran through him as he

thought of the pain to come. He could see what she meant – a guard waited beside the gates, his arms crossed as he watched them. Their presence this late at night, armed and with so many wounded, was bound to draw attention. They could not afford to wait while the guard questioned them.

Turning in her saddle, Inken whispered hurried instructions to the others, and then rode on towards the guard. They followed in tight formation, legs tensed in the stirrups. When they were still a dozen feet from the gate, Inken gave a shout and kicked her horse hard in the side. The gelding leapt forward, leaving the guard with barely enough time to dive clear.

Eric gritted his teeth and dashed after her. Briar's hooves pounded hard against the bricked road as they raced into the tunnel beneath the wall. Darkness fell across the company, but Eric did not glance back to check the others had made it. There was no time to hesitate, no time to think.

Then they were free, racing onto the plains beyond the city. The road stretched out ahead of them, straight and smooth beneath their horses' pounding hooves. This was the main road to Chole, along which most of the traffic in and out of the city passed. The paths from each of the four gates all turned north to converge on this road, though smaller trails such as the one through the desert branched off along the way. To the north, the desert eventually gave way to the grassy farmlands of southern Lonia.

Only when they were far from the lights of the city did Inken allow their pace to slow. Drawing back on her reins, she looked around to check they were all still with her, and then pushed on at an easier pace.

Taking a deep, shuddering breath, Eric allowed himself a glance at his side. In the pale light of the moonlight, he saw his shirt was wet with blood. He lifted his shirt and saw that half his stiches had burst, allowing blood to seep between the ragged folds of skin. A wave of dizziness swept through him, but somehow he felt almost no pain. Whatever potion Michael had given him while he slept had been strong.

Michael rode up alongside him, drawing Alastair's horse with him. Eric's eyes slid to his mentor's face. His eyes were still closed, and his skin was so pale he could have already been dead. Only the slight fluttering of his eyelids suggested otherwise.

The doctor must have seen the direction of his gaze, because he slowly shook his head. "I'm sorry, there's nothing more I can do for him," Michael's voice was gentle. "He doesn't have long."

"No," maybe it was the potion, but Eric felt strangely calm. Looking up at Michael, he met the doctor's eyes. "You said a Magicker might help him?"

Michael sighed. "I do not have magic myself, but I was trained in its basic principles. From what I can see, Alastair has expended his own magic, and begun to consume his own life force. Such a feat can only go so far before it becomes fatal."

"So there's nothing we can do?"

The doctor hesitated, eying Eric closely. "Well, it's possible another Magicker could give his life force a jolt of energy. All magic is connected, and while I believe it is an extremely dangerous feat, it could be enough to bring him back from the brink."

Eric sucked in a deep breath. "I'm a Magicker."

"No," Michael shook his head firmly. "Like I said, it's a dangerous act, and you're injured. We could lose both of you."

But Eric was already closing his eyes and shutting out the world. There was no time for hesitation – Alastair needed him, and he would do whatever it took to save his mentor.

Eric sank quickly into the trance, his mind already afloat

with the aid of Michael's medicine. Physical sensation faded away, and a flickering blue light rose to replace it. His magic's power lit the darkness of his mind, though it seemed weaker now, drained away with his life's blood. He hoped there was enough.

Reaching out, he drew the fickle energies to him, and cast himself into the sky. Opening his spirit eyes, he looked down at the trail of horses as they rode through the empty desert. Staring at them, his consciousness shivered. His comrades were oblivious to his ghostly presence, but each glowed with an inner light, their auras setting the night around them alight.

Their life force, Eric marvelled.

He stole a glance at Inken, admiring the fiery glow of her aura. It matched the red of her hair, though there was no menace to the light. But there was no time to linger on the wily bounty hunter, and turning his attention, Eric focused his mind on Alastair.

The old man's aura had all but vanished, reduced to a sickly green spark deep in his chest. Eric drifted closer, worry clouding his thoughts, and he felt the distant pull of his physical body. His magic slipped, but grimly he forced the emotion away and fixed his mind on the problem.

Grasping his magic in ethereal fingers, he spun it with his mind, and watched it thin and stretch into a long blue cord. It stretched out into the night, a thin tendril directed by his thoughts, and wrapped its way around Alastair. Slowly, the thread sunk into Alastair's core, until it met with the dying green spark at his heart.

As they met, light flashed across Eric's vision, and with a violent jerk, his soul was hurtled back into his body. He gasped as the pain returned. Exhaustion swept through his body and a dull ache began in his head. Silently cursing his failure, he forced his eyes open and looked around.

Beside him, Michael yelped as Alastair suddenly sat up on his horse. The doctor reeled back, almost toppling from his saddle before he recovered himself. Alastair gave him a curious look.

"What are you doing here, priest?" he asked in a gravelly voice.

"I… I… Elynbrigge sent me," Michael stammered.

Alastair nodded, his eyes sweeping over the rest of the company. "Inken, glad to see you've recovered. Did my old friend send you as well?"

Inken brushed a strand of scarlet hair from her face before shaking her head. "Afraid not. To be honest, I'm not sure why I'm here. Maybe I will leave you in the morning," she glanced at Eric. "Maybe not."

Alastair nodded. "Good enough," he pulled on Elcano's reins and dropped back beside Eric.

Eric grinned in greeting, his heart soaring at the sight of Alastair awake. The old man still looked like living death, his skin grey and eyes bloodshot, but the spark of life had returned to him.

"Thank you, Eric, for saving my life," as Alastair spoke, his face darkened. Before Eric could react, his hand flashed out and slapped Eric hard across the face.

Lurching back in his saddle, Eric cried out as he found himself falling. He screamed as he struck the ground and agony tore through his side. Gasping, he stared up at Alastair through blurry eyes, his mind reeling.

"Why?" he coughed.

"Never do that again, Eric," Alastair's voice shook. "What you just did… Even those who have truly mastered their magic rarely dare to attempt it. A little more energy, and you would have burnt me to a crisp – or worse, drained your own lifeforce dry."

Eric did not respond. He lay on the ground, speechless,

the pain from his side so great not even Michael's medicine could blunt its sting.

I was just trying to help! He wanted to say, but the words would not come.

Alastair closed his eyes. "I'm sorry I struck you," turning his horse, he rode past their stunned companions. "We'll make camp here. Morning's not far off, but we shouldn't go any further until we have light. We can't risk missing the signs if Enala has left the road. Michael, it looks like Balistor needs your attention."

The others dismounted and began to set up camp. Eric remained where he was, too shocked to move. The blow had rattled him, robbing him of his senses. Closing his eyes, he fought back tears, unable to believe the anger in Alastair's eyes.

Stones crunched as Inken moved across and sat beside him. She carried a bag over her shoulder. Reaching inside, she drew out a needle and thread, and then smiled at Eric. Eric blinked, his sluggish mind taking a moment to click what it was for.

"I think your wound might need some attention, Eric," Inken offered in a soft voice. "I'm sorry about the gallop, it couldn't have been easy."

Easy glanced at his blood-soaked shirt and sucked in a long breath. Gritting his teeth, he nodded, doing his best not to show his fear.

"It's not so bad," he said. "Michael's potion did its job, I barely feel it."

"Then I guess you won't mind this," Inken teased as she lifted up his shirt to look at his side.

Scowling, Eric looked away, not wanting to watch the procedure. But a morbid curiosity drew his eyes back down, and he watched in silence as Inken's hands moved with practiced ease. The thread trailed over her wrist, keeping it out of the dirt as she worked quickly with the needle.

"He shouldn't have hit you," Inken murmured as she worked. "You were only trying to help."

Eric didn't reply. He didn't want to think about it. Instead, he sat in silence, and watched as Inken went about her task with cool efficiency. It was an odd sensation, watching the needle pierce his skin. With the potion, he barely felt each pinprick, but he still had to force himself to relax with each new stitch.

"All done," Inken whispered a few minutes later.

Looking across at Eric, she offered a smile. Eric found himself smiling back, noticing now how close her lips were to his. Strands of her hair stirred as he inhaled, the scent of her filling his nostrils. Her eyes caught his, trapping his gaze in their hazel depths. He suddenly found himself very aware of everything around him: the pounding of his heart in his chest, her arm on his side, the closeness of her body.

"Why did you save us, Inken?" he whispered, so close his lips grazed her cheek.

"For you, Eric."

And she kissed him.

CHAPTER 20

Enala crouched in the damp grass and stared into the shadows beneath the trees. The first rays of the morning sun were just peeking above the treetops, and puffs of steam rose from the rain-soaked earth. The barren slopes of the volcanic peaks towered above the treeline that started where the earth finally flattened out.

A shiver ran through Enala as she straightened; not from the cold, but exhaustion. They had walked for two nights now, fighting to put as many miles as they could between themselves and Chole. They had finally crossed the mountains last night, walking the treacherous path in the cover of darkness. Her legs burned from the effort and her shoulders ached with the weight of her pack. They had filled their bags with enough supplies for a week on the road. If everything went to plan, that would be all they needed.

Taking a swig from her waterskin, Enala sent up a silent thanks to the Goddess that they had made it into the forest before sunrise. With the sun out, the mountain hike would now be unbearably hot.

Enala breathed in the fresh mountain air, savouring the

scent. It had been years since she'd last come this way with her parents, though once it had been an annual trip. The trail was almost indiscernible now, so overgrown she had almost missed it as they descended the treacherous slopes.

The way would be easier now, at least for the next few hours. The trees were thin around the base of the mountains, but would quickly grow denser as they worked their way into the rainforests on the floodplains of the Onyx River. That was their destination. Once they crossed the river, she doubted her unknown pursuers would dare to follow her further. It didn't matter who they were, few had the courage to brave Dragon Country.

Her thoughts darkened as she thought of her parent's murderer. Shaking her head, she turned her mind to Gabriel. They had said little during the three days they'd spent hiding in the abandoned house. They had wandered its empty corridors in silence, listening to the pounding rain outside, each lost in their own thoughts.

Slowly, Enala had risen from the chasm of her grief. Free of its weight, her wits had returned, and with them a plan had formed. Though she said little to Gabriel, she at least managed to break the silence between them, and together the two of them had prepared for their escape.

Now, while a gulf still stretched between them, Enala drew comfort from his presence. She feared being alone, feared her own mind. When she was alone, her thoughts would turn inwards, drawn into an unending cycle of self-interrogation and blame. In the quiet of the cellar, she had found herself trapped within her mind, lost in the darkness. Even now she feared to sleep, feared the nightmares it brought. Each night she woke screaming, desperate to escape the darkness, and the faceless men that stalked through her dreams.

Flicking the copper lock from her eyes, Enala pushed the

black thoughts away, and forced her mind back to Gabriel. The boy was an enigma. He had appeared from nowhere – with a *wolf* – and plucked her from the darkness. Then he had saved her from his own beast. And she still had no idea who he was, where he had come from.

"How are your legs?" she jumped as Gabriel sat up and stretched his arms.

"Fine," she replied.

An awkward silence followed, and Enala frowned, unable to find the words. Speaking with Gabriel inevitably returned her thoughts to the wolf, or the bloody nightmare that had becoming her living room floor.

"Enala, it's been five days. Enough. Listen, I know what you've gone through–"

"You know *nothing* of what I've been through," Enala found herself shrieking. Fists clenched, she turned on Gabriel. "How *dare* you. *My parents were murdered right above my head!*" the words tumbled from her mouth in a torrent, ending in a half-choked sob.

Enala turned away, running her hands through her filthy hair as she gasped for breath.

"I listened to them for hours," she went on, her voice barely a whisper. "For hours as they screamed and screamed and screamed. I listened to their murder, to the endless questions about children, about relatives. By the end, I was praying for their deaths, just so the nightmare would end," the words were out before she could take them back.

There was silence for a moment, and she looked back at Gabriel, daring him to speak.

"I'm sorry," he whispered.

"Sorry for what?" her words dripped with acid. "What do your sorries mean to me? My parents are dead. I *wished* them gone, and still they kept me a secret. Yet even that did not last, and now there are people *hunting me*. I can never go back, my life is over."

"I have no life to go back to either," Gabriel ventured.

Enala blinked, thrown off-balance. "What?"

Gabriel stared at the ground. "My home was destroyed by a storm. My parents, my fiancée, they didn't survive." He looked up then, and now there was steel in his voice. "I may not have lost them as you lost yours, but don't you *dare* tell me I have no idea of loss."

Enala watched as a tear streaked down Gabriel's cheek. She remembered him in the cellar then, the tears as he'd held her, and for the first time she felt a connection with him, a slender bridge spanning the chasm between them.

"I'm sorry," she spoke without thinking.

Gabriel laughed softly. "Ay. I guess in the end, we're both just sorry orphans. Friends?" he offered his hand.

Enala found herself smiling. Gabriel had a personality after all. In that brief moment, the day seemed just a little brighter. She took his hand. "Friends," she agreed. "It seems like a long time since I've had one."

"It is a lonely life without them."

"Yes. But then, before I had my parents," she frowned as her sorrow returned.

"We'll have to make do with each other now I guess," Gabriel forced a smile. "Shall we press on?"

Enala glanced at the sun, her anxiety returning. They had been sitting there for close to an hour. Gabriel was right. Though her body ached from the hike, they needed to move on. The hunters were coming.

She nodded, and swinging her pack onto her shoulders, started off down the overgrown track.

"Where are we going?" Gabriel asked from behind her.

"Somewhere safe."

Gabriel chuckled. "You know, that doesn't really tell me much. I thought we were friends now?"

"We are," Enala smiled to herself as they pushed deeper into the trees, leaving the morning sun behind. "It's just…"

"Aren't friends meant to trust each other?"

Enala sighed. She ducked her head to avoid a low hanging branch, and swore as her shirt and hair caught in the prickly scrub. Disentangling herself, she pulled up her hood, but it did little to protect her.

"I trust you," she grinned, though Gabriel could not see it. "Now trust me when I say it's better you don't know."

Gabriel fell silent then, and Enala could almost picture the frustration on his face as they continued through the forest. Even so, she didn't think he'd like to hear the truth. Though she was sure she could keep them safe, Dragon Country was not for the faint hearted.

Behind her, Gabriel quickly began to puff, his fitness nowhere close to measuring up to hers. He was no forester, and his heavy footsteps announced their presence to the forest creatures long before they appeared. The trees rustled in the morning breeze, and they heard the soft howls of monkeys in the distance. Tiny insects flew at their faces and bit wherever their clothes did not cover.

It was a few hours before Gabriel broke the silence again. "Can you at least tell me how far off we are?" he puffed. "This is not an easy trail!"

Enala laughed. The canopy was above their heads now, and they no longer had to fight their way through the undergrowth.

"It's a good day's walk through this forest. We should reach the river late tomorrow morning, if we can keep up the pace," she brushed a leafy branch from her face as she moved, and then ducked beneath it.

As she released it again, the branch swung back into place, and a yelp came from behind her.

Enala glanced back and chuckled. The branch must have struck Gabriel in the face. Somehow he had lost his footing and toppled to the ground. Dirt covered his clothing as he picked himself back up.

"Sorry!" Enala grinned. "But you shouldn't walk so close."

Shaking his head, Gabriel shot her a cheeky grin. "I'll get you for that one. And if I follow any further back, I'm afraid I'll lose you. I'm a smith, I'm not used to all these trees. I prefer *roads.*"

"Just wait until tomorrow. The trees near the river are younger. The seedlings grow thick beneath them. I doubt the path still exists by now, so we'll have to cut our way through."

Gabriel groaned. His discomfort was clear, but Enala could feel the weight lifting from her shoulders with every step. *This* was her home. Let them follow her here if they dared.

As the light faded and Enala's eyes began to droop, she finally allowed them to stop. Dropping her pack, she sank to the ground. They had hardly slept in the last two days, and she was beyond breaking point. The night settled in around them like a blanket, but she resisted the temptation to light a fire, and they settled for feasting on cold beef jerky.

"Enala," she started as Gabriel spoke. Shaking her head free of sleep, she looked at him as he continued. "I wanted to thank you. You saved me, back in the city."

"What do you mean?" Enala frowned. "*You* saved *me.* The wolf would have killed me if it wasn't for you."

"I wasn't talking about that, but I will add my thanks for the chair too," he paused, his eyes staring out into the night. "No, you saved my soul."

"What?" Enala asked.

"The wolf, it was given to me by a demon."

Enala's breath hissed between her teeth, and she saw again Gabriel drawing his sword on her. She had dismissed it from her mind, but now her heart began to race as she reached for her knife.

"Easy!" Gabriel offered his empty hands. "Let me explain. I think I've earned that much?"

Enala hesitated before nodding.

"The demon corrupted me," Gabriel sighed. "It placed me under some spell, made me something else. My memories were stolen. I'm only just starting to remember."

"That's horrible," Enala remained tense, but she sensed the truth behind his words.

"It was my own fault. The demon offered me aid, and I was desperate enough to take it. It gave me the wolf, although I can't remember why. It wanted you dead though, ordered me to kill you. But I couldn't do it; something about you broke its spell. *You saved me.*"

Enala frowned. "Who was this demon?"

"I don't know," Gabriel shivered, though the air was hot and humid beneath the trees. "I have never felt such evil. I don't know why I was so blind to accept its offer. It wasn't long after I lost my family. That time is all still a blur."

Enala watched the shadows. *Who am I to these demons?*

In a whisper, she asked. "What did it want? Why did it want me dead?"

"I don't know. I think you were unexpected though. I was meant to kill an old man – and a young one. Their faces are the clearest images I have left."

"I wonder who they are."

"Whoever they are, they're in mortal peril."

Like me, Enala thought. *Maybe they're just as terrified and confused as I am.*

"Your parents were incredibly brave," Gabriel changed the subject.

Enala shivered. "I don't know how they did it. They only managed to hide me a few seconds before they were found. They withstood torture to protect me. I don't think I could have done the same."

The leaf litter crunched as Gabriel eased himself down beside her. Gently he lifted his arm and settled it around her shoulders. "You were brave too."

"No, I wasn't. All I wanted to do was climb the ladder and save them. But I was too scared to move."

"It would have broken their hearts if you had. They died knowing they had protected their daughter, that you were safe. There was nothing you could have done for them."

The night pressed in around them. Enala closed her eyes, leaning into Gabriel's shoulder. She found some comfort in his words, though doubts still plagued her. Her parents had raised her to be strong, to never run from an enemy. Yet here she was, fleeing for her life.

You have no choice, she reasoned, *your enemies are ghosts. They are stronger and have the advantage of knowledge. There is no choice but to run.*

Even so, she wondered what her parents would have done. Their murder demanded justice, but she was powerless to seek it.

Enala felt the steady beat of Gabriel's heart beneath her head. Breathing in the earthly scent of his clothes, she closed her eyes and thought of sleep. Though she had been plagued by nightmares since the day in the cellar, suddenly the idea no longer seemed so frightening. She felt safe in Gabriel's arms, his heartbeat a lullaby in her ear.

She slept.

~

Enala stood on the banks of the Onyx river, her hands on her hips as she studied the flooded waters. To her horror they had slept late, and it was now well past noon, but they had finally arrived.

Unfortunately, the recent rain had swollen the river to heights beyond anything Enala had ever seen. The murky waters lapped at the edge of the banks, snatching at the overhanging branches of the nearby trees as it raced towards the distant ocean.

"We need to cross that?" Gabriel asked beside her.

"Yes," Enala nodded.

Silently she moved back under the shelter of the trees. Out here, so close to Dragon Country, there was more to be concerned with than those hunting them. While some dragon tribes were friendly with humanity, there were many that were best left to their own company. They would not take kindly to an invasion of their territory.

"How do you plan to do that? Can you swim?" Gabriel persisted about the river.

Grinning, Enala nodded. "I didn't live in Chole my entire life. Yes, I can swim. And I think I have a plan."

Enala moved back into the forest, and began searching for what they would need for the swim. She had never crossed when the river was so high, but her parents had taught her how. It would be dangerous, but it was possible.

She returned a few minutes later carrying a heavy tree branch over each shoulder. Both were around the length of her body, heavy and half-rotten. Nevertheless, they would float, and that was all they needed.

Gabriel relieved her of a branch as she walked up. "What are these for?"

"Think of it as your life saver. It'll keep you afloat in the river," she sat down and started taking off her boots.

"Are you insane? Those currents will drag us under in seconds."

Enala grinned. "We have two choices: cross, or wait here to be caught. You can stay if you want," she tucked her boots into her pack. "But I'm crossing."

Gabriel sighed and shook his head, before sitting down to copy her. Then he removed his sword belt and tied the pack closed with it.

"Let's hope the packs keep out the worst of the water," Enala commented as they moved back to the river's edge. "The river runs down from the mountains. We'll need dry clothes on the other side. Ready?"

She glanced at Gabriel, seeing the fear he was struggling to keep from his face.

He looked back at her and nodded. "Absolutely," he replied with forced bravado.

Enala laughed and threw herself out into the river. The racing waters caught her up and hauled her down. She struggled not to panic as the muddy water closed over her head, before the wood rose beneath her. She sucked in a deep breath as she broke the surface and looked around. Spying the opposite bank, she began to kick towards it, as a splash behind her announced Gabriel was following.

The cold water raced around her, dragging her downstream. Her arms grew numb and the currents threatened to pull her from the log, but she took a firmer grip and struggled on.

Enala was a long way downstream by the time she washed up on the far shore. Clambering up the bank, she gasped in the frigid air and dumped her pack to the muddy ground. Turning back, she searched the swirling waters for Gabriel.

He was still a few yards upstream, struggling against the current to reach her. He held his branch out in front of him and his feet churned the water, but his progress was slow. His face was pale and with each kick his movements grew weaker.

Watching him, Enala realised he wasn't going to make it. She quickly gathered up her branch and moved back towards the water's edge.

Before she could dive back in, an ear-splitting roar came from overhead. The hackles rose on Enala's neck as she shrank back against a tree. Peering up through the canopy, she glimpsed red scales glittering in the sunlight. The earth shook as the dragon landed, its hulking body shattering trees like toothpicks. Slitted nostrils expanded as it sniffed the air. The great yellow globes of its eyes searched the trees.

Enala slid around the tree trunk, still watching the water. Gabriel had gone still, his eyes wide as he stared at the dragon. The racing current was already dragging him back into the middle of the river. He would never make it now.

Their eyes met across the distance. *Go*, he mouthed.

Enala shook her head. She would not abandon her friend. Sliding forward, she edged closer to the river as the rumble of the dragon's breath came closer.

Go, now!

Enala could see his fear, his desperation. Ignoring him, she started to slip back into the water, preparing to follow him downstream.

"No!" Gabriel shouted.

In the middle of the river, he started to thrash, sending up a spray of foam.

Shrinking back into the shadows, Enala's eyes were drawn to the dragon. Its head had whipped around, and now the giant eyes stared at Gabriel's floundering figure. In the open water of the river, there was no escaping the dragon's glare. Trapped in the current, he had nowhere to go.

Tears ran down Enala's face as the dragon's wings beat down. This couldn't be happening, not again. She stood paralysed, her hands clenched at her side, powerless to help. Cracks spread through her fragile mind, madness threatening. Her eyes fixed on Gabriel, unable to look away.

The dragon took to the air, its scarlet wings carrying it towards her friend. Gabriel watched it come, eyes grim, silent now. The earth shook as the dragon roared, and dove towards the flooded river. Its bulk smashed the water, sending a wave rolling across the river and spilling out into the forest.

Enala gasped as the cold water swept her from her feet, while in the centre of the river, the dragon thrashed. Its jaws stretched and snapped shut. Then its great wings clawed the air once more, and it climbed above the river, circling still, before finally turning to disappear beyond the treetops.

Its roar slowly faded away.

Enala watched the roiling waters for a long time, but there was no sign of Gabriel. She sank to her knees, the cracks within her mind growing, spreading, until with a silent shriek, something shattered.

CHAPTER 21

Eric shifted in his saddle, watching as the waters racing past below. Leaves and branches floated in the current, rising to the surface and then disappearing back down into the murky depths. A cold wind blew off the water, offering a welcome respite from the humid valley air. Silt and dead leaves hung from the branches of the trees on the riverbank, revealing the height the floodwaters had reached before beginning to descend.

Glancing around, he waited for someone to speak. The sun was at their backs, fading quickly into the afternoon, and if they were to cross before dark they would have to move soon. But no one seemed eager to tackle the flooded river and what waited on the other side.

Dragon Country.

He shook his head. Why had Enala come here, of all places? Yesterday they had only made it another mile along the Gods' road before Inken called a stop. Dismounting, she had scouted around the road, her head bent low to the ground. Eric could not tell one stone from another, but the bounty hunter had insisted Enala and her companion had left the road there and headed east.

Looking at Inken now, Eric's stomach fluttered. The last few days had passed in a daze, and he was still struggling to catch up. Memories sprang into his mind, too vivid for fantasy. The taste of her mouth, the soft caress of her lips against his. Her hair tickling his cheek, filling her nostrils with her earthly scent. Her hand on his chest, his fingers entwined in her hair as he kissed her harder.

Yet when they had finally separated that first night, Inken had only smiled and winked at him, before moving away. The next morning she had been cold and distant, her brow creased as she studied the trail, and Eric was left wondering whether it had all been a pain induced fantasy.

The party had ridden in silence for most of that first day, each of them lost in their own thoughts. Balistor's wound had not been as bad as they'd first thought. His shoulder blade had prevented the arrow from penetrating deeper. Michael said he would heal quickly, though the Magicker silently fumed about his injury.

The doctor himself was quiet, clearly ill at ease in their presence. He had been dragged into this quest without a choice, and still had no idea what was going on. Caelin rode ahead with Inken, his keen eyes studying the trail ahead, ever alert for danger, while Alastair rode beside Michael. The old Magicker was slowly regaining his colour, though he seemed to have aged a dozen years in the past few days.

They had not made it far into the forests of the Onyx valley before the approach of night forced them to make camp. It was only then that Alastair had come to Eric, and offered to join him in meditation. The darkness had masked his expression, but Eric read the apology in his words, and nodded his acceptance.

Though they were too exhausted to touch their magic,

the meditation allowed them both a chance to regain their composure. As he sank into the familiar trance, Eric had felt his tension fade away. Concentrating on each inhalation of breath, he found he could set aside the shock and hurt of Alastair's blow. He could understand the old Magicker's reaction – he had seen the fear in his mentor's face.

Even so, the peace of his inner mind evaded him. To his surprise, he found it was Inken he could not put from his mind. When he finally shook his head and opened his eyes, he almost laughed when he saw Alastair had vanished.

In his place sat Inken, her hazel eyes watching him with interest. Smiling, she cocked her head to one side.

"What are you doing?" she asked.

Eric took a moment to stretch his neck and shoulders. "It's called meditation," he tried to keep his voice steady. "Alastair is teaching me to use it to control my magic."

Inken leaned in closer. "Can a normal person do it?"

Eric pulled back. "Am I not normal?"

A mischievous grin stretched across Inken's lips. "Hardly. Most people can't control the weather."

At that, she reached across and pulled him to her. A tremor swept through Eric as their lips met, and he could scarcely believe they were kissing again. The sweet tang of orange lingered on her tongue.

"And I don't do that with most people either," she whispered as she drew back.

Eric laughed, his heart still pounding in his ears. Grinning, he leaned across and kissed her again.

When they finally drew apart, Eric frowned, thinking back to her question. "I'm sure there's nothing stopping a 'normal' person from meditating. Come on, I'll show you."

For the next hour, they sat together, practicing the exercises Eric had first learned the night he'd met Inken. They were light hearted and playful at first, but as the night grew late, they quieted, becoming serious. As they both closed their eyes, Eric sought again the inner calm that had escaped him earlier. This time it came easily, his thoughts no longer distracted by doubt.

When he finally slipped from the trance and opened his eyes, he found Inken staring at him again. There was a softness to her eyes.

"You were so peaceful," she whispered. Reaching out, she stroked his cheek. "The sadness on your face was gone."

Eric shifted uneasily. "You should have roused me. How long was I out?"

"Long enough, but it's okay. It was calming to watch," she paused. "Eric, I have a question."

"Yes?"

"Who is Enala? Why are we tracking her?"

"That's two questions," Eric teased.

"I'm serious," Inken said.

Eric sighed and nodded. "I know, but I can't give you the answers you want. It's Alastair's secret to tell, though I can say he doesn't mean her any harm."

Inken frowned. Noticing a leaf in her hair, Eric reached out and brushed it away before continuing. "It's not my secret to tell," he repeated. "But without you, we would never have gotten this far. You deserve to know – I'll make Alastair tell you if necessary."

"Now?"

He nodded. They moved back through the woods to where the others sat. Balistor and Michael had already retired, but Caelin and Alastair were speaking softly to each other as they walked up.

"Ah, the young couple returns," Caelin grinned.

Eric flushed and Inken shot Caelin a warning glare, but Caelin only laughed.

Squaring his shoulders, Eric decided to ignore the

sergeant. "Inken wants to know about Enala," he stared at Alastair as he spoke, daring the man to refuse.

But Alastair only nodded. "I was wondering how long it would be. Inken, I have been speaking with Caelin about what happened in Chole. Without your skills, we would already be dead," he took a deep breath. "You have a right to know what you're fighting for – as does Michael."

Moving across to the doctor, he shook him awake. Michael grumbled at the disturbance, but his complaints quickly trailed off as Alastair began to speak. Slowly, Alastair laid out the tale Eric had put together over the last week.

Eric watched the two as the old man spoke, wondering how they would react. Archon was a nightmare whispered of by old men whose grandfathers had fought in the war. Only the Gods could rival the dark Magicker's power. If they failed, if Enala died, they would pay for their defiance. Eric could not blame them if they decided to turn back now.

Michael's mouth slowly dropped open as Alastair spoke, and open fear shone from his eyes. Inken's expression did not change as Alastair finished. Instead, she stood, silent, and offered Eric her hand. Drawing him up, she led him into the trees. Only when they passed beyond sight of camp did she turn and throw herself at him.

Shocked, Eric almost lost his balance. Pain lanced from his side, but then her mouth was pressed hard against his, and it no longer seemed to matter. She kissed him with an almost violent passion, and Eric felt himself swept away.

"You're either incredibly brave, or insane, Eric," she told him when they broke apart.

Eric couldn't help but smile. "When you work out which it is, could you let me know?" he paused then, staring into her big hazel eyes. "Will you help us?"

Inken smiled, laughter on her lips. "The Hunters Federation will be hunting for me by now. There is nothing for me to go back to. And even if that weren't the case, I couldn't leave this girl to die. She had no choice in any of this," she paused. "And I won't abandon you to this madness either."

Then they were in each other's arms, lips locked, tongues tasting, her body pressed hard against his. She groaned and a shiver ran through him. His arms encircled her, his blood throbbing in his ears. They fell, down, down, down…

Now, Eric sat staring at the river, his face growing hot at the memory. Watching the icy waters, he prayed to the Goddess that Enala and her companion had made it to the other side. According to Inken, they had entered the river several hours ago, when the flood waters would have been even higher. How they could have reached the other side without horses, he couldn't guess, but Inken had found no sign of other tracks on their side of the river.

And on the other side, Dragon Country waited. Few travellers came this way, and even less returned from adventures across the river. This was the last territory of the ancient dragon tribes – and most were no friend to humans. Only the Golds still honoured the pact that had been forged by the kings of old.

"Let's go," Alastair said finally.

Inken nodded and edged her mount forward. Eric followed close behind her, bracing himself as the glacial waters lapped at his boots. A shiver ran up his legs as the water climbed higher, drawing level with his waist. He tightened his grip on the reins as Briar's hooves left the riverbed, and the horse began to swim. Briar snorted beneath him and shook his head. The whites of his eyes showed, and Eric patted his neck, silently willing him on.

When they reached the far bank, Eric let out a long sigh of relief. Slipping from the saddle, he led Briar up into the trees and began to towel the horse dry with a blanket from the leather saddlebags. As he worked, he quietly whispered his thanks to the horse.

When he finally looked up from his task, the others had gathered around him, but Inken had vanished. He opened his mouth to call out for her, and then shut it again. This side of the Onyx river, it was best if they kept their presence quiet. Inken would be checking for Enala's tracks – he would have to trust the wily bounty hunter knew how to look after herself.

Even so, he couldn't help but worry, and when Inken finally returned almost an hour later, he was close to charging into the trees after her.

"Only the girl reached this side of the river," Inken announced as they gathered around her. "And there are signs of a dragon where she came ashore. Her tracks head east, but I'm afraid there may be a dragon on her trail."

"There was no sign of the boy at all?" Alastair asked.

"No. Do you know who he was?" Inken asked.

"Unfortunately, he is a mystery. We'll have to ask Enala when we find her. Let's go. If the dragon reaches her first…" there was no need for him to finish the sentence.

Inken took the lead until they reached Enala's trail. From there, she dismounted and continued on foot, her eyes fixed to the ground. She said little as she studied the signs, though it was obvious Enala was no longer attempting to hide her trail. She had left deep footprints in the soft soil, so clear even Eric could have followed them.

Even so, he could understand Inken's concern. A dragon was not to be trifled with.

Eric's eyes swept the forest as they rode, his hands tense on the reins. Around them, the woods had changed since crossing the river. Here the forest was untouched by the axes of man, and the trees grew to massive sizes. The canopy stretched high above, blotting out the sun and stunting the undergrow beneath, leaving wide open space between the trunks. The temperature fell as they climbed up from the river valley.

They made good time following Enala's erratic path through the giant trees, but it wasn't until the last light began to fade that Inken suddenly drew to a stop. Dropping to her hands and knees, she frantically inspected the earth around the trail.

"Stay back!" she warned.

Eric swatted away an insect buzzing at his neck. He stared as Inken searched the forest floor, his anxiety growing. The undergrowth was still; not even a breath of wind stirred the leaves beneath the canopy.

Scanning the trees, Eric started to notice signs of disturbance. To the right of the trail, a fern had been crushed against the ground, while bark had been scraped from the nearby trees. Freshly broken branches lay on the forest floor, and there, right next to the trail, a long indentation marked the soft earth.

Something big had crossed Enala's path.

"No, no, no!" Inken hissed. "Where did she go?"

Eric dismounted and moved to Inken's side. He placed a hand on her shoulder. She turned to face him, tears in her eyes.

"She's gone."

CHAPTER 22

Inken's words hung in the air, damning, irrefutable. Enala was gone, and with her, the last hope of the Three Nations. Their quest had failed before it had even begun. Eric held Inken tight to him, unable to find the words.

"It's over," Caelin whispered.

Above, branches rustled in the evening breeze, but beneath the canopy the air was still. A horse snorted, pawing at the ground. They did not like the smells here. From the distance came the crash of an animal in the undergrowth, too small to be a dragon. Even so, Eric stilled, his eyes scanning the woods for signs of movement.

Looking at his companions, he wilted at the despair in their eyes. Inken slumped against him, all the fight in her sucked away, while tears shone in the eyes of Michael and Caelin. Only the two Magickers managed to hide their emotion.

Without even meeting the young girl, Enala had become central to their lives. She was the princess they were meant to rescue, but they had failed her. This perilous land had claimed her – might claim them too, if they did not leave soon.

"We have to go back," Eric whispered.

Inken winced in his arms and a cloud darkened Caelin's face, but neither spoke.

"No." Alastair suddenly straightened. He shook his head. "We can't give up. Not all the tribes are violent. The Gold dragons may know what has happened to her. We can ask for their help."

No one replied, and Eric found himself wondering if Alastair had finally lost his mind. To continue now, without hope, was suicide. Yet no one spoke against him, and Eric could not find the strength to argue.

"What do you want us to do?" he asked.

"The Gold's nest on the coast," Inken cut in, her voice laced with misery. "They wouldn't have been here. The Reds or Blues would have found her first."

"Whatever the chance, we have to try. Without Enala, there is no hope," Alastair pressed. "Not for anyone."

Inken shivered. "You know the tales about the coast, about Malevolent Cove"

Alastair nodded. "I lived them."

"Malevolent Cove?" Eric whispered. The name called to him, and with a start he remembered where he had heard it. "That was where… that was where King Thomas disappeared?"

"Yes," Alastair looked away then, and his voice grew dull. "I have not returned since."

"It is the closest point on the coast to us," Inken murmured. "Going around would cost another day."

There was silence for a moment, before Alastair spoke again. "It is a dark place, but we cannot afford to delay," he paused. "I will go on, but it is up to each of you to decide whether you will follow."

"We can't abandon her," Eric echoed Inken's words from the night before. Beside him, Inken nodded.

Silently, Caelin and Balistor nodded their ascent. Together, they turned to see what the doctor would decide. Michael's eyes were wide and his lips were trembling. He still wore the green robes of his order, but this was no place for a priest.

"Elynbrigge asked me to help you, and so I will," he straightened. "I think this is folly, but I will follow you, Alastair."

Alastair nodded and closed his eyes. "It might be folly, but I cannot give up hope, Michael. I have searched for too long to surrender now."

After that, there was nothing left to say.

FIRELIGHT FLICKERED ACROSS THE CLEARING, casting shadows across the surrounding trees. They had left behind the humid valley, and now a cool breeze blew across the open grass. A pot sat over the open flames, a thick stew bubbling within. Eric's stomach growled as he watched it, breathing in the rich fumes. A hot meal would be a welcome change. Balistor had lit the fire with a flick of his hands after finding the clearing, and no one had bothered to disagree with the decision. They were all sick of caution.

Eric lay back in the grass and stared up at the tapestry of stars above. Balistor had assured them dragons returned to their nests at night, but his chest was still tight with anxiety. Dragon Country was a different world, ruled by creatures that were a law unto their own.

"Here, Eric," he sat up as Caelin offered him a bowl. "And one for you too, my lady," he grinned at Inken.

They accepted his offering with a word of thanks. Eric

took a long sip, enjoying the warmth of the spices Michael had added. Heat spread through his stomach as he devoured the meal, fighting back the cold night.

When Eric finished he handed back the bowl and glanced at Inken. She sat staring into the trees, her thoughts hidden by a grim mask. Her bowl was still half-full, the spoon dangling loosely from her fingers.

Eric put an arm round her waist. "What are you thinking about?"

Inken blinked and looked at him. "Sorry? I was lost in thought."

Eric kissed her. "I know the feeling. What were you thinking about?" he repeated.

She sighed. "Do you really believe she is alive?"

"Truthfully?" Eric spoke slowly, mulling over his words. "No. What chance did she stand against a dragon?"

"So we're chasing a ghost now. Why?"

Eric gazed into her eyes, feeling oddly at peace. "Because there's no other choice. Without her, he's already won."

"You're almost as stubborn as the old man, you know," she looked off into the trees again, and then stood suddenly. "Come on, there's something I want to show you."

"What is it?"

"I found it earlier, when I was searching for firewood. You'll like it. Come on!" she tugged at his arm, pulling him to his feet.

Eric stumbled as he stood, still exhausted from the day's ride. The stitches in his side pulled tight, but he tried to ignore them. All he wanted to do was lie down and sleep, but Inken was tugging at his hand, and there was no choice but to follow.

"There goes the couple again," Caelin teased as Inken led him to the edge of the trees.

Eric blushed, and ignored them. But as they entered the trees, he hesitated, pulling Inken back.

"Wait," he whispered. "It's not safe out here."

Inken looked at him and raised an eyebrow. Her breath hissed between her teeth, and shaking her head, she stalked past him back towards the fire. Wincing, Eric made to follow her.

"Stay there!" Inken shot him a warning glare. "I'll be back in a second."

She jogged into the campsite, gathered her gear and ran back. Now she carried her bow strung over one shoulder and wore the cavalry sabre at her side.

"Happy now?" she teased.

Eric nodded reluctantly, knowing this was the best he would get. It seemed they were going into the woods whether he liked it or not. Inken shot him a mischievous smirk as she took his hand again, and dragged him into the darkness.

He stumbled after her, tripping over roots and bumping into tree trunks in the pitch-black. He could barely make out the outline of Inken ahead of him, and without her warm hand in his, he would have been lost. Twice he almost fell, only for Inken's quick hands to steady him.

When they finally emerged from the trees, Eric was puffing and holding his injured side. But as he looked up to see where Inken had brought him, the pain fell away, and his mouth dropped open.

The giant trees had parted to reveal a patch of low-lying ferns. A soft glow seeped from the ferns, their gentle luminescence banishing the night. Tiny insects buzzed between them, and these too shone with light. A creek threaded its way through the clearing, the currents playing a warm melody against the coarse pebbles. Steam rose from the water, blanketing the ferns in a thin fog.

"There was only a faint glow when I found it," Inken spoke in a hushed voice. "I thought you might like it."

"It's… it's beautiful," Eric had no other words.

Inken turned to him, the scarlet curls of her hair ablaze. She took his hand and drew him further into the ferns. They sat beside the stream, arms around one another, savouring the closeness of their bodies, the warmth of their skin.

"Eric, I… I want to ask you something," she paused.

Eric leaned forward, reaching up to stroke her cheek. Her eyes closed at his touch. She shivered.

"What?" he breathed.

"What do you want, Eric? What are your dreams?"

The question took him by surprise and he looked away for a moment.

What do I want?

He had not thought about the question for a long time. It hadn't really mattered – not until Alastair.

"I don't know," he realised then how tragic it was. "I guess, to help Alastair…"

Inken reached up and entwined her fingers in his hair. She turned him to face her. "There must be something more. You had a life once, before the magic. What did *that* Eric want?"

He closed his eyes, unable to meet her fiery gaze.

"He was lost a long time ago."

"I know that's not true. When you were meditating, I saw him. Now, *what do you want*, Eric?"

Eric sighed, trying to think back, to remember the boy he had once been, before his magic had awakened. It seemed part of someone else's life now, too innocent to be his own. The memories took a long time to surface, but Inken waited in silence, ever patient.

"I wanted to be a *carpenter*," he laughed.

Inken rested her forehead against his. "Do you still want that?"

"I don't know…" he hesitated.

Inken kissed him. "Go on."

"I want to be *normal.* To finish this business and start a new life," Eric drew in a breath. "But if we can't find Enala, what is the point? Archon will tear the world apart."

"There is always a point, Eric. Life is a fickle thing, and it must be *lived.* Archon will attack, or he won't. It is no different to the farmer whose livelihood depends on the weather. He knows he may be ruined one day by a drought or a storm, but he battles on anyway. True bravery means pursuing what you want, no matter the obstacles. The world may end tomorrow, but what matters is what we do with the time we have left. Otherwise, we are already lost."

Warmth spread through Eric's chest as she spoke. He drew strength from her words, but knew they were not enough. "I can't put the past aside so easily," he looked away. "It is an anchor dragging me down. I cannot move on until I have redeemed myself."

"And you think saving Enala will do that?"

Eric nodded.

"Oh Eric," she hugged him. "I think you have already redeemed yourself. You're learning to control your power. You're doing all you can to prevent the past repeating itself. And you used it to heal Chole. What more can you do?"

"I don't know, but it's not enough."

Inken sighed. "I understand. Maybe there is nothing you can do to put those ghosts to bed. But you still have to live, Eric."

"I know," he smiled as he looked at her. "There's something else I want, you know."

"Oh?"

"I want *you*, Inken."

She stood then, her eyes still locked to his. "Well I'm right here, Eric Storm. Come and get me," she teased, walking backwards towards the stream. As she moved she pulled off her leather jacket, then the shirt beneath. The rest of her clothing quickly followed, until she stood there grinning, wearing nothing but the soft curves of her sun-touched skin.

"What are you doing?" he asked, his eyes feasting.

"Going for a swim," Inken grinned. "This stream is fed by a thermal spring. Are you going to join me?"

Springing to his feet, Eric followed her into the steaming waters.

CHAPTER 23

Eric and Inken lay wrapped in each other's arms, eyes closed, the hot water streaming over their naked bodies. Neither had spoken for a long time, and Eric lay at peace in the tranquil silence. Warmth wrapped around his stomach, and for just a moment, he forgot about the world waiting beyond the luminescent clearing.

Then a roar shattered the darkness.

Inken reacted instantly, rolling from Eric's arms and leaping to the bank in one fluid movement. Scrambling in their pile of clothes, she came up a second later with her bow. Eric clambered after her, his eyes scanning the canopy overhead as the roar came again.

The camp!

Barely pausing to pull on their clothes, Eric and Inken took off towards the campsite. The darkness fed their panic, as terrified screams came from ahead of them. Eric hardly noticed the pain in his side as he stumbled through the trees, only Inken's steadying hand keeping him on his feet.

Inken emerged from the trees first, exploding through the undergrowth and out into the long grass. Eric followed a second later, his arms still raised to protect himself from the low-lying branches. Ahead, Inken came to a sudden halt, and before he could stop himself, he slammed into her back. Reaching out a hand, he caught Inken before she fell. Then they turned together to take in the clearing.

The others stood in the centre of the campsite, weapons held at the ready, eyes fixed to the sky. Flames leapt across the long grass, stretching up into the night. Looking up, Eric caught a flash of red as something huge passed across the moon.

Then the sky erupted into flames, revealing the beast hurtling towards them. Fire licked from jaws large enough to swallow a horse whole, and bloody fangs flickered in and out of sight. The black orbs of its eyes swept the clearing, lingering on the group of men cowering in its centre.

The ground shook as it landed, flinging them from their feet. The horses screamed and tore free of their ties. The thunder of their fleeing hooves echoed in the darkness.

Lying on the ground, Eric stared up at the dragon, scarcely daring to breath. It crouched on all fours, its scaly red hide filling half the clearing, as claws the size of men raked deep grooves in the earth. Giant wings splayed out on either side, blacking out the moon. Its tail flickered out behind it like a snake, and a stench like rotting meat carried to Eric's nose. A blast of heat struck him like a furnace as it turned towards them, its tongue sliding out to taste the air.

It roared again, and fire gushed from its jaws. The grass burst into flames as Inken dragged him to his feet. Together they stumbled backwards.

Across the clearing, Alastair stepped away from the others. His cloak spun out around him, the silver embroidered lines glowing in the light of the moon. The air shimmered as he pointed a hand, and a dull ache began in the back of Eric's skull as power surged across the clearing.

The Red dragon shrieked as Alastair's magic struck, picking it up and flinging it into the trees. The ancient trunks groaned and toppled backwards under the beast's weight. The dragon thrashed, limbs tearing at earth and wood, before its wings beat down.

Bounding into the air, it circled the clearing, then folded its wings and dived. Fire gushed from its jaws as it roared. The inferno raced across the grass towards Alastair and the others.

Alastair spread his arms, and flung the blaze back on itself. Burning wood crackled as the trees around the clearing burst into flames. Smoke drifted low to the grass, and Eric bent in two, choking on the acrid air. He staggered, straining to hear the crack of the dragon's wings over the roar of the flames.

It appeared suddenly through the smoke, catching Alastair off-guard. He raised a hand in defiance – but too slow. The dragon slammed into the ground, knocking the old man from his feet, and unleashed a torrent of flame.

"No!" Eric screamed as fire engulfed Alastair.

Unbidden, his magic boiled up from the depths of his body. For once, he did not try to stop it. He let it grow, feeding it with his rage. High above, the wind stirred, and gusts swirled down into the clearing, whipping up the flames. They gathered around him, converging in a thunderous gale.

Squinting through the smoke, Eric searched out the dragon. It still stood over Alastair, fire streaming from its mouth. To his shock, Alastair was on his feet again, his arms outstretched in defiance of the flames. Roaring, the dragon lifted its claws and lashed out, but the monstrous talons ground to a halt a foot above Alastair's head.

Drawing himself up, Eric pointed at the dragon, and unleashed the gale. The air rushed away from him and cascaded into the beast. The wind caught in its wings, lifting it from the ground and hurling it towards the trees. Before it struck, the great wings beat down, carrying it over the treetops.

Beside him, Inken groaned as the dragon turned towards them, but Eric was not finished yet. He gathered the winds, encircling the creature with their fury. Gritting his teeth, Eric pressed down with everything he had, and watched in triumph as the red wings folded and the beast toppled into the forest.

Eric's shoulders slumped and letting out a long breath, he released his power. The strength fled from him in a rush, and he sank to his knees, an empty feeling in the pit of his stomach. A tremor went through him. The brief exertion had drained his already weakened strength.

"Eric, stop it!" he gasped as Inken grabbed him by the shoulders and shook him.

"What?" he cried over the whistling wind.

Inken pointed.

The blood froze in Eric's veins as he looked up. The wind had not dissipated. Instead, they raced around the clearing, sucking flames into the air. A column of fire was taking shape above the clearing, whirring around with the circling currents. Tree trunks groaned as it gathered force, and saplings were torn from the ground and hurled up into the tornado, where the flames quickly devoured them.

Eric gaped as Inken shook him again, wrenching him from his shock. Reaching down, he sought out his magic. But the pool of blue was gone, and only a spark remained to light the darkness. His strength was gone, his magic depleted – there was nothing he could do.

"I can't… my magic… not strong enough," the wind tore away Eric's words.

Inken's eyes widened and her knuckles tightened around her bow. Reaching down, she grasped him by the shirt and hauled him to his feet. "Then we've got to go. *Run!*" she yelled, trying to signal the others through the smoke and flames. "Run for the cove!"

Then they were on their feet, running, fleeing the burning air, the smouldering heat. Gusts of wind sucked at their backs as the inferno chased them, the crackling flames leaping between the trees. There was no trouble seeing the way now – the fire was everywhere.

A roar came from overhead as the canopy exploded, and the dragon came crashing down. Its wings shredded the bark from the trees as it landed with a thud, halting their desperate flight.

Eric dug in his heels and his hand whipped out to catch Inken's collar, hauling her back. The dragon stood across their path, its eyes glowing with a visceral hatred. The flames raced through the undergrowth to either side of them, and the tornado howled at their back. They were trapped.

The dragon crept towards them, its black tongue flicking out in rapid succession. Then it paused, hesitant, and Eric realised it had been wounded in the battle. A thick branch had impaled one leg, and the webbing of its wings hung in shreds. Thick blood ran down its scales.

But it did not need to attack to finish them. The tornado was drawing closer, and the air was hot and suffocating. Flames flooded the forest floor, taking light amidst the leaf litter. Eric could feel his skin beginning to burn.

Beside him, Inken nocked an arrow and loosed it at the beast. It shot upwards and bounced off its hardened scales. The dragon roared and took another step, its confidence growing.

Eric's heart sank as Inken drew another arrow. He searched again for a trace of magic, but found nothing. Around them the fire roared. They only had minutes left now. He prayed the others had made it clear.

Inken squinted through the smoky light. This time she took long seconds to take aim. Then she let out a slow breath, and loosed. The shaft arced up towards the dragon's face, and plunged into its giant eye.

The beast screamed and staggered back, but Inken did not pause. She had already nocked another arrow, and drawing back her bowstring, she loosed again.

The dragon bellowed as the second arrow buried itself in its other eye.

Eric gaped, unable to believe what he had just witnessed. But the beast had had enough. Dropping its head, it charged.

Inken drew another arrow, but this time there would be no stopping it. Seeing a chance, Eric tackled Inken to the ground. Pain tore through his side as they rolled, carrying them clear of the dragon's path, and the blinded beast charged past.

They sat up and Inken shot him a glare, but Eric only smiled back. Without speaking, they climbed to their feet and ran on. The forest around them was alive with flames, leaving them only one direction to flee.

Finally they left the flames behind, and the growl of the tornado died away as they left it behind. The forest grew dark again, lit only by the distant flickering of the forest fire.

Exhausted, they collapsed to the ground, clinging to each other in fear and pain and sorrow. The wound in Eric's side throbbed, and he knew he had burst his stitches again, but he was too exhausted to care. He hugged Inken to him, drawing solace from her touch. He marvelled at her courage, to have found the calm to halt the dragon. They had been so, so lucky.

They lay in the darkness, silent but for their laboured gasps and half-choked sobs. Slowly, Inken's breathing settled into a gentle rhythm as she drifted into sleep. Closing his eyes, Eric willed himself to do the same.

Instead, questions raced through his mind. *Were the others okay? Had they heard Inken's shout?*

There was only one way to find the answers to his questions. In the morning, they would continue on to Malevolent Cove, to the place where the old king Thomas had vanished. The thought chilled him, filled him with a sense of foreboding, though he could not say why.

He no longer cared about the Gold dragons, no longer held out hope for Enala. Alastair's plan had been folly – all that mattered now was gathering the shattered remains of their company, and fleeing this cursed land.

Enala was gone.

CHAPTER 24

Eric heard the crashing of waves long before they reached the dark shores of Malevolent Cove. The sound called to him, drawing him on through the dense trees. So close to the coast, they had become twisted and misshapen things, utterly unlike their towering siblings further inland. They tugged at his clothes, slowing him and draining his energy. But they were close, and he pressed on, eager to find their friends.

At the edge of the treeline, he stumbled to a stop, and looked out at the infamous cove. They stood at the edge of a beach, its black sands running down into the swirling waters. Elsewhere, sheer cliffs ringed the bay. White-capped waves churned the murky waters, and shadows lurked beneath the surface, a hidden graveyard to many a ship. Rocky spires sprouted from the black sands, their jagged tips like the claws of some buried giant. The air stank of rotten fish and the tang of salt.

Staring down at the black beach, Eric reached out and took Inken's hand. Cold fingers wrapped around his heart as he looked at her, then back to the beach, and the dark-cloaked figure standing on the black sands.

The figure stood like a statue, his features obscured by a hood, staring out at the raging waters. The outline of two swords stood out against his cloak, and his hands were clenched tight, his skin a deathly white.

Lingering in the trees, Eric stared at the figure, searching for some hint of his identity. Though almost completely concealed by the black cloak, there was something distinctly inhuman about the stranger, something dark and threatening.

Shivering, Eric fought to keep his feet. It had taken them several hours to reach the coast, and he was at the end of his strength. Only the hope of finding the others had kept him going, but there was no sign of their companions.

Eric shivered as a whispery laugh carried across the beach. Slowly, the figure turned towards them, and Eric caught the glint of black gemstones in the pommels of the stranger's swords.

"Why do you lurk in the shadows?" a voice slivered through the air.

Eric gasped as his foot took an involuntary step forward. He grasped at Inken's hand, struggling to stop himself, but she was moving too. Their eyes caught, and he saw the naked terror in her eyes. Step by step, they made their unwilling way down onto the black sands.

"Welcome," laughter mingled with the word.

Teeth clenched, Eric watched the figure, struggling to pierce the shadows beneath its hood. His mind raced, searching for answers, clutching at ideas. Who was this man, this creature? Where had it come from? What was happening?

Beside him, Inken straightened and reached for her sabre. "Who are you?" she growled. "What are you doing here?"

The hidden face beneath the hood turned to stare at her. "Wait… and see."

Eric swallowed. He still clutched Inken's hand in his, and silently he gave her fingers a squeeze. The figure had turned back to the trees, resuming its silent vigil. Helpless, they stood beside it, breaths held, and waited.

Within minutes, a crash came from somewhere in the forest. Looking up, Eric watched as Caelin emerged from the trees, stumbling onto the sand like a dead man. The others followed one by one, a trail of burnt and bloodied bodies. Alastair came last, hobbling and leaning heavily on a branch. His eyes widened as he looked down and saw them waiting beside the black-cloaked figure.

"*Alastair*," Eric turned as the word whispered across the cove, his neck tingling as he finally recognised the voice.

Slowly, the figure reached up to pull back its hood, revealing the creature beneath. Stark white hair whipped across a smooth grey face, and jet-black eyes swept the beach, burning with hate. He had lost his eyebrows and beard, but Eric still recognised the man from the vision Antonia had shown him.

"*Thomas*," Alastair hissed.

Alastair seemed to shrink as the king's black eyes found him. The laughter came again, echoing off the cliffs and casting a shadow across the beach.

Eric shook his head, unable to speak. The thing standing before them was Thomas, the king who had saved the Three Nations, who had stood with the Gods and defied Archon's wrath. The same king whose descendants had wielded the Sword of Light down the decades. The king who had disappeared on this very shore, all those years ago. Yet it was clear there was nothing left of the man he had once been.

"Ah, Alastair," the fiend spoke in a voice so low Eric

strained to catch the words. "How good it is to see you again. You have aged poorly, old friend."

"*Do not call me that!*" Alastair cried.

"Why not? You named me Thomas, did you not?"

"What did Archon do to you?"

"Archon?" Thomas laughed. "This was never his doing, old friend. Thomas was weak, dying. He let the magic win. He set the beast loose."

"No." Alastair closed his eyes as pain swept across his face. "It's not possible."

The creature cackled, the sound grating on their ears in a mockery of the old king's vibrant laughter.

"Oh, Alastair, did you truly never consider it?" The demon spread its arms. "I guess not, or you would have searched for me. I have been here all along, waiting. Decades have passed, and my natural born magic has long since given way to the darkness, but finally you have come."

"You are not him," Alastair shook his head. "There is nothing left here of the man I once knew."

"Why are you here?" Balistor cut in.

The dark eyes turned to stare at the fire Magicker. "Of course, how could I have forgotten?" the demon grinned. "Archon grows tired of failure. His human servants have disappointed him at every turn, forcing his hand. It is time I prepared for his arrival. When he finally marches south, I will ensure there is no one left to resist him. The Three Nations will fall like leaves before the autumn breeze."

"You are here to kill us?" Alastair asked.

Laughter answered Alastair's question, as the demon reached down and drew a sword from its scabbard. Steel rasped against leather as the blade slid clear. Runes shone along the length of the dark blade, and it glowed with a sickly aura.

"Do you know what this is?" Thomas whispered as he looked at Alastair.

Lips clenched tight, the old Magicker shook his head, and a smile spread across the demon's face.

"Then let me show you."

Before anyone could react, Thomas vanished.

Eric had no time to search for their missing foe. He gasped as a sudden, terrible pain ripped through his back and burst from his chest. A half-choked scream tore from his throat, and looking down, he stared at the black tip of the demon's blade stabbing from his torso. His body convulsed, and a dark sensation swept through his veins. He could feel the strength draining from him, as though sucked a way by some black vortex. His knees gave way, but an iron grip on his shoulder held him up. Behind him, the demon cackled.

He heard Inken scream, but she sounded distant, as though she were miles away. He looked up, searching for her, but shadows swept across his vision. He glimpsed five figures standing on the beach, but he could not separate them, could not find her.

Another blow struck him in the back, pushing him from the sword. Eric toppled to the ground, landing with a thud. He coughed, choking on the taste of blood. Agony swept through him in waves, and the dark threads spread, enveloping him in an otherworldly pain. He reached for the last drop of his magic, desperate to defend himself, but the power had vanished.

Through the fog, he heard the demon speak. "Such power for one so young. I am glad to take it off his hands," the boom of lightning followed.

Eric cracked open his eyes. Darkness swirled at edge of his vision, but the demon's sword stood out stark and clear. Lightning danced along the blade.

The demon stalked towards his companions. Eric closed

his eyes, unable to watch. His breath came in ragged gasps. The dark energy continued to envelop him, tearing at his soul, and he had nothing left to fight it with. Oblivion loomed. He wished for Inken.

Then Michael was at his side.

~

A SCREAM BUILT in Inken's chest as Eric fell, crawling up from some dark recess within her. Hot tears ran down her cheeks and her knees shook, the strength fleeing her legs. In her mind, a voice screamed for her to run to him, to save him. But the demon stood between them, laughing.

Hands trembling, her vision blurred by tears, Inken struggled to nock an arrow to her bow. But she missed the string, and the arrow tumbled to the sand. Shrieking, Inken hurled the bow to the ground and drew her sabre. An icy hand took hold of her heart as she stepped towards the demon.

It turned towards her, but Alastair attacked first, leaping across her path. His sword lashed out at his old friend, but the demon's blade swept up to meet it. Steel clashed and lightning jumped between the them. Electricity raced along Alastair's blade and vanished into the cool metal. Alastair sneered and lashed out again.

Caelin raced in from the right. The demon turned aside a decapitating blow from Alastair and struck out with its boot. The blow caught Alastair in the chest and flung him backwards into a rocky spire, and the old king spun in time to avoid Caelin's wild slash.

Now the demon turned its sword on the young soldier. Lightning leapt from the blade, but Caelin was already moving, and the bolt struck empty ground. The air erupted, the sand boiling where he'd just stood. Rolling with a smooth grace, Caelin regained his feet and swung at the demon's face.

The fiend leaned back to avoid the blow, but Caelin pressed the attack, his sword reversing its sweep. This time the demon caught his blade on its own. Lightning danced between the weapons, followed by a terrible boom, and Caelin's sword shattered like glass. The blast sent Caelin bouncing across the sand like a ragdoll.

Inken threw herself into the battle, and Balistor charged in beside her. The demon turned to meet them, leaving Alastair and Caelin to recover – or so she prayed.

Black steel flashed for her face and Inken hurled herself aside. The blade sliced the air, its razor-sharp edge shearing off a few fiery strands of her hair. Rolling, Inken struggled to lift her sabre as the fiend swung again. But before the blow could land, a ball of flame smashed into its chest. Embers exploded from its cloak, but the demon shrugged off the attack and turned to grin at Balistor.

Balistor launched another fireball, but the fiend's cloak was already aflame and it didn't seem to care. He began to retreat as it advanced on him. Inken saw her chance as the demon turned its back, and sprinting forward, she brought her sabre down on the demon's neck.

The blade struck home, and came to a sudden, jarring halt. A bone numbing shock ran up her arm and the sword slipped from her fingers. It was as though she'd struck solid rock, but the blade had not even pierced the demon's skin.

The demon turned on her, flames leaping from its cloak, and lashed out with a fist. The blow caught her in the chest and flung her into the sand. She tumbled across the beach and crashed into a stone pillar. Groaning, she struggled to sit up. Pain lanced through her chest, but gritting her teeth she lurched to her feet. Drawing her hunting knife, she stumbled back towards the fight.

Alastair was back on his feet and wielding his sword two-handed. Jaw clenched, he swung at the demon, but their foe was too fast, and each time the black blade was there to turn aside his blow.

Inken dove in, feet unsteady, searching for an opening. The hunting knife had no reach, but she hoped she could distract it, and give Alastair an opening. The demon began to laugh, its rasping cackle ringing with the clash of blades. Only Alastair's sword could touch the black blade, protected by whatever spells had been cast on the weapon.

Alastair jumped back, chest heaving, hands trembling. Inken moved to stand with him, praying for the strength to continue. They crouched low, and then sprang forward to attack together.

Lightning arced from the demon's blade, colliding with the sand at their feet. The beach erupted, and the force of the explosion picked them up and hurled them through the air. The breath tore from Inken's lungs as she smashed into the sand, while Alastair flew backwards into the ocean and disappeared beneath the waves.

Inken coughed, choking, her body wracked with pain. She rolled onto her stomach and spat out a mouthful of sand. She glimpsed her dagger a few feet away and gathering her strength, began to crawl towards it.

Only Balistor fought on now. His face was black with soot, but his powers were useless against the demon. It advanced through his attacks, a dark grin on its pale face. Over the roar of the waves and flames, she heard Balistor shout. "Leave them, they're *mine!*"

Inken closed her eyes, willing strength to her weary limbs. Her fingers found the blade and clasped desperately at the hilt. She felt better with a weapon in her grasp, though it was little use to her.

Across the beach, the demon raised its sword to the sky,

dismissing Balistor with a contemptuous turn of its back. Above the clouds darkened, and then lightning lanced down, spearing the black sword. Another bolt followed, and another, and the beach shook with the boom of thunder.

The demon's laughter followed. "You are all traitors. Farewell!"

Inken clenched her eyes shut and braced herself for the lightning's burning touch. She wished for Eric, for one last chance to embrace him.

Then a roar sounded over the thunder. Looking up, Inken stared as a shadow passed across the sky. Golden scales glinted as the dragon folded its wings and dived. It streaked towards the beach, jaws wide, talons spread, and slammed into the demon. The energy gathered around the dark blade flashed away, the blasts leaving glassy marks in the sand where they struck.

The fiend twisted in the air and landed on its feet, sword held out before it. Dropping into a crouch, a scowl twisted its pale face.

On the ground, Inken could only stare, unable to believe her eyes. The Gold dragon towered over them all, twice the size of the Red from the night before. Its wings spread wide, casting a shadow across the beach as it prepared to take flight. The massive tail lashed out, shattering rocky spires like they were made from glass. Its diamond eyes shone as it faced the demon.

And on its back sat a girl with golden hair.

Her clothes were torn, her skin streaked with dirt, but she showed no sign of fear as she grasped the dragon's neck. Her sapphire eyes glared down at them, her lips twisted with fury. Lifting her hand, she pointed at the demon, and screamed.

White-hot flames leapt from the dragon's jaws, far fiercer than anything Balistor had summoned. Now fear showed on the demon's face, and it dove from the path of the flames, unable to stand before their cleansing heat.

The dragon came after it, claws ripping up the black sand. Fire encircled the demon, forcing it to turn. Its sword lashed out, and a bolt of lightning lanced for the girl. Inken's breath caught in her throat and the girl flinched back, but a golden wing rose to protect her. The lightning shattered on the thick scales.

Then the dragon was attacking again. An inferno licked at the heels of their foe, chasing the demon across the sand, leaving a path of glass in its wake. Roaring, the dragon leapt into the air, the great wings beating down.

On the beach, the fiend swung round and raised its sword. Lightning twitched along its length and lanced at the dragon's unprotected stomach. White fire rushed to meet it. The forces collided mid-air and exploded outwards. The shockwave whipped sand into Inken's face, but she squinted through the grit, and saw the flickering blue lightning succumb to the all-consuming fire. The demon disappeared into the conflagration.

A hideous scream rose from the flames, and within the inferno she saw a dark figure writhing. The dragon kept on, relentless.

A flash erupted across the beach, forcing Inken close her eyes and look away. Even then the light seeped through, burning. Then the light flickered, and died.

Opening her eyes, Inken blinked as her vision returned. The flames had vanished, but the dragon still towered on its hind legs, its great head scanning the beach. The ground where the demon had stood had turned to molten glass, but now Inken saw a trail of glass footprints burnt into the sand, heading for the forest. The demon had fled.

Inken looked up at the dragon and the girl.

Enala stared back at her.

CHAPTER 25

Caelin slowly pulled himself to his feet. The dragon loomed over him; scales gleaming, fangs bared, eyes glaring, but Caelin ignored it. Turning, he sprinted for the sea. The surf roared up to meet him as he dove over the waves. Salty water stung his eyes as he searched for Alastair.

He bobbed the surface moments later with Alastair slung over his shoulders. Straining beneath the old man's weight, he dragged himself back to the shore and up the beach. He dumped the old man to the sand and collapsed beside him, gasping for breath. Alastair gave a hacking cough as he fell, and water gushed from his mouth.

Balistor appeared at his side. "Is he okay?"

Caelin nodded, shivering in the brisk sea breeze. He glanced back at the dragon and the girl who rode it. It was an astonishing sight, and he couldn't help but appreciate the irony. After all they had gone through to find her, it had been Enala who'd saved them.

"Gods, what can't the old man survive?" Balistor muttered.

"I'm going to talk to her," Caelin nodded to Balistor. "Look after him."

Standing, he walked towards the dragon. The golden scales glistened in the morning sunlight as the giant head turned to watch him, its eyes alive with intelligence. The jaws cracked open, revealing rows of dagger-length teeth. A gust of wind carried with it the stench of rotting fish.

Caelin shivered. Alastair's blade lay on the sand nearby, and reaching down he scooped it up. The dragon growled in warning, but he lifted it slowly, an arm raised in submission, and slid it into his empty scabbard. Showing his hands, he continued forwards.

As he moved, his gaze drifted to where Eric lay. Michael and Inken crouched at his side, but even from this distance he could see the gaping wound, and the blood staining the sand. He fought off tears.

Summoning his resolve, he turned back to Enala. The girl glared down at him, her crystal eyes following his approach. Her blond hair fluttered in the breeze and he noticed now the copper lock dangling across her face. Dark circles ringed her eyes.

When Caelin reached the dragon, he dropped into a low bow. It had been a long time since anyone had visited the tribes, but he knew the courtesies expected.

"Who are you?" Enala demanded.

Caelin frowned, his curiosity mounting. As a rule, Gold dragons did not allow people to ride them. Even during Archon's war, it had been a rare occurrence. Even so, he knew the correct etiquette. Ignoring the girl's question, he addressed the dragon first.

"Dragon, my name is Caelin, Sergeant of the Plorsean army," he announced formally. "I know the name of the one you carry, but may I enquire as to yours?"

Air hissed from the dragon's nose in what might have

been laughter. "Well met, Sergeant," a rumble came from its throat. "I am Nerissa."

"Nerissa, pardon my curiosity; but why do you bear this girl?"

Again the snort. "Her parents visited this place often when she was young. Her blood is old. She may ride with us, for we still honour the pact made by her ancestors. She and I have flown together many times."

Caelin nodded. Nerissa spoke of the pact King Thomas had forged after Archon's war. The dragon had confirmed Enala was truly the relative of the ancient king.

"Who are you? Why are you here?" Enala grated, her eyes flashing dangerously.

He bent his head. "My apologies. As I have already said, my name is Caelin. But these are the hunter Inken, Magickers Balistor and Alastair, and the apprentice, Eric," he pointed to each of them in turn and then looked up at the girl. "And we are here for you, Enala."

The girl stiffened. The dragon dropped into a crouch, a low growl rumbling up from its chest. Sand crunched beneath its claws as it stepped towards him. A tongue of flame licked the sand.

Caelin raised his hands, fighting back the instinct to draw Alastair's sword. "*Wait!* We mean you no harm, Enala."

"That is *all* anyone wishes for me," her lips curled back in a snarl.

"Please, let me speak. We came here to help you!"

Enala paused, her nostrils flaring. She leaned closer, though she sat high above him, and her gaze seemed to look right through him. "And how did you plan to help me, Caelin? When you cannot even help yourselves?" she gave a cruel laugh.

Caelin's cheeks flushed, but he pushed on. "There are

people hunting for you, Enala. Servants of Archon who want you dead."

The laughter died. "Archon?"

"Yes."

"What would he want with me?" her voice was hesitant now, touched by fear.

"You're a threat to him," Caelin said softly. "You are the last descendent of Aria, sister to the old King Thomas. And you are the only one who can wield the Sword of Light."

Enala's eyes widened. "What?"

"You must come with us, Enala. The Three Nations need you."

Her eyes hardened. "There is nothing for me there now. Everything and everyone I ever loved is gone. I am safe here with Nerissa. So, Caelin, why should I care?"

Caelin gaped. He had come too far to care for the ravings of a selfish teenager. Whatever Enala had been through, he would not allow her to abandon her nation.

"Why should you care?" he shouted. "Because people will die. Because without you there is nothing to stop Archon from unleashing his terror on our world. Because if you don't, a thousand other children will lose their parents, just as you have."

Enala stared down at him, her face expressionless.

Balistor stared up at the arrogant young girl. She sat there on her dragon: beautiful, brave, naïve. Did she really believe she would be safe here from Archon? The dark Magicker had the power to turn a dragon to dust if he chose. There would be no escaping him once he came, and so long as Enala lived, she was a threat to his plans.

So she had to die.

Smiling, Balistor shook his head, still unable to believe his luck. He had finally found her. Not only that, her arrival had saved him from his master's wrath. Now, her death would redeem him. The only obstacle left to surmount was the dragon, and fortunately, he had a piece of dark magic that might just have the power he needed.

He looked down at Alastair, lying so weak at his feet. The deception had been easier than he could have believed. How desperate the old man had been for help – he had never even questioned Balistor's story.

His anger flared then, as he recalled the disaster at the inn. He had lost track of time, and the hunters had stormed the building before he had the information he'd needed. It wouldn't have mattered, except one of the fools had shot him in the back without recognising him. The fool had stopped him from burning them all alive in the haystack. Instead, the fire had caught the window as he slipped out, preventing the hunters from following them. By the time he'd recovered, they were a long way from his hired help, and there'd been no choice but to go along with the fools.

Even then, the bounty hunters might still have been successful if it weren't for Inken. For her betrayal, he would ensure she endured a long, painful death. He smiled, pausing to appreciate her heartbroken sobs.

"She's the one," Alastair coughed, a smile on his lips. Then the old man closed his eyes and drifted back into unconsciousness.

Balistor shook his head, suddenly thankful each of his traps had failed. They had shown him one thing – not to underestimate the old Magicker. His strength was phenomenal, even at the edge of exhaustion. He'd thought the ploy with the Red dragon, tricking the company into camping in its nest, would have finished him, but somehow the old man had survived.

It seemed whatever he faced, Alastair would find a way to triumph.

Not this time, Balistor smirked. *The girl's sweet throat will have to wait.*

Reaching down, he drew his sword.

~

INKEN'S EYES BURNED. Her throat was hoarse from crying, her shirt soaked with tears. Sitting on the soft sand, she cradled Eric's head in her lap and gently stroked his hair. His blue eyes stared blankly up at her, flickering with whatever waking dream had taken him. His body shook, and his skin was cold to touch. When he coughed, red foam dripped down his chin.

She wiped the blood away with her sleeve. "Please, Eric, stay with us."

Michael laid a hand on her shoulder. The doctor had done his best to stem the bleeding, but they all knew the wound was mortal. "I can give him something to ease his passing, Inken."

"*No!*" she screamed at him. "No, no, no!" she sobbed.

Michael shrank back from her wrath, and she instantly regretted the outburst. All she wanted was for someone to hold her, to tell her everything would be all right.

Eric coughed again, and his brow creased in pain. Then he blinked, and his gaze caught hers. "Don't worry, Inken," he gasped. "It's… going to be okay."

Inken leaned close and kissed him. "Don't you leave me," she whispered.

Eric's eyes slid down the beach. His skin was a pallid grey, his lips blue, but still he smiled. "We found her, Inken. Everything's going to be okay."

Inken couldn't bring herself to smile back. The demon's

blade had pierced Eric's lung, leaving him to drown in his own blood. The wound was beyond any doctor's skill to heal.

As she watched, Eric's grin faded. He struggled to raise his arm. A spasm swept through him, and a cough rattled up from his chest. Red flecks stained her shirt as he wheezed, but through his coughs, she made out one word.

"*Alastair!*"

Inken shook her head, not understanding. Turning, she looked at the rest of their fellowship.

Down the beach, above the raging surf, Balistor stood over Alastair. His sword was in his hand. She watched as he raised it above his head.

"*Caelin!*" she shrieked.

CAELIN HEARD his name over the roar of the surf. Looking up, he saw Inken pointing at him. No, not at him – behind him. He spun, driven by the stark terror on her face.

Balistor stood beside Alastair, his sword poised over the unconscious Magicker. He had frozen at Inken's cry, his eyes wide, uncertain. Then his gaze flickered to where Caelin stood, and a grin spread across his thin lips. The sword lanced down.

Time seemed to slow, and Caelin watched helpless as the sword descended. He heard the crash of a wave on the beach, the great whoosh of the dragon's breath, Enala's gasp, Inken's painful sob. He saw the hate in Balistor's eyes – the hate he should have seen long ago. A ray of sunlight pierced the clouds, catching on Balistor's sword, and for a second it seemed as though the traitor held the Sword of Light itself.

Then the blade plunged home, burying itself in Alastair's chest, and the light died.

Alastair lurched against the blade. One last gasp escaped him, and then he slumped against the black sand.

Balistor wrenched back his blade and began to cackle. Blood dripped from his sword tip and a pool was already gathering around Alastair. His laughter carried across the beach, fuel to Caelin's fury.

"*Traitor!*" he drew the sword he had gathered from the beach.

Balistor walked calmly towards him, his smile unchanged. "Traitor? No, I don't think so. Spy would be more apt. I never served your king – only Archon. Thankfully, you're a gullible fool, Caelin."

Caelin gritted his teeth, resisting the urge to attack. Nothing made sense here.

"Who are you?" he hissed.

Balistor smirked. "Perhaps Inken might recognise me," he waved a hand. His purple robes darkened to black.

"You!" Caelin heard Inken hiss, but he did not take his eyes from Balistor.

"Still cannot guess, Caelin? I am the one who hired Inken and her friends, the one who has been hunting you. And this time, you won't escape."

The pieces began to click together. "All this time?" he choked.

Balistor continued his march up the beach. "Yes, although I wanted to be done with you all at the inn. An unfortunate series of events ruined up my plan - Inken's interference most of all," his eyes swept across to where Inken crouched. "And believe me, Inken, you will scream for mercy before you die."

Inken growled. "Not if I kill you first."

Balistor laughed, ignoring her threat. "Still, things have worked out well in the end. You have helped to shame my rival, and led me straight to the girl."

"And do you think this girl is going to die so easily?" Enala hissed. Nerissa's jaws stretched wide, revealing row upon row of razor-sharp teeth.

Balistor only grinned. With his free hand, he reached inside his cloak. Caelin stepped towards him, but Balistor's hand whipped back out. Flames licked from his fingertips and rushed at him. Caelin threw himself back, and the ground at his feet exploded, sending sand sizzling through the air.

"Stay back, Caelin. Your turn will come." His hand disappeared back into the cloak and drew out a glass sphere.

Caelin stared at the alien object. Dark mist roiled within, clawing at the glass with smoky fingers. A sickly green glow seeped from it, and a dreadful humming rang in his ears.

"I've been waiting to use this for a long time. Here, Enala, a gift from Archon," he tossed the ball in her direction.

The globe tumbled through the air. Nerissa reared back as the globe shattered against her head. A muffled explosion rang out, and a black cloud rushed from the glass to engulf the dragon's head. Nerissa roared. Rising up on her hind legs, she clawed at the dark fog, her head shaking as she tried to dislodge the cloying magic. On her back, Enala lost her grip and screamed as she tumbled to the sand. Winded and gasping for air, she struggled to find her feet.

Above, the darkness still writhed around the dragon's head. Nerissa's claws slashed and tore at it, but the cloud was like a living thing, reforming with each attempt. It clung to the dragon's face, robbing her of sight, of smell, of air.

Her movements grew more violent and distressed. The great head shook, jaws opening to bellow her defiance. The greasy poison poured down her throat, cutting off the sound. She stumbled across the sand, wings clawing the air, her struggles growing ever weaker.

Caelin could only watch in helpless terror. Beneath the beast, Enala sat frozen, staring up at her dying dragon.

Suddenly Nerissa grew still, the last of her strength fading away. She began to sway. Then she was falling, toppling straight towards Enala. The girl did not move, did not seem bothered by her impending death. She looked up at the dragon, on her knees, and watched the massive body descend.

Caelin was already moving, the sand slipping beneath his feet, as he leapt at the girl. His neck tingled as the dragon's shadow fell on him, then he was tackling the girl, hurling them both from the path of the dragon's fall. A wave of coarse black sand billowed out as the beast crashed to the ground behind them. Caelin lay over the girl, shielding her from the dragon's death throws.

When the beast finally stilled, Caelin picked himself up, leaving Enala where she lay. The giant body of Nerissa lay nearby, still as a statue. The evil smoke had dissipated, and the glassy globes of her eyes stared at him, blank and devoid of life.

On the ground, Enala opened her eyes and saw Nerissa lying there. A wave swept through her tiny body, a great shuddering jolt, as though something within her had been shattered into a thousand pieces. Enala rolled into a ball and began to sob, the quiet whispers mere hints of her sorrow.

But Caelin had no time to worry about her grief. He picked up Alastair's sword and stood over the helpless girl, waiting for Balistor to come.

The traitor walked calmly up onto Nerissa's stomach, grinning as he saw them. Caelin gripped his sword tighter as the Magicker began to clap. His cold eyes watched them, his grin dismissing Caelin as a spider would a fly.

Yet Caelin would not back down – he would fight to his dying breath to protect the girl.

"Well done, Caelin. For a moment, I thought I'd killed two birds with one stone. As ever though, you do not fail to impress. Sadly though, it is time for this mockery to end," as he spoke, flames spread along his arm and leapt at Caelin.

Caelin flinched and lifted Alastair's sword. Fire crackled, filling the air, too fast for him to avoid. It struck Alastair's blade – and vanished.

A sudden silence stretched out as Caelin blinked, staring at the sword. He ran a finger along the steel, and found it cool to the touch.

Breath hissed between Balistor's teeth. "Ah, Alastair's sword. It will make a nice memento."

"Come and get it," Caelin grinned, slipping into a fighting stance and waving the Magicker on.

Balistor lifted his blade and touched a hand to it. Fire leapt along its length and spread across his arm and chest, until it covered his entire body in a blazing suit of armour. Heat radiated from him in waves, forcing Caelin back. He squinted against the flaming light, and laughed.

"Do you think those flames will stop my blade?" he mocked.

If Balistor replied, Caelin did not hear him over the flames. But his foe's sword flicked out, burning a streak across his vision. Metal clashed as he caught the blow on Alastair's blade and turned it aside. Embers sprayed across his face, and he raised an arm to protect his eyes from the smouldering rain. He slid backwards, sword slashing out to cover his retreat.

Balistor pressed his advantage. Heat radiated from him in a stifling cloud and smoke filled the air, making it a struggle just to breathe. Sweat trickled down Caelin's face and into his eyes. His clothes, drenched just minutes ago by the ocean, were already dry. But he focused his mind against the discomfort, and blocked each blow with cool efficiency.

Yet as the fight continued, he could feel the heat sapping his strength. His attacks were already growing feeble, and while Alastair's sword protected him from direct attacks, it could not be everywhere. Each time the blades met, flames erupted between them. The cinders caught in his shirt and left scorch marks on his skin, forcing him to retreat.

Then Inken appeared from nowhere, an arrow already nocked to her bow. Before either could react, she loosed. The arrow hissed through the air, coming within a foot of Balistor before a tongue of flame lashed out to catch it. The shaft fell to the ground as ash.

Balistor lashed out with his sword, forcing Caelin back, then spun and hurled a wave of fire at Inken. It struck her in the chest, throwing her to the ground. She spun through the sand, fighting to beat out the flames. When they finally died, she collapsed to the beach and did not rise again.

Caelin turned in time to block a decapitating blow. Heat swamped him. It was like fighting in a furnace. The flames sucked away all moisture, burning his skin and leaving his lips cracking with each inhalation. His strength was running out. He needed to end the fight quickly, or he would have nothing left to give.

The burning sword came at him again. Caelin leaned back and the blade sliced past. Then he spun on his heel, his own weapon seeking flesh. Balistor wrenched back – but not fast enough. Alastair's blade streaked through the flaming armour and found flesh. The stench of burning blood followed, but the wound was not mortal.

Now Balistor's blade lanced at his side, faster, harder, and Caelin barely had the strength to leap back. Balistor charged after him, angry now, and before Caelin could react the burning sword swept beneath his guard. The red-hot blade tore across his chest, burning as it went. Caelin screamed.

Agony swept through his body, chasing away the last of

his strength. Balistor raised his sword, and Caelin stumbled backwards, his legs trembling with each step.

Balistor laughed. "And now the mighty Caelin flees. Did I not tell you how useless a sword is amongst Magickers?"

Caelin staggered, the heat burning deeper into his chest. Gritting his teeth, he fought to keep his feet.

I cannot fail, but the thought alone was not enough, and his legs crumpled.

Looking up from his hands and knees, Caelin watched Balistor approach. "Ah, the great swordsman humbled. I am glad to see the day," he placed the burning sword against Caelin's neck.

Caelin shrieked as flames licked his flesh. He flinched away, his hands reaching down to scoop up a fistful of sand. As Balistor raised his sword, Caelin hurled the sand at his foe's face. It disappeared through the mask of fire.

Balistor reared back and an awful scream came from beneath the flames. His sword tumbled to the ground as he reached for his face. Another shriek echoed off the cliffs, and he fell to the ground, clawing at his face as though his eyes were aflame.

Caelin did not stop to question the turn of fortune. Staggering forward, he lifted Alastair's blade and drove it through the traitor's chest. The screams cut off suddenly, the flames dying away to nothing as he wrenched back the sword.

He gasped as Balistor's face was revealed. The sand he'd thrown had liquefied in the flames, covering Balistor's face in molten glass. It had congealed in his mouth and nose and eyes, the skin blistering beneath, his eyes burnt black. Caelin's stomach churned as he smelt the burning flesh and hair. Suppressing a scream of his own, he turned away.

Crouched on the black sand, he looked around the bloody battleground. The dragon's body loomed nearby, Enala still catatonic beside it. Beyond, Alastair lay alone on the sand, while further up the beach, Inken had managed to crawl back to Eric's side. A breeze blew across the beach, carrying with it the stench of ash, the reek of their ruin.

Caelin's eyes drifted back to Enala. She was the one they had sought, the one who would save them all. Yet in saving her, they had paid a toll beyond what anyone had expected. And who was Enala but a young, inexperienced girl? How was she to stand against the powers of Archon?

Was she really worth this?

CHAPTER 26

Waves crashed down on the black shores. The glow of the evening star shone on the horizon, its light beckoning them into the dark. Night was close. Eric would not live to see the sunrise.

Michael watched the young couple, his heart breaking. For the thousandth time in his short life, he wished the Goddess had gifted him the magic to heal. All his life he had studied the art of healing, but his skills were next to useless beside those with magic. A healer might save the boy – but Michael was powerless.

He was amazed the boy even still lived. Through sheer courage Eric fought on, his eyes locked with Inken's. The girl refused to leave his side. Young love, fleeting as it could be, was fierce. Even so, it would not be long now. Closing his eyes, Michael fought back tears.

I told them, he raged. *I told them it was folly, but I never imagined...*

Michael looked back at them. The boy fought for every breath now. Liquid rattled in his chest, blood drowning his lungs. The wound had been patched, but the bleeding continued within. He did not have the skill to repair such damage.

"Michael, help!" Inken cried, desperate.

The girl's voice tore Michael from his despair. He joined them and together they shifted Eric onto his side. His breathing eased, but a moment later he began to cough again. Michael saw the terror in Eric's eyes and glanced at Inken. The girl's eyes were red, but there were no more tears. Her face was burnt and bruised from battle. Her eyes pleaded for him to help.

"I'm sorry, Inken. I don't think it will be long now."

"No," she whispered.

Michael moved away, unable to bear her grief. He saw the accusation in her eyes.

Why?

He looked over at Enala, the girl who had drawn them to this place. She sat stone faced, hands around her knees, rocking back and forth on the sand. She had not spoken in hours. No one could break her from the trance, and Michael was not game to try again.

Moving into the trees, he sought the calming touch of nature. A cloud of insects rose to greet him as he sat, but he ignored their tiny bites, seeking to immerse himself in the sounds and smells of the earth, to reconnect with his Element. It felt as though years had passed since he'd left the temple. He missed the simplicity of his life there, the rareness of death. Today's slaughter made no sense to him.

"Why, Antonia? Why did this happen?" he whispered to the forest.

"Because I failed," a tiny voice spoke behind him, heavy with sorrow.

Michael turned his head. A young girl walked towards him, bathed in a faint green light. Her feet crunched on the hard leaves, her violet eyes staring at him from beneath a fringe of silky brown hair. Faint freckles spotted her cheeks and her lips were twisted in sadness. She looked nothing like the paintings in the temple, but there was no mistaking her.

This could only be Antonia, Goddess of Plorsea.

Michael fell to his knees, head bowed and arms out before him.

Elynbrigge told the truth! He could not believe it.

To his shock, Antonia began to sob. "Get up, you fool. Please, no more."

He looked up. There were tears on the Goddess' cheeks. He noticed now the rips and scorch marks on her blue dress, the shadows beneath her eyes. She staggered towards him, and started to fall.

Michael leaned forward and caught her before she struck the ground. She seemed to float in his hands, the fabric of her dress slipping through his fingers like mist.

Antonia sighed and her violet eyes caught his. "Thank you," she whispered. Her eyes closed again. He thought she had lost consciousness, until she spoke again. "I'm too late. This wasn't supposed to happen. Damn you, Archon."

She ran her hands through her hair, her fingers twisting violently in the long strands. Her voice was weary. "He attacked, testing what remains of the banishment we cast. He was only probing, toying with us – *but his strength!* We could hardly hold him back. And while we fought him, his demon struck. He knew, he planned it all," her voice cracked, but whether from rage or grief, he could not tell.

Michael sat speechless. He held her in his arms, cradling her as though she were some great treasure. It felt like blasphemy just to touch her.

Then he remembered Eric, lying in agony, so close to death. Yet Antonia was exhausted, at the end of her strength. Dare he ask?

He summoned his courage. "Antonia, there is a boy, Eric. He is dying. Can you save him?"

Antonia nodded and lifted herself from Michael's arms. "Yes, of course. It's not over yet. Take me to Eric, Michael. He I can save."

Michael's heart lurched. "Really?"

Antonia stalked past, dismissing his question. Her movements were steady now. She had shrugged off her fatigue, and now it was all Michael could do to stumble after her.

Eric and Inken lay where he had left them. Inken still knelt beside him, but Eric's eyes had closed, and Michael's chest clenched at the sight. Were they too late?

Inken spun as she heard their footsteps. Her eyes fixed on Antonia, and she started to stand, reaching for her hunting knife.

"Don't worry, Inken. Everything will be okay," Antonia reached out with her hand and tapped the girl's forehead. Inken slumped to the sand, fast asleep.

Antonia looked at Michael. "This may take some time. There is more than just Eric's physical injuries to heal. Help Caelin build up a fire and find some food. He will be hungry."

Then she turned her back and leaned over Eric. Reaching down, she placed both hands on his chest. Her eyes closed and light leapt from nowhere to bathe them both. The air hummed with power.

Michael drew a deep, shuddering breath and turned away. He moved to help Caelin.

~

ERIC WAS LOST.

Every way he turned, darkness rose to meet him. And in that darkness, creatures danced, just out of sight. A low growl sounded, and whirling, he ran – unsure where he was going, but knowing he must escape. From behind him came the clack of claws on stone, as the creatures gave chase.

A tide of anger washed over him, seeping from the shadows. He could sense the creatures hunting him, taste their bloodlust. Hatred swept through his core, though he knew it was not his own. It fed his terror, driving him on through the darkness.

His legs were like lead, and pain blossomed in his muscles, but he could not stop. He knew with a strange, undeniable certainty that if he stopped, the hounds would catch him – and his life would end.

He raced on, his surroundings unchanging. He saw no trees or boulders or landmarks, no sun or moon to distinguish direction, just the ever-shifting darkness. And the barking of the hounds, growing louder. He searched desperately for an escape. Somewhere in this nightmare, there must be salvation. An image of Inken rose in his mind and he clung to it like a lifeline.

Ahead, a shape loomed in the darkness. Despair touched him as he slowed, staring at the cliff stretching across his path. Its face was sheer, unclimbable. As he reached it he pressed his hands to the cold stone, shaking with fear. There was no going on. His body could go no farther anyway. Gasping for breath, he turned, and looked out into the empty darkness.

Except it was not empty. Movement came, and deep growls echoed from the stone cliffs. Glowing red eyes appeared, followed by the shaggy bodies of the wolves. They emerged from the shadows – the demon's slaves.

Eric watched them come, preparing himself for the end. There was no fight left in him, nothing left for him to give. His last glimmer of hope fluttered away. Leaning back against the cool stone, he closed his eyes, and waited.

The wolves howled. Eric shivered and scrunched his eyes tighter. Claws scraped on stone. They barked as they leapt.

A flash of light burst through Eric's eyelids. He squinted against the glare, and saw a shining figure stalk through the shadows. Tall and shimmering with power, robes of pure white spilled out around the figure. By the man's glow, Eric saw one wolf already lay dead. The others shrank back, growling.

Eric's stomach clenched as the figure turned towards him. Their eyes met, and Alastair smiled, his face filled with warmth. The lines of age were gone, his power restored. Looking back at the wolves, Alastair raised a hand. Light shone out, and the wolves leapt back. But they were too slow, and as the light touched them, they collapsed without sound.

With the beasts vanquished, Alastair moved to Eric's side. Raising a pale hand, he placed it on Eric's head. Warmth spread through his body. "You're safe now, Eric. Antonia has healed your wounds – life awaits you."

"And you?"

Alastair's smile faded. "My time is over. But yours is just beginning, Eric. Enjoy it; fill it with love and family and friendship. Do not repeat my mistakes. I wish you well," he began to fade away.

"Alastair, wait!" Eric cried out, desperate.

"Yes?"

"*Thank you!*"

Alastair smiled, and vanished.

Antonia walked from the gloom. She offered him a pale white hand. "Life waits, Eric."

ERIC GASPED AS HE WOKE, sucking in a breath of salty air. His hands went to his chest and found the tear in his shirt, but the skin beneath was whole. He looked up. Around him was a dome of light, its shimmering glow shutting off the outside world. Antonia sat beside him, dried tears on her cheeks. She smiled, but it did not touch her violet eyes.

"You saved me," it was not a question. "Thank you."

"I wasn't the only one there, Eric. I would have been too late."

"Is he still here?"

She shook her head, her voice breaking. "No, he's gone now."

Eric nodded. The dome faded, slowly revealing the world outside. He could hardly bear the thought of returning to it without Alastair. "I'm going to miss him, Antonia."

"We all will," she whispered. She wore her fatigue like a cloak.

"You're tired."

Antonia sighed. "Archon is mustering an army. It is taking all our strength to keep his magic from the Three Nations. Soon the last of our protections will fail, and his demons will be free to wreak havoc on us."

Eric sat up. "The demon!"

She laid a hand on his shoulder. "It has fled."

"Why was it here?"

Antonia shook her head. "The traitor was informing his master of your every move. But Archon must have grown tired of his failure, and unleashed the weapon he had secreted here."

Eric looked away, his hand feeling absently for where the blade had pierced him. He shivered, remembering the icy chill of the blade. "What did it do to me?"

"Thomas carried a *Soul Blade*, a dark creation of Archon's. When it inflicts a wound on a Magicker, the victim's magic is absorbed into the blade."

Eric shivered. "That's not all though, is it? I felt something from the blade… infect me."

"Yes. Your magic is intertwined with your soul. The blade allowed the demon to borrow your power, but it cannot last without your soul. So the blade's magic entered you, harrying your spirit, breaking down your will. Eventually, it would have engulfed everything you are, and the *Soul Blade* would have taken your soul."

Shuddering, Eric thought of the wolves hunting him through the darkness. If not for Alastair, they would have had him.

"Does this mean my magic will return?"

"Yes, you magic will replenish itself, while without your soul, the *Soul Blade* cannot. Its power will be gone by now. The demon will need a fresh victim," she smiled. "And I have rejuvenated your magic with my own strength."

"Thank you," he hesitated. "Was it truly Thomas?"

Antonia's face twisted with pain. "His body, yes. Such an awful fate, to be taken by his magic, to serve the darkness he once fought to prevent. But I will put an end to his suffering," she stood.

"Where are you going?"

"Nowhere, yet," she offered him a hand. "Come, I believe there are some people waiting to see you."

Eric smiled and stood. A fire burned farther down the beach, ringed by his companions. They stared into the golden flames, their backs to the night. He could hear the faint whisper of their conversation.

They were just a few steps away when Inken turned her head. Her eyes widened and a grin split her face. Then she was on her feet and sprinting towards him. There was no avoiding her as she tackled him to the ground.

His breath rushed from his lungs as they landed in a

tangle. He coughed and started to laugh. "Nice to see you too, Inken!"

She pinned him down and planted a kiss on his lips. There were tears in her eyes. Her breath was warm on his cheek. "Don't you *ever* do that to me again, Eric, or I swear I'll… I'll…"

Eric pressed his mouth to hers, silencing her threats.

When they broke apart, Inken bowed her head to Antonia. "Thank you, Goddess."

"It was my pleasure," Antonia laughed, "and please, call me Antonia. Come, let's return to the warmth of the fire."

Caelin rose and slapped Eric on the back as they joined the circle around the fire. "Welcome back to the world of the living, my friend."

"I'm glad you're healed," Michael offered.

Eric returned their greetings, and then noticed Enala sitting hunched by the fire. Her face was like steel, and her eyes did not seem to have registered him. He moved across to her and held out his hand.

"Hello, Enala. My name is Eric, it's nice to finally meet you," he introduced himself.

There was no response. Frowning, he turned to the others.

"Enala has retreated from the world, from the pain," Antonia answered his unspoken question. "It will take more than magic to bring her back. But that is a worry for tomorrow."

Silence fell. Despite Eric's recovery, a terrible grief still hung over them. He looked around at his circle of companions, sensing the hollow where Alastair should have sat. Grief rose inside him, but he pushed it down.

Beside him, Antonia stood. "I should leave now. The demon must be found and destroyed."

"Wait!" Michael cut in. "What do we do now?"

"You put your dead to rest," Antonia answered. "He always liked the idea of a burial at sea."

Eric climbed to his feet. "Stay, Antonia. You knew Alastair better than anyone. Say your farewells with us. Besides, you're exhausted."

Antonia offered a sad smile. "I have already said my goodbyes, Eric. And the demon must be stopped – before it finds more power. But I will leave you each with a farewell gift."

Light seeped from Antonia as she raised her hand. It crept to Caelin first. His burns vanished at its touch, and the rings beneath his eyes faded away. The light continued on, to Michael, and Inken, and finally Enala. The marks of battle vanished from each of them in turn.

When the light finally faded, they raised their arms in farewell.

But Antonia was already gone.

ALASTAIR'S EMERALD eyes stared up at Eric. His skin was grey, devoid of life, and Eric could hardly bear to look at him. His thoughts turned inwards, remembering the man Alastair had been. The man who had told him of his magic, and protected him from its darkness. The man he'd travelled with, laughed with, learnt from. Most of all, he remembered the man who had been his friend.

The wisps of his grey hair and beard shifted on the gentle ocean breeze. The wrinkles on his face had receded, restoring his lost youth. He looked almost at peace. Yet Eric's heart was breaking.

Inken stood beside him, offering her silent comfort. The others ringed the makeshift raft on which they had placed Alastair's body: Caelin, who had killed the traitor, and

Michael, who had helped Eric save his mentor just a few days ago. They had spent all night gathering driftwood for the raft, but now the morning had finally come.

Eric's eyes burned. He reached down and squeezed Alastair's cold hand. His heart ached, and he could hardly believe this wasn't all some horrible nightmare. Alastair was dead. After everything they'd been through, the trials they'd survived, Eric had almost come to believe the old man was invincible.

How wrong he'd been.

In the time Eric had known him, Alastair had bestowed on him the gift of knowledge; the ability to control his magic. Not once had he asked for anything in return. Yet Eric felt the debt all the same. Alastair had given his life in the fight against Archon. It was up to Eric to carry on that fight now. He would not rest until the Three Nations were safe again.

For now though, it was time to say goodbye.

Eric stepped up to the raft. His eyes brimmed as he placed his hands on the hard wood. Tears spilt down his cheeks. Inside he was breaking, but he had a job to do, final words to say.

He looked down at his mentor. "Thank you, Alastair, for all you have given us. Farewell."

His grief broke free then, and he began to sob. He pushed all the same, and his friends stepped up to help him. The raft crunched on the sand and slid into the ocean. There the fierce currents took hold. There were no waves now, but the water lapped at the sides as it drifted out into the bay.

Inken nocked an arrow to her bow and lit it in the fire. Her hands shook, but they steadied as she drew back the bowstring. Firelight sparkled in her damp eyes. She loosed.

The arrow arced out across the waters, a tiny shooting star, and then began to fall. Flames leapt across the raft as it struck Alastair's final resting place, catching in the wood and tinder they had stacked around him. The raft blazed into light, flames reflecting off water and heaven.

No one spoke. Eric felt an arm around his waist. He looked at Inken, saw his grief reflected in her eyes. They stood together and looked out across the cove, offering one last silent farewell to the great man.

"What now?" Inken whispered.

"Now, we live," Eric answered.

EPILOGUE

Antonia yawned and shook her head as her eyelids began to droop. Fighting back fatigue, she walked on, her hands outstretched to brush against the vegetation. The trees leaned towards her, branches and vines reaching out to embrace her. The thick tree trunks groaned, and their voice whispered in her mind, telling her of the demon's passage. It would not escape.

Her pace slowed as the chase stretched on. The day had taken its toll, and all she wanted now was to rest. The call of sleep beckoned. The thought scared her; she had not slept in decades. She could not afford to now.

Antonia pressed deeper into the forest. Sensing her weakness, the trees offered their strength, but she only took a drop. Winter was coming, and she knew they had little to spare.

The demon had not stopped to recover from its battle. She had already covered many miles, and still her prey showed no sign of slowing. The forest was broken and battered from its passage. The trees whispered of the demon's pain. The dragon had hurt it badly. That would make her task easier.

Her bare feet caught on a rock and sent her tumbling to the ground. Cursing, Antonia sat up. This method of travel was far too cumbersome for her liking. But it was the only way to track the demon.

If only I could rest!

Antonia closed her eyes, just for a moment, gathering her strength. Her spirit was weary, her limbs lethargic. Slowly, her thoughts drifted to her brother, Jurrien. She wondered how he was coping after their battle. His stamina was greater than her own, though he had borne the brunt of Archon's initial assault.

She let out a long breath, preparing to continue. Yet sleep clung to her, beckoning, tempting. She relaxed again, wriggling sideways so her back was against a tree. She would rest for an hour and then push on. The demon would not get far.

Her breathing slowed and her thoughts began to drift.

She slept.

THE DEMON WATCHED from the shadows. It wondered how long the Goddess had been sleeping. It had taken most of the night to circle back, and morning was fast approaching. It had to act quickly.

Slipping forward, it smiled with anticipation. Archon's plan had worked better than they could have imagined. The Goddess herself had come after it, and she was exhausted in both mind and magic. The battles of the last few days were too much, even for her. She should have rested before giving chase. The mistake would cost her dearly.

Silent as death, the demon slid between the trees.

Antonia slept on. Slowly it pulled one of the *Soul Blades* from its sheath.

The Goddess's chest rose and fell in steady succession. The magic in her chest had shrunk to a dim spark, fluttering with each breath. The *Soul Blade* would pierce both easily. Smiling, it raised the sword.

Antonia's eyes flickered open. Her mouth widened as the blade flashed down. It met a second's resistance as the God magic rose to defend her, before the dark magic sliced through it like butter. The blade slid home.

Antonia screamed, stiffening against the cold steel. Her eyes widened, her fingers clawing at the *Soul Blade*, cutting on the sharp edges. Her legs thrashed, unable to reach the demon. Her body fought to heal itself, but with the sword in place the Earth magic could not save her. Light flashed from her body, burning the demon's eyes. Each flash quickly died, sucked into the dark depths of the *Soul Blade*.

Slowly, the Goddess' struggles weakened. Her hands were bloody from their fight with the sword, her dress stained red. She screamed again, as though the sound itself could save her. The demon drank in her pain, savouring the taste, the sweet essence of her fear.

Finally her magic began to fail. Powerful as she was, the God magic could not sustain her mortal body forever. Her struggles grew feeble, her fingers slipping from the blade. Her purple eyes stared into the demon's, her chest heaving with tiny gasps. The demon could feel her magic raging against the sword's power, fighting with every inch of her will. The demon held on.

At last, her eyelids slid closed. A final breath hissed between her teeth as the Goddess of Plorsea gave herself over to death.

And her spirit went screaming into the *Soul Blade*.

BOOK TWO: FIRESTORM

PROLOGUE

They appeared as the first glow of the morning sun touched the horizon. Great wings thumped the cool air, golden scales glittering in the dawns light; one, two, six, a dozen. Bursts of flame licked the treetops as the beasts circled, great eyes staring down at them. Wind whipped about the cove, catching in their golden wings.

Below, the surf roared and waves rushed up onto the black sands. The tang of salt stung the air as a fine mist of sea spray settled on their clothes. A breath of wind whistled through the trees behind them, carrying with it the bite of winter. Beyond the breakers the sea raged on hidden reefs. Dark cliffs stared down at them, casting the cove in shadow.

Eric sat on the cool sand watching the dragons, his chest tight with dread. He knew what they were here for, what they wanted. The body of Nerissa lay nearby; her golden scales dull with death. The dragon's bravery had saved them all, her crimson flames driving off the demon. But Nerissa's defiance had come at a price. Now her kin had come to claim their own.

He just prayed that was all they sought.

His companions sat around him, watching the display in grim silence. Inken sat beside him, her arm resting gently against his back. Reaching down he squeezed her hand, drawing strength from her presence. She glanced at him with her hazel eyes, scarlet hair shining even in the shade. Tears and burns marked her clothing, but beneath her skin was whole; healed by the Goddess Antonia.

On either side of them rested Michael and Caelin, the doctor and the soldier. Caelin sat with his legs folded, muscles rippling as he tensed, ready to spring. A short sword lay across his lap, his fingers lingering on the blade. The sword did not belong to him, but to Eric's teacher, Alastair. Eric's eyes slid out over the water, memories of the night before returning. His chest clenched tight, but he kept the tears from his eyes. Alastair was at peace now; the same could not be said for them.

Michael also sat with his legs crossed, but he held only a small pack stuffed with what remained of his medical supplies. Little good they had done Alastair. But they had at least kept Eric alive long enough to be healed by Antonia's magic. Eric would never forget how the doctor's strength and skill had helped bring him through the darkness. Michael stared up at the circling dragons, his short-cropped hair and beard betraying nothing of the ordeals of the last two days.

A roar came from overhead, returning Eric's attention to the sky. A dragon dropped from formation and descended towards them. Swallowing his fears, Eric pulled himself to his feet. His companions followed suit, fingers hovering close to weapons. His hand lingered in Inken's. She gave it a squeeze and flashed him a smile.

The ground shook as the beast thumped onto the beach. The wings beat a final time, sending a cloud of sand billowing out around it. Eric raised a hand against the onslaught and struggled to keep the dragon in sight. Air hissed as its mouth opened to reveal rows of glittering teeth. The stench of rotten fish billowed across the beach, followed by a wave of heat.

Who are you who trespasses here? The voice reverberated through Eric's mind. The dragon towered over them, its bulk covering the black-sanded beach.

Eric's knees trembled, but through his fear he remembered Caelin's actions from the day before. Forcing his limbs to obey, Eric bowed to the dragon. There could be no mistakes here; one swipe of those giant claws could slice him in two.

Straightening, he looked the dragon in the eye. "Greetings, dragon. This is Inken, a bounty hunter from Chole. These are Caelin, sergeant of the Plorsean army, and the doctor Michael. My name is Eric. I am apprentice to the Magicker, Alastair," he paused. "Or I was, until he was killed last night by a traitor. May I ask, what is your name, dragon?"

He did not mention the fifth member of their party – Enala, the girl they had come all this way to find. She still sat catatonic amongst the trees behind them, unresponsive to the world around her.

My name is Enduran, and you are not welcome here, the dragon's nostrils widened as it sniffed the air. Its eyes scanned the beach until they settled on the body of Balistor, still lying where he had fallen. *The blood of our sister is on your hands.*

Caelin stepped forward. "No, Enduran. It is on the hands of that traitor. He was an agent of Archon – he tried to kill us all. I stopped him, though he had been my companion for many weeks. We are not your enemy."

It was you who brought him here, brought him into our midst. His actions fall on your shoulders, a growl rumbled up from deep in Enduran's chest. Eric braced himself, expecting flames to follow. *But you speak the truth – it was your blade that slew him.*

The dragon shifted on the beach, its claws digging great grooves into the sand. Its tail flicked out, shattering a spire of rock that stood amidst the dunes. It growled again. *Enough blood has been spilt on our land. We will not be responsible for any more. We will give you the day to leave our lands. Come nightfall, we will put our sister to rest. Her body, and all who remain on this beach, will be cleansed by dragon fire.*

Eric swallowed. "But we will not survive Dragon Country alone. We have no horses, no supplies. We are trapped on this beach."

Flames licked from between the dragon's lips. Eric shrank backwards, holding his breath.

There is a Lonian fishing vessel nearby. I shall tell the sailors of your presence. It is up to them whether they wish to rescue you. Either way, we will not wait, the wings began to beat again, sending sand flying across the beach.

Eric raised his arm again and squinted through the sandstorm, watching Enduran rise into the sky. As he drew above the height of the cliffs the other dragons joined him, their wings carrying them out across the ocean.

Eric watched them go and then turned to his companions. "What now?"

Caelin smiled. "We wait. And pray the dragons don't send the Lonians fleeing halfway across the ocean."

"They're not exactly known as a timid bunch," Inken countered. "I'd say our chances are good," she moved up the beach to where their scant possessions lay scattered.

Eric followed her, his boots sinking into the coarse sand. "Fishermen, or Lonians?" he asked.

"Both," Inken laughed. "Although I was referring to the Lonians. Gods' know, they held the Trolans to a standstill during the Great Wars."

"Although unlike the Trolans, they've settled down a little since those days," Caelin replied as they sat in a circle.

Eric spared a look at the bundle of rags lying nearby, where Enala still lay inert. She had not moved or said a word since the night before, when Balistor had killed the dragon she rode. Whatever bond had been shared by the dragon and the girl, its loss had tipped Enala over the edge.

A muffled sob came from the pile of cloth. Michael moved across and sat beside her. He began to speak to her, but Eric could not make out the words.

He shook his head. Enala was a problem for another day, when they had escaped this deadly land. He glanced out at the ocean, straining to make out the tell-tale sails of a ship, but the horizon remained empty.

"They're likely to be some distance away," Inken noticed the direction of his gaze. "The Lonians fish right down the east coast, but they stay well clear of these waters. The reefs are treacherous for the deeper hulls of their fishing vessels."

Eric nodded, but a rumble from his stomach gave away his impatience.

Caelin laughed. "I know, we're all hungry. But there's not much we can do about that for now," he eyed Inken. "Unless a certain bounty hunter thinks there could be game nearby?"

Inken gave a short smile. "Believe me, if there was, I wouldn't be lazing around here," she glanced at Eric, "even if I'm hesitant to leave. No, I haven't seen a single bird or rabbit in the trees since we arrived. For whatever reason, dragons or demon or curse, the forest around this cove is empty."

Caelin sighed. "That is a shame," then he smiled. "Still, I'm sure we can survive a few more hours. A fishing ship is bound to have plenty of food on board."

"If they come," Eric interjected, doubt still plaguing him.

"They'll come," Caelin grinned. "I have every faith in our Lonian neighbours."

CHAPTER 1

The captain glared down at the company, lips twisted in a frown. A thick black beard matted his face, giving him a fierceness that would send lesser men scurrying. He folded his arms, the short sleeves revealing bulging muscles criss-crossed by old red scars. Even standing below them on the beach, he still towered over the four of them.

Behind him, the dingy crunched on the sand as a wave rocked it. His crew milled around the vessel, eying their captain nervously.

Caelin had taken the initiative, offering the sailors a lie about their being Plorsean ambassadors who had come to treat with the Gold Dragons. Eric could not help but think the story was a hard sell, given the dead dragon lying on the sand behind them. Not to mention Balistor's body, which everyone seemed intent to ignore.

"Enough!" the captain finally cut across Caelin. "I've heard enough. Never in my life have I heard such a ridiculous tale."

Caelin's face turned scarlet. Eric guessed the sergeant did

not have a great amount of experience lying, and getting caught in one clearly left him uncomfortable.

He opened his mouth to reply, but the captain spoke again. "I don't know what the five of you are really doing here, but I don't really care," he waved a hand. "From what I can see, I can guess we want no part of it. I don't need this kind of trouble on my ship," he turned to leave.

"Wait!" Eric shouted.

He stepped after the sailors, reaching out to halt the captain's departure. The crew drew their swords and advanced on him, faces dark with anger.

Eric raised his empty hands in surrender. "Wait, wait! You're right, Caelin was lying," he paused as the captain turned. He shot Eric an impatient scowl and raised an eyebrow.

"Thank you. Like I said, Caelin lied, but I swear there is a reason. We are emissaries for the Goddess Antonia, it is for her that we are here."

The black eyes of the captain locked on Eric's. "Oh? And what did the Goddess want with a rugged bunch of no goods such as yourselves?"

Eric glanced at his companions, seeing them as the sailors must. Antonia had healed their injuries, but their clothes had still been reduced to an assortment of burnt and bloodied rags. He swallowed. Only the truth would convince here – no other tale could explain their presence.

He looked at the big man, studying him closely. "You seem like a trustworthy man, but our purpose is a great secret. We cannot risk word spreading. I will tell you, and you alone, if you swear to secrecy."

The captain laughed. "Bold, aren't you? Why should I swear to anything? I could leave you here for dead, for all I care."

"Here me out. You will understand the need when I have finished," Eric met his gaze, and held it.

The captain's face darkened. He gave a sharp nod. "You have five minutes to convince me. You alone. Come," he waved at the twisted trees. Eric nodded and followed the captain up the beach. His men made to protest, but their voices fell on deaf ears. The captain obviously felt Eric was small enough not to warrant caution.

Eric couldn't help but smile at the captain's error.

Even so, his heart quickened as they entered the trees. Silently he debated how much he would need to tell. This man would accept nothing but the truth, but *too* much truth could also prove dangerous here. Anyone who helped them on their quest risked the wrath of Archon; he could not risk alienating the man through fear.

The darkness beneath the trees drew them deeper into the forest, until finally the captain turned and glared down at him. "Your time starts now."

Eric ran a hand through his hair, trying to decide where to start. "How much do you know of the Sword of Light?"

The captain blinked. "The Sword? How does this have anything to do with that Trolan trinket?"

"*Everything*. That trinket and the power of the Gods are the only things keeping Archon banished in the Wasteland."

A shiver ran through the captain. "So the legends say. Though others say Archon is long dead."

"He isn't. His influence is everywhere now. He has been waiting – waiting for a seed he planted decades ago to take root," Eric took a breath to calm himself. "When the Gods and King Thomas unleashed the spell to banish Archon from our lands, Archon cast a curse of his own. He bound the spell to Thomas and his bloodline, and over the generations it has slowly stripped the magic from the Trolan royalty. The same magic they need to wield the Sword of Light."

The captain's hand drifted unconsciously towards his sword hilt. There was fear in his eyes. "What are you saying?"

Eric stared back. "That the magic of the Sword no longer protects the Three Nations. Archon is already preparing to invade. Yesterday, we were attacked by one of his demons; his first probe of our defences."

"You killed it?"

"No, the dragon drove it off. That was before we were betrayed by our companion Balistor, another of Archon's servants, who slew the dragon and my mentor, Alastair. Antonia is hunting the demon now – it won't survive her wrath."

The captain shook his head. "This can't be true. What you're saying… What you're saying means the end of everything…"

"I am telling the truth," Eric paused to let his words sink in, "but there is still hope. King Thomas had a sister, one who was never affected by the curse. Alastair tracked down her ancestors, but Archon's minions got to them first. Only one of them survived – Enala. Yesterday, we finally found her."

The big man blinked. "You mean the girl on the beach? The blond that's gone mad?"

Eric bowed his head and sighed. They would have to deal with Enala's state of mind eventually, but right now they had more pressing concerns. "Yes, that is Enala. And believe it or not, she is our last hope. Archon has hunted her across Plorsea, and it has almost driven her insane. But Antonia believes she will recover. It is our job to make sure she has the chance to do so."

Silence fell as the captain weighed up his words. This time Eric did not back down. He only had one chance to convince this man to help them. He would not fail.

Finally the captain gave a sharp nod. "Okay, Eric. I'm not

sure I believe you, but I will give you the benefit of the doubt. It would be a bold lie indeed to tell such a story. We are heading for the Lonian capital. I will take you that far. After that, you're on your own," he held out his hand. "The name's Loris."

Eric gave a grim smile. "Thank you, Loris. You won't regret this."

Loris shook his head. "Somehow, I doubt that."

THE BOW of the ship rose sharply into the swell and then crashed back down the other side. Wooden boards creaked as water rushed over the side to swamp the deck. Sailors walked through the water, shouting at men who dangled overhead. Wind cracked in the sails, driving them through the unbroken waters. The sun shone high above, its heat beating down on the exposed deck. The stench of fish seeped up from the cargo hold below.

Eric's stomach lurched with each rise and fall of the ship. He had never been at sea before, but he had heard of seasickness. He stumbled across the deck, grabbing for the railing, and lost the battle to keep the meagre contents of his stomach down.

Laughter came from above. He looked up in time to see a sailor dropping from the rigging. A grin split his bearded face as he joined Eric at the railings.

"It helps if you don't look at the ship," he pointed to the distant coastline. "Keep your eyes on the horizon. That way when the ship moves, the eyes and body both tell your mind the same story. If you look at the deck, it tricks your eyes into thinking you're stationary, even though your body can feel the ship lurching about."

Eric's head spun and he could hardly make sense of the

sailor's words, but he managed to look out at the rocky coastline. Even from a distance the jagged cliffs towered over their little vessel. Scraggly trees grew from the rock faces, their crooked branches reaching out for them like fingers. Behind them, the ocean stretched out to the horizon. He was glad they would not be venturing that way; the great expanse of water filled him with a dread he could not shake.

A white bird with grey wings cawed from the sky, landing in the ship's rigging. He tried to ignore it. Following the sailor's advice, his stomach had already begun to settle, so he risked a glance at the sailor. He realised they must be almost the same age – around eighteen. "How long have you worked at sea?"

The man leaned back against the railings, arms outstretched as he stared up at the sails. "Most of my life, but I only joined the captain a year ago. Before that I worked as a dingy rower in Lon. Where are your friends, our other unexpected cargo?"

"Sleeping," the others were making the most of the opportunity, but Eric's sickness had been much worse inside the tiny cabin. "What happens with the sickness when you close your eyes?"

"That works too sometimes, but makes it difficult to get any work done," he glanced around. "Speaking of which, I'd better get back to my post before the captain sees me slacking. Nice to meet you," he moved across to the mast and climbed back into the rigging.

Shaking his head, Eric moved away from the railing and looked around for a good place to sit. It was time to test his magic. He had not reached for it since he'd been stabbed. Shuddering, he remembered the pain of the *Soul Blade* piercing his stomach, the demon's cackle in his ear. If not for Antonia's magic, he would be dead.

He spotted a pile of crates stacked against the cabin and

moved towards them, stumbling as the vessel shifted beneath him. Righting himself against the mast, he moved more cautiously across the deck and climbed atop the nearest create. Eric crossed his legs, leaned against the crate behind him, and closed his eyes.

He drew a deep breath in preparation. Sadness clenched his heart as he remembered the last time he had meditated. The company had been whole then, Alastair still alive to guide him. Now he was alone. The thought terrified him.

Drawing another breath, he allowed his thoughts to drift on the gentle ebb of his conscious. He focused on each inhale and exhale, allowing all other sensation to drift away. In out, in out. The air hissed from his mouth as he blew out, his chest swelling with each inhalation.

Sound began to fade away. The lapping of water against wood, the flapping of the sails, even the shouts of the sailors drifted from his consciousness, leaving him alone in the silence of his mind.

His thoughts proved harder to tame. The last few days had been hell. The night before last was a blur, a convoluted mosaic of flames and darkness and flashing red scales as the dragon chased them through the forest. If not for Inken, he would have perished.

The thought of her set his heart racing in his chest. Images of their time spent in the glow of the clearing flashed by: the hot steam, the luminescent ferns, the splashing of water as they tumbled in the stream. Shaking his head with a smile, he let those images fade too.

Memories of Alastair he could not so easily let go. Even now he could see the old man's emerald eyes, the edges crinkled in amusement. He had been Eric's mentor, his saviour and friend. His death remained crystal clear in his mind: Balistor, poised over Alastair's unconscious body, the sword flashing in the sunlight, plunging down, down, down.

Tears ran down Eric's face, but he fought to let the image go, if only for a moment.

In out, in out.

Then only memory of Enala remained; of the brave girl sitting atop the gold dragon, their last hope. Then Enala mad, rocking in the sand, catatonic. She still had not eaten, would barely drink. If it kept up, their last hope would perish without any assistance from Archon and his minions.

Finally, the last of his thoughts drifted away and Eric found himself falling into the familiar calm of his inner mind. A blue light flickered in the distance. The glow seemed cool and calming, but he knew from experience it had a darker edge. Magic had a mind of its own, a will to be free. But he was strong now, strong enough to control it.

Moving towards the distant spark, he watched it grow until a great lake of magic stretched out beneath him. Lightning flashed across its surface, rising from the depths like a serpent. The blue glow warmed his soul.

He stretched out a phantom hand and watched a thread of light rise up in response. It drifted towards him, wrapping gently around his wrist. His mind tingled as the power filtered through him, but he did not release it. He would need every drop in the coming weeks, if they were to see Enala safely to the Sword of Light. The enemy facing them was legion, and without Alastair and Balistor he was now the last Magicker in their small fellowship. The power radiating from his magic gave him reassurance though, where for so long it had been a source of fear.

Beside him a door slammed and he felt a hand back on the ship grab him. Eric's concentration snapped as someone shook him.

"Eric, stop! What are you doing?" he heard Inken yell.

Eric's eyes snapped open. He looked around in shock, finding Inken standing over him. Her face was twisted in panic, her eyes wide with fear. Rain soaked her scarlet hair and poured down around them. It streamed down his face and with a start Eric realised he was soaked to the skin.

The ship pitched violently, almost toppling Eric from the crate. Inken stumbled forward and fell against him. He caught her before the rolling of the ship sent her tumbling. The wind howled through the rigging above, tearing at the sail. The sailors shouted over the gale, terror in their voices as they struggled with the sails. Storm clouds blackened the sky, while sheets of rain and hail lashed the deck.

They toppled from the crate as the ship lurched again. Eric struggled to stand, reaching for his power. His mind reeled with shock – he hadn't released his magic, had he?

"I don't think this is me!" he shouted, grasping for Inken's hand.

"What? How is that possible?"

Lightning crashed. Eric winced, instinct driving him down into his magic. Power flooded his mind. He opened his eyes and saw a bolt flashing towards the mast. He raised a hand and gripped it with his magic, hurling it into the raging sea. Thunder clapped and the air shook as it struck. Boiling water geysered into the air and crashed over the railings. It swept towards them.

Inken tackled him backwards into the cabin. Breath exploded from his chest as they tumbled from the water's path. Eric gasped, struggling to sit up, already searching out the next flash of lightning. Panic rose within him, swamping his concentration. His magic began to slip from his grasp. They could not afford that.

Eric closed his eyes and sank back into the abyss. He wrapped the magic threads in an iron grip and opened his spirit eyes. The storm raged around them, pulling his phantom body skywards. The air crackled with the energy of the Sky element, but he worked on instinct now – and desperation.

Threads of magic stretched out from him, forming hooks of blue light to grasp the surging wind and rain. Gritting his teeth, Eric unleashed a surge of energy, pushing them back from the ship.

Almost instantly, the air stilled and the sails sagged in their rigging. The violent crashing of the waves faded away, leaving the ship to settle back into a gentle rocking. The scent of rain was strong in their nostrils.

Eric drew in a breath of relief.

Then he felt a surge of energy burn through his mind, and the storm returned with renewed fury. The mast groaned, cracks appearing in the thick wood.

Eric stared in disbelief. It was not possible. His magic remained embedded in the storm that had struck them, holding it back from the ship. But this wind and rain had appeared from nowhere, as if summoned by some unnatural force. That was impossible – the first thing Alastair taught him was that Magickers could manipulate the Light, the Sky and the Earth, but they could not create.

Only the Gods could do that.

A sudden force struck Eric, hurling his soul back into his body. Gasping, he opened his eyes, searching for the words.

"*Where is she?*" a voice boomed over the roar of the storm.

Eric stood in the doorway of the cabin and watched in terror as a figure materialised on the bow of the ship. Wind and rain swirled around him. Thunder crackled as lightning struck the bow, the shock wave knocking sailors from their feet. The energy rippled along the figure's condensing arms and shoulders, gathering in his outstretched fist. The figure seemed to coalesce from the Sky itself, until a man stood on the deck, pure rage etched across his face.

Hair as white as snow hung down to the man's shoulders. His ice blue eyes glared across at Eric, dark patches hanging beneath them. Lines of stress marked his forehead, but his face was clean shaven. He wore clothes similar to the sailors – a dark blue shirt and tight black pants.

Eric knew him from the vision Antonia had once shown him.

Lightning crackled around the man as he took a step. "*Where. Is. She?*"

The sky turned white as lightning flashed, casting long shadows across the deck. It raced towards Eric, crackling as it went.

Panic and fear fought within him, but instinct took hold. He reached out with his magic, with his hands, to catch it. The lightning flared as it struck. Thunder clapped and a shock ran through his body.

The force of the blast threw him backwards into the wall of the cabin. His head crashed against the wood, sending a jolt of pain down his spine. His ears rang and his head spun. He tasted metal on his tongue, then burning.

"*Tell me where she is, now!*"

The man stood over him now, seeming to tower higher even than the mast of the ship. Lightning crackled again. He held a fist above Eric, energy dancing along his skin.

Eric stared up at the Storm God, fear making his heart thud in his chest. "Who, Jurrien?" he croaked.

"My sister, Antonia. *Where is she?*"

Eric struggled to understand his words. He wiped the streaming rain from his face. His body shook with pain. "Antonia? What do you mean?"

The God sucked in an angry breath. "She is gone. I can no longer sense her, feel her anywhere. But the taint of her magic is on you. You were with her, not long ago. *What has happened?*"

Eric shook his head. "She left. She wanted to hunt down the demon Archon sent to kill Enala."

"*What?* One of Archon's demons is *here?*" he swore. "How could she be so *foolish?* Going after it alone, in her state!"

"She seemed okay in the cove," Eric croaked.

Jurrien's icy eyes bored into Eric, his teeth grinding as he clenched his jaw. "She was exhausted. We barely held off Archon's last attack, and then she runs off babbling about *Alastair* and *Eric* and *Enala*. How she summoned the energy to heal the lot of you I do not know. But to then go chasing a demon…" he covered his face with his hands and turned away.

"Alastair is dead," Eric whispered. Jurrien had known his mentor as well.

Jurrien shook his head. "The old man was going to bite off more than he could chew sooner or later," he spoke the words with venom. "But I never thought he'd bring Antonia down with him."

Eric struggled to his feet. "Alastair had nothing to do with this, whatever *this* is!" he argued. "The demon was *your* responsibility, yours as well as Antonia's. It should never have stepped foot in Plorsea in the first place."

The Storm God stepped forward until only an inch separated them. He towered over Eric, his muscular stature no less intimidating for his silver hair. Eric looked into his eyes and saw the depth of power and wisdom there. He found himself remembering his first encounter with Antonia, the light hearted Goddess of the Earth. The fight went from him as he realised the meaning behind Jurrien's words.

"Are you saying she's gone?"

The God's eyes softened. His shoulders slumped. "I don't know. This has never happened before. I can always sense her, even those rare times when we sleep. But now – nothing. I need to find out what has happened," he waved a hand as he spoke.

The wind ceased with a sharp snap. The sails slumped and the rocking of the ship slowed, released from the violent grasp of the waves. The crackle of lightning around Jurrien died away, until he seemed to be just an ordinary man. A man weighed down by worry, one teetering on the brink of defeat. The last God standing.

Eric prayed it was not so. "She was with us last at Malevolent Cove. She headed into Dragon Country on the trail of the demon."

Jurrien nodded. "Okay. I will follow her path. I just hope I am wrong," he turned and walked to the railings. With a grunt he levered himself over the side. A gust of wind caught him as he fell, propelling him into the sky.

Eric released his breath and looked around the ship. Jurrien's appearance had left the wooden boards at the prow of the ship burnt and blackened, and a part of the sail had torn loose in the wind. The rigging hung in a tattered mess. Crates and supplies lay strewn across the deck, broken free by the raging waves and wind. Several barrels bobbed in the ocean around them, slowly drifting away. The creak of straining wood came from the mast.

His companions stood nearby, their clothes wet, faces bedraggled. They stared at him in shock, but one by one moved to stand with him. Inken placed a reassuring arm around his waist, while Caelin grasped his shoulder and gave it a squeeze. Michael only nodded. There was no sign of Enala. Together they looked across the deck to where Captain Loris stood amongst his spoiled supplies.

Slowly the crew gathered around Loris, voices whispering as they glanced in his direction. Eric recognised the look on their faces all too well – the mixture of terror and rage. Blame would soon follow, and – if they did not put the mutinous glances to rest – violence. He sought out the young sailor he had spoken to earlier. His heart sank when he found the man and saw the hate in his eyes.

But for once his magic had not been responsible for the havoc, and he did not intend to suffer the consequences.

Eric took a step forward. The captain opened his mouth to stop him, a purple vein popping on his forehead. Eric spoke over the top of him. "Well, I hope you all enjoyed your first meeting with Jurrien, the God of Lonia. He's not much for introductions, apparently."

His words had the desired effect. A shiver went through the crew and the captain's words died in his throat. These were Lonian sailors after all, which made Jurrien their God. Eric had never been to Lonia, so he was not sure how the people generally regarded the Storm God, but he doubted they were likely to argue with someone on speaking terms with him. Even if his conversation with Jurrien had largely revolved around dire threats on the God's part.

At last the captain drew in a breath and bellowed. "Okay, back to work everyone. I want this ship ready to sail within the hour," he banged his fist against the mast to emphasise his words.

Loris walked towards the rear of the ship to take over from the helmsman. He glanced at them as he swept passed. "Guess your tale had some truth to it after all. Just wish I'd been wrong about the trouble," the glare in his eyes could have melted iron.

As he passed, the others turned to stare at Eric.

"What happened?" they asked in unison.

JURRIEN SLUMPED AGAINST THE TREE, a dark weight crashing against his soul. Around him, the forest was silent, dead. All colour had leached from the trees, leaving the woods grey and lifeless. Not a single creature stirred. Birds and squirrels lay in silent death on the leafy ground, their tiny bodies twisted in agony. A rotten stench spread throughout the clearing. The taint of dark magic hung thick in the air.

A single tear ran down Jurrien's cheek. He let it fall, unable to believe, to comprehend what his eyes told him. Antonia lay amidst the fallen animals, eyes closed. Her auburn hair spread out around her head, her tiny lips parted slightly as though she still breathed. She could have been sleeping, if not for the blood staining her sky-blue dress. The blood had seeped out around her, soaking into the earth that had bourn her.

A groan rattled up from Jurrien's throat. His fists clenched on thin air. He closed his eyes, opened them again, but the image did not change. His soul reached out for his sister, for some last trace of her.

Nothing. She was dead, gone.

He was alone.

And Archon was coming.

CHAPTER 2

Inken rested her head against the wooden crate behind her and looked down at Eric. She smiled fondly as she watched him sleep. His head was nestled in her lap, a few wild tuffs of dark brown hair covering his eyes. His chest rose and fell in a steady rhythm, interrupted every few breaths by a muffled groan. The brief fight with Jurrien had clearly cost Eric more than he'd let on.

She reached down and wiped a streak of soot from his cheek, then brushed his fringe from his face. A gentle warmth filled her heart. Just yesterday he had teetered on the brink of death. She had come close to losing him forever. Then Antonia had come, had saved him.

Yet not a day later, Antonia's brother had almost reversed that blessing. Inken could not believe Jurrien had attacked them. With empty ocean all around, far from any spies or demons, Inken had allowed herself to relax – and the Storm God had taken her by surprise.

Now she realised the darkness could find them at any time. She would not be caught unawares again. Her bow lay within easy reach, her sabre strapped to her side. If they were attacked, she would be ready.

Across the deck she could see Caelin arguing with the captain. She knew it would take every ounce of diplomacy the young sergeant possessed to cool the man's temper, and even then it might not be enough. Eric's words may have averted a mutiny, but Inken could sense the crew's anger, festering just beneath the surface. They feared the power they had witnessed. The captain's command could only do so much to stop that fear from bubbling over.

It would be a long two days before they reached Lon.

Inken's hand brushed the hilt of her sword. Its leather grip felt reassuring, although hostility from the crew did not worry her. She was confident Caelin and herself could handle them if it came to it. After facing demons and Magickers, Inken would almost cherish a fair fight.

It was the aftermath she worried about, when they would be left stranded at sea. None of them knew how to sail a dingy, let alone a ship.

Behind her, silence blanketed the cabin. Inken sighed. Its only occupant was the girl, Enala. She had yet to speak a single word. It was past time that changed. They had to reach her, bring her back from the brink of whatever crevice she teetered on.

Inken gave a wry smile. The men did not have a clue about how to go about the task, so it seemed it would be up to her. It would be easier now. Before, in the cove, the fear of Eric's death had weighed on her mind.

She sat there a few minutes more, enjoying the warmth and closeness of Eric's body. How the young man had wormed his way into her heart remained a mystery, but she was not about to let him go now. The ship offered little privacy for a couple – the crew slept in hammocks beneath the deck while their company squeezed into the small cabin with the captain – so she had to savour every little moment.

Finally, she lifted Eric's head from her lap and tucked a rolled up jerkin underneath him for a pillow.

Eric stirred, his blue eyes flashing as they opened to watch her. "Where are you going?"

Inken leaned down and kissed him, lingering as their tongues met. It was a while before she pulled away. "I want to check on Enala. You get some sleep. We need you well rested."

Eric yawned and nodded, closing his eyes again.

Inken grinned and stood, climbing down from the crate and walking back to the cabin door. Pulling it open, she made her way into the darkness within. A single candle provided the only source of light in the small room, and it took a second for her eyes to adjust. A desk was crammed into the rear corner, making way for the sleeping rolls they'd squeezed into the cabin. A single bed took up the other wall.

Enala lay curled up on the bed, covers drawn around her head with only a few tuffs of blond hair showing. The covers shook as the door swung closed, and a half-choked sob came from the darkness. It was the only noise the girl had made for two days.

Inken moved across and sat on the foot of the bed. The pile of blankets grew still, so Inken scooted back on the mattress and leaned against the wall. Pulling her knees up to her chest, she sat in the darkness, contemplating what to say.

What *could* she say to this girl? In less than two weeks Enala had witnessed the brutal murder of her parents, the death of a friend, and the loss of the dragon she rode. Never mind the revelation that the ancient evil known as Archon was hunting her, wanted her dead.

It was too much for anyone to take, let alone a seventeen-year-old girl. Inken doubted she had the strength to cope any better – she would be in the same position as Enala if their positions were reversed.

Even so, Enala had to know she was not alone anymore. For Inken herself, the search for Enala had never been about the Sword of Light, but a girl who needed protection from evil. She had to convince Enala that, though they were strangers, they cared about her. She had to convince her to trust them.

Inken released a long breath as she realised she had no idea where to start. She chuckled, and decided not to mention to the others she was as clueless as them. Still, she had to try *something*.

Closing her eyes, Inken began to talk.

She began with the trivial, the mundane. She spoke of the white mare she had purchased just a few short weeks before, and how absurd she'd felt riding such a conspicuous animal. A bounty hunter riding a white horse would be the talk of the town – not an ideal situation for a profession requiring subtly. She spoke of her debt back in Chole, the cost of her equipment, her old friends and what they must think of her now, after she'd betrayed them to rescue Eric and the others.

Then Inken spoke of her childhood, of the time her mother finally decided she'd had enough. Cold to the end, the woman had walked away without looking back. Not a kiss or a hug goodbye for the five-year-old she left behind, just a wave and a door slammed in her face.

From then on it had been just Inken and her father.

And things had only grown worse. Her father was a notorious drunk, and with her mother gone his attention soon turned to Inken. He often returned drunk in the early afternoon, unleashing strings of profanities which quickly disintegrated into screaming fits; the kind that shook the walls and led to knocks on the door from neighbours. In his drunken rage, the man blamed Inken for everything from her mother's desertion, to their poverty.

Inken learned to keep her mouth shut in those early years. Eventually the neighbours stopped knocking.

For years Inken had suffered his insults, his curses and threats. She had grown thick skinned, deaf to all but the worst of his curses.

But on the first day he hit her, the ten-year-old Inken had walked out the door and never looked back.

Hot tears spilt from Inken's eyes and ran down her face. In all her years, she had never told a soul about her past. She had always thought of it as just that – her past, nobody's business but her own. She could not imagine what made her speak of it now. Not even Eric knew the story of her parents.

She heard a rustling come from the other end of the bed and tried not to look. She glimpsed movement from the corner of her eye, and then Enala was curling up beside her, lips still pursed tight. The young girl pulled the covers up around them and leaned her head against Inken's shoulder.

Inken stretched out her arm and wrapped it around the girl. They sat in silence for a while, each contemplating the various horrors which were their lives. Inken had lived on the streets for most of her teenage years, but she did not regret her decision to leave. She smiled to herself, thinking of the convoluted path she'd taken to become a bounty hunter.

But that was a story for another day.

"We may not seem like much, Enala, but we are all here for you," she whispered.

Enala wriggled closer. "How do you know?"

"They're like me. Eric, Caelin, Michael, they're good people. They want to help you, help everyone in the Three Nations. You can trust them."

Inken caught a flash of blue eyes in the darkness. "I hope so," she heard Enala's soft voice.

"You can," Inken repeated, then. "Are you hungry?"

For the first time Enala met her eyes. "Bloody starving," she flashed a smile.

Inken laughed. "I'll be right back."

"WHAT'S GOING ON HERE?" Caelin looked up as Michael interrupted his argument with the captain.

Captain Loris scowled at the doctor. "None of your business."

Caelin raised an eyebrow. "None of his business? I think the good doctor would be just as upset as the rest of us were you to abandon us on some deserted beach."

"What do you expect me to do?" the captain snapped. "The crew are an inch from mutiny. God or no, that *thing* almost sank us. And he was clearly not fond of the bunch of you. The men are *scared*."

"I don't think he's coming back," Michael put in. "He was looking for his sister, Antonia, and I can assure you we don't have the Goddess of the Earth tucked up our sleeves," he waved at the wide sleeves of his coat with a smile.

"That's all well and good, but the crew don't know what's going on. And from what I've heard, the less we tell them about the whole affair, the better," he shook his head. "They won't stand for this. This is your fight. I cannot risk the lives of my crew for your affairs. We are only simple fishermen."

Michael spread his hands. "And I am only a priest. Caelin is only a soldier. We are all *only* something, but this fight goes beyond who and what we are. It doesn't matter to Archon; to him we are just souls waiting to be enslaved."

Caelin glanced at the resolve on the doctor's face. Michael's words warmed his heart, gave him hope.

But the captain wasn't having any of it. His brow drew

down into a scowl as he glared at them. "Archon or no, it's *you* who are a threat to our lives just now. Won't matter a jot whether Archon comes or not if we're at the bottom of the ocean."

Anger swamped Caelin. He swore. "If you abandon us in the middle of nowhere, you risk the lives of everyone in the Three Nations," he took a breath. "This is your chance to be more than *just* fisherman, to make a difference in this world."

"And what about our world? Who will pay our wages if we lose our cargo? Who will feed our wives and family if the ship sinks?"

Caelin wanted to shake the man. Michael interrupted before he got the chance. "We understand your concern, Loris, and the concerns of your men. I assure you, you will be safe. Jurrien will not return, nor any other vengeful spirit. And if it's money that concerns you, then perhaps we could come to an arrangement?"

"What?" Caelin and Loris asked in unison.

The captain glanced at Caelin and then continued. "What sort of payment? A priest's blessing is all well and good, but it doesn't pay the bills."

Michael smiled. "The temples of the God's are not rich, but I am sure they have a few spare funds to reward the ship that provided us safe passage to Lon."

Caelin swallowed, wondering whether Michael was bluffing. If so, this was one man he did not want to play poker with.

The captain grunted. "And what about *our* safe passage? It would have to be a hefty sum to convince my men to continue with this business."

Michael grinned. "Gold is a strong motivator, I believe."

Straightening his shoulders, Michael began to negotiate with the captain what they considered a 'reasonable' price for their passage. Caelin could only shake his head in wonder.

He had not seen this side of Michael before. Until now the doctor had been withdrawn, and Caelin had assumed him to be a fearful and timid man.

Now he found his first assessment to be changing quickly. With his priestly upbringing, Michael might never be a fighter, but there was clearly more to the man than the green robe of his order.

Ten minutes later Caelin joined Michael at the railing, their passage to Lon assured. At least for now. They stood in silence for a while, staring out at the jagged coastline sweeping past them. A gull skimmed the waves, its high pitched caw carrying across the water.

Caelin glanced at Michael. "That was well done," he hesitated. "Is it true though, will the temple in Lon really pay?"

Michael smiled, running a hand through his greying hair. "I think so."

Caelin laughed, but Michael continued. "It's at least standard practice for the Earth Temples to have a stock of gold available to aid those doing Antonia's work. I can only assume the Sky Temples would be the same," he laughed himself. "Perhaps they even have a store to cover damages when the Storm God loses his temper."

Caelin chuckled. "I hope that was not a common occurrence."

Michael's face darkened. "I doubt it. Whatever is happening with Antonia, it must be serious. For Jurrien to lose control like that… I mean, his temper does have a reputation, but even so..."

Caelin glanced at the burnt timber at the bow of the ship. "Agreed."

Silence fell again. A sadness came over Michael's face. "I've been thinking; it might be best if I were to stay in Lon."

"What?" Caelin glanced at the doctor. "Why?"

"I don't know what part I can play in the coming battle. I

am not a fighter," Michael echoed Caelin's earlier thoughts. "I do not want to hold you back. Elynbrigge asked me to join you, but I don't know–"

"The choice is up to you, Michael," Caelin interrupted. "But I believe we all have a place in this company. You may not have magic, but you are a doctor, and a diplomat, apparently. There is no telling when we might need your skills. We need more than fighters on this quest."

Michael drew in a breath and nodded. "I will think on it."

They both looked up as the door to the cabin opened. Inken appeared, smiling in the afternoon sunshine. She moved across to join them.

"They'll take us as far as Lon, but it's going to cost the Sky temple an eye and a leg."

"That's good news," Inken's smile widened. "I have some news of my own. Enala is hungry."

They gaped at her. Inken laughed at their shock. "Do you think these sailors could be convinced to part with some supplies?"

Caelin grinned, feeling a little of the weight shift from his soul. Finally, some good news. With Alastair's death and Antonia's disappearance, it had begun to feel as though things were spinning out of control. If Enala recovered, they would at least have one thread of hope to cling too.

"For the amount of gold we've promised, she can have a feast if she wants," Caelin spun and marched towards the captain.

A cry from the rigging stopped him in his tracks.

"Man overboard!"

THE TREE BRANCH rose beneath him as the wave swept past,

carrying him high into the air. He looked around, desperate for a glimpse of land, but the ocean stretched out in all directions. Swells rolled across the dark blue water, white wash breaking at their tips. Sea spray misted the air, cutting off sight of the horizon.

The soft lapping of water against his log rocked him towards sleep. He struggled to hang on, just a little bit longer, but his strength had long since faded. Only minutes separated him from the dark depths of the ocean now. Soon he would slip beneath the waves, never to be seen again.

Gabriel swallowed, his mouth paper dry from the long hours in the salty water. He prayed his sacrifice had distracted the dragon long enough for Enala to escape. Otherwise his death would mean nothing.

A shiver racked his body as he remembered the beast; the gaping jaws, the teeth and crackling of flames as the dragon hurtled towards him. The deafening snap of its wings, the roar that sent prickles of terror running down his spine.

Knowing he had no chance on the surface, Gabriel had released his rotten branch and dived deep into the river. The current whirled him around, dragging his helpless body deeper as the dragon's bulk smashed into the water. A talon tore at his coat, ripping the skin beneath, and then the river had carried him from reach.

Lungs exploding, Gabriel clawed his way to the surface. In the muddy waters he struggled to tell the difference between up and down, and panic threatened to overwhelm him. Then his head burst into the sunlight.

He drew in one ragged breath before the current pulled him back under. The power of the river sent him tumbling head over heels. A rock struck his thigh, then knee and shoulders. Gabriel screamed, air gushing in bubbles from his mouth. He kicked out, desperate to reclaim the surface.

The next time he broke free he grasped at the water,

struggling to stay afloat. He glanced around, searching the sky for sign of the red scaled dragon. A roar came from the distance, but he could see nothing through the canopy of tree branches overhanging the water.

The trees on either side of the river rushed past as the current grew faster. He struggled against its pull, fighting to reach the far shore, but there was no making headway against the river's might. At last, gasping for breath, he rolled onto his back and let the current take him.

Branches flashed past overhead, sunlight glinting between them. Golden leaves hung from the trees, breaking lose and tumbling down with each gust of the wind. The freezing water spoke of winter's fast approach. With it would come the freeze, and months of hardship for the people of the land. At least it rarely snowed in Oaksville.

Oaksville, the name rang in his mind, carrying with it the image of a man standing before a raging forge, hammer in hand.

My father, he realised with crystal certainty.

He saw himself then, standing at his father's side, arms up to their elbows in thick leather gloves. Heat washed over him, bringing with it the ring of a hammer on iron bars, the roar of the bellows as they worked the forge.

As he drifted down the river, one by one his memories returned to him. His proposal to his fiancée, the day the old soldier had given his father a sword. The horror of the storm, of finding all he had loved destroyed, his family dead. His fiancée's last painful breaths. The agony washed over him anew, pulling him down into the darkness.

The demon.

He remembered the demon and its wolf, his slow decent into madness. His heart twisted with a brand new pain as he saw his murder of the guardsman at the gates of Chole. Guilt swept through him. He was no better than the two he had hunted.

Then he stood outside Enala's house, and he knew what came there. The discovery of her murdered parents, and the girl herself hiding in the basement. The fight with the terrified Enala, then their battle with the demon wolf. The flight from Chole, the days of trekking through the wilderness, all the way to the Onyx River.

And there, the red dragon.

By the time he returned from his memories the trees had vanished. Cliffs rose on either side of the river, funnelling the waters through a narrow gorge. The current picked up speed, leaving him battling to keep his head above the water. A heavy object knocked into him. He fumbled at the log, gasping as he pulled himself atop it.

Collapsing onto the sodden wood, he clung to its broken branches, overcome by the cold and exhaustion. The water turned white as it raced over hidden rocks. The log rocked as it bounced off unseen objects. Gabriel lay shivering, the cool wind providing little relief from the icy waters. He battled to stay conscious.

He could not remember when the log had finally left the river and drifted out to sea. The cliffs had continued all the way to the coast, hemming in the raging river. Eventually Gabriel had fallen into a kind of half-sleep, his arms still clutching at the log while his mind drifted.

Then the sky had widened as the rocky cliffs gave way to… nothing. When Gabriel raised his head to look around, he found himself drifting on the ocean, the cliffs of the shoreline already growing smaller.

Cold and exhausted, there was little he could do but watch as the current carried him farther out to sea.

How long he had drifted, Gabriel could not say. More than a

day, for night had come at least once. But whether it was one or two or three, his memory could not recall. His mind was awash, his head throbbing. He ground his knuckles into his temples, willing the pain of the migraine away. His tongue rasped across his parched mouth, every sense screaming out for water.

Shivering, he held on.

His mind drifted and his grasp on the log loosened. Tears formed in his eyes, but he would not give in. This was not his time to die – not yet.

No, it is not, a chill voice sent fear through his soul. *There are still things for you to do.*

Gabriel cracked open his eyes, dread seeping into his heart.

A dark figure hovered over the water, staring down at him. Cold seeped from the ethereal body, a ghostly wind that spoke of death. Black spirits raced about the spectre, covering it in a deathly cloak. It towered over his helpless body.

Gabriel closed his eyes. There was no mistaking it; this was the same entity which had come to him in the forests near Oaksville.

"What do you want, demon?" he croaked the words.

To help you, the spectre whispered, *as I once did before.*

"Go to hell, foul demon," Gabriel spat. "I will die before I take your help again."

And die you will, a chill ran down Gabriel's spine as its voice echoed in his head. *Soon you will slip beneath the dark waters.*

"So be it," Gabriel grated.

I can save you, Gabriel. You know I ask nothing in return.

Gabriel would have laughed if he'd had the strength. He knew now the demon lied, that its aid would cost his soul and more. He had sworn to Enala he would never allow himself be drawn in by evil again. If that meant his death…

You do not wish to die, honey laced the demon's voice. *Take my hand, Gabriel, and live.*

Gabriel looked up and saw the demon's outstretched hand. Purple veins lined the pale skin, and long white nails grew from its fingertips. He shuddered as it reached for him, his only lifeline in this grim ocean.

Temptation rose within Gabriel, temptation for the warm lure of life. If he took the offered hand, he would survive this nightmare. He could begin a new life, a better life. All he had to do was say yes.

He stared at the demon, watching the spirits roaming over its spectral form. A chill determination filled him, the temptation turning to dust. Death itself clothed this being; how could life come from such a creature?

Gabriel summoned the last of his strength. "No!" he shouted.

And the demon vanished.

A splash came from nearby. Gabriel looked up, his mind still reeling from the encounter. His vision blurred in and out of focus, but through the cloud he saw a ship surging towards him. Its prow cut through the waves and overhead men swung through the rigging like spiders. Its sails billowed out, filled by the ocean breeze.

Gabriel opened his mouth and tried to shout. The call came out as a croak, the wind catching it and whisking it away. He groaned and struggled to pull himself farther out of the water. Raising one hand he began to wave, praying they would see him. In desperation, he called again.

The ship drew level with him. Gabriel gritted his teeth in frustration, despair rising to swamp the fickle hope.

"Man overboard!" the cry carried across the water.

CHAPTER 3

Eric paced across the empty hall. His footsteps echoed from the stone walls as he wove between marble pillars. The massive columns stretched high above him to where the ceiling should have been; but here there was no roof to protect against the elements. The stars glittered overhead, staring down into the silent hall.

Midnight approached, and Eric doubted anyone else would be visiting the Sky temple at this time of night. Reaching the far wall he spun on his heel and began his third lap. It had taken two days and a night to reach Lon, during which time he had barely slept an hour.

Gabriel remained unconscious, but Eric knew it could not last. Michael said he was exhausted, dehydrated from his time in the ocean. But soon he would wake, and Eric would have to face the man who had hunted him halfway across the Three Nations. There would be a reckoning.

Questions spun through Eric's mind, each more difficult than the last. How had Gabriel survived the attack by the Baronians? How had he followed them across Plorsea, all the way to Dragon Country? And how had he found Enala, and rescued her from Chole?

Eric swung a fist at a column as he passed. He immediately regretted the reflex as pain shot up his arm.

Closing his eyes, Eric shrieked into the night. "Alastair, where are you? *I need you!*"

The wind caught Eric's words and swept them into the night sky. He was alone now; Alastair was gone and there would be no bringing him back.

He had told the old man of his fear; that Gabriel was the one person he could not face. How could he, when Gabriel embodied the very crimes for which he sought redemption. How could Eric defend himself against a man from whom he had taken everything?

Eric's magic had destroyed Oaksville, had robbed Gabriel of his life and his family. Now the man had returned from the grave to haunt him, to remind Eric there was nothing he could do to balance out the evil he'd brought to Oaksville.

Eric sank to his knees, guilt weighing on his soul. What could he say to the man? That it had been an accident? That every action he had taken since was to make up for the horror he had wrought?

It would not matter, could not. Eric had seen the hatred in his eyes when they'd last met; only revenge could quench that rage.

Inken had tried to reassure him on the ship, but there was nothing she or anyone else could say to make this right. When they arrived at the temple, he had held her tight, giving his silent thanks for her support. But he knew in his heart he would have to face this alone, that this was his battle to fight.

He excused himself after dinner and wandered out into the night. The ship had dropped them on the temple's private wharf, ensuring Lon's citizens did not notice their arrival. The sailors had been happy to see the backs of them, some even cheering as the company carried Gabriel ashore. The captain accompanied them for as long as it took to claim his payment.

Fortunately the Sky priests had been happy with the price Michael negotiated. Jurrien had apparently called on them before their arrival, and warned of their approach. A group of priests met them as they disembarked and led them to an empty dormitory usually reserved for apprentices.

The temple grounds consisted of the massive hall and a collection of smaller buildings and living quarters. After leaving the others, Eric had picked his way through the adjoining buildings until he reached the great hall.

Looking around, Eric imagined it during the day, when people flocked here seeking guidance from the Sky priests. He needed guidance now more than ever, but he doubted it was the kind the priests could offer. And from what he'd seen of Jurrien, the God did not seem to share his sister's approachable manner.

Reaching the centre of the hall, Eric stopped and sucked in a breath. Pacing would get him nowhere. Exhaustion had frazzled his mind. Thoughts bounced around his head like a broken wagon wheel, lost and confused. He needed to concentrate, to focus on the larger problems at hand. He could do nothing to change the current situation, at least not until Gabriel woke.

Letting out a long sigh, Eric sank to the ground and crossed his legs. Closing his eyes, he began to meditate. Alastair had taught him the technique as a way of controlling his emotions and learning self-control. Eric needed those skills now more than ever. His thoughts were chasing themselves around his mind in a self-destructive loop, always returning to the awful dread of the confrontation to come.

He breathed in again, seeking the calm centre amidst the

storm. Thoughts assailed him, but as each rose he fought to let them go, to set them aside, if only for a moment. Turmoil crashed against him and exhaustion rolled through him like the ocean tide. He needed sleep, desperately. He had to break this cycle of anxiety.

Eric sank deeper, thoughts drifting back over the last few days. The confrontation with Jurrien loomed, but he pushed it aside. Still, he felt a pang of curiosity from the thought, from something Jurrien had done. As he left, the Storm God had leapt from the deck of the ship, where the wind caught him and propelled him into the air.

Jurrien had *flown*.

Eric possessed the same magic as the God, and while he did not have the power to create, he *could* manipulate the winds as Jurrien had done. Could he also fly?

He smiled then, another memory leaping to mind. In Chole, Caelin had thrown him from a second story window and in his fear Eric's magic had summoned the wind to catch him. For a few seconds, he'd hovered several feet above the ground.

Sinking into his magic, Eric released his tethers to the physical realm and sent his spirit soaring. Reaching out, he sent feelers up into the clouds, seeking the great gusts which formed where land met ocean. Working his magic, he wound threads of power around the howling gales.

Grimacing, he syphoned his power into the threads, and drew them down, gathering the winds together as they came. The gusts fought him, pushing against the bonds holding them. Energy surged through his mind as he poured more magic into the fray, binding the air pockets tighter. With the city so close, he could not afford to allow such powerful gales to escape his grasp. The last thing he wanted was to start tearing the roofs off buildings.

Back in his body, he shivered as the first pocket of wind

reached him. The gale whipped around his seated form, tearing at his clothes and hair, carrying the icy chill of the air currents high above the city. Shivers ran down his spine, but he smiled, happy to have come this far.

Turning inwards, he focused, pulling the wind in tighter and tighter knots. The gusts grew stronger, striking with a force that threatened to knock him flat. Clenching his fists, he pushed the pockets of air down to the paving. His feet grew numb as the icy wind wrapped about his legs, but now the rest of him remained warm.

With a shock, he felt the pressure push him upwards, lifting him from the cool tiles. He opened his eyes and gasped as he saw a few feet now separated him from the ground.

The magic slipped from his control, and the wind erupted outwards, whistling across the empty hall and upwards into the sky. He fell to the ground with an undignified thump.

Eric grinned, worries forgotten. His heart thumped hard in this chest as he clapped his hands in excitement. This was something new, something useful. But he needed practice. Closing his eyes, he tried again.

LON GLOWED IN THE DARKNESS, lit by the light of a thousand torches. The capital of Lonia spread out beneath him, the central hub of the farming nation. Rooftops glistened in the moonlight, each holding a family, a handful of souls asleep to the world. To the east the calm waters of the harbour lapped at the seawall, the nation's ships rocking at anchor. The walls of the citadel rose to the south, towering over the city.

Eric swallowed hard, staring down at the lights far below.

The air jerked and he dropped several feet. Sweat dripped down his forehead, only to be whipped away by the swirling air. Goosebumps pricked his arms and a shiver ran through him. Within, his mind was in freefall, his vision spinning at the distance below him.

His fear of heights had come crashing back.

Stupid, stupid, stupid, the word danced about his head.

It had all been going fine. It had taken hours, but he had finally managed to keep himself aloft without losing control of the winds. He'd spent another hour floating around the great hall, then the temple grounds, lifting himself higher and higher as his confidence grew.

He had not noticed the fear at first, had not recognised the familiar tingle as it crept into his mind. Even as he soared higher, Eric reassured himself, convinced the wind would catch him if he fell. After all, it was the fall he feared, rather than the height itself. Nevertheless, the terror had trickled into his consciousness, slowly eroding his control. His movements grew jerky and erratic, and his panic began in earnest.

It was not until he tried to halt his ascent that he realised the magic had latched onto his fear, using it to take over. Now he rose faster than ever, as sudden judders threw him about each time the magic slipped. Terror rose in this throat, feeding strength to the winds. They twisted about him, converging from all around.

Eric sucked in a breath, wrestling for control. Within, the magic stalked his mind, a wolf in the darkness. He drew back, fear robbing him of strength. He could not face the beast now, suspended hundreds of feet in open air. If he lost, things would become far worse. Alastair was no longer here to protect him. There would be no coming back if the magic took control again. To lose would be to unleash his magic on Lon.

Wind swirled around him, gathering force and growing

stronger. The cold sent shivers through Eric's unprotected body, his thin clothing woefully inadequate. His teeth chattered as the wind sucked the last warmth from his skin. Eric wrapped his arms tight around his chest and looked down, stomach roiling from the height.

He watched with horror as the wind swirled faster. He could feel the pressure building, a tornado forming high above the city, with Eric at its centre. If he did not act soon the destruction would be unimaginable.

Summoning his courage, Eric reached again for his magic. At his touch the power surged, and the winds holding him ceased, sending Eric into free fall. He spun through the air, hurtling towards the city, and all thought of control vanished.

When they caught him again, Eric could barely find the strength to breathe.

The tornado howled, drawing in the surrounding clouds, dampening the air. Tears ran down Eric's face. He could not let this happen, not again. He could feel the magic flooding from him, a free flow drawing in more and more of the Sky element. The air above the city darkened, the black tail of the tornado stretching down. Soon it would reach the city, and chaos would rein unchecked.

He could not let that happen.

With a scream he reached inside, wrenching at the magic within. The wolf rose before him, swamping his conscious, its deep blue glow shining with an angry rage. He felt no comfort from the magic now, no gentle pool of energy to draw on. The wolf towered over him, his magic come to life, fed by his fear.

Eric drew on every ounce of courage remaining to him, determined to defeat the wild beast. The wolf growled and came closer. With every step it took, it grew. Its teeth glinted with the blue of his magic, jaws dripping bloody malice.

He shrank back in despair. As he turned to flee, Alastair's words from long ago raced through his mind. *Master your fear. That is its only weapon against you. If you do not fear it, your magic cannot harm you.*

Eric swallowed, turning back to face the beast. He remembered the fear he'd felt after the desert, the fear of his magic had threatened to overwhelm him. Knowing the risks, he had faced that fear and vanquished it. In doing so, he had returned the rains to Chole.

Now he must do the same, or his wild magic would destroy the city below. He could not allow that to happen.

He faced the beast, reaching out to grasp the glow rippling from its fur. Fear sent a tremor through his knees, but he squashed it down, baring his teeth at the beast before him. They stood facing one another, locked in a silent battle of wills.

Then Eric blinked, and watched as the wolf started to shrink. It growled and took a step towards him, raising hairs on his neck, but he stood strong. He knew he had won. The winds still buffeted him, throwing him about the sky, but the fear no longer crippled him.

Taking a firmer hold of his magic, he sent its tendrils out to bind the wolf. It screamed and leapt for him, but the magic grasped it tight, locking it in place. Eric smiled, and drew the beast back down within him, until it vanished into the glowing pool of light.

The air still raged about him. He reached out again with his magic, confident now he could halt the whirling twister. Gritting his teeth, he tore apart the binds holding the winds together. The swirling ceased as air erupted outwards into empty sky.

"*You fool!*" the air shook with the power in the voice, and then a dark body hurtled from the sky.

Eric caught a glimpse of white hair and a face twisted

with rage before Jurrien smashed into him. The breath whooshed from his lungs and he found himself suddenly in free fall, careering through the clouds towards the ground below.

As he reached for his magic, a fist crashed into his face.

"*Don't!*" Jurrien snapped, his hands digging into Eric's shirt.

Their plummet towards the earth ceased with a violent jerk. The wind reformed around them, controlled now by Jurrien. He looked up at the God, his face lit by the light of the city below. Fear tingled down Eric's spine as he saw the anger there.

When they reached the ground Jurrien tossed Eric to the grass. Before he could recover, the Storm God grasped Eric by the collar and wrenched him to his feet. Jurrien pulled him close, leaving Eric no choice but to look into those icy blue eyes.

"How could you be so reckless?" Jurrien hissed. "Did Alastair teach you *nothing?*"

"I… I don't know." Eric stuttered. Tears came to his eyes. "All I know is Alastair is gone. He's dead, and I… I'm lost," he waved his hand at the sky. "The magic… it just took control."

A tremor of rage swept through Jurrien. He tossed Eric back to the ground. Thunder clapped as Eric rolled and came to his feet.

"You are no Magicker. You do not even deserve the title of apprentice. If it was in my power, I would strip the magic from you here and now. I do not care what my sister thought of you. You are as likely to kill us all as save us!"

Eric shivered with cold and fear. "I had control of it, there at the end." His voice shook, but he stood his ground. "I may be a novice, but I will not let history repeat itself."

Jurrien turned his back, fingers raking his hair. "I cannot

afford this… these distractions," he spun. "Antonia is dead. I am the only one left to stand against Archon."

The breath caught in Eric's throat. "No," he choked. The tears came now, hot and fast. "How can that be possible?"

"She was weakened by our battle with Archon. The demon took her by surprise. And it used the *Soul Blade* to do the foul deed, which means it now has her powers. It must be found, and quickly, before it collects any other magic."

"How could you not have told us?" rage grew from Eric's sorrow. "Where have you been?"

"I have been everywhere: alerting King Fraser and King Jonathan to the threat, the council of Lonia too. Mustering our armies, spreading the word. Archon is coming, and the Three Nations must stand together if we are to have any chance of stopping him," he shook his head. "Even then, I do not believe it will be enough. Even with the Sword of Light, without Antonia we would lack the power to stop him," he clenched his fists. Lightning crackled along his arm.

"Where is the demon now?" Eric asked.

"I have Magickers hunting it. They will signal me when it reappears, though they will not have the power to stop it. If it collects any more magic, it may be beyond even my powers. Last signs showed it heading north into Lonia, towards us."

"It is coming here?"

Jurrien scowled. "How should I know what it will do next? Perhaps it is trying to return to the northern Wastelands. Perhaps it is hunting the last of the Sword wielders'. Or perhaps it is coming for me. I do not know. There is too much to consider."

"What can we do to help?"

Jurrien laughed, the sound harsh and mocking. "Help? *Help?* You could start by leaving my city be," he fell silent, and Eric thought he might finish with that. When Jurrien continued his tone was sombre. “Your priority must be getting Enala to the Sword. It lies in Kalgan, a long way from here. Archon’s agents will be looking for her now.”

“The best path to take would be a ship up the river to Ardath. From there you will have to continue on foot through the Branei pass into Trola, and then down the coast to Kalgan. It will take weeks. I only hope we have the strength to hold Archon back that long.”

“When can we leave?”

Jurrien shook his head. “It will take a few days to organise. My priests will take care of it. I must leave, there is much to be done,” he turned and walked into the night.

Eric opened his mouth to wish him farewell, but the God vanished before he could speak the words. Shaking his head, Eric sank to his knees. Exhaustion rose in his chest, sucking the strength from his limbs. His stomach twisted. He hung his head, taking a deep breath. He needed to return to the dormitory and sleep. Only then would he have the energy to take in everything Jurrien had said.

Footsteps came from nearby. Eric looked up in time to see a figure emerge from the shadows. A familiar voice greeted him.

“So, we meet again.”

CHAPTER 4

Gabriel woke in darkness, the last dredges of a nightmare clinging to him. Panic gripped his mind and sent him tumbling from the bed. Climbing to his feet, he stumbled across the unfamiliar room, fumbling for an exit as he struck a wall. He cursed as his elbow caught on a doorknob, and then slipped silently through the unlocked door.

Outside he hurried down an empty corridor, trying doors until he found one leading outside. Slipping into the night, he started across the grass, the dew cold on his bare feet.

Wind whipped at him and he heard a crash from overhead. Looking up, he froze, fear gripping his heart. The lights of the city lit the sky above, revealing black clouds spinning inexorably towards a whirling centre.

Gabriel took an involuntary step backwards. He gaped, unable to comprehend the vision. Light flickered across the underbellies of the clouds, and it seemed he looked into a portal to hell itself. The wind on the ground picked up as the tail of the twister grew closer.

Then another crash came, followed by the flicker of lightning, and the swirling ceased. The clouds drifted to a stop and the wind died away, returning the night to tranquil silence.

Gabriel stared as two figures tumbled from the sky, plummeting towards the grounds on which he stood. As they approached they slowed, finally landing close to where Gabriel waited. They did not appear to have seen him.

Taking a breath, Gabriel continued through the night, creeping towards where the two had landed. He shivered in the cool; even without the wind, winter was not far away, and the clothes he wore were thin, not made for the outdoors. A dull ache throbbed at the back of his skull and his knees shook, but he did not care.

Gabriel could hardly believe he lived. He had been just minutes away from sinking beneath the waves when the ship appeared.

It seemed someone, or something, was still looking out for him.

The faces of his rescuers had appeared only as blurs to his sunburnt eyes, but as he turned a corner and saw the two figures standing on the grass, he knew who they had been.

Gabriel stared at the young man, the same one he'd hunted halfway across Plorsea. He could hardly believe it. There he was, the demon boy who had burned Oaksville to the ground, who had murdered Gabriel's family and left him for dead.

He felt the familiar anger well up within him, the hate that had driven him so far. He watched as the older man turned away, vanishing into the night. Taking a breath, Gabriel walked into the light.

"So, we meet again."

The young man looked up, and Gabriel saw with surprise the lines of exhaustion stretching from his eyes. "Gabriel," he paused. "You're awake."

His words confirmed Gabriel's suspicions. "So it was you who rescued me at sea," he stared. "*Why?*"

"Because we could not leave you there to die. That is not who I am."

"We? Who else is with you?"

The young man smiled. "There are five of us, though you only know one – Enala."

Gabriel stared, the name echoing through his mind. *Enala?*

He shook his head, anger catching light. "You have Enala? What have you done with her?" he took a step closer.

The young man rolled his eyes and raised his hands in surrender. "We have done nothing with her. In fact, she saved our lives back in Dragon Country. And then we saved hers. We are protecting her against forces you cannot begin to understand."

"Oh really? And why should I believe a word you say, *demon*. Who are you? What do you want?"

Eric scowled. "My name is Eric, and I am no *demon*. I am a Magicker – or at least I have been for the last few weeks," he looked away, his voice dropping to barely a whisper. "Before Oaksville, before Alastair, I did not know what I was – only that I was cursed."

Gabriel watched the young man, his anger mounting. "What are you saying? That Oaksville was not you? That it was some accident?"

Eric met Gabriel's gaze, the lightning blue eyes piercing him. "I am sorry, Gabriel. There is nothing I can do to make it right, but I had no control of my magic then, no way to stop the forces that descended on Oaksville," he sucked in a gulp of winter air. "But as I once promised you, I have spent every moment since then trying to atone."

Tears welled in Gabriel's eyes as he listened to Eric's words. He could hear the pain in his voice, the regret. But he could not bring himself to believe the words, to believe it had all been a mistake. Everything he had sacrificed, it could not have been for nothing. He had sold his soul, had committed *murder,* all to bring justice for his family.

"My parents, my fiancée," his voice shook. "They are dead because of you."

Eric hung his head. "Yes."

Only a few feet separated the two now. Gabriel reached out and grabbed Eric by the shirt. His eyes widened as Gabriel lifted him into the air and shook him. "*They're dead!*"

Eric kicked out, striking Gabriel hard between the legs. Gabriel choked and tossed him to the ground. He stumbled back a few feet and glared at Eric.

Eric climbed to his feet, sadness on his face. "I cannot change the past, Gabriel, but I will do everything in my power to make the future better."

Gabriel answered with a cold laugh. He waved at the sky. "And that? Was that you making the future better?"

Eric paled. "Yes, it was me. I lost control, for a while. But I stopped it," he brushed dirt from his arm. "I am not perfect, but as I told Jurrien, I will never allow what happened in Oaksville to happen again."

A chill spread through Gabriel's stomach. "Jurrien?"

"Yes, the Storm God is not a great fan of me either. But we have bigger dangers to consider now, other threats to face. Even here, Enala is not safe from the ones who hunt her."

"What do you mean?" shaking his head, Gabriel looked around, realising he had no idea where they were. "Where are we, and who is hunting Enala?"

"We are in Lon. And Enala is being hunted by Archon. He wants her dead, Gabriel, and if he succeeds the rest of us will quickly follow."

Gabriel stared, his head spinning. "*What?*"

Eric grimaced and began to talk. Gabriel could only stare

as Eric told him of Enala's lineage, and the curse that had been placed on the Trolan king's bloodline. His head throbbed as his heart quickened with fear. He sank to the ground as he listened to Eric's tale of the events which had unfolded since he separated from Enala.

Swallowing hard, Gabriel tried to process what Eric was saying. He thought back to the cool, collected young woman he had fled with from Chole. Devastated by the loss of her family, she had nevertheless shown a steely courage in the face of her pursuers. She had been as at home in the jungles of Plorsea as in the dusty streets of Chole.

But the last hope of the Three Nations? It cannot be true. The thought whispered through Gabriel's mind.

"Archon's minions will not give up. If they succeed, the Three Nations will fall before Archon's magic. Jurrien has asked us to protect her at all costs, to take her to the Trolan capital. Until she picks up the Sword of Light, she is in terrible danger."

Gabriel swallowed, eyes fixed on Eric. There had to be more to this, something missing from the story. He would not, could not trust Eric.

"Where is she?"

"This way," Eric strode past and back towards the building Gabriel had woken in.

Gabriel followed, lost deep in his thoughts.

They entered the dormitory through a small set of doors in the front and found themselves in a modest entranceway. This was a different door from which Gabriel had fled. He looked around as they wiped their feet on the rug, taking in the bare stone walls and simple wooden floors. Beyond the entrance way he glimpsed an interior lounge furnished with couches and a table.

Eric picked his way through the lounge. Gabriel followed, the path lit by a fire burning low in its grate on the far wall. Eric did not look back, and Gabriel guessed he did not care much whether Gabriel followed or not. He moved slowly though, shoulders slumped in exhaustion.

Gabriel's own energy was quickly fading, his body still shattered from the time adrift. His mouth felt dry and his head pounded with a headache. He guessed it would take at least a week before he made a full recovery.

Together they made their way through a door at the end of the room and into a corridor Gabriel recognised. Eric strode down its length, glancing at the doors on their left until he reached the one he wanted. Reaching up, he tapped on the door. They waited.

Shifting on his feet, Gabriel glanced up and down the hallway, suddenly nervous. How would Enala react to seeing him again, after thinking him dead? Only a few days had passed since the river, but to Gabriel it felt like a lifetime. The world had changed while he drifted at sea, and his mind was still racing to catch up.

Eric reached up to knock again, but the door creaked open and a woman leaned out. Red hair hung across her face and she looked as though she'd just woken from a deep sleep, but she smiled when she saw Eric. She reached out and embraced him, then noticed Gabriel standing in the shadows. Her smile faded.

She stepped back and stared at him. "You must be Gabriel," it was not a question. "Glad to see you are awake."

Gabriel nodded. "Who are you?"

The woman hesitated and then held out her hand. "My name is Inken. You must be here to see Enala."

"Yes, is she awake?"

Another face appeared behind Inken. Dark rings hung below her eyes and her blond hair was unkempt, but her sapphire eyes brightened when she saw him. "Gabriel," her voice exploded into the corridor as she launched herself at him.

Gabriel laughed as she knocked him back a few steps. He held her tight against his chest, relief flooding him. He had never expected to see her again, not once the dragon attacked and the current dragged him under. To find her here, alive and well, was a miracle.

He heard Eric clear his throat and glanced up. "You two obviously have some catching up to do. We'll talk in the morning," he glanced at Inken. "Shall we find someplace else to rest?"

Inken laughed and leaned across to kiss him. "Let's."

They moved away down the corridor, leaving the two of them alone. Enala drew him into the room. Inside he found four wooden bunk beds and little else. Only two of the beds had been slept in, the ruffled covers suggesting Enala and Inken preferred the bottom bunks. Heavy curtains hung over the window at the end of the room. A thin sliver of moonlight shone through a slit between them, providing a touch of light.

Enala moved across to her bed and sat down. Gabriel followed suit, lowering himself onto the bed Inken had occupied. He looked across at her, just able to make out her smile in the darkness.

"I can't believe you're here," she whispered. She reached across the space between the beds and grasped his hand.

Gabriel smiled in return. "I can hardly believe it either. How did we get to Lon?"

Enala shrugged. "It's a long story," she shivered, and he saw the glint of tears in her eyes. "This was just where the ship was heading."

Gabriel hesitated. "Eric... he told me some of what happened. About your dragon?"

A sob cut the air. Before she could reply Gabriel moved

to sit beside her. He pulled her into a hug, offering his silent comfort.

So at least part of Eric's story was true.

"Her name was Nerissa," Enala spoke at last. "She found me not long after I lost you, as I knew she would. I have known her since I was a child, when my family used to bring me to Dragon Country. I always thought nothing could hurt me so long as I was with her. I thought…" her voice broke. "I thought she could protect me."

Enala trembled in his arms. He held her tight, lost for words. He knew next to nothing about this girl, had only known her a few days. But during their time together they had become friends, comrades in arms against the unknown force pursuing them.

At last, Enala broke away. She glanced up at Gabriel. "You remember now, don't you? What happened to you before the demon."

Gabriel took a deep, trembling breath. "Yes," slowly, he recounted his story, starting with the storm that had destroyed Oaksville. He did not hold back, made no attempt to cast himself in a better light. He had done so much wrong, made so many mistakes he could hardly bare to recall them. But after all she had been through, Enala deserved the truth.

When at last he finished, he drew in a deep breath and looked Enala in the eyes. "We cannot trust these people, Enala."

~

"Doesn't say much, does he?" Inken commented, lying on the bed beside Eric.

Eric smiled and pulled her closer, brushing a strand of hair from her face. "He had plenty to say earlier."

Inken smiled back, her skin tingling where Eric's fingers touched. "And?"

She felt a shiver run through Eric. "I said what I could. I don't think it made a difference," he hesitated. "I'm glad he's alive though, that I could apologise. I know it cannot make up for what happened, but maybe now I have a chance to show him who I really am, that I'm trying to put things right."

"I hope so too," she flashed him a sly smile. "Although I couldn't help but notice some strange goings on in the sky when I looked out the window earlier."

Eric groaned and Inken leaned across to kiss him. "What happened?"

"I wanted to try something, to copy what Jurrien did when he leapt off the ship."

"And?"

"It worked, but I pushed too far, too fast. The magic took me well above my limits, and I lost control," Inken heard the venom in his voice.

She smiled. "Stop being so hard on yourself, Eric. You took control again before anything happened, that's what matters."

Eric gave a sour laugh. "Small victory that," he paused. "I didn't really have time to think about it. Jurrien showed up again. He had a lot to say about me and my magic."

Inken's heart gave a lurch. She suddenly found herself wishing she had followed Eric earlier.

"Ouch," Eric flinched away and Inken realised her nails had dug into his arm.

She released him. "Sorry, Eric. I do not like Jurrien; he is not like his sister. He is shrouded in anger, where Antonia is a calming force."

"Was," Eric's voice cracked. "Antonia was... He found her in the forest. The demon killed her. She's... she's gone."

Inken stared, unable to speak. She felt hot tears in her eyes but made no effort to wipe them away. A sound rumbled up from her chest, a half-warped sob that she abruptly cut off. She shook her head. "No," she choked. "How could that happen?"

"I don't know," Eric's voice broke again. "But we have to go on, for her. It's up to us now, to ensure Enala gets to the Sword in time. Maybe it will be enough. Jurrien is preparing the Three Nations for war and hunting down the demon."

Silence fell then, the weight of responsibility settling around them like a lead weight. With Antonia gone, the likelihood any of them would survive the coming war seemed non-existent. Last time it had taken the powers of all three Gods to overcome Archon. With only Jurrien and the Sword of Light, could they even hold their own?

"We have to try," Inken whispered.

"I know. We can't give up. I won't rest until we finish the quest Alastair and Antonia started."

Inken pulled him close again, leaning over to kiss him. Their lips met, fierce and hard. She held him tight, desperate to feel the life within him. He had come so close to death on the beach. Just thinking of the danger to come filled her with fear – not for herself, but for the reckless young man she loved. Eric told the truth; he would not run from the peril they faced – he would rather die.

Inken feared it may come to that.

Unbidden, hot tears ran down her cheek. Sobbing, she broke away from Eric, turning her face to hide the tears.

He heard her grief anyway. She felt his hand reach up to stroke her hair. Closing her eyes, Inken took a deep breath to calm herself.

"It's going to be okay, Inken."

Inken felt a wild, insane laughter bubbling up within her. She held it back. They both knew the lie in Eric's words. If even the Goddess of the Earth could fall to Archon, what chance did they have? And if by some miracle they managed to defeat Archon, how many of them would survive the battle? How many souls would perish? Who of their company would live to see the dawn of a new peace?

It would be so easy to turn now and run, to find some hole in which the dark tendrils of the north would not find them. But she knew they could not. There was too much at stake, and if Archon conquered, the darkness would find them wherever they hid.

No, there was no choice but to fight.

Slowly the sobs subsided as she regained her composure. They lay there in silence, each lost in their own thoughts. Here in Jurrien's temple she felt safe, even if she now counted the Storm God amongst her adversaries. The darkness felt almost comforting with Eric beside her, as if it could hide them from the world without. But she knew it could not last, that morning would soon bring the light of day. Nor would the safety of the temple. If they remained, Archon would find them.

Only one option offered them hope. Get Enala to the Sword of Light, before all hell broke loose.

Inken closed her eyes and breathed in Eric's familiar scent. Whatever the future may bring, they still had this moment, right here, right now.

She resolved not to waste it.

CHAPTER 5

"You lied to me," Enala stood in the entrance to the lounge, arms folded across her chest.

They had been talking before she entered, but they broke off now, staring up at the two of them in the doorway. Silence settled like autumn leaves as Enala looked around the room, eyes lingering on each of them. Inken, Eric, Caelin, and Michael; she knew their names, though she had not spoken to half of them.

She and Gabriel had stayed up half the night talking. He had told her of the past he now remembered, of the storm which had destroyed Oaksville and killed his family. At first she had not believed him when he claimed Eric had brought the storm. She may not have spoken to the young man, but she could not believe he was a killer. But Gabriel was insistent, unwavering in his belief.

Now Enala wanted answers. Inken had said she could trust them, that they cared about her. But if Gabriel was right…

Eric shifted in his seat, looking like he was about to

speak, but Inken beat him to it. "No, we didn't. I know you trust Gabriel, that he saved your life in Chole. But there is more than one side to this story."

Enala glanced at Gabriel. He stood staring at Eric, his face blank, unreadable.

She looked back to Inken. "Tell me then."

Inken nodded. She glanced at the others. "Enala and I are going for a walk. Don't eat all the food," Enala caught the warning glance Inken shot Caelin as she stood.

Caelin raised his hands in surrender. "Don't look at me. I was thinking I'd get some exercise before breakfast anyway," he looked at the others. "Perhaps Gabriel and Eric will join me. You too, Michael, if you're interested?"

Enala picked her way across the room and joined Inken as she walked out into the cool morning air.

"I'm quite alright thank you, Caelin," she caught Michael's words as the door swung shut behind her.

Inken led the way across the grass and into the gardens surrounding the temple grounds. White frost crunched beneath their boots as they made their way through an archway hung with winter roses. Mist billowed from their mouths with every breath, but the sun had just peeked over the rooftops of the nearest buildings. As its rays reached them, warmth spread through Enala's limbs. The rich scent of roses hung in the air.

"I first met Eric and Alastair in the desert of Chole. I was dying; my horse had fled and I was unarmed and badly injured. If Eric had not spotted me, I would be dead," they left the grass and stepped onto a gravel path leading through the gardens.

"What does that prove? That he has a soft spot for you?"

Inken scowled and Enala felt her cheeks grow hot. "Perhaps you'll let me finish before you begin flinging accusations. There is far more to this story than Gabriel knows. Eric has never meant to hurt anyone with his power; he did not even know he possessed magic before Alastair found him in Oaksville."

"What do you mean?"

"Before Oaksville, Eric spent the better part of two years wandering the wilderness, afraid to return to civilisation for fear of what he thought of as his curse. He did not know it was magic, only that there was some power within him he could not control. But finally, he could no longer bear the isolation. He went to Oaksville to begin a new life, but within an hour of entering the town he was attacked by slavers," Inken spoke in a soft voice.

"When an emerging Magicker has not been properly trained, their magic is tied to their emotions. It is unleashed when they are overwhelmed. When Eric was attacked, his fear and anger took control, and his magic lashed out to protect him."

"What do you mean?"

Inken stopped, gravel crunching beneath her boots. The thorns of a nearby rose caught in Enala's coat as she turned to meet Inken's gaze. "Eric had no choice in what happened, not once attacked. He had every reason to fear for his life, to feel enraged at the men attacking him. He could not direct how his magic responded to those emotions, not without training."

Enala looked away, remembering her horror as she hid in the basement, while men murdered her parents upstairs. The anger had almost driven her to madness. She thought of Eric, unarmed and at the mercy of such thugs. Then she felt a pang of horror as she imagined the helplessness he must have felt once the power was unleashed. To know it was his doing, but being powerless to cease the destruction.

Tears sprang to her eyes. "Does Gabriel know this?"

Inken shook her head. "So far, he has not been too receptive to any explanation.

"Can you blame him?"

"No, of course not. But he is not the only one to have lost those he loves," she paused, choosing her next words carefully. "Eric's parents were the first victims of his wild magic."

Enala's heart twisted in pain. She opened her mouth, but found no words.

Inken nodded, a sad smile on her lips. "You, Gabriel and Eric have much in common. Like it or not, you are linked by tragedy, and will continue, I hope, to fight together on the side of good," she paused. "You should also know; Eric is determined to put right the debt he feels for Oaksville. That is why he used his magic to bring the rain back to Chole."

Enala gaped. "What?"

"That was when I knew he was not the demon everyone thought him, and when I decided I wanted to get to know him better," Inken winked.

Enala stared, lost again for words. Eric may have cursed Gabriel's town to ruin, but he had saved Chole, her city. How could anyone weigh the two deeds against one another, as great and as awful as they were?

Yet Enala could feel the truth in Inken's words, that Eric had never meant to harm Oaksville, that he'd had no control over what happened there.

"I'll try to talk to Gabriel," Enala finally offered. "But I don't know if he will listen. The two of them might have to work it out themselves."

Accident or not, Eric's magic had still caused the death of Gabriel's family. Whatever the circumstances, Enala could not blame him for hating the young man. But perhaps the truth might at least open a dialogue between them.

"Agreed," Inken smiled. "I think us girls had best stay out of this one."

Enala shot back a sly look. "You really love him, don't you?"

She saw Inken's cheeks redden, and laughed. Inken wagged a finger back at her. "That is none of your business, miss. You don't see me asking about what's between yourself and Gabriel!"

Enala felt her own cheeks warm. She opened her eyes wide. "Whatever are you talking about?" she asked. "We're friends, we slept in separate beds and everything."

Inken laughed. "I'll bet," she sniped, but let the subject drop.

They rounded the corner of a building and found themselves at the end of the garden. In the distance the dormitory's shale roof gleamed in the morning sun. The far-off ring of steel blades carried to their ears. Beside her, Inken straightened and reached for her sabre. Enala edged closer to the woman.

She searched the grassy lawns ahead, her eyes picking out two figures battling in front of the dormitory. They both stopped dead as they recognised the fighters. Gabriel and Eric were locked in furious combat, swords slashing at one another as they stumbled on the icy grass.

Inken moved first, her long legs eating up the distance. Enala trotted after her, reaching out to grab her shoulder. "Wait," she said, pointing.

Inken tore herself free, but glanced towards where Enala pointed.

Caelin stood nearby, arms folded as he watched the two with an amused grin. Enala could practically hear Inken's teeth grinding as she switched directions and headed for the sergeant.

Enala could not help but grin. "Like you said, Inken. Maybe they can work it out themselves."

~

ERIC RUBBED his hands against his arms, struggling to warm himself. A shiver ran down his back as the wind whipped past. "What are we doing?" he asked through chattering teeth.

Caelin stood with hands on his hips. "Jurrien paid me a visit this morning. Apparently you need another way to protect yourself, Eric," he turned to Gabriel. "And I'm sure you could use blowing off a little steam."

Eric glanced at Gabriel, heart sinking at the mention of Jurrien. The sun shone across the nearby rooftops, but they stood in the shade, the frost still thick at their feet. Eric already missed the gentle warmth of the fire burning in the lounge. The sky shone with the bright blue of morning, without a hint of cloud.

Caelin tossed a long bundle of cloth to the ground in front of them. It rattled as it struck, unravelling to reveal a collection of swords.

"These are practice blades. They're lead weighted, but the edges and tips have been blunted, so you shouldn't be able to damage each other too much."

As he spoke, he drew his own sword and beckoned Eric closer. Eric moved across to him, but stepped back as Caelin flicked the sword into the air and caught it by the blade.

He held it out to Eric. "First though, this is yours, Eric. It saved my life in Malevolent Cove, but I know Alastair would have wanted you to have it. Make him proud."

Heart pounding in his chest, Eric reached out and gripped the hilt. The worn leather felt warm and the short sword light in his hand. It shone in the morning sun, revealing the faint traces of runes etched in the metal. Eric looked closer, but could not make out the writing. He guessed it must be something to do with the spell on the blade, which protected its user from magic.

Remembering himself, he grinned up at Caelin. "Thank you, Caelin. I will."

"What did you want with me?" Gabriel asked.

Caelin's eyes turned on Gabriel. "I thought you might enjoy being Eric's sparring partner."

Eric made to object, but Gabriel beat him too it. "Why would I want to help *him?*"

Caelin met Gabriel's stare. Eric looked from one to another. "Maybe because we saved you, pulled you from the ocean waters rather than leave you to drown. Or because we rescued Enala, when you had failed her," Caelin paused, a sly look in his eyes. "Or perhaps you'd just like the chance to land a few blows on the boy."

Gabriel glared at Caelin, then shrugged his shoulders and approached the pile of weapons. Retrieving a practice blade, he stepped in front of Eric. "Well, let's see what you're made of then."

Eric scowled back. Gritting his teeth, he stepped around Gabriel and found a practice blade of his own. Lifting the heavy weapon, he laid Alastair's blade by the pile of swords. As he turned to face Gabriel, he drew in a deep breath of cool air. Bracing himself, he walked across the grass and squared off against his foe.

Caelin clapped. "Good! Now, before you begin, let me show you a few things about fighting with the sword," he picked up a blade for himself and moved between them. "The first thing a good swordsman needs to learn is how to stand in a fight. A true fighter will use any number of stances in a fight to overcome his opponent. Different stances allow you to move in and out of attacking range while maintaining your balance, and without overexposing yourself to an attack. I'm going to show you one or two, and hope that'll be enough for now."

He moved his feet so they were shoulder width apart and facing forward, with the right about a foot in front of the left. "This is called a forward stance. It doesn't matter which foot is in the front, so each time you move you can step straight into this stance. It gives a fighter a solid, balanced base to launch and defend against attacks."

Eric moved his feet to mimic Caelin's, feeling awkward with the heavy blade in hand. He followed the soldier's movements as he drilled them in the basics of thrusts, parries and blocks. Eric immediately began tripping over his own feet as he struggled to obey Caelin's instructions. His body ached from the brief scuffle the night before, and within his magic felt drained and weak.

He watched Gabriel swinging the practice blade to match Caelin's movements, a bored smile on his face. His large shoulders wielded the blade with ease, although his movements were slow and somewhat clumsy. Still, Eric could not help but think the power in his swing would leave a nasty bruise.

"Okay, that should be enough for now. How about the two of you show me what you can do," Caelin stepped back and folded his arms. "The practice blades may be dulled, but you will still need to be careful," he gave them each a hard stare. "Blows to the head are off-limits."

Gabriel grinned and raised his blade in mock salute. "It's about time," he crouched low and crept towards Eric.

Eric wiped sweat from his brow and took a firmer grim of his sword. He kept the tip pointing at Gabriel the way Caelin had shown them, and slid into the forwards stance. After half an hour of practice, it almost felt comfortable.

Pushing down his fear, he summoned an arrogance he did not feel, and waved Gabriel forward. "Come on then, let's see what you've got."

Gabriel grinned, and charged.

Eric held his ground until the last moment, and then ducked beneath Gabriel's wild swing. He leapt backwards as Gabriel attempted to reverse the cut, lashing out with his own blade to counterattack. The blow went wide, but Gabriel still flinched backwards in surprise.

They eyed each other. Eric smiled, masking his nerves, and motioned Gabriel forward again. The larger man scowled and edged his way to the left. Eric followed him, careful to keep his stance tight. His eyes narrowed as he searched for an opening. He held his sword low, ready to strike when Gabriel moved into range.

Gabriel struck again, more cautious now, aware he could not simply beat his way through Eric's guard. He slid forward, swinging his blade at Eric's side in an awkward cut. Eric danced backwards to avoid the blow, then leapt to the attack. His sword snaked out, biting at Gabriel's thigh.

Stumbling backwards, Gabriel swore and fixed Eric with a glare. Eric did not attempt to pursue his larger opponent, guessing it would be foolish to come within range of Gabriel's blade. Instead he dropped into a crouch, and waited.

Gabriel bared his teeth. "What, are you afraid?" he spat.

Eric only smiled, refusing to let Gabriel get under his skin.

With a scream, Gabriel charged across the open ground. Eric backtracked, raising his sword to fend off a wild blow. Their blades met with a dull ring and the blade vibrated in Eric's hand. Pain lanced down his arm as he blocked again. Gabriel was not holding back any longer; each blow carried the full force of his strength.

Ducking beneath a wicked swing, Eric leapt back out of Gabriel's reach. He brushed a hand through his hair, already feeling the heat of exertion burning off the morning chill. Gabriel paused to do the same, a grin on his face. He was enjoying this.

The break did not last long. Gabriel brought his sword about and returned to the attack. Eric swung to counter, but his feet slipped on the damp grass and his sword went wide. Pain lanced from his side as Gabriel's weapon struck his hip. Swearing, Eric kicked out, catching Gabriel on the knee. They both stumbled backwards.

Gabriel's grin widened. "There's more where that came from."

Eric did not waste energy replying. He panted heavily, breath fogging the crisp air, the exertions of the night already catching up to him.

This is exhausting! Eric now had a new respect for Caelin's endurance. He had watched the sergeant take on three men at once while hardly breaking a sweat.

The ache in his hip throbbed in time with the beat of his heart. Cursing his clumsiness, Eric allowed his anger to take hold. He gripped the practice blade tighter, and leapt to the attack.

Gabriel's eyes widened. He raised his sword in a clumsy block, but Eric's sword slipped beneath and struck him in the stomach. Gabriel staggered backwards, wheezing as he fought for breath. Eric stepped back, allowing him to recover.

When he did, Gabriel leapt at him with a roar. Eric stood his ground, fighting to hold his own as Gabriel unleashed a string of blows. His arm shook with each clash. He began to retreat, ducking and dodging, while making the occasional attack of his own. Several times Gabriel's blade snuck through, biting at Eric's flesh. Within minutes his arms and body stung from the kiss of Gabriel's sword.

Gabriel kept on, seeming to gain strength with every blow. Swearing, Eric fought on, his strength waning rapidly. His boots grew heavier, his weary legs unable to move with the same speed as earlier. He struggled to keep his blade moving, to jump from the path of Gabriel's blows. He all but gave up counterattacking.

His foe's grin widened with each swing. It seemed adrenaline now more than countered whatever fatigue he felt from his time adrift.

At least, even exhausted, Eric still moved faster than his opponent. He found himself studying Gabriel's movements, watching for the first clench of muscle or flicker in his eyes to reveal his next attack. Gabriel's bulk made him slow and his inexperience provided more than enough warning for Eric to avoid most of his blows.

Not all of them though, Eric winced as Gabriel's blade bounced from his own and smashed against his elbow. Arm numb, Eric backed away.

Sensing blood, Gabriel pressed the attack.

Eric swore, feet carrying him to safety as Gabriel's blade glanced from his shoulder. He lashed out to cover his retreat.

Gabriel knocked the blow aside, contempt on his face. "Not so tough without your magic, are you?" he mocked.

"Least I'm not a bumbling buffoon like you," Eric snapped back, pain driving his anger.

Gabriel only grinned, and struck again. Eric raised his sword but Gabriel knocked it aside, his shoulder driving into Eric's chest. The force of the collision knocked the wind from his lungs, sending Eric tumbling across the ground. The sword spun from his grip, landing a few feet from where he lay.

Gabriel laughed and raised his sword over Eric's head.

Dimly, Eric heard Caelin shouting something. His ears rang, making Caelin's voice seem distant and frail. He summoned the last of his strength and threw himself from the path of Gabriel's blade. A soft thud came from behind him as mud sprayed the air.

Gabriel wrenched his blade free of the earth and came after him. Eric gasped for breath, unable to summon the strength to move. The sword appeared overhead, already descending towards his head.

Eric raised an arm over his face in a feeble attempt to protect himself.

Metal shrieked on metal as another blade blocked the blow.

"Enough," Enala growled. "If you want a real contest, you'll fight me."

Enala studied Gabriel and Eric as they fought, wincing each time the heavy blades found flesh. Gabriel's bulk clearly gave him the edge, but both would have some nasty bruises come tomorrow. She herself was used to the harsh sting of practice blades; her parents had taught her from a young age how to fight. It was a pleasant change to see someone else suffering.

The two young men appeared almost equally incompetent, but she could see Gabriel slowly gaining the advantage. His strength and reach drove Eric backwards, and despite his speed, Enala could see Eric beginning to fade.

She could also see the rage masked behind Gabriel's eyes, that he would not stop should Eric fall. Moving away from Inken, she walked to the bundle of blades beside Caelin. Retrieving one, she crossed the field to where the fight was drawing to an end.

As Eric fell she leapt forward, her sword flicking out to catch Gabriel's blow. Her own anger caught light in her chest, rising from the depths of her pain. With everything they faced, how could these two still be fighting one another? A dark tide was sweeping towards them, and their only chance of survival was to stand together.

"Enough," she growled. "If you want a real contest, you'll fight me," it was all she could do to hold back her rage.

"What are you doing?" Gabriel snapped. "You know what he did!"

"I do – you don't. You don't have the whole story, so enough of this nonsense. If you had listened to anyone, you would know what truly happened. These people helped me, saved me. Some of them gave their lives for me. And the fight is not done yet. So if you want a piece of Eric, you'll have to go through me."

"Get out of my way, Enala. I don't want to hurt you."

Enala laughed and swiped out with her sword. The blade rapped across Gabriel's knuckles. He swore and dropped his weapon.

"Pick it up, and show me what you're made of."

Gabriel growled and swept up his blade. He made a few weak swings, clearly expecting the blows to knock the sword from Enala's hands. Enala swept them aside with contempt, and then slashed out with her own weapon. Gabriel yelped as it connected with his elbow. The sword slipped from his numb fingers.

"Pick it up," she nodded to the blade.

Five minutes later Gabriel sat on his knees, gasping for breath and cradling his right arm. Purple marks spotted his skin where bruises had already begun to swell. His sword lay discarded on the ground nearby. He looked up at Enala, hurt in his eyes.

Enala stared down, anger still boiling within. It raged against her restraint, screaming for her to teach Gabriel a lesson. He had almost killed Eric, almost struck him down while he lay unarmed and helpless. What good would that have done any of them? Inexperienced or not, Eric was the only Magicker their little company had left.

She grated her teeth, fingers clenched around the pommel of her sword. The blade trembled in her hand. Pressure swelled in her chest, her frustration bubbling within.

Then she took a deep breath, and it vanished.

Enala stood, panting softly. She felt a slight sheen of sweat on her forehead, but otherwise she showed little sign of exertion. Despite Gabriel's strength and her small size, the blacksmith had not been hard to tame. Gabriel might be brave, but his skill with a sword left a lot to be desired.

Turning, Enala walked back to where Caelin and Inken stood watching and tossed her blade back onto the pile.

"Who trained you to fight like that?" Caelin asked.

Enala shrugged. "My parents. They taught me how to fight when I was young," she glanced at them. "Perhaps they knew more about all this than they let on."

"Maybe," Caelin eyed her closely. "We have a few days here in Lon before the ship can set sail. If you're interested, I'm sure Inken or myself would be happy to have you as a sparring partner. The Gods know those two aren't up to it," he nodded to where Eric and Gabriel still sat nursing their bruises.

Eric laughed as he stood. "Agreed. Gabriel was bad enough," he held out his hand. "Thank you."

Enala shook her head. "No, thank you," she looked around. "Thank you all. I had no idea what you went through to find me. If not for you, I don't think I would be alive right now. That Balistor, he would have found me, one way or another. I am sorry for how I've acted," she stepped up and hugged Eric.

"You're welcome," Eric smiled back as they drew apart.

They turned at the sound of Gabriel climbing to his feet.

Enala's heart sank as he stared at her, his face twisted with emotion. He clenched his fists and closed his eyes. He opened his mouth to speak, and then closed it again. Spinning on his heel, he stalked from the field.

Enala glanced at the others. "I'll talk to him."

CHAPTER 6

Gabriel looked up as the door to his room opened. Before he could object, Enala slipped into the dormitory, eyes downcast. She clenched her fists, sucked in a breath, and then crossed to sit on the bunk opposite him.

Neither of them spoke. They sat quietly in the dark, the silence stretching out into an unbearable tension. Gabriel gritted his teeth, the bruises to his body and pride feeding his anger. He made to speak, and then thought better of it. With a stubborn grunt, he rolled over on the bed, turning his back to Enala.

"I'm sorry," he heard her whisper. "I lost my temper. There is so much happening here, Gabriel. So much to take in," her voice cracked.

Hearing the sorrow, the loneliness in her voice, Gabriel took a breath and turned back to her. "You betrayed me."

Anger flashed in Enala's eyes, burning away the tears. She took a deep, shuddering breath, and shook her head. "No, I was not betraying you. I was stopping you from doing something stupid, something you would regret."

Gabriel sat up on the bed, staring hard at Enala. "I would not regret killing him," he struggled to contain his anger. "It is all that has kept me going since I left Oaksville."

"Yes," Enala replied. "Hate is a strong force. But it is also an evil one – it has already driven you to make awful choices, to commit murder. Or do I need to remind you what you told me last night?"

Gabriel saw again the dying guard in Chole, choking in his own blood. He looked away, unable to face the fire in Enala's eyes. "No, you don't need to remind me," he took a breath and looked back. "But Eric is no innocent. He killed my family, you know this!"

"Do I? Do you? Have you given even a moment to consider everything may not have been as it seemed in Oaksville?"

"You mean that it was an accident?" he shook his head. "I don't believe it."

"Don't, or won't?" Enala asked.

Gabriel bared his teeth. "Both!" he snapped, and made to stand.

Enala was on her feet first. She shoved him backwards onto the bed, landing on top of him and pinning him flat. "You will listen to what I have to say!" she grated through clenched teeth. "Then you can go or stay, it is up to you."

Looking into her crystal blue eyes, Gabriel almost thought he saw their colour change, tainted red by the fire of her rage. He swallowed and nodded.

Enala's expression softened. She released him and retreated to her bunk. "I hope you will stay though, Gabriel," she sucked in a mouthful of air and blew out. "I need you."

Warmth flooded Gabriel's chest, filling him with an urge to go to her, to hold her tight. He pushed it down, determined to keep the anger in his voice. "Speak."

Hurt spread across Enala's face and her eyes hardened.

"Very well then," slowly, she began to repeat Eric's story, of the first emergence of his wild magic.

Gabriel listened in shock as Enala explained Eric had lost his own parents that first night, and had then spent almost two years in self-imposed banishment, haunting the back-roads of rural Plorsea. He struggled to block out Enala's words as she spoke of Eric's decision to begin a new life in the town of Oaksville, and her account of the slavers who had accosted him within an hour of entering the town.

He knew what was coming next, and try as he might, he heard the truth in Enala's words.

By the time Enala finished, Gabriel was quietly sobbing to himself, torn again by the loss of his parents, his fiancée's death.

Could it all have been an accident? He questioned himself. *Could this all have been for nothing?*

"Are you okay?" Enala whispered, reaching out a comforting hand.

"Leave me!" Gabriel batted away her arm. "Get out, leave me!"

Enala drew back, her eyes watering. She gave a curt nod and stood. Making her way to the door, she turned back at the last minute. "I'm sorry, Gabriel," she murmured.

Then she was gone.

ENALA TWIRLED the practice blade in her hands, taking measure of its weight. It was heavier than the weapon she'd used over the last couple of days, and much heavier than the real sword Caelin had presented her with earlier.

She smiled; its weight would be perfect for building a little more strength and speed into her strikes. Across from her, Inken grinned back.

The older woman moved to position herself in the centre of the practice field. Enala squared off against her, as she had for the last two days. So far they had kept to light sparring, but even then Enala had been hard pressed to hold her own. Inken's reputation as a bounty hunter was obviously hard earned. She provided a much better challenge than Gabriel, and today Inken promised there would be no holding back. It would provide a good distraction from Gabriel's continued absence.

"Try not to hurt each other too much," Caelin joked from nearby.

"Wouldn't dream of it," Enala replied.

Inken laughed. "Confident aren't we?" she motioned Enala forward. "Show me what you've got then."

Enala shifted her feet and leapt, swinging her blade low at Inken's elbow. Inken stepped back, bringing her own sword down to counter. Enala dodged to the side, reversing her swing to catch Inken's blade on her own. Steel rang as the two separated.

Inken brushed hair from her face. "Very good."

Without warning Inken struck out, her practice blade sweeping towards Enala's head. Heart pounding, Enala blocked high, wincing at the force of the blow. Then Inken's foot swept up to strike her in the chest. The kick sent Enala crashing to the ground.

Enala gasped but refused to stay down. She rolled backwards, coming to her feet in a single movement before Inken could follow up her attack.

"Dirty move," Enala commented.

"No such thing in a fight to the death," Inken replied.

They clashed again, blades ringing as they circled one another. Enala soon realised the truth of Inken's words. The bounty hunter treated her blade as just one tool in her arsenal– she was just as likely to lash out with hand or foot as she was her sword. This was a new brand of combat for Enala. Her parents had taught her to fight, but they had never taught her to fight dirty.

Fortunately for her, Enala was a quick learner. After half an hour she began to adjust to Inken's sudden attacks, learning how to avoid the fists and feet lashing at her. Finally, when she thought she might have a grasp of Inken's unorthodox style, she launched a counter of her own.

Ducking beneath Inken's swing, Enala lashed out with her foot, driving the bounty hunter backwards. Bringing up her sword, she feinted low. Inken's blade leapt to meet it, but Enala pulled back and spun on her heel, reversing her sword's cut. The blow bounced off Inken's shoulder.

Inken cursed, pulling back, but Enala did not cease her attack. She pressed on, her sword slashing in a series of brutal swipes. Several times her weapon came within a hair's breath of contact, but Inken was no longer playing around. Lines of concentration were etched across her face, her eyes coolly studying Enala's every movement. The air rang with the clash of metal.

Then Inken calmly swiped her blade aside and lurched forwards. Caught off-guard by the sudden counter, Enala walked straight into Inken's head-butt.

Pain lanced from her nose, forcing her back a step. She stumbled, tripping over her own feet and toppling to the ground.

Enala gasped, tasting blood on her tongue. Rage surged through her, a burning in her chest that screamed for vengeance. It built inside, heat spreading through her limbs until all she could see was red. Fists clenched, a low growl echoed from her throat. The sword hilt felt hot in her hand. The tension grew, building until it seemed she must explode.

"Okay, I think that's enough for today," Caelin interrupted, stepping between them.

Enala blinked, and the heat vanished. She looked up as Inken offered her a hand.

"Sorry about that, Enala. I got a little carried away."

Enala nodded, wiping her arm across her face. Blood ran from her nose. Wincing, she took Inken's hand.

Michael joined them and handed her a towel. "Here, this will help with the blood," he leaned in for a closer inspection, reaching up with gentle fingers to test it. "Doesn't look like she broke it. Just a little nose bleed. Keep your head down and don't worry about messing up the towel. It should stop shortly."

"Thank you, Michael," she glanced across at Eric. "Let that be a lesson to you, Eric. Never mess with your girlfriend."

Eric grinned back. "Don't worry, I figured that one out pretty quickly. Just last week she shot a Red Dragon through both eyes."

Enala blinked, unsure whether Eric was joking. Then again, after the fight she'd just had, she wouldn't put anything past the bounty hunter. The woman was tough.

"Eric," they all swung round at Gabriel's voice. Enala's heart sank. She had hardly seen him for two days, since she had tried to explain what Inken had told her. What he wanted now, she could only guess.

"Eric," Gabriel said again. "Could we speak? In private?"

Eric looked from Inken to Enala, and then back to Gabriel. He frowned, uncertainty on his face, and then nodded. Gabriel waved a hand at the dormitory and the two moved off towards the building.

"To be a fly on the wall for that conversation," Caelin muttered.

~

Gabriel's heart thudded in his chest as he led Eric across the field. His mouth felt dry, his tongue parched even though he'd just drunk water. His knees shook and a sick feeling twisted his stomach. He could hear Eric behind him, sense the young man's nerves as he followed Gabriel into the dormitory.

Closing his eyes, Gabriel struggled to summon his courage. *Who knew an apology could be so hard?*

He hadn't wanted to listen, hadn't wanted to believe what Eric had told him. But he could not ignore Enala, not after everything they'd been through. It had been her courage, her innocence that freed him from the demon's grip. If not for her, who knew what monster he would have become.

Even if she was too late, he thought. He looked at his hands, remembering the blood of the innocent man he had killed. *Who am I to judge, I am no better.*

He looked up at Eric, standing across the room from him. This was the one he had hunted all this time, had sworn vengeance on. Even now, a part of him wanted to lash out, to drive a sword through Eric's chest and watch the life drain from his eyes. As he had watched his fiancée's life drain away.

But he could not, not now.

He breathed out a long sigh. "I'm sorry," he whispered.

Eric blinked. "What?"

"Enala told me everything. About Oaksville, about your magic, about why it was unleashed. She told me everything you have done since, everything you and your friends did to help her."

"And you believed her?" Eric walked across and slumped onto one of the couches, a look of disbelief in his eyes.

Gabriel shrugged. "I must. Enala brought me back to the light, freed me from a demon's spell. I owe her. If she believes your story, so must I."

Eric closed his eyes, and then looked up to meet Gabriel's

stare. "I am truly sorry for your family, Gabriel. If I could go back…"

Gabriel raised his hand to silence him. A tremor ran through him as he fought down his grief, his anger. "I won't pretend this is easy. I won't pretend I can forgive you. But I am sorry for attacking you, for hunting you. And I should not have tried to kill you while we sparred," he took a deep, shuddering breath. "I don't know if I trust you, but I do know I am tired of hate and anger. So, let there be peace between us," he offered his hand.

Eric hesitated, staring at the offered hand. Gabriel could not blame his mistrust; in truth he had spent the last few days debating whether to offer Eric his hand, or a dagger. But he spoke the truth now; the hate must end. He could not live his life beneath the shadow of the past.

Finally Eric gave a cautious smile and took his hand. "Okay, truce it is."

A long silence stretched out. Gabriel coughed, struggling to find the words. Then he shrugged. "Well, shall we go practice with those swords?"

Eric laughed. "Don't think it'll be so easy this time. I'm ready for you now," he waved towards the door, clearly doing his best to hide his nerves.

Gabriel smiled as Eric opened the door and let in a fresh blast of icy air. Outside the sky had opened up, and rain now bucketed down, leaving water pooling across the grassy fields. The wind caught the door and threw it back against the wall before Eric could catch it. Thunder rumbled in the distance.

Inken and Enala had just walked up the steps and quickly ducked inside. Caelin still stood in the rain, arms folded, eyes catching theirs. He beckoned.

Gabriel's heart sank as he looked out at the rain. He stepped out the door, allowing the cool water to run down his face. His hair and clothes were instantly drenched.

Gabriel shivered as he followed Eric to where Caelin waited, already regretting his apology. Or at least the timing of it.

"Good luck," he heard Inken call from the doorway.

"Think I'll need it?" Eric shouted back over the rain.

"Most definitely," she called. Laughing, she and Enala disappeared into the house.

"That doesn't bode well," Eric observed, glancing at Gabriel.

When they reached Caelin, the sergeant wasted no time tossing them each a practice sword. "If you two are done making up, perhaps today you can learn to work together. It's time I showed you how a real swordsman fights," he waved a practice blade of his own. "Touch me if you can."

"What?" Gabriel asked.

In response Caelin leapt forward, sword sweeping out at Gabriel's weapon. The blow knocked the blade from his loose fingers and sent it tumbling. Gabriel flinched back as Caelin rapped him lightly on the arm.

"You will both work together to fight me. Let's see what the two of you can do," Caelin grinned.

Gabriel gritted his teeth, glancing at Eric as he retrieved his sword. Eric gave a quick nod and then looked back to Caelin. It seemed the young man was willing to test their fragile new trust.

Raising his sword, Eric edged sideways away from Gabriel. Realising Eric was trying to divide Caelin's attention, Gabriel moved in the opposite direction. Together they attempted to encircle their foe.

Caelin grinned. "Very good. Let's see just how fast you can move," he stepped forward, blade slicing towards Eric.

As Eric jumped back, Gabriel sprang to the attack. Eric's sword rose to block Caelin's blow as Gabriel stabbed out with his own weapon, aiming for Caelin's exposed back. Caelin's sword slid through Eric's guard and struck his arm, then the soldier was spinning on his heel, sword already raised to parry Gabriel's blow.

Gabriel's blade rang as their weapons met, then pain shot from his shoulder as Caelin's sword slid up to sting him.

Next thing Gabriel knew, he was toppling to the muddy ground, tripped by a blow from Caelin's foot. He swore as water soaked through his cloak and touched his skin. Shivering, he climbed back to his feet, mud dripping from his clothes. Eric moved to his side and shot him a glance.

"Together?" he whispered.

Gabriel nodded and they launched themselves at the sergeant. Eric's blade found only empty air, but the ring of steel and shock down Gabriel's arm told him his had at least connected. Reversing his weapon, he stabbed for Caelin's side, even as Eric struck again.

Caelin spun in place and Gabriel's thrust swept past. His fist swung out, connecting with Gabriel's head to send him reeling backwards. He kept his feet this time, but his vision spun and blurred around the edges. He backed away, shaking his head to clear it.

Across the muddy grass, Eric fought on, lashing out with wild swings at their wily foe. Caelin slipped past each attack like an eel through water, his sword licking out every so often to parry a blow which came too close. The grin he wore told them both he was enjoying this far too much.

Gabriel took a tighter grip of his sword and threw himself back into the battle, determined to wipe the smile off Caelin's face. They attacked together, swords flashing as the rain poured down around them. They swung at Caelin's face, his legs, his arms, anywhere they could.

Not once did their blades touch skin.

To his left Gabriel saw the frustration building on Eric's face. His own anger bubbled towards the surface. Then Eric lurched forward, blade raised high. Grinning Caelin moved to block, just as Eric dove forward, ducking beneath Caelin's attack and coming up within the sergeant's guard. He raised his sword to strike.

Caelin's knee rose up to smash Eric in the face. The younger man reared backwards, sword dropping from his limp fingers. He swayed, head lolling to either side, and then toppled to the ground.

~

ERIC'S VISION spun as Caelin's blow staggered him. Pain lanced through his head as he dropped to his knees. He swayed, a sudden weakness spreading down his body. He glanced up at Caelin, opened his mouth to speak.

Then darkness rose to swallow him.

But he was not alone there.

Eric shuddered as another presence slithered into his mind. The foreign touch sent a tremor down to the foundations of his consciousness. Shadowy fingers rose around his thoughts, dark claws slicing into him.

"Hello, Eric," *the voice sounded triumphant, ecstatic.*

Eric shivered. It knew his name. He could feel the dark tendrils digging deeper, searching out his secrets, seeking to claim them.

Eric shrank back, reaching out for… what? Memory escaped him, slipping through his fingers like water. How could he fight such a force?

The image of Enala mounted atop her dragon drifted through his thoughts.

"Ahhh, so that is her, the hunted one," dread sank deep into Eric's soul. It knew!

"Where are you taking her?"

Eric fought against the shadow's grip. Pain twisted its way through his being as the claws dug deeper. Slowly, visions of the coming journey slid from his conscious, and the outline of a ship began to take form.

Still he struggled, clinging to the slightest distraction, to a mystery within his conversation with Jurrien. Why had he spoken to the God? What had happened that night? Jurrien had come, stopped him, hated him.

For what?

Magic!

Lightning crackled as the spell broke, memory of his magic bubbling up within. Blue fire raced through his thoughts, lightning in the darkness. Gritting his teeth, he turned it on the intruder.

A blast of white light lit the confines of his mind. He heard a dark, angry cackle, and then silence resumed.

"Eric, are you okay? Caelin asked.

Eric cracked open his eyes, groaning as the light set his skull afire. Like a dream, memory of his internal battle quickly faded away, vanishing from his thoughts.

"What happened?"

Caelin offered a hand. "You pulled a bold move, but made the mistake of placing your head in range of my knee."

The contents of Eric's stomach threatened to come up as he took Caelin's hand. "What?" he mumbled.

Caelin placed a steadying hand on his shoulder. "While in a fight, it's almost always a terrible idea to lower your head. It makes a very tempting target."

Eric nodded, holding back another groan. His stomach swirled again but he fought it down. Mud soaked his clothes, and he wanted nothing more than to be dry again. Swallowing the nausea, he looked around for this sword. His legs shook when he tried to take a step.

Caelin laughed. "I think that's enough for today, you've

both taken quite the beating. Anymore and Inken might just kill me. Come on, let's get out of this rain."

They made their way to the dormitory and pushed open the wooden doors. As they crossed the threshold a wave of warm air swept over them. Eric closed his eyes in relief, already feeling halfway better. Looking inside he spotted Inken and Enala sitting on the couches in quiet conversation, each holding a steaming mug. A fire blazed in the hearth, casting a warm red glow across the lounge. The scent of roasting meat wafted over from somewhere deeper in the building.

Inken frowned when she saw Eric. She rose and made her way over. "That looks like a nasty bump."

Eric raised a hand to his forehead, wincing as his fingers brushed across the bruise. "Blame Caelin."

He grinned as Caelin shot him a glare.

The look Inken shot back was far worse. "Oh I will," she growled, taking Eric's shoulder. "For now though, let's find you some clean clothes."

"I can look after myself you know," Eric attempted to take his own weight and stumbled sideways into the wall. The room began to spin.

"Oh really?" Inken raised her eyebrow.

Eric fought back a laugh. "I guess you could help, just this once."

Inken smiled and took his arm again. Together they made it up the hall and into their bedroom, where he struggled into a clean set of clothes. When they returned to the living room they found everyone already seated and dry, each with a glass of the steaming red liquid.

"What are you drinking?" Eric asked.

"It's mulled wine," Enala answered. "Apparently somewhat of a Lonian specialty. Warms the stomach on cold winter days like this," she picked up an empty mug from the coffee table and poured more wine. "Here, try it."

Eric took the offered glass and sank onto the spare couch. As Inken joined him he took a sip of the wine. The rich red was coupled with the spice of cloves and cinnamon, and when he swallowed warmth flowed down his chest. He took another sip.

"I have some herbs that could help with the pain, Eric," Michael offered. "Or some ice might help," he tossed a bag across the room.

"Thanks, Michael," Eric placed the icy bag against his forehead. "The wine and ice will do for now."

He looked around the room at his friends. Michael and Caelin sat opposite him, while Gabriel had taken the seat beside Enala. Inken leaned into him and sipped from her own mug. They all looked worn out from the day's exertions. Through the clouded glass window behind Enala, he saw darkness had fallen outside. They would need to light the lamps soon.

"You must be the only one who won't be hurting tonight, Michael," Eric offered.

"Agreed," Enala groaned. "I'll be staying on Inken's good side from now on."

Inken laughed. "You did pretty well yourself. You almost had me a few times. Whoever trained you was very good."

"I don't know, I could have used a few more rounds myself," Caelin teased.

Gabriel scowled and muttered under his breath. Eric could only agree – they hadn't even come close to touching the sergeant.

"Don't worry, Caelin," there was ice in Inken's voice. "I wouldn't mind switching sparring partner's tomorrow."

Caelin didn't even have the good grace to look abashed. He shot Inken a grin, but Eric guessed it wouldn't last long tomorrow. If anyone could beat the wily soldier, it was Inken. If not in a fair fight, certainly in an unfair one.

"Do we know when the ship leaves yet?" Michael asked. "Has anyone heard from Jurrien or the priests? It's been a few days."

Caelin shook his head. "Silence. All they've said is to stay on the temple grounds. They don't want anyone to know we're here, in case Archon's servants get wind of us. The fewer who know about Enala, the better."

Eric looked around the room, a thought dancing just out of reach. The others turned to him, waiting for him to speak, but the memory eluded him. He shook his head, and immediately regretted the action as the pain returned.

"Makes sense," Gabriel continued Caelin's train of thought, then. "So, does anyone know what there is for dinner?"

Michael grinned. "Well, as luck would have it I used my time somewhat productively today. I rummaged around the priest's storage shed, and actually managed to find the ingredients to put together a decent meat pie. It should be ready right about now," he rose and made his way into the adjoining kitchen.

As he opened the copper stove door, steam billowed out and the aroma of roasting meat became overwhelming. The steam rolled into the lounge, rising to the ceiling where it began to dissipate. Caelin followed him into the kitchen and took out plates and cutlery. Before long they were each presented with large slices of meat pie. Thick gravy and chunks of mushrooms overflowed from the pastry onto the porcelain plates, mixing with the steamed vegetables.

"Another Lonian delicacy. Once upon a time the shepherds here began making use of their tougher leftover meats by baking it inside the pastry of a pie, along with various spices. Today they've become a staple here, and most just use regular meat. I learnt the recipe during my apprenticeship," Michael offered.

Eric's stomach growled. He couldn't even remember what he'd had for lunch, but it was well past time for a hot meal. He grabbed his knife and fork, glancing around to ensure everyone had a plate of their own.

As he raised the first chunk of meat and pastry to his mouth the front door burst open and crashed into the wall. Eric leapt from his seat, his food tumbling to the ground. Outside lightning flashed, casting strange shadows across the lounge. He saw Caelin fumbling for his sword, felt Inken rising beside him. He was reaching for his magic when he realised who had invaded the quiet of their gathering.

Jurrien strode into the room, his footsteps slow and measured, but his face alive with power. The door slammed shut behind him.

"The ship is ready," he announced. "You leave at dawn."

CHAPTER 7

Eric sat on the deck of the ship and watched the trees on the river bank slide past. Branches stretched out towards them, long limbs mirrored in the water beneath. But here the Hall river was wide and its current slow, leaving long yards between themselves and the banks. Below the oars rose and fell in quick succession, crewed by the mariners Jurrien had sent. With each heave the ship surged forward, carrying them up the river towards the distant lake city of Ardath.

Birds swooped past, chasing the insects which swarmed about the ship, biting wherever they found flesh. Eric slapped another and felt a satisfying squelch as the mosquito died. Flicking it over the side, he wished the birds well on their hunt.

The forest on either side of the river appeared dense, but he knew from their maps that the farmlands of Lonia lay just beyond the treeline. The farmers here cultivated the forest along the riverbanks to keep their cattle from the swift currents. The trees also served to keep the waters clean of the runoff from their livestock. They had travelled well into the

Lonian floodplains now, where pasture flourished and cows ran in great herds, but the river remained a deep, clear blue.

They had left Lon three days ago. On the first day the ship made its way across Jurrien's Inlet, and the following morning had started up the Hall river. Now they were drawing close to Sitton – the port city marking the halfway point along the river.

So far, their progress had felt unbearably slow, the minutes whittling away like hours. Restless nerves plagued Eric, and he knew the others were just as eager to reach the end of their quest. But Kalgan remained a distant prospect – first they must reach Sitton, then Ardath, before making their way on foot through the mountains into the nation of Trola. There, if all went to plan, they would find the Sword of Light.

The weak winds didn't help, but Jurrien had warned not to use magic to speed along their journey. Fellow Magickers could sense when someone released powerful magic, and they did not want to broadcast their passage to Archon's minions.

The boredom made matters worse. Other than some limited training with Caelin, they had little to do but sit and stew over the struggles to come. Eric rubbed a bruise on his leg, another of Caelin's lessons – to never stop moving in a fight. His whole body ached as though it had been put through a meat grinder, but at least his skills were finally improving. Caelin praised his speed and reflexes, but Eric had yet to develop the intuition needed for an actual sword fight.

Eric used the quiet to meditate, practicing his control and ability to draw on his power. He kept his magic suppressed, but he hoped the practice would still prove valuable.

He ran his fingers over the hilt of his sword. Its weight felt awkward on his belt, but he now wore it at all times. He felt a sense of pride, that he might be worthy of carrying Alastair's blade, the same weapon his mentor had wielded in the war against Archon. He hoped he might one day live up to that legacy.

"Still nursing your bruises?" Caelin joined Eric at the rails.

"Just a few," Eric gave a sour reply. "Actually, I was thinking how much more enjoyable sailing on a river is. No seasickness, no raging Gods, no vengeful castaways to collect."

Caelin laughed. "We're not there yet, although we'll sleep in Sitton tonight. We'll collect some supplies and enjoy some solid ground beneath our feet, then press on first thing in the morning."

"Thank the Gods, I'm going crazy on this ship," he glanced at the sun. Noon had long since passed and the days were steadily growing shorter with winter's approach. "Will we arrive before dark?"

"If all goes well."

Eric laughed. "And when does that ever happen?"

Nevertheless, a few hours later the evening sun found them pulling into the sleepy port of Sitton. Wooden docks stretched out into the river to greet them, empty but for a few barges and the odd fishing rig. The city spread out from the docks and up into the foothills of the river. The nearest buildings looked old and showed signs of wear, while the white roof tiles of those behind gleamed red in the dying sun.

Eric stretched his neck, taking in the city. It appeared to rise from the river itself, old stone walls hedging the waterfront revealing the settlement's violent past. Sitton had not been spared the wars which had once torn the land apart. But new buildings now rose above the old, spreading up the hill above the city. Great spires of marble and domes of shimmering metal stood amidst the stone houses, revealing the wealth of trade passing daily through Sitton.

Their ship drifted up to the docks where men waited with ropes to pull them closer. As they drew alongside their own sailors leapt across the gap and began helping those ashore. They tossed ropes to those remaining on the ship and pulled the vessel tight against the wharf. Eric could not help but be impressed by the speed with which they accomplished the task.

Inken joined him as he moved to where the sailors were lowering a plank down to the docks, allowing the less nimble passengers to disembark. She swung up onto the railings beside him. "Not going to jump?" she asked as she leapt to the wharf.

Eric raised an eyebrow, feeling no desire to take a spill into the river. Turning he strode along the deck and wandered across the plank, much to Inken's amusement.

"Sorry," she offered. "I just couldn't wait to be ashore. I've never spent so much time on the water. It almost makes me miss that damn white horse I bought back in Chole," Inken whispered in a conspirational tone.

Eric smiled. Earlier he'd had the same thought about his horse, Briar. It'd taken him a week to get used to riding, but he had almost enjoyed it after that. The ship might move faster, but it was boring, offering little to do but sleep and watch the riverbanks.

They followed Caelin down the dock. They knew which inn the crew would be staying in, but they had no desire to wait for the mariners to gather their gear. Fresh beds and dry land beckoned.

As they wound their way through the thin crowd of people around the docks, Inken tucked her arm under his. "It feels good to have solid ground beneath my feet again," she whispered in his ear. "I was going crazy, cramped up on that ship."

Eric waved away a fly and smiled. "Me too. I didn't realise Jurrien would be sending quite so many marines – I felt like a sardine packed in a barrel."

Inken squeezed his arm. "I miss you," she looked around. "I think they will be okay without us for an hour. The marines are right behind us. How about we go explore a little. It would be nice to have some time to ourselves while we're ashore."

Eric's hand drifted to the pommel of Alastair's blade as his eyes scanned the crowd. There was a calm air to the way people moved here, a peace missing from other towns and cities he'd visited. He nodded to Inken. "You know the way to the inn?"

"I heard the captain giving Caelin the directions. Now come on!" she tugged at his arm. Smiling, Eric allowed her to pull him into the crowd and into one of the side streets leading farther up the hill.

"Have you been here before?" Eric asked.

"No, but I've heard about the place. The temple here is said to be quite unique. Since the river marks the border between Lonia and Plorsea, the temple is dedicated to both Antonia and Jurrien."

Two storied buildings lined the street, but through the gaps overhead they made out the spire of a temple. Inken took his hand and they made their way towards it. The buildings closed in around them, growing larger as they climbed the hill. The dirt roads close to the port soon gave way to bricked streets, worn smooth by the passage of wagon wheels.

Eventually the afternoon crowds heading to and from the markets gave way as they entered into quieter streets. Eric wrapped his arm around Inken's waist and exhaled with relief. After spending two years in the wilderness, crowds still unnerved him. Even without the usual bustling rush of larger cities.

The temple surprised them when they finally stumbled across it. The overlapping walls of the surrounding buildings hid the towering spire as they drew near, forcing them to circle the spot where they guessed it must be. Knowing its general direction, they persisted until they reached the tiny street in which it hid.

The temple's sheer marble walls stretched across one side of the street, the rich stone streaked by faults of blue and green. Where the architects had found such a variety of marble, Eric could only guess. The spire stretched high into the sky, vines of ivy clinging from the enamels. As they approached a bell high in the tower started to ring. Its shrill clang echoed loudly in the street.

They made their way to the entrance, where the oaken gates stood open.

Inken glanced at Eric. "Do you think they know about Antonia? That she's gone?"

"I don't know. But either way, we better not say anything. We don't want to draw attention to ourselves."

Inken smiled, nodding to their swords and her bow. "We might be a little too well-armed for that. I'm not sure many citizens take a casual stroll to a temple with this sort of weaponry."

Eric glanced down at his own blade. "Would be nice if we didn't need them."

He felt Inken's hand on his head and looked up. "One day, Eric. Remember what we said, we will get through this. Don't lose sight of what we're fighting for, don't lose hope. We will finish this quest of Alastair's and find peace again. Then you can put up that sword, and live your own life."

Eric leaned across and kissed her. As their tongues met a shiver ran across his skin. His heart beat faster as he pulled her hard against him. Her fingers curled in his hair and he felt a pinch as she bit his lip. When they separated the taste of cinnamon lingered on his tongue.

"Are the two of you in the right place?" a man in sky blue robes asked, emerging from a doorway.

His face was lined and his eyes careworn, but he wore an amused smile. He carried a walking staff of oak, which he leaned on heavily as he approached them.

Inken's cheeks reddened and Eric felt his own grow warm. "Sorry, sir," he offered. "It's been a long and crowded ride up the river."

The priest waved a hand. "Not at all. We are used to couples passing through, and seeking some quiet with each other. We do not judge – that is not the way of the Gods," he smiled. "So what brings two young lovers to the Temple of the Earth and Sky."

"We heard it was the place to visit in Sitton," Inken offered. "Although we really just needed to get away from the rest of our company for a time."

"Understandable. I remember my youth all too well. Welcome, anyway. You will find all the peace you could want in the courtyard," he turned and waved for them to follow.

They made their way down a short corridor and back out into the lengthening shadows. There they found themselves in the midst of a tamed jungle. Vines grew up the walls and hung from dense trees. The last calls of the evening chorus faded away as they walked between the trees. The scent of azalea flowers and chamomile drifted in the air. Chimes hung from the branches, ringing in the afternoon breeze. Lanterns lined the marble walls, the strange flames within casting a flickering blue light beneath the trees, as though lightning flashed overhead.

The priest bowed and disappeared back through the doorway, leaving them alone in the strange courtyard.

Eric smiled, the glow of the lanterns bringing back memories of their night at the hot springs in Dragon Country. It could not have been much more than a week ago, but already it seemed a lifetime. The trials they'd suffered since had strengthened the bond between them more than he could ever have imagined.

"What life would you want to live, Inken, when this is finished?"

Inken lifted her bow off her shoulder and held it in her hands. "I don't know. This used to matter to me, this life on the road, the thrill of hunting down criminals, testing my skill against theirs. But I don't know any more, not after this, after doing something so much more meaningful. Now..." she shook her head, returning the bow to her shoulder. "I think it would be nice to try something new," she smiled, "maybe something less life threatening."

"Like fishing?"

Inken chuckled, nodding her head in amusement. "Like fishing."

They sat together in silence for a while, watching a red finch hop its way along a nearby branch to its nest in the tree trunk. Quiet settled over the courtyard like a mist, blocking out the world outside, the worries of tomorrow. They sat there, relishing the quiet, the chance just to be with each other. Eric felt his heart swell, fed by the warmth of Inken at his side, and knew he loved this girl more than anything else in this world.

He had finally found peace.

Somehow, he knew it could not last.

A dim rumble carried from outside. Dread swept through Eric, washing away the peace. The sound swelled, as though whatever caused it was growing larger.

Or coming closer.

The rumble erupted into a roar as the ground started to shake.

They leapt from the bench and stumbled as the tiles shifted beneath them. Eric clutched at Inken, desperate to keep his feet as the earthquake shook the world. The walls of the courtyard groaned, cracks racing through the marble. He glimpsed the spire through the treetops, swaying in the dying sunlight.

Eric could sense the magic in the quake, the power surging through the air, boiling the ground with a force unlike any he had felt before. He could almost touch it, almost taste its metallic tang.

This nightmare could have only one source.

Terrified, they held each other and waited for the world to end.

With a sound like air being sucked from the room, the shaking ceased. But the groans continued, the buildings around them straining beneath their own weight. The cracks in the walls widened, spreading around the courtyard.

The priest reappeared in the doorway. "You must get out of here, now. The temple, the tower, it won't survive another one."

Eric and Inken swept up their belongings and sprinted for the doorway. They ducked into the corridor after the priest, desperate to make the street outside. Dust trickled from the ceiling and tiny pebbles bounced onto the cobbled floor. A mosaic of spider webbed factures criss-crossed the walls. The old man moved quickly now, fear adding speed to his limp. The clack clacking of his staff echoed loudly in the dark corridor.

As they emerged into the street they were greeted by the blood red light of sunset. Eric turned to Inken. "It's him. Thomas, the demon, whatever it is. I could feel the magic in the air, like Antonia's, but *tainted,* dark."

"The demon?" Inken pressed her hand to his chest. They both remembered all too well what had happened the last time they'd met it. "It's here?"

Eric nodded, his hand clutched around his sword. "Yes, or close. That was no natural earthquake. Its power, it could only have been caused by God magic."

Inken knelt and strung her bow. "We have to find the others," straightening, she looked down the street.

Pandemonium had engulfed the city around them. People poured from the surrounding buildings, mingling on the road in horror and confusion. Nearby several buildings had collapsed, sending bricks tumbling into the street. Eric glimpsed an arm amidst the rubble and quickly looked away.

But there was no avoiding the chaos. Everywhere he looked, people stumbled through the broken bricks and mortar, dust coating their clothing as they pleaded for help. Others had already begun to pick their way through the debris, pulling survivors from the broken buildings.

Closing his eyes, Eric struggled to think. The desperate cries of the villagers assailed him, begging for help. Swallowing his guilt, he closed his heart to them. They could not stop to help these people; they had to find Enala, had to get her to safety. They did not have the power to stop the demon – with Antonia's power, only Jurrien stood a chance against it.

"The inn is this way," Inken started to pick her way through the rubble, glancing back at Eric.

Eric nodded and they began to run. His mind raced and the world seemed to slow. As they dodged through the wreckage, he glimpsed the horror on the faces of the villagers, the blood streaming down their faces, heard the boom as another building crumpled.

How did the demon find us? The question raced through his mind. Or was it just here by coincidence?

Either way, Enala was in grave danger. They had to find her, now.

Together they leapt over the broken bricks in the street and ducked beneath shattered walls. People ran in every direction, hindering their headlong rush through the city.

Another rumble came from the distance but they did not stop. Shoulders tensed with expectation, they ran on.

A sharp crack came from ahead. Eric glanced up and saw a wave rippling through the very earth, tearing the bricked road to pieces as it rolled towards them. The street rose up beneath them and tossed them from their feet. Nearby buildings seemed to crumble at the seams as the earth shook them to pieces.

A sharp crack came from behind them. Eric looked back in time to see the tower of the temple topple into the street. Metal shrieked on stone as the bell struck the ground. Dust billowed out in all directions, spilling into the surrounding streets.

Eric coughed, holding his shirt across his face. But the quake had passed, and he struggled to stand.

Dark laughter echoed from the crumpled buildings. Eric spun, eyes searching the clouds of dust, seeking the source. But the sound came from all around, chasing the people through the ruins of the city, bringing fresh terror to the populace.

Ice slid through Eric's veins. He looked across as Inken grabbed his hand.

"*Run!*"

CHAPTER 8

"I'm glad you came," Caelin slapped Michael's back as he joined him at the bar.

Michael grinned. "Didn't think you could handle all these young folk without me?" he slid a draft of ale across to the soldier with a laugh.

Caelin shook his head. He would never admit it, but there was some truth to Michael's words. "No, no, I just figured we would need a doctor around if I'm going to continue beating them every day."

Michael took a swig from his mug. "You're pressing them hard."

The mood turned sombre. "Ay, I am. Enala is tough, far tougher than I expected. And Eric has his magic. But we have seen ourselves that neither is always enough. They need to be prepared for anything. I won't always be there to protect them."

"You're a good man, Caelin. So long as we have men like you around to fight the good fight, men like me will continue to hope."

Caelin grimaced. "You sell yourself short, Michael. If not for your skill, Eric would have bled to death on that beach before Antonia had any hope of healing him. And it was your quick thinking that got us to Lon in the first place," he paused. "How are you, now… you know, with Antonia gone?"

Michael shrugged, face hidden in his mug. "I cannot believe she is gone, not for good. Once Jurrien destroys that demon, he will free her from the *Soul Blade* and restore her to life. I have faith things will work out."

Shaking his head, Caelin glanced at the older man. "I am glad we have you, Michael. For myself, I'm finding it harder and harder to hold out hope. Enala is strong, but can she truly wield the Sword? And without Antonia, will that even matter?" he swallowed another mouthful of the cool ale. "But as you say, we must have faith. Jurrien will come through."

"He will. And I am glad I came too. I don't know if I could have stayed in Lon, not knowing your fates. Thank you for convincing me."

Caelin gave him another slap on the back. "My pleasure," as he stood a rumble came from the floor.

Then the ground began to shake.

Caelin stumbled as cracks spread through the wooden floor boards. Struggling to keep his feet, he grabbed for the bar as Michael toppled from his stool. The other patrons screamed, lurching from their tables towards the doorway. Burning lanterns fell from their brackets and shattered on the floor.

Instinct screamed for Caelin to follow the townsfolk outside, but Gabriel and Enala were asleep upstairs. If the building went up in flames, they would be trapped, and their quest would all be for naught.

As the shaking subsided he turned to the nearest lantern,

where oily flames were already licking at the varnished wood. Pulling off his cloak he beat at the flames, attempting to smother them.

"Michael, get the others! We have to get out of this building," he cried.

Michael pulled himself to his feet and raced for the stairs.

The flames caught at Caelin's cloak and heat washed over his face. He tossed it to the ground, spinning in search of a better weapon against the fire. A whoosh came from across the room as the blaze raced up the curtains. Then the bartender was there, dousing it with a bucket of water.

Caelin looked across the counter and glimpsed a barrel of water sitting at the back. Grabbing a bucket from beside the door, he raced to join the bartender. Water hissed as it struck the flames. Steam and smoke billowed across the room, but within a few minutes they had the blaze under control.

Michael appeared at the top of the stairwell leading Gabriel and Enala. They carried a bag over each shoulder and their swords strapped at their waists. Each wore a grim expression of terror.

"This cannot be coincidence," Michael coughed through the smoke. "This has to be Earth magic. The demon has found us."

"How?" Gabriel asked. "No one but Jurrien and his priests knew we were travelling up the river. Could it not just have been an earthquake, no more than that?"

"Either way, we had better get out of this building," Enala observed. "I've never felt one like that, but we used to have earthquakes in Chole. There are usually aftershocks. Every so often buildings would collapse, so it's best to move outside while you have the chance."

Caelin nodded. "Okay, let's get out of here," he moved for the door. The innkeeper, satisfied his property was at least safe from the flames, had already fled.

Moving through the swinging doors, Caelin found the streets outside the inn empty. He looked around, surprised, and glimpsed the innkeeper disappearing round the corner at the top of the hill. The others followed him outside as he turned to look downhill towards the port.

He took a step backwards, fear sending a chill right down to his toes.

A dark forest now blocked the road, black trunks towering above the buildings. Vines wrapped around the trees and slivered like snakes through the branches. The grey leaves whistled with the wind, dagger-like twigs stretching out towards them. Thorns stabbed from every surface of the vegetation. Not a hint of life came from the dark forest.

Caelin saw the trees were marked by faces, their mouths open, twisted in pain. He watched as new vegetation sprang from the ground, the forest advancing towards them. He shuddered, dread gripping his very soul. There was no mistaking what they faced now.

The demon had arrived.

"We need to get to the ship," Michael whispered beside him.

"I know. That's in our way," he nodded towards the dark forest.

"Then we cut our way through," Gabriel insisted.

"No," Caelin glanced around, "nothing that goes in there is coming out alive."

"Can we go around then?"

"I doubt it," Enala's face had paled, but she remained resolute. "The demon cannot know exactly where we are, or we'd be dead already. It is just making sure we can't get to the river."

The rumbling came again, followed by a second quake. This time the earth itself rippled. The power of its movement knocked them from their feet. They crouched on the bricked road, eyes squeezed shut, and endured.

When the shaking stopped, little remained of the city around them. Fortunately, the buildings in this area of Sitton were made of wood, so most had collapsed inwards on themselves rather than toppling into the street. But flames were already taking light in the ruins, the smouldering remains of fireplaces and lanterns catching amidst the fresh kindling. Smoke drifted in the air.

Then the laughter began; a bleak, evil sound that sucked the hope from their souls and the strength from their limbs. It echoed around the city, bouncing from the ruins to encircle them.

"Come on, we have to try," Caelin fought against the laughter's pull, hauling himself to his feet.

The others stood with him.

"Where do we –?" the crackle of thunder interrupted Gabriel.

They turned together to look at the forest. A bolt of lightning fell from the sky, disappearing somewhere amidst the blackened trees and leaving a white streak in Caelin's vision. He stared, breath held, waiting.

"Eric?" Michael whispered.

The laughter chased them through the crumbling streets, haunting their footsteps like the ghosts of the past, driving them on. Eric felt a pain in his chest, an icy fist clenching hard around where the *Soul Blade* had pierced him. It grew stronger as they approached the inn.

When they turned the final corner they slammed to a halt, shocked to find a murky forest stretching across their path. Faces of terror stared out from the trunks of the trees, red eyes alive with pain. Thorny vines waved at them, reaching out, *alive*, searching for prey. The forest itself stood dead, no birds or animals in sight, a perverted mirror of the temple courtyard.

"The inn is on the other side, I think," Inken murmured. "What do we do?"

"Not far now," Eric whispered back, already moving, instinct taking over.

He reached out with his magic, summoning the power of a distant storm cloud. Thunder crashed and lightning flashed from the sky to strike his outstretched arm. A blue arc of energy took shape in his hand. With a scream of rage, he pointed it at the forest.

Blue fire leapt from his fingers, burning its way through the dark apparitions. A strange, eerie scream sounded as the lightning touched the trees. The red vanished from the haunted eyes as the electric glow bathed them, and the vines curled back to wither and die. In seconds he had burnt a path through the evil forest.

Eric grabbed Inken's hand. "Let's go!"

They sprinted down the path as the lightning continued to burn its way closer to the inn. Vines and branches reached for them, thorny fingers grasping at their hair and clothes. Inken drew her sword and struck back without breaking stride, wild swings keeping the dark limbs at bay. Seconds later they burst through the other side of the forest, into the last light of the dying sun.

Except burning buildings now lit the city streets. By their light they saw their four companions, eyes wide, mouths open in astonishment. Inken and Eric raced towards them, eager to put distance between themselves and the twisted trees.

"About time you two showed up," Caelin wore an anxious smile. "We were getting worried."

"Sorry, we didn't expect company here in Sitton. The demon is coming; we have to go. We can't fight it."

"Agreed," Caelin pointed behind them. "Think you can blast your way back out, Eric?"

Eric turned, cursing to see the path had already closed.

"Stay back," he moved closer to the forest, gathering more lightning to him. The air crackled as the power danced in his hands, raising hairs on his arms. Pointing his finger, he unleashed the pent up force. The trees of the forest again gave way, burnt to ash.

They moved quickly, shepparding Enala between them, Caelin bringing up the rear. They struck at the vines with their blades, ducking through the tangled assault. Only Michael was unarmed, although Eric had yet to draw his blade. Lightning crackled in his palm; that was all he needed.

Halfway through the trees, a scream came from behind Eric. He spun, hand raised to strike, but a vine shot from the thicket and wrapped itself about his wrist. He gasped as thorns bit deep into his skin. Before he could react the vine gave a jolt, and began to drag him towards the darkness beneath the trees. In horror he glimpsed one of the faces in the trees waiting for him, its eyes now warped with hunger, the dark mouth opening wide to reveal its twisted teeth.

He fought against the vine's pull, digging in his heels as he searched for help. But the others were also trapped, engulfed in a fury of whirling green. Two vines wrapped about Enala, dragging her towards the thicket as Inken struggled to cut herself free and reach the younger girl. Only Caelin held his own, his sword a far more dangerous viper than those assailing him.

Eric gritted his teeth. He could not use the lightning to aid his friends in fear of hurting them, but he could free himself. Blood gushed down his arm where the thorns pierced him and the gaping mouth was growing steadily closer, but he had no intention of feeding it. As another vine shot towards him, he closed his eyes and willed the lightning outwards. A flash of blue burned through his eyelids to the crash of thunder.

Opening his eyes, he found nothing but scorched earth and ash. Nodding in satisfaction, he drew Alastair's blade and leapt to Enala's aid. The sword flicked out, slicing through the vine holding her sword arm. Free again to swing her weapon, Enala cut away her other bindings and leapt back to the safety of the path. The others joined them, staring out at the writhing wall of vegetation.

"What now?" Michael shouted.

"Now, the game is over," a rasping voice came from the shadows.

A figure stepped into the light, black cloak billowing about him as the vines drew back. He held a sword clenched in one hand, a dark green glow seeping from the blade like blood. Beneath his cloak Eric glimpsed the pommel of a second sword. A pale hand reached up to pull back the hood, revealing the face of the old King Thomas. His demon black eyes stared across at them, their empty horror sending a chill to Eric's stomach.

Thomas, the demon, whatever he was now, began to laugh. "You did not think you could really escape, did you? That I would not find you? Archon's minions are everywhere, his dark tendrils seeping into the minds of your people. Without the Gods to protect you, there is nowhere in the Three Nations you can hide, *Enala*."

A chill swept through Eric as the demon spoke Enala's name. *How does he know her?* A memory rose, just out of reach, and then faded into the darkness.

Caelin stepped forward, waving them back. "Run, get Enala out of here. I will try to hold it," he turned to the demon. "You will not have her, *demon*."

The demon laughed, Thomas' face twisting beyond recognition. "You think you can stop me, *mortal*? You think I could not kill any one of you in an instant?" It twirled the *Soul Blade*. "I do not even need Antonia's magic, you are nothing before my power."

Caelin spat, waving his sword. "I hear you were a great fighter once, one who did not need to use magic as a crutch in his battles. Are you too much a coward to fight me?"

"A coward? No," the demon loomed over Caelin. "But I am no fool either. You will not distract me, mortal," he raised a hand and swung. An invisible force gripped Caelin by the shoulders and hurled him back into the others.

The laughter came again, curling around them, stealing their courage.

Eric stood against it, lightning crackling in his palm. "Leave now, demon."

The demon stared down at him. "So we meet again, Magicker. Your power was most exquisite. A shame I could not keep it," it's head twisted. "Perhaps this time," it disappeared with a blink.

Time stood still for Eric. He tried to move, to throw himself aside, but his feet seemed stuck, frozen in place. He knew what would come next, could almost feel the deathly touch of the *Soul Blade*. The breath whooshed from his lungs as he watched his companions, saw the horror on their faces.

Except Michael's. Somehow the doctor was already moving, his shoulder crashing into Eric, smashing him from his feet. Eric tumbled backwards, eyes locked on Michael's, his fear turning to dread.

Michael stared back, and smiled.

His eyes widened as the *Soul Blade* pierced his heart, but the smile did not falter. The black metal tore through his chest, the demon's cackle ringing from the trees. A gurgling cough came from the doctor's throat. Then the demon pulled back its blade, and sent Michael toppling to the ground beside him. Tears ran down Eric's cheeks as the light faded from his friend's eyes.

"*No!*" he turned on the demon, lightning surging through his body. Without thought, he unleashed it on the creature.

The bolt struck Thomas' body and hurled him backwards into the thicket. Eric climbed to his feet, energy crackling in his fists, but the demon had vanished.

Its voice echoed from all around. "Another foolish mortal," it whispered. "Giving away his life for yours. But then, what use is a priest without his God, I wonder? Perhaps he simply wished to join her," the cackle came again.

Anger surged within Eric. He made no effort to control it, feeling the power building inside him, the raw energies of his wild magic. Ruin had already come to this city; his magic could not make things worse now. The demon had to be stopped.

The magic rushed from him, summoning the elements of the Sky, binding them together in a conflagration of wind and hail and lightning.

The rage washed all thought from Eric's mind, leaving only the single, burning desire to destroy Archon's dark servant.

When the demon stepped back into the light, he unleashed his magic. The very air shook at its coming. With a crash it struck the demon, light flashing and wind gusting as it hurled the dark thing backwards. An explosion rang out, a blast of wind knocking them flat.

Eric rolled across the ground, struggling to force his magic back into its cage, to protect his comrades from its wrath. He braced himself against the wind, squinting through the dust. Smoke hung where the demon had stood.

The blast had blown Michael's body clear. He lay face down, unmoving, blood pooling around him.

The smoke began to clear, drifting away with the dying gusts of wind.

The soft cackle of the demon echoed through the forest.

CHAPTER 9

Inken nocked an arrow, spinning to search the woods for the laughter's source. A shiver ran through her soul, but she refused to bend. The bowstring twanged as she loosed into the smoke still drifting in the street. Before the arrow vanished she had already nocked another.

"Caelin, Gabriel, get Enala out of here!" she yelled.

She spared a glance for Michael, a lump catching in her throat as she took in the pool of blood surrounding him. He lay motionless, his bag discarded, medicines scattered across the broken road. She fought back tears; there would be time later to grieve. Or so she prayed.

Caelin grabbed Enala and they retreated down the burnt path. Eric stepped up beside Inken, lightning still crackling in his hands. The sight raised hackles on her neck – she doubted she'd ever become used to it. But just now Eric's magic offered their only chance of holding their own. They had learned in Malevolent Cove just how ineffective mortal weapons were against this foe.

Stones cracked as the demon stepped from the shadows, arms raised. Before they could react, the ground shook, throwing them from their feet. A crack split the earth, racing towards them, and Inken reached desperately for Eric's hand. But the fissure tore between them, ripping them apart, and she found only empty air.

Inken struggled to her feet, gripping her bow tight as the ground continued to shift. Across the chasm now separating them, she watched Eric fighting for his life, the deadly vines all around. Lightning flashed, but it no longer seemed so effective. The vines wrapped about his torso, thorns tearing into flesh.

Then there was no more time to think about Eric. The demon stood before her, sword raised, and it was all she could do throw herself backwards. The razor edged blade swept past her eyes, slicing through a stray wisp of hair. She already knew her sword was useless against this foe. She could only hope to distract it long enough for the others to get free.

"Why do you resist? You cannot hope to defeat me. Do you really think you can save her, that I would allow her to escape?" the demon waved a hand.

Inken risked a glance back. Lead settled in the pit of her stomach. The forest had already claimed her comrades, trapping their arms and legs in the thorny thicket. Blood ran down the dark tendrils, the monstrous tree trunks standing in wait, mouths stretched wide.

Tears brimmed in Inken's eyes as her strength evaporated. She sank to her knees and stared up at the demon, grief blurring her vision.

"Good girl. You know when you are finished. I will enjoy watching the girl die, after what her *dragon* did to me," the demon growled the last words.

"Pity the beast did not finish the job," a voice boomed from overhead.

Inken's heart surged as Jurrien plummeted from the sky,

energy crackling around him. Blue fire fell with him, it's almost tender touch burning through the black forest. Her companions regained their freedom as the vines holding them crumbled to nothing. They stood in a daze, staring at the Storm God, blood running from their limbs.

"You did not think you could fool me forever, did you *Thomas?*" the God growled, his voice crackling with power.

The demon king laughed. "Ah Jurrien, I was wondering when you would arrive. Late as usual, my old friend. Although I admit, I had been hoping to take care of our companions here before you arrived. I'm sure they will wait though."

"No, this ends here, *Thomas*. I should have guessed the magic had taken you long ago. I should have hunted you down then, put you out of your misery. But no longer," Jurrien pointed a finger. "Your suffering ends today, old friend."

The demon drew the second *Soul Blade* and waved it at Jurrien. "This one's for you, old man. Archon forged them himself," he held up the first blade, staring into its sickly green glow. "He was very pleased to see how well they worked. Your sister put up quite the fight."

Jurrien's face darkened. Inken backed away as the air crackled. A dull pain shot through her skull and her ears popped as the air pressure plummeted. Storm clouds took shape and began to circle Jurrien. Lightning lit the black clouds and wind howled through the trees. Inken braced herself against the tiny hurricane as the very earth shook with its power.

In the eye of the storm, Jurrien released his pent up fury, screaming as he threw out his hands. A ball of lightning gathered between them. Jurrien drew back an arm, and hurled it at his foe.

The demon was already moving, retreating into what

shelter remained of its dark forest. But Jurrien would not be deterred. He wrenched his hands apart and the ball exploded outwards. A rain of lightning tore apart the forest, burning the trees to dust. The dark powers of the earth retreated before the Storm God's rage.

Jurrien stalked into the smoking remains, the hurricane still swirling about him. His ice blue eyes searched the ruin, seeking the demon.

But his foe was not defeated yet. The earth beneath Jurrien tore open, revealing a vast gulf stretching down to a red glow far below. The God dropped several feet before the wind caught him and propelled him upwards.

Inken stumbled as the earth shook. With a roar the pit snapped closed, entombing Jurrien in solid rock.

Panic gripped Inken. Then a blue light pierced the broken cobbles, streaming up into the night. A bright flash forced her to look away. A groan came from the ground, then a boom. When she turned back a crater marked the street, and Jurrien now hovered several feet above the ground. A purple bruise marked his face, but he scowled down at the demon, undeterred.

The demon raised a sword in mock salute. "You are a wily foe. At least you put up more of a fight than your sister."

Vines burst from the street, ensnaring the God's legs. The demon leapt as they dragged Jurrien lower, the *Soul Blade* aimed for his chest. A spear of lightning materialised in Jurrien's hand, sweeping down to block the blow. Swinging it further, he burned himself free and spun in the air. Roaring in defiance, he hurled the spear at the demon.

Sparks erupted outwards as the spear struck home. The full power of the God's rage hurled the demon backwards, sending it bouncing across the rubble. Thunder rumbled as another spear of energy appeared in Jurrien's hand. As he hurled it the demon rolled, and the lightning scorched only bare earth.

Jurrien dropped to the ground, wind swirling in his frost white hair.

Inken turned and stumbled back towards her companions, thunder ringing in her ears. Together they retreated from the fight, the flashes of lightning crashing around them, the fallout from the battle coming dangerously close to killing them all.

Twenty feet further down the pockmarked road, they drew to a stop, hedged in by the last trees of the demon's forest. Eric drew Inken into an embrace before they faced the others. Despite the Storm God's efforts, the demon still seemed unstoppable. And its forest, decimated as it was, still surrounded them.

"What do we do?" Caelin shouted over the shriek of the battle.

"There's nothing we can do for him. This is his fight," Eric replied. "The lightning I control is nothing to that creature, only Jurrien seems to have the power to harm it."

"We have to get out of here," Gabriel spoke up, casting a nervous glance at the two titans. "Just in case things don't go our way."

"Can you burn another path?" Inken asked.

Eric shook his head. "I've already tried. The vines are growing resistant, and regenerating themselves faster than I can cut my way through. The demon does not want us going anywhere."

Inken hesitated, an idea coming to her. It was dangerous, but it might be their only way out. "What if we fly?" she asked.

Eric paled. "I've only tried that a couple of times since it went wrong in Lon. Jurrien warned me…"

"I think Jurrien has other things on his mind right now," Enala offered.

Inken eyed the Storm God. The battle had closed to weapons now, *Soul Blade* against Jurrien's spear of lightning. Jurrien looked hard pressed to hold the demon at bay, its dark blade coming closer and closer. Sweat dripped from his brow and Inken wondered how much energy the Storm God had already spent.

Eric ran a hand through his sweat-soaked hair. "Okay, maybe. Let me see," he closed his eyes, forehead creased in concentration.

The forest began to sway in the rising air currents. Then the roar of the wind arrived, drowning out the clashing blades. It tore at Inken's hair, flicking leaves and stones at their faces as a vortex gathered around them.

A shiver ran down Inken's neck as the pressure lifted her half a foot off the ground. Her arms windmilled, struggling to keep her upright, and her heart beat hard in her chest. But the wind pushed all around her, keeping her stable.

But there she stayed, hovering only two feet from the earth. A minute passed, then another. Sweat beaded Eric's forehead, until at last he released his breath and they dropped gently back to the ground. She looked at Eric, heart sinking.

"There's too many of us," his voice was a whisper. "I can't concentrate the wind enough to carry us all."

Inken closed her eyes, fighting back tears. She summoned the image of the temple courtyard, drawing strength from the few quiet moments they had stolen together. She knew what they had to do, but it took all her courage to speak the words. "Then you have to take her. You have to take Enala, and leave the rest of us behind. She's all that matters now."

"No," Inken did not miss the tremor in Eric's voice. "I won't leave you," he shook his head, looking around the circle. "Any of you."

Inken reached out and grasped his shoulders. She kissed him, and drew back. "You have too, Eric. You have to get her as far from here as possible."

"We can't just leave you here," Enala interrupted. "We can't abandon you!"

"You can, and you will," Caelin stepped in. "Inken's right, your life must be our priority. If you die, we are as good as dead anyway," he turned to Eric. "Do it, Eric."

Inken nodded. "You can do it, Eric. You must."

He looked into her eyes for a long moment. She saw the pain there, the uncertainty. But they both knew this was their only option. It had to be done. They could only pray Jurrien would emerge victorious.

Finally, Eric closed his eyes, forehead scrunched with lines of worry. "Okay. Come on, Enala. Let's see if this works."

Enala stepped up beside him and the wind gathered again. This time the currents did not buffer Inken or the others. They watched from without the whirling tempest as Enala's hair whipped in the air, the red lock caught beneath her ear.

Inken's eyes fixed on Eric's. His face grew grim and her own heart twisted with despair. She struggled to keep it from her face though, least Eric turn back. Instead she blew him a kiss.

This time it did not take long for Eric's magic to work. The two lifted from the ground, rising higher and higher into the air. Enala gripped Eric's hand, holding them together as they drifted over the forest towards the river.

Inken stretched up on her toes to watch them go. She raised a hand above her head in farewell, and saw Eric and Enala do the same. Then they were gone, vanishing over the distant rooftops, and all she felt was the pain of loss. Tears came unbidden to her eyes, but she fought them off.

She took a great, shuddering breath, struggling for composure.

Fists clenched, she turned to the others. "Now what?"

JURRIEN GRITTED his teeth and took a step back. Exhaustion crept through his soul and a dull ache throbbed in the muscles of his back. Blood ran down his arms and chest from a dozen small cuts. The kiss of the *Soul Blade* stung, sucking at his life force. Lightning crackled in his hand, the pain feeding his anger.

Thomas stood across from him, the same sly smile on his face. *It is not Thomas,* he reminded himself. The man who had been Thomas was long gone. Sadly, the old king's proficiency with the blade had not been lost with him. Jurrien would not win this battle of blades, but so far the demon had evaded each of his attacks.

"Take all the time you need, Jurrien. The *Soul Blade* will wait," again the soft cackle.

Jurrien scowled back, reaching deep for the strength he needed. He heard the silent cries of his people from all around, the pleading of the townsfolk suffering the wrath of this monster's magic.

"Are you ready to die, demon?" he growled.

Thomas swung the *Soul Blade* in a lazy ark and yawned. "I'll admit, Jurrien, I do enjoy the contest. Not many have held their own against me. Of all Archon's warriors, I am the greatest. His champion, as Alastair once was to me," he shook his head. "I am disappointed the old Magicker did not meet his end at my hand. Alastair deserved better than a death to one so low as Balistor."

Jurrien closed his eyes, the demon's words drowning in the sea of misery echoing from his people.

I cannot let my sister's magic be perverted like this, the thought spurred him on.

He launched himself at Thomas, lightning arcing from his arms.

Thomas threw himself to the side, and his magic burned a path deep into the cursed forest. The *Soul Blade* flashed out, striking for Jurrien's throat. He raised his spear, thunder crashing as the blades met. Then Thomas' foot rose to smash Jurrien in the chest, forcing him back. He brought his spear up to block the next blow, but still felt the lick of the cursed steel on his cheek.

Cold spread from the wound and Jurrien sensed another trickle of power sucked from his soul. This could not go on; his magic bleeding away drop by drop. He spun on his foot, summoning the wind to blast the demon. Thomas hurtled backwards through the air before a vine reached out to catch him.

Magic surged as Jurrien spun the currents into a vortex, attempting to launch Thomas into the sky, away from the source of his power. If he could pin him in the sky, the demon could not avoid a killing blow.

But more vines shot out and wrapped themselves about Thomas, pinning him to the earth. The ground beneath Jurrien split open once more, heat billowing up from the flames far below. He drew the wind back to himself and rose into the sky, feeling the whoosh of air as the crevice snapped shut below him

"Nice try, old friend," Thomas growled.

Jurrien threw a bolt of lightning in response. He was tired of talking to the creature wearing his friend's body.

Thomas vanished and Jurrien threw himself to the side, already familiar with the demon's trick. The hiss of the *Soul Blade* as it sliced past raised hackles on his neck, but his hands were already moving to strike back. He heard a satisfying crackle as his spear found flesh.

Twisting, he attacked again, but Thomas had already retreated out of range.

"You will pay for that," Thomas growled, anger twisting his face beyond all recognition. Even the voice had lost all resemblance to Thomas'. "I grow tired of this game, Jurrien. It is time it ended."

Jurrien shivered. The demon's cloak billowed out, growing until it seemed darkness itself clothed the fiend. The earth shook and Jurrien quickly summoned the wind to lift him to safety.

Before he could rise five feet, a vine tore from the dirt to wrap itself about his wrist. He growled as thorns bit deep into his mortal flesh. Before he could swing the spear another snatched at him, and another and another, as a mass of cruel tendrils blackened out the sky. He struggled within the thicket as the thorns tore through his defences.

Concentrating, he drew lightning from the air, magic flooding from his body. His skin crackled with energy, burning away the vines. Relief swept through Jurrien as they fell away like spent tinder.

Then fresh panic surged as he felt the piercing sting of their return. He opened his mouth to cry out, but a thorny tendril wrapped about his head, cutting off his scream.

Jurrien struggled to control his dread. The familiar magic of his sister surged around him, usually so soothing but tainted now by darkness. His own power coursed within, battling with the dark forces, drawing energy from the air itself to burn at his earthly entrapments. Yet his body remained imprisoned, the godly strength of the vines threatening to tear him apart.

But that was not how the demon wished for him to die.

"Do you see now, Jurrien? Do you see how weak you

really are; how much stronger your sister was? Gentle, sweet Antonia. Always the light-hearted one, the beacon of hope. But this power of hers, it can level cities. How she must suffer, locked away in the blade, knowing the death her magic now brings."

The demon appeared through the thicket, the darkness around it merging with the forest Antonia's magic had brought forth. The pale face looked up at him, blank eyes showing no hint of life.

"But your power, your power will be welcome too."

Jurrien wanted to curse the creature, but the vines choked the response from him. He reached again for his power, to summon all his strength and strike him down. With shock he found only a tiny pool remaining. The rest had withered, trickling away with each drop of his blood, spent in the battle to free himself. There was maybe enough for one last attack, but he knew now it would be futile.

"Relax, Jurrien, you must relax. It will not be so bad. You will have a blade all to yourself, see?" It held up a *Soul Blade*, the steel still black, empty. The demon grinned. "Now your sister, she fought it. The process did not go well for her."

Rage boiled up within Jurrien. He shrieked against the gag, teeth tearing at the vine. He tried to swing his arms, to kick out with his legs, anything to free himself. But his struggles were futile, the vines refusing to budge an inch. There was no escape this time, not for himself at least.

Closing his eyes, Jurrien opened his spirit mind and soared into the sky, seeking the fellowship. Elation rose in his soul as he saw Enala and Eric had already fled. Following the scent of Eric's magic, he found them racing across the farmlands to the south.

Jurrien reached out with his mind to Eric. *I am done, Eric. Do not turn back!*

His message sent, he turned back to the city. There he

found the others still trapped by the forest, helpless before the demon's magic. A shiver went through Jurrien's soul. They had given everything for this quest. He must give them a chance to run. He had magic left for that, at least.

Summoning the final reserves of his strength, Jurrien sent lightning rippling through the forest beside the company. Such an easy task, yet exhaustion swept through him as the last drop of his magic trickled away.

As the energy burnt its way through the nightmarish trees, Jurrien plummeted back to his body.

He gasped as pain exploded from his chest. A cool black tide swept into his body, seeking out his soul. In despair he reached for his magic, desperate to resist, but found only emptiness.

No! he screamed in the confines of his mind.

Then Jurrien slumped against the black blade piercing his heart.

And the Storm God's soul went screaming into the *Soul Blade.*

CHAPTER 10

"What do we do now?" Enala shouted over the howling wind.

"I don't know," Eric called back, fighting to keep the despair from his voice. Jurrien's final words rang in his mind. "We were meant to head for Ardath, but I don't think I can take us that far."

Eric could sense his pool of magic shrinking; keeping them airborne was sapping his strength at a shocking rate. But at least they were making good time. They had already travelled over a league upriver, although it was difficult to tell for sure in the darkness. The stars glittered overhead, but the half-moon failed to cast enough light to illuminate more than the dim reflection of water below. It was eerie, flying through the night, unable to see where they might end up. At least Eric could not tell how high they were; somehow that seemed to have kept his fear at bay.

"It may have been a trick," Enala suggested. He had told her of Jurrien's message.

Eric shook his head. "No, I don't think so. If it was the demon, it would have told us to turn back. No, Jurrien is gone," he closed his eyes, his heart twisting as he thought of Inken and the others. He should not have left them, should have found a way to save them all. But there was no turning back now. "We're on our own now."

"They may have escaped, Eric," there was strength in Enala's voice, enough to almost give him hope.

Tears spilt from Eric's eyes. Angrily he wiped them away. "I don't see how; if Jurrien could not even save himself."

How could you have left them? The question raced through his head, haunting him.

Clenching his fists, Eric forced it to the back of his mind. He had to focus, think of what to do next. They had to assume the demon now had Jurrien's magic. That meant it could wield the God powers of the Earth and Sky. No one could stand against such forces. Their only chance was to put as much distance between themselves and the demon as possible.

"If it has Jurrien's power, will it be able to fly now?" Enala asked.

A chill swept through Eric. "Maybe. Let's just pray it first has to learn how to use the Sky magic. That could be why it hasn't shown its face until now; it had to master Antonia's powers first."

Enala nodded. "That makes sense. But when it does, it will head this way. It knows we have to go to Kalgan; the Sword is there. Do you think we can outrun it, once it learns to wield the Sky magic?"

"No," Eric's power was still fading fast. The God magic would not have the same limitations. "In fact, I don't think I can carry us much further."

"How long can you last?"

"Maybe another hour, no more than that," Eric shrugged. "We won't get as far as Ardath."

He caught the glimpse of water away to their right and

altered course to keep with the river. So long as they followed it, they would eventually arrive in the lake city of Ardath, capital of Plorsea. But if the demon knew their plans, it would be on their trail within hours. Even without mastery of the Sky, intuition told Eric it would catch them long before they reached the city.

Eric coaxed a little more magic into the winds, driving them faster. Emotion swirled in his chest, fear and sorrow battling within. He closed his eyes, seeing again Michael's face as he pushed Eric from the path of the blade. The short smile of farewell. He had sacrificed himself to save Eric, and who knew whether the others had followed him.

I left them to die.

Eric glanced up at a squeeze from Enala's hand. "It was their choice, Eric. Whatever happens, we have to honour them, Michael and the others. We will make it to Kalgan, and turn the Sword against that demon and whatever other creatures Archon sends," Enala drew a deep, shuddering breath. "We will not let their deaths be in vain."

Tears blurred Eric's eyes again, but in the darkness he no longer cared. "Okay," he whispered, the winds whipping the word away.

"So do we go to Ardath?" Enala asked.

Eric swallowed, thinking hard. "No," he replied. "The demon must know we would head that way. If it can fly now, it would overtake us within hours."

"Then where? We have to get to Kalgan and the Sword, and Ardath guards the only passage through the mountains for leagues around. What other choice do we have?"

Frowning, Eric searched for an answer. A chill iced his heart as the answer came to him. There was another way to Kalgan, one that did not pass through the mountains. Antonia had shown him the way, in the vision of Alastair and Thomas fighting during Archon's war. There was a secret passage to Kalgan, one guarded by a creature which might prove more dangerous than the demon behind them.

"We must go to Chole," Eric whispered.

"What?" Enala shouted back, confusion sweeping across her face. "Chole is in the wrong direction!"

"Exactly. The demon will never guess to look for us there."

"But the Sword of Light is in Kalgan."

Eric nodded. "I know. But there is an ancient passage between the two cities, a magical path called The Way. Unfortunately, as far as I know, only two people have used it in the last five hundred years and lived."

Enala fell silent. Finally, she turned to him. "Who were they?"

"Alastair and Thomas."

Enala gave a grim nod. "Okay, we go to Chole."

Eric's sense of dread grew. Silently, he reached for the winds and directed them away from the river. The image of the skeleton's grin as it attacked Alastair appeared in his mind's eye. He fought down his fear, but in truth he did not hold out much hope for their new plan. His mentor had only survived through sheer luck. What chance did they have?

But then, they didn't stand a chance against the demon either.

Eric closed his eyes and sent a desperate prayer to whatever entity remained that Inken and the others had survived. Every inch of his being screamed for him to turn back, but he kept on, jaw locked, neck straining, hands clenched so hard his fingernails bit into his palms. There was no choice, they had to keep going.

They flew on for another hour, then a second as Eric strained every mile he could get from his magic. Below they caught glimpses of open farmland in the dim moonlight. Patches of forest flashed by, and the odd stream, but otherwise they saw little. They held each other close, shivering as the wind drew the heat from their bodies.

Eric felt his concentration waning with his fading strength. His eyes drooped, the chill creeping through his body. Finally he could go no further, and they drifted lower in the sky. With the trickle of magic remaining, he directed them towards the ground in a downwards spiral.

He could see no roads or buildings, only the gently rolling hills of northern Plorsea and a flock of sheep huddled together in the pasture. A few looked up at their approach, and then returned to their slumber. Apparently two humans falling from the sky did not bother them overly much.

Despite his best efforts, they were still moving too fast when they hit the ground. Their feet went out from under them, a final gust of wind sending them rolling across the dry grass. Eric bit back a curse as his shoulder struck a rock buried in the field. When they finally came to a stop, he was thankful just to be in one piece.

They lay there a while then, taking stock of their bruises and checking for broken bones. Eric took a deep breath, savouring the grassy scent of the field. Nearby several sheep finally climbed to their feet and trotted away, their angry grunts loud in the night's silence. Exhaustion washed through Eric's body as his muscles began to ache. The flight had pushed him too far; he had spent some of his own life-force to bolster his magic. Now he would suffer the after-effects.

"Are you okay?" Enala asked as she stood.

Eric took stock of his body, the twinging pain already spreading to his arms. Soon they would start to cramp and seize. Then the real pain would begin. If he was lucky he might still be able to move. Either way, they needed to find shelter before he was completely immobilised. He pushed himself to his feet, his injured shoulder shrieking in protest.

"For now. But we had better get out of the open. Who knows what's out here."

"Easier said than done. It's pitch black, we have no torches, and all I could see as we landed was farmland," she glanced at the stars. "From what I can tell, Chole is in that direction," she pointed to where he guessed was south.

"That's a start. We should probably avoid the roads anyway," he took a step down the hill. His leg crumpled as pain tore into his calf. He would have fallen if Enala had not caught him.

"I don't think you'll be going anywhere in this condition," Enala observed.

Eric ran a hand through his hair. "We don't have much choice; we need to find shelter."

Enala shook her head, forehead creased with worry. "I don't know much about magic, but you don't look good, Eric. You're pale as a ghost. And we're not going to get far in the dark anyway. It must be almost midnight," she looked around. "At least we seem to be on the leeward side of the hill here. There doesn't seem to be much wind."

"Where did you learn so much about the outdoors?" Eric glanced at the younger girl. Blond hair hung across her face and her copper lock had caught on her nose.

Enala made a face. "My parents, remember. They taught me how to survive."

"Okay, so what do we do? We didn't exactly have time to grab supplies before we left."

"No, and you're in no condition to go anywhere. It's going to be a rough night. But you rest, I'll see if I can find some wood for a fire."

"Is that a good idea? The demon might not be far behind."

"If it is, I don't think it'll need a fire to find us. But if our plan worked, it shouldn't be anywhere near us. We should be safe here, I hope."

Raising his hands in surrender, Eric sank back to the grass. "You win. But I lived in the wilderness too, remember. There are other things out here, dangerous creatures and people. A fire might attract them."

"Maybe, but there are others it will keep at bay," she laughed suddenly. "And I'm *cold*," the laughter overtook her then, her whole body shaking as she bent in two, hysterical tears running down her face.

Eric couldn't help but laugh himself; a painful, hopeless laughter rising up from the gulf inside him. Michael was dead, another friend lost to the darkness. And Jurrien had followed, the last God standing against Archon's power, and their companions had probably gone with him. They were alone, fleeing for their lives from a mad, unstoppable demon.

And here they were, worrying about thieves and the wildlife.

Finally the laughter subsided. Eric wiped his eyes, offering Enala a gentle pat on the back. "Okay, good plan. Let's at least be *warm*."

Enala took a deep breath, cooling her last bout of laughter, and straightened. She wore a small smile, reflecting the self-directed mirth. With a wink she made her way into the darkness and disappeared around the bend in the hill.

Lying back, Eric tried not to second guess the decision. Worry gnawed at his conscience; whatever Enala said, he should not have let her wander off alone. If she was lost…

"Okay, sleepyhead. We have fire."

Eric snapped awake, shocked he'd drifted off to sleep. The exhaustion had crept up on him, stealing him away the second he closed his eyes.

Enala sat across from him, smiling happily in the light of

the small fire. She held her hands out to the blaze, her grin growing. A pile of wood and kindling lay beside her.

Stretching, Eric tried to hide his surprise. "How did you light it?" he asked.

"It wasn't hard. An old trick I learned when I was young. If you're lucky, I'll show you one day. We were just fortunate I found a dead tree with plenty of firewood."

"Another time," Eric nodded. Holding his hands out to the flames, he let the warmth seep into his frozen joints. The cold had crept into his bones while he slept. A sharp pain lanced through his body as he moved. He tried to stifle a groan, and failed.

Enala moved across to sit beside him. "Are you okay?"

"Nothing a bit of sleep and food won't fix," he paused. "We don't have any food, do we?" His stomach rumbled.

"Afraid not. It was too dark to look properly; in the morning we might be able to find berries or something. Oh, and the firewood will probably only last an hour or so. Enjoy it while it lasts."

Eric groaned and lay back again, trying to rest his aching body. He closed his eyes, the light of the fire flickering across his eyelids. Its heat provided some scant comfort against the night's chill. At least the hill sheltered them from the cursed wind. He'd had more than enough after their flight.

Eric flinched when he felt Enala's body lie down next to him. Instinctively, he reached out an arm and drew her closer. It would be a long night; they would need each other's body heat to keep out the cold. They held each other close, silent, eyes closed, and listened to the chirping of the crickets and the crackle of the fire.

Before long Eric felt himself drifting back towards sleep. This time he made no effort to resist…

Eric's eyes shot open. He stared up at the stars, feeling the cold wash over him. He had no idea how long he had slept, but he sensed the fire was cold and dead. There was only Enala's warmth beside him now.

He frowned, exhaustion threatening to pull him back down into sleep. What had woken him? The growl of an animal? The wind? Or the muffled whisper of a footstep?

Fog clouded his mind, the lure of sleep reassuring him they were safe. But something had woken him. Groaning, he tore himself from the clutches of sleep and sat up.

The sound of movement came from nearby. Eric struggled to his feet, alert now but his aching body refusing to obey.

He looked up in time to see the club descend. He opened his mouth to cry out, then pain exploded through his skull, and he fell back into darkness.

"Go!" Inken screamed.

There was no time to stand there in shock. Just a moment before a bolt of lightning had erupted from thin air to dance amongst the forest in front of them. The rotten stench of burning meat and wood reached them as the trees burnt, clearing a path to safety. For a precious second Inken stood shocked, searching for Eric, expecting the young Magicker to drop from the sky.

Then, with a sick sense of dread, Inken realised this was Jurrien's final gift to them.

"Go!" Inken screamed again and sprang forward. She raced into the gap left by the lightning, not stopping to check if Gabriel or Caelin followed. They could not afford to hesitate now. The demon remained preoccupied with Jurrien, but that might not last long. They needed to get as far away as possible, while they still could.

As she ran, Inken glanced at the writhing mass

surrounding them. Already the blackened shoots were beginning to regenerate, shooting from the earth to chase them down the narrow alley. She picked up the pace. Fear bordering on panic drove her onwards, concern for her companions coming a distant second.

The path before them narrowed as the vines reached for them. But the end was close, the walls of a broken building beckoning through the unnatural forest.

They burst from the last of the trees, vines tearing at their skin as they made their escape. Inken lashed out with her blade to free herself and pressed on. Their respite would not last long, not if they remained in Sitton. Ahead the street sloped down towards the river. The ship was their only chance.

She glanced back to check on Gabriel and Caelin. They nodded back, their faces strained and haggard. Inken guessed hers did not look much better. They jogged down the street, dodging through the ruined buildings and rubble littering their path. Any faster and they would break an ankle in the darkness. If not for the burning buildings, their pace would have been even slower.

As they neared the waterfront, a flash of light lit the sky behind them. They looked back in time to see a blue glow erupt from where Jurrien and the demon had fought. A rumble of thunder followed, then a blast of wind struck them, forcing them to their knees.

As quickly as it had appeared, the conflagration vanished, and a deathly silence fell over the company. No one spoke. They knew what had just happened.

Jurrien, God of the Sky, was dead.

They were alone now, the only ones left to stand against the darkness.

Inken swallowed hard and picked up the pace. The ship could not be much further, but with every step she expected the laughter to begin anew, as the demon came for them. She glanced back over her shoulder, searching for the first sign of pursuit. She prayed to whatever force of good remaining that Eric and Enala were a long way from here by now.

A surge of relief swept through her as they turned a corner and found the river waiting for them. Their ship still bobbed on the water, alone now in the docks, the other vessels long since fled. The contingent of marines they'd left behind stood guard at the dock, faces grim. Terrified villagers packed the railings of their vessels, eyes glancing up at the city.

The marines parted as they approached, the captain offering Caelin a salute.

"Sir, everyone but your party is aboard. I don't know what's happening up there, but we took as many villagers on board as we could and then closed the dock," the man hesitated, eyes drifting up to where the light had appeared. "Where are the others?"

Caelin shook his head. "Dead or gone. There's no time to discuss things now. Get the ship ready to depart. We have to be gone five minutes ago."

"Already done, sir," the captain announced as they boarded. "Everybody hold on! Throw ropes, we're underway!"

Men leapt to obey the captain's command, as eager as anyone to leave the doomed city. Ropes were cut and oars shipped as they pushed off the dock. Minutes later the ship was surging up the river, the frantic beat of the oars driving them onwards at a rapid pace.

Inken could not tear her eyes from the broken city. Flames lit the shattered buildings and the thick smoke rising from the once beautiful city blacked out the stars. She could see little chance of survival for any soul remaining within its walls.

As the ship raced around the first bend in the river, the burning city slowly disappeared from view.

Closing her eyes, Inken let the first tears begin to fall.

THOMAS CLOSED HIS EYES, feeling the new power coursing through him. It twisted with the dark magic that now ruled his mortal body, joining with the green tendrils of Earth magic. This was a wild force, this Sky element, a power he had never wielded before. It fought him, surged against his will, fighting for freedom.

The demon inside grinned at the challenge. Antonia's power had come easily; as a mortal he had possessed Earth magic for decades. Yet the Sky was different: unwieldy, demanding, struggling for control. It would take time to master.

Ah, but when he did.

Thomas lifted his face to the sky, breathing in the destruction. His tongue darted out, tasting the ash of his conquest. Closing his eyes, he savoured the screams of the dying echoing up from the city. The destruction was almost complete. As was his mission.

He frowned then, sensing an absence. His quarry had escaped, the girl fleeing with the boy who wielded Sky magic of his own. And Jurrien had saved the others.

Shaking his head, Thomas dismissed them. The mortals were of no consequence. The other two though, he would hunt them to the ends of the earth.

He smiled. It would not come to that. No one remained to stand against Archon's magic now. The Three Nations lay open before his master's power. His taint would spread, and those who grew tired of the yoke of the Gods would rise up against their rulers. This time, there would be no resistance, no Gods to unite the people against his master's crusade.

And whispers of the two he hunted would spread. They could not go undetected for long. Word of their passage would soon reach the ears of Archon's servants.

But of course, he knew where they must go anyway. The kingdom of Trola lay far to the west. In its capital, the Sword of Light waited for its rightful wielder. The Sword was their only hope now, the only God power remaining to protect the Three Nations. They would claim it if they could.

Thomas grinned. But not if he claimed it first. He began to march through the ruins of Sitton, following the taint of magic the boy had left behind. It was already fading, and soon all sign of their passage would vanish. It did not matter. He would wait for them in Kalgan.

He glanced at the night's sky. The boy and Jurrien could fly. A useful skill, even if the dark magic already allowed him to travel faster than any mortal. He would need to discover the secret to their flight. With the strength of the Storm God's magic, he had no doubt he could outpace the boy.

Thomas laughed, basking in the power of the two *Soul Blades*. A surge of joy throbbed in his veins as he reached for Antonia's power. He felt the dim shriek of her soul as he tapped into its destructive force. A tremor raced out from him, buckling the earth in one final wave of destruction. With a roar and a whoosh of dust, the last of Sitton toppled to the ground.

Thomas walked from the ruin, into darkness.

CHAPTER 11

Enala wriggled on the hard floor, struggling to find a more comfortable position. The task was almost impossible with the wagon lurching through every pothole in the rutted road. The rope tying her hands behind her back also didn't help, or the dirty rag that had been shoved in her mouth. She winced as the wheels struck a rock, tossing her into the air. Canvas sides covered the rear of the wagon, leaving her blind to the world outside.

Eric lay across from her, unconscious. His breath was laboured and a purple bruise marked his forehead. Sweat beaded his brow, while grass stains covered his clothes. He groaned as the wagon bounced again, but still did not wake.

His warning call had woken her, but before she could even draw her sword rough hands had grabbed her and thrown her to the ground. There had been at least six, too many for her to fight alone. She had been overpowered in seconds, then stripped of her sword and dagger. Then they had then been lugged overland for hours in the darkness, finally arriving at a faint track where a wagon waited.

Sunlight had begun to seep through the canvas cloth

hours ago, and Eric still showed no sign of stirring. Enala pulled at her bonds again, hoping to stretch the rope enough to free herself. The coarse threads cut into her wrists, refusing to yield. It seemed their only hope was if Eric could regain the strength to summon his magic.

That's if he wakes at all, a cynical voice whispered in her head. She shook herself, forcing her mind to other thoughts. There had to be another way out.

The banging of the wagon wheels lessened as their pace slowed. When they drew to a stop she shifted herself to watch the flap at the back. She fixed a scowl on her face, wishing she wasn't gagged so she could curse whoever entered. Anger boiled up within, surging through her veins. Her heart thudded and pressure built in her chest, a white hot heat begging to be released.

Enala clenched her fists, fighting the anger. She could not afford to be reckless.

Stones rattled outside as boots approached the rear of the wagon. A shadow appeared against the canvas, then the flaps were drawn aside and a woman carrying a bucket pulled herself into sight. Her grey eyes surveyed them as she brushed short black hair from her face. She wore the long pants and leather jerkin of a man, both stained a deep black. A scar stretched from her jaw down to the collar of her shirt.

The woman paid no attention to Enala. Instead she hoisted the bucket with two hands and poured it over Eric, a wicked grin fixed on her freckled face.

"*Arghhh!*" Eric screamed and seemed to rise into the air. He gasped as he tripped over his bonds, tumbling face first to the floor. He shrieked again, the whites of his eyes showing as he looked around in panic.

"Good, you're awake," the woman ignored the string of curses which followed, "the chief wants to meet you."

She reached back and pulled the cover across. Sunlight

streamed in before a large man stepped up to block it out. Enala swallowed as he stepped into the wagon, already reassessing her first impression. The man wasn't large, he was huge; towering over them in the confined space. He had to bend just to stop his broad shoulders from touching the roof. Thick leather armour covered his barrel-like chest, painted black in a match of the woman's clothing. His hair had been pulled back in a ponytail, which draped over his shoulder and a matted beard covered his face. He wore a great two-handed sword strapped to his back.

His black eyes stared down at them. Enala shivered as they lingered on her, seeing the naked greed there, the black soul of a man used to having whatever he wanted.

"What have we here?" the man boomed. "I expected only the Magicker."

"They were together when we found them, Thaster. I thought you might like to talk to both."

The man nodded. He waved at Eric. "And he is secure?"

The woman grinned. "Absolutely. He used too much of his power anyway, he'll be no problem to control."

"Good, I don't want any trouble from him," the man turned back to them. "I am Thaster, chief of this Baronian tribe. You are my captives. If you are lucky, we will find some use for you. So long as you cooperate," his voice turned hard. "Or, if you do not, perhaps we will collect the bounty on your head, boy," he stared at Eric.

Groaning, Eric struggled to his feet. He spoke through gritted teeth. "Or perhaps you would like to let us go, before I burn all you own to ash."

Hope surged in Enala's chest. Had Eric recovered enough to save them?

Thaster only laughed. "Go ahead. Laurel here has taken care of that," he waved a hand at the woman with the bucket.

Enala's hope curdled in her stomach as Eric paled. "What have you done? Why can't I find my power?"

"Allow me to explain," Laurel stepped forward and grabbed Eric by the collar. Next second, her knife was at Eric's throat. With his arms tied behind his back, Eric could do nothing but stare into her eyes as she pressed the dagger harder. Blood began to trickle down his neck.

"I am a Magicker too," she growled. "One of very bad repute, you might say. Even if my powers come from the Light element. I sensed your magic earlier and tracked you down. Something told me it might be worth it. And now my magic will keep yours under check for as long as we care to have you as our guests. Understand?" she threw Eric to the floor.

Eric stared up, eyes boiling with hate. He gave a curt nod.

"Good," the woman shrugged. "Look on the bright side, boy. At least here you won't be burning any towns to the ground," she gave a dark cackle. "Or at least not the ones who are good to us."

Thaster folded his arms. "Then we have an understanding. The Magicker will be good. If you're lucky, I might just keep you around. A power like yours could prove very useful. If not, well, then we will enjoy the gold for your head," he turned to Enala and a dark terror filled her heart. "As for your friend, I'm sure there will be a place for another slave in our camp."

Just then, Enala would have given anything for her sword. The pleasure of driving the sharp blade through the man's stomach would be worth the beating. She struggled to keep the hate from her face, helpless as she was.

Thaster waved a hand. "I will leave you to your prisoners, Laurel. You can remove the girl's gag. Let me know if she has anything interesting to say," he turned and left the wagon, leaving them alone with the Magicker.

Laurel moved across and untied the gag from Enala's head. "There you go, my lady," she smirked. "How is that?"

Enala spat at her face, but she ducked out of range and grinned. "Feisty, I see," she sat on a crate at the rear of the wagon, ignoring Enala's dark glare. "So, what are your names?"

Enala clenched her mouth shut. Eric did the same. Laurel only lay back and crossed her legs. After a few minutes she cleared her throat. "I'm afraid we're going to be spending quite some time together, my friends. I can't very well go around calling you 'boy' and 'girl' now, can I?"

"Do what you like," Enala growled, her fury spreading. A ringing started in her ears, growing as the pressure built.

"Why should we make your life easier?" Eric snapped.

Laurel shrugged, up ending her bucket to use as a foot rest. "My life is easy whether you cooperate or not. But it's up to me whether I untie you, or let you spend the next three weeks trussed up like pigs," her knife appeared again. She tossed it casually into the air and caught it by the blade. "Either way, don't think there'll be any hope of escape," the knife flashed across the wagon, burying itself in one of the wooden supports holding up the canvas.

"My name is Eric," Enala turned in surprise as Eric grated out the words. "this is Kathryn. We don't want any trouble."

"Okay, Eric and Kathryn, it's nice to meet you," Laurel stood and moved across the wagon. Pulling her knife from the wood, she quickly cut their bonds. "Let it not be said I let a good deed go unrewarded. Make yourselves comfortable. We'll be travelling most of the day," as she spoke the carriage began to move again.

Enala rubbed her wrists, pain tingling the tips of her fingers as the blood returned. "Where are we going?"

"South," Laurel answered. "That's all you need to know. Thaster likes to keep his plans quiet, you understand," she spread her hands. "Where were the two of you going in such a hurry?"

Outside the rumble of the wheels told Enala they were picking up speed. "South," she answered. "That's all we can tell you, you understand."

Laurel laughed, a wheezing snort from her skinny nose. "Not like it matters now. Oh well, no doubt you'll tell us one day," she turned to Eric. "Now Eric, what about your powers? Where did you learn to use them? From what I hear, you caused quite a bit of carnage in Oaksville. But you seemed in control when I sensed you earlier."

"A friend taught me," Eric smirked. "Release my magic, and I'll show you just how well."

Laurel wagged her finger. "Now, now, we were getting along so well. Besides, you're in no condition for a fight. I can tell, remember?"

Eric shrugged and leaned back against a strut, his defiance spent. Enala refused to be deterred so easily. With Eric exhausted, it was up to her to get them out of this mess.

"So what makes a Magicker want to join a bunch of thugs like the Baronians?" she asked.

Laurel paused, her grey eyes catching Enala's gaze, searching for a motive behind the question. "A means to an end," she said at last. "I was never the priestly kind, but it was the Temple of the Light who found me when I was young and taught me to use my magic. The Baronians offered an escape, and a little more adventure."

Enala nodded, pleased with the new information. She thought she had recognised a Trolan tang to Laurel's accent. The Temples of the Light worshipped Darius, the God of

Trola. Or former God, since he had vanished over a hundred years ago. "I hardly think murder and theft were your only options for adventure."

Laurel's eyes flashed. "No, but they were the most profitable. Besides, I was bonded to the temple until I turned twenty-five. I would still have a year of service left had I not escaped. Here, I am free to come and go as I please. Here, I am valued."

"Free?" Enala raised an eyebrow. "You're saying Thaster would just let you leave tomorrow if you wished? You think he would let a power like yours walk out the door?" she laughed, her voice taking on a mocking tone. "Not that you exactly have a door. Is this what you call 'home'?"

Laurel's face darkened and her eyes took on a dangerous glint. She rose, towering over Enala, dagger still in hand. Enala made no effort to move. She met Laurel's glare with a smirk of her own.

"You should watch what you say around me," Laurel growled.

"Oh should I now? And what would Thaster say if you were to damage his new prizes?" she laughed. "You don't fool me, Laurel. You're no more free than either of us. Thaster is in charge here, and whatever Thaster wants, Thaster gets," she eyed Laurel. "You all bow to his will."

Laurel lurched forward, hands reaching out to jerk Enala to her feet. She pulled Enala close, face to face, the breath hissing between her teeth. Enala forced herself to remain still, even as the stench of Laurel's breath caught in her nose. She struggled to stop herself from gagging.

Finally, Laurel growled and grabbed Enala's wrists in hands of steel. She picked up the rope and bound her even tighter than before. Then she marched to the flap at the rear of the wagon.

"Tell Thaster I would like to speak with him," Enala

shouted as Laurel swung out of the moving wagon. She glimpsed the rutted trail through the gap as Laurel clambered around the side and made her way to the front of the wagon. Enala watched Laurel's silhouette through the canvas as she took a seat beside the driver.

She glanced at Eric. He raised an eyebrow. "Now what?" he asked.

Enala had no idea.

CAELIN STOOD at the bow of the ship, watching as they passed beyond the last bend in the river. Ahead, the great expanse of lake Ardath lay revealed. The vast body of water stretched out before them, rolling green hills rising up on all sides. The noon day sun shone high above, vanishing occasionally behind the white clouds racing across the sky. The wind howled, rolling in off the surrounding hills. In the distance, white cliffs rose from the blue waters of the lake. At the top towered the spires of Ardath, beckoning them closer.

The rigging creaked as the wind took hold in the sails, propelling them out onto the lake. A collective sigh of relief rose from the marines below as they shipped oars. Caelin closed his eyes, a lump catching in his throat. The same scene ran through his mind, again and again. Two days had passed and still Michael's face haunted him, staring up from the pool of blood, dead eyes accusing.

A groan rattled from Caelin's throat. "*Why?*" he whispered to the wind. "Why did you do it?"

The wind offered no answer, and the thoughts continued to chase him. Why had he been so selfish? Why had he convinced the doctor to come? His foolish desire for Michael's company in this insane quest had led his friend to his death. Guilt weighed on Caelin's soul. Tears filled his eyes, not for the first time since they had escaped Chole.

The refugees of Sitton packed the deck, staring out with expressions of awe and apprehension. The ship sped through the water, rocking gently as small waves lapped at the sides. Caelin shivered as a finger of cool air reached down his neck, raising goose bumps on his skin.

He looked up as Inken joined him at the railing. "We're almost there," she looked at him, her hazel eyes showing strength. "They'll be there, waiting for us."

Caelin stared into her eyes, and nodded. "I hope so."

He tried to keep the sorrow from his voice, but Inken was not easily fooled. "No one could have stopped it, Caelin," she closed her eyes. "But I will never forget him, could never thank him enough for saving Eric."

Caelin barely heard her words. "It is my fault," he croaked. "I convinced him to come, told him we needed him."

Inken fell silent, looking out across the choppy waters. "It was his choice," she said at last. "And no one else's. You may have given him a purpose, but it was Michael who decided to come," she closed her eyes. "It was Michael who decided to give his life for Eric's."

"I don't know," Inken's words rang within, trickling against the flow of self-destructive thoughts. He took a deep breath, his frustration coming to the fore. "I just don't know anymore. What is the point of any of this now? The Sword of Light will not be enough without Jurrien and Antonia. We cannot even hope to stop the demon without them, let alone Archon himself."

A strong hand grasped his shoulder and shook him. "Get a hold of yourself, Caelin," Inken snapped. He flinched back at the fire in her eyes. "No matter what, it is up to us to go on now. Michael gave his life for this fight. Jurrien's last act in this world was to save us. So we must take strength from their faith in us, in their belief that we could win this fight."

The courage in Inken's voice bolstered Caelin. He straightened and gave her a nod, pushing his self-pity down to the depths of his mind. Inken was right; they had to continue, had to find a way to win this battle.

He looked around and saw they were almost upon the city. Onlookers packed the docks at the bottom of the cliffs, staring out at the strange ship approaching. Their war galley had outpaced the other refugee ships from Sitton; they would be the first survivors to reach the capital.

The crowd on the docks clambered for a view as the ship pulled up to its mooring. The marines were the first ashore, bellowing orders for people to make room for the passengers to disembark while others secured the ship. They waited patiently on-board as the refugees unloaded first, happy for them to distract the crowd.

At last they walked down the plank to the wharf. They allowed the marines to guide them through the milling crowds, and then Caelin took the lead as they reached the marble staircase leading up to the city. Gabriel and Inken stayed close as he waved to their escort, telling them to return to the ship. He knew the way from here. The men looked relieved to see the back of them. Caelin could not blame them after all they had witnessed in Sitton.

Together the three of them began the long climb to the top. Caelin knew from experience there were over five hundred steps to the stairwell. It was an impressive feat of engineering; some of the steps had been cut from the cliffs themselves, while other parts led them through caves deep in the stone. It was a long climb, but the view from the top would reveal the wide expanse of water stretching out all around them.

The refugees of Sitton had left some time ahead of them,

but they still found themselves caught behind some of the slower climbers. Caelin did not mind the delay; when they reached the citadel it would be his duty to inform the king of the current state of affairs. He struggled to put the story together in his mind, but could not even begin to explain the deaths of Alastair and Balistor, never mind the murder of both Antonia and Jurrien. He had even lost Enala, the very reason King Fraser had sent him from the city in the first place.

They stopped to rest halfway up in a viewpoint carved from the cliff. Looking back towards the Hall river, Caelin saw that a host of smaller vessels now spotted the lake, making their way for Ardath. More citizens of Sitton come to seek refuge. He prayed the capital had the resources to cope with the sudden influx of people. Ardath was rich, but the island was small and could not support a large population.

When they finally reached the top they found the outer gates standing open, beckoning the last stragglers of their ship into the city. Caelin wiped sweat from his brow and made for the cool shade of the wall. Despite the winter winds, the midday sun still provided ample heat.

They walked beneath the granite walls which ringed the clifftops and entered the city. As they entered the square, Caelin looked around for a welcoming party. If Eric and Enala had made it this far, the king would surely know who the ship carried. His heart sank when he saw only city guards herding refugees down a side street. He saw no sign of the scarlet embroidered jackets of the councillors or their body-guards, nor the blue tunics of the royal family.

He caught Inken's eye and saw she shared his concern. Shrugging, he took point again, brushing off the city guards and heading up the road he knew led to the citadel.

As they made their way deeper into the city, Caelin felt his heart lighten. This had been his home since birth; he knew these streets, knew every marble mansion, every carefully crafted fountain. He knew the stories depicted in the murals decorating the walls, the tales they told of the creation of Ardath. This was the first of the cities Antonia had founded with her followers; to be a buffer between the bitter rivalry of Trola and Lonia. She had led her people into the waste that had been this no-man's land, destroyed by decades of war. Here they had watched the land flourish at her magic's touch.

Now Ardath sat on the crossroads of the main trading routes between the Three Nations, providing protection to travellers and collecting tax from the passing merchants. The city had grown rich off trade, and flourished.

Ahead the citadel loomed, the smooth marble walls glittering in the afternoon sunlight. Soldiers manned the battlements. They stared out over the lake, alert for the first sign of trouble. The Baronian raiders continued to grow bolder, especially since the fall of Oaksville. But the king would suffer no interference to the trading routes between Lonia and Trola.

The gates to the citadel stood barred when they arrived, the soldiers on guard moving to block their passage. They wore steel plated armour and helmets with the visors down, prepared for any attack. They each carried a steel-tipped spear and short swords strapped to their sides.

Caelin marched up and offered a salute. "Good morning, men. I am Caelin, sergeant of the Plorsean army. We have just arrived from Lonia, and have urgent news for the king."

At Caelin's words the foremost soldier raised his visor, revealing a well-trimmed beard and brown eyes. His face lit up with recognition. "Caelin? It's been weeks since anyone heard from you, where have you been?"

Caelin gave a quick smile. "Elton, my old friend. I have

been away on the king's business, business which I am afraid still continues. I must speak to King Fraser."

Elton nodded, hesitating a moment. "The king… has not been the most receptive to guests lately. You may find your presence is not so well received in the throne room," he paused, and then continued in a whisper. "The men say the stress has gotten to the king. He speaks to us less and less, and when he does it seems as though his mind carries a great burden."

Caelin rubbed his forehead. "I am afraid my news will only make matters worse then, but it must be given. May we pass?"

"Of course. But as I said, tread carefully, Caelin," he glanced at the other guards. "I won't be long. Do not let anyone else enter while I am gone," he turned to Caelin. "Sergeant, you and your friends can follow me. I will take you to the king."

The wheels of the gatehouse groaned as the portcullis rose ponderously into the air. The wooden gates swung open behind it.

Caelin felt a tingling run down his neck as Elton beckoned for them to follow. He shook his head, forcing down his nerves, and nodded to his friend.

"Lead on."

CHAPTER 12

Eric swallowed hard. The chief towered above them, arms crossed, his giant two-handed blade sticking up over one shoulder. His eyes burned with rage or amusement, there was no telling which with this man.

They stood before him, tiny but defiant. The wagons had stopped for the night an hour ago, but Laurel had only just appeared with the chief. Eric could see the amusement on her face, and he did not like the wicked twist to her grin. The man standing before them was not someone to trifle with – especially with Laurel suppressing his magic.

To make matters worse, he still had no idea what Enala was planning.

If she even had a plan.

"Well," Thaster growled. "Laurel said you wanted to speak, girl. So speak."

Enala lifted her head and looked him in the eye. "I do," she smiled, adding a sweet curl to her lips Eric had not once seen her wear.

He held his tongue, deciding it would be best to remain silent.

Thaster stepped closer. "And?"

Enala tilted her head and leaned in, the copper lock hanging across her eyes. "We have decided we will be good. It would be an honour to serve a man of your power."

The chief squinted down at her. Eric swallowed again. What was Enala playing at? This man would not be fooled so easily.

Eric jumped as the chief threw back his head and unleashed a booming laugh. The sounds sent a shiver of dread through Eric and he shrank back, reaching unconsciously for his magic but finding only a black wall stretching across his mind.

Thaster's mirth drew the attention of the Baronians nearby. He waved a hand for them to listen. "You hear that?" he cackled. "This lovely young girl would like to *cooperate* with me," he laughed again. "Says it would be an *honour*."

The other Baronians joined in with Thaster's laughter, and a crowd gathered round to watch them.

Beside him, Enala's face reddened. Her shoulders shook as she clenched her fists. Before anyone could react, she stepped across the space separating them from the chief. Her knee flashed up, striking Thaster squarely between the legs. As the giant of a man doubled over, she brought her elbow down on the back of his head. He went down like a log.

A second later Laurel had her arm around Enala's throat and a dagger at her side. "Don't move," she hissed.

It took a long minute for Thaster to regain his feet. When he stood his face had turned a beet red and purple veins bulged in his forehead. He looked down at Enala, the rage in his eyes terrifying to behold. He raised a fist above her head, ready to strike her down.

Enala made no move to avoid the blow. Instead, she laughed. "What a man! A girl knocks you low, and the best you can do is beat her while your lackey holds her still. What a leader!"

Thaster hesitated, eyes glancing at the crowd of Baronians. These were his people, his followers, but Eric guessed there must be those within these ranks who aspired to replace him. Enala had just shown them all Thaster's mortality, showed them he could be laid low by a mere girl. If he let things stand, the vultures would soon be circling.

"Why don't you show your people just how much of a man you *really* are, Thaster. I challenge you to a fight to the death. Give me my sword, and I'll show everyone here just how much of a man you are," she laughed again. "Unless you're afraid to fight a girl."

Thaster's face had progressed from red to a dark purple. His whole body trembled, his fist still hovering over Enala's head. It looked as though it was taking all his will not to beat her to death right there. The crowd held their breath, eyes fixed on their leader, waiting for him to react.

A long moment passed before he lowered his fist. He began to laugh again, softly at first, but it quickly grew to a roar. The other Baronians joined him, though some turned away, disappearing back into the crowd. Eric guessed they had much to ponder.

The noise buffeted them, and made Eric want to shrink away and hide, but beside him Enala stood strong, staring hard into Thaster's eyes.

Finally Thaster raised an arm and the laughter died. He met Enala's gaze. "Tomorrow, at midnight. That should give you some time to contemplate your fate. Laurel!" he snapped. "Take them to their wagon. Make sure they're well fed tomorrow, the girl will need all her strength," at that he began to cackle. With a wave of his hand he dismissed them, turning his back and disappearing into the crowd.

Laurel grasped them by the scruff of their shirts and pushed them away from the crowd.

"You just couldn't play nice, could you?" she growled in their ears.

Enala pursed her lips but did not reply. When they reached the wagon, Laurel all but threw them through the flap. Eric stumbled to the back and slumped against one of the struts. His heart thumped at a hundred miles an hour.

"What the hell were you thinking?" Laurel and Eric asked in unison.

Eric glanced at the older woman, then waved a hand.

Enala answered before either of them could repeat the question. "I acted. You may be happy trapped here, Laurel, but I won't be. I won't live a day longer than I have too with the likes of men like Thaster."

Laurel grabbed Enala's tunic and thrust her against the canvas wall. "Listen here, you little *fool.* That man is going to kill you tomorrow. You have no idea what you are up against. In battle he is more a force of nature than mortal man," she paused. "And he uses black magic."

"*What?*" Eric made to stand.

"Stop!" Laurel fixed him with a glare. "Don't say a word. I should not have told you that, but perhaps now you might be convinced to give up this folly," she shook her head and released Enala.

Enala glared up at her. "*Coward.* How could you serve such a man? Your magic comes from the *Light.* How could you allow it to be corrupted by the twisted wants of one who works with that perverted force?"

Laurel's hand snapped out. The slap of her hand striking Enala's cheek rang through the wagon. Eric winced. "Shut your mouth, girl. You'd better write a letter to your family, since you're never going to see them again," she glanced at Eric. "And good luck avoiding the hangman's noose now.

Thaster will deliver you straight to the authorities when we arrive in Chole. Gold is a much better investment than a troublesome Magicker," she shook her head. "Enjoy your sleep. Tomorrow will be a bumpy day, and likely your final one on earth. I'll be sure to bring you a fine last meal," with that she turned and left the wagon.

When she was gone, Eric looked at Enala. "Well? Care to elaborate?"

Enala stared at the canvas wall. She looked up at Eric's words, a blank look in her eyes, her mind clearly someplace else. She shook her head, slowly returning to reality.

"Actually, I was just trying to figure out the date. It's my birthday the day after tomorrow," she smiled. "So whatever happens, at least I'll get to see eighteen," then she laughed. "Maybe that will bring me some luck."

A chill swept through Eric at her words. A memory pricked at the back of his mind, something Alastair had once said to him. He stared into space, struggling to recall the words, but it lingered just out of reach.

Finally, he groaned and leaned his head back against the canvas wall. His thoughts turned to Inken, whether she still lived, where she might be. Her smile flickered in his mind, warming him. With a sigh, he closed his eyes.

It was a long time before either slept that night.

Inken stood before the gold embossed doors of the throne room, arms folded, foot tapping with impatience. Half an hour had already gone, and she was tired of waiting. Her nerves grew with the passage of each minute. She struggled to maintain a calm outward appearance. All she wanted to do was scream the question bouncing around in her head.

Where is Eric?

Caelin stood to her right, shoulders staunch and a blank expression on his face. She smiled, proud of the sergeant's strength. Despite his doubt and guilt, she knew he would not falter now. Whatever ghosts haunted him, they could rely on his courage to get them through.

To her left Gabriel stood with his hands in his pockets, looking uncomfortable amidst the riches of the citadel. He had said little since the events in Sitton and Inken was not sure what to make of him. Though his desire to find Enala was clear, there was a darkness in him, a haunted look to his face. And she still did not trust him after his attack on Eric.

Inken shook her head, her attention caught by a creak from the great doors. A crack appeared between them as the golden metal swung outward, revealing a manservant on the other side. He surveyed the waiting room before his gaze settled on the guard who had escorted them from the gates.

"The king will see your guests now, Elton. I hope it is important, the council is not in the best of moods," the man spoke in a haughty tone.

Elton nodded and turned to the three of them. "Time to tell your tale, Caelin," he waved for them to enter.

Inken followed Caelin through the doors into the chamber beyond. Guards stood to either side of the entrance, spears held at the vertical position. Inken took a deep breath as they made their way down the red carpet, trying to keep the strain from her face.

The walls of the throne room were made of wood rather than marble, and the rich red of the timber glowed against the flickering torches. Tapestries hung from the tall ceilings, each depicting a different time period from Plorsea's history. White glass windows ringed the room, their crystal panels looking out over the lake encircling the city.

A table stood on a raised platform at the end of the chamber, and a granite throne loomed behind it. Several men and women sat around the table, their quiet conversation buzzing about the room. Guards stood to attention in front of them, forming a human shield. Those at the table looked up as the company entered, and Inken got her first glance of the Plorsean King.

King Fraser wore a platinum crown and sat at the head of the table, but otherwise there was little to identify him as the most powerful man in Plorsea. His navy blue tunic with gold embossed buttons marked him as a member of the royal family, but others at the table wore the same blue – brothers and uncles who sat on the council. Grey streaked his hair and beard, both of which had been cropped short like the soldiers outside. She'd heard King Fraser served in the army when he was younger; apparently some of their customs had stuck. His dark brown eyes caught hers as they followed their approach.

"What is this we have here?" the king stood, his voice ringing out across the room. "Caelin, my champion, returned at last," open scorn laced his voice.

Caelin faltered midstride and Inken caught panic in his eyes. Then his face closed over and he continued his march towards the king. When he reached the ring of guards he sank to one knee.

"Aye, I have returned, my king, though my quest is not yet done," he tried to keep his tone neutral, but Inken caught the hint of defiance in his voice.

Inken grasped Gabriel's arm and led him to stand with Caelin. Together they knelt beside the sergeant.

"Ah, so you have not found the family I sent you to protect? Why, then, are you here? Where is Alastair?"

Caelin swallowed. "I am sorry, your majesty. The family are dead but for one girl. As is Alastair. He died protecting their last child, at the hand of one of our own, the traitor Balistor."

Whispers rushed around the room at Balistor's name. The king raised a hand, and silence fell. He walked around the table until he stood at the edge of the dais.

"Balistor was a traitor? Who are you to make such an accusation?"

Rage flashed across Caelin's face and then vanished. He continued in a calm tone. "I saw it with my own eyes, heard it from his own mouth. He slew Alastair, Antonia's champion, and then tried to kill the last descendent of Aria. If I had not stopped him, he would have succeeded."

The whispers grew to shouts. Some of the council stood, their chairs grating on the stone floor and banging to the ground. Glasses spilt across the wide table, and others cursed as wine dribbled onto their scarlet jackets. Though he had been a battle Magicker, Balistor had clearly been popular amongst the king's council.

King Fraser raised his hand again. This time silence did not fall until the guards thumped the butts of their spears on the stone floor.

"It sounds like you have quite the tale to tell, Caelin. Perhaps you could start at the beginning," his tone was calm, but Inken could not miss the warning in his voice. They were on thin ice; if the king did not like Caelin's story, who knew where they would end up.

Inken licked her lips, and kept quiet.

Caelin had paled, obviously surprised by the councillors' reaction. Nevertheless, he looked to the king and began to recite their story from the beginning, when he had met Alastair in Chole.

Ten minutes later, the room was silent as Caelin told of how Balistor had betrayed them. His voice shook with emotion when he described how he had confronted the traitor, and faced him with Alastair's blade.

When Caelin finished, no one spoke. They stared at him

with awe, a collection of fear and anger on the faces at the table. Inken could see some believed the story, but others were not so easily convinced. She looked to the king, trying to read the blank expression on the man's face. He alone held their fate in his hands.

"And where is Enala now?" the king asked, giving no hint of his verdict.

Caelin swallowed. "I am sorry, your majesty. My news grows worse. We were ambushed by the same demon in Sitton, where we had come ashore for supplies. We were separated from Enala, who was able to flee with Alastair's apprentice. We had hoped they might have arrived before us..." he looked around and found only blank expressions in response. "And... and worse still, the demon slew Jurrien in Sitton. We are alone in this fight now."

The room exploded, swallowing Caelin's final words in a cacophony of sound. Panic swept through the chamber and even the guards were caught up in its current. For a moment, it looked as though total chaos might break loose.

The king turned and walked to the meeting table. Drawing his greatsword, he raised it above his head and brought it down. A great crack ran through the throne room. He swung again, the metal blade slicing through the thick wood. On the third strike, the table folded in two, collapsing to the ground with a boom. The sound reverberated around the room, silencing the councillors.

"Silence!" Fraser roared, tossing his sword to the ground. He walked to the edge of the dais and sprang down to the red carpet. Caelin bowed his head as the king approached, and Inken quickly followed suit. Glancing at Gabriel, she nudged him to do the same.

"So what you are telling me, my champion, is that the last wielder of the Sword of Light is missing. That you yourself have witnessed the deaths of our beloved Goddess Antonia, and the Storm God Jurrien? These are evil tidings indeed you bring, ones so dark one might question the truth of your tale. Or the allegiance of the messenger."

Inken looked up, anger pushing her beyond caution. "He speaks the truth, your majesty. I witnessed all of it. As have others. The priests in Lon will verify everything we have said; they worked with Jurrien to send us here."

She glared at the king, refusing to drop her gaze. Their eyes locked, the silence stretching out, until at last Fraser waved a hand. "Well, we shall see then. I will send messengers to Lon, of course. And to whatever remains of Sitton. We will have the truth."

"You cannot allow our men to engage with that demon," Caelin spoke up. "It is beyond mortal might now, not unless we mount a host of Magickers against it," anger was written on Caelin's face now, masking the fear hidden just below the surface.

The king stared at Caelin. "You forget yourself, sergeant. Do not interrupt me. As for your advice, I do not need lecturing by a foot soldier in the business of magic. Now, what of the girl? Where has this companion of yours taken her, if not here?"

Caelin shrugged. "I do not know. We thought they would have arrived by now. I can only pray the demon has not found them. Either way, they fled using Sky magic, leaving no way to track them. But I believe if anyone can get Enala to the Sword, it is Eric."

The king nodded. "Very well. You have given us much to think about. Jurrien was here only a week ago, telling us of the peril faced by the Three Nations. We recalled our armies at his request; even now they are mustering at stationing points around the lake."

Caelin bowed his head. "That is welcome news, your majesty. Only the might of men is left now to protect us from Archon. We must march immediately for Fort Fall to reinforce the garrison, or the war will be lost before it begins."

Silence fell as Caelin's words echoed off the high ceilings. The councillors looked from one to another, open fear on their faces.

At last a woman stood. "There is wisdom in your words, Caelin, but we cannot act rashly. To do so would only be to play into Archon's hands. Marching north is but one option we have to discuss."

"*What?*" Gabriel snapped, raising his voice in protest. "That is the *only* option," he made to step forward, but Inken grasped his shoulder and pulled him back.

The king's guards advanced a step, hands on the pommels of their swords.

"Careful how you speak, boy," the king's voice was hard. "That is Katya, one of my most trusted councillors," he paused. "That was done once before, was it not? The armies of the Three Nations marched north to stand united at Fort Fall, to defend our people against Archon. And they were decimated. I will not so recklessly march my armies to the same fate," he looked to Caelin. "Thank you for bringing this news. I have not yet decided whether to believe your tale, but the priests in Lon will have the truth of it. For now, you may have your free run of the city, but the guards will not allow you to leave the outer walls," he waved a hand to dismiss them. "Elton will find room for you and your companions. You are dismissed."

CHAPTER 13

Enala tried to conceal the trembling in her legs as they walked through the Baronian camp. Around her the men and women stared, fear and pity in their eyes. A few might have shown a hint of awe, but it was quickly hidden when she turned their way, and left her wondering if it was just her imagination.

She gave a mental shake of her head. It didn't matter. These people were slaves to this life, trapped by the black garments they wore to represent their 'freedom.' They were blind to the poverty in which they lived, the pitiful state of their holy tents and wretched wagon village. Their tattered clothes would be useless in the winter, and she guessed many would not live to see the spring.

Enala refused to be trapped in their cycle of suffering. She would fight and win, or die.

Ahead the crowds parted, revealing a circle of brown grass lit by bonfires. The moon and stars hid behind dark clouds, the sky a blank canvas. They would fight by the light of the flames. Enala made a mental note to be wary; she could easily be blinded by their light.

Eric walked beside her, his face blank, unreadable. Enala rubbed her hands together to ward off the chill, still trying to hide her nerves. She could show no fear here. Thaster would feed on it, and he needed no extra advantage. Although in truth, her fear was more for Eric than herself. She held his life in her hands as well as her own. One stumble, and it would cost them both.

Laurel came behind, her boots scuffing on the hard ground. Enala could almost feel her anger, prickling at her back like needles. It hung over them like a blanket, suffocating. That at least she could shrug off. The Magicker meant nothing to her.

As they entered the ring, Enala turned to Eric and hugged him. She felt the trembling in his body, and knew hers must be shaking too. She hoped no one else could see it.

"Don't go dying on me," Eric whispered.

Enala struggled to hold back tears. "I won't," the words caught in her throat. She gave a quick nod and turned away. She had to focus. From behind her she heard the thud of Eric and Laurel's footsteps as they moved away.

She walked into the circle, eyes flicking around in search of her opponent. She did not have to look far.

Thaster came marching into the light, dust rising up behind him as his boots thumped the dry grass. The dust glistened in the firelight, casting it in red and orange, and it seemed a cloud of embers trailed in his wake. He held his greatsword in one hand, its five-foot blade reaching for her. The other hand he raised above his head, as though this fight had already been won. Which, Enala had to admit as she stared up at him, might be as good as true.

But she refused to be cowed. She flashed the brute a toothy grin, knowing she must look a madwoman. Reaching down, she drew the blade Laurel had given her earlier. She looked at the short sword in her hand, and couldn't help but feel foolish wielding such a tiny weapon against the monstrous blade held by Thaster. It was not her sword, but Eric's, the one that had passed to him from Alastair. But its weight felt good in her hand, its balance similar to her own weapon.

When Thaster saw her weapon, his laughter shook the circle, silencing the crowd. "Would you like a bigger toothpick, girl?" he mocked. "I will break that toy with my first swing."

Enala bit her tongue and gave a curt shake of her head. A bigger sword would take time to adjust too, time she did not have. She knew the quality of the blade she held, had heard the others speak of the man who once wielded it. Alastair was a legend, and she felt honoured to hold his sword. It would be foolish to switch now.

The chief looked down at her. "Very well then," he grinned and passed his blade to his left hand. "Just for you, I shall use my left hand tonight. Perhaps that will make a fair fight of this contest."

The crowd's laughter began again, but Enala blocked them out. She stared up at the giant, taking in the massive shoulders, the legs like tree trunks, the muscles bulging in his arms. He held the greatsword in one arm as though it weighed no more than a feather.

Then she began to chuckle herself, a memory of her father emerging through the fear. He had always been fond of the old proverb – *the bigger they are, the harder they fall.* Grinning, she looked up at Thaster, the thought giving her strength.

Gods, I hope you were right, dad, she grinned, crouching in a fighting stance, sword out before her. *Otherwise this will be my last birthday.*

Around them, the laughter of the crowd ceased. Even the chief looked unsettled by her sudden change. He stared at her, the surprise in his eyes turning to suspicion. He glanced at the blade in his left hand, and then shook his head.

Enala raised an eyebrow. "You can use your right if you like," if he was debating whether to switch hands again, she had definitely succeeded in unsettling him. But she knew with all those watching, such an act would be viewed as cowardly. Changing back now would undermine his position in the tribe, and worse, dent his own confidence.

"I don't need it," he growled, forcing a grin. "Let the fight begin!"

Roaring, he started towards her, feet thumping as he moved at an almost casual stroll. Yet his pace was deceptive, his long legs narrowing the gap between them in two steps. His blade lanced out, seeking her head.

Enala was faster. She only had one hope of prevailing – keep out of reach of Thaster's blade until its weight began to wear on him. With such a large weapon, Enala hoped it would not take long. Exhaustion would flood his muscles with acid and his arms would start to ach. Then she would strike.

But first she had to survive.

The greatsword swept through empty air as she darted towards the nearest bonfire. Placing it at her back, she spun in time to deflect a second blow. As their blades met sparks flew and a shock from the impact ran down her arm. Enala cried out, stumbling back a step, grasping desperately at the pommel of her sword to keep from dropping it.

Fortunately, the fire caught in Thaster's eyes as he moved in for the kill. He hesitated, squinting against the burning light, giving Enala time to dodge to the side. Again his blade descended on empty space.

Spinning, Enala saw Thaster struggling to find her, blinking as he tried to recover his night vision. Seeing an opportunity, she leapt forward, short sword stabbing for his side. Enala almost dropped the blade in surprise when it connected, tearing through his thick leather armour and piercing flesh. She had not really expected the blow to find its mark.

Thaster bellowed in pain and the crowd gasped. His right arm lashed out, his iron fist catching her on the shoulder and flinging her from her feet. Somehow she kept hold of her blade as it tore from his side.

Enala rolled as she landed, holding the bloody weapon out at a safe distance. Shaking off the blow, she stumbled to her feet, sword at the ready as she looked for her opponent.

Thaster charged across the ring, silent now, rage burning in his eyes and the greatsword held overhead. The wound did not seem to have slowed him at all, and Enala found herself shrinking before the strength of his anger. His blade whistled as he swung it with enough force to split her in two.

Enala side stepped the blow, and the blade thudded deep into the hard earth. As Thaster wrenched at the blade, Enala kicked out, catching him in the groin for the second time in two days.

The chief roared again, half-doubling over while still clutching his blade in one hand. Enala swung her short sword, and cursed as Thaster managed to wrench his greatsword up in time to block it. A bloody fist lashed out as she retreated from range. As it sliced past she hacked out with her sword. Her blade bit into his wrist, and the scent of blood quickly followed.

The chief cursed. She retreated a few steps, expecting him to lash out, but this time Thaster did not pursue her. He held his ground, glancing down to inspect the cut in his arm. When he looked up again, the anger in his eyes had cooled to a simmer, but she sensed the berserker rage still lurked just below the surface. He studied her, taking her in, reassessing his foe.

Enala swallowed. She did not like this change of events. Thaster had finally decided to take her seriously, that she might actually pose a threat to him. There would be no more reckless charges now.

"So you know how to fight," Thaster smiled. "Well, isn't that something."

Enala scowled back, showing a courage she did not feel. As least she had injured his right arm; there would be no switching sword hands now. She raised her blade and offered him a mock salute, hoping to reignite his reckless rage. Blood dripped from her sword to her arm, but she did not waste a second to wipe it off. She kept her eyes fixed on Thaster, daring him to attack.

Instead, Thaster dropped into a fighting crouch of his own and edged his way towards her. Enala shuffled sideways, searching for a better position, or at least to get her back to the flames again.

Thaster smiled and shifted direction to head her off, trapping her near the centre of the circle. Enala glared, catching the hint of a smile at the corner of his mouth.

Realising she could no longer wait for him to make a mistake, Enala swallowed caution and drove herself forward. Her sword flicked for Thaster's face. The chief leaned back, his own blade raised to deflect the blow. Enala did not pull back, allowing her momentum to carry her forward. She attacked again, knowing her proximity would make it difficult for Thaster to bring his long blade around. Her short sword had no such limitations.

The chief grunted as her blade stung his shoulder, but his sword came down to knock hers away before she could drive it deeper. Then his fist crashed into her face, driving Enala to her knees. Stars streaked across her vision, but she knew Thaster would not allow her time to regain her sight. Half-blind, Enala flung herself forward.

Her shoulder crashed into Thaster's knees. With her small size she almost bounced off, but so far below his centre of mass the blow still managed to knock him off balance. Thaster stumbled backwards, arms wind-milling. His blade came within an inch of her head as it swung wildly through the air.

Enala rolled backwards out of range and regained her feet. She held her blade out before her, wishing for just one opening to drive it through the chief's black heart.

They circled one another, wary now, each suffering from the blows they'd exchanged. Enala's head ached from the punches she'd taken. She prayed the blood trickling from Thaster's wounds would soon leave him too weak to fight. She looked him up and down, searching for sign of exhaustion, sure no man could lose so much blood and continue to fight.

Yet the chief still towered over her, showing no sign of his slowing.

His legs, Enala decided. *That should stop him.*

She danced sideways and then darted at him, sword lancing for his face. As he raised his blade to defend himself, Enala withdrew her feint and swung at his legs. To her shock, Thaster leapt and her sword sliced beneath his boots.

Leaping sideways, Enala struck again. This time Thaster caught the blow easily with his own blade.

"Nice try, *Kathryn*. Would you like to try that one last time?" Thaster laughed.

Enala gritted her teeth. "My name is Enala, you moron," remembering too late Eric had given her a false name.

Ignoring her slip, Enala launched herself at Thaster, blade slashing out like a viper, seeking the taste of flesh. Thaster skipped backwards, his great blade keeping her at bay with surprising ease. She struck high then low, stabbed straight, dodged to the side before launching an attack. Each time his steel rose to meet her.

At last she stepped back, panting hard, cursing herself a fool for using so much energy.

Thaster's eyes flashed. "My turn."

Enala looked up at his words, and barely managed to sidestep the first blow. Even then, his sword sliced through the fabric of her coat, the steel coming within inches of her skin. Thaster left her no room to counter. He reversed his sword as it swept past, raising it high to strike her down.

Throwing herself to the side, Enala heard the thunk as the greatsword bit the hard earth. Spinning, she raised her short sword to attack, and instead found herself deflecting the behemoth's next blow. Steel shrieked and a jolt ran through her arm. The force of the blow drove her back a step, but Thaster followed, the blows coming one after another now, leaving her no time to think. Instinct alone kept her alive.

With no chance to counter, Enala fought to defend herself, and barely managed that. Thaster had found another level of skill, as though he were pulling energy from thin air to use against her. He showed no sign of pain or exhaustion from wielding the greatsword, only strength, power.

How is this possible?

Enala remember Laurel's warning – that Thaster used black magic – and knew the answer.

Anger flared in her then; that this man would resort to using such a vile force against her. Rage fed energy to her tiring limbs, giving her the strength to turn aside his next blow. Then with a scream she kicked out the way Inken had taught her, seeking to drive him backwards.

With supernatural speed, Thaster's hand shot out and caught her boot. He grinned down at her, contempt in his eyes. Grunting, he lifted her above his head and hurled her across the circle.

Enala spun through the air, the sword slipping from her grasp. With a sudden thud she crashed to the ground. Air whooshed from her lungs, leaving her winded, gasping as dust billowed out around her. Pain shot through her body and she struggled to take a breath. She lay there for a minute, sure she must be dying, choking, waiting for Thaster's blade.

At last she managed to inhale. Oxygen flooded her lungs, feeding strength to her burning muscles. Tears of pain ran down her cheeks, but she wiped them away, angry at her weakness. She managed to get her knees beneath her before she looked up.

Thaster stood over her, a mocking grin on his lips. He held her sword in one hand, his greatsword in the other.

"Would you like your toothpick back, little girl?" he laughed.

Enala closed her eyes as the rage took light, boiling through her like wildfire. Hate rose to overwhelm her, a red hot energy that left no room for sanity. Her chest burned and power surged through her veins, rising up from somewhere deep within, until her whole body shook with it. A buzzing began in her ears as the pressure built, pressing against her skull, unrelenting.

A scream rose within her, beginning in her chest and shrieking up from her throat. As it split the air, Enala felt some barrier in her mind shatter.

She opened her eyes. A brilliant red light lit the circle, and for a second she thought someone had added fuel to the bonfires. Then she saw the sudden fear in Thaster's face, his panic as he looked around the circle, his mouth opening to cry out. Screams of terror came from around them. The Baronians started to edge away, some already turning to flee.

Finally Enala looked down and saw the flames. Fire

covered her body, leaping from her clothes, her arms, *everything*. It roared from her, tongues of flame taking light in the dry grass and racing out towards Thaster and the crowd. The chief did not even have the chance to run before they reached him.

His scream sent a shiver down Enala's spine. She watched as flames caught on his leggings, burning as they went. He turned and tried to run, but the fire danced all around him now. He had nowhere to go. In seconds it covered him, the inferno scorching through cloth, burning deep into his flesh.

Thaster screamed again, beating at the hungry flames, his movements already growing feeble. Enala tried to cover her ears, but flinched back from the fire dancing along her arms.

Panic took her, and she struggled backwards, fighting to escape the blaze, unable to understand where it had come from. Had Eric broken Laurel's hold on his magic? But she had heard no thunder, seen no lightning.

And why was she not burning with Thaster?

Then she heard the shrieks from the crowd. She looked up and saw the Baronians fleeing in panic. The blaze leapt among them, uncontrolled, wild, burning wherever it touched. Wagons turned to bonfires in the night as people stumbled amidst the ruin, desperate to escape. Thaster's struggles had already ceased; all that remained of the chief was a pile of ash amidst the flames.

Enala gaped, a slow dread spreading through her. She could think of only one impossible explanation – magic. Her own magic.

But how? She had never had power before, never even considered the possibility. How could this have happened?

Chaos swept through the Baronians. They fled, leaderless, defenceless against her wild magic. Ice ran down Enala's spine as she realised Eric was somewhere amongst them. She looked at her hands, searching within for a way to make it stop, to halt the destruction. Staring at the flames, she willed them to die, but she could not begin to contemplate how to control such a force.

Enala spun in a circle, but all she could see now was fire, racing out in all directions.

What have I done?

THE GLINT of red on the horizon alerted Eric to the arrival of dawn. He released a sigh of relief, looking down from his perch on the hill. Soon it would be safe to return, to search for Enala amidst the wreckage of the camp. Until now the dying flames had been the only light to see by.

He was still struggling to comprehend what he had witnessed. One moment Enala had knelt on the ground, at the mercy of the chief. The next she was alight, flames racing out to engulf her foe.

There had been no time to think, only run. Eric had sensed the surge of energy the second Enala's magic was released. Her magic crackled on the air, wild and out of control. He knew then what was about to happen. He remembered it all too well from his own past.

Magic always awakens on the anniversary of our births, Alastair's words rose from his memory.

Eric was already running by the time the flames reached the chief.

Knowing Laurel must also sense the magic, Eric wondered why she had not stopped Enala. But there was no time to ask questions. From behind he heard the first screams of the crowd. Their fear drove him on.

As one, the crowd turned and fled in his direction. Watching them, Eric reached for his own magic, sure Laurel would be too distracted to keep it suppressed now. His power rose within him, still weak, but enough for what he needed. He launched himself into the sky, beyond the reach of the firestorm below.

Now as the sun cleared the horizon, Eric saw the scorched patch of earth marking the Baronian campsite. He swallowed hard. Nothing remained of the wagons and tents. There was not a soul in sight; the Baronians either long gone or dead. No one, except for the pale figure of a girl lying at the centre of the conflagration.

Eric stood, eyes fixed on the girl. The winds whipped at his clothing, lifting him into the sky. It could only be Enala. He shot towards her, straining to make out details, searching for sign of movement, of life.

The earth cracked as he landed, his foot breaking through the hard crust of ash which had formed on the surface. He stumbled before righting himself, then made his way closer to Enala. As he approached, he glimpsed a sheen of metal and saw Alastair's sword still lying where Thaster had dropped it. Detouring, he retrieved the blade. Its weight felt reassuring in his hand.

When he turned back to Enala, he saw her chest rise and let out a long sigh.

"You're alive," he whispered.

Enala lifted her head from where she lay. Relief flooded her eyes as she saw him. Tears cut through the ash covering her face. She struggled to her feet, kicking at the ash piled up around her.

"Eric, you're alive!" she made as if to run to him, then froze.

Eric frowned. "What's wrong, are you okay?"

Enala's face went white and her eyes rolled in her head, as though searching for someone behind her. She opened her mouth, but no words came out.

"Enala?" Eric made to step towards her.

"That's quite close enough, Eric," Laurel's voice hissed from somewhere behind Enala. "One more step, and your little friend dies."

Eric froze, frantically searching the ashes for sign of the Magicker.

He heard Laurel laugh. "Does this help?"

Eric lurched back as Laurel materialised behind Enala. She held her dagger to Enala's throat, her other arm holding the younger girl tight. A sly grin spread across her face.

"Hello again, Eric, Enala. Did you miss me?"

CHAPTER 14

Gabriel raised his mug of ale. "To Michael," he said, his voice solemn.

Glass clinked as Inken and Caelin's joined him in the toast. "To Michael," they repeated.

Gabriel took a long swig, the cool liquid refreshing after the day they'd had. And truth be told, his nerves could use calming. If the ale could wash away the anxiety he'd experienced as Caelin spoke to the king, it would be no small miracle. He was surprised they'd avoided the execution block, let alone the dungeons.

It was mid-afternoon and the bar was almost empty, but when Inken suggested a drink after their appearance before the king, none of them had argued. A few other patrons sat at the bar while they huddled together at a table in the corner. A chandelier lit the room, the flickering light of the candles casting shadows across the walls.

"He was a good man," Inken added. "Braver than any of us, to come on such a journey without even a dagger to protect himself. But that was Michael: a healer, even if he did not have magic."

Caelin nodded, taking another swig. "Agreed. Sometimes I wish I had his courage. The world needs more men like him."

Gabriel raised an eyebrow. "Really? Right now I think what we need are fighters. How many men and women will it take to hold back Archon's armies?"

"Thousands," Caelin grunted. "But what happens afterwards; if we reduce our people to numbers and swords, if we praise a man's fighting ability above all else? Or a woman's," he added at a look from Inken. "Whatever happens, we need men like Michael: doctors and builders, farmers and fishermen. Men who do not rely on violence to make their way in the world. Men like me, we do not build. We can only give our lives to protect what we already have."

"Or we can change," Inken added.

Gabriel looked at his glass, remembering his days in the forge with his father. "What if we have already changed? Picked up a sword and turned our back on peace?" he paused. "I don't know if I could go back."

Caelin shrugged. "A worry for another day. As you say, the Three Nations need warriors now more than ever. But believe me, war will make you sick to your stomach. It is the worst of man's demons."

"That may be so," Gabriel looked up. "But it is necessary, for now at least. Plorsea cannot just stand by and wait for Archon to come."

"No, we can't," Inken agreed. "Whatever alternative the councillors are considering, it won't work. Only the magic of the God's was able to banish Archon last time. Now we only have the Sword of Light, if we are lucky. It will take every ounce of might the Three Nations can muster to fight him to a standstill."

"More," Caelin added grimly.

"No," Inken shook her head. "I have to believe it's possible, that if we all stand together we can match him. The Sword is powerful, and there are hundreds of Magickers in our lands to help combat Archon's magic. There has to be a chance."

"I wish I had your optimism, Inken," Gabriel gave a short smile. "What's your secret?"

Inken met his eyes. "I think I got it from Eric."

Gabriel scowled, fighting down the anger Eric's name still brought. He may have decided to let go of his hate and join them, but the act was easier said than done. He shook his head, forcing a smile. "I'm glad Enala has him then. They're going to need all the courage they can get."

Silence fell around the table as they nursed their drinks. When Caelin finally spoke again, there was frustration in his voice. "Elton did not lie; the king has changed," he shook his head. "How could he just dismiss us like that, after all we've done... after all *I've* done for him?"

Gabriel stared at the sergeant, surprised by the venom in the words. "What do you mean?"

Caelin rubbed his eyes. "I have served Fraser for years, long before I won the king's tournament. This is not the first quest I have undertaken for him," his eyes took on a haunted look. "He has always trusted me. Though I can't say an assignment has ever unravelled this badly."

"I do not know the man," Inken offered. "But his manner did not seem to match the tales told of him."

"No," Gabriel added. "From what we heard of the king in Oaksville, he was a kind man, not quick to anger."

"He's different, there's no doubting that," Caelin accepted. "But to all but accuse *me* of treachery? To suggest I could have killed one of our own?" his words drifted off into a growl.

Inken leaned across the table, eyes flashing a warning.

"Careful, Caelin," she warned. "We are being watched," she sat back in her seat and took another swallow of ale.

Caelin's eyes widened and Gabriel would have turned to look around the bar, had Inken's foot not connected with his shin.

"Don't, you'll give us away," the hunter fixed him with a glare. "The man at the bar, the one nearest to the bartender, he's been following us since the citadel. Someone is keeping tabs on us."

From the corner of his eye, Gabriel glanced a man in an indistinct green tunic and black leggings, with a sword strapped to his side. His eyes were in his drink, ignoring the other men at the bar. There was nothing to the way he sat suggesting he might be interested in the three patrons in the corner.

Caelin swore softly beneath his breath. "Damnit. If that's true, things are worse than I thought."

Inken shrugged, but Gabriel glimpsed the same concern reflected in her eyes. "It's what I expected, after our reception. They don't want us going anywhere…" she paused. "Or, perhaps they do not want us looking around too much."

"What do you mean?"

"What do I mean?" she looked around the table. "I mean things may not be all as they appear here in Ardath. Balistor was a trusted Magicker here, and he obviously had many friends on the council. Maybe they weren't all as shocked as they seemed when you told them of Balistor's betrayal. Maybe there are other traitors amidst the king's advisors," she took a breath. "Maybe they've turned the king."

The hairs on Gabriel's arms stood up. He watched as a tremor swept through Caelin. "No, that's not possible," the sergeant growled. "I know the man; he would never betray Plorsea. He loves his people."

"Even so, how else can we explain the way he greeted you, one of his most loyal soldiers?"

Caelin fell silent, his eyes haunted. Gabriel stared at him, struggling to find some words of comfort. "What about Katya?" he said at last. Caelin and Inken turned to stare. "She seemed pretty determined to prevent the army marching north. Could she be the traitor? From what the king said, she is one of his most trusted advisors. She could be steering him down the wrong path."

Inken frowned. "It's possible. No one is beyond suspicion; they could all be traitors for all we know."

"If they were, it would certainly explain the king's despair, listening to their dark whispers all day," Gabriel said in a hollow voice.

Caelin still had not looked up from his drink. "How do we figure out who is friend and who is foe?" his voice cracked. "You say Katya could be the traitor, but how do we know if she's not just incompetent? That she truly believes holding back from the Gap is the best strategy?"

"We don't," Inken replied. "We can't. All we can do is hope to convince them otherwise. If the king is truly uncorrupted, we at least have a chance of persuading him. Same with the other councillors, if they truly serve the interests of Plorsea."

"You want to go to the king again? To the councillors?" Gabriel shuddered, remembering the detached eyes of the council staring down at him. "Who are they anyway, the councillors? How did Katya become so close to the king?"

"They are the king's advisors, elected by the people of Ardath and other provinces. They are meant to offer innovation and differing opinions to the rulers of Plorsea. They also help to govern different parts of the nation: trade, agriculture, mining, even parts of the army. Katya has been a councillor for years, and is one of the few Fraser trusts absolutely. She commands the city's defence."

"Maybe that's why she wanted the army here, to bolster Ardath's protection against Archon?" Inken asked.

"It's possible," Caelin answered. "But it wouldn't make sense. The Plorsean army cannot stand against the armies Archon will muster. Alone, we would be overwhelmed."

"And if Trola and Lonia stand alone at Fort Fall, the battle there won't last long either," Inken added.

"Agreed," Caelin replied, sitting straighter in his seat. "So we had better hope your plan works, Inken. Our only chance is to get the council to see reason. I just pray there are more loyalists than traitors in their midst."

A silence fell around the table, as each realised there was no one left to pray too. "They might be gone, but we're still here," Gabriel swallowed. "Michael believed in us, believed we could win; it's up to us to prove his words true."

"Agreed," Inken and Caelin added in unison.

They raised their mugs again, offering one last toast to their fallen comrade.

"What about Enala and Eric?" Gabriel whispered after a moment's silence. "Where are they?"

Sadness crept into Inken's face with the mention of Eric, though she tried to hide it. Gabriel watched her swallow the lump in her throat. "We must have faith. I believe they're still alive. For whatever reason, they must have decided to carry on their quest alone. Eric will get Enala to the Sword. It's up to us to keep the Three Nations together long enough for it to matter."

"Agreed," Caelin whispered.

"Agreed," Gabriel repeated.

~

"Don't worry about your magic, either of you," Laurel growled. "This time I've got you *both* nicely under wraps," she bared her teeth, pressing the dagger hard against Enala's throat. "Who knew this one was a latent Magicker? Certainly not Thaster!" she laughed.

Eric wiped ash from his tunic, fighting to remain calm. "What do you want from us, Laurel?"

"Not much," she shrugged. "Just the bounty on your head, Eric."

Ice wrapped around Eric's heart and he struggled to keep the fear from his face. "You don't ask for much, do you?"

Laurel grasped Enala's hair and pulled back her head. The dagger sliced a shallow cut across Enala's throat. Blood trickled down her neck. "I don't really need her alive, you know. Now throw down your sword, Eric."

Hands shaking, Eric tossed Alastair's sword to the ground. Quick as a Raptor, Laurel threw Enala aside and scooped up the blade. She held it out before her, warning Eric to come no closer. He held his hands up in surrender.

"Excellent, there you go. I knew you could listen," she waved Alastair's sword at them. "Well, Chole is about one day in that direction. I suggest you start walking," she swiped the sword for emphasis.

Enala fell in beside Eric as they began to march in the direction Laurel indicated. The Baronian's footsteps followed close behind them.

"Be good, and maybe I'll let Enala live when we reach Chole," Laurel laughed.

Eric's mind raced, searching for a solution. They had come so far; he could not believe their escape could fail at this last hurdle. Yet now they found themselves unarmed and powerless against the Magicker; with the sword at her side and Eric's own blade, Laurel held all the cards.

He shot a glance sideways and saw Enala looking back at

him. Blood still seeped from the wound at her throat, turning her shirt to a red mess, but there was defiance in her eyes. He smiled back. After what Enala had accomplished last night, he would not want to be the one left standing between the girl and freedom.

They just needed the right opportunity.

ERIC SLUMPED to the grass with a groan. The volcanic peaks of Chole were just peaking above the rolling hills, towering on the distant horizon. But with night setting they could go no further. So close to the desert, who knew what lurked in the darkness. Especially now, with Antonia gone.

Beside him Enala sat with slightly more grace. Laurel had pushed them hard and with no food, they were close to breaking. Eric's legs trembled and a sharp pain pricked his spine. He lay back, inhaling a deep breath to fight the ache.

"Anyone would think you two weren't used to walking," Laurel smirked, crouching down beside them.

"Maybe it's the lack of food and water," Enala snapped back.

Laurel laughed and pulled a water skin from her belt. She tossed it down between them. "There you are, drink up," she sat nearby, casting her eye over them. "I'll admit, the two of you interest me. For starters, why give Enala a fake name?"

Enala glared back, lips shut tight. Eric answered in her stead. "Why do you care? You'll be done with us come tomorrow."

"True, true," Laurel grinned, "but still I've been wondering. Maybe there's a bounty on your head too, Enala?"

"Wouldn't you like to know," Enala grated.

Laurel sighed. "I thought we'd gotten past this. After all,

we don't want to take the hard route, do we?" her dagger slid from its sheath, glittering in the last rays of the dying sun.

Eric gritted his teeth. Then an idea came to him. "That depends on whose side you're on now, Laurel."

"What do you mean?"

Eric leaned forward, staring deep into her grey eyes. "Are you still Baronian? Is that your plan, once you dispose of us? To find another tribe and volunteer yourself back into slavery?"

Laurel scowled, waving the dagger. "Watch what you say, Eric. I don't need you alive. What do my plans matter to you?"

"He's just wondering where your allegiances lie," Enala joined in. "Are you still tied up with the trappings of that cult, or do you want to be your own person again?"

"You're still chirping on about that rubbish," Laurel cackled. "Of course I'm free, I always was, I told you," even to Eric her words sounded weak, lacking belief. After a moment's silence she stood and started to pace. Finally she spun. "I don't know what I'll do now, but it's nothing to you!"

Eric laughed. "Coward."

He reeled back as Laurel's fist smashed him in the face. His teeth rattled and his nose went *crunch* before her weight slammed him into the ground. She crashed down on top of him, hands grasping for his throat, eyes just an inch from his own. He choked for breath as she began to squeeze.

Laurel smiled at him. "As I said, the bounty for you is dead or alive, Eric. The only reason you're alive is to make my life easier. Better you walk yourself to the noose, rather than me carrying you. So let this be your final warning," the pressure on his throat eased. "Do not test me."

Eric coughed as she released him and stood up. "Now,"

she walked towards Enala, her sword sliding from its sheath. "Why, Enala, did you give a fake name?"

Enala stood her ground, glaring up at the taller woman, fists clenched at her side. She would die before she gave the secret away.

Closing his eyes in defeat, Eric croaked out an answer. "Because she is being hunted."

Laurel looked back. "By who?" greed flickered in her eyes.

Eric shook his head, pausing for a heartbeat to weigh the wisdom of his next decision. Laurel might be out for herself, but he had not mistaken the disgust in her eyes when she spoke of Thaster's dark magic. "She is not hunted by any mortal force. She is pursued by the servants of Archon himself."

Laurel's face paled in the twilight. "What?" she looked from Eric to Enala. "What the hell are you talking about?"

"You heard him," Enala glared back.

"You're joking?" fear shook Laurel's voice.

Eric regained his feet. "It's no joke. Enala happens to be the last person alive who can wield the Sword of Light. She is the only one left who can stop Archon. So unless you enjoy the thought of a world ruled by dark magic, I suggest hers is one bounty you don't collect."

Silence fell. At last Laurel spoke again. "This is some trick…"

"It's not," they replied in unison.

Laurel glanced between them again, uncertainty written on her face. Then she shook her head. "You're both delusional."

"It's the truth," Eric replied, resolute. "Antonia and Jurrien have already fallen. It won't be long before Archon comes. Then everyone will have a decision to make. The dark or the light. Sooner or later, you will have to pick a side, Laurel."

Laurel waved a hand, as though trying to dismiss his words. "Be quiet, the both of you. I've heard enough of your nonsense for one night. Sleep, or don't. I'm going to rest. And don't bother trying anything, I don't need to be awake to keep a couple of unruly Magicker's under control," with that Laurel turned and walked a few paces down the hill and slumped to the grass.

Despite what she'd said about sleep, she sat with her legs pulled up to her chest and her head on her knees, staring out into the darkness.

Eric looked at Enala. This was the closest they'd come to privacy in days, and there were things they needed to discuss.

She answered his first question before he could ask it. "Where did it come from, the magic? How…?"

So he'd been right, Enala had no idea. "It came from you. Just like your ancestors, you have powerful magic within you. As for why it chose last night to appear, well, we were lucky. Alastair once told me magic only emerges on a Magicker's birthday. The age varies, depending on the person and what they experience growing up. Happy coincidence that Thaster chose today to fight you," he paused and smiled. "Happy birthday, by the way."

Enala nodded. "The last few days I kept feeling this pressure within me, whenever I was angry. Last night, it just snapped, like something within had shattered. And for the first time, that pressure was released."

"I'm just glad it happened," he smiled. "Whatever dark magic Thaster was using, it was no longer a fair fight. I think we'd both be dead by now if you hadn't taken them by surprise."

To his shock, Enala began to sob. "But there were so

many people, so many that had nothing to do with the fight. How many died because of me?"

"Enala, it was not your fault," he reached out and gripped her wrist. "You could not have controlled your power without training. I can barely restrain mine, even with everything Alastair taught me. And besides," his face hardened. "It's not like they were innocent. They knew what was happening, that we were slaves fighting for our very lives. They made their decision when they joined that man."

Enala's sobs started to subside. When she finally looked up her eyes still watered, but her voice was strong. "Will you teach me, Eric?"

Eric smiled. "I can try. Now?"

Enala shrugged. "At least it might take our minds off our stomachs."

Eric nodded. "Okay. Well, the first thing a Magicker must learn is meditation…"

Laurel sat in the darkness, listening to the rhythmic breathing of the two young Magickers. She could feel their magic; powerful, bubbling below the surface, seeking its freedom as they sank deeper into their minds. Even so, it took little effort to keep the blue and red glows in check.

It left her mind free to wander.

Who are these two? The question bounced around her head. Had they actually spoken the truth? Could Enala wield the infamous Sword of Light? Was Archon really hunting her?

An icy breeze swept across the hilltop. She shivered, pulling the cloak tighter around her and burying her head into her knees. It could not be true: the tribe had heard nothing of their tale, and as nomads the Baronians picked up most of the gossip in the Three Nations.

She shook her head, her thoughts changing direction. In less than twenty-four hours, her world had collapsed. The girl's latent magic had been undetectable until the moment she released it – and by then it was far too late to stop. Laurel's magic only prevented a Magicker from tapping into their powers; once unleashed, there was nothing she could do but flee.

It had taken all she had to outrun the flames. Only the head start provided by her magic's warning allowed her to get clear. The other Baronians had not been so lucky. She guessed less than half their number had escaped the firestorm which followed.

Still though, more than enough to carry word to the other tribes. To carry word of Laurel's failure.

The other chiefs would not take Thaster's death lightly. They would be out for blood, out to show the world they were not to be trifled with. The word would go out, a list of those responsible made. The heads of Eric and Enala would be at the top of that list. For her failure, Laurel would come a close second.

Regardless of her own desires, Laurel would not be welcomed back into the fold. Yet who else would want a disgraced Magicker such as herself? Who would be powerful enough to protect her from the wrath of the Baronian chiefs?

No, she would have to disappear.

Thankfully, the bounty on Eric's head would go a long way towards accomplishing that task.

CHAPTER 15

Eric hesitated before the gates of Chole, shrinking back from the great stone walls. The giant blocks of granite stood stark and forbidding, a grim reminder of the fate waiting for him within. Behind him, Laurel gave him a shove, propelling him through the open gates. Enala walked beside him, head held high as she returned to the city of her birth.

Inhaling, Eric struggled for calm and forced himself to continue. Tears leapt unbidden as memories of Inken rose in his mind. It was here they had met, here where he'd first discovered his love for the feisty bounty hunter. Their first kiss had not been far from this very gate. Now five hundred miles separated them and for all he knew, Inken was already dead.

He rubbed his eyes to wipe away the hot tears, determined to hide his weakness from Laurel. Sniffing back his sorrow, he forced down the memories. They had other things to worry about now.

Even so, Eric could not help but pause again as they emerged from the shadow of the gate, overwhelmed by the change a few weeks had brought to Chole. This was a different city from the one they'd left behind. Everywhere he looked shoots of green now sprang from the earth, where before there had been only dust. Grass grew between the street tiles and vines dangled from drainage pipes, swaying in the breeze. A drizzle of rain swept through the streets, sending people scrambling for shelter.

Eric blinked, seeing then the other change to the city. Before Chole had been empty – the Dying City people called it – and all but the hardiest of men stayed clear. The city was left to the desperate and the criminal.

Now, everywhere Eric looked people moved through the streets, hurrying about their business. Even here by the gates, in what had been the poorest districts, civilisation had returned. It seemed news of the rain's return had spread fast, and many a brave soul had decided to gamble on the city's resurrection.

"So it's true," Eric turned at Laurel's words. "I could hardly believe the stories, but the rain has returned."

"It has," Enala's voice cracked with emotion and Eric saw the tears in her eyes. "It has changed so much, in such a little time. I only wish my parents had lived to see it. Thank you, Eric," she smiled at him.

Eric nodded and flashed a smile back.

"This was you?" Laurel asked, raising an eyebrow.

"A first step in a long journey," Eric shrugged.

Laurel shook her head and Eric thought he glimpsed a flash of compassion in her eyes. Then she turned away. "Come, we need to move. With all these people you might be recognised. I wouldn't want someone else trying to claim your bounty."

Eric sighed, glancing at Enala. They were running out of time, but an opportunity to flee had yet to come. He reached within, but his magic remained tantalisingly out of reach. They were powerless against Laurel.

Laurel led them through the bustling streets, her eagerness to leave behind the crowds betrayed by the pace she set. Eric searched for familiar landmarks as they moved, but the maze of Chole's streets seemed to have only grown worse with the newcomers. At least he could see from Enala's smile she at least knew where they were.

Laurel, however, was struggling. Baronians were not welcome in most cities, even one with a reputation like Chole's. But Laurel must have been here at least a few times, as she finally led them into the more prosperous streets around the central square. The crowds grew larger and the streets bristled with street venders plying their food and wares.

"Don't suppose you could spare me a last meal?" Eric asked, nodding towards a stand with chicken on the grill. His stomach rumbled; they had not eaten in days.

"No!" Eric looked up in surprise at the anger in her voice. He had missed the growing frustration in Laurel's movements. "There's no time. We need to get off the streets."

Eric frowned as Laurel gave him a hard shove. What was she so nervous about? Surely she did not really think someone would recognise him. Unless he used his magic, there was nothing to mark him as the so called 'demon boy' of Oaksville.

No, it had to be something else.

"What are you running from, Laurel?" Enala asked from beside him.

"Quiet!" Laurel snapped. "I told you, I won't have my prize stolen from me."

"You don't really expect us to believe that, do you?" Enala persisted.

Laurel spun, her hand drifting towards her dagger. "I warned you –"

"Laurel!" a shout from nearby cut her off.

Their captor spun at the sound of her name, hand switching from the dagger to the hilt of her short sword.

Eric looked across and saw three men muscling their way through the crowd towards them. Straggled beards covered their faces and scars crisscrossed their arms. Each sported a black arm band and held greatswords in their meaty hands. The thugs wore plain clothes, but Eric guessed their usual attire was the black armour of the Baronians.

"The Hawk would like a word with you, Laurel. About Thaster's untimely demise," the first of the men growled.

The blood fled from Laurel's face. Whoever Hawk was, he clearly terrified her. Drawing her sword, she held it tight in front of her, hands trembling. She glanced at Eric and Enala, regret flashing in her eyes.

Then she vanished.

The men paused, and then started to laugh. "Well, well, look lads, I told you so. See the coward run?" they looked around the street, searching for the Magicker. "Or perhaps she just likes to fight dirty," they laughed again.

Goosebumps rose on Eric's neck as a dark light seeped from the man who led. "Come on then, Laurel. Come and get us. We shall see which magic is greater – the dark or the light."

The men edged into a circle, blades out, the darkness encircling them. Their eyes roamed the street, searching for Laurel. Eric had no idea what dark magic they were employing, but he guessed its touch would leave a mark.

Either way, the men had not yet taken notice of Eric or Enala. They backed away together, trying to put the crowd between themselves and the Baronian thugs. They moved slowly, doing their best not to draw attention to themselves.

When they reached a nearby alley, they turned and sprinted between the buildings.

Enala took the lead, Eric struggling to keep up as she raced through the twisting nooks and alleyways of Chole. Her knowledge of the city was priceless now – within minutes they had left the Baronians far behind. Eric glanced back as they ran, searching for sign of pursuit, but all looked quiet.

They raced on all the same, eager to extend their lead and lose any invisible followers.

Half an hour later they drew to a stop in the shadow of a library.

"Who were those men?" Enala asked.

"Baronians, I'm guessing. Laurel must have made a few enemies when she didn't protect the Baronian camp from your magic. We're just lucky they didn't recognise us," he paused and turned his mind inwards. His magic surged at his touch, free at last. "Speaking of which, I think we've lost her as well. My magic is back," he felt a pang of sadness at the thought of leaving Alastair's blade in Laurel's hands, but he could do little about it now.

Enala grinned. "Well that's something, because we're now unarmed and alone in a city of thieves. A few weeks can't have changed it *that* much. Where are we going?"

Eric quickly described what he remembered from Antonia's vision: the steps down from the ramparts, the narrow path which separated the buildings from the city walls, and the vines that had covered the granite blocks, hiding a dark secret beneath them.

At the end Enala nodded. "I think I know the place, but last I heard the vines had withered and died. Although now that I think of it, they've been there as long as anyone can remember."

"Hopefully there is still a way past them," Eric whispered.

They started off again, moving at a slower place this time, neither eager to reach the gateway and the cursed world waiting for them. Eric remembered all too well the deadly land beyond, and the creature lurking there. They still had no idea how to defeat it; he just hoped his magic would be enough.

It took half an hour to cross the city, but they managed it without incident. The streets grew quiet as they approached their destination, the citizens retreating into their homes to wait out the night. Whatever changes had enveloped Chole, the growing fear on the faces of passers-by suggested the night still belonged to the unsavoury.

They stood together beneath the wall, staring up at the ancient granite blocks. Vines hung from the battlements high above, but Enala had been right – they were long dead. Whatever magic had sustained them through the centuries, it had not been enough to save them from the drought. Yet somehow, their death did not seem to have been permanent. Fresh green shoots now sprang from the dry husks of the old vines, and white flowers sprinkled the wall. Their aroma drifted down, their rich honey-like scent lingering in their noses.

"What do we do?" Enala asked.

Eric leaned back, trying to see how high the vines went. "I'm not sure. Alastair said only those with Earth magic could control the vines. But maybe there is another way through."

Enala gave a wry grin. "Like burning them?"

Chuckling, Eric shrugged. "Maybe, but we'll use my magic for now. There is a lot you need to learn before you try to use your magic consciously. But we'll save that lesson for another day."

Lightning crackled as Eric drew a bolt of energy from the sky. It struck the vines with a crash and a roar. Blue fire raced along the half-dead tendrils, burning up browned leaves and new growth alike.

As the flames died out, the remains of the vines fell to ash around them. Beneath, the empty abyss of the portal beckoned. They bathed in its flickering glow, its light swirling away into infinity. The dark energy danced in their eyes, drawing them into its embrace. The power tugged at Eric's soul, but remembering Antonia's warning, he resisted.

Beside him, Enala leaned towards the portal. He grasped her hand and pulled her back.

"Careful, Enala. Archon cursed this place a long time ago. His taint is everywhere, do not let it tempt you, or you risk being corrupted."

She gave a wan smile, her face pale. "Okay," she looked up. "At least that was easy."

Eric closed his eyes, summoning his courage. "No, this is just the beginning. Beyond, the real battle begins. Brace yourself."

They leapt together into the abyss.

LAUREL WATCHED as the two stepped into the portal, heart thudding hard in her chest. It had been no easy task following them through the city – in fact, she had lost them a few blocks back. Only the surge of Eric's magic allowed her to find them again.

Now she wished she hadn't. She could not believe what she was witnessing. The power emanating from the abyss reached her even in the shadows of the nearby alley. Its dark taint spoke to her, called to her. But she had overheard Eric's words, and struggled to close herself to its power.

So they told the truth, Laurel could deny it no longer.

The truth of their tale stood before her – an ancient

magic leading to the Gods only knew where. It changed everything. Perhaps she could find more than just gold on the other side of that portal. Whoever Eric and Enala answered too, they were obviously powerful. Powerful enough to resist the forces commanded by Hawk.

She needed protection now more than ever.

Unsure quite what she planned, but knowing she could not stay in Chole, Laurel slipped from the shadows. Moving towards the portal, Laurel saw the vines stirring, fresh shoots regenerating from the ashes. They crawled across the stony surface, covering the portal. In seconds it would shut, closing her off from the two young Magickers.

Taking a breath, Laurel dove for the portal

And the world began to spin.

CAELIN STRODE down the streets of Ardath, ignorant to the bustle of the city around him. Frustration bubbled in his chest. It had been two days since they had seen the king, two days spent petitioning to see the council again. But their every effort had been met by blank stares and stony silence. It was becoming increasingly clear the king and council did not wish to see them.

Swinging around a corner, Caelin picked up speed. Looking back, he caught a glimpse of the man following him. Today they had separated after leaving the inn, knowing their ghost could only tail one of them. There were people Caelin wanted to speak too, and he did not want anyone interrupting their conversation.

Outside the city the army continued to muster, but they showed no sign of being ready to march. The king had not even sent an advanced party out to reinforce Fort Fall. The standing garrison at the fortress was meant to keep out the banished and odd raiding party – it would stand no chance against an army. If something did not change soon, the Plorseans would arrive too late to make a difference.

Likewise, the situation in Ardath grew worse with each passing day. Fear spread through the city, infecting its citizens with a terror not seen since Archon's war. All knew of the attack on Sitton, and many said in whispers it could only be a matter of time before the same fate befell Ardath. Even the city guards were affected, and whispers of the king's isolation only made matters worse.

Caelin still could not bring himself to believe his king had been swayed to Archon's cause. He had always been a good man, loyal to the Gods and his people. But there was no doubting it – something had changed in the man. Caelin's homecoming still rankled him. He had expected disappointment from the king, not open scorn.

He broke into a run as he rounded the next corner, sprinting for the alleyway halfway down the street. Water splashed beneath his feet, the remains of last night's rain. The wind whistled in his ears as he picked up speed, his boots thumping the bricked street. Leaning low, he ducked into the alleyway and out of sight.

Once hidden, he did not stop to check if the tracker had seen him. He picked his way through the alley, jumping over discarded garbage and a dead rat, before swinging round the next corner. Quickly, he made his way through the network of alleyways connecting the streets of Ardath, heading for a nondescript building where the others waited.

The owner of the building did not know he was coming.

When he emerged back into the open streets, Gabriel and Inken stood across the street waiting for him. The street was quiet, cast in the shadow of the city walls looming behind the houses.

Inken smiled when she saw Caelin and moved across to join him. "Looks like you drew the short straw."

"I thought he might choose me. I'm the one they know. A good thing, since I know these streets better than either of you."

"That's a bold statement," Inken laughed. "You'd be surprised where my hunts have taken me."

"If you too are done competing with one another, shouldn't we get this over with – before someone figures us out?" Gabriel suggested.

Caelin nodded and they moved towards one of the houses. At first glance the building looked non-descript, with plain stone walls and a tile roof. But as they approached, Caelin saw small hints of the owner's wealth. Well-kept gardens suggested the house had full-time help, and the trimmings of the eaves were edged with marble. The door stood closed, the thick oak shining in the cool sun. An intricate mural dedicated to the earth had been carved into the wood, another sign of the occupant's wealth.

Inside was the one councillor they knew more about than any other. Unfortunately, she was also the councillor whose loyalty they doubted more than any other.

The house belonged to Katya.

Raising his hand, Caelin banged on the door, and waited.

Silence came from within, followed by the creak of wooden floorboards and the faint shuffle of somebody moving inside. The sounds ceased when they reached the door, as the person inside placed their eye to the spyhole.

Caelin smiled and waved.

After several long seconds, there came a clack as the bolt was unlocked and the door swung open.

Katya stood in the door way, arms folded across her chest. She scowled at Caelin, eyebrow raised. She wore tight fitting clothing that hugged her supple frame and long black boots stretching up to her knees.

"Caelin, I wasn't expecting you," Katya growled. "How can I help you?" she stood stiff, clearly angry at the unexpected intrusion.

Swallowing his doubts, Caelin answered. "Katya, I know things went poorly with you and the king in the throne room. But I am here to ask you for another chance. Please, help us to see King Fraser, help me explain."

"And why would I do that?" she snapped, one hand clenched on the door, prepared to slam it in their faces. "If you wish to go before the council again, you will have to book an appointment with the clerks."

Caelin raised his hands, heart pounding in his chest. "Wait, don't, please. Look, I know you don't want to listen. I know you have a different plan. But at least hear us out first. Let us sit down like adults and weigh up the options. If yours is truly the better approach, then let the king see that for himself."

Katya stepped from the house, anger flashing in her eyes. "You have no idea what the king is planning. Who are you, a mere sergeant, to advise him on the most sensitive of military matters?

Caelin stared her down. "I may be young, and only a sergeant. But I am no green kid enlisted in the army. This is my life. And I have seen the enemy, I have seen the power of just one of his servants. It is beyond anything I have ever witnessed from the Magickers at your command. Greater even than Alastair. And the demon grows stronger by the day."

Katya paused, uncertainty flashing across her face. Then she bared her teeth, the steel returning to her eyes. "Even so, if you wish to see the king, this is not the way –"

"They have locked us out," Caelin interrupted. "The

clerks ignore our petitions and we are followed day and night. Someone does not wish us to see the king," he paused, studying the woman before him, weighing her up. Could she be trusted, or was there more behind her anger. Taking a breath, he risked a gamble. "We believe there are traitors in the council; others like Balistor who have been turned by Archon."

Katya stared him down. "And do you think I am one of these traitors."

"I don't know," Caelin replied.

The silence stretched out, their gazes locked in a mental war. Caelin stared deep into her hazel eyes, searching for a hint of doubt. But he could see no sign of treachery there.

At last Katya blinked and looked away. She opened her mouth to speak.

A shout came from above, drowning out her words. Caelin looked up and saw guardsmen racing across the battlements atop the wall.

Even from this distance, he could see the panic in their eyes.

CHAPTER 16

Enala's stomach swirled as solid ground materialised beneath her feet and her body lurched to a sudden stop. Red hot pain streaked through her head. Her knees crumpled, the strength fleeing from her trembling muscles. Another heave of her stomach, and Enala threw up the measly remainders of her last meal.

A few minutes later, Enala finally took a great shuddering breath and sat back. Groaning, she wiped her mouth and stood on shaky legs. Looking around, she very nearly threw up again.

Piles of human bones littered the barren earth. The empty eye sockets of broken skulls glared up at them. Rusty blades and broken bows lay scattered amidst the piles, but not a shred of cloth or flesh remained. A blood red sky stretched overhead and the air smelt of baked dirt and death.

Enala stumbled backwards, a shiver running through her, fear screaming for her to flee this defiled place. She sucked in a breath, the air stifling, not a trace of wind to be felt. Stark white cliffs rose on either side of them, hedging them in. A single path cut through the bones, leading deeper into the narrow valley.

A rattle came from nearby as Eric stood. Enala's heart sank when she saw the fear on his face.

"What's wrong?" she whispered, unwilling to disturb the slumber of the dead surrounding them.

"My magic, it's not going to help us here."

"*What?*" Enala tried to control the tremor in her voice, but failed. "What do you mean? Laurel couldn't be..."

"No, not Laurel. It's this place. I can't sense anything of the Sky here – no rain or wind or *anything*. It's empty. I'm powerless in this place."

Enala stared. "What do we do?"

Eric hesitated, and then a hardness replaced the fear in his eyes. "Whatever we have too. There's no going back. We have no weapons, so our only chance is to evade the creature that lurks here. If it comes to it though, I will distract it while you run. There is a granite arch at the end of the valley. It leads to Kalgan. No matter what happens, you have to reach it," Enala opened her mouth to argue, but Eric raised his hand. "There's no time to fight about this. Come on, time passes strangely here and the longer we hesitate the more likely it is the fiend will find us."

He walked past her and started down the track into the valley. Bone fragments and gravel crunched beneath his feet, raising the hackles on Enala's neck. Shivering, she pushed down her fear and followed after him.

It took them ten long minutes to escape the boneyard. Enala winced with every step, disgust at their trespass rising up from the depths of her soul. A cold sweat stuck to her skin, useless in the stifling heat. She walked carefully, shuddering at the grinding of bones beneath her boots.

When they finally made it clear the going became easier, although gravel still slid beneath their feet on the treacherous slope. The cliffs closed in on either side, the valley narrowing to a thin canyon. Boulders dotted the hillslope, as though dropped there by giants. In places they clumped together to block the canyon, forcing them to clamber over the colossal rocks. Elsewhere they had to hold their breath to squeeze between them.

Enala soon realised the path had once been a stream bed, its waters long vanished with whatever magic had cursed this world. She saw then where the racing waters had sliced into the cliffs, leaving deep underhangs in the white rock.

She shivered. *What happened to this place?*

They continued on. Without the sun there was no knowing what bearing they travelled on, but it made no difference here. There was only one direction for them to go. They must have walked for hours, but the empty sky gave no indication of the passage of time. Enala's lungs burned, the air suffocating, the heat overwhelming. The little water in their skins was all but gone.

Ahead, Eric came to a sudden halt. Enala joined him, a grim dread settling in her stomach. Before them the path fell away, as though someone had taken a knife to the earth itself. A near sheer drop plummeted to the valley floor more than a hundred feet below. Loose gravel covered the slope all the way to the bottom.

As Enala stepped back from the edge a chunk of stones broke loose. They tumbled down the slope, picking up speed and disturbing more as they went. Their clatter echoed from the canyon walls, the rumble quickly growing to a roar. Enala winced as the landslide reached the bottom and spread out across the valley floor.

"This wasn't here when Alastair and Thomas passed this way," Eric whispered. "What do we do?"

Enala grimaced. "There's only one way to traverse a gravel

slope. We have them in the mountains of Chole, though I've never seen one so steep. We have to run."

"*What?*"

"It's the only way to take them. If you try to walk down, the gravel will give way and you'll fall. If you're lucky, you'll only hurt your backside. If not, you might fall all the way to the bottom or be buried by the gravel. When you run, you're less likely to slip backwards. And even if you trip, your other foot can still catch you before you fall."

Eric eyed her, disbelief written across his face. "You cannot be serious?"

"Trust me, it's the only way," she smiled. "I'll go first."

Eric inhaled. "Just looking at it from here, the height has my head spinning. I hope you're right."

"Me too," she grinned. "Wait until I reach the bottom before you follow. Otherwise the rocks you dislodge might catch up to me," she glanced at him. "See you on the other side."

Without another word, she leapt from the edge.

The air whipped through her hair and her stomach twisted as she dropped several feet. When she struck the gravel slope, her legs almost crumpled under the shock of the impact. Stones erupted around her, slipping beneath her boots, and she began to slide. She waved her arms outwards, struggling for balance as stones scattered in every direction.

When she began to slow, Enala leapt again. Twisting in the air, she turned her hips to land with one foot stretched out in front. Dust billowed up with the impact, but an instant later she was airborne again, propelling herself back into clear air. Sweat beaded her forehead and dripped into her eyes, but she could not afford a second to wipe it away.

Squinting through the dust and tears, she continued down.

Gravel filled her boots, but with no time to dislodge it,

she gritted her teeth and ignored its sharp bite. Every bound sent her flying, plummeting in free fall for long seconds before she crashed back down. She fought to keep her balance, instinct spinning her to absorb the shock of each landing. A single mistake and she would be done.

When she finally reached the bottom, Enala sank to her knees and sucked in a long breath. Dust rushed down her throat, sending her into a coughing fit. Stumbling to her feet she retreated down the valley, away from the dust. Once clear she turned and looked back up the slope.

Eric still stood at the top, his expression unreadable from such a distance. She waved a hand and he gave a short nod. After a moment's hesitation, he jumped from the edge. His first bound did not carry him far, but stones still exploded outward as his boots struck the slope. His arms windmilled as he slid, struggling to keep his balance.

Just as Enala thought he would stop, Eric leapt again, further this time. The dust rose up, concealing him in a cloud before he whipped back into view, picking up speed as he raced towards her. With each leap and bound he drew closer, his feet barely touching the gravel before sending him soaring again. A grin flashed on his face.

Enala couldn't believe it; Eric was enjoying his headlong race down the slope.

Then as Eric drew close to halfway, his smile turned to sudden terror. As he landed, Eric shrieked and his feet collapsed beneath him. He toppled forwards, his foot caught on some hidden obstruction. His face struck the gravel and he started to slide, arms thrust out in a hopeless attempt to regain his feet.

"No!" Enala shouted. "Get up, Eric!"

But it was too late. Even as he tumbled down the jagged stones, the hillside above him gave way. The landslide began as a dim rumble, a rattle of stones, but it quickly grew to a roar as the tonne of rocks rushed towards Eric.

Eric looked up and raised an arm in a vain attempt to protect himself.

Then the landslide struck.

Enala screamed as the tumbling mountain of rocks and stones swallowed Eric. She caught one last panicked look from him, then he was gone.

She took a trembling step towards the slope, arm stretched out in desperation, then stopped. Her eyes locked on the avalanche now rushing towards her. If she tried to reach Eric now, she would be buried along with him. Stealing herself, Enala backed away. Closing her eyes, fighting back tears, she waited for the rumbling to cease.

When she finally looked up again, the slope was empty. Not a sign remained of their passage – no hint of their foot-steps or of Eric. A mound of gravel lay at the bottom of the slope, the only sign remaining of the landslide.

Swallowing her fear, Enala picked her way through the gravel and began to climb. She moved slowly, taking care not to disturb the loose stones. That quickly proved impossible. With every step she took, her boot sank deep into the shifting surface. Her heart pounded painfully in her chest as hooks of despair tore into her soul. Gritting her teeth, she struggled higher, sliding back a step for every two she took.

Eric had to be here somewhere, buried beneath the gravel. But the landslide had wiped away all sign of his passage. There was no telling where he had disappeared, or whether the landslide had carried him further down the slope.

Even so, Enala refused to surrender. She toiled her way up, her panic growing with each step.

"This cannot be happening," Enala whispered to herself, her breath coming in ragged gasps.

Dread clutched her heart in its icy hands, turning her muscles to dust. Eric had to be alive. He would not abandon her. She could not go on alone, could not bear to lose another friend. Cracks raced through her consciousness, the madness rearing up within her.

She stumbled across the slope, searching in a mindless panic for her fallen friend.

Finally, Enala collapsed to the ground, defeated. A scream rumbled up from her chest, coming out as a choked squeak as she wrapped her arms around her knees and began to rock.

"*No, no, no, no,*" she whispered to herself. Tears spilt down her cheeks.

He can't be gone! Enala screamed to herself, muscles burning with exertion.

She glanced up the slope, seeking movement, desperate for a sign.

There was nothing but empty stones.

Eric was gone.

She was alone.

Enala looked down the slope, breath quivering in her throat. The madness rose again, threatening to overwhelm her, but she clung to Eric's words. She knew what he would want her to do. He would tell her to go on, that it was up to her now. The fate of the Three Nations rested on her shoulders. She could not let them down now, not after so many had given their lives to protect her.

Summoning her courage, Enala made her way back down the treacherous slope.

She did not look back.

~

"Well, this was a terrible mistake," Laurel muttered to herself, watching Enala from the edge of the cliff.

From the moment she had stepped from the portal, it had been the only thought on her mind. The boneyard marking the entrance to this nightmare realm was enough to send any intruder fleeing for their lives.

As soon as she appeared, Laurel had reached within to ensure her magic still concealed her. While her power felt thin and weak, she was pleased to find it still worked. Creeping closer, she had overheard Eric's grim pronouncement about his own magic.

At least that was something going for her. That, and the two swords she still wore at her side.

As the two made their way down the canyon, Laurel followed close behind. She fought to keep her movements silent – there was little point in revealing herself just yet. A plan had begun to take shape in her mind, but it could wait until they escaped this wasteland.

Then Eric had gone and gotten himself killed.

It had happened so quickly, Laurel almost missed it. One second the boy was picking up speed, his confidence growing with each bound. Then before anyone could so much as cry out, he was gone, buried beneath the landslide.

Now Laurel stood and watched Enala making her way back up the slope. The futility of the search was already obvious; she was risking her life for nothing. Eric was gone. Laurel almost revealed herself, if only to spare Enala the same fate as Eric.

But Enala would flee if she saw Laurel and in her precarious position that would be disastrous. Whatever happened, the girl could not die. At least not until Laurel had the chance to complete her plan.

Finally, crying in despair, Enala surrendered to the impossible task and made her way down. Laurel waited until she disappeared around a bend in the canyon before attempting to follow. Her invisibility would not hide the disturbance caused by her descent. Just as the two had done before her, she made her way down in leaps and bounds. Unlike Eric, she did not have any problems.

When she reached the bottom, Laurel spared a glance back up the slope, surprised to feel a touch of sadness for the boy's death. She had planned to see him hang, but it had never been personal. In truth, she felt a touch of respect for Eric and Enala's feisty resistance, for their courage in the face of death. But despite their youthful audacity, they were not immortal.

Laurel glanced down the canyon after Enala. The girl was made from the same cloth as Eric – her courage bordering on the edge of stupidity. Challenging Thaster to single combat had been pure insanity, and only her innate magic had saved Enala from death. Magic she had not even been aware of.

Laurel shook her head, still unable to believe the luck.

Taking one final glance up the slope, Laurel sent an old prayer to Darius for the boy's soul. She may not have been a very good apprentice of the Light, but she still remembered a few things. It was the least she could offer Eric.

Then she turned her back on the graveyard, and broke into a jog.

Somewhere ahead, Enala waited.

CHAPTER 17

Enala stood alone in the centre of the valley, the heat of the baked earth seeping through her boots. Cracks crisscrossed the valley floor and the white cliffs still towered overhead. The air was still and sweat soaked her clothes, leaving them sticking to her skin. She stared at the granite arch stretching across the end of the canyon. The flowers etched into the grey stone were exactly as Eric had described.

A thin mist swirled beyond the arch, beckoning her, promising freedom.

But before her stood the cursed creature that haunted this realm. It, too, was exactly as Eric described. Its yellowed bones gleamed in the light of the blood red sky. Joints clacked as it moved, a bony arm reaching down to wrap bare knuckles around the hilt of its scimitar. Metal shrieked as it drew the rusted blade. The skull's empty eye sockets bored into her, jaws set in a toothy grin.

"Ahhh, a visitor," its head tilted to the side. "And one who is familiar. I know your scent – you are the descendent of one who escaped me…" it took a step towards her.

Enala reached for a blade that was not there. Panic rose in her chest but she forced it down. "What do you want, monster?" she asked, trying to stall, searching for a plan.

The skeleton laughed, the dull whisper echoing from the cliffs. "To hear you scream. Your death will be slow, for your ancestor's defiance," it took another step.

Enala bent down and swept up a rock. Bracing herself, she pulled back her fist to hurl the missile. Before she could swing, the skeleton froze. It stood deathly still, one bony toe clacking on the sunburnt ground. Then the skull turned on its naked spine, staring into space a few feet to Enala's right.

"I see you," it laughed. "Come out, Magicker, or I will make your death as long as hers."

A tremor of intuition ran down Enala's neck an instant before Laurel materialised.

She followed us!

Laurel puffed out her cheeks and exhaled, as though she had just run a long distance. Grimacing at the skeleton, she spared Enala a glance. "I think we might have a common enemy," she held a sword in each hand and without further word, tossed one to Enala.

Enala reached up and caught the blade by the hilt, smiling when she realised it was Alastair's. Still shaking with the shock of Laurel's reappearance, she turned to face the skeleton. Questions would have to wait.

It felt good to have a sword back in her hands. She switched to a two-handed grip and smiled. At least now she stood a fighting chance.

The skeleton laughed, and surged towards them.

THE FIRST THING Eric became aware of was the pressure. It pressed in from all around, steady, unrelenting, reducing each breath to short, quick gasps. An ache came from his spine, and as awareness returned he found himself curled into a ball, legs crushed up against his chest.

A dull grinding came from all around, as though the darkness itself was moving. Eric listened to the sound, struggling to recall its source. Memory came slowly, trickling back from the depths of his mind. The boneyard, the scree slope, *the landslide!*

Had he been able to move, Eric would have thrashed about in panic then. But the weight of a mountain had settled on him, trapping him in place. Coarse stones dug into his skin and a dusty darkness met him when he opened his eyes. Already the air tasted stale, his panicked gasps quickly using up what little remained.

How deep am I buried? A suffocating fear swelled within him. He held it down, struggling for calm. Panic would serve no use now. He had to think.

Gritting his teeth, Eric tried moving different parts of his body. Another bout of terror threatened to overwhelm him as he realised the pressure had locked his legs in place. He clenched a fist and found he could at least move an arm. Stones rattled and he realised where the sound came from – the slow, unrelenting crawl of gravel down towards the valley floor.

Still on the verge of panic, Eric tried to move again. A shiver ran up his arm as stones tore through his skin. Curled into a ball, he attempted to lift his arms, trying to dislodge the stones either side of his body.

Time passed and his efforts grew weaker, but he knew he was making progress. The stones pressed down on his back, the pressure growing with every strained breath. Finally, he managed create enough space to move his arms with relative freedom. Reaching out, he began to clear space beneath him so he could straighten his legs.

Sharp points stabbed him, slicing through his clothes and grinding against raw flesh. Fear dulled the pain and drove him on. Exhaustion slowed him, but there in the darkness he had only one goal: to escape. As the stones slid away, he twisted, levering himself into a better position. Taking another breath of stale air, he started digging in the direction he prayed was up.

Suddenly the stones to his right gave way, his movement undermining the slope's fragile balance. He shrank back as earth roared and the slope collapsed. Light flooded the darkness. Eric sucked in a breath of fresh air and levered his arms beneath him. Using every ounce of his strength, he pulled himself from the scree and back to his feet.

His boots sank to his ankles and stones rattled away from him, another landslide already threatening. Eric did not stop to think. He leapt, fear propelling him downwards. Each bound carried him closer to safety. Stones slipped beneath him with each crash landing, the force of impact flinging them up at his face.

When he reached the bottom, Eric almost dropped to his knees to kiss the ground. Puffing, he resisted and continued into the valley until sure he was beyond range of stray rocks. Then he collapsed to the ground and looked back at the slope. It towered over him, giving no hint anyone had ever passed that way.

How long was I buried? He wondered, looking for sign of Enala.

The hairs on his neck prickled when he saw no sign of her.

Turning to face the valley, he climbed to his feet and began to run.

~

Enala ducked beneath a decapitating blow and threw herself backwards. To her left Laurel darted in and swung at the skeleton. It spun with almost casual speed, its rusted scimitar turning aside the blow. A contemptuous backhand sent Laurel reeling.

Driving herself forwards, Enala stabbed at the yellowed skull. The skeleton leaned back and her sword fell short. Instinct kicked in, sending Enala sideways as the scimitar sliced through the air she had just occupied.

Laurel regained her feet and threw herself back into the fight. They shared a glance, then attacked together, blades slashing out like vipers. Using every scrap of strength they could muster, they forced the demonic creature back – one step, then two. Yet still the ancient blade blocked their every attack, the dull ring of its steel mocking them.

Enala could not help but think it was toying with them.

Then as Enala launched herself forward, slicing low at its legs, the skeleton stepped up to meet her. It turned her blow away with ease, then the rusted scimitar flashed out, driving into her side.

Enala screamed and lurched backwards. Laurel charged in to halt the creature's next attack, her frantic blows keeping it at bay.

Enala's hand groped to her side and felt hot blood. Pain throbbed from the wound, sending tremors down to her knees. She clenched her teeth and pressed hard against the gash. She risked a glance at their foe and quickly looked away.

Two steps away, Laurel was fighting for her life. It was clear the creature had her hopelessly outmatched. The skeleton cackled each time she swung her sword, batting away her attacks like a cat playing with a mouse. Without aid, Laurel would not last thirty seconds.

Swallowing her pain, Enala released her side and gripped

Alastair's sword in both hands. Blood rushed from the wound and ran down her leg, but she drew on her courage and dove back into the fight.

The skeleton's grin widened as it watched her approach.

"I see you enjoy pain, young one," it's laughter sent shivers down her spine.

Enala ignored the taunt. She gritted her teeth, fighting to keep her feet as agony swept through her body.

The skeleton cackled and spun towards her. Enala brought up her sword and swung it at the deathly skull with all her strength.

The creature reached up and caught it in one skeletal hand.

Enala gasped as ice swept the blood from her face.

Before either of them could react, the skeleton drove its rusted blade up into her unprotected body.

Whatever pain Enala had felt before, it now fled before the white hot agony sweeping from her stomach. It spread down her legs and along her arms, overwhelming all other sensation. She heard a distant ring of metal on stone, and wondered if she had dropped her sword. She tried to clench her fist, and realised she could not feel her hands.

Enala stumbled backwards, collapsing to her knees. A strange ringing started in her ears, a bell tolling with each thump of her heart.

The skeleton stepped towards her.

Laurel looked between them, eyes wide with shock and terror, and vanished.

Head bobbing, Enala watched her foe approach. Tears sprang to her eyes as she struggled to control her body, determined at least to defy this creature to her last dying breath. A gurgle rose in her chest and she tasted blood, but she looked at her foe in defiance.

Pain radiated through every fibre of her being. She felt something else rising with it.

The creature looked down at her, skeletal fingers clenched around the hilt of its ancient weapon. From so close, she could see the blood of long dead foes congealed on the rust-flecked metal. It held the weapon poised over her, ready to slash the head from her shoulders.

Then it withdrew the blade, and a whispering cackle echoed up from somewhere in its yellowed skull. "Not so easy for you, young one. Did I not say your death would take an eon?"

Slowly, the creature's words sank in, seeping through the agony of her fractured mind. Fear chilled the pain spreading through her body. Looking up at the creature, hands clenched to her gut, Enala felt her terror take light. She glared at the creature, allowing the power within her to grow, letting its mocking grin feed the flames within. Energy pulsed through her veins, throwing back the shackles of her pain.

Enala felt heat in the palms of her hands.

With a scream of defiance, she threw her arms out at the creature.

Flames roared and raced towards the monster.

Eric sprinted down the ancient stream bed, rocks slipping beneath his booted feet. Several times he came close to twisting his ankle as he leapt between boulders, the broken surface threatening to send him tumbling. He paid little heed. His lungs burned and his heart pumped hard in his chest.

Please don't be too late!

The ring of blades carried to his ears, echoing off the

white-washed cliffs. There was no way of telling how far off they were, but he pushed himself harder, picking up speed. He did not stop to question how Enala had gotten a weapon.

The empty sky stretched out, unbroken, giving no hint to the passage of time. Hours could have passed since the landslide buried him. Eric recalled the power of the creature they faced all too well. Not even Alastair could stand against it; Enala would not stand a chance.

His foot landed awkwardly on a loose rock and sent him spinning across the ground. Gravel sliced at his skin, but he rolled and came up running again. He dodged around a bend in the canyon, his foot striking the opposite cliff to make the turn without slowing.

Ahead the canyon straightened. At its end he caught a glimpse of Enala, on her knees and staring up at the dark skeleton he remembered all too well from Antonia's vision.

As he watched, flames erupted from the girl to engulf the skeleton.

Putting down his head, Eric sprinted for the conflagration. His spirit soared as he sensed the swelling of magic. Enala's magic had responded again to her need, summoning heat from the scorching wasteland to burn the skeleton from their path. Perhaps her power could do what Alastair's could not.

Or perhaps not.

Eric ran harder, determined to reach Enala and do what he could to help. He just hoped her magic did not spread as it had in the Baronian camp; there was no wind here to carry him from harms reach.

With a gasp of relief, he drew to a stop behind Enala. He raised a hand to shield his face from the heat, taking in the scene in a single glance. Enala knelt on the ground, flames pouring from her small frame to envelop their foe.

But now Eric saw the blood staining the ground beneath

her, saw Enala swaying and the tremble in her arms. A gasp gurgled from her throat and she dropped one hand, halving the flow of fire. A chill swept through him as he realised Enala could lose consciousness at any moment.

Laughter came from the conflagration enveloping the skeleton. Its dark shadow appeared against the flames. The pop of stones shattering beneath its feet sounded unbelievably loud to Eric's ears. He heard Enala sob in frustration, saw her other arm begin to dip.

Eric stood behind her, fists clenched in rage. He had no weapon to fight with, but he could not just stand by and watch the cursed skeleton prevail. In desperation, he reached for his magic, for any power that might offer them salvation.

His magic rose at his touch, his fear feeding it strength. Before he could pull back he saw it changing, morphing into the wolf that still haunted his dreams. It stood before his inner mind, teeth bared, fur flickering with the blue light of his magic. It growled, towering over his feeble mind.

But Eric was stronger now, and he knew he could best this beast. He stared back, pushing down his fear, seeking to drive the wolf back into its cage.

It stepped towards him, already shrinking before his courage. Grinning, he approached it, confident in his strength.

It leapt, teeth bared, and struck his spirit form. Its teeth tore into him, sending pain lancing through his soul. The fear returned, stealing away his strength and feeding the wolf's. He fought back, pressing out with his mind, struggling to force the beast from him.

A voice whispered in his mind then, cold and devoid of life. *Stop, you fool. This is the only chance we have.*

Eric froze at the urgency in the voice, his defences slipping. The speaker seemed familiar, though he was sure he had never heard it before. Too late, he realised it came from the wolf. Its jaws ripped out, enveloping his conscious.

Eric's eyes opened and the magic stared out, taking in the skeleton emerging from the flames. It stalked towards Enala, scimitar in one hand, the other stretched out to fend off her attack. A tremor ran through Eric's body as energy surged into his veins

Eric smiled – or rather the magic forced a twisted grin to his lips. It knew how to handle this foe. The answers lay not in the wasteland without, devoid of any force capable of harming it, but with the power hidden within. Reaching into the pool of magic at their core, it searched for the power Eric had buried there so long ago.

Lightning flickered in Eric's inner eye, rising from deep within. The same lightning he had pulled inside all that time ago, in the desert of Chole. The lightning Alastair had once told him might one day save his life.

With a roar of thunder, it returned to the mortal world. The hairs on Eric's arms rose as it crept along his skin, crackling as it went, eager to finally be spent. Blue light flickered in Eric's eyes. A surge of greed overtook him as he looked on the raw energy. He shivered at the raw thirst of the magic, its demand for more.

The skeleton turned to stare at him. Somehow, he could see now the fear in its empty eyes. The skull's grin faded against the lightning's glare.

Eric laughed, the sound a dull imitation of his usual baritone. He pointed a finger. Lightning flickered along its tip, and leapt for the skeleton. The blue energy merged with the flames still streaming from Enala, and struck the skeleton. A roar echoed from the cliffs, followed by a dull boom.

The skeleton screamed, stumbling back before the combined force of their magic. It screamed again, jaw hanging wide as the heat took hold. As they watched, the bones of its face started to melt, the yellowed bone blackening before their eyes. Energy crackled in the air.

Scimitar raised, the skeleton stepped towards them, but its leg gave way, snapping beneath its weight. The creature fell to the ground, blue and red flames still flickering over its body. It clawed at the stones, reaching for them.

They watched as its yellowed bones melted away to nothing.

The magic within Eric looked around in triumph, its power swelling, spreading through his body. Eric shrank before it, feeling himself being thrust back from the world. Sight and sound retreated against the roar of its might.

"Eric," Enala croaked, "help me!"

Enala's words pierced the fog, slicing through the magic's spell. His conscious rose, fighting back against the power that controlled him. The pressure in his skull grew, soul and magic vying for supremacy. But its desperation shone through, feeding him strength, even as its claws dragged through his mind.

"Help…" Enala's voice was growing weaker.

The magic's hold snapped and Eric found himself returned to his body. Turning the hooks on the magic which bore them, he hurled it back into the depths of his mind.

He stumbled towards Enala. Her torn shirt hid the full extent of her injuries, but the pool of blood told the story for him. She needed help, and quickly. Alastair's sword lay beside her, and he quickly slipped it into his belt. Then Eric crouched beside her and swept her into his arms.

He stumbled towards the arch, strength fading, and prayed salvation waited for them on the other side.

CHAPTER 18

Gabriel's footsteps pounded down the bricked road, fear sending strength to his limbs. Somewhere in the city a bell tolled, calling the soldiers to war. Terrified citizens leapt from their path, hurrying back into the scant shelter of their houses. He was closing on Caelin now, though Inken and Katya were only a few steps behind.

A single question tumbled through Gabriel's mind as he chased after Caelin.

Is it the demon?

The wall loomed ahead, the pale figures of the city guard scurrying across the ramparts. Their movements seemed panicked, chaotic.

"What's happening up there?" Gabriel shouted over the clang of bells.

"Nothing good," Inken hissed as she drew level with him.

"If it's the demon, we don't stand a chance," Gabriel whispered, half to himself.

A chill dread crept into his stomach as they reached the walls. Caelin bounded up the steps, Inken not far behind. Gabriel followed, heart pounding, waking nightmares of the demon sending terror through his very soul. Never before had he felt so helpless; to stand before the dark magic wielded by the creature, and know he could do nothing to save Enala from its wrath.

Even so, he would not bend now. As long as he lived, he would fight.

Their boots thumped on the stone stairs, tiny pebbles scattering beneath their feet. The cries from the guards grew more frantic as they approached. Gabriel struggled to stop the shaking in his legs, pushing down his fear.

At the top they did not pause, the three of them and Katya spilling out onto the battlements. Men milled about them, staring out over the dark waters of the lake. Gabriel held a hand over his eyes to shield them from the autumn sun, squinting at the distant hills. The sun's warmth returned some of the feeling to his hands, frozen by the cool air.

Together they looked out over the lake, expecting to see the dark silhouette of the demon soaring towards them.

Instead, Gabriel found his fear turning to awe. Across the lake, a dozen golden specks marred the horizon, miles away still, but coming closer with each passing second. Gabriel stared, not quite believing what his eyes told him.

He had never seen the Gold Dragons before, only the vicious Red which had almost killed him. His heart soared all the same, his thoughts turning to Enala, and the sudden hope she might be with the creatures.

The specks continued to grow, until soon Gabriel could make out each beat of their golden wings, see the flick of their tails and the rows of teeth glinting in the sun. Reptilian tongues flicked out as they approached, flames licking the air before them.

Gabriel held his breath. Not one of them could believe it. They could only stand there and stare in wonder, unable to comprehend this miracle, but thankful beyond measure. The

Gold Dragons could only be here to help in the fight against Archon, to fulfil their part in the ancient treaty.

Beside him, Caelin thrust his fist into the air in silent joy.

Gabriel grinned. Now, surely, they might just stand a chance.

"Men, stand to!" Gabriel felt his hopes curdling as Katya's voice bellowed across the wall.

AN ICY BREEZE swept over Eric as he stepped from the portal onto the neatly manicured lawns of the citadel. He shivered in the frigid air, turning to stare at the stone walls rising up about him. Torches burned in brackets around the courtyard, their light casting an orange glow across the snowy grass. Stars lit the sky and somewhere in the darkness an owl called.

Eric stumbled as he shifted Enala's weight to his other shoulder. He squinted against the torchlight, searching for an exit.

Shouts came from around them and the steel doors at the end of the yard burst open. Guards appeared, spears held at the ready. They charged across the slippery grass, voices raised against the intruders. Steel armour rattled beneath their woollen cloaks.

Eric made no move to run. He would not get two steps carrying Enala's dead weight. Even so, only their obvious distress stopped the guards from killing them on the spot. Eric stood helpless with Enala in his arms and waited as the guards surrounded them, spear points bristling.

A man barked orders and the guards closed ranks, cutting off any chance of escape. Then the man stepped towards them.

"Who are you? How did you get into the citadel?" he demanded.

"We're friends," Eric's voice shook with the cold. "I can explain everything, but you have to help her. She's been stabbed. If she doesn't get to a healer soon, she'll die."

The man hesitated, his eyes taking in the blood seeping from Enala's cloak, already staining the snow beneath them. The truth of Eric's words was clear for all to see.

"Please," Eric whispered. "She's important. You cannot let her die."

The leader took a deep breath, then nodded. He barked out a string of orders. Two men lowered their spears and approached Eric. Two others joined them, their spears aimed in his direction. Eric reluctantly allowed them to take Enala's weight. Carrying her between them, the men retreated from the circle and disappeared through the steel doors.

"Thank you," Eric croaked to the leader.

The man nodded. "Explain yourself."

Rubbing his arms to ward off the cold, Eric gave a quick summary of who they were and how they had come to be there. The soldiers stared back, eyes hard and unforgiving. With their woollen cloaks, the cold did not seem to affect them. Eric could read the scepticism in their eyes, and doubted they believed a word of his tale.

When he finished he spread his hands. "Do what you want with me, just make sure Enala survives."

The leader stared at him, eyes unreadable. At last he nodded. "The council did receive word from Jurrien some time ago about a company who would bring a girl to us. No doubt the council would like to be the ones to judge the truth of your tale. They do not convene until morning."

Eric nodded. His teeth began to chatter and to his surprise the man laughed. "Until your story is verified, we cannot trust you. But let it not be said we Trolan's do not know how to treat a guest."

He retrieved a pair of iron cuffs from his cloak and tossed them to Eric. "Put those on, and we will show you to someplace warmer where you can wait out the morning."

The cuffs must have been deep within his cloak, because the metal still felt warm. Shivering, Eric locked them about his wrists and nodded to the guard.

The man gave a short smile and waved Eric towards the doors. "Follow me."

SHAME WELLED up in Laurel's chest as she watched Enala's healing. An hour had already passed, the air crackling with the magic of the three healers. Light flowed from their hands to wrap Enala in a blanket of power. It seeped into her skin, seeking out the injuries within. But healing did not come without cost; Laurel knew that from experience.

Enala had spent the last hour writhing in agony. Her shrieks would have sent grown men reeling, and only the strength of two guards had been able to hold her in place. Sweat beaded her pale face and her blond hair hung dull and limp. The copper lock burned a bright red, hinting at the power locked within. But Laurel kept a tight hold on Enala's magic, ensuring the Magickers could work in safety.

Laurel listened, unseen, to the whispers of the healers. They were worried the magic might not take, that Enala would not survive the night. Laurel smiled at their concern; they did not know this girl like she did. If she could survive the horrors of that creature, she would survive this.

It took another hour before the worst had passed. Her skin slowly regained its colour, a healthy pink returning to her cheeks. The shrieks started to subside as Enala settled into sleep, a gentle frown replacing the scowl.

At last the healers declared her healthy. Laurel smiled, wishing she could thank them. It was clear the effort had cost them; exhaustion ringed their eyes and haggard lines were etched across their faces. Shoulders slumped but smiling in triumph, they left the room one by one.

Then Laurel was alone with Enala. Closing her eyes, she slumped into the chair beside the girl's bed. The skeleton's cackle rang in her mind. Shivering, she wrapped her arms around herself, the fear rising within her. The creature had unmanned her, her strength evaporating before its overwhelming power. When Enala fell, the last shred of her courage evaporated.

With the creature intent on Enala, Laurel had cloaked herself in magic and fled for the archway. Enala's screams and the skeleton's dread laughter chased after her, but she closed her ears to the girl's plight. She sensed the surge of magic as Enala unleashed her power, but knew it would not be enough to overcome the monster.

Laurel had done what she'd always done. She had taken care of herself. She had left the girl to die.

So why do I feel so guilty? She shivered, watching Enala sleep. *How did you survive? How did Eric survive? What the hell happened in there?*

Laurel shook her head, still trying to come to grips with what had unfolded. When the portal dumped her in the citadel, she'd had no idea where she had escaped too. Remaining invisible, she slid through the courtyard, listening to the guards.

When she learned she was in Kalgan, she could not help but smile. It would take a long time for the Hawk to find her here.

Then the two Magickers had stepped from the portal, and all hell had broken loose.

Now Laurel found herself conflicted. When she had followed them into the portal, she'd thought to use Enala as leverage against the Trolan's. No doubt they would pay a steep ransom for her life.

But here in the citadel, the height of Trolan power, she knew such a plan could only end in disaster. Even if the Trolan's eventually recognised Enala and were willing to pay for her life, Laurel would stand little chance of escaping with her ransom. While she possessed a few unique abilities, she was not powerful. The Battle Magickers of Trola would hunt her down within hours.

Nor could Laurel ignore the shift in position between herself and Enala. They had stood together against the cursed skeleton, fought side by side to survive its relentless attack. Enala's bravery had saved Laurel a dozen times in the short minutes of the battle.

In return, Laurel had left the girl to die.

Taking a deep breath, Laurel released her magic and reached out to touch the sleeping girl.

Enala's eyelids fluttered and a low crackle came from her throat. Then her sapphire eyes opened and looked up at Laurel. She did not miss the suspicious glint in their murky depths.

"What are you doing here?" she croaked.

Laurel bowed her head. "I followed you from Chole. I thought it might be the best way to escape the Baronian thugs hunting me. I… I'm sorry I ran when it stabbed you."

Enala's mouth twisted in a frown. "You… yes, you vanished," she shook her head. "No, *I* should be thanking *you*. You were the one who gave me a fighting chance in the first place."

"The creature made it clear the only way either of us

would survive was to work together… I should not have abandoned you."

Enala smiled. "There was nothing more you could have done. As you say, we only stood a chance if we stood together. I was finished…" she shuddered. "If not for Eric…"

"How did Eric help you? His magic should not have worked there; there was nothing of the Sky element in that world."

"I don't know, but somehow he summoned lightning. Combined with my fire magic, it was enough to destroy the creature."

Laurel stared at Enala, wondering if she had dreamt the whole thing. Eric was powerful, but he was no God. He could not have created lightning from nothing.

"So," Enala interrupted her thoughts. "What will you do now? You aren't thinking of kidnapping us again, are you?" she looked at Laurel with humour in her eyes.

Laurel laughed, but before she could answer a knock came from outside. She wrapped herself in magic once more, vanishing from sight.

The door opened and a man with greying hair entered. His face looked haggard, with wrinkles lining his forehead and he sported a patchy beard. He wore a plain brown doublet, long black pants and a scarf wrapped around his neck. He carried a jacket over one arm and a sprinkling of snow dotted his shoulders. A sword was strapped to his waist. He carried a small pack in one hand and a thin golden crown nestled on his temple.

His pale green eyes surveyed the room, passing over the hidden Laurel and settling on Enala.

"Ahh, awake I see, and healed too! I am so glad," the man smiled, moving to stand at Enala's bedside. His voice was a rich bass tone. It could have come from a man twenty years his junior.

Enala stared up at him, confusion written across her face. "Who are you?"

The man gave a booming laugh. "Why, I am the king of course. And my guards tell me that *you* are Enala."

The girl nodded, struggling to sit up in the bed. "Yes, I'm Enala," she stammered. "It's ah… an honour to meet you, your majesty?" unable to do anything else, she offered her hand.

The king laughed again and accepted the gesture. Laurel watched the exchange in silence, hardly daring to breath.

"Nice to meet you too, Enala. And you can call me Jonathan. We are family, after all."

Enala swallowed visibly. "You know?"

Jonathan grinned. "I do. Your companion told my guards an abridged version of your story, and given your rather miraculous appearance, I at least am predisposed to believe it."

"I see," Enala looked lost for words. "I… I… What happens now?"

"That depends on you," he hesitated. "How do you feel?"

Enala's hand drifted to her stomach. Surprise flashed across her face when she found the skin whole. Laurel suppressed a shudder, remembering the gaping wound left by the skeleton's scimitar.

Enala smiled at the king. "Looks like I'm fine."

"Excellent!" the king clapped his hands. "In that case, we can talk. I would not have wanted to disturb your healing," he moved across to the bedside chair and sat down. "I'm not sure whether you know much about Trola, but all is not well in my kingdom. Since my magic failed a few months ago, I have lost the faith of my council, and with them, my people."

"What do you mean?"

"Despite our many decades of peace, the Trolan people still place a great amount of value on the strength of their leaders. When my magic failed, I became the first king to rule Trola without magic. The council saw that as a sign of weakness, saw me as a failure with no right to rule. Over the last few months they have used their power to undermine me. Today, I have little power or control over my own kingdom, other than a few men who remain faithful. The council rules in Kalgan now."

Enala stared at the king. Laurel shifted on tired legs, closing her eyes as the silence stretched out.

"And I am not entirely sure the council still serves the Trolan people," Jonathan whispered.

"What do you mean?"

"I believe there are some on the council who have been corrupted, who now work in the thrall of Archon."

Laurel shivered. Ever since these two had come into her life, the whispers of Archon had been unrelenting. Even here, in the greatest city in the Three Nations, it seemed dark powers still lurked in the shadows. Not even the Trolan council was immune.

"Where are the council now?" Enala asked.

"Fortunately, you arrived late in the evening and they had already retired for the day. Word of your arrival will have spread by now, but they will not reconvene until morning. They will summon you and your friend then. Whether they will believe your story or not, I do not know."

Enala made to get out of the bed and then hesitated, the sheets drawn up around her. She blushed, realising the healers had taken her clothes, that she was naked beneath the covers. "But they have to believe us!" she insisted. "You have no idea what we've been through, the sacrifices we've made to get here."

"It might not matter. There has been no word from Jurrien or Antonia in weeks. They know there is a girl called

Enala who is meant to wield the Sword of Light, but that does not mean they will believe you are that girl."

"There is an easy way to test that! Let me hold the Sword. If I survive, then they'll know they have the right girl."

"The Sword is not here though," the king replied, voice grim.

"*What?* Where is it? It's meant to be here!"

"When I lost my powers the council had it moved to Witchcliffe Island. For safekeeping, they said. No one is allowed there. A powerful magic was cast to keep people out."

"They must allow me to go there, to try it," Enala argued.

"I do not think they will," the king hesitated. "I can argue on your account, but they hold little respect for me now. It will not do much good. I think they will lock you up, at least until someone verifies your story."

Enala's eyes flickered to where Laurel hid. "What do we do?"

The king stood. "You can come with me. I can get you out of the citadel, take you to the island. My few remaining men have secured keys which will allow us to pass through the magic protecting the Sword. But we have to go now, before the council can stop us."

"Are you sure?" Enala frowned. "What if they can be convinced?"

"It's a possibility," he paused. "But is it worth the risk? Better to ask forgiveness, than permission."

Enala stared at the older man. Laurel held her breath, thinking over what had been said. It was a difficult decision, with both options fraught with risk. If they caught Enala attempting to escape, they would never let her near the Sword. But if they were going to lock her up anyway…

Enala finally nodded. "Okay," she looked around. "But I have no clothes… and we need Eric."

The king reached into his rucksack and tossed some clothing on the bed. "I hope they fit. As for your friend, I'm not sure where they are holding him. My man followed you to this room. By the time he returned to seek out your friend, guards loyal to the council had already taken him. He could be anywhere in the keep."

"We may need his magic."

"We may. But the keep is massive and we don't have the time to search for him. We would be caught for sure."

The girl took a deep breath. "Okay. I'm sure he will figure out what's happening, somehow."

Laurel smiled at the obvious message in Enala's words. She nodded her silent agreement. She wondered how Eric would react to her sudden appearance.

"Good. I'll wait outside while you get changed. Be quick!" he slipped out the door and closed it behind him.

Enala rolled out of bed and slipped into the fresh clothing. The jacket hung loosely off her small shoulders and the breaches needed a belt, but they would protect her from the icy weather outside. Laurel's own jacket was far too thin for the Trolan climate.

"Don't worry, I'll tell him," Laurel whispered. "Good luck!"

Enala grimaced in her direction. "Thank you. I think I'm going to need it."

CHAPTER 19

Gabriel turned to see Katya moving through the crowd of soldiers. She swung her sword as she moved, laying into the fleeing men with the flat edge of the blade. Her eyes burned, her face a mask of rage.

"Any man that abandons his post will see the noose," she growled, and her words finally sank in. The men slowed, glancing back at the approaching dragons, as though weighing their chances.

Gabriel could not help but smile. Dragons had not been seen in the skies of Plorsea in decades – who could blame the men for panicking? Even so, he stifled his grin. The councillor was right, this was a time of war. Plorsea could not allow the fear of cowards to cripple its army.

Beside him, Caelin stepped forward. "Do not worry, men," his parade ground voice boomed over the clamour. He waved a hand at the approaching dragons. "Those are Gold Dragons, the last tribe allied with men. They mean us no harm; they are here to help. I spoke with them in Dragon Country, they are no threat."

Katya cut her way through the crowd of soldiers. When

she reached them, Gabriel saw her anger had not abated since their unexpected visit. "Did you bring these beasts here, Caelin? Did you know they would come?"

Caelin met her frosty stare. "No, I did not bring them here."

"But you did not think to mention to the king that you had spoken with these creatures?"

"You will have to forgive me, it was a rather brief meeting and I had more pressing things to discuss. Perhaps if someone had allowed us another audience, I could have told you."

Katya shook her head. "What are they doing here, unannounced?"

"You will have to ask them that yourself," Caelin offered.

"You think we can just *talk* to those beasts?" Katya growled. "Those are *dragons*, you fool, in case you hadn't noticed. I can't just have them flying up to the city uninvited. Who knows what their true motives are."

Gabriel's stomach twisted. "What do you mean?" he interrupted. "Those are Gold Dragons – they're our allies, friends of Enala."

Katya turned her frosty eyes on him. "And where is this 'Enala' I keep hearing about? Vanished, dead for all we know. As for the alliance, there are few who even remember it exists. It is a forgotten treaty forged by a long dead king. You are both fools if you think we should allow such powerful creatures to fly right up to the city," she waved an arm to encompass the buildings behind them. "You would entrust all those lives to an outdated piece of paper?"

Gabriel made to reply, but Inken's elbow in his side cut him off. Simmering, he pursed his lips and bit back his response. It would not do to lose his temper now, not while the situation on the wall still hung on the edge. Air hissed from his nostrils as he breathed out and looked to Caelin.

But Caelin did not reply. He stood stiff as a board, staring at Katya, panic in his eyes.

Katya shook her head. "Nothing. Unsurprising. You are a fool, Caelin, and I won't risk everything we have on the word of fool," she turned to the men and raised a fist. "Men, to arms! Prepare the catapults. Archers to the fore. You there, find me a speaking trumpet. Perhaps we can persuade these creatures to leave without bloodshed."

Gabriel gaped, unable to believe what he was hearing. He opened his mouth to scream at Caelin, to demand why the sergeant had frozen, but his tongue twisted in his throat and only a strangled squeak came out. He choked, his mouth dry, unable to form coherent words.

Gabriel stood rigid, staring at Katya, at Caelin. He made to move, to grab Caelin and shake him, but found his muscles locked in place. His whole body stood frozen. With growing horror, he realised Inken and Caelin were in a similar state.

Around them the soldiers began to move, rushing for weapon stashes and manning the great war machines mounted to the battlements.

His eyes flicked to Inken and Caelin and saw his panic reflected in their eyes. Swallowing, Gabriel glanced at Katya, watching as she strode through the men, bellowing at the top of her voice. Her eyes found them, and Gabriel thought he saw her lips twitch in the slightest smile.

Dark magic, the thought swept through Gabriel's mind.

He stared at Katya as she swept through the Plorsean ranks. They had been wrong to trust her, to try and make her see reason. She had been Archon's agent all along. Being a senior councillor, it was not hard to see how Katya might have influenced the king. Who knew what dark magic she had worked in Ardath.

Gabriel closed his eyes and gritted his teeth, fighting against whatever magic held his body. His muscles trembled and his knees creaked, but nothing changed. He could almost feel the dark forces surrounding him, the ghostly tendrils binding his limbs in iron. Only his eyes remained untouched, leaving him free to watch, horrified, as the dragons grew ever closer.

This cannot be happening.

"Dragons!" Katya's voice boomed out. Someone had found her the speaking trumpet. "Why do you enter Plorsean lands uninvited. Turn back now, you are not welcome here."

Gabriel sucked in a breath, his muscles straining to break free. His eyes flicked to the men nearest them, praying one would realise something was amiss. But no one was watching them; all eyes were on the approaching dragons. Soldiers raced along the parapet, taking up positions at regular intervals and crouching to string their bows. A catapult groaned as it turned to face the oncoming threat.

In the distance, the dragons roared and fire criss-crossed the sky.

No! Gabriel swore to himself. This had to be stopped. He clenched his fists, eyes flicking again to his companions. It took a moment for him to realise he had moved his hand. Hope blossomed in his chest and he struggled to bring feeling back to the rest of his arm.

Katya returned to where they stood frozen, a sad look on her face. "I have to admit, I'm disappointed you were wrong, Caelin," her eyes looked distant. "Dragon's would have been a welcome ally, but those beasts have not come to make peace."

Gabriel felt the blood flee his face. *This cannot be happening!* Plorsea was about to fire on their most powerful allies. The dragons believed they were approaching friends; the surprise attack would decimate them – along with any future chance of alliance.

And those who survived the carnage would wreak bloody revenge on Ardath.

Katya still stood close by, her grim eyes watching the dragons approach. Gabriel felt another surge of hope as a tremor ran through his arm. He strained his muscles further, seeking every inch of give he could find. Then, slowly, he lowered his hand to the pommel of his sword.

Golden scales flashed with the beating of wings. The dragons had already crossed the halfway mark of the lake and were closing fast on the city. They would be within range in seconds.

"Men, prepare to fire!" Katya called.

Gabriel stood rigid as Katya paced past, shouting orders to the men on the catapult. Her eyes glittered, studying the dragons' approach, ignorant now to the three of them. His fingers found the pommel of his sword and wrapped around the leather hilt. As he clenched it tight, a shock ran from his arm into his body, and a pressure snapped in his mind.

Shaking his head, Gabriel risked a glance at Caelin and nodded. His sword rasped from its scabbard.

In front of them, Katya raised an arm, eyes fixed on the advancing dragons. She opened her mouth to give the order.

Stepping up behind her, Gabriel drove his blade through the councillor's back. The sharp steel slid in to the hilt and lodged there. Katya stiffened on the blade, her sharp groan echoing across the battlements. Her head half-turned, staring in shock at Gabriel. Her mouth opened, but only blood came out.

Staring into Katya's eyes, Gabriel felt ice grow in his chest. In that moment, he had a terrible thought – maybe he'd been wrong, maybe Katya was not the traitor. Heart pounding hard against his ribs, he released the blade. Katya toppled to the ground.

Her dead eyes stared up at him, accusing.

Caelin stumbled as the spell broke and Inken shuddered beside him. Then she was swinging the bow off her shoulder and into her hand. She had an arrow nocked before Caelin had even drawn his sword. Together they stepped up on either side of Gabriel, weapons at the ready.

Around them the soldiers stared, unable to comprehend the sudden death of their commander. It only took another second for that to change. Almost as one, a hundred bows turned in their direction.

Yet all Gabriel could do was stand and stare at the dead woman at his feet.

ERIC PACED ACROSS THE BEDROOM, the soft carpet yielding beneath his sandaled feet. Incensed candles in the chandelier above cast their flicking light across the walls and left a citrus tang in his nostrils. A cushioned bed sat in the centre of the room, beckoning. But he could not sleep, not now, not while Enala's fate still hung in the balance.

He glanced towards the heavy wooden doors barring his exit. They opened into a corridor where two guards waited, ensuring Eric did not make any unaccompanied trips into the citadel. Taking a breath, he moved towards the doors and then stopped, knowing it was useless. He had already tried that route. The guards had said in no uncertain terms he was to remain in this room until morning.

At least he could be thankful for their treatment of him. The first thing they'd done on reaching his makeshift prison was to un-cuff him and usher him into an adjoining room. There a hot bath waited. Still shivering from the cold outside,

Eric had not needed any further encouragement. He pulled off his bloodstained clothing and slid into the hot water. The guards took his ruined clothes and quickly departed. To his surprise, they left Alastair's sword where he had discarded it.

He returned to the bedroom wearing only a towel, where he found a white bathrobe and thin pair of sandals waiting for him.

Now hours had passed and still there was no word of Enala. Eric moved to the bed and sat down. He ran his hands through his hair, desperate to know if she had survived. Kalgan was the richest city in the Three Nations; surely they must have healers.

She will be okay, Eric reassured himself.

A fire burned in the grate on one wall, the flames casting a warm glow to mix with the candlelight. The walls were plain and windowless, there would be no escape there. Of course, with his magic he was confident he could fight his way out if necessary. But it would not come to that. These people were their allies, it would not be prudent to start blasting through walls just yet.

He lay back on his bed, the soft cushion yielding beneath him. With a wry grin, Eric realised this was the most comfortable bed he had ever lain on. Whether they believed him or not, the guards had not joked about making him feel welcome. He just hoped Enala was receiving the same attention.

Swallowing a lump in his throat, Eric closed his eyes. Inken's face drifted through his mind, her wry grin flashing beneath her fiery red hair. How many days had it been now? How many nights since he'd left her in the ruin of Sitton. Even without the time warp of the Way, he'd lost count.

Staring up at the high ceiling, Eric prayed she still lived.

Then, exhaling, Eric began to meditate.

He wasn't sure how long he lay there before a bang on

the door woke him. A guard entered carrying a steaming plate of food. He placed it on the bedside table and flicked Eric a smile.

"Sorry to wake you, but I thought you could use an early breakfast. Glad you got some sleep, you're looking better than when we found you," he waved at the door. "Sorry for the lock and key too. If what you say is true, it's a relief to have you. Without the king's magic and the Sword, things have grown…dark here in Trola."

"Is my friend okay?" Eric asked.

The guard nodded. "I heard the healers have given her the all clear. Must have taken them a bit of magic, she looked a bad way when you arrived," he turned and moved back to the door. "Enjoy your breakfast, the council will want to see you within the hour."

Eric's shoulders loosened as relief undid the knots in his stomach. *She's okay!*

As the door closed he turned to the plate of food. It held a generous portion of bacon, eggs and beans, along with sausages made from a darker meat than he'd seen in Plorsea. He guessed it would be lamb or sheep – the mountainous countryside of Trola was good for little else.

Ignoring his cutlery, Eric picked up one of the sausages and took a bite. Red juice ran down his chin as the charred meat touched his tongue.

Somewhere in the room, a woman laughed.

Eric jumped, spilling beans across the bedsheets.

"Didn't anyone ever teach you to eat like a gentleman?" Laurel laughed again, appearing next to him on the bed.

Eric scrambled backwards, but Laurel's hand flashed out to cover his mouth.

"Ssssh ssshh, Eric. We don't want to alert the guards. Enala has a message for you."

THE DEMON SUCKED in a deep breath of air, tasting the salt on the ocean breeze. It looked down at the city of Kalgan, nestled in the curve of the Trolan coastline. Rugged beaches stretched out to either side, and in the north forest grew right to the city walls. Waves smashed against the seawalls, driving salt spray into the air to cover the city with mist. In the distance an island sat in the deep waters of the bay.

A smile twisted its lips as it looked down on its old home. Slowly the winds holding the demon aloft dissipated and it dropped lower in the sky. It had taken some time to gain control of Jurrien's magic, forcing the demon to travel much of the journey on foot. But when it finally mastered the Storm God's power, the final hundred miles had flashed by in hours.

The demon had hesitated at Ardath, reaching out to check for the presence of its prey. There was no trace of them, but still it paused to consider the city's destruction. But it had sensed the power of its comrades, other emissaries of Archon. The demon smiled. They were specks compared to the power it now wielded, but their presence meant Archon had other plans for the city.

There had been no sign of its prey elsewhere either. It listened for word from Archon's spies, but the trail had gone cold. It seemed the two had vanished.

It did not matter now though. Somewhere below, the Sword of Light waited. It would find the blade and reclaim Thomas' ancient birth right. They could not hide the Sword; it would tear the city apart brick by brick if necessary. Then, finally, the power Thomas had once wielded would be restored.

The wind roared and its cloak flapped out. Lightning flickered along the blade in its left hand. He grinned.

Before the demon could unleash the power, it felt a familiar magic stir in the city below.

The demon frowned. *Now how did you get here?*

"This is a bad idea," Eric whispered.

"A bit late to turn back now," Laurel hissed back as she relieved the unconscious guards of their swords.

"Thanks, so glad you pointed that out," he replied in a bland voice.

He hoped Enala knew what game she was playing at, trusting Laurel. But he had little choice but to go along with the plan. It had apparently taken most of the night for Laurel to discover where they were keeping him, and even longer waiting for a chance to slip into his room undetected. Enala and King Jonathan were a long way ahead of them by now.

Eric glanced up and down the corridor, his nerves fraught. The sun was up and the council could send for him at any minute. They must know Enala was missing by now. There was no more time to waste; they needed to get out of the citadel, now.

But first, he needed proper clothes. He winced as Laurel tossed him a pair of pants. These were followed by the guard's jerkin, cloak and boots. Using the robe to shield himself and keeping a wary eye on Laurel, he began slipping into the clothing.

Laurel laughed when she saw him watching her. "Don't worry, you're not my type," she still didn't turn away.

Eric flushed but finished pulling on the clothes. They were too large for him, but at least he would have some protection from the cold air outside. Together they dragged the guards into the bedroom and locked the door behind them.

Laurel slipped past him. "This way," she whispered.

Swallowing, Eric glanced back at the doors. *Too late now.*

Taking a firmer grip of Alastair's sword, he followed after her, slipping down the silent corridors. Eric glanced through open doors as they moved, surprised by how empty the citadel seemed. They did not encounter a single soul as they made their way through the keep.

Eric shook his head, worry gnawing at him. Despite the early hour, there should have been people, servants and workers moving about to prepare the citadel for the day ahead.

"Where is everybody?"

Laurel shrugged. "The place is all but empty. I checked too many rooms to count looking for you – there's nobody here. It seems the occupants of the citadel have gone elsewhere."

Eric frowned. Something didn't add up. *Where have they gone?* The empty corridors offered no answers. Even the guards were sparse, absent.

It took ten minutes for Laurel to lead them back to the courtyard where they'd first arrived. There were no guards in sight now, and Eric guessed they had only been drawn there by the crash of their arrival. In the dawn's light he saw a few scraggly trees growing up the walls, but otherwise the lawn was empty.

"This is where your magic comes in, Eric," Laurel gave a wry smile. "Just don't drop me."

Eric shot her a glare. "Don't tempt me."

Closing his eyes, he reached for his power. It rose with intent, made bold by its conquest in the wasteland of The Way. But Eric had no patience for its mischief; Enala needed his help and he was not about to let his magic get in the way. He crushed down his doubt and brushed aside the growls of the magic's wolf.

Wrapping the magic in his command, he reached out and drew the winds to them.

Eric held out his hand to Laurel as the winds gathered. She took it, and an instant later they lifted ponderously off the snowy grass. He grinned at the pale fear on Laurel's face as the ground fell away beneath them. They soared up into the heavens, far higher than necessary.

The city of Kalgan stretched out beneath them, slate rooftops shining in the morning sun. The domed towers of two temples shone golden at either end of the city, while the citadel towered on a hill at the centre. On the coast, docks stretched out into the harbour. Ships rocked at their berths, the rare westerly wind driving waves straight in from the ocean. Witchcliffe island loomed in the distance.

As he reached again for his magic, he sensed a tremor of disturbance in the sky. Another power tingled at the back of his neck, racing closer. It felt hauntingly familiar.

God magic, Eric realised, an instant before the demon rose into view.

CHAPTER 20

The scrape of the wooden keel on gravel jolted Enala from her dreams. She looked around, eyes struggling to adjust to the darkness staining the world, and glimpsed the vague outline of the king as he leapt from the stern. Stones crunched again as Jonathan dragged the dingy farther up the beach.

Enala toyed with the silver bracelets cuffed around her wrists. The emeralds embedded in the precious metal seemed to glow with a light of their own, and in the pale moonlight she caught the glint of strange symbols etched along their length. Jonathan had given them to her as protection from the magic that had been cast over the island. Their spells would kill anyone who stepped foot there without permission.

She just hoped the bracelets worked.

"Come on, quickly," Jonathan shouted above the crashing waves.

Enala struggled over the wooden benches and leapt down to the beach. The stones sank beneath her feet as she landed, and a wave rushed up to drench her boots. She swore, stumbling farther up the dunes and away from the ocean. The bracelets burned hot for half a second and then cooled once more.

She turned to watch Jonathan tie the boat to a post in the beach. He still carried his duffle bag, clutching it close as though his life depended on it. On the journey here she had watched the king, her first impressions of him quickly changing. Jonathan was not the confident man he had appeared back in the citadel. He spent most of his time casting nervous glances behind them, and jumping as water lapped over the sides of the row boat.

Enala shook her head. She could already see why the people might have lost confidence in this king. His nervous ticks made him seem weak, but perhaps she was not giving him enough credit. He had defied the council and spirited her out of Kalgan – that had to count for something.

Swallowing her worries, Enala decided to do her best to ignore his behaviour. She just hoped he knew what he was doing.

Together they trekked up the beach, the stones giving way to soft sand. Overhead the red cliffs of Witchcliffe island loomed as shadows against the dark sky. The wind whistled through the wiry branches of the trees dangling from the sheer walls. A faint glow lit the distant horizon, signalling the approach of dawn.

Jonathan led her off the beach and up a trail through the long grass growing on the sand dunes. Without a torch they relied on the moonlight to guide them. Enala soon found herself tripping on the thin grass roots criss-crossing the trail, and cursed Jonathan's lack of foresight. Insects buzzed around her head and flew at her face, the vicious flies biting wherever they discovered flesh. Enala swore and swatted them away as best she could.

It did not take long to reach the first fork in the trail. A left turn continued along the beach, while the right led to the base of the cliffs where Enala glimpsed a narrow staircase carved into the rock. As they drew closer, Enala saw that wind and rain had worn the stairs smooth. Someone had strung a rope through hoops hammered into the cliff-face, but there was little else to prevent them plummeting to their deaths.

At least it's something, she thought, fighting down her nerves.

Jonathan paused when they reached the bottom and turned back. His face was pale and sweat beaded his forehead.

"These steps are treacherous, so be careful. Halfway up we will encounter the second protection spell. It will not be visible until we are right in front of it, but it encases the top of the island in a dome of magic. Only those who carry the correct keys can enter."

"Your bracelets are spelled to let you pass through the dome unharmed. Inside is a third protection, a maze which we must navigate together. The magic there is strange, ever changing to stop any threat powerful enough to bypass the first two traps. The bracelets may not protect you from everything," he pulled down his shirt to reveal a gold and emerald necklace. "Nor will my amulet. We will have to work together to survive. Are you ready?"

Enala ran her fingers over one of the bracelets, feeling the small indentations the emeralds made. She nodded. "Let's go."

They made their way up, step by cautious step. Loose stones littered the stairs, rattling as their stray feet kicked them from the edge. After a few minutes of climbing, they were too high to hear the thud as they struck the ground below.

They continued up, clambering over branches where the

scraggly trees overgrew the path. Small thorns crisscrossed the trunks and pointy leaves sliced at their skin as they squeezed between the branches.

It did not take long for Enala's legs to start burning from the upwards march. After half an hour still the steep incline offered no pause. Enala's lungs stung, but she pressed on. She panted along behind Jonathan, surprised by the large man's stamina. The dim light offered no sign of the beach below, but by now it must be far beneath them.

It took another half hour before Jonathan finally came to a stop.

"This is it," he announced.

Enala leaned against to the cliff, panting for breath as she peered over his shoulder. Her eyes widened. Ahead a transparent bubble enveloped the path. Colours swirled across its surface, while beyond the path continued, winding its way up through the ghastly trees. The bubble stretched outwards in all directions, disappearing into the sky far above.

"How high does it go?" Enala asked.

"As I said, it forms a dome around the top of the island, to ensure none can pass unchallenged," Jonathan answered. "When we enter, you must stop on the other side. We will need to take our bearings before continuing into the maze. Even with the keys, it is designed to confuse the mind. And there are dark creatures lurking there."

Enala stared at the barrier. "What maze? I can see the path on the other side."

"You'll see," was Jonathan's only answer before he stepped into the bubble.

Enala watched, expecting him to continue walking along the path on the other side. Instead, he vanished. Staring into the barrier, Enala bit the side of her cheek, wondering where the magic led.

Taking a deep breath, she stepped after Jonathan.

The bubble bent inwards as she entered, it's cool surface pressing to her skin. Then a screech ran through her ears and the world spun. The barrier snapped closed and a strange wetness enveloped her body. Fighting down panic, Enala held her breath and took another step. The ground still felt solid, even as her eyes watched the world continue to spin.

Lungs screaming, Enala pressed on, unsure whether she could breathe in the strange material. Her stomach twisted and her chest strained with the desire for air, but her feet did not betray her. A heartbeat later the spinning ceased and she stepped from the wetness into the maze.

The air howled, tearing at her clothes and threatening to push her from the path. Sand or something like it whipped at her face as she tried to make sense of what she saw. Shadows spread out through a world tinted blue, some just beginning to form as others faded into the misty ether. Ahead the path splintered out in a dozen different directions, each trailing away into the ghostly landscape.

One path called to her, and without thinking she made to step towards it.

A firm hand grasped her by the shoulder. "Stop," Jonathan whispered in her ear. "Wait. We must stick together if we are to survive. The maze is alive, and it lies. If it draws you in, you will never see the real world again. Do not trust what your senses tell you."

Enala felt a fog enveloping her mind, slowing her thoughts. After a time, Jonathan's words seeped into her consciousness. She shook her head, trying to clear her thoughts. "Then which path do we take?"

Jonathan raised a finger to his lips. He pointed at the shadows. They continued to shift, some growing while others shrank, but bit by bit the maze grew clearer. Through the apparitions she saw ceilings and stairwells which seemed to fold back on one another, and in places the trails led straight up walls. Her stomach twisted at the impossibilities of the maze before her.

The bracelets burned at her wrists, and some of the queerness faded away. One pathway grew clearer, though the others criss-crossed it like tangled wool.

"Do you see it?" Jonathan whispered.

"I think so," Enala nodded.

"Good. We must take care. The magic of our keys might not last the trip. If it runs out, we will have to rely on our own cunning to escape," he paused. "Whatever you do, do not touch the shadows that surround us. They are death. And keep quiet, we are not alone here. Dark creatures roam these corridors. It would be best if we avoided them."

Jonathan swallowed. "Follow me," he stepped onto the path.

Enala could not miss the fear in Jonathan's eyes. Biting her lip, she braced herself against the wind and followed in his footsteps. She prayed his courage would hold. Whatever lurked in these shadows, she did not wish to face it alone. But she had a feeling Jonathan's hands were not the safest in which to place one's life.

Still, he was the only guide she had. They made their way deeper into the maze, shadows pressing in on them. Enala kept her arms close to her sides, mindful of Jonathan's warning. Her fingers brushed across the bracelets, drawing scant comfort from the warmth of their touch.

Her thoughts turned to Eric, and whether Laurel had found him. It did not feel right to continue without him, not after they had been through so much. She had watched him die – and somehow come back to life. She thought she was dreaming as Eric stumbled towards her, his clothes brown with dust and lightning leaping from his fingers to join her flames. She would feel better with him at her side.

But he was not here. It was up to her to find the Sword, to bring it back to Kalgan.

Time stretched on as they passed through the strange realm. Bit by bit the wind died away, leaving silence in its wake. Not even their boots made a sound as they trod the dark path. The fog slowly returned to her mind, turning her thoughts to porridge. She kneaded her forehead and tried to focus on the true path. Jonathan walked ahead of her, his stride becoming hesitant.

With the maze all around, they did not stop for food or rest. The path led inexorably upwards, staircases and steep tracks carrying them further into the ghostly sky. The shadows drifted like clouds, moving across the path to slow their passage. Somewhere outside, Enala guessed they must be nearing the summit of the island. But the maze stretched on, endless.

"Almost there," Jonathan whispered after what seemed like hours.

Enala grunted, too exhausted to reply. Her body ached and she had come to the end of her strength. The Magickers may have healed her body, but they had not restored her completely. Her stamina was gone.

A chill wind blew from behind them. The hackles on Enala's neck stood as she smelt the stench of rotting carrion. Her stomach swirled and she slowed, turning to search for the source of the deathly tang.

Behind, a beast stood on the path, its hungry red eyes following them. Saliva dripped from its gapping maw and rows of dagger-like teeth glinted in the shadow light. Long arms reached for them, claws stretched wide. It crouched, the knotted muscles taut and ready to spring. A broad tail flicked out behind it. Jet-black scales covered its body from head to foot.

Enala knew enough of the dark tales told in Chole to

recognise a Raptor. She could not fathom how one had come to be here, so far from the desert, but there was no mistaking the greed in its eyes. Moving carefully, she edged her way backwards up the path.

A shout came from behind her. She glanced back in time to see the colour flee the king's face. Terror overtook him as he screamed again. He turned and bolted, leaving Enala for dead.

Enala swore and raced after him. Behind, the Raptor roared, turning her stomach to ice. Jonathan's long legs quickly outpaced her, while Enala felt her strength fading with each step. Before she could catch him, Jonathan disappeared around a corner in the maze. Another roar came, right behind her now.

Goosebumps prickled on Enala's neck and instinct shrieked for her to move. She dove, the ground rising up to meet her as a shape whistled past. Claws caught in her cloak, almost tearing it from her neck. Then the fabric ripped and the creature's momentum carried it past.

Springing to her feet, Enala searched the shadows for a weapon. Jonathan wore a sword, but that would do her little good now. The cowardly king was long gone. Her search came up empty – this world held nothing but shadows.

And the Raptor. It had regained its feet and now stalked towards her, head bent low and outstretched, teeth glistening. Its slitted nostrils widened as it scented her. A low rumble came from its throat.

Enala backed away, fear making her heart thump painfully in her chest. She could not flee this thing, that much was clear. Nor could she fight it with her bare hands. That left only one option – magic.

Staring at the beast, Enala sought to summon her fear, her rage; anything that might bring the magic forth. The fear was easy, bubbling beneath the surface, threatening to steal away the last vestiges of her strength.

The rage followed, festering at the king's cowardice. With his sword they might have stood a chance, might have overcome the beast. Instead, he had fled, leaving her there to die.

Enala growled, anger stirring as she stepped towards the beast. It burned through her body, searing away her fears. The creature stilled, staring at her, the hunger in its eyes turning to doubt. She felt the power rising within her and made no attempt to control it. She needed it now and did not care if it wreaked havoc in this phantom realm.

The power throbbed in her chest, burning as it spread through her skin.

Enala closed her eyes and willed the fire forth.

Heat encircled her arms, burning into her wrists. For a moment, she thought the flame magic had taken light but when she looked her hands were empty. Instead the bracelets shone bright on her arms, their heat scorching her skin. Pain lanced from her wrists, bringing tears to her eyes. She gasped, concentration snapping, and the power sank back into the depths of her subconscious.

She looked up in panic and knew the Raptor could sense the change. Its jaws widened in a reptilian grin. It started forward again, unstoppable.

Enala wiped the tears from her eyes and turned to flee. She raced down a random path, mind racing as she searched for a new plan.

What happened to my magic?

But there was no time to dwell on that question. From behind came the monster's roar as it leapt after her. She could not avoid it for long, and who knew which path she now tread. Jonathan had warned her to stay on the true one – though his word suddenly held little value to her.

Ahead a shadow loomed and Jonathan's words came back to her.

To touch them is death!

An idea flashed through her thoughts and she ran on. The shadow wall loomed, a ghostly barrier blocking the way. Half her mind urged her to spring through, to test the truth of Jonathan's warning. But there would be no second chances here and out of options, she put her faith in the cowardly king.

At the last moment, Enala spun to face the creature. It bounded towards her, claws outstretched, mouth wide to tear her head from her shoulders. It roared – and sprang.

Enala only had a split second to react. She dove for the ground, as she had earlier. The beast's momentum carried it past once more, straight for the shadow wall blocking the path. But this time the Raptor was ready. Its claws lashed out, biting deep into the flesh of her arm. She screamed as the beast's weight caught her, almost tearing her arm from its socket.

Then the beast struck the shadow. The wall disintegrated at the Raptor's touch, collapsing down to envelop the creature in darkness. It thrashed, jaws gaping as the shadow engulfed its head. The red eyes rolled back in its skull and its legs kicked helplessly.

As the Raptor weakened, Enala struggled to free herself from its claws. Pain tore into her, unbearable, but the shadow was crawling over the beast towards her. She guessed if it reached her, she would soon join the Raptor in its suffocating death. Claw grated on bone as Enala fought to break away.

Steel flashed as a blade descended towards her. Enala flinched as it struck the creature's arm: once, twice, three times. On the final blow the limb snapped and Enala tore herself free.

She stumbled backwards, looking around for her saviour.

She found Jonathan standing over her, his brow wet with sweat and his breath coming in heavy gasps. His eyes still shivered with panic, but somehow he had summoned the courage to return.

Enala could not decide whether to embrace the king, or punch him in the face.

Then the maze collapsed around them, and there was no time for either.

CHAPTER 21

An involuntary tremor ran through Eric as the demon laughed at them. Panic shook his hold on his magic and they dropped half a foot. Laurel shrieked and gripped his hand tighter. Eric grimaced and steadied the winds.

"Ah, my old benefactor, however did you come to be here?" the demon's voice crackled with power.

Eric did not bother to reply. He reached out to the swirling winds, then turned and fled for the city. His racing heart thrust him onwards – he knew this was not a fight they could win. Their only hope was to find shelter in the buildings below. He tightened his hold on Laurel's arm, dragging her with him.

Then the winds gave an abrupt *crack,* and disappeared as though sucked into a vacuum of nothingness. Eric found himself falling, tumbling towards the city below. The rooftops raced up, the spires of a nearby church beckoning.

Eric reached desperately for his magic, fighting back fear as his stomach climbed into his chest. He reached for the wind, cords of magic seeking any parcel of air. But the sky was empty – there was nothing, nothing, noth – *there!*

The wind howled as it caught them, halting their freefall. Looking down Eric hesitated, then drove them towards the pavement, eager to regain solid earth. The demon now ruled the sky. Its laughter came from behind, its magic hot on their heels.

Eric sucked in a breath of relief as they touched down, but there was no time to waste. Laurel tugged at his arm, dragging him down the street. She could not know what they faced, but nor was she a fool. There was no mistaking the power of the demon.

Before they could take five steps a roar came from behind them. Eric felt his ears pop with the release of energy. The earth in front of them split open, the bricked road tumbled into the chasm. Houses on either side of the road tore in two with a violent crack. Screams came from nearby citizens as the earth shook them from their feet.

The demon's cackle rose above the chaos. Eric spun in time to see it touch down, the black cloak billowing in the breeze. It held a sword in either hand, one dark green, the other blue. Energy rippled in the depths of those blades, a dark power which sent a chill to his very soul.

"Stick around a while, won't you," the demon smirked.

Summoning his courage, Eric took a step towards it. "Stay back," he growled.

The demon ignored him, striding forward, dark eyes locked on them. "I don't believe I will, mortal. Now, where is the girl? Where is the Sword?"

Eric answered with lightning.

The air crackled as he unleashed the bolt. Then a surge of energy struck Eric, sending him reeling back, and the lightning stopped dead a few feet from the demon. It hung there, frozen in place, and yet still sizzling with power. The demon laughed and waved a hand.

The blue fire reversed direction, slamming into Eric's chest and flinging him backwards. Air exploded from his lungs as he struck the ground and went tumbling across the ground. The chasm loomed up before him. He grasped for purchase, his body plunging over the edge.

Laurel's hand found his, halting his fall. Grunting, she managed to pull him back from the brink. Together they scrambled clear. He stood, accepting a shoulder from Laurel. They looked across at the demon, helpless fear taking hold. Eric clenched his teeth against the pain rippling through his body.

"Where is the girl? Where is the Sword?" the demon ground out.

It stalked towards them, cracks radiating from where its boots struck the road. The air shimmered, rings of heat seeping from the *Soul Blades*. The earth shook again, driving them to their knees.

Vines erupted from the ground around them. Laurel lashed out with her blade, struggling to hold them back, but to no avail. In seconds they held her immobile. Eric did not even have time to draw Alastair's sword before he found himself trapped in their iron grasp. Thorns stabbed deep into his skin and his chest ached as they began to squeeze.

"*Where?*"

Air exploded between Eric's teeth as the breath was crushed from him. Hot blood ran from his wrists and he shuddered as the thorns scraped against bone. He opened his mouth to scream, but his lungs were already empty.

"Please," he croaked.

The demon stood just two feet away now. It sheathed the blue sword and reached out with a pale hand. Cold fingers grasped Eric's chin and tilted back his face, forcing him to look into the dark depths of what had once been Thomas' eyes. The pressure on his chest eased a little. He sucked in a breath of precious oxygen.

"Well?" the demon growled.

"You're too late," he rasped. "Enala has the Sword, she's gone."

The demon's fingers dug into his cheeks. "Liar."

Eric screamed as its fingernails tore his skin. The vines began to move, dragging their thorny tips through his flesh. He shrieked again as they cut long gashes down his body. Blood dripped from his chest, soaking into the earth beneath him. Agony swept through him in waves. He could almost feel his mind breaking before the onslaught.

The demon drew back its hand. Blood stained its fingertips. "Ah, how I would love to feel Antonia's pain, to see her magic used against one of hers. She has been quiet for so long now, subdued by the blade's magic. But perhaps she can still taste your blood," it ran one bloody finger down the green *Soul Blade*.

Light erupted from the sword at the demon's touch. Eric closed his eyes, but even so a bright track blazed across his vision. The light burned through his eyelids, but trapped in the vines he could not turn away. The demon cursed and stumbled back, shaking the sword as though it had scorched him. But its fist remained locked around the pommel, the demon either unable or unwilling to release it.

As the light blazed stronger, a voice whispered in Eric's mind.

Eric, can you hear me?

Eric's spirit soared at Antonia's voice. "Yes!"

Then listen, I cannot hold him long. I have been saving my strength for this moment, but even so, it is not much. I cannot escape.

Eric's hope shrivelled away, but he remained silent.

There is much you don't know, much Alastair and I were meant to tell you before things went so wrong. Secrets we kept for the safety of all, to ensure Archon did not discover the truth. Enala is not the only ancestor of Thomas' sister, Aria. Watch, and you shall see.

Eric's vision faded to black, before a new image took shape in his mind's eye. A cross-roads materialised, the streets obscured by the darkness of night. Buildings ringed the intersection. A single lantern burned on the corner, illuminating a pale circle of light. A man stood beneath the lantern, his hands deep in the pockets of his trench coat. He turned to look down the street, waiting.

A couple appeared from the shadows, their breath steaming in the cold. The woman held a bundle of cloth in her arms, clutching it close to her chest. The man wore a sword at his side and strode with the confidence of a fighter. Their faces were familiar, calling to Eric from the depths of his memory.

With a chill, he realised they were Enala's parents.

The man at the cross-roads turned to watch the approaching couple. They met beneath the glow of the lamp, faces huddled close to hide the whispered words.

Eric heard them anyway.

"Thank you for coming," Enala's father began. "You don't know how hard this is for us."

"Then why are you doing it? Why choose me?" the other man's voice was familiar too.

Eric struggled to place it as the woman replied. "We do this because we must. Our custom demands it," she smiled, her voice filled with warmth. "And we chose you, Allan, because we know you. You and your wife. You are the ones we want."

No, no, no, the words raced through Eric's mind as the scene faded. The last thing he glimpsed was of Enala's mother passing the bundle to the man called Allan. *It cannot be true!*

Allan was his father's name.

Yes, Eric, it is the truth. You are Enala's twin brother, you too have the royal blood, Antonia's voice returned, but it was fainter now, diminished.

"*How?*" Eric's mind reeled, unable to comprehend the vision. "*Why?*"

Aria and her children were hunted from the moment Alastair took them into hiding. Archon was desperate to see them dead, and only the most desperate of measures could keep the line safe. Over generations, it became tradition for your ancestors to separate their children at birth, to adopt one into a worthy family. You were such a child.

Eric shook. "No, no I knew my parents. This cannot be possible."

The light from the *Soul Blade* shivered. *You saw the truth, Eric. Both Enala and yourself have the blood to wield the Sword,* she paused. *But you must be strong to use it. You must have conquered your own power if you are to stand a chance of wielding the Sword.*

"Enala has only just begun to learn," Eric whispered.

Then it must be you, Eric, though you too are still learning. You must not die here.

Eric's mind still whirled, still fought against Antonia's words. "How can this be? Did Alastair know this?"

I never told him, though he may have guessed when I sent him to you.

Eric choked back tears. He struggled to concentrate, though pain still rippled from where the vines were embedded in his flesh. "None of this matters, Antonia. It's too powerful, I cannot escape."

Do not worry about that. But we are out of time; the demon will soon take control of my powers again. I give you my blessing, Eric. Good luck.

With her last words, warmth flooded into Eric's body. As it spread the vines drew back, falling to the ground where they withered and died. The warmth spread, encircling his wounds and drawing out the pain. He watched as gashes in his flesh closed over, the skin knitting itself back together.

As the last of his wounds healed, the warmth vanished.

Eric looked up to see the demon's dark eyes watching him. The emerald light of the *Soul Blade* had returned to a sickly green. Purple veins stood out on the demon's arms as it gripped the sword hard.

"What did she tell you, boy?" Rage burned in its eyes.

Eric summoned his magic, bracing himself for another round. *What is Antonia playing at? She knows I cannot win this fight.*

"Do not worry yourself about that, demon," Laurel stepped between them.

Eric stared at the ex-Baronian, shocked by her interference. She too had been freed, her wounds healed by Antonia's magic. She looked sideways at him and flashed a smile. She no longer held her sword, but she stood with a strange confidence, defying the demon.

"She spoke to me too," a shiver ran through Eric as she faced the demon. "I know what I have to do," she raised an arm. It flared bright white as she summoned her own power.

The demon laughed. "You think you have the strength to challenge God magic?" the other *Soul Blade* scraped from its sheath.

Laurel shook her head. "No, I do not have the power to challenge your stolen magic. But you cannot wield them without your own dark magic, *demon!*" she spat.

The demon froze, the light from the *Soul Blades* dying away. Its face twisted with hatred. The dark eyes bored into

Laurel, its body trembling as it fought to break the spell. The same spell the Magicker had cast over Eric and Enala.

Laurel stared back, arms outstretched, concentration etched into the lines of her mouth. Light flashed again and her eyes glowed with power.

Eric stared, frozen with indecision. What had Antonia told Laurel? What had she done?

Teeth gritted, Laurel turned to him. "What are you waiting for?" she ground out. "I cannot hold it for long. *Go!*"

Still Eric hesitated, tears springing to his eyes. There was no denying the truth behind Laurel's words. "Why are you doing this?" he whispered.

Laurel gave a sad smile. "That's between me and Antonia," her face softened. "Go, Eric. Find Enala, get the Sword, save the world. *Go!*"

Eric leapt for the sky.

~

LAUREL STARED AT THE DEMON, arms trembling. She blinked back tears, unable to take her eyes from its hateful glare. Only Antonia's warmth kept her strong, unwavering before its fury.

"You cannot hold me, mortal," the demon grated.

Laurel bowed her head, tearing her eyes from the deathly face. It was, she knew, the face of her death. She could feel her pool of magic withering; the energy it took to hold the demon was sucking it dry at an alarming rate. She did not have much longer.

She prayed to the Goddess it would be long enough.

She had told Eric the Goddess' words were between herself and Antonia, but in truth the decision had been a simple one. They could not hope to destroy this demon, not without aid. But bolstered by Antonia's final gift, she had the strength to hold it, at least for a time. Her Light magic, against the darkness swirling at its core.

If not for Antonia, Laurel would never have had the strength to hold it back. Even without the *Soul Blades*, the demon was unbearably strong. Its magic surged against her, fighting to pierce the Light magic smothering it. One second's lapse, and it would be free.

But for now it remained trapped in the blanket of Laurel's magic. Without its dark magic, the demon could not access the power of the *Soul Blades,* could not even move the body it possessed. It was helpless, for so long as Laurel could hold it.

Or almost helpless. Antonia had warned her that the *Soul Blades* had power of their own – power to defend their wielder. If Laurel or Eric attacked the demon directly, their power would be unleashed and the demon freed.

Antonia had given her the strength to stop the demon, but they still had no way to kill it. Their only hope to stop it was the Sword of Light, but the Sword was far beyond reach. That left only one option. Laurel had to hold the demon, to give Eric the chance to escape.

There was no other alternative; if she did not hold it, it would kill them all.

"I can feel you weakening, girl. You're dying. Release me and I will let you live," the demon whispered, its voice seductive.

Laurel looked up and laughed. Darkness radiated from the demon's soul, the falsehood of its words clear in her mind's eye. There would be no mercy from this creature, not once its magic was free of her binding.

Closing her eyes, Laurel took a deep breath to calm her racing heart.

Standing amidst the ruin, she waited for death.

CHAPTER 22

Inken held the bowstring tight against her cheek, arrow nocked and sighted at the nearest soldier. She glimpsed Caelin taking up position on the other side of Gabriel, sword in hand. Gabriel himself stood motionless, staring down at Katya, his sword still embedded in her back. The councillor lay dead at their feet, her empty eyes staring up at them.

A heavy tension hung in the air as the men edged closer, weapons held at the ready. One false move and the three of them would be peppered by arrows. Indecision held them back for now, but it would only take one raised voice to break the spell.

Inken swallowed hard, her eyes sweeping the battlements, reading the odds. They faced at least two dozen archers. There could be no resistance here, only a pointless death. Taking a breath, Inken slowly released the tension on her bowstring and removed the arrow. Crouching, she laid her bow on the ground and raised her hands. Caelin followed suit.

A man forced his way through the gathered soldiers. She

recognised him as Elton, the man who had greeted them at the gate and seen them to the king. His face held no cheer now, only anger and fear. As he approached, she saw his eyes flick back towards the oncoming dragons.

"How could you do this, Caelin?" he hissed. His voice shook with anger.

Caelin let out a long sigh. "She was working for Archon, was about to fire on our allies. We couldn't let that happen."

"How can you say that?" Elton shook his head. "She has served our king and nation faithfully for years! I know her, *knew her!*"

"And do you not know me?" Caelin stared hard at his brother soldier. "Was it not you who said the king had been acting strangely, that he had not been himself? He was under Katya's influence, under the spell of her black magic. Even now she was using it, freezing us helpless. Only Gabriel managed to break free of the spell, to stop her."

Inken glanced at Gabriel, seeing the uncertainty in his eyes. She could read the guilt there. He was second guessing his actions, questioning whether Katya had really been the traitor they believed. Yet the proof was before them; the councillor had been about to fire on their allies, and the spell had broken with her death.

Yet one question still rang in her head.

How did Gabriel break the spell?

Before she could contemplate the matter further, the soldiers around them began to scream, drowning out her thoughts. Inken swung around, and found herself taking a step back in sudden fear.

A dragon alighted on the battlements, its great wings spread wide to cast the wall in shadow. It towered over the trembling soldiers, golden scales glittering in the midday sun. The giant head leaned down towards them, the intelligent eyes inspecting them in detached curiosity. The long tail rose up behind it, poised as though to strike.

Where is the one who addressed us with such uncouth language? the dragon's voice echoed in her mind as it bared its teeth.

Inken covered a smile, watching Elton's face pale. He gaped like a fish caught out of water, staring in terror at the beast perched above him. A sudden sweat beaded his forehead.

Across the wall, weapons bristled as the soldiers pointed arrows and crossbows at the dragon. Arms shook and eyes widened with fear. The men stood in terrified silence, waiting for an order.

Realising they were seconds from disaster, Inken nudged Caelin. "Speak, sergeant, before these men get us all killed."

Caelin's lips tightened. "Hold your fire," he bellowed. "These are our *allies!* See how they have not rained fire down upon us?" he swept his arm out at the dragons hovering overhead.

He glanced then at Elton. Inken caught the unspoken question in the look. When no answer was forthcoming, Caelin turned to address the dragon.

"Greetings, Enduran. It is good to see you again," he bowed. "Welcome to Ardath. What brings you here?"

Surprised, Inken looked closer and realised Caelin was right. This was the same dragon they had spoken too in Malevolent Cove.

Jurrien came to us, asked my tribe to stand again with the humans. We have spent many days debating his request. At first, some refused to come, but when we discovered what Archon's demon had wrought in our land, even they joined us. There is no more neutral ground now. All must fight, or die.

Caelin nodded. "We are glad to have you. I must apologise for the greeting," Caelin continued. "It seems Archon's servants are a plague in our nation. This woman," he waved a hand at Katya, "was his agent. She is the one who offered you insult. I am glad you still wished to talk with us."

Enduran's head twisted to stare at the dead woman. *You are a strange people, to allow traitors to grow so easily in your midst.*

Inken suppressed a laugh as Caelin bowed his head. "Agreed. It is our great shame to admit it. I am sure my king will be more diligent in who he seeks council from in the future."

A crackling rose from Enduran's chest which Inken interpreted as laughter. *I should hope so,* the great head turned to survey the soldiers. *Such fragile creatures, you should not be wasting your energy fighting one another*, the dragon yawned, flashing its giant teeth at the men.

As one, the Plorsean guards took a trembling step backwards.

Caelin smiled. "Try not to terrify them too much, Enduran. Most have never seen a dragon before," he paused before moving on. "Your aid is sorely needed in this fight. I am sure the king will welcome your arrival. We will speak to him presently. Elton here will see about making arrangements for your people's comfort."

Inken looked up at the circling dragons and gave a quiet chuckle. Enduran's head turned at the sound. *I agree, little one,* she jumped as the dragon addressed her. *We are too large for this city. But there is plenty of space in the hills. We will camp at the lake's edge. Please send our regards to the king, Caelin, and offer him our invitation to speak further of the coming war*, at that Enduran's wings beat downwards and he lifted from the battlements. He soared up to re-join his tribe.

Inken turned to Elton. "You can thank me later for getting you out of that one."

Elton looked from her to Caelin, his eyes wide, his

mouth twisted with indecision. Inken almost laughed again, unable to decide herself how the change of positions had come about.

Caelin took pity on him. "Elton, there is no need for you to make a decision on our guilt. We surrender ourselves freely to you. Take us to the king, and allow him to decide our fate. We will bring the dragon's words with us."

Elton breathed a sigh of relief. "You're right, Caelin. I don't know what's going on, but the king will know the right of it," he gestured to a couple of nearby soldiers. "Bring their weapons, and keep a close eye on them," raising his voice he called to the other guards. "Stand down, the threat has passed, for now."

Inken smiled to herself as Elton led them down the stairs. *Well, that's one way to get an audience with the king.*

THE DAWN HAD BROKEN. That was the first thing Enala noticed as the shadow maze dissolved. The golden globe of the sun hung low on the horizon, its light banishing the chill in her bones. She held her arm as it throbbed with the beat of her heart, fighting to stem the bleeding.

She stood and looked around as the last shadows faded into the ground. Somewhere in her reckless sprint through the maze, she had finally reached the top of the cliffs. Soft, short cropped grass grew out around them, covering the peak. A flock of sheep grazed nearby, a few looking up to study the intruders on their private mountaintop. In the distance, the pasture gave way to small trees. The forest led down a gentle slope, where the rest of the island spread out beneath them.

Enala found her gaze drawn across the pasture to where a rundown building overlooked the harbour. Fragile sandstone walls stood against the mountain breeze, decorated with faded murals of the sun and stars. In each painting a figure stood in the light, a silent guide against the darkness. Cracks riddled the walls and the roof had long since collapsed.

Granite pillars lay strewn amongst the grass and across the steps leading up to the temple. Broken stone marked where they had once stood, bordering the temple stairs. Moss grew on the leeward surfaces of the stone, rusted braziers still attached to the top of each.

"This was a Temple of the Light," Enala whispered. She looked round again. "But what happened to the maze?"

Jonathan shrugged. "I do not believe the creatures and the shadows were ever meant to come into contact. They were polar opposites of the same spell. When you tricked the Raptor into charging the shadows, it triggered a chain reaction which twisted the protection back in on itself. Either way, we are here."

Enala scowled. "No thanks to you," she snapped, her anger flaring to life. "You ran."

Jonathan hung his head. "I know," he clenched the sword tight in his hand. "I am sorry, I allowed my terror to overwhelm me. That place… it unmanned me," he took a breath. "Can you forgive me?"

Enala looked away, tempted to tell the cowardly king to leave. *At least he came back*, she reasoned.

At last she nodded. "The Sword is in there?" she asked.

"Yes, I believe so. We have passed the last of the protections. All that is left is for you to claim the Sword," he held out an arm, indicating she should lead.

Enala drew in a breath of mountain air, setting aside her doubts. She was here for a reason; she could not afford to be side-tracked. The soft ground sank beneath her feet as she crossed the field, mud sticking to her boots. The sheep cast jumpy glances at them as they weaved between them, their nervous *baas* coming from all directions.

Stepping over the fallen columns, Enala climbed the staircase to where the open doorway beckoned. She walked through the musty shade of the anteroom and continued into what must once have been a great chamber filled with priests and worshipers. Now though, the place was a ruin.

Stone tiles from the fallen roof lay in disordered piles and rotted wooden beams littered the floor. The chamber now appeared as an open air courtyard, although signs of the temple remained. Four stone pillars stood untouched near the centre. Images representing the Light were carved into each: flames and stars, the sun and moon. Furtive eyes watched from the top of the pillars, looking inwards to a stone altar in the centre of the room.

It was to the altar Enala's eyes were drawn. There, hovering point down, was the Sword of Light. The steel blade glowed like the noonday sun, its light streaming across the broken courtyard to cast off the shadows of dawn. The great blade extended at least three feet. Above the two-handed grip a diamond sat in the pommel, shining with a golden light.

Enala swallowed, frozen with awe.

She glanced back at Jonathan, a sudden fear giving her pause. She had heard tales of the Sword's power, how it was deadly to all but a chosen few.

What if they had been wrong?

"What now?" she asked.

Jonathan attempted a smile, but could not keep the nerves from his face. His eyes flickered to the Sword and he shook his head. Enala followed his gaze. For a moment, she allowed its light to wash over her, feasting on the sight of it, feeling its power tugging at her soul.

Then doubt snapped her back to reality and she retreated a step. She shuddered and would have turned back then, if not for the sacrifices her friends had made to get her there. This was not what she wanted, what she dreamed of.

But she had no choice. Seeing there would be no more aid from Jonathan, Enala glanced down and realised she still stood within the anteroom, on the threshold of the inner chamber. Closing her eyes, she summoned her courage, and stepped forward.

As her foot crossed the wooden level marking the perimeter of the chamber, a dread swept over her. Hairs prickled on the back of her neck and ice fed her veins. In that instant she knew she'd made a mistake, that something had just gone terribly wrong. Something lurked in the shadows of this place, some other magic.

The bracelets on her wrists blazed to life. Their angry red glow bathed the sandstone walls, battling with the light of the Sword. She gasped as the bands contracted, shrinking until the hot silver cut into her skin. Their heat seared at her wrists, wrapping them in cuffs of flame.

With a scream she dove backwards, desperate to escape the courtyard. But an invisible force took hold of the bracelets, trapping her in place. They held fast against her, oblivious to her shrieks.

Then she felt the first tug, as they began to draw her inexorably into the temple.

Enala fought to free her wrists from the fiery grasp, crying out for help, twisting to look for Jonathan. Her boots slid beneath her, scrambling for purchase on the broken floor.

Bit by bit, the cuffs dragged her towards the centre of the broken chamber.

"Help!" she yelled, trying to jolt Jonathan into action. "Jonathan, *do something!*"

An icy hand crawled inside her chest as she heard Jonathan's laughter. He strode past her to stand beside the stone alter, eyes fixed on her now, an eager hunger on his face.

Enala shook her head, mouthed the word 'no,' but could not find her voice. She kicked at the wooden beams, pushing back against the steady pull of the bracelets. Tears burned her eyes as she fought, determined to resist. The pain of the Raptor injury felt dull compared to the agony of her wrists.

The cuffs drew her to one of the stone pillars. Her back thudded against the cool marble as the bracelets struck. Then they continued their relentless crawl upwards, lifting her from the ground as the metal welded to stone. She dangled in the air, boots scrambling for a foothold against the smooth stone at her back. The cuffs bit deeper as the burning metal took all her weight. Blood ran down her arm from the gash left by the Raptor.

Enala kicked out, furious, desperate to free herself from the entrapment. The stench of burning flesh reached her nose as she bit back a sob. Her chest contracted and she struggled for breath, her weight pushing down on her lungs.

Jonathan walked forwards, raising a hand in mock solute. "We arrive at last, kinswoman!"

ERIC FLASHED ACROSS THE SKY, the white caps of the raging ocean far below. Ahead Witchcliffe Island grew steadily larger, its peaks obscured by a dome of shimmering air. His heart beat hard in his chest, Laurel's final words still ringing in his ears.

What had Antonia told her? What could the Goddess have said to convince Laurel to take on the demon alone? She had no hope of winning, of that Eric had no doubt.

She was giving her life for his.

The wind whipped away his tears. They had been

enemies since the day they'd met, yet she had made the ultimate sacrifice for him. The woman had changed, or perhaps he had simply missed the good within her. He had seen it when she stood alone against the demon though, when she had told him to flee.

Pulling more energy from within, he pushed the winds faster. He would not allow her sacrifice to be in vain.

Light flashed as an explosion tore the sky over the island. Eric dropped like a stone as the shock wave struck him, disrupting his magic and ripping the wind from his grasp. A brilliant light rushed from the top of Witchcliffe Island, casting the ocean below in a patchwork of angry shadows.

Eric shielded his eyes against the glare. Pushing down his fear, he took a firmer grasp of the wind and halted his free fall.

What just happened?

Slowly the light faded to a dim glimmer, then died away. He stared ahead at the island. The veil of haze had lifted, revealing red cliffs stretching up into the sky. Above the peaks he made out a distant building, sun glinting off the brown walls. Another light seemed to come from within, seeping out through the broken roof. Blinking his eyes, he tried to make out the source.

He was still some distance away, but his gut told him it was the place.

Eric just prayed the explosion had not come from Enala attempting to wield the Sword.

My sister, he was still struggling with Antonia's revelation. But however he felt about Antonia and her secrets, he was not going to let Enala throw her life away. Not after all she had scarified for the Three Nations.

And certainly not before he broke the news to her.

I'm coming, sis.

CHAPTER 23

"What are you doing?" Enala spat, writhing against the pillar. Anger helped to dull the pain, but there was no breaking the hold of the silver bracelets.

"What I have been planning for months, my dear. You see, this place does not belong to the council, the magic protecting it was not theirs. I created all this long ago, before my magic was lost. I designed it to protect the Sword from everyone but me."

"Why?" Enala grated. "The Sword is the only thing left to protect us from Archon. And you cannot even use it without your magic."

"Yes, yes, you are right, of course. Try not to rub it in," he wagged a finger. "But I could not simply pass its power to another. The Sword is *mine!*"

Enala struggled to breathe as her weight pulled down on her arms, constricting her chest. She tried to calm herself, but her heart refused to slow and the lack of air made her head swim. Her feet beat at the pillar, trying to take some weight from her arms.

"This doesn't make any sense, Jonathan," she gasped. "Why are you doing this?"

"All will be clear soon, my dear," he walked round the alter, pulling materials from his pack as he went. "I suppose you deserve some explanation before you die though. You don't mind if I work while we talk, do you? I imagine the council will have noticed your absence by now. I must be ready for when they arrive," he flashed her a grin.

His words froze Enala in place. "You're going to kill me? *Why?*" her shout came out as a weak cough.

She stared at the objects as he arranged them on the alter. A pestle and mortar lay alongside a small velvet bag. Vials of strange liquids joined them, the dark red of one looking suspiciously like blood.

"You have no idea what it is like," Jonathan's voice had a bitter tang, "to be born with such a gift as magic, only to feel it slowly shrivel and die in your hands," he took up the mortar and began pouring in measurements of the different liquids.

"My greatest fear was that one day it would vanish completely. I may have never been as powerful as the likes of *Alastair*," he spat the name. "Who never once tried to save the magic of my line. But it was mine, and gave me happiness in an otherwise joyless life."

"So, coward that you are, you hid the Sword away, so no one could use it?" Enala growled.

"Yes, yes, yes, but that is not the end of it," Jonathan snapped back. "I made plans, you see. Plans that required the Sword, plans for which you are the final piece of the puzzle."

Enala struggled to think through the pain, battled against her own weight to breathe. She locked her eyes to Jonathan, willing him to die. Her magic bubbled up within, straining just below the surface, until she was gasping from the pressure of its unspent force. Then the cuffs flashed brighter and the power sank back into the depths of her mind. She shrank back against the stone, tears streaming down her face.

"Good girl, Enala. Don't worry, this will all be over soon," he moved back to the alter.

Enala spat, wanting nothing more than to tear his head from his shoulders.

"For years I searched for a cure, for a way to break Archon's curse. But his magic was too great and my own too weak for such a task. So I turned my studies to other matters. Like how to restore lost powers."

"You are trying to bring back your own magic?"

Jonathan pursed his lips. "Would that I could, but unfortunately such a feat also proved impossible. However, through my studies I did discover that Magickers can link their power, though it is very dangerous. One might accidently suck the very life force from another, or be overcome by the influx of power. It was not much good to me, but the discovery put me on the right track."

"Finally, I found the spells which would allow me to use that connection to rob another Magicker of their power, and transfer it to me. Of course, it does require the donation of the other Magicker's life to complete the process."

Enala stared at the mad king, unable to believe what she was hearing. "But why me? Surely you could have taken any Magicker?"

"Yes, yes, yes, I know. But what would be the *point*? It is our *family's* magic that allows us to wield the Sword. So I had to be patient, had to bide my time and wait for you to arrive," he grinned, "but I did not lie idle. As I said, I had this place created, protected so that I could work unhindered. And I moved the Sword here, so when you arrived you would be forced to enter my rabbit warren."

"You're insane. Eric, the council, they'll kill you for this!" Enala pulled against her bonds, hot tears in her eyes. Her arms ached, blood still running from the wound left by the Raptor. She watched as Jonathan continued preparing whatever mad potion his spell required.

Her head pounded, her thoughts growing foggy from blood loss. Straining her arms, Enala hauled herself up to relieve the pressure on her lungs and sucked in a breath. The cool tang of salt carried strength back to her muscles, but she could not hold herself up for long. She collapsed back against the restraints and the pressure returned.

Jonathan finished grinding up his concoction and moved across to her, mortar in hand.

"I need you to drink this."

No way am I drinking that, Enala glared back, turning her head and clamping her jaw shut.

Jonathan reached out and grabbed her by the neck. As he squeezed Enala kicked out, aiming for his groin. The king twisted away, raising a knee to protect himself. Then he pressed up against her, his weight holding her tight against the rock. With his spare hand he grabbed her jaw and tilted her head back.

Enala stared into his eyes, mustering every ounce of hate she possessed, and clenched her jaw tighter. Grunting, he pinched her nose, cutting off her meagre supply of air.

Lungs shrieking, Enala squirmed against Jonathan's hold. Her head spun but she held on, determined to defy him to the last. Jonathan's grin widened as the seconds ticked away. Her lungs cried out for air, her brain demanded it.

She fought against the urge, but it was unconscious, instinctive. She gasped a lungful of air, and screamed in pain and hatred. Her cry was cut off as Jonathan poured the noxious contents of the bowl down her throat. She choked and coughed, trying to spit it out, but he clamped a hand over her mouth until she was force to swallow. It burned right down to her stomach, leaving a bitter, furry taste in her mouth. Tears ran down her face.

"Good girl. Don't worry, it will be over soon," Jonathan said at last, moving back to the altar.

"Coward," she spat, coughing in a feeble attempt to throw up the awful concoction. She felt half-suffocated. A numb tingling spread through her muscles and she almost wished herself dead, just to end the suffering. "Why don't you remove these cuffs and we'll see how brave you are," she growled. "You couldn't even stand against your own creature in that maze."

Jonathan glared at her. "Yes, well, sometimes magic takes on a life of its own. Especially when mine was no longer there to hold its form."

An uncontrollable tremor ran through Enala. How she wished she'd pushed Jonathan into the shadows of the maze when there'd been a chance. Or off the side of the cliff. But it was too late now. Jonathan had won. Despair grew in her chest, mixing with the burning strain from her lungs.

To her shame, Enala started to sob. "Please, don't do this. I never wanted any of this!"

Jonathan turned his back and continued his work. "Sorry, my dear. Really, neither of us have any choice in this matter. I must regain my magic and my Sword, and you are the only one who can help me with that," he shrugged. "Such is life."

Silence fell, broken only by Enala's laboured breathing and the grinding of the pestle. The sun crept above the lip of the walls, casting its warmth across the Temple of Light. As it struck the Sword, the blade's light grew to match it, blazing across the courtyard.

What can I do? Enala felt her courage breaking, the insanity rising from within. She prayed Laurel had found Eric – he was her only hope now. Yet there was no sign of him, no hint of his approach. A steady pain wracked her body, feeding the madness within.

"Please, let me breath! I'm dying!" Enala choked.

Jonathan chuckled. "Sorry about that. When I made them, I had no idea who I would be using them on. They were designed for a larger person. I'm afraid I cannot control them without my magic. But not to worry, I'll be sure to fix that right up when I have it back."

Jonathan's laughter fed fuel to her fury. Enala gave herself to it, thrashing against the pillar, kicking and screaming her hatred at the king's back. She strained against the bracelets until it felt like they would cut right to the bone. Still they remained fixed, immovable, and her rage soon succumbed to exhaustion. Collapsing against the cold stone, Enala fell silent, staring at the mad king.

Tears blurred her eyes and her mouth was dry. She could feel the desperate thud of her heart against her chest, the throb of blood in the numbness of her fingers.

Jonathan turned and raised the mortar to his mouth. He drank quickly, a scowl fixed to his face. Apparently his brew tasted no better. Its horrid smell wafted to Enala's nostrils and her stomach wrenched, but nothing came up. The last of her strength faded away. She began to sob again, knowing each choked breath brought her closer to death.

Then he stood straight and stretched out an arm across the alter. His meaty fingers wrapped around the leather hilt of the Sword of Light. He pulled it to him, smiling as he looked into the glimmering metal. The light of the diamond glowed in his eyes. There was open greed on his face when he looked from the Sword to Enala.

"Almost there," he walked towards her, blade in hand. "Soon I will be whole again."

Enala watched him come, limp against the pillar, hanging helpless from her cuffs. There was no more fight left in her.

"Thank you, Enala, for your sacrifice."

Enala thought he almost sounded sincere. She would have laughed, if she could breathe.

He raised the weapon, the deadly point poised to strike. Enala stared into the glimmering light of the Sword. Time seemed to hang still as dread clutched at her soul. She could find no hope in that fabled light, no power to conquer this darkness. This was the magic meant to save the Three Nations, to save them all from Archon.

Instead, it was about to end her life.

Enala clamped her eyes shut, and waited for death.

ERIC RACED ACROSS THE SKY, desperate to reach the building sitting atop the cliffs. He squinted against the sun's glare, unable to make out more than the broken roof. A sick feeling in his gut drove him faster. Enala had only to touch the Sword for its magic to overwhelm her; he prayed he was not too late.

What was that explosion? He asked again, his instincts screaming.

The beach flashed past far below as he reached the island and dropped towards the clifftops. From above he could make out little detail of the building, but as he approached he realised it could only be a temple. The broken roof revealed the ruined interior, where a stone altar lay amidst the rubble. A man stood beside the alter, leaning out to grasp the source of light in the makeshift courtyard.

The Sword! Eric realised as the blade came into focus. *But where is Enala?*

Eric dropped lower, watching as the man grasped the Sword and pulled it to him. The man paused for a heartbeat to stare at the fabled blade, then turned and approached one of the standing stones. Eric stared, trying to understand what was happening. The man could only be King Jonathan, but he could not see Enala anywhere.

Drawing closer, he noticed something different about the pillar Jonathan was making for. He squinted, trying to identify the difference, and with a jolt he realised someone had been tied to the pillar.

"*Enala!*" he screamed, but the wind caught the word and stole it away.

Confusion gave way to panic. Discarding caution, Eric plummeted from the sky, racing towards the temple. Jonathan stood poised before Enala now, the Sword of Light extended towards the girl's prone form. She did not move as the blade drew closer. Light shone from the Sword, its glow casting shadows across courtyard.

"Enala!" Eric called again, closer now.

Jonathan looked up, his face pale in the Sword's light. His eyes widened at the sight of Eric hurtling towards him and panic twisted his face. His head whipped around and for a second Eric thought the king would flee.

Then Jonathan looked back at Enala, and raised the Sword to strike.

"*No!*" Eric yelled.

With no time to think, Eric grabbed for the closest weapon at hand – the winds holding him aloft – and hurled them at Jonathan. His stomach lurched as the power of flight abandoned him, while the winds shrieked towards the king. Eric barely noticed his body go into freefall; his mind flew with the winds, driving them onwards, directing them with all his strength at the traitor.

The Sword shone as it plunged towards Enala, the deadly tip aimed straight for her heart. The wind howled and there came a muffled thump as the gale smashed Jonathan from his feet. He tumbled across the rubble strewn ground, skimming like a pebble across water.

But the force of the blow had knocked the Sword from his grasp. The blade spun through the air, tip flashing with the magic within, and plunged into Enala's chest. As it struck a shriek of pain exploded from Enala and her eyes widened in shock.

Then she slumped against her restraints and her eyes flickered closed.

"*No!*" Eric screamed.

And the ground rushed up to meet him.

CHAPTER 24

Eric woke with a groan, every muscle in his body aching. Opening his eyes, he pushed himself into a sitting position. When he moved to put weight on his leg, agony lanced from his shin and something in his leg went *crack*. He collapsed back to the ground, muffling a shriek, and looked for Enala.

"*You fool!*" Jonathan screamed. Before Eric could move rough hands grabbed him, dragging him up. The king shook him. "*What have you done?*"

Eric's leg smashed against a pillar and this time he could not bite back his scream. Struggling in the king's grasp, he struck out blindly with his fist. It connected with what felt like a chin, but did not seem to make any difference to the madman's iron grip.

The king lifted Eric above his head and tossed him like a ragdoll into a nearby wall. Eric raised his arms to protect himself as he crashed into the stone and landed in a pile of roofing tiles. Their jagged edges cut his skin as he rolled aside.

Heavy footsteps came from nearby, driving him up onto

his good leg. He managed to bring himself to a half-stand before a meaty fist slammed into his stomach. Air whooshed from his mouth and he stumbled backwards, pain lancing from his broken leg as it took his weight.

Looking up, he tried to avoid the next blow.

Scarlet fury twisted the king's face as he swung again, this time aiming for his head. The air rustled in Eric's hair as he ducked and reached for his sword. His hand scrambled at the empty sheath. Dread caught in Eric's throat; Alastair's sword must have slid free when he crashed.

Jonathan did not miss the futile gesture. Stepping back, he spun to look where Eric had fallen. They both saw the blade at the same time. Eric managed one stumbling hop before Jonathan reached the weapon. Reaching down, he wrapped his thick fingers around the hilt and raised it in front of him.

"You will pay for what you've done," the king growled.

Eric mustered his strength and dove into his magic. Reaching for the sky, he searched out the nearest storm. Energy crackled and black clouds appeared overhead. Thunder roared as lightning fell. It struck Eric's outstretched hand and danced along his arm, banishing his fear.

"Give up. Don't make me do this."

The king scowled and stepped towards him. Lightning leapt from Eric's fingers.

Jonathan flinched back and raised Alastair's sword to protect himself. The lightning flashed as it struck the blade, followed by a roar and sucking sound as it disappeared into the cool metal.

The king blinked, holding the weapon out in front of him as though it were a snake about to bite him. Then he laughed and flashed Eric a wicked grin. "What an interesting sword. Very useful," he stalked towards Eric.

Eric stumbled backwards, trying to put a pile of rubble

between himself and Jonathan. He flung another bolt at the traitor, but the king only raised the blade, and the energy vanished again into the weapon. Apparently whatever spell Alastair had cast on the sword still held, protecting its wielder from magical attack.

As Eric retreated he glanced at Enala, then quickly looked away. She still hung by her arms, silver manacles chained tight to her wrists. The Sword of Light had impaled her high in the chest, pinning her to the column. Blood stained her shirt and ran down the stone behind her. He bit back a sob, unable to believe she might still live.

Jonathan screamed and swung Alastair's blade in his direction. Eric was well out of the king's range, but he still ducked behind another of the stone columns, eager to put as many obstacles between them as possible. His mind raced, searching desperately for a way to overcome the madman.

"Come out, come out, little Magicker," the king hissed. "Don't you want to help your friend? She's bleeding to death over there, you know," he chuckled, leaping out from behind the column.

Eric swallowed hard, still staggering backwards, broken leg dragging on the ground.

What do I do?

Changing tactics, Eric reached for a gust of wind and threw it at the king. It rushed through the broken ceiling and struck Alastair's blade, whistling as the protection sucked it into the abyss. But the blade could not completely block the more dispersed attack, and the king staggered backwards. Eric took advantage of the extra moments to place the altar between himself and Jonathan.

"Come here!" the king shouted, swinging the sword through the gusts. He staggered around the altar towards Eric.

Eric watched him come, realising the king was limping as

well. His earlier attack must have caused more damage than he'd realised. A spark of hope returned as he considered how to take advantage.

"Who are you, imposter?" Eric shouted, trying to stall. "What do you want with Enala?"

Jonathan smiled. "I am no imposter, you fool. I am King Jonathan, and I want her *magic*," he slashed at Eric, but another gust forced him back.

They stood facing each other, locked in a desperate stalemate. Jonathan was panting heavily and sweat ran down his face. Eric fought down his own pain, struggling just to keep his feet. He had to fight on, had to end this now if there was to be any possibility of saving Enala.

"Then I'll give you one last chance to surrender, Jonathan. Put down the sword, and I'll spare your life," Eric warned.

Jonathan's laughter rang from the stone walls. "And how do you plan on killing me, young Eric? With your broken leg and worthless powers?" he raised Alastair's sword. "Why don't *you* give up, and maybe I'll give you a quick death," he glanced at Enala. "If she is still alive, I believe it's in both our interests to finish this quickly," he observed.

Thunder rumbled as Eric summoned the power of the storm. He was thinking back to what Alastair had taught him about magic, about how his own magic worked. Alastair had once said magic was finite – that if he drew on too much of his own, he would eventually expend his own life force. Staring at the sword in Jonathan's hands, a plan had come to him.

He did not know how the spell had been cast on Alastair's sword, but surely it could not absorb an infinite amount of power, especially without someone to refresh it's magic. Perhaps if he threw enough energy into the blade, the spell would shatter.

Jonathan strode towards him, sword at the ready. There was no way of knowing if his theory would work, but Eric had run out of options. Throwing out his arms, he released the lightning.

Blue fire surged through the Temple of Light, casting shadows across the room. The roar as it came was deafening. Jonathan flinched back from its might, face lit with fear. Despite his words, he too was unsure of the blade's power.

As the lightning struck Alastair's sword, Eric gritted his teeth and pressed on, unleashing a continuous stream at the weapon. Blue light burned across his vision, all but blinding him. Jonathan disappeared behind the fury of the lightning's dance, until all he could feel was the strange vacuum where his power vanished into the sword.

Blinded by his own attack, Eric did not see the first blow coming as Jonathan's fist lashed at him. Eric reeled back, losing his grip on the magic. The lightning flashed and died away, abandoning him to the king's fury.

Jonathan struck again, knocking Eric from his feet. He stared up at the hateful monarch, unable to believe the king had fought his way through the onslaught. Before he could move the king's foot crashed down on his chest, pinning him to the ground. Alastair's blade hovered overhead, poised to strike.

"Goodbye, Eric."

Eric rolled as the blade flashed towards him, sending the king tumbling. He bit back a cry as rubble struck his broken leg. Coming to a rest against one of the pillars, he used it to stagger to his feet.

Well that didn't work, Eric cursed.

Returning to the wind, he hauled it down from far above. At least that would slow the coward.

Gusts whipped about him, carrying cool air from high above. Goosebumps pricked Eric's skin. He tucked his hands into his cloak to ward off the cold. Then an idea, a memory, came to him.

Drawing on more power, he sent his magic further afield, reaching higher than ever before. There he grasped at every whisper, every gust he could find and drew it down. Taking a breath, he directed the swirling mass at the approaching king.

Jonathan paused as the gale struck. It tugged at his cloak and whipped around him, shrieking in his ears. Eric could sense Alastair's sword working its magic, but drawing on his own power, he redoubled his efforts.

Even from ten feet away, Eric could feel it working.

Jonathan stared at him. "Wha– what are you doing?" he stammered, the cold winds sucking the words from his chest.

A shiver ran through the king. Ice began to gather in his beard and settle on his shoulders. His face took on a blue tint and his jaw clenched. He waved Alastair's sword around his head, as though it's magic could ward off the air itself. Beneath him, a frost formed on the broken tiles.

When the sword finally slipped from the king's numb fingers, Eric was ready.

Throwing out his hand, he released one final bolt of energy. Lightning flashed across the space between them, taking Jonathan full in the chest. The air crackled as the blast knocked the king from his feet. He did not get back up.

Alastair's blade struck the ground, and shattered.

Eric turned and staggered towards Enala. His heart twisted in agony as he drew closer, unable to bare the horrifying sight of his sister.

The Sword had sliced clean through Enala's chest and struck the pillar behind her. Blood still seeped from the wound and had begun to congeal around the blade. It's light bathed her face, her jaw locked in a painful grimace. Her eyes were closed.

Eric reached her, struggling for breath. When he had last

seen her, she had just been stabbed by the cursed skeleton, barely able to stand. This was much, much worse. He closed his eyes, hope fading.

A half-choked sob rattled from his chest. He reached for her hand, trying to prize the cool metal from the rock. The silver bracelets refused to budge, the metal so tight around her wrists they seemed almost fused to her skin. Blood trickled from where they bit into her flesh.

"Eric," Enala croaked.

He jumped, so shocked by her voice he thought for a second Jonathan had recovered. He looked around, but the king still lay where he had fallen.

"Eric," Enala whispered again.

Eric allowed a wild hope to take hold as he turned to her. "Yes, I'm here."

"Eric," he leaned close to catch her words. "Get me off this damned pillar," Enala coughed, and blood bubbled from her mouth. She groaned, head leaning back against the cold stone.

Eric nodded. He ran to where Jonathan had fallen and swept up the hilt of Alastair's sword. Part of the shattered blade still remained in place. He returned to Enala and held the weapon at the ready.

"Let's hope this works."

With cautious movements, Eric wrapped an arm around Enala's waist and took her weight from the cuffs. A rattle came from her chest as she sucked in a breath. Hot blood stained his hands but he ignored it, aiming the ruined sword at her right cuff. Silently he prayed Alastair's sword still contained enough magic to counteract whatever spell Jonathan had cast. He stabbed the jagged edge of the blade against the silver band.

The silver gave way almost instantly, the soft metal crumbling beneath Alastair's sword. He repeated the procedure with her other arm and took her weight as she slumped against him. Clutching the broken sword under his arm, he carried her to the altar and gently laid her on the stone. Alastair's blade clattered down beside her, but he did his best not to disturb the Sword of Light still lodged in her chest. He distantly remembered Caelin's advice from so long ago – *leave it in, or you'll bleed to death.*

"Thank you," Enala croaked.

"Just stay still, Enala. You're going to be okay."

A dry laugh wracked her body, followed by a groan. "You don't give up, do you?" she gasped.

Eric shook his head. "Neither do you, remember?" tears spilt from his eyes. Thoughts raced through his head as he searched for a way out. "I guess it must run in the family," he whispered.

Enala's eyes opened to stare at him. "What?"

Eric smiled through his tears. "Turns out I'm adopted. I'm your long lost brother, Enala."

Enala groaned and gave a weak smile. She opened her mouth to respond, but dark laughter cut her off. It echoed around them as a shadow fell across the alter. A shudder ran through Enala, her pupils dilating with fear. The hairs on Eric's neck rose in warning. Dread filled his veins as he spun.

The demon hung overhead, a dark grin spreading across its face.

"So you are the other one. My master has been looking for you, Eric."

CHAPTER 25

King Fraser sat on his throne and stared down at them. A sword lay across his lap, his hands resting lightly on the hilt. His lips pursed in a tight scowl, jaw jutting as he clenched his teeth. The other council members sat around the table on the dais, but silence filled the king's court – no one dared so much as breath.

Caelin licked his lips, trying to ignore the vein throbbing on the king's forehead. He was more than aware of their perilous position; justified or not, they had killed a councillor in cold blood. If they could not talk their way out of this, their heads would not be far from the chopping block.

So far he had explained their suspicions, and their meeting with councillor before disaster had struck on the wall. The king had made no attempt to interrupt, his face remaining stony and impassive.

Beside him Gabriel shifted from foot to foot, his nervous fear betrayed by the way his eyes flicked from the councillors to the king. Inken stood on his other side, her casual stance in stark contrast to the blacksmith. Her eyes flicked to him and he caught the briefest of smiles. He found her confidence reassuring.

When he finally reached the magical paralysis that had frozen the three of them, the king broke him off mid-sentence.

"Enough!" he saw Gabriel jump at the king's shout. "I have heard enough of these stories, Caelin. I can assure you I have been under no spell. No dark magic has been worked on me. But this is the second 'agent' of Archon you claim to have killed – who until this moment I had regarded as a trusted member of my council. I shall need proof if you expect me to believe Katya was a traitor."

Caelin's heart sank as he stared down the king. From the corner of his eye he caught a moment's panic come over Inken's face, quickly hidden. His response caught in his mouth, his words retreating before King Fraser's rage.

"We will search Katya's apartment and belongings for sign of this alleged betrayal. And I would speak with these dragons, who claim to have come to aid us," he hesitated, eyes looking around the court. "I do not know what happened on that wall. But from what I have heard, the men were panicked and close to breaking before Katya arrived. I do not know why she decided to fire on the beasts, but at this point my belief is she thought the action justified. For her courage alone in holding the walls, I would praise her," he shook his head, glaring down at them. "But she is dead."

Caelin shrank as the king's eyes found him. He stared into his monarch's face, willing him to retract the words, searching for the man Fraser had once been. Surely with Katya dead, reason should have returned to the king. But there was only rage in those dark eyes.

Then the king let out a long breath and some of the anger went out of him. "I do not know what to do with you. I find myself doubting your story more and more, Caelin.

Up to this moment, there is still no proof of anything you have claimed, either with Balistor or Katya. I gave you the benefit of the doubt, gave you free rein of the castle. In payment, you stained the city walls with the blood of my most trusted councillor. You have left me no choice."

"Your majesty," Caelin interrupted.

King Fraser raised a hand. "*Silence!*" his gaze swept the room, taking in each of them. "You have said enough. You and your two companions cannot be trusted to have free rein of the city, or the citadel. You leave me no choice but to lock you away until the truth of this matter becomes clear."

Before Caelin could raise his voice in argument, the king waved a hand. Iron hands grasped him by the shoulder, holding him tight. He glanced back at the two guards behind him, taking in the grim determination in their eyes. The sick dread of treachery swept through him, washing away all thought of resistance.

For all his years of service, King Fraser had repaid him with betrayal.

Caelin went limp, eyes falling to the ground. There would be no fighting their way out of this. Guardsmen ringed the throne room, spears at the ready.

Inken did not see things the same way. Her calm had vanished, swept away by a red hot rage. Growling, she pushed the first guard away and spun to face the king.

"*Your majesty!*" she shouted. "We have come a long way to help you, have given everything for Plorsea, for the Three Nations. Who are you to judge us, sitting safe up there on your throne. How *dare* you try to lock us away."

The king scowled. "Silence, woman. Men, get them out of my sight."

Inken screamed and leapt for the dais. Before she could take two steps a guard tackled her to the ground. She went down, kicking and screaming as another man joined the fray.

It took a third before she finally subsided, going limp on the tiled floor. Together the men dragged Inken to her feet. Blood ran from her nose, staining her white top, but she glared around the throne room in defiance.

"This is a mistake, Fraser!" she shouted.

The king waved a hand and turned back to the table of councillors. As the guards led him from the room, Caelin saw the king take his seat at the head of the table.

Outside, the guards pushed them together and took up positions ahead and behind them. A jab in the back told Caelin to move. They marched down the wide corridors of the citadel, footsteps dragging on the soft carpets. The hallways were empty now – everyone who could be spared had been called to man the walls. Allies or not, dragons were fearful beasts, and the citizens would rest easier seeing the soldiers manning the walls.

A few minutes later they turned from the well-lit passageways down a stairwell leading into the depths of the keep. A cold sweat broke out on Caelin's forehead as his mind began to work again. A cool wind blew up from the dark depths below. He knew this staircase – they were not being taken to a tower keep or warded room. They were being led to the dungeons.

One of the guards took a torch from a wall bracket, providing a thin circle of light in against the darkness. They continued down the staircase, the light of the flames only carrying a few steps ahead. Caelin moved slowly, taking care on the slick steps. He thought of all those who had come before, the centuries of men and women who had disappeared into this darkness.

Caelin shuddered, suffocating in the pitch black. He could feel it pressing in on him, drawing away the light, smothering hope. The warmth fled from his face and his fingertips grew numb with the cold. He glanced back at the guards, but they stared straight ahead, all but ignoring their prisoners but for the odd shove to keep them moving.

The cold seeped deeper, creeping into Caelin's skin and sending shivers down his spine. He looked across at his companions in the darkness, and saw his own fear reflected in their pale faces. They could sense it too – the wrongness about this place. But the guards still held them fast, ushering them downwards, leaving no opportunity to flee.

Four or five stories beneath the keep, the staircase came to a sudden end.

At the bottom was a single corridor lined by thick wooden doors, disappearing beyond the reach of their torch. There was nothing else to light the space. Caelin shuddered as he realised they would be left alone in the darkness. The empty black beckoned and he felt his courage melting. He turned back to the guards, ready to beg for them to leave the torch.

Beside him, Gabriel jumped as a rat skittered past. The guards chuckled and pushed him forwards. He stumbled into Caelin, knocking them both to the ground. From the floor he watched the panic catch in Inken's eyes, saw her turn to flee, but a steel gauntlet struck her in the face and sent her stumbling backwards. Caelin reached out to catch her as she fell.

They lay together on the icy stone, looking up at the grim faces of the guards. Chainmail rattled as their captors drew their swords.

"Stop, please, we won't struggle," Caelin raised his hands. "There's no need for that."

The lead guard stepped forward. He held an iron key in his gauntleted fist. "Here," he tossed it to Caelin. "There is a cell at the end of the corridor. You will unlock it. You will leave the key in the door and enter the cell. Do not try anything."

Caelin caught the key and nodded. "Okay."

Together they backed down the corridor. The guards pressed forward, swords extended to block their escape, leaving nothing to chance. To either side of the corridor the doors stood barred, but there was no escape there anyway. The only exit from the dungeons was through the men facing them. Caelin shivered as the dark swarmed him.

Caelin froze as his back brushed against the door at the end of the corridor. Heart pounding, he turned slowly and felt for the lock. His back felt exposed, unprotected from the approaching guards. He fumbled for the keyhole, struggling to place the key in the dim light of the torch, then a click came as the mechanism within the door drew back the bolt. The hinges creaked as it opened.

"Get in," the guard ordered, his sword glinting in the torchlight.

Caelin swallowed, biting back a response. The full truth of the king's betrayal crashed down around him, as he realised with sick certainty they would never leave this hole in the ground. The absolute darkness of the cell beckoned, but his feet refused to obey. Beside him, Gabriel and Inken were also frozen, unable to take that final step into captivity. He could almost sense the pain radiating from the cell, the waves of despair crashing down upon him.

He yelled as the sharp tip of a sword prodded his back. Biting his tongue, Caelin strode into the cell. In the pitch-black he did not look back, but heard movement as Inken and Gabriel joined him. With another groan of rusty hinges, the door slammed shut behind them, leaving them alone in the darkness.

Panic rose in Caelin's chest as the empty black crowded him. He fought for control, for a moment's sanity. Every instinct shrieked for him to turn and pound on the door, to beg for release, for light. The darkness hung over them, absolute, overwhelming, pressing down on his very soul. He struggled for breath, the black almost like liquid, suffocating him. A scream rose up within him, tearing at his chest as he fought to stifle it.

"This seems like a place you go to be forgotten," Inken's words echoed in the small space.

"Or a place where no one will ever find you," a voice replied from the darkness.

ERIC STARED up at the demon. He felt strangely detached, without fear or panic. He crouched beside Enala, a defiant anger bubbling in his chest. Its heat crawled through his veins, pushing away the pain, feeding strength to his desperate body. Enala's hand was warm in his. He gave it a squeeze and stood. They had gone through too much, beaten the odds too many times to fail now.

The demon dropped from the sky. Dust billowed out as it crashed to the tiled floor. It straightened and looked around the ruined temple, a strange look in its demonic eyes.

"Curious. When I ruled, *his* temple was a place of pilgrimage. People would travel here from all over Trola, to beg for *his* return," he laughed. "No longer, it seems! The people have all but forgotten Darius."

Eric faced the demon. "You heard what I said, demon," he growled. "I am Enala's brother, descended from Aria herself, sister to the man whose body you possess. I wield the Sword of Light. You had better run, if you wish to live."

The demon grinned. It raised its hands and gave a slow clap. Then it drew back its cloak to reveal the green and blue stained crystals set in the pommels of its *Soul Blades*. "I have mastered the God powers of Earth and Sky. I am not afraid of the Sword of Light. No, I will prise it from your cold dead fingers."

Eric looked down at Enala, watching her laboured breathing. Indecision gripped him. The Sword was the only thing stopping her from bleeding to death. If he pulled it free, she would die in minutes. There would be no chance of returning her to the healers in Kalgan. He would be condemning her to death.

Yet he did not stand a chance without it.

"Eric," Enala croaked. "Take the Sword and finish the damn thing."

Eric shook his head. "No, I can't!"

Enala gritted her teeth, eyes clenched closed. "Eric, you know what's at stake. Demon or not, Thomas was the first to use the Sword. You cannot let it fall into his hands," she coughed the words. "*Take it!*"

Eric wiped tears from his eyes. "I can't lose you too, Enala," he took a steadying breath. "So just stay with me, okay?" his voice cracked, but he reached down to clasp the hilt of the Sword.

Closing his eyes, he began to pull. Enala screamed as the blade shifted. The sound tore at his soul, but he could not turn back now. Biting back tears, he drew the Sword of Light from her chest. Enala thrashed against the altar as the blade slid clear. Blood began to bubble from the naked wound.

Enala's shrieks died away and her head sank back against the alter.

Holding the Sword of Light in his hand, Eric hardly noticed. He could feel its power as it flowed down his arm, swirling within him, seeking out every dark crevice of his soul. He stood before it like a leaf in a flood, overwhelmed, helpless before its power. Light shone through his mind, a threatening edge to its touch.

Eric focused on the light, feeling out its power, fighting

the lure of its pull. It wound its way deeper, curling around his soul. Within, his own magic rose in response, its blue glow mingling with the pure white – one feeding the other, or fighting for control, he could not tell.

Then, anxiety driving him, Eric reached out with steely resolve and grasped the flickering lights. The blue of his own magic succumbed easily, but the white reared back, fighting against him. The Sword's magic turned red hot, threatening to burn his mind to a crisp.

But Eric had no patience for the unruly force, no time to waste. Threads of power spun from his magic, blue ropes that wrapped their way around the white light. Twisting and turning, the Light fought against him, but he left it no place to go. With a final flash of red, the light settled, trapped in the bindings of his power.

Opening his eyes, Eric smiled. The Sword glowed in his hand, its brilliance banishing all but the deepest shadows in the temple. The power of the Light, returned to Witchcliffe Island.

"This ends now, demon," he swore.

"You are strong, to overcome the pull of the Sword. Still, it will do you no good now," reaching down, the demon drew its *Soul Blades*.

Eric leaned down and kissed Enala on the cheek. "Stay with me," he whispered.

The power of the Sword thrummed in his ears, burning away pain and feeding strength to his limbs. Even so, Eric could not move quickly on his broken leg, and the demon had two swords to his one. He could not let this become a battle of blades.

The demon's cloak cracked as it strode towards Eric, a dark grin on Thomas' worn face. It had fought this battle twice already; both times Eric had been overwhelmed in moments. Even with the Sword of Light, he knew the odds were against him.

Even so, he would fight on. This monster's terror had to end – here and now. However slim, the Sword at least gave him a chance.

Reaching down, Eric sought to draw on the Sword's power. The light fled at his touch, slipping free of his magic. Clenching his fist around the Sword's hilt, Eric followed the power as it retreated into the blade. There he wrapped it again in his magic and pulled the bindings tight.

White flames raced along the length of the blade, burning bright as the noonday sun. Heat seared at Eric's face, far fiercer than any mortal flame. He flinched away, unable to bear it, until the Sword's magic seeped back into his body. His skin cooled as it spread through his limbs.

Eric smiled across to where the demon stood watching him. A weariness lurked in its eyes now, a grim smirk on its lips. It held the *Soul Blades* stretched out towards Eric. He remembered how Thomas had required instruction from the Gods to wield the Sword of Light, and grinned.

"I'm a fast learner," he mocked. "Unlike some."

He flicked out the Sword and a column of white hot flame leapt towards his foe. Where dragon flame had once been hot enough to drive the demon from Malevolent Cove, the Sword's fire was fiercer still. It swept towards the demon, stone melting beneath its touch.

The demon hurtled sideways, a gust of wind carrying it skywards.

"Impressive," it growled. "But you are a mere novice, injured and exhausted. You will perish here, boy!"

Then it fell, hurtling towards Eric with blades extended. Energy flashed within the tainted steel, the green and blue glows reaching out to mix with the white of the Sword.

Eric raised his arm and hurled another inferno at the

demon. It lurched in the air and came on, but Eric was already moving. The winds cast him into the sky. Behind him the familiar vines exploded through the pavement, engulfing the space where he'd just stood.

Smiling, Eric allowed the wind to carry him higher. He would not be caught in the same trap twice. His breath came faster as he felt the power flooding his body. It swept through his muscles, washing away all pain, all sensation, leaving him free to tackle the demon. The white of the Sword fed his magic, its unlimited energy recharging his own.

He lashed out with the fire again, eager to destroy the jungle below. The flames roared as they devoured the demon's creations. Directing the wind, Eric landed atop one of the pillars and watched as the demon settled opposite.

It hissed, teeth bared, pale fingers gripped hard around its blades. Thick smoke rose from the temple, turning the space between them black. Eric raised the Sword as the demon disappeared into the smoke. His clothes whipped in the wind as he prepared to take flight.

The crackle of lightning leant Eric precious seconds. He dove from the pillar as blue fire turned the granite to molten stone. The winds propelled him up through the acrid smoke. He coughed as black soot caught in his throat, then he rose above the burning stench.

Air whooshed as a blade flashed for his face. Eric ducked, dropping a foot, and the sword swept overhead. He lashed out at the demon's feet but Thomas shot backwards out of range.

They circled one another, air crackling with energy as they soared higher. Eric drew on the Sword's power and unleashed a wave of white fire. The demon drew back. Then the blue blade crackled. Lightning flashed and the wind howled as the Sky elements lashed out to halt the flame's advance.

A blast exploded outwards, smashing into Eric and spinning him through the air. He struggled to keep hold of the wind, drawing the gusts into a tighter spiral. Flames flashed and thunder clapped as blue lightning smashed the temple below. He prayed Enala had not been hit.

Eric looked up to see white fire licking at the demon's cloak. It beat at the flames, face twisting with pain. Shielding his eyes against the glare, Eric watched its pale flesh blacken and burn.

It still has no defence against the Light, Eric thought with a smile. If only he knew more about what the Sword could do.

The demon screamed and tore the flaming cloak from its body. It scowled at him, lightning crackling along the blue blade. A dark green glow came from the other. Beneath, the earth shook with its rage.

"Is that all you have, boy?" it growled.

Eric glared back, frustrated by his own limitations. He knew the Sword was capable of so much more than simple fire. The God magic controlled all aspects of the Light. It was capable of feats he could not begin to imagine. But there was no time to learn now. The fire would have to do.

Across from him, the demon dropped into the smoke and vanished from view. Eric swore, eyes searching the roiling clouds below. The blaze was everywhere now, flames catching at the rotten walls. He could hardly make out the building through the smoke and fire. He hoped Enala was still safe at the centre of the courtyard where the flames had not yet reached.

Reaching out with his senses, he searched for his foe, for the tell-tale whisper of magic.

A sudden gust pushed him down as the winds holding him aloft gave way. He fell, tumbling into the acrid smoke towards the distant earth. Panic gripped him, but a few feet above the ground the winds returned and he caught himself.

As he touched down, vines sprang from all around, their thorny tendrils shooting out to catch his fragile body. The demon charged through the smoke, *Soul Blade* raised to strike Eric down.

But the Sword of Light moved faster. Flames danced out from him, turning the vines to ash and flinging the demon into a nearby pillar.

Eric grinned as the demon climbed to its feet. Gripping the wind still spinning through the temple, he sent it out in a blast of fury. It caught the smoke and carried it upwards, blowing it from the building and into the sky. The temple reappeared as the wind died away.

But the demon had vanished. Eric spun, searching the ruins. Its laughter came from the shadows to his right, then left, always moving. He glared around him, chasing ghosts through the empty temple. He caught sight of Enala, still lying on the altar but conscious now, clutching her cloak to her chest. He caught the glint of metal and saw her other hand wrapped about the hilt of Alastair's shattered blade.

Stones rattled from behind. Eric spun in time to parry the demon's blow, energy crackling as the blue and white blades clashed. Then Eric slashed out with the greatsword, feeling a satisfying crunch as the blade caught flesh.

The demon stumbled, its growl echoing from the temple walls. The face of Thomas constricted, grey lines creeping through the pale skin. Burns scorched his flesh and as Eric watched, dark shadows began to creep beneath his skin.

"*Enough!*" the thing that had been Thomas hissed.

Fear caught Eric as the demon surged forward, faster than thought. Instinct screamed for him to move, but his broken leg caught beneath him and he tripped. Eric shrieked in agony as the demon's blade drove into his stomach. A deathly cold hand grasped his throat and pulled, dragging him further onto the blade. He gasped as the demonic steel tore into him.

"Goodbye, Eric," the demon's lips pressed against his ear. "Say hello to Antonia for me."

With a casual smirk, the demon shoved him to the ground. The *Soul Blade* slid free, its dark green glow flickering in the sunlight. The Sword of Light slipped from Eric's hands, scattering across the tiles. Sparks of flame burst from the blade with each bounce.

The Sword's magic fled Eric's body. Without it, the pain returned to strike him down. A chill spread from his stomach and the same dark shadows he had sensed in Malevolent Cove reached out to claw at his soul. The edges of his vision blurred and he felt hot blood pooling beneath him. He clutched at his stomach, struggling to stem the bleeding.

Rubble crunched beneath the demon's boots as it walked towards the Sword of Light. Sheathing Jurrien's blade, it reached out to pluck the Sword from the broken ground.

"*No!*" the demon swung at Enala's cry.

As it turned, the shattered remnants of Alastair's blade took it through the eye.

Eric gaped, staring at Enala's heaving body. She collapsed back to the alter, the last of her energy spent with the effort it had taken to hurl the blade. A convulsion tore through her, lifting her body from the hard stone. Blood bubbled from her lips and spread across the altar beneath her. A gurgling groan came from her chest.

Beside him, the demon screamed. The sound tore at Eric's ears; it's shriek like a hundred nails on a chalk board. He fought through the sound, through the pain in his leg, through the chill spreading from his stomach as his lifeblood leaked away. This was his chance – if only he had the strength to take it.

Clenching his fists, Eric fought back against the shadows

clinging to his soul. He gathered the last of his courage and lunged for the Sword of Light. His fingers scrambled at the hilt, pulling it to him, though he had lost the strength to lift it.

The Sword ignited at his touch, feeding new strength to his dying body. Its power burned through him, extinguishing the shadows of the *Soul Blade*. The pain faded until it became just a dull throbbing within, a distant reminder of his impending death. Drawing on the Sword's power, Eric stood.

The demon staggered across the temple floor, blindly clutching at the broken sword still piercing its skull. Dark magic flashed about it, shadows racing around its warped body to vanish into Alastair's blade. Some part of Alastair's enchantment still held. Yet Eric could already see the shadows gaining power, as more and more escaped the clutch of the sword.

Eric had no idea what the demon was trying to do, but clearly the blow had not been fatal. It was distracted though, and that was all he needed.

Stepping up behind the demon, Eric raised the Sword. Energy blazed from its depths, not flames this time but a pure white light which cast the shadows from the demon. It started to turn, must have felt the gathering power, poised to strike it down.

Eric swung the Sword with all his strength. The Sword blazed as it sliced through the creature's robes and pierced the body beneath, the body that had once belonged to the king of Trola. A blood curdling cry bellowed from the twisted mouth. Then energy erupted from the Sword, engulfing the demon and cutting off its final scream.

The light spread across the old king's body, raising red welts wherever it touched. The demon shuddered and a gasp echoed from the pale lips. The head slumped, then turned to look at Eric.

Eric stumbled backwards as he glimpsed the demon's eyes. Hazel had replaced the black, and the man from Antonia's vision stared back at him.

"*Thank you,*" Thomas' words whispered through the temple.

Then light exploded from the blade, engulfing them both in its power.

EPILOGUE

Enala dragged herself across the broken floor towards Eric. She locked her eyes on the young Magicker, fighting back pain, struggling for breath. Her chest gurgled with each gasp, as though filled with liquid, as though she were drowning in her own blood. Fire burned in her heart and sleep beckoned, it's cool depths offering sweet relief.

But she could not give in. Not while Eric, not while *her brother,* lay dying.

She crawled on. Flames flickered nearby, their heat washing across her broken body. Smoke drifted overhead, but where she lay the air remained clear. A crash came from nearby as another part of the roof collapsed, the orange flames consuming the crumbling ruins of the temple.

Closing her eyes, Enala pressed on.

Rubble ground against her skin, but she hardly felt it – sensation had long since fled with the lifeblood trailing behind her. All that remained was the slowing thud of her heart, the searing in her lungs, the slow suffocation of her body.

It seemed an eternity had past when she finally reached his side. He lay amidst the ash that had been the demon, body bleeding and broken. She stretched out a hand and grasped his arm. His eyes opened at her touch. He attempted a smile, but it came out as a grimace.

"Enala," he croaked.

"I'm here. You did it, Eric, you beat it."

His eyes closed again as he groaned. "That's something at least."

Tears blurred in Enala's eyes – not for herself, but for the sight of Eric lying there dying. She remembered Inken, the kindness she had given Enala, to bring her back from the madness. She remembered the love the two shared.

Enala shut her eyes. She had nothing and nobody left in this world, but Eric had someone who loved him, a future after all this. She could not bear to watch him die.

Gritting her teeth, she squinted through the smoke, searching for something, anything. Her eyes swept the burning courtyard, catching on the Sword of Light. But the Sword was no good to them now – the Light did not encompass healing powers.

Then Enala noticed the dark sheen of the *Soul Blades*. Somehow they had survived the conflagration unleashed by the Sword of Light. They lay in the rubble, discarded. The green glow of Antonia's sword danced in her eyes, drawing her in.

Antonia was the Goddess of the Earth, and the *Soul Blade* held all the power that entailed. Enala vaguely remembered the little Goddess, from when she had retreated into a catatonic state. Earth magic could heal – Antonia had healed them all on that dark beach so long ago.

Summoning the last dredges of her strength, Enala started to crawl again. The *Soul Blades* were close, but the distance could have been miles for all it mattered to her. She was dying. She could feel the last of her life bubbling from her chest, strangling her every gasp. Agony swept through her body, but she persevered.

Reaching out, Enala wrapped her fingers around the leather pommel of the *Soul Blade.*

Antonia, help us! she screamed in the confines of her mind.

There was no answer, only the gentle ebb and flow of light from the sword.

"Please, Antonia," she whispered, fading fast. "*Help us.*"

Still nothing happened. A sob tore through Enala. She struggled for another breath, but found herself choking, drowning. Tears poured from her eyes as she strained for one last mouthful of air. Heat radiated at her back and the air shimmered, the fire coming closer. Even so, a cold was spreading through her limbs. She could no longer feel her legs.

Enala clutched the *Soul Blade* tighter, dragging it across the tiles. The Goddess was right there, so close, so powerful, yet it seemed she was helpless to aid them.

In desperation, Enala reach out with her mind, the way Eric had explained while they meditated. Darkness blurred the edges of her vision, the light fading from her eyes. With a final push, she reached outwards, seeking the Goddess.

Enala felt the last sensation of her body fall away. She drifted up into the air, floating aimlessly.

Is this death? she wondered.

Yet there was the *Soul Blade*, glowing with a brilliant green light edged with black. Trapped within was the one being who could save them. Dead or not, Enala had to try. Staring at the sword, she stretched out an arm. Her spirit fingers sank into the cool metal and she dove deeper, throwing caution aside in her desperation to reach the Goddess.

Antonia, help us! Her cry rang out across the spirit plane. *Please!*

Enala shivered as a force rose at her words, brushing against her soul. At its touch, she was flung back from the blade. Crashing into her body, sparks flew across her vision. The pain returned, and the desperate need for air.

Then a gentle warmth blossomed around Enala, spreading from the arm that still clutched the *Soul Blade*. A light grew around her, expanding to encompass Eric, until they were both surrounded by a dome of energy. Its power bathed their broken bodies, seeping deep into their skin, seeking out the wounds within.

The burning at Enala's wrists faded away. She glanced down to see the red rings vanish, disappearing without so much as a scar. Sucking in a breath, air rushed into her lungs, sending strength flooding back to her muscles. The gurgling died to a tremor as the liquid fled before the magic. The pain from her chest came last, falling away until only a dull ache remained. Slowly, that too began to fade.

Reaching up, Enala wiped tears from her eyes. She looked across at Eric, witnessing the magic's touch there too. The wound in his stomach healed before her eyes, the skin knotting itself together as though stitched by an invisible hand.

The magic was working. She could feel its power, thrumming through her blood.

Eric opened his eyes and looked at her, wonder on his face. She smiled back, then coughed in the acrid smoke. But it was nothing now, compared with the slow, creeping suffocation of a few moments ago.

"Antonia?" he asked.

Enala shook her head. "I don't know."

Then, deep inside, Enala felt something go horribly wrong.

~

ERIC COULD NOT BRING himself to believe what he was feeling. Magic surged around him, powerful and healing, its touch so familiar he would have recognised it anywhere. The Goddess, Antonia, had returned.

Opening his eyes, he saw Enala staring at him. She wore a sad smile on her face, but he could see the worst of her wounds had already healed.

"Antonia?" he asked.

"I don't know."

Enala shook her head, and then her eyes widened. A tremor shook her, her body convulsing against the hard tiles. She stiffened, and he saw her fingers were wrapped tight about the *Soul Blade*. Energy crackled along the steel, flickering in sparks and bursts, shooting up into the dome surrounding them.

With a whoosh the magic went out, vanishing back into the blade, leaving them alone in the burning temple.

Eric pulled himself into a sitting position as Enala rose, Antonia's *Soul Blade* still clutched in her hands. Her wounds had healed – not a scratch remained on her – but Eric could sense a wrongness about her, a difference. She stood stiff and straight, her movements disjoined, like a puppet on strings.

Putting his arms beneath him, Eric stumbled to his feet. Standing opposite Enala, his sister, he stared hard into her sapphire eyes. Except now he saw they were no longer blue, but a deep, emerald green.

"Enala?" he whispered.

A tremor went through her as he spoke her name. Her face twisted, as though in pain, and he saw a flash of blue rise from the depths of her eyes.

"Eri–" Enala croaked, cutting herself off.

The green returned stronger than ever, glowing with

some internal power. The shivering ceased. She stood straight as a pin, staring at Eric as though he were the strangest of creatures.

"Enala?" he tried again.

There was no tremor this time. Enala tipped her head to the side, watching him with detached curiosity. She did not speak. The light in her eyes brightened, the green flickering across her pale skin and mixing with the flames.

"Enala, what's happening?" he stepped towards her.

"Stop," Enala spoke, the word coming out as a crackling, metallic shriek.

She raised her arm and pointed the *Soul Blade* at Eric's chest. Green light flashed. Plants burst from the tiles between them. Saplings sprang from the earth, growing to great redwoods in the time it took Eric to retreat a step. Vines curled their way up the massive trunks and dense shrubbery spread across the temple floor, smothering the flames in a sea of green.

Enala laughed, a harsh, soulless shriek like the grinding of metal on stone. The sound rattled through the forest, sending a shiver to the depths of Eric's soul.

"Enala, please! Something's wrong, this is not you! It's the *Soul Blade*, you have to fight it, to stop it before it destroys you!"

The *Soul Blade* crackled, blinding him with its light. The laughter came again, grating in his ears. The forest trembled and groaned as the tree trunks bent towards him.

Enala stood amidst it all, bathed in the power of the Goddess, a dark look of torment cast across her face.

She stared at Eric. "Don't look for me."

Then she vanished into the forest.

BOOK THREE: SOUL BLADE

PROLOGUE

May strode along the silent battlements, her sharp eyes sweeping out to search the night. Stars sprinkled the sky overhead and torches lit the frozen stones beneath her feet. Darkness gripped the world around her, concealing the wasteland to the north.

Her short sword slapped against her leg as she walked and her breath misted in the winter air. The cold enveloped her, eating its way through the thick woollen coat she wore. Ice crunched beneath her boots as she made her rounds.

Shivering, May picked up the pace.

Ahead, a guard looked up at her approach. A thin frost sprinkled his white beard, but the smile he flashed her was genuine. Lowering the giant war hammer he carried, he stood to attention and offered a short salute.

"Commander May, what brings you to the outer wall at this time of night?" He spoke in a gruff voice, but the tone was soft.

May smiled back. "At ease, Alan," the man was a familiar face in the fortress, and a legend amongst the Lonians. Tales of his exploits as a youth had been circulating for weeks, and if even half of them were true, May was glad to have him. "If anything, I should be saluting you."

She moved to stand beside him, looking out into the darkness. After a moment's silence, she addressed his question. "I couldn't sleep."

"The reinforcements will come," the old soldier offered.

May glanced at him, raising an eyebrow.

Alan laughed. "It doesn't take much to guess what would keep the commander of Fort Fall up at night," his smile faded as he looked out to the north.

May followed his gaze, unable to find a response. Men and women had been trickling in for weeks now, answering Jurrien's call to arms. Alan had been amongst the first to appear – an old man with his hammer. Yet his arrival had been greeted with a hushed silence. Even at sixty years of age, Alan dwarfed most of the garrison, and he was a legend amongst the Lonians. In his youth he had strode these very walls, and ridden out to quash the small rebellions amongst the banished. Tales of his exploits were still told around the campfires of the young.

"What if they're not enough?"

"They will be," Alan replied.

Listening to his confidence, May could almost believe him. Silence fell then, and together they stared out into the empty darkness. Except they both knew it was not truly empty. Somewhere out in that wasteland, the banished waited. Centuries' worth of criminals and exiled, those deemed unworthy of living amongst the citizens of the Three Nations. Yet left on their own, those banished had formed a civilisation of their own, of sorts. Towns had grown from the rocky hills, the inhabitants surviving on what little water and food they could find.

That was all well and good. As far as May was concerned, they could have their lawless civilisation. So long as they kept to the north. Far from the Three Nations, they could do whatever they wished.

Unfortunately, she knew things would never be that simple. North of Fort Fall the land was a wasteland, barren of life. The people there craved something better, to escape the deathly plains of their existence. They wanted the land of the Three Nations for themselves.

And it was her duty to stop them.

At least with the massive walls of Fort Fall, that task had never been particularly difficult. Three walls stood between the towering citadel and the northern wasteland, each higher than the last. With the standing guard of five hundred men, few enemies had ever come close to mounting a successful attack. It would take an army ten times their number to breach those walls.

Only once had the unthinkable happened – the last time Archon marched south.

And now the whispers spoke of Archon's return.

May shuddered, struggling to find the courage that drove men like Alan to join such a war. She glanced at the big man, and found herself caught in his grey eyes.

He smiled. "Is that the sword?"

May's eyes widened, her thoughts thrown off by the question. "What?"

"The sword, missy. The one the king gave you. Is that it?"

May looked down at the short sword sheathed at her side and nodded. "Yes, it's the one King Fraser gave me when I was awarded this appointment," she sighed. "The sword of the Commander. It seems so long ago now."

"Good," she looked up at the tone in his voice. "A magic sword might be useful right about now."

May stared as he reached down and pulled the horn from his belt. Before she could speak he had lifted it to his lips.

Three long, pealing blasts rang out through the night. Lowering it, he flashed her a grin.

"Just doing my duty," tossing aside the horn, he picked up his war hammer. "They're coming, Commander. Best prepare yourself."

Even as Alan's horn had sounded, May had caught the glint of metal below, reflecting from the light of the defenders' torches. She nodded back at Alan, the hackles on her neck rising. Reaching down, she drew her blade as the first men below appeared in the light of their torches.

Torchlight flickered on the grizzled faces of the enemy, revealing their matted beards and unkempt hair. Hard eyes stared up at them, alerted by the horn, their lips drawn back in scowls. Scar-crossed hands gripped hard around the hilts of swords and axes.

The final ring of the horn faded away, returning the night to silence.

Then, almost as one, the men below charged.

Staring down at the enemy, May struggled to guess at their numbers. But in the darkness the task was impossible, the enemy beyond count. May sent a quick prayer for the Gods to grant her soldiers speed. Half the garrison slept below them at the foot of the wall. In her mind's eye she pictured them leaping from their beds and sliding into their chainmail; sweeping up swords and helmets as they rushed for the door. With luck they would reach the battlements in minutes.

In the meantime, it was up to the night guard of fifty to see off the first attack.

Returning her attention to the invaders, May clenched her sword tight in her fist. She glanced at Alan, surprised to find his presence comforting.

She smiled. "Are you ready, soldier?"

Alan hefted his hammer. "Always."

Light burst across the plains below as the guards tossed bales of hay into their flaming barrels. The glow caught the shadows of the men below, revealing the stark truth of the challenge they faced. May forced herself to stand still as she heard whispers from the men around her.

"Stand strong!" she called out over the thumping of the enemy's boots.

Turning her eyes back to the force below, May swallowed hard. This was no raiding party, that much was clear. They were too numerous and too well-equipped for that.

Where did they get chainmail and steel weapons?

Sharing a glance with the aging warrior beside her, she gave him a nod. She could trust him to hold the men together here. Her presence would be needed elsewhere though; to add steel to the backbone of the defenders. Turning, she strode along the battlements, shouting encouragement to her men as she went.

Sixty feet down the line May found a space and stepped back up to the crenulations. Mouth dry, she cast a glance to her left and right. The fifty men of the guard lined up either side of her, their faces grim but determined. She felt a rush of pride when she saw their fear had retreated behind masks of courage. Whatever challenge they faced, these men and women would stand to the last against the enemy.

Below, the enemy roared and rushed across the last patch of ground before the wall. Swords and axes crashed against shields and a wave of sound swept up over the defenders.

May stepped up as a grappling hook clunked onto the stone battlements. Sword in hand, she waited until the rope went taut before slicing down. A shout rose up from below as the rope split on the second swing, sending the climber toppling back into his companions. All along the wall, the other guards did the same.

Moments later, the first scream of a defender split the

night. She looked up in time to watch two axemen dispatching the guard to her right. They had clambered up one rope while he sliced at another, taking him unawares before he could defend himself. Another foe had appeared at the top of the rope and more would no doubt be following behind him. If they were not stopped now, the wall would be lost long before the reinforcements arrived.

Screaming a battle cry, May leapt at the nearest axeman. Grinning, he watched her come, the axe held loosely in his thick hands. May allowed herself a smile of her own, glad to be underestimated. But you did not become commander of Fort Fall without earning the position.

As the man hefted his axe May moved to the side, ducking his first clumsy swing. Then she slid forward beneath the man's guard and stabbed out with her short sword. The blade crunched through the gap in the chainmail beneath the man's arm.

The man swore and swung his gauntleted fist, but swift as a cat she moved back out of range. He tried to follow, but only managed two steps before he collapsed to the ground, blood bubbling from his lips.

May sprang past the man, eyes already studying the second axeman. The man on the rope joined him and they eyed her warily, apparently realising now the threat she posed.

Smiling, May beckoned them forward. Blood pounded in her head, adrenaline feeding strength to her limbs. In her three years as commander, she'd had little practice in real combat. She had almost forgotten the thrill that came with it.

As the axeman stepped towards her, May danced sideways out of range, eager to engage the smaller swordsman first. The axeman made to follow her, but suddenly found himself tangling with his comrade. The swordsman stumbled, pushing back as he turned to swear at the larger man.

May's blade slammed into his exposed back and the words never left his mouth. He toppled without a sound.

The remaining fighter roared and swung his double-headed axe, forcing May back a step. But the man was a novice and the force of the blow carried the blade past, burying it in the body of his fallen comrade. Another curse echoed through the cool night air, but he tore the blade free before May could close on him.

The thug eyed her closely now, edging back to give himself room to swing. May laughed, hoping to ignite the rage she glimpsed behind the man's eyes. She was not disappointed.

In silent fury he stepped forward, axe raised in a two-handed grip. May almost laughed again, pleased by the man's lack of skill. While someone had clearly taken great effort to arm these men, their preparations had obviously not extended to training. Stepping sideways to avoid the blow, she thrust out with her blade. The tip slipped beneath the man's guard and sliced through his exposed throat.

As she leapt past, the man gave a gurgling cry and staggered backwards. He managed a single step before his feet gave way beneath him and he collapsed to the bloody ramparts.

Looking up, May grinned as she saw another guard had reached the rope. Steel rang on steel as he fended off the next man attempting to reach the battlements. She moved towards him, eager to offer her aid, but the man suddenly reared backwards. He staggered, the sword slipping from his fingers as something pushed him back from the ramparts.

May swore as he twisted, revealing the dagger buried in his throat. She reached out to catch him, but she was still too far away and he pitched to the ground before she could reach him. He gave one last gurgling cry, and lay still.

Turning back to the rope, May felt an icy hand wrap about her heart. A figure clambered into view, pausing to straighten and survey the battlements. Black robes flapped in the wind, revealing the pale flesh of the creature beneath. Black eyes stared out from a deathly face and a host of shadows clung to the figure, rippling against the light of the torches.

Demon, the word sent a tremor through May's soul, but there was no denying the truth. The creature standing atop the wall wore the body of a human, but there was no humanity left in those eyes. Her mind reeled at the implications.

The demon turned, its black eyes finding hers, and grinned. Its head tilted to the side in detached curiosity.

"Commander," its gravelly voice carried through the night. "What brings you here on a night like this?"

May shuddered, and gripped the sword her king had given her tighter.

The creature laughed, the sound sending dread down to the pit of her stomach. Her knees shook, but she stood her ground, determined to do her duty to the last.

The thing cackled again and stepped towards her.

With a roar of defiance, May shook herself free of her fear, and attacked. Silently she prayed whatever spells had been cast over her blade would be enough to combat the creature's power.

A blade slid into the demon's hand and shot out to parry May's attack. Steel screeched on steel and she felt a reverberation go through her arms, but the sword held firm. Surprise flashed in the demon's eyes and it drew back, suddenly hesitant.

Drawing courage from its surprise, May pressed the

attack, unleashing a string of blows that drove the creature backwards across the wall. But its hesitation was short-lived, and with supernatural speed its blade moved to fend off her attacks. Then it spun, black cloak sweeping out around it, and its blade flashed for her stomach.

Twisting, May threw herself sideways, but even her speed was not enough to avoid the blow. A sharp pain lanced from her side and then she was clear, dancing backward out of range. Instinctively, her hand dropped to her hip. It came away streaked with blood, but she was relieved to find the wound was not serious.

Keeping her eyes on the dark creature, May began to circle. It smiled and mimicked her, wary too of the skill she had shown. Her eyes narrowed as she studied it, seeking a chink in its defence. She was confident now this was not one of Archon's more powerful demons – she would be long dead if that were the case. Nevertheless, its skill with the sword was phenomenal, and who knew what other magic it might possess. She needed to finish it now, before it could work any further mischief.

Sliding into a fighting stance, May beckoned the creature forward. It growled and leapt for her. She sprang to meet it and their blades rang as they came together, flashing in the firelight. Stepping to the side, she made to stab for the dark thing's head.

As the black sword swept up to parry her blow, May pulled back, then hurled herself at the demon's legs. Her shoulder struck first, driving straight into the creature's knee. She heard a satisfying crack as the joint shattered beneath her weight. Then her momentum carried her forward, sending the two of them toppling to the ground, limbs and weapons flailing.

Gritting her teeth, May fought to free herself from the entanglement. A hand clawed at her neck and the demon's iron fingers grasped at her wrist, but she refused to give in. The thing had not made a sound as its leg broke. The demon within was well beyond the realm of mortal pain, but the damage had still done its job, crippling the demon's movement.

Swinging her sword, the blade finally found flesh. Roaring, the demon released her and she broke free, rolling away and scrambling to her feet. She fumbled to bring her sword to bear as the demon writhed on the ground. It struggled to regain its feet, but the shattered knee would no longer take its weight and it collapsed back to the stone.

Springing forward, May drove her blade down through its back. She felt a satisfying crunch as the tip slid home. Then a hideous cry shattered the night, ringing from the towers of the citadel behind them. May clapped her hands over her ears as pain sheared through her head, the high-pitch scream cutting to her very soul. Strength fled from her legs and she sank to her knees.

When the noise finally ceased, a fragile silence fell over the ramparts. Across from her the demon had rolled onto its back, driving the blade through its chest. The black eyes found hers, its face twisted with hate. Its chest still rose and fell, but she could see it was finished, its energy spent.

May edged closer, drawing the dagger at her side. It watched her come, breath still coming in ragged gasps.

When she reached its side she raised the blade, ready to plunge it through the black skull. Before she could strike, a pale arm shot out to catch her by the shirt. She gasped at the icy touch, struggling to free herself, but even dying its grip was like iron. It pulled her closer, a deathly grin on its pale lips.

Sucking in a breath, May ceased to resist the demon's pull. She still had the dagger and she raised it to strike.

The demon laughed and released her.

May hesitated, the dagger hovering over the creature's head.

Their eyes locked and a shudder went through her soul. There was no fear in the depths of its black stare. Instead, she saw triumph.

"Archon has come," the words rose from its lips like death itself.

Almost without thought, May plunged the blade into the demon's skull. But she felt no joy at the victory now, no pleasure. Despair crept through her heart, the demon's words hovering like a ghost in the air around her. She did not hear its last gurgling gasp. Her mind was already far away, lost on a tide of dread.

The demon's words meant the end of peace, the end of the Three Nations, the end of life as they knew it.

The cries of the reinforcements as they finally reached the wall came from around her as the defenders swept the last of the enemy from the battlements. May hardly noticed, her mind consumed, lost in the grip of the demon's final words.

Archon has come.

CHAPTER 1

Eric staggered as a stray root caught his boot. Before he could right himself he found himself falling, toppling to the muddy ground. The breath whooshed from his lungs and he choked, thrashing in the puddle he'd landed in. When he finally managed to suck in a breath of air he swore, pulling himself to his knees.

Climbing back to his feet, he tried to wipe the brown muck from his clothes. It coated him from head to toe now, the result of days spent trekking through the untamed wilderness. Looking around, he took stock of his progress up the steep hill.

Thick forest rose all around him, making it difficult to determine how far he'd come. Lichen clung to the branches overhead, thriving in the cool damp climate of Witchcliffe Island. Dense ferns dominated the undergrowth and low-lying vines threaded their way through the mossy carpet, making movement anywhere within the forest a constant battle.

If he'd had a choice, Eric would have been a long way from the cursed island by now. Yet over a week had passed since he'd slain the demon, the cool days giving way to freezing nights, and still he remained. His clothes were torn and filthy and he'd hardly eaten for days, but he refused to quit. He would not leave his friend, would not abandon Enala to the forces that had taken her.

Of course, she was more than a friend now – though he doubted he would ever adjust to their true relationship.

"*Sister*," he whispered the word to himself. "Where are you?"

Even now the revelation still shocked him, though there were more pressing concerns to distract him from that now.

Despair clutched his heart. It had grown with each passing day, weighing on his soul as he marched through the dense forest, clambering up the muddy hills and searching the empty forest. In the week that had passed, he had not glimpsed a single sign of his sister, not a footprint or stray thread of clothing.

Nothing.

He saw again the burning temple, his last glimpse of the girl as she disappeared into the trees. Earth magic had radiated out around her, surging from the *Soul Blade* clutched in her hand. Its power had taken her, and Eric had been powerless to stop it.

Shuddering, he prayed for the thousandth time that he would find her in time. The longer the magic held her in its thrall, the less chance there was Enala could be saved.

For all he knew, it might already be too late.

Pushing down the thought, Eric sucked in a breath and started off again. The pommel of the sword strapped to his back struck him in the neck with his first step, forcing him to reach back and readjust it. As his fingers brushed across the leather grip he felt a crackling of power race down his arm.

He flinched back, his chest constricting with fear. He'd almost forgotten it was the Sword of Light he carried, not some ordinary blade. The weapon possessed power far beyond his understanding, and was not to be taken lightly. Only members of the royal bloodline of Trola could touch the blade – though their direct line had now come to an end.

Thankfully, Eric and Enala were distant relatives.

Even so, he had hesitated to touch the blade since his battle with Archon's demon. Its power was overwhelming and only his desperation had given him the strength to wield it. Now though, fear made him pause. He had no wish to suffer the same fate as his sister.

Worse yet, the demon's second *Soul Blade* slapped at his side. *That* he had absolutely no desire to touch. It contained the Storm God, Jurrien, and if Enala's transformation was anything to go by, to touch it meant a fate worse than death. Enala had awakened the Earth magic of the other *Soul Blade* in time to heal them, but before she could release it, the God magic within the blade had overwhelmed her.

Willingly or not, she had sacrificed herself to save him.

Eric could not let that stand.

Reaching out, he tore aside another fern frond, anger fuelling his limbs. For days he had eaten nothing but berries and beetles; in his desperate flight from Kalgan, he had not thought to pack supplies. At least the two years he'd spent in self-imposed banishment had taught him how to survive in the wilderness.

Pressing on, he reached out with his senses – sight, sound, *magic*. He was desperate to catch any whiff of Enala or the magic controlling her. Even inexperienced as he was, he had sensed the magic of others before and knew its taste. Yet he had felt little of the God magic within the *Soul Blade* – only flashes of power now and then. It gave little hint of his sister's location.

Eric smashed his way through the trees, unconcerned by the noise he made. As far as he could tell, Witchcliffe Island was deserted. That was probably why the traitorous King Jonathan had hidden the Sword of Light here in the first place.

A breeze rustled the branches overhead, catching in his hair, and he was again tempted to fling himself skyward. His own magic gave him power over the weather, and with a little effort the wind could carry him high above the island. Unfortunately the island's dense vegetation made searching from the air an all but impossible task.

Eric stumbled again as the ferns ahead of him gave way to an open field. He breathed a sigh of relief, pleased for a moment's break from the fight with the dense undergrowth. He strode forward, eyes searching the open grass.

He paused as the hairs on his neck rose in sudden warning. Closing his eyes he reached for his magic, felt its power rising at his touch.

"*Don't,*" a voice challenged from the treeline opposite him.

Goosebumps pricked Eric's skin. He hesitated, searching the trees. "Why? Who are you? *Show yourself!*"

Movement came from across the clearing as men stepped from the trees. Eric's eyes raced over the men, counting ten in all. Each held a bow with arrows nocked, their tips pointing in Eric's direction.

Except for one, he realised, his eyes returning to the man at their centre.

His white robes had been stained by the muck of the forest, but there was still no mistaking the markings of a priest of the Light. His face was lined with the beginnings of age and his fiery red eyes were locked on Eric. He wore a sword at his side and Eric guessed from his stance he knew how to use it.

"Who are you?" he asked again. Despite the presence of

the priest, he was not about to trust the strangers. He had been betrayed too many times for that.

"Who are you?" the man in the white robe replied. His voice was gruff, but Eric recognised it as that of the original speaker. "You are trespassing on royal land."

Eric hesitated, uncertain of his next move. The priest was clearly a Magicker – and he had already sensed Eric reaching for his magic. There was no way to know what powers he might possess, but from prior experience he knew it was best not to guess.

Then, of course, there were the archers.

Still, despite his fear of the weapon, he had the Sword of Light. Its magic was more than enough to deal with a Magicker, and its power would incinerate any arrow before it came close. His fingers twitched as he weighed up his options.

"I warn you, trespasser, our patience is short. We have other matters to attend to. Tell us your name, now."

Eric grimaced, making his decision. For all he knew these were Archon's men, or King Jonathan's. Quick as lightning, he reached up and drew the Sword of Light clear. The blade ignited at his touch, bathing the clearing in its brilliant light. Heat washed across his face as he pulled it down and held it in front of him.

He swallowed as the first wave of magic washed through him. White fire swept up his arm, spreading to fill his body, to flood his mind. It burned within him, lighting up the darkest confines of his mind, illuminating his every secret regret. Eric shrunk before its strength, withering beneath its glare.

Then his own magic flared, its stormy blue glow erupting outward to mingle with the white. The sight gave him strength. He had mastered that dark force – now he would use it as a weapon against this new power. Reaching out with his mind, he gripped his magic and pulled it to him, twisting it into ropes of power.

Staring at the white flame, Eric gathered his courage and unleashed the threads of his magic. They raced from him, wrapping about the power of the Sword. Flashes of white erupted through his mind as it fought for freedom, blinding his inner eye, but he held strong. Slowly, the strands of blue wrapped around the white, binding it to his will.

At last Eric opened his eyes. Though only a second had passed, the clearing had changed, bathed now by the white fire of the Sword.

"I am Eric," he announced.

As one, the men who faced him dropped to their knees, heads bowed.

Eric blinked, turning to look behind him to ensure it was not a ploy. But the clearing remained empty but for himself and the kneeling men.

He turned back to the leader, the Sword gripped tight in his hand. He could feel its power writhing within, fighting at its bonds.

"Who are you?" he growled through gritted teeth. "I will not ask again."

The priest looked up from the ground. "I am Christopher, priest of the Temple of the Light. I am here representing the Trolan council," he waved at the other men. "We are here to find King Jonathan and the girl known as Enala. The Magicker, Eric, too – though I guess we have found him," he trailed off. "But how? How is this possible?"

Shaking his head, Eric allowed himself a smile. He could hardly think with the power wrapping about his insides. Without another thought, he extinguished the Sword's flames and sheathed it.

"That is a long story – but the short of it is Enala and I are twins, separated at birth by our parents to protect Aria's line. When Jonathan betrayed us and injured Enala, I was forced to take up the Sword."

The man stood as the light of the Sword died away, his head still bent. "I am sorry; we did not know. Please, allow us to start over. I am one of the few remaining councillors left in Kalgan. We were sent to rein in our wayward king. But we had no idea how far he had sank."

"I would say he was far more than wayward," Eric growled.

Christopher raised his hands. "I would have to agree. From the signs I saw at the temple, it appears he tried to steal your… sister's magic. We found his body and guessed one of you had put an end to him," a hint of uncertainty hung in his voice.

Eric almost smiled. If they had been to the temple, they had also seen the forest created by Enala as she fled. It had taken him an hour to cut himself free; even healed he'd been too exhausted to use his magic. More than enough time for her to vanish.

"I killed him," he answered Christopher's unspoken question. "He didn't leave me much choice. He stabbed Enala in the chest and would have done the same to me if he'd had the chance."

Whispers spread amongst the men and Christopher bowed his head again. "I am sorry for your loss."

"My loss?" Eric shook his head. "Enala is not dead. She saved us both. She was able to use the Earth magic trapped within the *Soul Blade* carried by Archon's demon to heal us."

Christopher frowned. "So that's where the trees in the temple came from, why there was such evil in the air. I could not begin to decipher what had happened there. Where is she then?"

Eric clenched a fist. "Lost. She has not even learnt to use her own magic. The God magic in the *Soul Blade* overwhelmed her and she fled before I could stop her. I have been searching for her, but…" he trailed off, his voice trembling.

Christopher glanced at his men. "I might be able to help you. I have felt the power shaking through the island. From its strength, I thought it was the Sword at first. But it moved too quickly and did not feel like Light magic. Together, I'm sure we could track it though."

"I've tried," Eric ran a hand through his hair. "I have only sensed flashes. And there's been no trace of her anywhere."

"Like I said, together we may have more luck," Eric looked up as the priest stepped closer. "A magic like that cannot hide, not while it possesses your sister. We will find her."

Eric felt a surge of hope, but crushed it down. "Why should I trust you?"

King Jonathan had warned them about the council, and though obviously his word meant little now, Eric was still wary.

Christopher's face darkened at Eric's implication. "I don't know what our dear king told you of the council, but they have done their best to fill the void left by his melancholia. While he vanished with the Sword, we have provided Trola with what leadership and guidance we could. And when Jurrien came to us, desperate for aid, we mustered our armies and sent them north. Did you not notice Kalgan is all but abandoned?"

Eric nodded, remembering the empty corridors of the citadel.

"I was one of the only Magickers left in the city. Without me, the Kalgan is all but defenceless to magic, but I came all the same."

Eric took a breath and nodded, shamed by the fire in Christopher's eyes. He could read the truth there, his sense of betrayal that Eric and Enala had fled their custody. Jonathan had tricked them all with his lies. Thinking back, he remembered the kindness the guards had shown him, the comfortable room he'd been left in. They had not even taken his sword.

Shaking his head at his own stupidity, Eric met Christopher's gaze. "I'm sorry. I should have guessed the truth."

Christopher gave a sad smile. "He fooled us all, had us believing he was a broken man when all along he was scheming," he waved a hand. "But we must put that in the past. Come, tell me all you know of Enala and this *Soul Blade*. If she remains on Witchcliffe Island, we will find her. You have my word."

Nodding, Eric began to tell him their tale.

CHAPTER 2

Elton stifled a yawn and then swore as the horse shifted beneath him. The creature was eager to return to its stable and it took a firm tug of the reins to put the animal back on track. In truth, he could not blame the gelding's nerves. They were close now, and even his own heart had begun to thump hard in his chest.

Raising a hand, he squinted up the hill, seeking for a glimpse of their quarry. The first rays of the morning sun peaked over the horizon behind them, casting shadows across the rolling hills. Below, their ship still bobbed at anchor, awaiting their return. The ride across the lake had been rough, the winter winds tearing at their clothes and flinging freezing water over the sides. It was a relief to escape, though it did not seem to have helped King Fraser's mood.

He stared at the king's broad back, wondering again at the change in the man. His temper on the journey across the lake had set the men on edge. Glancing around, Elton glimpsed nervous fingers lingering close to swords and swore silently to himself. This was not the disposition one would expect of a welcoming party.

Especially not when treating with creatures as sensitive as gold dragons.

Swallowing, Elton resolved to ignore the tingle of warning raising the hairs on his neck. Memory of the dragons' arrival was still fresh in his mind. Their appearance over the waters of Lake Ardath had sent panic through the ranks of men manning the city walls. Unsure of their intentions, the city defenders had come within seconds of firing on the dragons. Only his friend Caelin had prevented the disaster.

If only he had done it without bloodshed. Elton closed his eyes, seeing again the body of Katya, the blood pooling around her. The king's rage at the woman's death had been terrifying to behold. In his anger he had locked away Caelin and his companions, at least until their true allegiance could be determined.

Shaking his head, he returned his thoughts to the present. Before the dragons had departed they'd invited the king to join them and plan for the war to come. Elton had expected King Fraser to meet with them within a day, but it had now been over a week since their arrival. He hoped the dragons did not consider the delay an insult.

Ahead the winding trail was finally approaching the top of the hills surrounding the lake. Long grass grew up on either side of them and the mud-streaked trail had made the trek difficult for the horses. It had clearly not been used for some time. Even so, the trip had taken less than an hour and the scouts reported the dragons were nesting at the top of these hills.

A low growl came from overhead and Elton felt a tremor run through his horse. Craning his neck, he looked up at the ridge and saw a massive head rise into view. Sunlight glittered off golden scales as the blue globes of its eyes shifted to stare at them. Another rumble carried down to them as the jaws opened, revealing rows of sword-like teeth. It shifted again, dragging one giant claw into view, then another. Bit by bit the lumbering body appeared as it pulled itself onto the ridge.

Stretching out its wings, the dragon watched their approach, intelligence glistening in its eyes.

Elton's horse shied as they drew level with the ridge. He tugged at the reins, struggling to keep the horse in line, and cursed as it jostled against his control. Around him the other guards were experiencing similar problems. Glancing at the dragon, he swore he caught a glint of amusement in the curl of its jaw.

The king's horse had no such problems. It trotted between the scattered guards and drew up beneath the dragon. The king glanced back from the saddle, anger in his eyes as he surveyed them.

"When you're ready, men," he growled.

Elton ignored the king's barb and kicked his horse forward. The others followed, white fists now wrapped tight around their sword hilts. Elton resisted the urge to copy them, his nerve wilting beneath the shadow of the dragon.

"Dragon!" Fraser boomed. "I am King Fraser. I have travelled here to meet with your leader. He is called Enduran, I am told."

Elton winced at the king's lack of courtesy. A rumbling came from the dragon's throat as it lowered its head to their level.

We do not have leaders, King of Men, the dragon's voice vibrated through their minds. *But Enduran seems to have developed a patience for your kind.* At that, the dragon turned away and moved down the other side of the ridge. *A patience I do not share,* its voice carried back to them.

The king dismounted from his horse, muttering under his breath as the others moved to join him. Elton hoped the man would keep his temper – it would not do to alienate their allies any further than they already had. They needed all the help they could muster against Archon's forces, and the dragons were more powerful than most.

Climbing down from his own horse, Elton handed the reins to another of the guards and walked to the edge of the ridge. His mouth dropped as he looked down the other side. Dragons lay strewn across the open field below, basking in the warm rays of the morning sun. Gold glittered wherever he looked, all but blinding him, but he thought he counted around forty of the beasts.

The dragon who had greeted them had already disappeared amongst the crowd, but another now climbed towards them. Though there was little to differentiate between the creatures, Elton felt a tingle of recognition. This could only be Enduran, the dragon that had spoken to them on the wall.

"He's coming," he turned back to the king.

Fraser nodded and waved for him to join the other guards. Elton hesitated a moment, wondering if he should offer his assistance, but a scowl from Fraser sent him on his way.

King of Man, Enduran's voice echoed in their minds as the dragon reached the ridge. *You are late.*

"My apologies, dragon," the king replied. "I had pressing matters to deal with. We have a war to fight, after all."

Elton winced at the abrupt tone to Fraser's voice. There were courtesies to be observed when speaking with the gold dragon tribe, and the king had all but ignored them.

Enduran gave a slight nod. *Very well,* he turned, surveying their company. Elton shrank as the eyes found him. *You, I know you. You were on the wall. Where are the others, the ones I spoke with in Dragon Country?*

"They could not be here," the king answered for Elton. "They send their regards."

Smoke puffed from the dragon's nose. *You are a busy*

people, it seems, Enduran paused, staring down at the king. *So how can my people assist in the war to come?*

Fraser waved a hand. "A good question. You are mighty creatures, but it seems your numbers are few. How many of you remain?"

Forty-five joined me in this journey. There are others, old or with child, who remained behind. But we are a great deal more steadfast than you brittle creatures.

"I have no doubt," Fraser nodded. "Even so, I must consider how best to employ your people. Our armies have gathered, but we have not yet decided on the best course of action."

A rumble came from Enduran's chest. *It was our understanding that Jurrien wished the armies of the Three Nations to march north, and defend Fort Fall against Archon's forces.*

"Yes," Fraser snapped. "But that was before the Storm God went and got himself killed and left us without the protection of the Gods."

A dim growl escaped Enduran's jaws, and there was no missing the flash of anger in the dragon's eyes. The king's tone clearly did not agree with it. The great head lifted back, the globes of its eyes studying the king.

The passing of the Gods only means the rest of us must stand together, Enduran rumbled. *You cannot hope to defeat Archon alone?*

The king smiled. "As I said, dragon, we have not yet decided. But our plans are our concern, not yours."

An awful silence stretched out at the king's words. Elton exchanged a quick glance with his fellow guards and saw his own confusion reflected there. The king's anger was clear, his tone brisk. But whatever the reason, the stakes were too great for him to address Plorsea's ally in such a fashion.

And then there was the matter of his plan. Did he truly mean to hold their army back?

Elton shook his head. He knew this man, had served under him for years. He would not abandon the other nations in their time of need.

A wave of heat swept over them as the dragon let out a long breath. Its eyes glittered and Elton saw the anger there, bubbling beneath the surface. The great claws shifted, slicing massive grooves through the soft ground.

Very well, Enduran's words came at last. *When you decide your course, we would be pleased to know your plans. But do not delay long, king. We will not wait forever.*

"Very well, dragon," Fraser nodded his head. "Until next time."

Without another word, Fraser turned his horse and rode back down the hill. Elton stared as the king passed through the men, searching for sign of… what? He kept waiting for the man he knew to appear, the kind soul edged with strength, the man who had ruled Plorsea for more than a decade.

Can this truly be the same man?

Their eyes met as he rode past and for an instant Elton thought he glimpsed a smile on the king's lips. His stomach clenched with anger, and he felt a desperate need to speak his mind, but he held back. Fraser would not welcome open criticism, and it would not do to alienate himself now. He had already seen what became of those who crossed the man.

Yet doubt clung to the back of his mind. Questions whirred through his thoughts, feeding his uncertainty.

He shook his head, trying to ignore them. Yet as he mounted and turned his horse down the hill, a single thought clung to him, persistent and undisputable.

This cannot be the same man.

~

INKEN WRAPPED her arms around her knees and rocked herself in the darkness. It stretched out all around, endless in the tiny space of the cell, wrapping them in its doom. Beneath her the damp stone seeped through her thin pants, sending a shiver through her body. Despair hung around her like a blanket, dragging her down.

A steady stream of tears ran down her cheeks, but she did not make a sound, determined to keep her sorrow to herself. Somewhere in the empty darkness sat her companions: Caelin and Gabriel, and the other one. The one who had sucked the last droplets of hope from her soul.

Sucking in a breath, Inken fought down another bout of sickness. She had hardly eaten in… she could not say how long had passed since the events in the throne room. The darkness offered no hint; only her steady pangs of hunger suggested the passage of time. Food had come once, a tray sliding through a slot in the bottom of the door, but that seemed a long time ago now.

Panic gripped at the edges of her mind as she scrunched her eyes closed. It made no difference, but at least it stemmed the tears. She could feel herself teetering on the brink of some abyss, one from which she would never return. Around her the silence stretched out, thick with its own presence, filled with a dark promise.

This will be your tomb, it whispered to her.

A long, drawn out groan came from her left. Gabriel, she guessed. He had been the first to break, to lose his mind to the lure of the darkness. His whispers woke her sometimes as she slept, though it grew harder each day to distinguish between reality and dream. He spoke to some creature in the darkness, one only he could see.

Inken released her legs, drawing another lungful of air from the suffocating dark, as if that alone could sustain her.

The nausea came again and she retched, though there was nothing in her stomach. Her chest ached and her throat burned as she spat bile onto the grimy stones.

She struggled to stay strong, to keep herself from the madness which had claimed her friend. But knowledge of the man in the cells with them drove away all thought of hope. A scream rose up within her, but she fought it down.

In the darkness the world seemed to spin, drawing her further from reality. She grasped at the ground, her fingernails scraping through the muck coating the bricks. She felt a stab of pain as a fingernail caught and broke, but the ache at least drew her back from the edge.

Gasping, she looked around again, desperately seeking some break in the darkness. But there was only the unrelenting nothingness.

She swallowed and felt the action catch in her parched throat. Her chest heaved and she began to cough, the sound coming out like a bark in the tiny cell. Shuddering, she swallowed again, desperate to stop the fit.

When it finally subsided, Inken leaned her head against the wall. The cold bricks collected what little moisture was present, providing a small supply of water. It was all that sustained them now. She licked at a droplet, biting the inside of her cheek to keep herself from choking at the taste.

Her stomach growled and she wondered if they would ever be fed again. Their new companion said food came occasionally, but they had no way of knowing how long had passed since the last delivery. It would not be enough to sustain them anyway. She could feel her strength fading away.

Inken struggled to think, to keep her mind occupied. How many days now since Eric and Enala fled? Since they had lost Michael? How many days had the Three Nations survived without their Gods? How many more would they last?

Frustration grew in her chest, rising up to fight down the fear. They could not remain locked up in this wasting darkness; she would not allow it. The world outside hung in the balance, the threat of Archon pressing in from all around. His servants were everywhere, could get to anyone. The presence of their new cellmate proved that.

She needed to get out.

Rising, Inken felt her way to the door and slammed a fist into the wood. The dull thud echoed in the darkness, but the panels did not move an inch. She was not surprised – this was not the first time she'd tried. Even so, anger flashed within her and she lashed out with her boot. Then, with a screech of rage, she threw herself at the heavy door.

When her rage finally subsided, Inken leaned against the door and slid to the floor. She panted heavily, exhausted from even that brief exertion. A shudder went through her as the despair returned. No one had come; no one had even acknowledged her screams. They did not post guards in this dungeon; there was no need.

Caelin had already told them where they were. This was not the citadel's regular dungeon and this was no ordinary cell. This place had been created a century ago for a single purpose – to hold the dark creatures Archon had unleashed upon their world. The darkness still stank with their evil.

"Are you finished then?" a voice came from the darkness.

Inken closed her eyes and forced her breathing to slow. She clenched her fists, feeling the sticky wet of blood on her palms. She had done far more than break a nail in her mad fit. Turning, her eyes searched the dark, drifting to the empty space where the voice had come from. She knew where he sat, where he had sat for untold weeks and months before their arrival. He was a broken man, of that she was sure. The fight had gone from him, stolen away by the black cell.

"No, Fraser," Inken hissed. "I will never be finished. I will not allow the darkness to win. Never!"

"So be it," replied the king.

CHAPTER 3

Eric stared across the sunlit clearing. His heart thumped hard against his ribcage and he struggled to swallow the lump crawling its way up his throat. His eyes flickered sideways as Christopher and the others stepped up beside him, but they quickly returned to the vision in the centre of the field. Silence hung in the air, thick and heavy.

Enala stood opposite them, her face bathed in the sickly green glow of the *Soul Blade*. Long strands of grass rose up around her, twining their way around her legs and knitting through her blond hair. She held her arms open, the *Soul Blade* clutched in one, the other clenched tight in a fist. Her eyes were closed, her face lined with concentration.

Sucking in another breath, Eric fought down his panic. He could hardly believe they had found her. With Christopher's help they had sought out the tendrils of God magic seeping across the island, finally tracing them back to this clearing high on the mountainside.

Except now they had finally found her, Eric had no idea what to do next. Unclenching his fists, he wiped the cloying sweat from his fingers and glanced at Christopher. A chill fog hung on the morning air, hovering just above the treeline. His chest heaved and he could feel the blood thumping in his head, but he knew they could not afford to hesitate. If Enala fled, they might never find her again.

Looking back to Enala, Eric stepped towards his sister.

As his feet touched the damp grass, Enala's eyes snapped open. Eric froze as their unnatural green glow found him. Not a trace remained of Enala's usual sapphire blue, and with a wrench in his stomach Eric felt another trickle of hope leave him.

When she did not speak, he gathered his courage and took another step.

"*Stop*," his sister's voice screeched like steel on stone.

Ice spread through Eric's stomach, doing nothing to slow his racing heart.

Even so, he locked eyes with Enala, willing the girl within to break free. "Why?"

"I told you not to follow me," the forces holding Enala ignored his question. "I told you –"

"I will not abandon you, Enala," Eric interrupted.

Watching her closely, Eric thought he glimpsed a trace of recognition sweep across his sister's face. Then the iron glare returned and her teeth flashed, her lips drawing back into a scowl.

"Leave, *now*," the rasping voice growled.

"No," Eric took another step forward, alone in the clearing. He stared at the thing possessing his sister, refusing to back down. "I will never leave you, Enala."

"Then you will *die!*" the voice roared.

The hairs on Eric's arms stood up as he felt the crackling of magic. Then the clearing erupted into chaos. Screams came from behind him as tree branches swung down to smash the Trolan soldiers from their feet. He heard Christopher cry out, and then he had no more time to worry about their fate. Grass erupted beneath his feet, twisting up to bind his legs in place.

Eric acted without thought, his hand already reaching up to draw the Sword of Light. He knew from bitter experience only God magic could match God magic. Steel hissed on leather as the Sword slid free of its makeshift scabbard, white flames igniting at his desperate touch. Heat washed across his face, and then the flames were all around him, burning the green tendrils to ash.

Turning quickly, Eric risked a glance at the Trolans. The men huddled in a circle with Christopher at their centre. Flames leapt from his hands, incinerating any branch that came near. Together they retreated backwards from the clearing and their mad princess.

Glad they at least were safe, Eric turned back to Enala. Thoughts twisted in his head as he searched for a plan to free her. Looking at her expressionless face, the haunting green eyes, Eric felt pain twist in his heart.

Are you still in there, sister?

Enala strode towards him, the long grass billowing out in waves around her. Green light flooded from the *Soul Blade*, contorting the features of her face, revealing the wild magic within. Purple veins stood out stark against her pale skin, her muscles tensed with the power of the *Soul Blade.*

With a roar, Eric pushed back his emotion and slashed through the grass, stepping up to stand before her. He stared into the emerald green eyes, seeing the power swirling within but seeking out the girl he knew so well. But there was only the madness of power there. The same power he felt each time he touched his own magic, but magnified a thousand times by the ancient might of the Gods.

She is gone, the thought hissed in his ear, trickling into his soul.

Yet Eric would not give up. He could not abandon her to this fate. Somehow, he would find a way through.

"Enala!" he yelled through the chaos of the clearing.

This time his cries seemed to give the wild magic strength. A twisted grin spread across Enala's face and a dark laughter followed.

"There is no Enala here," she raised the *Soul Blade* and swung at Eric.

It was a clumsy swing but Eric leapt back all the same, terror in his heart. The God magic was gaining strength, driving Enala deeper inside, away from the light of life. If that light went out, there would be no coming back for the girl within.

She would become a demon.

They had already witnessed the destructive powers of one such creature. In his old age their ancestor Thomas had been overwhelmed by his magic, losing his soul to the dark depths of the power within him. The demon that took his place had wreaked havoc across the Three Nations, slaying the Gods of Earth and Sky before Eric finally destroyed him using the Sword of Light.

Eric had no intention of watching the same fate take Enala. In his heart, he knew he did not have the strength to do the same to her as he had to Thomas.

"Enala, you have to listen. This is not you, you do not need this power. *Fight it!*"

The laughter came again. This time when she raised the *Soul Blade* it was not the grass that came for Eric. The ground shook, and with a roar it tore apart beneath his feet. He leapt, reaching now for his own magic and its power over the Sky.

Winds raced around him, his magic leaping at his desperate need to propel him into the sky. Looking down, Eric watched the crevice tear its way through the forest. Trees groaned as the fissure widened, sending them tumbling into the depths below.

Wiping sweat from his brow, Eric turned and searched for Enala. His eyes swept the shattered clearing and found her hanging over the crevice, suspended there by a host of vegetation springing from the earth below. Her murky green eyes watched him, the breeze toying with the copper lock hanging across her face.

Tears stung Eric's eyes as he watched her. "Enala, please, please, you have to break free!"

This time he caught a flicker of doubt in his sister's eyes. A surge of hope washed through him – he had not imagined that! It could only have been Enala. Somewhere in the dark depths of her mind, her soul still fought for freedom. He just had to find a way to help her break free

But the wild magic had other plans.

"*Die!*" the voice screeched, and green light flashed across the clearing.

Eric gripped the winds in threads of magic and drove himself higher as vines flashed towards him. He ducked as a tree branch swung for his head, then he was clear of the trees, racing upwards as the vines chased after him.

Then, growling, he spun in the air and raised the Sword of Light. White fire swept down, incinerating the vegetation below. He coughed as smoke wafted up to catch in his nose. Rising higher, he searched again for his sister, eyes watering.

She rose through the smoke, the vines lifting her above the treetops. Gripping the Sword hard in his hand, Eric drew more power from the blade. The white of its magic blazed within him, but his magic wrapped it tight. A grin tugged at his lips as he revelled in its power.

The grin faded as he stared at his sister. He could not allow the magic to corrupt him, not if he wanted to keep his sanity. His joy faded as he realised raw power could not free

Enala. He could not fight the power possessing her, not without risking her in the process.

The Sword could draw on any aspect of the Light element, but he had yet to master even the simplest aspects of its power. Without that mastery, it offered little more than protection against the power possessing Enala. The rest was up to him.

Taking hold of the winds, he dropped towards Enala. The emerald eyes watched him come, the power behind them studying his descent. The corner of her lips rose in a deathly smile.

Eric shuddered as he saw the demon within, its confidence growing with every clash. If it was allowed to escape, the God magic it possessed would wreak untold havoc.

Lightning flickered as Eric drew on the power of a distant storm. A bolt raced across the sky, striking his outstretched hand with a crash of thunder. It flickered in his palm and danced up his arm, a faint numbness lingering with its touch. He watched it with detached curiosity and then turned his gaze to Enala. Silently he prayed the lightning and the Sword would be enough to protect him.

The earth below them groaned and snapped shut with a dull boom. The vines holding Enala began to contract, lowering her back to the ground. Letting out a breath, Eric followed her down until they both stood again in the clearing. The silence stretched out as they stared across the broken clearing.

"I will not allow you to be born, demon," he addressed the magic for the first time. "Fight it, Enala!"

"*Oh, Eric*," the thing within his sister cackled, mimicking Enala's true voice. "You are already too late."

Eric stared into the depths of his sister's eyes as she raised the *Soul Blade*, searching for a hint of recognition. His stomach twisted in a knot as the truth of her words crept through the cracks in his mind. The magic was too powerful. For more than a week it had burned its way through Enala's body, tearing at her soul, driving her deep into the depths of her conscious.

"Not yet," he breathed as he recalled his battle within the otherworld known as The Way.

There, Eric's magic had come close to possessing him. Only Enala's desperate, dying cries for help had given him the strength to beat it back.

Closing his eyes, Eric lowered his head.

The risk is too great, the thought whispered in his mind. If things went wrong, both of them would be lost. They were the only ones left who could wield the Sword of Light. Without them, the Three Nations would fall to Archon.

Yet he could not turn his back now, not if there was still a chance to save her.

Eric's hand trembled, his thumb running along the diamond embedded in the hilt of the Sword. He could sense the power throbbing within Enala, preparing for another attack. He had only seconds to react now, mere moments to change his mind. But even as dread spread through his chest, he knew he would take the risk.

Enala would come through for him. He knew the girl's strength, the courage she possessed.

She would not let him die.

Closing his eyes, Eric felt the weight lift from his soul. Right or wrong, the die had been cast. A smile tugged at his lips as he unclenched his hand and released the Sword.

The snake-like tendrils were on him before the blade had even touched the ground. They whipped from all around, rippling out from Enala in a wave of earthly power. The strands twisted around him, binding him tight.

The lightning died in Eric's palm as the pressure grew, stealing the breath from his lungs. He stared through the writhing mass of green, seeking out Enala, seeking out those haunted eyes. Blood throbbed in his arms, trapped by his bindings.

As the last vines wrapped about him the air cleared, revealing Enala's approach. She stared across at him, hate twisting the features of her face, a smirk on her lips. Arms folded, she held the *Soul Blade* in a casual grip, and watched as her creatures squeezed the life from her brother.

Summoning the last of his strength, Eric sucked in one last breath.

"Enala," he gasped. "*Help me!*"

A shadow crossed Enala's face, her eyes widening. For a second he thought he saw a flicker of blue in her eyes, and to his surprise the vines around him loosened. He sucked in another gulp of air and screamed. "You can do it, Enala. Don't let it kill me!"

A tremor swept through his sister and her irises swelled, reducing the whites of her eyes to thin circles. Blue swirled amidst the green and she stumbled back a step. The *Soul Blade* trembled in her hand.

"Come on, sis. You can do it," he mouthed.

His bindings loosened further, almost freeing him. He did not move, knowing Enala was locked in a desperate struggle with the force within her. Any change might shift the balance, destroy the desperate strength with which she fought.

Slowly the colour in his sister's eyes shifted, the green retreating before the sapphire blue. Her lips quivered and her breath came in great, gulping gasps. Yet still her fist remained clenched around the hilt of the *Soul Blade*. So long as she held it, the flow of Earth magic would not cease.

Swallowing caution, Eric spoke again. "You're almost there, Enala! You can do it, just let it go. Cast out the God magic!"

Enala's eyes drifted back to Eric and for the first time he saw again the girl he knew in their crystal depths. Fear lined her face, matched by a great, all-consuming fatigue. But the steely determination he knew all too well was there too. It just had to hold out a few more seconds, for one final push.

Their eyes caught and Eric gave a short nod.

Enala's eyes closed as she summoned whatever strength remained to her. Her shoulders heaved and she raised the *Soul Blade* above her head. Then, with a final scream, she hurled it from her. The weapon spun in the air, sunlight glinting from the suddenly dark metal. It slammed point first into the ground and quivered there.

The vines around Eric collapsed to the ground as one, freeing him from their grasp.

He looked up in time to see Enala's eyes roll back in her skull. He stepped forward and caught her as she fell. Holding her close, he pulled her tight against him.

"You did it, Enala. You're safe."

ENALA GROANED as sensation returned to her, agony lancing through every muscle of her body. Light burned into her skull as she opened her eyes, struggling to take in the world around her. A thumping pain came from the back of her head and a sharp jolt came from her neck as she tried to move. She fell back to the ground with a whimper, surrendering to the waves of agony.

"Enala?" she heard Eric's voice from nearby. "Are you okay?"

She cracked open an eye, squinting against the fiery light. Her brother's face hovered nearby and branches clawed across the sky behind him. Concern touched his lightning blue eyes and his auburn hair was slick with oil. Dirt streaked his face and his tunic was stretched and torn. Even so, the sight of him warmed her heart.

"Where are we?" she croaked.

Eric smiled. "Someplace on Witchcliffe Island. How do you feel?"

Memory was slowly returning to her as she lay there. She shivered, recalling the helpless horror she'd felt in the clutches of the traitorous King Jonathan. Images flashed in her mind: Eric falling from the sky, the Sword of Light spinning towards her, the agony as it tore through her chest.

Enala shuddered. "I don't know," she whispered, still caught in the tide of memories.

She recalled with horror Eric's battle with the king, then the arrival of the demon, Thomas, and a final surge of elation as the Sword burnt the creature to ash. She watched with growing dread her desperate crawl across the temple floor, her helpless cry as she reached for the *Soul Blade*.

She remembered the healing light that had shone from the weapon, and then the wave of power that surged from the blade. It burned through her veins, flooding her mind and washing her soul away in its current.

Enala shot upright, a deep, rattling gasp rising from her lungs. She felt Eric's touch on her arm and flinched away, a scream on her lips. She could still *feel* the shadow of the power within her, the God magic burning at her soul, her helpless fear as it tore away control.

If not for Eric, she would never have found the strength to overcome it.

Sanity returning, Enala opened her eyes and reached for her brother, desperate to feel his touch, to reassure herself the nightmare was truly over. Pulling him close, she held him for dear life, drawing comfort in the solidness of his skin, his body.

"It's okay, Enala. You're safe."

Another tremor took her. "I've never felt anything like it, Eric. It was like a wave, sweeping me away, taking everything that was me and leaving only the magic. I thought I would drown in it."

"I know," Eric drew back from her. Enala looked into his eyes and saw her own fear reflected there. "It is the same with all magic. It has a life of its own, a longing for freedom. When you touch it consciously with your mind, even your own magic will try to overwhelm you. I can only imagine the strength it would take to fend off God magic."

Enala took a deep breath and forced herself to look around. Her eyes took in the clearing around them. She remembered it from before, though the memories were distant, as though she had dreamt them. Several people stood nearby, doing their best to ignore them.

"Who are they?" she murmured.

"Trolans," Eric answered. "They helped me find you. The council sent them. Turns out Jonathan misled us all along. It was the king who abandoned Trola, forcing the council to step in and govern the nation."

Enala nodded, the last pieces of the puzzle falling into place. "I'm glad he's dead."

Leaning on Eric's shoulder, she pulled herself to her feet.

"Thank you for your help," she looked around at the Trolans. "I am sorry we fled the city. We should not have run."

A man wearing the white robes of a priest smiled as he walked up to them. "Do not worry, we place the blame squarely on Jonathan's shoulders. The man did not deserve the title of king."

Enala smiled. "I can agree on that."

Something in the corner of her eye drew Enala's attention. Turning, she stumbled back a step as her eyes fell on the *Soul Blade*. It still lay on the grass where it had fallen, a faint green seeping like water from the black blade. An icy hand gripped her heart and a cold sweat dampened her forehead. She gripped Eric's shoulder tight, her hands like claws.

Eric followed her gaze and squeezed her hand. "It's okay, it's gone, you're free. You don't have to worry about ever touching that foul thing again."

Relief swept through Enala, but before she could reply the priest spoke. "I'm not so sure, Eric," Christopher paused as she turned on him. He raised his hands, and went on. "We have no way of knowing how to free either Jurrien or Antonia from those blades, and the Three Nations are desperately short of God powers just now. If we cannot find a way to free them, someone will need to confront the power of those blades."

"I will never touch that thing again," Enala hissed.

Christopher stared back, his face grim. "I pray you won't have to."

CHAPTER 4

Elton strode down the dimly lit corridors of the citadel, his thoughts lost in a whirlwind of questions. Two days had passed since the king's meeting with the dragons, and nothing he'd seen or heard since had lessoned his suspicions. There was no longer any doubt in his mind – something was very wrong with the king.

He had done his best to find Caelin and the others, but they had not been seen since the king ordered them imprisoned. They were not in the dungeons or locked away in any of the towers reserved for noble 'guests', and the king had yet to set a date for their trial. To make matters worse, as far as the councillors knew, no one had come forward yet to corroborate their tale.

Yet Elton knew that could not be true. Yesterday he had spoken with the guards on the stairwell up from the lake and heard from them that a Lonian priest had arrived several days ago. The priest's presence could only mean the Sky temple in Lon had sent someone to verify his old friend's story. But still there was nothing.

The more Elton searched, the less he could deny the

truth of Caelin's suspicions. Something was wrong in Ardath, and it seemed the king sat at the middle of it all.

What has happened to him?

Still, Elton could not bring himself to believe Fraser could be at the centre of such a conspiracy. No, he had to be under some spell, some corruption cast by one of Archon's agents. Caelin had already slain two of the creatures; there had to be more.

He had considered going to the king himself, but so far had held back. He was no Magicker and had no way of breaking the king free of such a spell. And what if he was wrong?

No, he could not risk it. Not if somehow, impossibly, the king had truly been turned.

Thankfully, as a soldier, Elton had plenty of friends amongst the guards and soldiers of the Plorsean army. The councillor's might not know a priest had arrived in the capital, but all news in the city eventually made it to ears of the guards. It had not taken long for him to discover a small pool of men had been assigned to guard a room deep within the citadel.

It only took a few pints of ale to convince one of the guards to exchange shifts.

Picking up the pace, Elton took the next right and turned into a poorly lit corridor. It had taken longer than expected to navigate the maze of hallways in this section of the citadel, and he was running late. Ahead he glimpsed the shadow of a man in the light of a single lantern and smiled. He had arrived.

The guard turned and flashed a grin as he saw Elton approaching. "Ah, Elton, good to see you. I heard you changed shifts with Alexandar. I think you pulled the short straw on that one; nothing to do but stare at this here wall."

Elton laughed. "Sorry I'm late, I haven't been back here

often," he shrugged. "Truth to tell, after a few run-ins with those dragons, I could use a little quiet."

Chuckling, the guard shook his head. "True, true. I'll not forget the sight of that beast landing on the walls till my dying day," he clicked his neck and groaned. "But that's me for the night. Best of luck. Hope you find something to keep yourself entertained."

With that he turned and wandered away down the corridor. Elton waited a few minutes after he'd turned the corner before facing the door. Reaching up, he thumped on the heavy wood. He wondered how the priest had taken the reception here in Ardath – it was not exactly customary to post guards outside a guest's door.

He didn't have to wait long for his answer.

"*What?*" a woman's voice growled from inside the room.

There came a scrambling from the door and then the creak of hinges as it opened. A woman stood in the doorway, her blue robes scrunched with lines as though she'd just pulled them on. Angry eyes glared up at him, blinking in the lantern light, her long white hair muddled with sleep.

"What do you want?" she growled. "Has the king finally given up this nonsense?"

"Nonsense?"

"About whether he believes the news I brought?" the priest snapped. "I am tired of this room. It was not my intention to spend my days in Plorsea locked in the citadel. Do you treat all your guests like prisoners, or is this treatment reserved just for priests?"

Elton held his hands up in surrender. "My apologies, ma'am. I am just a simple soldier – I am afraid I do not know the king's mind. But I am interested in your story. I believe you may know my friend, Caelin?"

The old woman nodded. "I do, though we did not speak much with the bunch of them. We were busy preparing the soldiers and equipment for their expedition," she eyed him closely. "What did you say your name was?"

"I didn't," Elton nodded to the room. "But perhaps this is a conversation better had in privacy, away from any prying ears."

The priest studied him for a long moment before finally stepping from the doorway and beckoning him inside. "Very well. I take it you are *not* here at the request of the king then."

"No," Elton moved into the room, his eyes sweeping the interior. An unmade bed had been pushed into the far corner, while a table took up the opposite side of the room. Otherwise the room was unadorned.

"I'm afraid I can't offer you anything to drink..." the priest spoke in a wry voice.

"My apologies..." Elton shook his head, realising he did not know the woman's name. He held out his hand. "My name is Elton."

"Lynda," she took his hand in hers.

Elton lowered himself into a chair at the table. "Nice to meet you, Lynda," he sighed. "I am afraid I don't know why you're here. I don't know what is happening in this city, what is happening to the king."

Lynda sat opposite him. "Perhaps you could start from the beginning."

"You're right," Elton shook his head. "I'm afraid there is something very, very wrong happening here in Ardath."

Bit by bit, he explained how the king's demeanour had changed over the past weeks and months. It had started with the occasional outburst and rages, but with the arrival of Caelin and his companions, things had quickly descended into madness. The tale of his friend's reception by the king rushed out, followed by the arrival of the dragons and the insanity that had almost shattered the ancient alliance between the beasts and man. As he spoke he could feel a burden lifting from his shoulders, the weight of his suspicions fading away in the warmth of the woman's gaze.

When he finished he fell silent, looking up at Lynda for a response.

She took a long time to reply, her old eyes studying him closely. At last she gave a short nod.

"I am afraid my part to this story will only confirm your suspicions. I spoke to the king two days ago in his private chambers. Everything Caelin and his friends said was true – I confirmed as much to the king. He told me he would consider my words and sent me away. I have been locked in this room ever since."

"How can this be?" Elton lowered his head into his hands. "He has always been a good king. Could he be under the control of one of Archon's servants?"

Lynda shrugged. "I do not know. I did not sense anything from him myself. But there are many ways for the dark to turn the light. For now though, we must get to the bottom of this rabbit hole," her voice was firm, resolute.

"How? I cannot accuse the king of treachery. Even with your word to support me, the council is clearly with him. His power is indisputable. What can I do?"

"You could free Caelin and his companions. That would be a start. We will need allies if we are to wrestle control of Plorsea back from whatever influence Archon has over the throne."

"I do not even know where they are being kept," Elton groaned.

"I believe I do," Lynda offered. "When I met with the king, he mentioned they were being held in the dungeons."

"No, I already checked. There's only the usual thieves and riff-raff down there."

"Are you sure?" she frowned. "The king mentioned it

several times. He was angry, refused to take my news as fact. He insisted they could not be trusted after murdering his councillor, that they were exactly where they deserved to be."

"Strange," Elton stood and started to pace.

He had checked most of the citadel in his search, but there had been no sign of the company. And he could not have missed their presence in the dungeons.

Pausing mid-stride, Elton turned to face the door.

They are not the only dungeons, the thought whispered in his mind. There were others, ones far older than those used today. As far as he knew, the black cells had not been used in decades. They were from another time, a darker time. They had been used to hold the prisoners of Archon's war – beasts and humans alike.

Elton shuddered, thinking of the cursed cells far below the keep. Untold horrors had transpired in those cells and darkness clung to the air itself. He had walked down the stairs once, but had never made it to the bottom. The darkness had driven him back, and not even the warmth of the torch in his hands could convince him to return. There was a presence about the place, a creeping evil that chilled the soul.

They are exactly where they deserve to be…

With sudden clarity, Elton knew his suspicion was right. If the king had truly been turned to Archon's cause, then those dungeons made a chilling sort of sense, offering a perverse revenge for the dark things that had once taken place down there.

"I know where they are," Elton breathed.

Lynda nodded. "Good. Then let us go find them."

"Us?" Elton questioned. "You can't come with me, you're a priest…"

"Ay, I am," there was steel in Lynda's voice now. "A priest entasked by the Gods to defend this world from darkness. I will not stand here, trapped in this room, and wait for that darkness to triumph. This is my fight as much as yours, young Elton. Besides, you may need my help," as she spoke a wind whirled through the room.

The hairs stood up on Elton's arms as he felt the bitter kiss of winter on the air. "You are a Magicker?"

"I am," Lynda smiled. "I have a gift with the wind. Perhaps it will help in the fight to come."

Elton stared at the priest, trying to guess her age. Beneath the blue robes her body looked frail, the skin of her hands thin and wrinkled. She must be well past sixty. But there was no denying the strength of resolve in the woman's grey eyes. And he did not know if he could continue this fight alone, not against the men and women he had served beside for the better part of a decade.

She was right, he would need her help.

"You're right," he nodded and moved to the door. "Let's go find our friends."

Give in, the demon's voice hissed in the darkness.

A groan crackled up from Gabriel's parched throat as he tried to block his ears to the whispers. But the voice came from all around him, reverberating through the deepest confines of his mind.

Give in, and I will free you from this place, it persisted, tempting, irresistible.

Gritting his teeth, he fought the call. Dried blood congealed beneath his fingertips from where he had dragged them down the stone walls, desperate for distraction. The pain cut through the haze, offering a brief respite from the lure of the demon's call. But as the pain faded the voice would return, unceasing.

"*No!*" he screamed again, no longer caring what his

companions thought. In truth, he hardly remembered their presence. There was only the darkness now, only death.

And the voice.

"No, no, no," he sobbed.

He swung his fist and jumped when it connected with flesh. "Gabriel, stop," Caelin's voice echoed off the stone walls. Strong hands grabbed his wrists. "Stop this, get a hold of yourself!"

"Leave me!" Gabriel screamed, wrenching himself free, hardly aware it was Caelin who grabbed him and not the phantom stalking the darkness. "Just leave me alone," he sobbed.

"Gabriel," sadness tinged Caelin's voice, but the word was followed by scuffling as the sergeant retreated further into the cell.

Gabriel slumped back against the wall, closing his eyes, trying to close his ears.

They do not understand, the voice came again. *These mortals, they do not understand your greatness. Surrender, and I will free you from their presence.*

Tears welled in Gabriel's eyes. Why had it returned? Why would it not leave him be? Its presence radiated through the cell, its perverse evil sending chills down to his very soul. He reached inside for some defence, for some weapon with which to fight it, but there was nothing. Its thoughts crept through his mind, whispering dark secrets, washing away his sanity.

It's too late, Gabriel. You will never be one of them. It is not your destiny. There is blood on your hands, innocent blood. Join me…

Gabriel bit his tongue to keep from crying out again. Guilt swept through him. The voice was right; he had made a terrible mistake. Katya had not been the traitor. The truth had been before them all along. Some foul impersonator sat on the throne in place of the king. Katya had been no more than a pawn.

And he had killed her. The blood of an innocent woman was on his hands.

Fool, fool, fool, the words rang in his head, digging deeper until only pity and hate remained. *I swore, I swore to do good. And I failed.*

It is only your nature, the demon's voice twisted through his thoughts. *You cannot deny what you are, the darkness in your heart. Surrender, and I will give you the world.*

"Who are you?" Gabriel cried. "Leave me!"

"Gabriel, it is only us, your friends," Inken spoke now, her voice soft but weak. "We are here, only us, only ever us. Whatever speaks to you, leave it be."

"Inken?" Gabriel groaned. "What have I done? I killed her… She was innocent, and I killed her!"

"It was not your fault," her voice was sad. "We all thought it was her. The way she acted, the spell that was cast over us. You could not have known."

"Ay," it was King Fraser who spoke now, his words thick with despair. "It is a treacherous creature, well-versed in deception. It spent weeks in our court, garbed in the body of one of my councillors. I suspected something was amiss, but it whispered in my ear, sending me after the wrong suspect. I did not realize my mistake until it was too late. The man it had impersonated was waiting in here for me. It killed him once it had me."

"It doesn't matter," Gabriel replied. "Her blood is on my hands, mine alone. I deserve to be here."

For a while there was silence.

Then the whispers of the demon returned.

CHAPTER 5

Enala rolled onto her back, sighing as her head sank into the soft pillow. The bed beneath her was more comfortable than anything she could remember, but sleep would not come. Closing her eyes, she tried to lose herself in the crackling of the fireplace, in the gentle snoring coming from the other bed. Struggling to relax, she allowed her thoughts to drift over the events of the past few days. The revelations rose one after another – though her mind kept returning to the one, inconceivable fact.

I have a brother.

The word still felt strange on her tongue, the notion beyond belief. A twist of pain swept through her as she remembered her parents and the fierce love they had given her. Even amidst the poverty-stricken streets of Chole, she had never wanted for much.

More than anything, she cherished the time they had spent together amongst the Gold dragon tribes to the east, the summers spent in the wilderness of Dragon Country.

She could only imagine the pain they must have felt to

give up their child, to pass Eric into the arms of another family.

Where did you find the strength, Mum, Dad?

A tear ran down her cheek. She would never get to ask them. Eric would never get to meet the ones who had brought him into this world, who had given everything they had to protect him. He would never share in the joy her parents had given her.

Enala rolled in her blankets again, desperate for sleep but knowing now it would not come. Her restless mind ate away at the long hours, the passage of time marked by the dying light of the fireplace. Exhaustion clung to her mind, but her fear kept her awake.

"What if I have to use it, Mum, Dad?" she breathed to herself.

"Then you will pick it up and conquer it," Eric's voice came from across the room.

She turned to see him watching her, the firelight reflecting in his blue eyes. Eyes that matched her own.

"How long have you been awake?"

"I've been drifting in and out of sleep," he glanced at the window, and Enala noticed a hint of light had appeared on the horizon. "Did you sleep?"

Enala shook her head. She sat up in the bed, staring down at the covers. "What if it happens again, Eric? What happens if I can't come back this time?"

"It won't," Eric's voice was strong. "Next time, you'll be ready," he shook his head then. "Anyway, it won't come to that. Christopher will find a way to free them."

Enala should have taken heart from Eric's confidence, but the dread in her chest whispered a different song. In a flash of intuition, she knew the priest would not succeed. Even so, she smiled and nodded at her brother.

"Come on," Eric said, pulling himself from the bed.

"We're awake; we may as well get ready. We're meant to meet the council at dawn."

With a groan, Enala followed Eric's lead, rolling from the bed. She cursed her whirling mind for keeping her from sleep. She needed it desperately, and the soft bed was difficult to leave behind.

An hour later, they moved slowly up the red carpet of the throne room. Enala's feet dragged as she walked, an entirely new sense of dread wrapping around her throat. She had betrayed the Trolan council's trust when she fled with Jonathan, spitting on their hospitality. Now she had to face that same council, and beg for their aid.

Without the help of the Trolan Magickers, Eric would never master the true power of the Sword.

Eric stood beside her, his lips pursed tight. He carried the *Soul Blades* wrapped in a bundle – neither of them had any desire to touch the cursed things – and the Sword of Light strapped to his back.

A raised stone ceiling stretched high overhead, carrying echoes of the councillor's whispers across the hall. Sunlight streamed through the wide windows to their left. Enala attempted a smile as the warmth caught in her hair, her eyes drifting to the table at the end of the room. A dozen seats ringed the wooden slab, though only four were occupied. Enala guessed those who had marched north with the army usually filled the empty chairs. She felt another twist of guilt in her stomach but shook it off. Crossing the last strip of red carpet, they drew to a stop and stared at the collection of men and women facing them.

She recognised Christopher in his white robes immediately, and felt a surge of relief to see the smile on his face. The relief faded as her gaze swept across the others: another man and two women. Each wore neutral expressions, though the thin line of their lips suggested they were not impressed by their presence.

Biting her lip, Enala held her hands behind her back and gave a short bow of her head. Eric followed, and then there was nothing left to do but talk.

Enala opened her mouth to introduce herself, but broke off as one of the woman stood and walked around the table towards her. Her hair was grey and her face aged, but her eyes were sharp. They caught Enala's gaze and held her. The words in Enala's throat shrivelled and died as the woman drew to a stop in front of her.

"Welcome," the older woman spoke in a soft voice. Even so, it carried to the furthest corners of the room. She raised an eyebrow. "Again."

Enala winced, looking away from the iron in the woman's eyes. Then a surge of anger gripped her and she looked up into the woman's amber gaze.

"We have already apologised to Christopher, and the soldiers you sent. Must we bow and grovel for your forgiveness too?" her eyes flashed. "Or will you apologise for the actions of your king, for allowing such a man to wander your citadel unsupervised?"

To her surprise, the woman chuckled. Warmth spread to her face as she smiled. "I see my fellow councillor did not exaggerate when he spoke of you," she gestured them towards the table. "Come, let us leave the past in the past. My name is Angela. Christopher you already know, and this is Heather and David. Please, join us."

Enala hesitated as Eric moved past her, then nodded. Striding across to the table, she lowered herself into the chair beside Eric.

"These are dark days indeed," Angela looked around the table, as though expecting someone to disagree. "With the Gods gone, the world is descending into chaos. In truth, I see little hope for our nation's survival without divine intervention. It is a welcome sight to see the Sword of Light back in the hands of one who can wield it."

Beside her Eric nodded, and Enala tried to relax. She managed a short smile. "We were lucky things turned out in the end," she paused. "I am sorry that we ran. It was a costly mistake."

Angela smiled. "As I said, it's in the past."

"So, are you all Magickers?" Enala decided to change the subject. "The king... he told me his people no longer respected him as a ruler when he lost his magic. Or was that another lie of his?"

"A half-truth, at best," the woman named Heather answered. "Jonathan was the one who abdicated his duties and left the council with the burden of governance. Although myself and Christopher are Magickers, it is by no means a requirement."

"No," Angela added. "For myself, I am glad not to carry that burden. Most of our Magickers marched north with the army, along with half the council. We have been left rather short-staffed, as you may have noticed."

"That was why the citadel was empty when we... left," Eric's cheeks reddened as he stumbled on the last word. "Is the guard... the one outside my room, is he okay?"

Christopher chuckled. "Ay, although a little embarrassed about letting someone half his size get the better of him."

Eric smiled. "I had help, from a Magicker by the name of Laurel," his smile faded. "She was a Light Magicker."

Christopher's eyes widened. "Laurel, you say?" when Eric nodded he turned to Heather. "Could it be the same Laurel?

"What?" Enala asked. "You knew her?"

"I believe so," Christopher nodded. "I knew a Laurel once, when I was a senior apprentice to the Temple of Light. She vanished several years ago, not long before I graduated.

We have always wondered what happened. How did you come to know her?"

An image of the feisty Baronian woman drifted through Enala's thoughts, and the smile faded from her lips. Eric had told her of the woman's sacrifice, that she had held the demon long enough for Eric to escape.

Making a decision, she interrupted Eric's reply. "We would never have made it here alive without her," she nodded at Eric. "And she sacrificed her life to save Eric from the foul demon Archon sent to hunt us."

Eric's eyes widened at her omission of Laurel's unsavoury past, but said nothing.

Christopher's eyes wrinkled in sadness. "A brave woman. Would that she had lived, we could have used her skills now. Despite lacking the Light's more aggressive powers, she was rather adept in its subtleties," he nodded at Eric. "You will need such skills if you are to wield the Sword against Archon."

Enala shivered at the name. Even now she could not bring herself to think of the confrontation to come, though it seemed all but inevitable now. Without the Gods to aid them, there would be no spell to banish the dark Magicker from their lands. No, it would be up to the men and women of the Three Nations to confront Archon.

"Is there anyone left here who *does* wield the Light?" Eric asked.

Christopher chuckled. "Well, as you might have guessed from my robes, my magic comes from the Light. It allows me to manipulate fire."

"I think I've got that one fairly well under control," Eric grinned.

"Yes, I noticed," Christopher sighed. "I do still remember most of the theory from my years as an apprentice. That may have to be enough."

"What about you, Heather?" Enala jumped in, turning to the older woman.

Her face wrinkled as she smiled back. "I am just a simple healer, I am afraid. I was one of the ones who worked on you when you first arrived."

Enala felt a sudden welling of tears. "Thank you," she murmured, blinking rapidly to clear her eyes.

After a moment of silence, Eric spoke again. "At least you'll be able to help with Enala's magic too, Christopher."

Enala's brow knitted at the thought of her power. In truth, she wanted nothing more to do with the force within her – not after everything that had happened on the island.

But Christopher was already nodding. "Yes, a budding fire Magicker I can help."

"What about the *Soul Blade*?" Enala cut in a little too sharply. Taking a deep breath, she continued. "Are you going to look at them, to see if you can free Jurrien and Antonia?"

The eyes of everyone at the table slid across to the bundle Eric had placed on the table in front of him.

"We will," Heather answered. "If you allow it, Christopher and myself will take them and do what we can to inspect them. I suspect it will take stronger powers than our own to break such a curse though."

Enala bit her lip, finding the kind eyes of the healer. "Do you think the same as Christopher? Do you think I will need to wield it?"

Heather stared back. "It may very well come to that, Enala."

Shuddering, Enala turned away. "What if I'm not strong enough?"

"You will be," Christopher spoke into the silence following her question. "I will make sure of it."

"How?" Enala hissed, still unable to meet his eyes.

Christopher stood and walked around the table until he

stood beside Eric. Reaching down, he flicked the cover off the *Soul Blades.* Enala suppressed a shudder as the faint blue and green lights bathed their faces.

"It is my theory that these blades can only be used by anyone with magic strong enough to control them," he looked across at Enala. "From what I saw on the island, I believe the magic of the *Soul Blade* overwhelmed you because you could not summon your own magic to protect yourself. From what Eric has told me, you have never consciously tapped into your power. Without that preparation, you never stood a chance against the God magic trapped in the *Soul Blade.*"

"So what are you suggesting?"

"That before you even go *near* this sword again, I will train you to use your own magic."

Enala bit her lower lip, her thoughts turning to the fire magic that had appeared within her such a short time ago. It terrified her still, though it was nothing compared to the force waiting in the *Soul Blade*. At least this power was a part of her, had aided her when she had been threatened. But could it truly protect her against the God magic?

Only time will tell.

Taking a breath, she met Christopher's eyes. "When do we start?"

"WHAT DO YOU THINK?" Eric sat up as Christopher walked into the snowy courtyard.

He stretched as Christopher approached, then rubbed his arms to fight off the chill. Even in the woollen clothing they'd given him, the Trolan winter was bitterly cold. He would rather have waited near the large fireplace in his room, but the old Magicker had asked to meet him here.

Shivering, Eric wiped the sprinkles of snow from his shoulders.

"She is a fast learner," Christopher replied. "But she's not ready yet. It can take months before a Magicker is able to make the final leap with their powers."

"We don't have months. We don't even have weeks."

"I know," Christopher raised his hands. "But I will not push her before she is ready. I can sense her fear; it holds her back. And who could blame her, after what happened…"

They both fell silent then, remembering the scene in the clearing, the demonic distortion of Enala's face.

Shuddering, Eric nodded. "Okay, you're the teacher."

Christopher chuckled, shaking his head. "There's a first time for everything. I was never much of a student; I guess I'm going to learn how my teachers felt. Are you ready?"

Eric glanced down at the Sword of Light. He held it by the scabbard, the soft leather separating him from its power. Even so, light seeped from the diamond in the blade's pommel, dancing across the snowflakes falling around them.

"Well?"

Glancing up, Eric caught Christopher's eye and smiled by way of reply. Then he reached down, wrapped his frozen fingers around the pommel, and drew the blade from its sheath.

The familiar power raced up his arm, burning away the tingles of ice in his fingers. The warmth spread through his chest, pulsing with the beat of his heart. He could feel its light touching every part of him, seeping into every shadow of his mind. A shiver of fear touched him and he reached for his magic, eager to bind it to his will.

Eric breathed a sigh of relief as the blue lines of his power wrapped about the white, pulling it back from his mind. He felt the warmth of the Sword's flame and opened his eyes with a satisfied smile.

Looking up, he saw Christopher staring. "I don't think I'll ever get used to that," the Magicker offered. "I can feel the power radiating from it. Like a second sun. Unbelievable."

"I'm just glad it's under control," Eric gave a sad smile. "I have wreaked enough havoc with my own magic. I can only imagine what this would do."

"The destruction would be beyond anyone's imagination," shaking his head, Christopher clapped his hands. "But enough of such thoughts. There is much you must learn about the Light. As you may know, the Light is the most powerful of the three elements. It controls the raw energies of nature – the heat of fire being just one of them."

Eric nodded. "I saw Laurel become invisible several times – so it also controls the light itself?"

"That's correct. Although invisibility is just the beginning. A true master can also project illusions, make others see whatever the Magicker *wants* them to see."

"And Alastair's power?"

"Yes. While I only met him a few times, Alastair's power to move objects also came from the Light. With the Sword, you can do the same," Christopher took a breath. "Even more than that, the Light has dominion over magic itself. True mastery of the Sword would allow you to suppress the magic of others."

Eric gave a sad smile. "Laurel was rather adept at that particular skill," he frowned then, thoughts turning to the confrontation to come. "Could I do the same as she did – use the power of the Sword to steal the magic from Archon?"

Christopher took a while to answer. "It could be possible, but I don't think it would work. I believe it would take knowledge beyond mortal comprehension to bind dark magic as great as Archon's. Darius himself could possibly do so, but with just his raw power?" he shook his head. "If it was possible, I would have thought Thomas or one of his ancestors would have done so."

Eric bit his lip, struggling to hide his disappointment. Even so, he would keep the idea in mind. "When I was fighting the demon, I could feel the sword giving me energy, giving me the strength to keep going."

"That's not surprising," Christopher replied. "As you know, the Sword is God magic. Unlike our own power, it can create energy from nothing. It does not need to draw heat from the air or manipulate what is already there. In theory, you could draw unlimited energy from the Sword, though I would not recommend it."

"Why not?"

Christopher looked down at him, a hint of fear in his eyes. "We are not immortal creatures. Our souls are fragile, unlike the spirits of the entities we know as Jurrien, Antonia and Darius. We are not meant to wield such power. If you draw on the Sword's magic too much, there is no way of telling what the side effects might be."

Eric's stomach clenched in a knot, but he asked his next question anyway. "So in theory, I could use the energy of the Sword to recharge my own stores of magic?"

"It should be possible," Christopher sighed, then shook his head and grinned. "But enough with the questions. Let's see what you can do."

Eric hefted the Sword and grinned. "Let's begin."

CHAPTER 6

Elton paused at the top of the stairs, glancing back at Lynda. A few steps below, the light of the torch came to an end, engulfing the world in shadow. Staring at that darkness, he was suddenly glad he'd brought the old priest with him. He did not know whether he had the courage to continue down those steps alone.

"We had better move quickly," Lynda hissed. "Before someone comes."

Drawing in a deep breath, Elton nodded and took his first step down into the darkness. He shivered as the icy air touched him, the warmth of the torch in his hand providing scant comfort. Together they moved downwards, the darkness swallowing them up, reducing their world to the globe of light cast by the torch.

Beside him Lynda's footsteps were soft on the stone, a stark contrast to the rhythmic thud of his own boots. He glanced at her, taking strength from the courage on her stern face. Whatever the consequences, the woman intended to see this out to the end. Swallowing the lump in his chest, Elton continued their downward march.

Minutes dragged by, punctuated only by the scuffling of their feet on stone and the rhythmic thump of his heart. As they reached each landing he found himself praying they were finally at the bottom, finally within reach of his friend. But with each turn they would find another empty wall, and see another set of stairs continuing down. Down into the never-ending darkness.

"How far do they go?" Lynda whispered.

"I don't know. This dungeon was built to hold the worst of Archon's followers; those creatures and Magickers captured after his defeat in the last war. There were many who escaped the net cast by the Gods' spell, and our people were all too eager to extract their revenge."

He heard the priest swallow. "No wonder you can almost taste the evil on the air. The actions of our own people, let alone the stink of those creatures, it will never come out."

Feeling the swirling shadows around him, Elton couldn't help but agree. But there was no time to reply now – ahead, the torch had finally illuminated the bottom of the staircase. The stone steps came to an abrupt halt, replaced by a smooth, unlit corridor disappearing into the darkness. Their light reached the first of the cells, but there was no telling how far they stretched.

"This is it," Lynda murmured.

Elton looked around as a breath of wind stirred his clothing. Glancing at the priest, he stepped back in shock to see her robes flapping around her, caught in the grip of a great gale. But other than the briefest of whispers, the air in the dungeons was still, dead.

Lynda smiled. "I thought I'd call the wind now, in case we are cut off from the surface. You never know what we might find down here."

Forcing his mouth shut, Elton nodded. Lynda must be more powerful than he'd thought, to summon wind from so far above them, into a place as dark as this. Then he shook his head, returning his thoughts to the task at hand.

Somewhere down here, Caelin and his companions waited.

Stepping into the corridor, Elton made his way to the door of the first cell. Reaching up, he pounded the wood with his fist, then stepped back, waiting anxiously for a hint of life within.

After a few moments of silence, he moved to the next door, heart clutched tight in his chest. Down in this darkness with no source of light or heat, Caelin and the others could easily have succumbed already. It had been almost two weeks since the incident on the wall; he could only imagine the horror they had suffered in this place.

They made their way quietly down the corridor, Elton's hopes fading with every silent door. Lynda walked beside him, lips pursed, silent but for the gentle flapping of her robes. But he could see the determination in her eyes. If they did not find anything, he had no doubt she would blow every door from its hinges before she gave up.

Finally, they reached the door at the end of the corridor, the only one left unchecked. Elton's head throbbed with the cold, the beginnings of a migraine starting in the back of his skull. Icy despair touched his heart, but he pushed it back and held the torch aloft to cast its light over the door. From the outside it looked the same as the others. There was no sign of recent use.

Holding his breath, he reached up and banged his fist on the wood.

They waited together, breath held, the only sound in the darkness the gentle whirring of Lynda's wind. Elton closed his eyes, fighting the racing of his heart, and tried to push his panic down. The seconds stretched out, slipping away like sand from an hour-glass. And still no sound came from within.

At last Elton released his breath, the weight of defeat heavy on his shoulders.

"They're not here," he hissed.

As he spoke, the faintest of taps came from beyond the door.

Elton almost jumped, reaching for his sword before reason could take hold. In this dark place, the faintest of noises was as loud as a drum. He glanced at Lynda, eyes wide in question.

She nodded, and raised her hand.

The wind roared in the narrow corridor, rushing outwards to slam against the door. Wood groaned as the bottled up fury of the Sky crashed against it, followed by the scraping of hinges on stone. Elton stumbled back a step, sparing a glance at the priest. A vein throbbed on her forehead and her teeth were bared with exertion.

Then with a heavy crunch, the door buckled inwards, the wood splintering before the fury of the Sky. A second later it vanished into the black depths of the cell.

Elton stared, eyes searching the darkness within for a hint of movement. For a moment there was nothing, then he glimpsed a shadow in the light of the torch. He stared, waiting with anxious breath to see who would emerge.

The shadows shifted again, a figure taking shape within. It stepped closer, stumbling as it moved towards the light. Elton glimpsed an upraised arm, warding off the brilliance of the torch, and cursed his own stupidity. After so long in the darkness, the flame would be blinding. Shuttering the torch to just a slit, he waited for the figure to emerge.

The figure took the final step from the cell, and the slit of light fell across his face.

The air went from Elton's mouth in a sudden hiss. He stared, mouth agape and eyes wide, unable to comprehend this vision in the darkness.

Matted hair covered the man's face and his grey hair hung in a tangled mess. Dark brown eyes squinted out from beneath bushy eyebrows, struggling with the light. Lines marked his forehead and his limbs were shrunken and thin, starved of the power they had once wielded. The long weeks had reduced his clothes to little more than rags.

Yet even filthy and unkempt, there could be no mistaking the King of Plorsea.

"Elton," the king's words were barely a whisper. "So glad you came. You're a little late."

Deep in his thoughts, Caelin did not notice the first knock on the door. The sound echoed in the tiny room, trickling slowly into his conscious. It found him there, locked away where the darkness outside could not find him.

He studied the noise, curious as to what could have disturbed him. Certainly it could be nothing within the cell: he had long since filtered out Gabriel's mad rambling and the quiet sobs from Inken's corner.

What could it be?

The question continued to bother him. Had the guards finally returned with food? Or were they here to take them up again, to go before the imposter on the throne and plead their innocence?

Yet he had long since given up that hope. There was no reason for the creature to return them to the light, not now that they knew the truth.

No, they were meant to wither and die here in the darkness.

But there had been a sound, an echo of the outside world. The knowledge seeped through him, growing and spreading out to light the candles of his mind.

What could it be?

His mind was waking now, searching out the answer. It would not be the guards – they did not knock. The only time they had come, a tray had slid through the slit beneath the door.

Someone else then.

The thought finally gave him the strength to open his eyes and move. The darkness greeted him once more, but then, even his dreams were of the darkness now. The light seemed but a distant memory, a lifetime ago. Only the Gods could guess how long they had been here.

But then, they were dead too.

Drawing on the last dredges of his will, Caelin pulled himself back to his feet. In a daze he stumbled to where he knew the door stood. Reaching out, he tapped at the hard wood.

The noise seemed unbelievably loud in the narrow confines of their cell. Or perhaps that was because it had been so long since there had been noise.

Staring into space, Caelin found his energy withering, trickling back down to the depths of his soul.

It was nothing – a rat or nothing.

Then the darkness roared, and before he could think he was throwing himself to the side as the shattered remains of the door bounced past where he'd stood.

Light split the darkness, burning his eyes with the intensity of the sun. Tears spilt down Caelin's face but he could not look away from the light. The wonderful, unbelievable light. Around him the shadows peeled away, lifting from his soul. Strength flowed back to his muscles, lifting him from the ground. Light could mean only one thing.

Freedom.

Looking around the room, he saw the others blinking back. Inken wore a sort of wonder on her pale face, her hazel eyes glistening with tears and her fiery red hair shining in the light. Grease marked her face but he could see the strength there, flooding back to wash away the despair.

Gabriel sat beside her, but where Caelin had welcomed the golden glow, Gabriel flinched away, curling up and turning away from the doorway. His black hair was thick with oil and his forehead wet with sweat. But Caelin could not spare the young man his help yet. His thoughts were returning now, the memories rising up to meet the light. And with them, questions.

To his surprise, the king was already standing and staggering towards the doorway. The ravages of Fraser's captivity were clear in the light, his body shrunken almost beyond recognition. But despite it, there was a light in the man's eyes now, one Caelin had not expected after the man's earlier despair.

Perhaps the king was not broken yet.

Fraser was the first to reach the light, stumbling through the doorway to the corridor beyond. Gasps came from outside and Caelin's suspicions were confirmed; whoever was out there had not been sent by the false king.

Listening to the voices, Caelin drew on his last reserves of energy and stumbled out after his king. He heard Inken behind him, offering Gabriel her hand, and hoped the young man would find the strength to bring himself back from the grip of madness. It would take all they had to overthrow the demon on the throne.

Pain stabbed at his eyes as he emerged, though he saw the lantern held by their rescuers had been reduced to a slit. He stared at the man with the light, struggling to make out his features. A priest stood beside him, that much was clear from the blue robes. The woman's face appeared as a blur, but he guessed she was from the temple back in Lon. Probably the one they'd sent to verify their story.

Hope rose in his chest as the man's face came into focus.

"Elton, you found us," he croaked, his throat rough from thirst.

"Caelin," his old friend's voice shook. "How… how is this possible?"

Caelin gave a weak shake of his head. "I do not know," sorrow clung to his voice. "Archon's reach has stretched further than any of us could have imagined."

"Ay," the priest spoke now. "Without the Gods to protect us, there is little to stop the dark tendrils of his power spreading south. Us mere mortals are easy pickings for the likes of him. And it seems this time, he does not intend to be slowed by the armies of the Three Nations."

"What can we do?" Inken emerged with Gabriel on her shoulder. Her face was a sickly white, but she stood straight. "What will *you* do, Fraser?"

Elton winced at the casual way Inken addressed the king, but he had not been locked in that cell with them. Whatever happened now, they were bound by the shared horrors of the darkness.

Fraser stared back, his eyes pits in the shadow of his brow. He had lost so much to the darkness. Anyone who saw him now would call him imposter to the demon upstairs. There appeared to be little left of the man Caelin knew.

But he prayed the darkness had not taken everything, that a spark of the man still remained.

Staring at the king, Caelin held his breath and waited.

Fraser looked back, his breath misting in the icy dungeon air. The flames of the lantern reflected in his eyes, reminding Caelin of the man that had sent him to find Alastair so long ago. He was in there somewhere; they just needed to find him.

"Fraser," he whispered. "We need you."

The king drew in a great breath and looked around, his eyes lingering on each of them.

He took another breath. "I guess… I guess we go to war."

CHAPTER 7

Light, light everywhere. Emptiness, a vast open void, stretching out to eternity. And it burned, burned wherever it touched, consuming him, devouring him.

Eric opened his mouth to scream, and woke.

He snapped upright, struggling to bite off his cry before he woke Enala. His chest heaved and a cold sweat ran down his brow. He turned his head, his desperate eyes searching the room. But there was no one, nothing but the gentle snores of his sister from across the room.

Slowly his panic began to subside. He took another breath, trying to still his racing heart.

The memory of the Sword's magic lingered in his mind. His eyes drifted across the room until they found the blade leaning against the foot of his bed. He shivered. It had just been a dream; the vision had not been real. The blade remained out of reach, its magic locked within.

Yet the memory of its touch lingered in his mind. They had been training for days now, and Christopher's warning about the Sword's magic was becoming all too real. Its magic was never far from his thoughts.

Each time Eric touched it he felt its hunger, its harsh light burning away the shadows of his mind, searching for a weakness. And each time he touched it, he feared it would find it.

Shivering, Eric pulled back the covers and stood. His legs trembled and his mouth stretched in a yawn, but the dream still clung to him. He would not sleep now.

"Eric?" he heard the sleep in his sister's voice. "Are you okay?"

He saw her sitting up in bed and sighed. Sinking back onto his bed, he looked across at her.

"Sorry, I didn't mean to wake you."

"It's okay. I was hardly asleep," she shrugged, hesitating. "The magic, it scares me. Every time I close my eyes I can feel it, waiting. It may not be the same as the power in the *Soul Blade*, but it still terrifies me. I am afraid to close my eyes."

Eric rubbed his hands together and glanced at the fire. It had burned down to embers, and without its heat the room was beginning to cool. Without speaking he moved across the room and tossed one of the smaller pieces of firewood onto the ashes. Flames licked at the wood as he crouched down in front of it, hands out to the heat.

"I know how you feel," he spoke without turning, his voice soft. "Before we reached Chole, Alastair began to teach me how to use my magic. I began to meditate, to look within the shadows of my inner mind. Before Alastair could prepare me, I found my magic. Not knowing the risks, I reached out and touched it. When I did, my magic took me. If not for Alastair…" Eric shook his head. "Afterwards, I was gripped with the same terror you feel now. But you cannot let it rule you, Enala. If you let it fester the fear will only grow, until it becomes a beast you can never face."

He turned and saw tears in Enala's eyes. "Why is this happening to us, Eric?" she whispered. "How can we possibly hope to defeat Archon, when even the Gods have failed?"

Standing, Eric moved across to his sister and drew her to her feet. "We take one step at a time," drawing her across to the fire, they sat on the fur rug. "You need to face the beast within you, Enala. You need to prove to yourself you have the strength to face it. Remember, your fear is the only weapon it has against you."

He watched Enala take a shuddering breath, and then her sapphire eyes met his. Eric added another log to the fire, closing his eyes as the flames licked up the fresh morsel and the heat washed over him.

"Are you ready?" he asked in a whisper.

"ARE YOU READY?" Eric asked.

Enala smiled back at her brother, glad for his support. "I'm ready."

Without another word, she closed her eyes and turned her thoughts inward. She had spent the last few days practicing meditation with Christopher, but it still took time to concentrate. Thoughts rose to distract her, the bitter tang of fear at the forefront. Swallowing, she pushed them down, focusing on the rise and fall of her chest.

In, out. In, out, she breathed.

Slowly, her thoughts faded away, the simple words rising up to swallow them. Sensation fell with them, until all that remained was the gentle in and out of her breath. She found herself drifting in a world of shadows, alone, free from the trappings of her earthly worries.

Then, in the distance, she glimpsed the faint flicker of light. Curious, she turned towards it. The darkness slipped past her, as though she were soaring through a night sky, and the light grew. Within seconds it had turned from a dim speck to a vast pool of flame. It flickered beneath her, tongues of fire leaping up from its depths. And she knew she had found what she needed.

My magic, the words echoed all around her, as though spoken aloud.

Drawing on her strength, Enala cast aside her hesitation and reached for the light. A flame licked up in response, a finger of power reaching out to meet her. A tingle swept through her as it touched, curling up to wrap around her.

She gasped as the power drew suddenly tight, trapping her in its heat. Red flashed before her eyes and then it was burning, its touch searing through her spirit form. In the empty darkness, she screamed.

The pool of flame beneath her twisted, turning in upon itself. It rose in a column before her, shifting, changing from benign light to a creature of fire. Great jaws took form within the darkness and fangs of fire reached for her. The sleek body of a lioness grew out from the jaws, its sharp ears flat to its head, the wicked tale flicking out behind it.

Enala's fear came rushing back and she shuddered in the bonds of flame. The lioness swelled, drawing strength from her fear. It stepped towards her, fangs and claws poised to strike.

You can do it, Enala, from someplace far away, she heard her brother's words. *Face it; defeat it.*

Enala stared at the beast, the fear within her alive, swelling to engulf her. She clung to Eric's words, her lifeline in the darkness. The fear swelled, seeking to consume her, but as she stared at the lioness she found her courage returning.

Clenching her fists, Enala looked into the eyes of the beast.

You are nothing, she hissed.

To her shock, she felt the bonds of fire loosen. The lioness growled and took another step towards her. Enala ignored it. Summoning her own strength, she stepped towards it. The flames around her roared as she stepped into their midst, their hungry tongues licking at her spirit. But Enala pulled her courage around her like a cloak and took another step forward.

As she emerged from the flame she saw the lioness shrinking, withering before the power of her courage. A house cat now stood before her, hissing as she approached it. Its paws swiped out in rage and its hair stood on end, but she felt no fear now. Reaching down, she grasped it in her hands.

And the flames went out.

With a rush of warmth, she felt the magic surging within her, flowing through her veins. It swept through her soul, carrying with it images of smoke and flame. But it was hers to command now, and she would not release it.

Smiling, Enala opened her eyes.

"Welcome back, Enala. You did well," Eric grinned back at her.

Reaching up, Enala wiped the sweat from her brow. Her body felt hot, far hotter than the fire burning in the grate.

"Thank you, Eric," she shook her head. "Thank you for your belief in me. I could not have defeated the lion without it."

"I have every confidence you could have. You are the bravest person I know, Enala. If anyone could conquer their fear, it's you. And without fear the magic has no hold on you," he paused. "Although personally, my magic takes the form of a wolf. Much scarier," he winked.

Enala sucked in a breath. "Maybe, but I think I still have a lot to learn. Whatever you think, it almost had me. It will take time to master it," she paused. "And the *Soul Blade*..."

"One step at a time, remember."

"I know," even so, Enala could not stop her thoughts turning forwards. "Do you think we'll be able to free them? Antonia and Jurrien?" It seemed that was the only way she could avoid touching the cursed blade.

Eric shook his head. "Not here. I don't think the Magickers remaining in the capital have the power. In Fort Fall, maybe…" his voice trailed off.

Enala found herself biting back tears, the worry in her heart rising up to overwhelm her. It seemed that with every challenge they overcame, a greater one waited to take its place. She may have conquered her magic this one time, but she could not even enjoy that triumph, knowing the *Soul Blade* lurked in her future.

She felt Eric's hand on her shoulder and looked up. "It's not fair, I know."

A great, shuddering sob tore through Enala and she buried herself in his shoulder. "I can't do it, Eric. I can't face that *thing*, whatever it is in that sword."

Eric said nothing, just held her there in the light of the fire, offering his silent comfort. There was nothing he could say, nothing either of them could do to escape the destinies waiting for them. It was as Eric had said – unfair.

At last her sobs started to subside and she pulled back from her brother. She attempted to smile through her tears. "You know, I bet we find Inken and the others at Fort Fall," she said the words to give Eric cheer, but felt a warmth swell in her own chest at the thought of a reunion with Gabriel.

Eric smiled back. "I hope so. The Gods know we could use their help."

"There will be a lot of catching up to do," Enala nodded at the Sword of Light. "How do you think Inken will react to *that*?"

Laughing, Eric shook his head. "She'll probably ask what took us so long."

"When will we go?"

Eric frowned, watching as an ember rose from the fire to settle on his sleeve. "I don't know. Soon, I guess. We cannot afford to wait. Archon won't. Without the Gods holding him back, there is nothing left to stop him from marching south."

Enala nodded, her mind distant, thinking of the men and women manning that lonely fortress far in the north. "No," she whispered. "You're right; we can't linger here for long. As much as we need the rest, Fort Fall needs every soul they can get."

"We had better talk to Christopher and the others in the morning. Perhaps we can take a ship up the coast to the Gap."

A shadow wrapped around Enala's heart at the words, but she nodded all the same.

Silence fell between them then, as their thoughts turned inwards. Enala stared into the fire, her mind a thousand miles away, consumed by a fortress she had never seen.

Fort Fall.

She prayed the place would not live up to its name.

ERIC FROWNED as the muffled *whoosh* of flames erupting against stone echoed through the courtyard. Wiping the sweat from his forehead, he looked up at the two combatants as they fought their way through the heavy snow. The clash of steel followed as they closed on each other, the blades little more than blurs in their hands.

Sighing, Eric shook his head. It was good to see Enala making progress; he only wished he could say the same for himself. He sat on a stone bench at the other end of the courtyard, the Sword of Light lying across his lap. So far he had achieved little more than the first time he'd felt the rush of its power. It was galling to think unlimited power lay in his lap, yet he could do little more than create fire.

He watched Enala dive sideways into the snow to avoid a column of flame. It had been three days now since their midnight lesson, but they had made little progress with their plans to travel north. A blizzard had moved in over the city that night, burying the citadel in white and freezing the harbour solid. Things had only begun to thaw today, though Eric could still taste the ice on the air.

At least they had made the most of the extra time. He could see Enala's confidence growing each day, the fear lurking behind her eyes retreating before it. Christopher was proving to be a good teacher, although he'd had less luck with Eric. The Magicker had explained the basic techniques to wielding the different parts of the Light element, but so far Eric had failed to grasp even the most basic of them.

Across the courtyard, Enala rolled and regained her feet. Flames flickered along her arms, the snow coating her clothes turning to steam. She glared across at Christopher and with a scream, swept out her arm.

The flames roared and rushed towards her opponent, the snow sizzling at its touch. Across from her, Christopher raised both arms and a wall of orange fire leapt up in front of him. A dull boom rang across the courtyard as the two forces came together.

But Enala was already moving, sprinting across the burning stone with sword in one hand, fire in the other. Christopher waved a hand and the tangling flames went out with a rush, then Enala was there, flaming hand swinging for his face. Before the blow could land Christopher leaned backwards and her fist swept past, finding only empty air.

Then a burst of orange roared from Christopher's open

hand, taking Enala full in the stomach, and suddenly she was airborne.

Eric suppressed a chuckle as his sister tumbled backwards, disappearing into a mound of snow.

A groan came from somewhere within, followed by a string of curses. Her head reappeared, flushed with anger.

"You couldn't have pulled your blow?"

Christopher laughed. "I *did* pull my blow."

Enala swore again and shook her head. Eric could see the attack had rattled her. She still struggled to focus on both her magic and physical combat, a skill he himself had yet to even attempt. He did not envy her the challenge.

"I think I'm getting the hang of it," Enala offered as she climbed to her feet and brushed snow from her jacket. "It's a difficult balance."

"It takes practice," Christopher agreed. "But it is also an excellent way to help you get a grip on your power quickly. And I imagine it could prove useful in the north."

"I know. It's just *hard*."

Smiling, Eric shook his head. Turning back to the Sword of Light, he let out a deep breath and began again. Sinking into the confines of his mind, he reached out for the magic of the blade. The white flames leapt at his touch, their heat searing at his thoughts, but his own magic quickly rose to combat it. The blue lines of his power wrapped about the white, binding it tight.

Taking another breath, Eric opened his spirit eyes and allowed his soul to take flight. Rising from his body, he drew the white fire with him, holding it firm in his grasp. Looking now at Enala and Christopher, he saw the burning red within them, bright as torches in the darkness.

Eric had already attempted to suppress their magic as Laurel had done to his, but without success. Now as he reached out he decided on another course. It seemed an age ago now, but he had watched Alastair work his magic a hundred times. His mentor's strength had been prodigious, but Eric only needed the gentlest of touches for what he intended.

Drawing the Sword's power with him, Eric drifted across to where Christopher stood watching Enala's approach. Lines of power wrapped around the Magicker, some flashing red with the power burning at his core, while others seemed to appear from the air itself. Praying he knew what he was doing, Eric reached out and pressed the white fire of the Sword to the lines of power.

Light flared as the two forces met, then pale fire raced down the line towards Christopher. Eric's spirit shivered as the power reached the priest. The air popped as they met, but nothing changed, and Christopher stepped forward to knock aside Enala's next attack.

Frowning, Eric repeated the process sure he must be onto something. The lines had to be connected to some part of the Light – otherwise the Sword's magic would not be able to interact with them. Some intuition told Eric they must be related to how Alastair's power had worked.

This time as the white swept along the line, Eric reached out and gripped it with his mind. To his surprise, the surging white froze, its energy tingling beneath the soft touch of his conscious. Then, almost by instinct, Eric drove the energy into Christopher and gave one final, gentle push.

Christopher gave a shout of surprise as his legs whipped out from beneath him, tripped by some invisible force. The flames in this hand died away as his concentration snapped, and Enala leapt in to tap his chest with her practice blade.

Chuckling to himself, Eric retreated into his body and stretched his arms. His chest swelled with pride, that he had managed to replicate the magic of his mentor. Smiling, he stood and sheathed the Sword of Light, then walked across to join the others.

He laughed out loud as he caught Christopher's glare.

"Made some progress at last I see," the priest raised an eyebrow.

Eric grinned back. "Slowly but surely."

"A bit of warning would have been nice," Christopher shook his head. "But well done. You will need every skill you can muster to face Archon."

"I thought the scales could use a bit of balancing. Enala looked a little outmatched."

His sister scowled. "I didn't need you to cheat for me, Eric."

Eric raised his hands in surrender, but could not keep the smile from his face. "I just hope I'll have time to learn the rest. I want to at least *try* and use the Sword to suppress Archon's power."

Christopher sighed. "Would that it could be so easy. Only time will tell I guess."

"How goes the training?" they all looked up at Angela's voice.

"Progressing better than I had hoped," Christopher answered with a thin smile.

Angela nodded. "I have news. Heather and the other Magickers have finished inspecting the *Soul Blade*. It is as you suspected, Christopher. They are not powerful enough to break the enchantments. Unless we find someone stronger, the Gods will remain trapped in the weapons."

Eric's heart sank. He shot a glance at Enala and caught the despair sweep across her face. She masked it quickly, but not before their eyes caught. She looked away before he could say anything.

"There's still hope, Enala," Christopher spoke from between them. "By the time you reach Fort Fall, the greatest

Magickers of the Three Nations will be there. If anyone can free the Gods, it will be them."

"That is my other news," Angela interrupted.

Eric looked up, catching the hint of warning in her voice. "What is it?"

He saw then the weariness in Angela's eyes, the rings of exhaustion lining her face. She held her shoulders tensed and her fists were clenched tightly around a scrap of paper.

"This just arrived by pigeon," Angela paused for a breath. "It's from Fort Fall…" her voiced faded off.

A wave of weariness swept through Eric's legs. He stumbled a step, struggling to find the strength to keep his feet. "What's happened?"

"The invasion has begun," the old councillor's voice trembled. "Fort Fall is under siege, and the majority of our armies have yet to reach them. With the standing guard and the advance parties from Plorsea and Trola, they only have a thousand men."

"How far off are the rest of our forces?" Christopher's forehead creased with worry.

"The last word we had from our army put them a week out from the fortress. The Lonians are likely closer. But with only a thousand men, Fort Fall will be hard-pressed to hold on long enough for reinforcements to arrive."

"We will leave today," Eric growled, a desperate idea taking form in his mind.

Angela shook her head. "Even if you leave now, it will take weeks for the ship to traverse the Trolan coastline. It could be all over by then…"

Beside him Enala cursed, but Eric was already shaking his head. "You're right; there's no time for that now. We will not go by ship," he tapped the pommel of the Sword of Light. "We will fly. The Sword can give me the energy I need to make the journey. We could be there in days."

Christopher shook his head. "Remember what I said, Eric? Using the Sword for such a long period of time… there is no telling what the consequences would be."

Eric drew in a breath of the icy air. "It doesn't matter; we have to take the risk. If we don't we'll be too late to make a difference anyway."

"What about the Plorsean army?" Enala interrupted. "Could they be closer?"

"We have heard nothing from King Fraser," Angela answered. "But even if they marched as soon as Jurrien sent out word, the Lonians would still be closer."

Eric swallowed. "Then we have no choice."

"Are you sure?" Angela stared at him. "There will be no second chances here. You know what waits for you up there."

Eric nodded. "I know. But I doubt I could ever be ready for what is to come – not if I had a decade to prepare. Either way, it doesn't matter now. Our time is up."

"He's right," Enala added. "Ready or not, we have to do this. Archon will not wait for us."

Tears in her eyes, Angela stepped forward and drew them both into her arms. "Then good luck, my king, my queen. How I wish you had come to us sooner."

"May the Gods bless your journey," Christopher murmured from beside them.

CHAPTER 8

Inken staggered down the corridor, Gabriel and the priest Lynda at her side. Gabriel had regained some of his colour and now walked unsupported, but the haunted look remained and she still feared for his sanity.

Ahead Caelin, Elton and Fraser strode through the door of the barracks. Swallowing her doubts, Inken moved after them. They were taking a terrible risk, but there was no arguing with Caelin's logic. Circumstances left them little choice – they needed reinforcements. She just prayed Caelin and Fraser could convince the guards to follow them.

Stepping through the doorway, she reached unconsciously for her sabre and then swore at its absence. Elton had not been able to arm them, and he held their only sword. Not that it mattered; if they were forced to draw their blades now, they had already lost.

Even so, the sight of a dozen men stepping towards them with blades drawn did not give her much confidence in their plan.

Caelin and the others raised their hands and the guards

paused, exchanging uncertain looks between themselves. That was all the time they needed.

"Men, you know me," Fraser spoke now, his voice soft but with a quiet confidence Inken had not expected. "You know my face, beneath the filth. I have fought beside many of you, spilt my blood to defend you. I am Fraser, your king."

Swords wavered in indecisive hands as the men stared hard at the filthy beggars who had invaded their barracks.

Finally one of the guards stepped forward. "What is going on here?" he growled. "You *look* like our king, but it cannot be. I was in the throne room not an hour ago. The king was as strong and *clean* as I have ever seen him. You, you look as though you have not eaten in weeks, *imposter.*"

Fraser bowed his head, and for a second it looked as though their cause was lost. Then he looked up, and saw the fire in his eyes. "*Ay*, I have not eaten in weeks, Robin. No, I have been locked in the old dungeons, shut away from the world, starved and kept alive for the Gods only know why. And in my place has sat a demon, or some other cursed creature of Archon."

The man reeled back before the king's fury, but others were not so easily cowed. Another man stepped forward and waved a hand. "Yet another traitor named by Caelin?" he shook his head. "No, I will not believe the words from this man's mouth, not with this murderer standing beside him," his voice broke. "I will not believe Katya was a traitor."

Inken sensed the sorrow behind the man's words and guessed the councillor had meant more to him than most.

"I am sorry, truly, Antony. I know you two were close," Caelin drew in a breath. "And I fear you are right, we were tricked. I now believe Katya truly was innocent, that the creature sitting on the throne manipulated us into believing she was the one wielding the dark magic against us."

"But the truth stands before you now. This man is your king, filthy and withered from starvation as he may be. If you wish for me to suffer, let it come later. For now, believe the truth of your own eyes, the whispers of your conscious. You know the king has not been himself, and he has not. A traitor sits on our throne, one who means to see our nation fall before the might of Archon. We cannot let that happen."

Antony's eyes swept the room, lingering on each of them in turn. He settled on the priest standing beside her and raised an eyebrow.

"What's your place in all this, priest?"

Lynda bowed her head. "I was sent from Lon to verify their story," she waved at Caelin. "Everything he has said is true. The thing on the throne had me locked up before I could confirm their story to the council. Elton freed me, and together we found where they had been imprisoned. We were as surprised as you to find the true king locked away with them."

As her words spread around the room, Antony's shoulders slumped. Inken held her breath, hand twitching with anticipation. If Antony denied Lynda's words, it would come to bloodshed. She could see the anger in his eyes, his desire to revenge the fallen councillor.

Air hissed between Antony's lips and he bowed his head. "Okay," when he looked back up, the rage had faded. "But this is not the end of this discussion, Caelin," he turned to Fraser then. "Your majesty, please, forgive us. We should have seen through the creature's deception long ago. Things have been… wrong… for weeks."

The others in the room nodded, and Inken breathed a sigh of relief as swords were returned to their sheaths.

Fraser waved a hand, dismissing the soldiers' guilt. "The fault is not yours, but Archon's."

"Well that's a relief," Lynda smiled beside Inken as the soldiers gathered around Fraser and began to discuss their next move.

Inken nodded, the tension fleeing her shoulders. "That's half the battle won."

"The easy half, I imagine," Gabriel's voice was thick with self-loathing.

Inken glared at him. He turned away, unable to meet her eyes. "If we can convince the guards in the throne room the same way, there won't be a battle at all."

Gabriel nodded, his eyes to the floor. Inken reached out and grasped his chin, forcing him to look at her.

"We will make this right, Gabriel," she stared into his eyes, refusing to flinch at the darkness she saw there. "You understand?"

"How?" he croaked.

"By banishing this evil, by sending that creature screaming into the void," she paused, taking a breath. "But it will take everything we have to do it, Gabriel. We cannot afford to hesitate. We need you, Gabriel, all of you. So, are you with us?"

Inken glimpsed a spark of light in the young man's eyes and smiled as Gabriel nodded.

Before she could respond a roar went through the room, and then the soldiers were sweeping past her, Fraser in the lead. Caelin tossed her a sheathed sword and she reached up to catch it, nodding her thanks. She glanced at Lynda and raised an eyebrow in question.

The priest shook her head. "I have my magic. It will be enough. Shall we join them?"

Inken smiled. "Let's go to war."

~

GABRIEL SQUEEZED HIS EYES SHUT, swallowing his fear as he followed the others from the barracks. The whispers came in a constant stream now, the shadow of the demon hovering always just out of sight. He pushed them down. He needed to concentrate, to find the strength to fight. His friends needed him.

At least day had finally broken, the light of dawn streaming in through the windows of the corridors. The sun's warmth offered him comfort, banishing the icy chill clenched around his soul.

Ahead, Caelin, Fraser and Elton led the group of guards. They had been armed from the stockpile of weapons in the barracks, though the sword Gabriel now carried felt heavy in his hand. His stomach rumbled and he wished they'd eaten more than the scraps they'd pilfered from the kitchens earlier. Even with the food he felt exhausted, his muscles starved of energy.

Hopefully we won't need to fight, he thought to himself. Twelve guards had joined them in the barracks, yet he wondered whether they would have the courage for such a fight. If they could not sway those protecting the false king, they would be forced to kill their own comrades. Such a decision was not to be taken lightly.

They encountered few people on the short march to the throne room. Those who spotted them were easily fooled though – after all, it was clear the guards were escorting a group of prisoners to the king for judgement. Fortunately, no one bothered to give them a closer inspection. If they had, they would have noticed Gabriel and the other prisoners were armed.

Gabriel kept his sword low and tucked out of sight beneath his old coat. The muck from the dungeons still clung to him, leaving his skin itchy and raw. Still, at least they had left the darkness behind. Though the light hurt his eyes, it also gave him hope, and the strength to push back the voice.

The guards in front reached the great double doors of the throne room and thrust them open. The gold-embossed doors swung open without so much as a creak, the hinges obviously well-oiled by whichever servant was in charge of maintaining the throne room. Gabriel held his breath as the company raced inside, and waited for the shouts to start.

It was not a long wait. As he strode after his friends the first cry of rage came from the dais. The false king stood on the dais, towering over the room from his position at the head of the council table. His eyes swept the room, anger burning in their depths – though it quickly turned to shock as he found Fraser in their midst.

"What is the meaning of this?" the false king shouted. "Guards, why have you bought these beggars before me?"

Fraser stepped forward and pointed at the false king. "I am no beggar, foul creature. I am Fraser, the true king of Plorsea. You are naught but some foul beast of Archon, sent here to betray our land."

Shouts raced around the room as councillors leapt to their feet. The guards surrounding the dais wavered, looking from the false king to Fraser and his circle of men. He saw the indecision on their faces. But it seemed clear to Gabriel which king they would pick. Fraser still wore the ruined clothes of his imprisonment, while the false king stood atop the dais in all his finery, the picture of royalty.

If they chose the false king, it did not bode well for their chances. The guards in the throne room outnumbered them two to one.

Fraser turned to the ring of guards, his eyes filled with fire. "You know me; you know who I am. Do you truly believe that thing on my throne is your king? You know the truth; you've seen it each day with your own eyes. That is not the king; that is not *me*."

The words swept through the ranks of men and Gabriel saw the doubt in their eyes. Then a slow clap carried through the hall, echoing down from the false king. As the eyes of every man and woman turned to him, he reached down and drew his sword.

"You know your true king, men. And it is not this traitorous beast. Let us put an end to the lies of this foul imposter."

With a roar the false king leapt from the dais. Gabriel's heart sank as the guards fanned out around him. They had lost the war of words; it would come to blades now. Outnumbered and drained by starvation, Gabriel feared he and his companions would not fare well.

"*Stop!*" Lynda's voice cracked through the room. She moved through the soldiers until she stood beside Fraser. "Stop," she repeated. "And listen."

"No," the false king growled. "We will hear no more of your lies," with a roar, he leapt towards them.

Lynda smiled and raised a hand. A howling whistle filled the room as wind rushed through the open windows. With a nod from the priest, the wind struck the false king and his men, forcing them backwards.

"You will listen," Lynda snapped. She waved at Caelin and the others. "Caelin and Fraser speak the truth. It is here for all of you to see. Why would a creature of Archon come before you as a beggar? Why would your fellow soldiers join him, if not for the truth of his claim?"

"Who are you?" Gabriel looked up to see a councillor still standing atop the dais.

"I am Lynda, the Lonian priest you sent for to verify the story of Caelin and his companions."

"Where have you been?" the councillor moved closer to the edge of the dais.

"That *thing* had me locked away," Lynda nodded to the false king.

The councillor stood silent, staring down at them with a strange look on his face. Gabriel held his breath, praying this might be the turning point they needed. The councillor's red robes rustled in the breeze still whipping about the room. Then the man crossed his arms and smiled.

"I do not believe you," before any of them could react he threw out a hand.

A beam of light lanced across the room and caught Lynda in its brilliance. The old priestess raised a hand as the light reached her and the wind roared once more. It billowed up over the heads of the soldiers, up to the councillor atop the dais. There came a muffled thud as it caught him, followed by a sickening crack as he spun head-first into the wall.

Then the light spiralled around Lynda, and she threw back her head and screamed. Gabriel stumbled back, staring in horror as her body began to convulse. Lines of purple spread across her face, and the sound of her screams drove splinters into his head. But he could not look away. The woman stood frozen, her eyes filled with pain and fear.

Then the screaming stopped and an awful silence fell over the throne room. As one Caelin and Elton stepped towards the woman, but before they could take two steps she crumpled to the ground and lay still.

Gabriel looked away as Caelin reached her and searched for sign of life. In his heart he already knew the truth – Lynda had given her life to protect them from the other Magicker. Turning to face the false king, he resolved to make her sacrifice count. To his relief, the others in their party did the same. Not a man wavered; each had made their decision, and now they were determined to see it through.

The same could not be said of those opposing them. Already some of the false king's guards were stepping back, retreating to the far wall and taking themselves out of the fight. None of them made a move to join Fraser, but it was clear they had no wish to fight their comrades for a cause they did not quite believe in.

Even so, there were still some twenty guards left supporting the false king. Even counting their weakened fighters, they remained outnumbered and outmatched.

Gabriel's eyes found the false king and locked on the greatsword he carried one-handed. If he fell, would his true identity be revealed? Even if it did not, surely his death would rob his remaining supporters of motivation, and stop the slaughter of innocent men.

That has to be our best chance, Gabriel resolved, and began to inch his way around the ring of guards, searching for an opening.

As the first clash of steel rang through the throne room, Gabriel leapt at the nearest guard. His sword swept for the man's helmet, but found only empty space as the man leaned backwards. Then Gabriel was jumping back as the man's sword stabbed out for his stomach. He heard the tearing of cloth as the blade sliced through his cloak and swore at his feeble movements.

The man smiled as Gabriel retreated out of range, but stayed in formation with his fellow guards.

Swallowing, Gabriel edged forward with more caution now. These men were accomplished fighters and even at full strength he would have trouble besting one of them. His heart sank as he realised there was only one way through the guards. This was a fight to the end, and each would give their lives to protect the false king.

Not that the false king appeared to need protecting. He had stepped into his ring of guards and now swung his greatsword as though it weighed no more than a feather. Already one of their side had fallen to his blows, the heavy blade shearing through chainmail and flesh alike. If he was not stopped soon, their resistance would be over before it began.

The guard facing him sneered as Gabriel closed on him, the contempt plain on his face. His sword flicked out and Gabriel struggled to deflect the blow from his throat. His arm already felt heavy and his chest burned with the exertion. He was no expert in the best of conditions, but he usually relied on the strength he'd built from years in the forge to defeat his opponents.

Now that strength was failing him. He felt a tingle of fear in his spine as the man came for him again.

I can give you back your strength, the demon's whispers came again, but there was no time to consider the words.

His opponent hacked at him with his short sword, driving Gabriel backwards. As he retreated his foot caught on the edge of the carpet and he stumbled. The guard could have killed him then and there if he had not hesitated to leave the circle of men.

Gritting his teeth, Gabriel straightened and threw himself back into the battle. A dozen men were already down between the two sides, their blood staining the royal floor, but so far Caelin and Fraser still held their own. Gabriel knew it could not last. A few more losses, and their remaining fighters would be overwhelmed by sheer numbers.

They had to end this, now.

Tightening his grip on his blade, Gabriel charged at his opponent, determined to smash his way through to the demon beyond. There at least was a guilty soul, the one truly responsible for the chaos hovering over the capital.

The guard grinned as Gabriel came at him, blade at the ready. Drawing on every ounce of his strength, Gabriel swung for the man's helmet again. The guard raised his sword to deflect the blow but stumbled as one of his comrades staggered into him. Knocked off balance, the guard's sword went wide and Gabriel's blow crunched home.

The guard's eyes widened. A trickle of blood ran down his forehead as a low groan hissed from his mouth. Then he dropped without another sound.

Gabriel released the hilt of his sword, its blade still embedded in the iron helmet. He stared at the dead man, the familiar guilt rising up within him. Looking down, he looked at the blood speckling his hands.

You have to move, a voice hissed in his mind, returning him to reality. *Slay the king!*

Sweeping up the fallen guard's sword, Gabriel leapt through the gap left by the man's absence. The guards to either side were caught up in battle and he passed unnoticed. Ahead the false king stepped back from the line and wiped sweat from his forehead, grinning as his men slayed another of Gabriel's comrades. He froze as he turned and saw Gabriel approaching.

His hesitation did not last long. His eyes studied Gabriel and he began to laugh, clearly unimpressed.

Swallowing, Gabriel closed the gap between them. He held his sword straight, ready for anything the massive man might throw at him. Even so, the greatsword wielded by the imposter made Gabriel's blade look like a toothpick by comparison.

"Come on then, boy, try your luck. Let's see the kind of man you would have been," before Gabriel could reply, the imposter charged at him, swinging his blade like an axe.

Fear ran down Gabriel's spine as he ducked the blow. Then he leapt to the attack, his sword snaking out in search of flesh. The imposter grinned and batted his blows away with a gauntleted fist. Bringing his sword around, he swung again, attempting to split Gabriel in two.

Gabriel stepped to the side, feeling the breath of the blade's passage as it sliced past. His hackles rose on the back of his neck but he pressed on. All that mattered now was destroying this creature, before it led Plorsea into the abyss. Fist clenched around his sword, Gabriel attacked again.

The false king stood waiting for him, sword held in a casual grip. As Gabriel attacked, the greatsword came sweeping down to block the blow. Pain shot through Gabriel's hands at the impact and the blade slipped from his numb fingers. Gabriel retreated backwards as his sword clattered to the ground.

The imposter strode after him, the greatsword raised for the final blow. Gabriel scrambled for the dagger he'd slid into his belt back in the barracks. The air hissed as the greatsword sought his flesh. Without looking, Gabriel hurled himself to the side.

He struck the edge of the dais as the greatsword smashed into the ground where he had stood. Chips of tile scattered across the room and a jagged piece sliced across Gabriel's face. Then his dagger finally came loose. He raised it before him like a talisman, looking up to see the false king preparing to swing again. Before the blow could descend, he hurled the dagger at the traitor.

The imposter screamed as the blade caught him in the shoulder and sent him staggering backwards. His greatsword clattered to the ground as he reached up and grasped the hilt of Gabriel's blade. With another cry he tore it loose. Blood splattered across the tiles as he turned and glared at Gabriel.

"You will pay for that," he raised his empty hand.

Gabriel's stomach twisted as darkness began to gather in the man's palm. It swirled between his fingers, gathering force.

"What?" he whispered, scrambling to find his feet. He glimpsed the fallen greatsword nearby and swept it up, turning to face the king. His body ached, battered from his fall. He was utterly exhausted, but he strained to keep the massive blade pointed at the imposter.

"Die," the false king growled, and Gabriel saw his eyes had darkened to pure black. He pointed his fist and a ray of darkness shot towards Gabriel.

There was no time to move or think, only react. Gabriel drove himself forward, the greatsword raised to strike down the imposter.

The wave of darkness rushed towards him and caught him in the chest. At its touch sickness swept through him, sucking the strength from his failing body. Gabriel's advance slowed, yet even as the sickness spread he could feel the dark force weakening.

With a cry of defiance, Gabriel forced his way forward and to his surprise, the darkness fell away.

Gabriel glimpsed panic on the imposter's face a second before his blow struck. The greatsword swept out, sliding beneath the king's outstretched fist to take him in the chest. Without armour or chainmail there was little resistance, and he drove the blade in to the hilt. Then he stepped back, watching the rage turn to fear in the traitor's eyes.

The false king tried to take a step towards him, but his legs suddenly gave way. He collapsed to the ground, a thick blackness spreading out around him. Then, as every soul present turned to stare, a sickly black fog rose to cover the creature's body. A foul smell filled the room, sending grown men staggering backwards in disgust.

As quickly as it had appeared, the fog vanished.

Gabriel stared at the spot where the false king had fallen. There was nothing left of the creature but a dark scorch staining the white tiles.

Taking a breath, Gabriel turned to Fraser and sank to his knees.

One by one, the guards and councillors did the same.

"All hail the king," the cry rose up from around the room.

Head bowed, Gabriel stared at where the imposter had fallen, and smiled.

CHAPTER 9

"We must march north," Caelin sat at the council table and looked around at the assembled faces.

Only a day had passed since the events in the throne room, but all signs of the battle had already been removed. The blood had been cleansed from the tiles and the ruined carpet removed. If he looked closely he could spot where the tiles had been cracked by stray blows, but otherwise the room was clean. Even the black stain left after the traitor's death had been scrubbed spotless.

Yet despite their best efforts, a darkness still hung over the capital. Their victory may have given them a chance, but the damage caused by the traitorous creature might yet prove irreparable. Men and women ringed the council table, many of whom had sat in judgement of them only two weeks ago. These were the same people that had left them to rot in the darkness, who had supported the false king to his dying breath. It was difficult to ignore that fact.

"Of course," Fraser replied, his tired eyes scanning the table. "There is no other option. Alone, we cannot hope to match the forces Archon will muster; we found that out last time when Fort Fall was lost," he turned to Caelin. "But even with the army mustered, it could take a week or more to be ready to march. And with winter setting in, the journey itself will take weeks."

Caelin swallowed. The demonic king had done its job well, delaying their forces to the point where their arrival at Fort Fall would likely come too late to make a difference. A letter had just arrived from the north – Archon's forces had arrived and were now preparing to make siege on the fortress.

"Even so, we cannot abandon our allies at Fort Fall."

"Of course," Fraser eyed the room again. "And anyone who thinks otherwise can join the traitor who replaced me," he growled. Several men winced and dropped their gazes, unable to meet Fraser's eyes.

Beside him Inken chuckled. He glanced at her, glad to see the colour back in her face. Cleaned and fed, they were all looking better after a good night's sleep. Though in truth he had slept with a lantern lit near his bedside. It would be a long time before he was ready to face the darkness again.

Despite the rest, Fraser still looked weary. Caelin saw through the man's facade, seeing the darkness he hid from his councillors. That he could sit here and give orders at all was a minor miracle. The man had spent weeks locked alone in the pitch black of that cell. The mind of a lesser man would have been shattered into pieces.

Even a man such as Fraser had come close.

But there was no time for weakness now. Archon would not wait and they had no time to spare. They needed the king Caelin remembered, the one the people knew and respected. Only that man could get them through the coming days.

"Okay, what do we do then?" Fraser questioned the table. "How do we reinforce Fort Fall in time for it to matter?"

"The dragons," Inken surprised Caelin. She blushed as the table turned to look at her. "Unless the imposter managed to insult them beyond repair, the dragons could reach Fort Fall within a few days. If we are lucky, they might be able to carry a hundred men between them. It may not be much, but it's better than nothing. And the dragons themselves would also be a formidable boost to Fort Fall's defences."

As whispers spread around the table, one of the councillors came to his feet. Caelin recognised him as one of those who had supported their imprisonment. "But can we trust them? They are beasts; what is to stop them from turning on us?"

Caelin's anger stirred in his chest and he struggled to keep his voice even. "Sir… despite what you might think, the gold dragons are for all intents far more civil than our own species. Certainly more polite than some humans I have met."

The man's face coloured and he made to respond, but Fraser spoke over him. "Oh get out, Councillor Richard. And do not come back, or I will have my guards introduce you to my accommodation from the last few months."

The councillor paled. He stared at the king, his chest heaving as he fought to keep his rage in check. Then with a final exhalation of breath he spun on his heel and stamped from the room.

Fraser waited until the doors at the end of the hall swung shut before he continued. "I like your idea, Inken. You and I shall visit the dragons today and offer my apologies for the insults my… predecessor gave them. I just pray the damage he caused was not permanent."

Inken smiled. "They are a prickly bunch, but they are also reasonable creatures. I am sure we can convince them to forgive us."

"What about the rest of the army? Can we send an advance party now?" Caelin asked. "A thousand men a week earlier may mean the difference between finding Fort Fall in our ally's possession, or Archon's when the rest of our forces arrive."

"But what if they're still too late?" another councillor spoke. She looked around the room, her face apologetic. "If Archon's forces have already broken through they would come on our men in the open. A thousand men would be slaughtered for nothing."

Fraser passed a hand across his face, his exhaustion palpable. "You're right, of course… both of you. But there are no good choices here. We have been robbed of the time we needed to do this right. But even so, I have to agree with Caelin. It's a gamble, but if we lose Fort Fall, we are doomed whether our army is separated or not. We will send a thousand men as an advance party. They will leave first thing in the morning."

He turned to Elton, who had sat quietly through the meeting, clearly uncomfortable with his sudden elevation to the council. "Elton, there are few I trust now more than you. I want you to lead the advance force."

Elton blinked. "But your majesty, I have never led men in open battle! I am only a guard captain; how can I lead a thousand men? There must be others… better suited."

The king nodded. "Ay, there might be. But none I trust, not now. I have other plans for Caelin, so it must be you. Can you do it?"

Elton swallowed, eyes wide, and nodded.

"Good. Go and prepare your men. I award you now with the rank of Commander. I will leave you to choose which men to take with you. I suggest you talk to the sergeants of each unit and go from there."

Elton rose and saluted. "Thank you, my king. I will."

Fraser nodded back. "Good luck, Elton. Do not let us down."

As Elton left the room, Fraser turned his attention back to the council. "Well, we have a plan. Let's get to it. Caelin, you are to select a hundred of our best fighters and have them ready to depart at a moment's notice. If Inken and I are successful, you and the men you select will be flying north by the day's end," his gaze swept the table. "The rest of you know your roles. I want the army ready to march within the week. Get to it."

Caelin took a breath as he watched the others stand and file out of the room. Gabriel, Inken and himself remained at the table, sitting in silent thought.

He watched Gabriel closely as the last of the councillors disappeared. Gabriel had hardly spoken since slaying the false king, and Caelin still wondered how the youngster had managed it. The thing had been a demon or worse, a dark creature that no doubt possessed an equally dark magic.

So how had Gabriel, an unskilled youth weak with starvation, managed to best it? Starved of his strength, Caelin himself had hardly been able to hold his own against the royal guard, let alone go up against the false king.

But that was a mystery for another day. For now, they had work to do. All going well, they would be a-dragon-back come nightfall.

He glanced at Inken. "Do you want one of us to go with you?"

She flashed him a wry smile. "I think I'll be fine, Caelin. And don't worry, I'll look after Fraser," she winked at the king.

Fraser scowled back. "Watch yourself, Inken."

Inken only laughed and stood. "Don't worry, I will. Come on, let's go see the dragons."

Caelin smiled as the two left trading barbs. Inken had a

knack for getting the best out of people, for bringing them back from the darkness. Her strength had helped him keep fighting after his friend Michael had been killed in Sitton, and he had not missed the talk she had given Gabriel. If anyone could keep the king on his feet, it was her.

Standing, he nodded to Gabriel and followed them out. They were already disappearing down the corridor as Caelin pushed through the great double doors, a host of guards at their back. Caelin made to follow them, already thinking ahead to what he would say when he reached the barracks. He would need to find men with a particular breed of courage if they were to ride the gold dragons to Fort Fall.

"Caelin," a voice came from the shadows to his left.

Caelin turned, his heart sinking as Antony stepped forward to block his path. He knew the man from his days as a recruit. They had never been more than friendly rivals, but he could see the hate on the man's face now.

"Katya wasn't a traitor," he croaked, and Caelin saw there were tears in the guard's eyes. "I knew her. She never changed, not like the king. It was *her.*"

Caelin bowed his head. He'd been dreading this confrontation, but knew there was no avoiding it. Raising his chin, he looked Antony in the eye. "As I said yesterday. I was wrong. You're right. She was not a traitor."

"Then why did she have to die? *Why?*"

"I don't know," Caelin shook his head, guilt eating him from within. Since the battle he had heard more from the other guards about the relationship between Antony and the councillor. "I know you loved her, Antony."

"Do you?" he took a step towards Caelin. "How could you? How could you know what it's like to see someone you love killed by her own people?"

"I have seen my fair share of treachery, Antony. But this

was an accident, and the only one to blame was that creature."

"And that boy, Gabriel," Antony growled, taking another step. "He was the one who killed her. I cannot let him get away with it."

"No," Caelin stopped Antony with a word. "It was not his fault; he did what he thought was right. And he did the same thing when he killed that treacherous creature. If anything, you should thank him for avenging Katya's death."

Antony stared at Caelin, his arms trembling with anger. Caelin met his eyes, refusing to waver. He would not let this man anywhere near his friend. Slowly, the rage in Antony's eyes cooled and they started to water. The man took a great, shuddering inhalation and bowed his head.

"Fine," he breathed, then looked back up. "Then take me with you, Caelin. I heard the others talking as they went past; I know what you're doing. Take me with you to Fort Fall. Let me avenge Katya's death with the blood of Archon's people."

Caelin looked into the man's eyes and saw the desperation behind his rage. In that instant, he knew the truth. Antony wanted to die. He sighed, wanting to refuse the man's demand but knowing he could not. Antony was one of the best fighters they had. His skill would be needed in the north.

"Very well, Antony. You can join us."

With that he pushed past Antony and moved away down the corridor. Guilt hung in his throat, the weight of the man's life heavy on his shoulders.

Inken dropped to her knees on the damp grass, struggling to keep the measly remains of her breakfast down. The rough ride across the lake had not been kind, and it was a relief to have solid ground beneath her again. She had already thrown up once as they neared the shore, but she was determined not to repeat the event.

"You okay?" Fraser asked from nearby.

Inken forced a smile. "Fine," they were alone now on the shore. The small sailboat rocked on the beach, the sailor who manned it leaning back against the mast with his eyes closed. Fraser had ordered him to remain in the boat while they went ashore. He had left his usual guards in the city, already growing weary of their constant presence. That, and he claimed it would be difficult enough to apologise to the dragons without marching up to their camp with a small army at his back.

"Okay, whenever you're ready then," Fraser grinned, no doubt drawing some satisfaction from her discomfort after her joke earlier in the throne room.

Her stomach swirled again, but Inken pushed it down and stood. Nodding, she strode past Fraser and began the short trek up the hill. Despite the seasickness, it was a relief to be in the fresh air again. Overhead the sky seemed huge after her time in the cell, filled with the untold vastness of nature. A bird flew past and she smiled, setting aside the unpleasant feeling in her stomach and deciding to do her best to enjoy herself.

Yet she knew it would take more than the open sky and sun to lift the darkness from her soul. It clung to each of them still, waiting in the backs of their minds to strike. Not for the first time that day she found herself missing Eric's quiet confidence. She prayed he had survived whatever trials had come his way since they separated.

"There doesn't seem to have been any word of them," Fraser appeared to read her thoughts. "Eric or Enala. Although we cannot be sure the creature did not hide news of them."

Inken nodded. "Eric is used to travelling in the wild, and Enala's parents trained her for this – whether she knew it or not. They would know how to go unnoticed."

"Good. As we've seen, Archon's people are everywhere now."

They fell silent as the top of the hill loomed. Elton had given them an account of the false king's encounter with the dragons and they did not expect a friendly welcome. Inken was surprised the creatures had stayed at all.

The breath caught in her throat as a golden head lifted into view. Her heart thudded hard against her ribs and the nausea in her stomach was suddenly forgotten.

It's okay, but despite her own reassurance, she could feel the fear sweeping through her. Faced with the giant creature, it was all she could do to force herself to stand still.

Fraser, however, seemed to suffer no such fear. He continued on a few more steps before noticing her hesitation. He glanced back and grinned. "After all we've been through, don't tell me you're afraid of a little dragon?"

Inken scowled. Biting her tongue, she forced down her instinctive fear and continued up the slope. The dragon watched them come in silence.

As they mounted the rise, Inken could not suppress a gasp. Even Fraser seemed taken aback, though he hid it well. The dragon camp lay spread out below them, stretching away for miles across the green fields. The hulking forms of the gold dragons sprinkled the grass, the light reflecting from their scales almost blinding. Each dragon appeared to have a range of its own; an area the size of a small village which the others avoided. A few lay in pairs, but the majority appeared to prefer their own space.

Welcome, humans, the dragon on watch growled, moving to block their view of the camp.

Inken turned to look at the creature and found its eyes

looking back. She could almost imagine the hunger there, the desire of a wild beast to consume such lesser creatures.

Shaking her head, she dismissed the thought. This was no beast. As far as she was concerned, the dragons seemed to be far more intelligent than any man she'd ever met. Woman, however…

Before she could finish the thought, Fraser bowed low to the dragon. Inken quickly followed suit, cursing the king for beating her to the act. The dragon watched them with an amused tilt to its head.

You have suddenly found your manners, oh king of man?

Fraser straightened, a sad frown on his lips. "Would that it had truly been me to greet you last time, dragon. Alas, it was an imposter who came to your camp and offered you insult. I was imprisoned beneath the keep, and have only just managed to find my freedom once more."

The dragon leaned closer, the great slits of its nostrils opening to sniff them. *Ay, there is a different smell about you,* the dragon straightened. *I am Enduran. It was I who spoke with your imposter,* there was a threatening edge to the dragon's tone.

Fraser bowed again and Inken followed suit. "My deepest apologies, Enduran. My people were tricked and I was imprisoned while the creature took my form and stole control of the kingdom."

A growl rumbled up from Enduran's chest and sent tremors down to Inken's stomach. The dragon took a step closer, its claws digging grooves in the untouched earth.

Another? there was open anger in the dragon's tone now. *What creatures are you, to allow such things into your midst?*

Fraser met the dragon's gaze, unflinching. "We are weak, all of us. But do not forget, mighty Enduran, the creature tricked you as well. No one was immune to its guile."

Silence fell, and then another rumble came from

Enduran's chest. Inken smiled as she recognised the sound as laughter. *You speak the truth, king of man.*

Fraser smiled back and continued. "The creature has done us great damage, but it is not irreparable, not yet. I am sorry for the way you and your kind were treated, Enduran, but from this day forth I promise to treat your people with respect. We need you."

Enduran's head twisted down until it hovered eye level with the king. *And what do you need of us, king of man?*

Inken struggled to hide her grin as Fraser gaped, taken off-guard by the question. *Definitely smarter than men*, she chuckled softly to herself.

Enduran's eyes turned her way. *Do not think I have forgotten you, little one*, there was humour in the dragon's voice. *It is good to see you again. You have progressed.*

Inken blinked, staring at the dragon in confusion. "Progressed?"

Your child, the dragon answered. *I could not be sure when last we spoke, but I smell the change in you now.*

Gaping, Inken looked from the dragon to the king. "Wh… *What?*" she all but shrieked.

The dragon looked to Fraser. *She did not know?*

Open mirth sparkled in Fraser's eyes as he turned to her. "The dragon is telling you you're pregnant, Inken," he grinned. "It seems congratulations are in order."

Inken would have beaten the smile from Fraser's face if she could have found the will to move. She stood frozen on the hilltop, staring at the king and the dragon, unable to form the thoughts to speak. Her heart hammered in her chest like a runaway wagon and she struggled to catch her breath.

Sinking to her knees, she was surprised to find Fraser suddenly beside her, his hand firm on her shoulder.

"Are you okay, Inken?" he murmured, concern in his eyes.

She nodded, and found herself smiling up at the king. A warm fluttering spread through her stomach, washing away the illness that curdled there. Her eyes watered.

Oh, Eric, where are you? She whispered to the void.

When she finally caught her breath, she looked up at the dragon. "Are you sure, Enduran?"

Yes, child. We are not wrong about such things, she could almost imagine a grin on the dragon's giant jaws.

"Then can you take me to Fort Fall?" she asked, desperate now to reach the fortress. "If Eric is alive, he will be there."

The dragon's head dropped down to stare at the two of them. *Is that what you wish as well, king of man?*

Fraser nodded. "It is, Enduran. Archon's forces have reached the fortress. They desperately need reinforcements. My man, Caelin, is gathering our best fighters as we speak. If you agree, I would have you carry them north to bolster the defences at Fort Fall. Together, you could make all the difference..."

Fraser's words trailed away as Enduran stood and spread his wings. At full height he towered over them, casting the hilltop in shadow. Stretching back his head, the dragon opened its jaws and roared. The sound echoed across the hills, rebounding and growing louder with each second. Flames licked from Enduran's lips as he turned to look down at them.

Then let us fly, little one.

CHAPTER 10

Eric stared down at the fortress far below, a creeping awe spreading through his chest. Fort Fall stretched out beneath them; a behemoth of sprawling walls and towers nestled on the narrow straight of land known as The Gap. Its three massive walls carved across the barren land, standing in silent defiance to the forces of the north. The outmost wall stood fifty feet high, and each grew larger than the last. To the east and west they came to an abrupt halt atop the ocean cliffs, impassable by even the most skilled of climbers.

The rumble of the waves smashing into the cliffs of The Gap carried up to them, covering the fortress in a fine mist. From so far above the men and women manning the ramparts appeared as ants, scurrying about their business with an insect-like determination. Yet even from their vantage point, there did not appear to be enough soldiers manning the walls.

The towers of the citadel stood behind the third wall, the stone spires reaching up towards them. This was the fortress' final defence, though in truth, the battle was already lost if the third wall fell.

Beside him, Enala hung in silent contemplation, the wind ruffling her golden hair and sending her single scarlet lock fluttering across her face.

"There's a lot of them," she said as she noticed his gaze.

Eric nodded, his eyes drifting to the north. There the forces of the enemy waited, the light of their fires stretching out to the horizon. Bathed in the crimson red of sunset, it appeared as though the land itself were bleeding.

Swallowing, Eric pushed the dark thoughts from his mind. His strength was flagging, his body aching with the power he'd spent in the three days of flight. They had stopped only to eat and sleep, with Eric drawing on the power of the Sword to replenish his own store of magic.

Yet despite its support, Eric felt weary to his very soul. Each time he used the Sword's magic the white fire would sweep through him, burning at his spirit, eating at him in a way he could not quite explain. And even with the Sword's heat, he would find himself shivering, clinging to the warmth of Enala's hand. But he had little choice; they could not afford to wait for his magic to recover on its own.

Eric took another breath, preparing to descend, but the winds lurched suddenly in his grasp. The air stilled and then they were falling, plummeting towards the ground far below. Heart hammering in his chest, Eric sent his magic racing outwards, regathering the winds and catching them mid-air.

"Eric!" Enala shrieked, her face white with fear. "What was that?"

Eric shook his head, his thoughts turning inwards, gripping the swirling ropes of blue tighter. He could sense a change in the air, the presence of another magic. With a curse he wrapped his fingers around the hilt of the Sword, prepared to summon its power if necessary.

"Who approaches?" the voice boomed from all around them.

Enala glanced at him, her question clear. *Is it our side, or theirs?*

Taking a risk, Eric shouted over the cracking of the wind, unwilling to test his fading strength against the might of whoever faced them. "We are Eric and Enala of Plorsea. We have come to aid Fort Fall," he did not mention the Sword of Light.

There was a long pause before the voice answered. *"If you speak the truth, you are welcome. You may land to the south of the fortress, not within. Approach the gates and we will speak more."*

The voice cut off and Eric guessed they would hear no more from the Magicker – unless they disobeyed the command.

With a sigh of relief, Eric directed them down towards the small southward wall. The gates stood closed, but he could see a group standing on the ramparts in the shadows of the gate-house. As they closed he began to make out individuals, and saw a mixture of concern and relief on their faces. Only a woman in the centre of the group kept her expression neutral, her arms folded across her chest as her dark eyes followed their approach. She stood a foot taller than her companions and wore a red cape and tunic of the Plorsean army. Her fingers hovered close to the hilt of the gold-embossed sword she wore at her side.

From the way the others glanced at her, Eric guessed her to be Commander May. Christopher and Angela had spoken of her before they left, and had nothing but praise for the woman.

Keeping a tight grip on the wind, Eric settled them gently to the ground. Even in the dim light of sunset, he could see that the northern wasteland had extended south of the fortress. The ground beneath their feet was hard and dry and there was no sign of vegetation.

"You're getting better at that," Enala commented.

Eric grinned, remembering their first crash landing after they had fled Sitton. It was a cheering thought, to think he had improved in such a short span of time.

"At least we'll have beds to sleep in tonight," he pointed out as they started the short walk to the gates.

Enala rubbed her back. "Thank the Gods, my back couldn't take another night on the cold ground."

Eric laughed. "And no more frostbite," that morning they had woken in their blankets to a world of white. A thin ice had settled around them over night, coating their hair in a white frosting. The cold had seeped into Eric's very bones and his teeth had chattered halfway to the fortress. For the hundredth time in three days, he wished he'd had the strength to carry a tent with them.

But at least they'd made it.

Ahead the southern wall loomed with its waiting company of men and women. Eric and Enala walked with their swords sheathed and the *Soul Blades* hidden in their bundle of blankets. They had eaten the last remnants of their food for lunch and Eric was looking forward to a hot meal.

They came to a halt before the wooden gates and looked up at their welcome party. The group stood at the edge of the ramparts, looking down at the strangers below. Eric glimpsed curiosity in the eyes of some, wariness in others. This was a fortress under siege and it was clear they would not allow them through the gates unchallenged.

"Who are you?" the woman he'd guessed to be Commander May shouted down. "Who sent you?"

Eric stepped forward. "My name is Eric, and this is Enala. Your letter about the attack reached us in Kalgan. We came as fast as we could."

"Well, Eric and Enala, welcome. You must excuse my suspicion, but how, pray, did you come here so quickly? Kalgan is a long way from here," she paused, then shook her head. "And I am rather confused as to why our Trolan brothers would send us two children as reinforcements."

Eric grimaced, his patience wearing thin. Obviously talk was not going to get them far here – these people would never believe their tale. And May was right, there was no way any ordinary Magicker could have come so far so fast. His magic would have run out long ago without the Sword.

No, he would have to show them. Drawing on the last of his strength, Eric reached up and pulled the Sword of Light from its scabbard. Above, the guards nocked arrows to their bows and he sensed the power of the Magickers beginning to gather, but he was not overly concerned.

Light swept across the wall as the blade slid free and ignited in the crisp winter air. The warmth of its flame flickered across Eric's face as he looked up at those gathered above.

"Commander May," he boomed. "We have come a long way and I am tired. This is the Sword of Light and I am its wielder. By blood and by magic, we claim the Trolan throne. Open the gates, if you please."

The colour had fled May's face and her mouth hung open. He gave her a second for his words to sink in, then smiled as she finally came back to life. Looking around, she shouted an order and a moment later the gates gave a groan and began to open.

Below, Eric glanced at Enala and grinned.

Together they walked through the gates, and into greatest fortress in the Three Nations.

~

Enala groaned as she sank into the chair nearest the fire, her joints aching from the icy cold. Even with the thick woollen clothes Angela and Christopher had given them, the winds holding them aloft had still sucked the warmth from her. The nights had been worse still, the ice creeping across the clearing each evening to freeze their sleeping bodies solid. Or so it seemed when they woke in the mornings.

It was more than a relief to be indoors again.

Eric's knees cracked as he took a seat across from her and stretched his hands out towards the flames. A shiver racked his body and his face was pale, but he was looking far better than the first time she'd flown with him. He'd hardly been able to move that day. The memory seemed an age ago now.

Commander May stood between them, shifting nervously from one foot to the other. She had dismissed the rest of her people and brought them here – her private meeting room deep within the citadel.

Her discretion came as a welcome relief. Enala did not have the energy to be interrogated by half the fortress. Although the eager look on May's face suggested she had more than enough questions of her own.

"Please sit down," Enala sighed, to weary for manners.

May straightened. "If you are who you say you are, I should stand, ma'am."

Enala would have laughed if not for her utter exhaustion. "Oh Gods, please, Commander, just take a seat. We're too tired for pleasantries. As you said, it's a long journey from Kalgan to here."

Eric nodded and May finally gave in. As she sank into her chair Enala could not help but smile. They had been told of the woman's fierceness in battle – apparently she had even defeated a demon in the first attack on the wall – but now she seemed almost a child, eager to please her guests, if only to get the answers to her questions.

Her eyes slid to where Eric had discarded the Sword of Light beside his chair. "It's true then, the Sword is back? What happened to the old king, Jonathan?"

"He's dead," Enala growled. "He was a traitor, tried to kill me and steal my magic. Eric killed him."

May swallowed and sat back in her chair. "It seems treachery is everywhere now. What has happened to our land?"

"Archon," Eric answered. "Without the Gods to protect us, we have little to defend us against his subversions. Only the strength of our own courage can protect the Three Nations now."

"And the Sword?" May raised an eyebrow. "Is it as powerful as they say?"

"It is, and it isn't," Eric answered, then continued at the confused look on May's face. "I am yet to master most of its power."

"It's better than we had this morning," May shrugged.

Enala looked from Eric to May and then swallowed her hesitation. "We may have more than that," reaching down, she unwrapped the bundle at her feet. The green and blue glow of the *Soul Blades* rose up from the blankets. "These… these are the *Soul Blades* that killed Antonia and Jurrien. They contain their magic, the God powers of the Earth and Sky. We are hoping that the Magickers here might be able to free them."

May stared at her, eyes wide, and gave a slow nod. "You're saying we can bring them back?"

"Maybe," Eric corrected. "The Magickers in Kalgan could not, but their strongest had already marched north. Perhaps those here can."

May swallowed, her eyes shining in the light of the fire. "That's all we needed last time – the Sword and the two Gods," her eyes shone with hope. "Thank you for coming."

Enala gave a soft laugh. "Do not get ahead of yourself, May. The Magicker, Christopher, did not think it would be possible. Not without knowledge of the spell first used to summon their spirits."

The Commander waved a hand. "Even so…" her eyes were drawn to the creeping glow of the *Soul Blades*. "Could we use their power still, if we cannot free them?"

Pain twisted in Enala's stomach and she dropped her eyes. May had a sharp mind; she had seen their problem and was already looking for an alternative plan. Enala just wished that plan did not inevitably include her.

"Enala already has," Eric murmured over the crackling of the fire. "She was able to draw on Antonia's magic and heal us. But it was too powerful, and she was overwhelmed. We almost lost her."

"But it is possible," May mused.

"It is a terrible risk," Enala said grimly. "To the Magicker and everyone around them."

"I take it you do not wish to try again?"

Enala's heart sank as she looked into the Commander's eyes, but she refused to look away. "I will do anything I can to help my brother," she looked down at the *Soul Blades,* her blood curdling at the sight. "I am stronger now. I can control my power. I will try, if it comes to it."

May nodded. "You are a brave girl."

"No. The thought terrifies me. But I will do what I must."

"Let's hope it won't come to that," Eric put an end to the discussion.

"Of course," May leaned back in her chair. "I shall have our Magickers begin examining them in the morning. But I will also make enquiries for the other blade, in case it *does* come to that."

"What about your forces here?" Enala changed the course of the discussion. "How many defenders do you have?"

"Just over a thousand," May answered. "The standing guard, plus the advance force Lonia sent, and volunteers that have been arriving for the last few weeks."

"Not enough," Eric said grimly. "I cannot even guess how many men are waiting to the north."

"No, but the rest of the Lonian army is close. And word from the Trolans put their army less than a week away."

"Will it be enough?" Enala asked.

"By ourselves, I do not think the combined might of every man, woman and child in the Three Nations would be enough. But with the Sword, and these *Soul Blades…* maybe," she let out a long sigh and seemed to shrink in her chair. "In truth, I was beginning to lose hope. We have suffered terrible losses these last few days. We did not even have the men to hold the outer gates; we were forced to seal them with rubble to prevent the enemy from smashing their way through."

Standing, the Commander moved to a cupboard and reached inside. Enala smiled when she saw her hand emerge with a wine jar. She stood and retrieved some glasses as May unstopped the jar.

"It's a Lonian red," May offered as she poured. "I've been saving it for a special occasion. We might not have won the war yet, but I think your arrival is worthy of the vintage. Cheers," she offered when their glasses were full.

"Cheers," they echoed her, joining their glasses to May's.

Enala took a sip, enjoying its dry touch and fruity richness. "We heard you were on the wall during the first attack?"

May nodded with a shudder. "Our cause was almost lost before it began. Despite our best preparations, the enemy still took us by surprise. If the outer wall had fallen…"

"But you held," Eric interrupted her. "You're still here.

Fort Fall still stands because of you. The Three Nations owes you a great debt for that."

Enala frowned as she took another sip of wine. "Why do they call it Fort Fall? I've always wondered."

"From the last war," there was sadness in May's eyes. "Archon's final attack, when he rained fire from the sky, became known as 'The Fall'. Somehow the name stuck when the fortress was rebuilt."

Enala stared into the fire, imagining the fear and horror of the defenders as the sky turned to flame. She shuddered. "How can we stop magic like that?"

"I don't know," Eric replied. His eyes were fixed on his glass of wine, but she saw them flicker as he glanced at the Sword.

"You will find a way," May replied, her voice firm.

"What about his army?" Enala asked. "Who are these people, how did he gather so many to him?"

"They live in the wasteland, surviving off what little food and water exists up there," May swirled her glass of wine, deep in thought. "For centuries we have banished the worst of our criminals to the north. It always seemed a good solution – remove them from our society, wash our hands of their evil," she paused. "We did not expect them to thrive. They have built a society of sorts, and their numbers have grown. But locked in that wasteland, we have given them no hope of redemption, no reason to change. And so they and their children have grown to hate us. In truth, I cannot truly blame them."

"There are children up there?" Enala asked, surprised.

"There are entire *cities*," May replied. "Though we only know of a few, I am sure there are more hidden in those lands. Many of the families there have survived for generations, scavenging a meagre living from the harsh land," her eyes shone in the firelight. "But they wish for more, for the plentiful lands to the south. They want our food and water and wood, and will flock to whoever offers it to them."

Enala's stomach twisted with guilt as she thought of the struggles of her own people in Chole. But they had at least chosen to stay. Her family could have left for greener lands at any time, but Chole was their home and they would not abandon it. The enemy did not have the same choice.

"In truth, we gave Archon this army," May whispered.

Enala almost laughed at the harsh truth of May's words. She shook her head. "Maybe so," she looked around the room. "But if we win, this time things must change. We cannot let this happen again. If we win, we must find a way to put things right."

Eric nodded. "Agreed. But first, we have to win."

CHAPTER 11

Eric's chest heaved as he sucked in another breath and stumbled up the last of the stairs. His eyes teared in the salty air as he bent in two and gasped for another lungful of air. His muscles burned from the brief exertion and he cursed himself for making the trek to the outer wall. A single night of sleep had not been close to enough to restore him after the three days of flight, although it had certainly helped.

He felt the pommel of the Sword of Light against his neck and resisted the temptation to draw it. One touch and his weariness would flee, washed away by the fire of the blade's magic. The aches and pain would fade away to nothing before the thrill of its power.

Shaking his head, Eric straightened, chilled by the compulsion. The magic of the Sword was addicting, but he did his best to fight its temptation. Straightening, he looked across the ramparts of the wall, surprised to see flakes of snow drifting in the air. He shivered, pulling his woollen cloak tighter, glad for the gift Angela had made of it. It was far warmer than anything he'd ever owned.

"Looks like you could use a bit of exercise, sonny," a ruff voice came from nearby.

Eric scowled as he caught the eyes of the speaker. The man stood nearby, his broad shoulders and massive arms dwarfing Eric's small frame. Lines stretched across the man's face as he flashed Eric a smile, humour showing in his amber eyes. A massive war hammer hung across his shoulders and must have weighed at least ten pounds, though he did not appear to notice its weight. He was a monster of a man but his greying hair and the speckles of white in his beard suggested he must be at least sixty years of age.

"It was a long journey," Eric wheezed, walking over to join the man at the battlements. "I'm Eric, I only arrived yesterday."

"Alan," the giant offered his hand. "Welcome to Fort Fall, sonny. What brings you here? You look a little young for this business."

Eric grimaced, thinking of the path that had led him here. "That is a long story," he glanced at the soldier and grinned. "What about you, you seem a little old for this business."

To his surprise, the man threw back his head and unleashed a booming laugh. "Ay, ain't that the truth!" he wiped a tear from his eye. "You've got some nerve, sonny. No, I volunteered when I heard the news. Got here a few days before the first attack," he shook his head. "Sixty-six and still at the business of war. Who would have thought. But what is a man to do when evil knocks on his door?"

Smiling, Eric found himself taking a liking to the old warrior. "Why the hammer?"

Alan chuckled again, the sound ringing across the wall. Reaching up, he lifted the hammer from his shoulders and hefted it as though it weighed no more than a sword. "Old *kanker* has been with me since the beginning. We've won our fair share of fights, she and I. Wouldn't go to battle without her. And certainly not my last."

Sadness swelled in Eric's chest. "You think we'll lose?"

Alan stared out at the wasteland and then looked back to Eric. "Perhaps, sonny. That will be up to you young folk; whether you have the strength to hold them. As for myself, I know when I've come to the end. I can feel it in here," he patted his chest. "It's time I left this world, time I surrendered my place to the young. But at least I know my passing will have meaning, that my death might give others the chance to live."

Eric stood stunned, unable to find the words to answer the man's honesty. The moment stretched out, the silence punctuated by sadness.

"We will," Eric said at last. "We will hold them."

Eric met the amber glow of Alan's eyes and the old warrior smiled. "Ay, I believe you," he laughed then, and the sadness left the air, passing like an autumn cloud. "And what of that fancy sword of yours, sonny? You know how to use it?"

Eric's cheeks flushed. "I've won a few fights… Sort of," he replied. "Truthfully, I'm a Magicker, though I'm still learning that too. I usually use my magic instead of a sword."

Alan nodded. "That's all well and good. But from my experience, a Magicker is only as good as his stamina. More than a few rogue Magickers fell to my hammer when I was younger. I would suggest holding back your power until you really need it."

Eric sighed. "The Commander already mentioned that. We're to save our strength for the enemy Magickers and the beasts, if they come."

"Well keep close to me then, sonny," he reached down and picked up his hammer from where he'd leaned it against the ramparts.

"What?"

Alan nodded out towards the wasteland. "Here they come."

Eric stared as men began to emerge through the falling snow, their black cloaks staining the white ground below. They slid across the wasteland, silent as death, swords and axes held at the ready. Their eyes flashed as they looked up at the defenders, catching in the light of their torches.

Along the wall, the first blast of the trumpets rang out, sounding the call for the defenders to stand at the ready. The outer wall was already fully manned, but they would need the reserves soon enough.

Glancing to either side, Eric watched as the guards drew their weapons and strapped on their helmets. The red, green and blue cloaks of the Three Nations stood out crisp and clear amidst the snow. Eric felt a surge of pride at the sight, though the Lonian green outnumbered the others two to one. That would soon change once the other armies arrived.

Together they stood atop the wall and waited for the horde to descend.

Swallowing his fear, Eric reached up and drew the Sword of Light. Its fire flared at his touch and its power surged down his arm, but he pressed it back, fighting the rush of desire that came with it. He knew its power could decimate the enemy below, but May had warned him against using its magic too soon. If Archon sensed the Sword he might be provoked to attack with his own power, and they were not ready for that. Not yet.

The flames died away, though there was no stopping the white glow seeping from the blade.

"So, the rumours are true. The Sword of Light has returned," Alan grinned and winked at Eric. "Well, it's no *kanker*, but extra swords are always welcome up here."

"I'll do my best," Eric replied, heart thudding in his

chest. His legs shook and a voice in his mind shouted for him to run, that he had no place amongst these warriors. Gritting his teeth, he stood his ground.

Alan laughed. "Like I said, stay close to me, sonny. I'll keep you safe," he eyed the men below. "Don't worry how many of them are down there. It's the ones who make it up *here* that matter," he hefted his hammer. "I'll try to save some for you."

Eric grinned. "Hope I can keep up with an old fella like you."

"Don't you worry about that, sonny," Alan replied. "You just focus on whoever is trying to cut ya."

Eric swallowed, the big man's words slicing through his bravado. Beneath them the men were closing on the wall, and now their shouts and curses carried up to them. He spotted a dozen ladders amongst their ranks and cast a nervous glance at Alan.

Along the wall the first volley of arrows rose into the sky and plunged down into the enemy. Dozens fell but the rest came on, fresh men quickly taking the place of the fallen.

Alan pulled him back as the enemy returned fire. Their arrows clanged on stone as they retreated below the crenulations. A few seconds later there came a crash as the first ladder struck the wall. Eric made to grab for it but the larger man held him back.

"Don't bother. There's already enough weight on that thing that neither you nor I have the strength to push it back," he reached down and removed a length of rope from his belt.

Before Eric could ask its purpose he tossed the looped end over the top of the ladder and moved to the side. Flashing Eric another grin, he gave two massive heaves on the rope. On the third pull the ladder shifted, the wood scraping on the rock as it slid across the battlements. Then suddenly it was gone, disappearing sideways as it toppled back to the ground. Screams carried up to them as the climbers fell.

Puffing slightly, Alan returned to his station. "That's how you do it," he answered the unspoken question. "Though soon they'll be coming too quick and fast to have time for that."

Even so, Alan managed to dislodge two more ladders before the first of the enemy reached them. Eric shuddered as he imagined the slaughter below as the enemy waited to gain a foothold atop the wall. The walls of the fortress curved in towards the keep, leaving the men below exposed on all sides to the defenders' arrows.

But then there was no more time to think of those below. Summoning his courage, he leapt to aid the aging warrior as the first of the enemy reached the battlements. Not that Alan showed any sign of his years.

As the first man leapt from a ladder and sprang across the crenulations, Alan surged forwards. Their foe hardly had time to raise his sword before *kanker* struck, smashing in his chest with a sickening crunch. The man collapsed to the cold stone, blood bubbling from his mouth to stain the snow.

Eric shuddered at his fate, but there was little time to spare the man a second thought. Another ladder crashed onto the stone beside him and he forced himself to focus on the battle. Crouching low in the forward stance Caelin had shown him so long ago, he waited, the Sword of Light poised to strike.

His first opponent surged into view, rolling across the stone to land on his feet in a single movement. His sword was already in motion as Eric stepped up to meet him, arcing towards his head. Instinct alone saved him, the Sword sweeping up to deflect the blow as though directed by a mind of its own. Then he was moving, stepping sideways to avoid the next attack and slicing out with the Sword in a clumsy strike.

The warrior laughed as he deflected the blow, then his eyes widened. Eric stumbled back as the man crumpled, the back of his helmet caved in by a casual sweep of Alan's hammer. The big man nodded in Eric's direction and then turned back to his ladder.

Returning to his position, Eric took a deep breath, then threw himself at the next enemy to appear. This time he was prepared, and his blade caught the attacker in the chest before he could even raise his weapon.

As he fell, Eric caught the sound of a boot on stone and spun, deflecting the sword of another attacker. The defender to Eric's left lay dead, the ladder beside him unguarded. A second attacker was already clambering onto the ramparts, but Eric had no time to act. The warrior facing him growled and surged toward him.

Eric slid backwards, using a forward stance to maintain his balance, and caught the blow on the hilt of the Sword. Teeth gritted, he pushed forward so their blades locked together, leaving them face to face, each straining to overpower the other. Despite his small size, Eric remembered Caelin's training and came in low, using his lower centre to push the man off balance.

The man cursed and retreated back a step, then cried out as he tripped against the edge of the crenulations. The man's arms windmilled as he fought to regain his balance. Seeing his chance, Eric quickly stepped up and kicked him in the chest. The man toppled backwards off the wall and vanished from view.

Taking a breath, Eric stepped back and turned where the man had forced his way through their defences, but reinforcements had already plugged the gap.

Gasping in the cold air, he struggled to hold down the

sickness of utter exhaustion. His vision swirled and he stumbled for a second. Only a few minutes of battle had passed, and he was shocked by the fatigue already gripping him.

But still the enemy came on, clambering up the ladders in an endless tide. Eric straightened as the next appeared. Panting, he allowed the man to come to him now, hoping the Sword of Light's long reach would give him an advantage against the man's axe.

The axeman grinned as he dropped to the walkway, seeing only an exhausted boy opposing him. Eric swallowed and gripped the Sword tighter, prepared to summon its magic if necessary. The screams of the dying came from all around, but Eric's vision narrowed now to a single point, focused only on the axeman. He glimpsed the slightest movement of the man's boot and leapt forward, even as the man raised his axe and charged.

The man's eyes widened as the Sword of Light lanced up into his unprotected chest. The axe clattered to the pavement as Eric pulled back his blade, allowing the man to topple to the ground. His blood streamed across the snow, one more body to add to the mounting pile atop the wall.

"That was well done," Alan observed. "Told you I saw a fighter in you, sonny."

Eric nodded back, unable to find the breath to reply. He could not begin to understand how men fought for hours in battle.

Alan laughed at the expression on Eric's face and stepped back from the edge, allowing other men to take his place. "Rest, sonny, you've earned a break. The reinforcements have arrived," he gestured with his hammer to indicate the stream of men now bolstering their ranks.

Looking around, Eric felt a wave of relief to see their forces holding strong. The defenders were disciplined and well-armed, waiting out of sight of the archers below before dispatching the enemy as they reached the top.

"They won't take the outer wall today," Alan observed. "We're still fresh; it'll take a few more days to wear us down."

"How long do you think we have?" Eric asked over the ring of steel, staring at the mounting dead.

Despite their advantage atop the wall, Eric counted far too many of their own amongst the dead. From what he'd seen the day before, the enemy numbered in the tens of thousands. Fort Fall only had a thousand defenders; they could not afford to lose a single soul.

"A few days, a week. It depends how often they attack and when the reinforcements arrive. So far we've been lucky. They've only launched a handful of assaults each day. But they're just probes, from what I've seen. When the real assault begins, we'll struggle to find time for a jug of ale between the fighting."

Eric swallowed. He was about to reply when a roar came from behind them. The hairs on Eric's neck prickled with warning as Alan swore. Spinning, Eric raised the Sword of Light and reached for its magic, ready to unleash it against whatever foul creature Archon had sent.

Instead, he found himself staring in wonder as gold dragons dropped from the southern sky. He lowered the Sword of Light and released its power, watching as the beasts swept past and dove towards their foes.

Below the enemy had also seen the beasts, though they seemed unsure of their allegiance. The uncertainty did not last long. As one the dragons turned in the sky and roared. Columns of fire erupted from their massive jaws, streaming down to burn through the massed ranks below. A barrage of arrows followed, and Eric saw that men and women in Plorsean green clung to the dragons' backs.

Alan and Eric moved to the edge of the wall and stared

down at the devastation. The enemy were in full flight, the flames dancing amongst them like a living thing. Streaks of black marked the land below, growing as the flames spread through the black-garbed ranks.

Atop the wall, the defenders burst into applause, cheering as the dragons swept by for another pass. Men embraced, their eyes lit by the glow of hope.

As the last of the attackers vanished into the snow, the dragons swung around and headed back towards the land south of the fortress. All but one. Overhead the crack of wings drew Eric's eyes up, catching on the descending dragon. Somehow he knew the dragon, though it had been many long weeks since Malevolent Cove.

Eric, my eyes did not deceive me, he heard Enduran's voice in his head.

Grinning, Eric sheathed the Sword of Light and raised his arm in greeting. His heart surged at the sight of the familiar dragon, already seeing the happiness on Enala's face when she heard the news. Around him the soldiers retreated to make room for the dragon. With casual ease the great body settled on the battlements, its golden tale draping over the edge like a discarded cloak.

Folding his wings, Enduran lowered his head to inspect Eric. *You are looking well, little one. Your power has grown*, a rumble rose from Enduran's chest and Eric recognised the sound as laughter. *Yes, yes, get down then,* the dragon eyed Eric. *I believe you know my passengers.*

Eric's eyes slid to the figures who sat atop the dragon's back. One was already sliding down the dragon's side, clambering onto its knee and then dropping to the battlements.

Eric glimpsed a flash of scarlet hair and a long bow clenched in a pale fist. Then he was moving, racing across the short distance between them, his eyes blind to everything but her face. The icy stone slid beneath his feet but he did not slow. He watched as she turned and her eyes found his, and he knew he was right.

Inken managed two steps before he reached her, his arms wrapping around her, drawing her to him. Her lips pushed against his and warmth surged through his chest. Her body pressed against him, her fingers twining in his hair, her tongue dancing with his to a music only they could hear.

They clutched each other close, as though they would never let go, as though their very lives depended on it.

And in Eric's mind, a single word repeated itself, over and over.

Hope.

CHAPTER 12

Inken lay on the soft bed, eyes closed, listening to the gentle in, out of Eric's breath. Reaching down, she entwined her fingers with his and felt a gentle squeeze in return. She smiled, a tingling warmth spreading from her heart to her head, washing away all thought of the world outside.

It didn't matter. Tonight was theirs and the world could wait until the light of morning. For now, she wanted nothing more than to lie there with Eric and enjoy the miracle of their reunion.

Eric gave her fingers another squeeze and she looked over to see his blue eyes on her. Reaching over, she ran a hand across his brow and up through his hair. He closed his eyes, the creases of worry falling from his face.

"You're awake," she breathed.

Their only light came from the dying embers of the fire, though with Eric beside her the darkness no longer held the same terror. Even so, she would have to get up and add more wood soon. A storm had descended over the fortress and the temperature had plummeted.

"I am," he smiled. "Sorry I drifted off. It was… a long day before you arrived."

"From what I hear, you fought well," she leaned across and kissed him. "Caelin taught you well."

A shadow passed across Eric's face as she pulled away. "It was not the first time I've had to fight since..." he shook his head. "So much has happened… since I left you."

"You did not leave me, Eric. You did what you had to do. We all did," she embraced him. "You cannot second guess what happened. It was the only way. If you had not run with Enala, none of us would be here right now."

A tear spilt down Eric's cheek but he nodded. "It's been a long couple of weeks."

"Agreed," Inken shuddered, then pressed the memories down. There was no place for sorrow now. Grinning, she gave Eric a jab in the side. "So, how did *you* end up being the one wielding the Sword of Light?" she nodded to the blade leaning against the foot of the bed.

Laughing, Eric grabbed her hand and pulled her close. Before she could squirm free, his fingers began to tickle her side and she burst into laughter. "*Stop!*" she gasped.

Eric refused to relent until there were breathless tears in her eyes. He grinned at her, his smile infectious. "You'll pay for that," she threatened.

Eric only laughed. Finally he took a deep breath and answered her question. "Enala… is my sister. Antonia showed me a vision, from her prison within the *Soul Blade*. Enala and I are twins, but Aria's descendants took on a tradition of separating siblings at birth, so our family would survive even if Archon's hunters found them. Who knows how many other descendants of Aria there are now, lost on secret branches of our family."

Inken's eyes widened and her hand drifted to her stomach. She could not imagine the strength it must have taken

Eric's parents to give up their child. It had only been three days since Enduran had broken the news to her, but even so…

Fortunately Eric did not notice her unconscious gesture. She had not told him yet, though she could not explain her hesitation.

"Incredible," she whispered, then hesitated. "What… what is it like, the Sword?"

Eric shook his head and she saw a shadow cross his face. "It's… like my own magic, but stronger, fiercer. It fights me every time I use it, flooding me with its power, searching for a weakness. Only my own magic keeps it in check."

Inken shuddered. Eric had already told her what had happened to Enala. It seemed clear to her that the powers of the Gods were not meant for mortals. It terrified her to imagine Eric lost to the Sword's magic; that it might burn away his soul and reduce him to an empty shell. She remembered the demon Thomas had become, the empty darkness in his eyes, and prayed Eric had the strength to resist the pull of the Sword.

"What about you?" Eric interrupted her thoughts. "What happened to you and the others?"

Inken bit her lip, staring up at the stone ceiling. Memories raced through her mind and it was a minute before she found her voice. Eric's eyes did not leave her face as she recalled their escape from Sitton and their strange reception by the king in Ardath, nor as she spoke of the arrival of the gold dragons.

But as she spoke of their imprisonment in the black cells beneath the lake city, he reached across and drew her into his arms. She cracked then, the tears coming hot and fast as she struggled for breath. A groan rose in her throat and she sobbed in his arms, the horror of the darkness returning. The fear came rushing back, the helpless terror of their imprisonment.

Eric rubbed her back, his silent presence giving her comfort, and slowly her sobs subsided. At last Inken drew in a deep breath and wiped the tears from her eyes. She flashed Eric a smile, giving him her silent thanks.

"I'm here, Inken," Eric smiled back. "I won't leave again."

Inken suppressed another sob, still trying to get a hold of her emotions. "Sorry," she whispered. "I… I've never felt so helpless."

Eric squeezed her arm but said nothing.

Together they lay back on the bed and held each other close. Inken rested her head on his chest, listening to the steady thump of his heart and feeling the rhythmic rise and fall of his chest.

Closing her eyes, Inken released her fear. The painful throb of her heart slowed and exhaustion spread through her aching limbs. She fought the lure of sleep, unwilling to let the moment slip away. But its call was irresistible and within minutes she had slipped into a dreamless slumber.

Gabriel could not keep himself from staring, still unable to believe his eyes. Enala sat across the table from him, her blond hair aglow in the light of the torches. Her single lock of scarlet hair drooped lazily across her face, begging him to reach out and tuck it behind her ear. He resisted, contenting himself to watch her eyes as she recounted her journey with Eric.

It was late now and the dining hall was all but empty, the other benches and tables vacant but for a few stragglers. He had hardly noticed the others leaving the hall, so intent had they been on their conversation.

Even the voice in his head had quieted, reduced to faint whispers in the back of his mind.

He shivered though at Enala's tale. It seemed her journey had taken her through more strife than even his own ordeal. She had almost died a dozen times. He could hardly believe her courage to sit here now, ready to face the might of Archon and his armies.

Most surprising of all, she now possessed magic. He would not have believed it had she not shown him, had he not seen it with his own eyes.

Now her voice shook as she described falling under the spell of the *Soul Blade's* power. Silently he reached across the table and grasped her hand. She broke off her story and gave a soft smile, squeezing his fingers tight.

"Thank you, Gabriel," she breathed.

He smiled. "I'm sorry I wasn't there," he paused, struggling to get the next words out. "I'm glad Eric was there for you though, truly," it surprised him to realise it was the truth.

Enala let out a long breath. "He's my brother, Gabriel. My twin."

Gabriel was surprised to find himself smiling, sharing in the joy on Enala's face. It warmed him to hear she had found family, even after the tragedy that had befallen her parents. Then sadness touched him as an image of his own parents and fiancée drifted through his thoughts.

Revenge, the angry whisper rose from the back of his mind.

He shook it off, ignoring the voice and looking back to Enala. "What happens now then, with Eric wielding the Sword? Will you leave, now that it is no longer your 'destiny'?"

"No," Enala sighed. "No, I think I have a different 'destiny' now. If they cannot free the Gods from the *Soul Blades*, it may…" her voice broke and she shook her head, unable to finish.

"Enala?" Gabriel stood and moved around the table to sit beside her. He pulled her into his arms, smiling as he felt her head nestle beneath his chin. "What is it?"

"I may have to use it again, the *Soul Blade*," she shuddered in his arms. "Last time… Last time it *destroyed* me, Gabriel. If not for Eric…"

"Why?" he could not believe anyone would ask such a sacrifice of this girl, not after everything she had been through. "Why you?"

"Because I have already used it. We know it will not kill me, that my magic is powerful enough for that at least. The Magickers in Kalgan thought that it was only my inexperience that allowed the God magic to possess me. Now… now I might at least stand a chance of controlling it."

"What if they're wrong?" Gabriel whispered, terrified for the girl in his arms.

Enala stiffened and push away from him. Fire flashed in her eyes. "Do not say that, Gabriel," she growled. "I don't need any more doubt, I have enough of my own. Don't you see, I'm *terrified*," tears sprang to her eyes. "But I don't have a choice; I have to do this. I can't let Eric face him alone!"

"Surely another Magicker –"

"*No*," Enala snapped. "If it comes to it, I won't let someone else risk death because I was *scared*. I can do this; I *will* do this."

"Okay, I understand," Gabriel held up his hands in surrender. "But what about the other one, the *Soul Blade* with Jurrien's magic?"

Take it! The whispers in his mind suddenly turned into a roar. *Take it and embrace your destiny!*

Gabriel shuddered as shadows danced just beyond his vision. The voice was stronger than he'd ever felt it before, drilling its way deep into his mind. Groaning, he slumped on the bench, his hands clutching at his face.

"*No!*" he ground out through clenched teeth.

"Gabriel?" panic rose in Enala's voice. "What's wrong?"

But her words were a whisper now, carrying to him from some great distance. He could hardly hear her over the screeching in his ears.

Take it! Take it and you will have more power than you could ever have dreamed.

He pressed his hands to his ears and shook his head, but it made no difference. The voice came from within, seeping through his conscious, reaching down to the darkness within him. A shadow stirred in his soul, claws reaching up, desperate to be free.

"Gabriel!" Enala shook him. "Gabriel, what's happening?"

Gabriel tasted blood as his teeth clenched on the inside of his cheek. Slowly, he pulled back from the edge of the abyss and the voice retreated to a whisper.

He looked up into Enala's sapphire eyes, saw the concern there, the fear.

"It's back."

~

"You're looking bright this morning, Commander May," Caelin grinned as the woman moved through the dining hall and sat across the table from him.

"Yes, well I'm enjoying my good mood while it lasts," she waved to a server, who nodded and raced to bring her food. He caught her eyes on his plate and pulled it out of reach. May raised an eyebrow. "You know, it would be polite to offer your food to your superior."

Caelin laughed and scooped a spoonful of beans into his

mouth. "Not on your life," he swallowed. "Flying on a dragon's back may look like fun, but it gets uncomfortable after a few days. And we didn't exactly stop long enough for hot meals along the way."

May waved a hand, grinning as the servant placed a plate of food in front of her. "Just in the nick of time," the plate was heaped with beans, bacon and eggs.

Grinning, Caelin shook his head. "I'm glad you're the one in charge here, May," the woman had been a legend even when he'd been training to join the army. He doubted there was anyone he would trust more with the defence of the fortress. "How are the defences looking?"

May finished chewing her mouthful before answering. "Better than a few days ago, that's for sure. The Lonian army arrived not long after your somewhat eventful entrance. That gives us another five thousand swords. The Trolans are still a few days out, but their birds say they have another ten thousand. And we now have the Sword and forty dragons."

"But you don't wish to use them?" he was still confused by May's decision.

"Not yet," she shook her head. "Archon's army may outnumber us, but his human forces alone are not likely to take even the outer wall. Now that we've been reinforced, they will not break us. But his beasts are another matter. I don't want to lose a single dragon before they are needed, and make no mistake, we will need them if we are to hold back Archon's creatures. The last time Archon came, those beasts swept us from the outer wall like we were no more than children."

"And what about the Magickers?"

"I have them stationed on the walls in case they are needed, but they are under strict instruction not to use their magic unless they absolutely must."

Caelin nodded and suppressed a yawn. He had spent

much of the night surveying the fortress' defences for himself, and couldn't help but agree with May's plan.

Looking around the dining room, he spotted Eric and Inken moving towards them. He smiled, warmed by the sight of their reunion. Joy radiated from their faces as they joined them at the table. Gabriel and Enala appeared next, but Caelin was disappointed to see the haunted look still darkened Gabriel's face. If anything, he seemed to have lost more colour.

Looking around the table, he took stock of their reunited company. He smiled, though a sadness stirred in his heart as he remembered those they'd lost. The gap left by Michael and Alastair was plain, but they would never be forgotten. Their sacrifice spurred them on, giving them the strength they needed to face the challenges still to come.

"It's good to see you two again," Caelin nodded at Enala and Eric. "You seem to have gotten yourselves into quite a bit of trouble since you left us."

Eric grinned. "I heard you got yourself thrown in prison, Caelin, and had to be rescued."

"It was all part of the plan," Caelin laughed. "But what's this I hear about you two being siblings now?"

"Believe me, it was just as much of a surprise to us," Eric looked around the room. "I'm glad to see you too, all of you," his eyes lingered on Gabriel.

Gabriel looked away and his face darkened. Caelin raised an eyebrow. He'd thought Gabriel might have finally forgiven Eric, though he understood the young man's pain. To Eric's credit, he let the slight pass.

Enala did not. She reached out and squeezed Gabriel's wrist, then turned to the room. "He's glad to see you too, Eric. But there is more here, something Gabriel has kept from the rest of you."

Gabriel shuddered and Caelin glimpsed the gleam of

tears in his eyes. "It won't leave me alone," he hissed. "It won't stop."

A shiver raised the hairs on the back of Caelin's neck. "What won't leave you alone?"

"The demon," Gabriel hissed. "The thing that came to me in the forests of Oaksville all that time ago."

"Demon?" May half-rose from her seat, her hand going to her sword.

Gabriel nodded. "That's what I've always thought it to be. It… it came to me after my men were slaughtered by the Baronians outside Oaksville, when I'd come so close… to killing you, Eric."

Eric swallowed, clearly uncomfortable with the memory, but Gabriel continued.

"I knew it was evil. It appeared as a shadow in the forest, cloaked in the spirits of the dead. Somehow, *somehow*, it convinced me to listen to it, to take its gift. It offered me resistance to magic, though I never tested it. Not until Ardath," quietly he explained how the dark magic cast by the false king had slid from him like butter.

"But its gift came with a price. It stole my thoughts, my memories, my very soul, until I had nothing left but hatred. Only my encounter with Enala broke the spell, when it told me to kill her."

"I thought I had rid myself of it then, but in the cell it returned. It has been with me ever since, whispering in my mind, driving me towards the darkness," Gabriel hung his head as he finished.

Caelin stared, mouth open in shock. He'd thought it had been madness haunting Gabriel, but now he shuddered at the memory of the darkness in their cell. An evil presence had hovered over them, drawing away their strength. Could it have been Gabriel's demon all along?

"What –?" the ring of trumpets cut May off before she could finish the question.

A shadow swept over the dining hall. Caelin's heart sank as he glanced down at his half-finished plate. Then he stood, lifting his sword belt from his chair and strapping it around his waist.

His eyes found Gabriel's. "We will speak of this after the battle, Gabriel. For now though, I think it's best if you sit out this fight. Afterwards, we will find a way to help you," he reached down and squeezed Gabriel's shoulder. "I swear it."

Gabriel nodded back, the despair in his eyes unmistakable. But there was no time to offer the young man further comfort now.

The evil at their gates would not wait.

CHAPTER 13

Adrenaline swept through Inken as she picked up her bow and followed the others from the hall. This was why she'd first become a bounty hunter: the thrill of combat, the exhilaration as she tested her skill against another's. Her strength had returned over the last few days and she was eager to prove she had lost nothing to the darkness of her imprisonment.

She had already decided she would not back down from the battle. Every sword and bow was needed now, and if Fort Fall was lost, the Three Nations would soon follow. There would be nowhere for her to run, no place left to keep a child safe. No, it was all or nothing, and if she had to give her life so others could raise their children in peace, so be it.

Their boots cracked against the brick path as they raced for the outer wall. The mess hall where they had been eating adjoined to the outermost barracks between the middle and outer wall, so it did not take long for them to reach the staircase leading up to the front line. Behind them others were rushing to their respective stations, ensuring the other two walls were manned in case the first fell.

But that would not be today, not if she had anything to say about it.

May led the way, striding up the stairs while keeping her pace in check. Inken smiled at the woman's self-control. It would not do for the defenders to see their commander panicked, but May seemed to have little difficulty maintaining an outward calm.

At the top May moved off along the wall, her voice bellowing out as she gave orders for the archers to form up. Inken slid her bow off her shoulder and strung it, then stepped into the front line. She sensed the presence of her comrades as they moved in behind her, but she only had eyes for the enemy now. Looking down, she searched for her first target.

Below, a wave of men surged towards the wall, weapons raised in defiance. The snow had cleared during the night but the ground remained frozen white, slowly giving way to the incoming tide of black. The screams of the enemy and the banging of shields carried up to the defenders, breaking on the steel of their courage.

Inken smiled, proud to stand amidst the best of the Three Nations. But as the sunlight glinted off the weapons of the enemy, Inken felt a trickle of fear slide through her chest. Her hand drifted to her stomach and she found herself retreating a step before she caught herself. She bit her tongue, struggling to find the nerve to step back to the edge. Within, a voice was screaming for her to flee.

"There's more of em today," an old warrior stepped up beside her, his amber eyes looking down at the oncoming enemy. He held a massive war hammer casually in one hand.

"Seems that way," Inken swallowed.

"Won't matter much, so long as they stay down there," the giant commented.

Inken found herself grinning, her fear falling away. Reaching up she drew an arrow from her quiver.

"That's what you said yesterday, Alan," Eric muttered from behind her. "And my arms are still hurting."

Inken jumped as Alan's laughter boomed out across the wall. "You'll get used to it, sonny. I expect they'll be throwing the anvil at us now, after yesterday. And whatever else they can get their hands on."

Caelin nodded. "Ay, they'll want a win after yesterday's slaughter."

"Well, sonny, they won't have any luck while I still stand," Alan grinned. "*Kanker* here and I have never lost a fight, and I don't intend to start today," he hefted the great hammer in both hands.

"Is that so?" Caelin grinned at the older man. "Well, just see if you can keep up with me then, old man."

Inken chuckled as Alan replied with a toothy grin. She eyed the older warrior with a professional eye, and guessed Caelin might find himself outmatched on this occasion. Despite the greying hair and lines on his face, Alan held the war hammer seemingly without effort and he moved with the natural grace of a fighter.

"Here they come," Enala commented.

Turning back, Inken swore and nocked her bow.

From down the line she heard the call from May. "Archers: draw, *loose!*"

Sighting down the arrow shaft, Inken found a man at the forefront of the charge and fired. Along the wall the other archers did the same and a volley of arrows swept out to meet the incoming tide. The enemy ranks faltered as it struck, the front line disappearing beneath the deadly rain.

Screams carried up to the wall, but despite the devastation at the front, the men behind came on.

"Archers, nock, draw, *loose!*" May's voice rang out again.

Inken drew a breath and released it, losing herself in the rhythm of the bow. With each volley she reached for her next arrow before the last had even found its target. They managed a dozen volleys before the first of the enemy reached the base of the wall.

"Fire at will! Fighters, at the ladders!"

Then the enemy were firing back and Inken hardly heard May's words as she ducked beneath the crenulations. The hiss of an arrow's passage raised the hairs on her neck and she swore, rolling sideways to come up in a new position. Leaping to her feet, she quickly sighted on an enemy archer, loosed, and ducked back out of view.

Glancing around, she saw the first of the enemy had reached the battlements and were leaping from their ladders to engage with the defenders. Their shaggy coats and black leather armour stood out in stark contrast to the red, blue and green of the defenders. So far, none had managed to gain a foothold on the walkway.

Yet there was no stopping the flood of men racing up the ladders.

A crash came from nearby and she looked up in time to see a man climb into view. Without thinking she drew back her bowstring and loosed her arrow. The bolt struck the man in the chest and flung him backwards. He toppled out of view.

Inken reached for another arrow and found her quiver empty. Cursing, she realised they had spilt from the quiver as she rolled. Tossing aside her bow, she drew her sabre. The next man to clamber onto the parapets was met with steel, his skull shattered by her first swing. As he fell, Inken took up position to the side of the ladder and waited for the next attacker.

A roar came from her left and she looked up in time to see Alan charge into a cluster of three black-garbed enemies. She turned to help him, but quickly realised there was no need. The war hammer caught the first man mid-charge, smashing him from his feet, even as the giant's fist crashed into the face of a second man. The man's head bounced backwards into the stone with an audible *crack*. Panic swept across the face of the last man and he turned to run.

Dropping his hammer, Alan leapt after the man. Grabbing him by the neck, Alan hoisted the man over his head and tossed him at two enemy warriors who had just gained the battlements. The man screamed as he flew into his comrades, knocking them backwards off the wall.

Alan swept up his hammer and turned to see her staring. "Watch yourself, missy," he nodded to another enemy who had just appeared.

Inken grinned back, pleased her assessment of the old warrior had proven true. She doubted even Caelin could keep up with such a man. His strength was prodigious and with that war hammer he appeared to be all but unstoppable.

The enemy approaching her had no such skill and in two breaths she had speared him through the heart. Stepping back, she swung to check on Eric. A tingle of fear went through her as she saw him facing two men.

Before she could move to his aid, Enala leapt in from the side, her short sword stabbing out to catch one of the men in the stomach. As the other turned towards her, Eric surged forward and the Sword of Light crunched through bone. The man crumpled beside his comrade.

"Well done," Inken commented as she joined them.

"Thanks," Eric panted, flashing a weary smile.

As the next wave of enemies swept over the battlements they leapt together to meet them, swords flashing in the morning sun. Inken's heart thudded hard in her chest, strength warming her arms as another enemy fell to her blade and she ducked beneath a swinging axe.

Yet even as she fought, regret touched her. This had been her life as a bounty hunter, an existence filled with excitement and danger. But that life seemed a thousand years ago, and it felt now as though she were reaching back to a past long gone. Sadness stirred in her stomach as she realised how empty that existence had been.

She had been drifting through life before, living each week for the thrill of the hunt, but now she had finally found her purpose. Not for the first time, she thanked the Gods she'd made the right decision all that time ago, when she had sided with the company and joined their quest, when she had joined the fight to save their world from Archon.

And as she slashed past another enemy, she realised with a smile that this war would be her last fight. Not because of the life growing within her, but because she knew she could not return to her old life. After this, she could find no joy in such an existence.

No, there had to be more. Glancing at Eric, warmth rose in her throat at the thought of starting a life with him. It would be an adventure all of its own.

She swore as a blade sliced past her face, coming far too close, and then brought her sabre around to block the next attack. The hilt rung in her hand, but she did not flinch back from the power in the blow. Reversing her swing, she hammered her blade into the man's skull. Wrenching her sword back, she kicked the man through the gap between the crenulations.

Swinging around, Inken surveyed the wall, ready to aid her friends if necessary. A tingle of panic started in her stomach as she saw the enemy were beginning to gain the upper hand. The black-garbed warriors had won purchase atop the battlements in several places and now more were pushing up the ladders behind them. Around them the defenders were falling in greater numbers, their coloured cloaks dotting the walkway amidst the hordes of fallen enemy.

Then she saw the old warrior Alan, still standing his ground amidst the slaughter, a calm centre amidst the storm. Where others were being forced back he stood like a boulder, immovable as the enemy pressed forward around him. Black-cloaked bodies lay strewn about him.

Yet Alan's defiance also threatened to cut him off from the other defenders as they retreated beneath the enemy's weight.

Seeing the threat, Inken screamed to the others. "Follow me!"

Knowing Eric, Enala and Caelin would not let her down, she charged into the ring of men gathering around the old warrior. She took the first one in the back, bearing him to the ground as her momentum carried her forward. Pulling back her blade, she leapt to her feet, her steel finding a second victim before the others could turn to face her.

Then Caelin was there, his sword like lightning, dancing amidst the enemy, too quick for thought. His foot lashed out, knocking an axeman off balance as he parried the sword of another. Eric followed him in, the long blade of the Sword of Light cleaving into the enemy ranks, and Enala too, her short sword stabbing low beneath the enemy's guard.

In seconds the fight was over, the enemy overwhelmed before they had a chance to regroup.

Together they re-joined with Alan, helping him to dispatch the last few enemy on his other side. As one they faced the next wave of attackers, their weapons red with the blood of the fallen.

Inken's heart raced, her movements beyond reason now,

beyond thought. She attacked with a primal instinct, developed from her years of combat. The enemy fell like autumn leaves before their fury, and though her lungs heaved and she could hear the laboured gasps of her comrades, Inken knew not one of them would back down.

Around them the other defenders took courage from their defiance and began to press back against the enemy, making them pay for every inch of bloody stone. Where the enemy had gained footholds their numbers quickly shrank, falling away beneath the fury of the defenders' blades. Together, the men and women of the Three Nations stood atop the wall, and defied the might of Archon.

Inken heard May's roars of encouragement from further down the wall. Bit by bit, the defenders drove the enemy back.

Slowly the tide turned and the anger in the eyes of the enemy turned to fear. They had been winning, had been within an inch of claiming the wall, but now that triumph was slipping through their fingers.

Inken smiled as panic spread through the enemy ranks and they began to retreat back towards their ladders. But with men still surging up from below, they had nowhere to go, and there on the battlements they were slaughtered.

It took a few minutes for Inken to realise there were no more enemies left to fight. Blinking in the bright sun, she looked around and saw the last of the enemy had fallen to the defender's blades. Below, the black tide was retreating and men were leaping down from the ladders in panic, desperate to escape the fury of the defenders above.

Her friends stood around her, wide smiles on their faces.

"We did it," she laughed.

"Ay, we did," Alan smiled. "But I am afraid this is just the beginning."

GABRIEL WATCHED from a distant window as the defenders began to clean up in the aftermath of the battle. They started with the enemy, with defenders taking it in turns to lift the lifeless bodies between them and toss them back out into the wasteland. There were more than he could possibly count, though he knew in his heart it was still not enough. Archon had countless warriors at his disposal, along with whatever nightmarish creatures waited out in that vast wasteland.

When the defenders started with their own fallen, Gabriel could hardly watch. They brought them down one by one, carried solemnly on stretchers to be laid out on the ground below. There a great pit had been prepared, although men were already working to make it larger. The losses today had far exceeded anyone's expectations.

Yet even that was not the worst of it.

Screams echoed up from below him, the cries of the injured and dying rising through the floorboards. They had been carrying them down throughout the battle, clearing the wall for fresh defenders. Some had even brought themselves, hobbling down on shattered legs or cradling broken limbs.

They had set up a makeshift hospital in the large hall beside the mess hall to treat the worst of the injured, to stabilise them before moving them to the main infirmary inside the keep. Gabriel had stumbled down earlier, desperate to make a difference, but the cacophony of sound and smell had driven him back.

Never before had he felt so powerless, so helpless to aid his friends.

And still the whispers would not stop.

You can help them, Gabriel, the voice came from the shadows. In the corner of his eye, Gabriel could glimpse the demon, the flickering of ghosts whirling around it. But he refused to face it, to acknowledge its presence. *You could be more powerful than you ever dreamed.*

Gabriel closed his eyes, struggling to ignore the words. They clawed at him, dragging hooks of guilt through his soul. Could he truly help them? Could he use that sword and use it to drive back the enemy?

"No," he growled to himself. "It lies. You know what it is, *what it wants!*"

I want nothing, the demon's voice came again. *You are my child, Gabriel, do you not see? I only wish to free you.*

"I am no child of yours, demon!" Gabriel finally swung to face the creature.

The demon emerged from the shadows, its slow, gliding movements revealing its insubstantial form. The strength fled Gabriel's legs as he watched it approach. He sank to his knees and looked up into the pale face of the demon. Death hung around the thing like a cloak, drawing the life from him.

It seemed more solid now, more powerful. As though it had fed, had grown stronger.

I only wish to help you, Gabriel, to give you strength. Do you not wish to aid your comrades?

Gabriel shuddered as the creature reached down and grasped his shoulder. Its touch felt like ice, its chill spreading out to engulf him. Tears ran down his face and he felt the darkness inside him rising from where he had banished it. This time, desperate and alone, he could not find the strength to fight it.

The shadow leaned closer, until the deathly lips were an inch from his ear. *You know who you are, Gabriel, what you must do. Return to the girl's room and take up the Soul Blade. Only it can give you the strength you need. Go!*

Hot tears burned in his eyes as Gabriel found himself standing. The darkness spread out within him, pushing him back, swamping him. He faced the creature one last time, looked into the infinite depths of those black eyes. But there was no breaking its spell now, and with a twist of terror he found himself turning and walking from the room.

Somewhere below, the *Soul Blade* waited for him.

CHAPTER 14

The slow thump of Gabriel's boots on the wooden stairs echoed in the narrow space. The descent seemed to take an age, though less than a minute had passed since the demon had come. Gabriel's head burned as he struggled to stop himself, but each thump brought him one step closer to the *Soul Blade*, closer to some dark fate he could only imagine.

The darkness within him swirled, rejoicing at its triumph, and Gabriel felt himself slipping away. He struggled against the emotions rising within him, the rage and hate he had thought long buried. Greed coloured his thoughts, and a desire rose in his chest, a craving for the power offered by the *Soul Blade.* He closed his eyes, trying to deny the darkness within.

But he could not close it off any longer, could not control it.

Then he was standing within Enala's room, crossing to where a burlap sack lay carelessly discarded at the foot of the bed. He could feel the power radiating from within the sack, the aching taint of the *Soul Blades*. Reaching down, Gabriel upended the contents onto the floor.

The *Soul Blades* tumbled out, their blue and green glow spilling across the room. Gabriel staggered backwards as a tingle of fear caught him, cutting through the hate and greed. For a second he stood frozen, the dark and the light warring within.

But fear alone was not enough. The darkness roared and his soul shrank, retreating back to the depths of his conscious. With a long sigh, he straightened and stepped towards the swords.

The blue glow of Jurrien's *Soul Blade* washed across the room, beckoning him. Voices whispered their warning in his mind, but the call of the blade was everything now. He was beyond reason, beyond thought. He shivered, his skin tingling with the power of the sword.

All the power of the Sky lay at his fingertips; the very magic Eric had used to destroy his life.

A dark grin crossed Gabriel's lips as he reached for the *Soul Blade*.

"*Gabriel!*" Enala's shriek pierced the mist around his thoughts.

Gabriel looked up, eyes widening to see Enala standing in the doorway. Blood stained her clothing and her hair hung limp across her eyes. Brown and red streaks marked her skin, but there was no mistaking the fear on her face.

"What are you doing?" she stared, mouth agape, fingers hovering on the hilt of her sword.

"I – I –" Gabriel looked from her to the *Soul Blade*, but whatever hold the demon had over him, Enala's presence had not freed him. He felt tears sting his eyes. "I'm sorry," he breathed.

Then he lunged forward and wrapped his fingers around the hilt of the *Soul Blade*. A surge of energy raced up his arm as he lifted it. He stiffened as the power reached his chest, the blue fire burning down to his very core. His fingers clenched tight to the hilt of the *Soul Blade*, locking it in an iron grip. From somewhere far away, he heard a girl scream.

A grin pulled at Gabriel's lips as the power spread and a euphoric joy lit his mind, banishing doubt and fear. He had never felt such power, such strength.

His eyes opened and Gabriel found himself looking out at the world through a haze of blue. Energy crackled in the air, the raw potential of the Sky begging to be unleashed. He had only to wish it, and he could use its power to wipe the fortress from existence. Winds would tear the stones from the walls and lightning would fall from above, burning rock and steel alike to ash.

A mad smile split his lips. Reaching out, he touched a swirling ring of light. Thunder boomed as lightning materialised within the room. The blue threads of power crackled and danced across the wooden floorboards. A shriek came from somewhere and he turned to see a figure flee through the open door.

A trickle of regret touched him, quickly gone, and then there was only the magic of the *Soul Blade*, the thrill of its power.

Gabriel, the voice was so soft, so faint he would not have heard it if not for the shiver it sent through his soul. He shook his head, trying to dismiss the whisper, but a part of him clung to it, to the comfort of the voice. It hung in stark contrast to the demon's whispers.

Yet the room was empty, his only company the roar of lightning and the crackle of flames now licking the walls. Slowly, the feeling fell away, tumbling back into the depths within. A dark joy throbbed in his head as the magic filled him. It raced through his mind, burning away thought and reason, and Gabriel felt himself slipping away.

Looking down, he watched lightning take form in his hands, crackling between his fingertips. His fingers clenched as though by a will of their own, and Gabriel suddenly felt like a spectator in his own body. His throat quivered as laughter filled the room.

Gabriel, this is not your destiny, the voice came again, stronger now.

A growl rose from Gabriel's chest as his eyes searched the room. He spun, throwing out his arms. Lightning leapt outwards, catching on the bed, the wardrobe, the walls. It raged around him, burning away the meagre contents of Enala's room.

"*Where are you?*" he raged.

Someplace you can never harm me, sadness touched the voice.

The voice cut through the power, finding Gabriel deep within his conscious. A tingle of recognition touched him and he clung to the words, pulling himself back towards the light. He struggled to remember the speaker, but his memories came in bursts now, burned away by the throb of magic.

"*Who are you?*" words grated from his mouth in a metallic screech.

Gabriel's eyes slid to the *Soul Blade*, fighting the pull of the magic. The veins of his arm stood out stark against his skin, glowing blue in the light of the sword. But he saw now the colour of the *Soul Blade* had changed, the blue of the Sky tainted by darkness.

And still the power raced up his arm, crashing upon his consciousness, pushing him down.

What is happening to me? He screamed in his mind, his jaw clamped shut, locked by the forces surging within him.

It will take you, Gabriel, the voice came again, a desperate edge to its tone. *Unless you let me help you.*

How? Gabriel could feel himself teetering on the edge, an infinite precipice dangling beneath him.

Relax your mind, and let me in, the voice demanded.

Gabriel swallowed, struggling to breathe as energy crackled in his chest. The God magic was everywhere now, burning, crackling, overwhelming. He fought it still, desperate to break free. Slowly the voice's command seeped through to him.

No, Gabriel cried into the emptiness within. *I will be lost.*

It is the only way.

Shuddering, Gabriel felt the magic welling again, the power gathering to sweep him away. Unable to fight any longer, Gabriel succumbed to the voice's command, and let go.

As his mind relaxed, a brilliant flash erupted behind his eyes. He felt the God power flee before it, racing back into the darkness of the *Soul Blade*, and then the world turned white.

For a long time Gabriel drifted, his mind afloat on the empty white. He knew he was lost, adrift in a foreign land, but somehow he could not find the will to care. He felt no worry, no dark touch of emotion to colour his thoughts. There was only the light, the unending space. It had been a long time since he'd felt such peace.

Closing his eyes, Gabriel gave himself to the feeling.

"Gabriel," it was the voice again, calm now, the panic gone.

Reluctantly, Gabriel opened his eyes to search out the source. The absolute white still stretched out in every direction, but he was no longer alone. A man walked towards him, striding through the emptiness as though a bricked path lay beneath his booted feet. He wore a blue shirt and tight black pants in the fashion of a sailor, though his white hair was well kept and his face clean-shaven. His ice blue eyes found Gabriel's, and held them.

"Jurrien", he whispered, remembering the God from the battle in Sitton. "What happened? How are you here?"

Jurrien's face darkened. "What one might expect, when someone without magic tangles with such an artefact. You have no power of your own, Gabriel, not even a touch of magic waiting to be born. Without it, your body had no defence against the magic within the *Soul Blade.*"

Gabriel shuddered. "Enala… the same thing happened to her when she touched the other blade. But Antonia did not come to her. Why?"

Jurrien frowned. "I do not know. I cannot sense much of the outside world; only what the wielder of the *Soul Blade* allows. But I have been saving my strength, preparing myself for a moment when I might be needed. When I felt the God magic taking you I thought it would be best to intervene. But my power is all but spent now…"

"Antonia had already come once, for Eric," Gabriel breathed. "She had nothing left to save Enala."

"Ay, my sister has always had a soft spot for the descendants of Aria's line. I cannot imagine her willingly sitting by while one of Aria's children was lost to her God magic."

Gabriel smiled. "Thank you, Jurrien. I hope you don't come to regret using your strength to save me. But you will not be in here much longer. The fortress' Magickers are working on a way to free you from the *Soul Blade.*"

"They will not succeed. Not unless…" the God trailed off, then waved a hand. "No, our bodies have been destroyed, returned to the earth as we have returned to spirit. We are Gods no longer."

Despair touched Gabriel then, seeping up from wherever his body lay back in reality. "But we need you, Jurrien. We cannot defeat Archon without you."

"You will find a way. You humans have never ceased to amaze us, even when we watched you only as spirits."

"How?" Gabriel shook his head. "Archon is too powerful."

Jurrien only smiled. "Together. You will defeat him together, Gabriel. The Three Nations joined as one."

Gabriel's shoulders slumped as he looked into the God's icy eyes. "We cannot leave you here, trapped forever," he looked around "Wherever here is."

"This is the spirit realm, of sorts," Jurrien answered. "Though it has been warped, a part of it twisted and broken off into the *Soul Blade*, ensuring a spirit can never truly depart."

"Am I trapped here too then?" Gabriel swallowed at the thought.

"No," Jurrien shook his head. "You are not truly here. Your body still waits for you back in Fort Fall. I only brought your spirit here to protect it from the God magic."

Gabriel breathed a long sigh. "Thank you, Jurrien. Thank you for sacrificing the last of your strength to save me," he paused, sensing the God still held something back. "Are you sure we cannot free you?"

Jurrien smiled. "Forget us, Gabriel. Our time is done. We cannot return, not without sacrificing more than I am prepared to ask. I will offer you only this: if the time comes when you have nowhere left to turn, nowhere to run, look again to the *Soul Blade*. The answer will come to you then," the God raised his hand. "Farewell, Gabriel."

Gabriel opened his mouth to argue, but Jurrien was already fading, the white world falling away.

Enala's heart raced as she fled the room, the mad laughter

of her friend chasing after her. A boom came from behind, followed by a wave of heat. She spun around a corner and leapt for the stairwell, thumping down the wooden steps as flames licked at her heels.

Another boom shook the air and a wave rippled down the stairs, shattering the boards beneath her feet. She stumbled on a jagged edge and went tumbling down the last flight, arms raised to protect herself. Then she was up, swinging herself into the corridor and racing for the outer doors.

Other men and women filled the hall, stumbling towards the exit, the healthy carrying the injured. Most of the army remained on the wall awaiting the next attack though, and Enala realised there were not enough able-bodied to carry all the wounded. Panic gripped her chest as another roar came from overhead.

Racing outside, Enala spun to face the building. Flames poured from the upstairs windows and thick smoke stained the sky. A crash came from inside as walls began to collapse. The blaze was spreading far too quickly – the building would collapse long before it could be evacuated.

Enala cursed her hesitation when she'd seen Gabriel standing over the *Soul Blades.* She should have grabbed him, tackled him, done whatever it took to stop him. But she had not even had time to grab the other *Soul Blade*. Now they had lost the God power it contained, and only the Sword of Light could match the power flooding through Gabriel's body.

Overhead the noonday sun streamed down on the clearing between the walls, but its heat was nothing compared to that of the burning building. Screams came from within and Enala knew she could not hesitate any longer. Something had to be done, or innocent lives would be lost.

As people streamed past her, fleeing the burning building, Enala reached down to the power burning within her. Its red light rose at her touch, snapping at her mind, but she had no patience for its wilful nature now. Clenching it with a will of iron, she released her mind and opened her spirit eyes.

Staring at the building, she saw the eerie glow of the flames and reached out for it with her magic. Taking a firm grip of her power, she soared closer. Lines of magic stretched out from her, wrapping around the flames and binding them to her will. They fought against her, desperate for freedom, to feed their ravenous hunger, but Enala refused to give in. Gritting her teeth, she pulled the ropes tighter, and hurled them skyward.

Screams came from around her as flames rose from the barracks and took to the sky, soaring over their heads towards the wall. Embers drifted down and the crowd flinched back as one, panic spreading through their ranks. But the flames did not fall, and a moment later they disappeared beyond the curve of the wall, tumbling into the wasteland beyond.

"What's happening?" Eric's shout came from beside her.

Enala drew back to her body. "It's Gabriel," she gasped, her thoughts still half with her magic. "He picked up the *Soul Blade.*"

Eric swore and reached for the Sword of Light. Flames lit the blade as he drew it, sizzling in the air, and she raised an eyebrow. "I don't think we need more of that," she offered.

Shaking his head, Eric closed his eyes and the white fire died away. Beads of sweat sprang out on Eric's forehead and his breathing quickened.

"Are you okay?" she sensed the tingle of power from the building and knew the flames were growing again.

Eric shook his head. "No. I… I'm still exhausted from the fight. But I have it under control. It's just a good thing I didn't use my magic in the battle."

"Can you help?" Enala asked, nodding at the glow of fire coming from the upper windows.

Eric flashed a smile. "We'll find out soon enough."

He lifted the Sword and pointed it at the building. Enala closed her eyes and released her spirit again, pulling her magic with her. The fire leapt as her magic touched it, hungry to devour everything within reach. She sensed the surge of magic thumping in her ears and knew Eric was using the Sword's power to do the same.

Together they wrapped their magic about the fire. A muffled roar came from the building as the roof collapsed and the flames rushed outwards, breaking free of their grasp. Enala raced after them, flinging out hooks of energy to pull them back. Slowly the flames began to calm, surrendering to their will.

As one they pulled the flames skyward and hurled them across the wall. As they disappeared beyond the wall the air grew still. Voices whispered around them as the injured continued to be carried from the building. Then another boom of thunder came and Enala sensed fresh flames take light.

Sweat beading her forehead, Enala threw her spirit back into the conflict. Beside her she sensed Eric's own determination, but worried for his soul. Whatever he said, using the Sword clearly cost him. And her own strength was already wavering. They could not keep this up forever.

Still they kept on, determined to save the injured souls still fleeing the building. Overhead a river of fire streaked the sky, rising from the barracks to fall on the desert beyond the wall. Enala panted for breath, desperate for water in the sweltering heat of the flames. The air was growing thin and her muscles burned as though she had run a hundred miles. Her mind swam, crying out for relief.

Then with a final boom, the lightning died away to nothing. Silence fell as the last of the flames disappeared and a hush fell across the crowd. As one they turned to the building, waiting to see what would come next.

Enala sank to her knees, swallowing a mouthful of air, her throat like sandpaper. Eric sat down beside her, his fingers clenched on the dry ground. He gasped, his face pale and his eyes ringed by shadow.

"What happened?" Inken appeared beside them, sweat running down her forehead.

"Gabriel," Enala croaked.

Before Inken could reply a whisper spread through the crowd. Enala turned, seeking out the source of the disruption. They sat at the front of the gathering, nearest to the barracks, so it only took Gabriel two steps to reach them. His eyes were clear now, empty of the darkness from earlier, though they were ringed by exhaustion. His clothes had all but burned away and his skin had bubbled in places, unprotected against the fire.

He stumbled as he reached them, almost falling before staggering to a halt. He looked down at them, his eyes filled with fear and wonder.

"Jurrien," he murmured. "I saw him."

CHAPTER 15

Inken strode down the empty stone corridors of Fort Fall, shivering as a cool breeze swept through an open window. Three days had passed since Gabriel had picked up the *Soul Blade,* and the mood of the fortress was now teetering on a fine balance. Hundreds had witnessed the power wielded by Eric and Enala to save the barracks and those inside from the fire, but others whispered about what had happened afterwards, of the man who had been last to stumble from the building.

Even May had taken some convincing just to keep Gabriel from the hangman's noose. As it was he had been locked away until the Magickers could confirm the dark magic had truly left him. Eric and Enala had not had the strength for the task. The magic they'd spent saving the infirmary had cost them dearly and the two had spent the last few days confined to their beds.

For the rest of them though, the last three days had been filled with the ring of blades and screams of combat. Archon's forces hardly paused for breath now, the enemy coming night and day to climb the walls and die beneath the defenders' blades. Each attack would continue for long, gruelling hours. And each time the enemy would be fresh, while Inken struggled to find the strength to lift her blade again.

Exhaustion clung to her very bones now. They fought in shifts, rosters of men and women taking turns to hold the wall, but even so the defenders were lagging. Even with the extra soldiers from Lonia, there were only so many of them, and the long hours of battle sucked the strength from her soul.

Their only source of hope was the impending arrival of the Trolan army. The ten thousand swords they brought would provide a welcome relief, and the Trolans were renown throughout the Three Nations as fighters. Word from their army said they would arrive tomorrow.

Until then though, it was up to their weary arms to hold back the black tide outside. Inken clenched her bow tight, drawing comfort from the firm wood. Her sabre slapped at her side as she moved. She had lost count of the number of men that had fallen to her blade. It was all a daze now. All that mattered was staying alive, keeping out of reach of the swords and axes of the enemy, and the arrows flashing up from below.

In truth, even with her skill she would have fallen long ago without Caelin and Alan. They fought together as a unit, smashing through any resistance the enemy could mount, the big man's strength providing them an anchor in the chaos.

She saw him now, a wide grin spreading above his greying beard. Caelin stood beside him in the gates from the citadel, waiting for her arrival. It was their shift again, their turn to hold the fortress against the evil of the north. Feeling the weight of her bow in her hand, Inken hoped she had enough strength left to survive the day.

"You okay, missy?" concern edged Alan's voice as his soft eyes inspected her.

Inken shook her head and straightened. “Only tired. I hope the Trolans arrive early; it’s about time they had a turn against the buggers.”

She felt a hand on her shoulder. She looked up, expecting Alan to dismiss her back to the citadel. But the big man only smiled. “Just remember, stay close, missy.”

Inken opened her mouth and then closed it, fighting back tears. There was such a kindness in Alan’s eyes she found herself lost for words, unable to respond to the compassion there. Choking out an unintelligible response, she pushed past them, wiping tears from her eyes when she thought they would not see.

Where did that come from? She cursed her weakness and swallowed the emotion. Turning, she called back to them. “Well, what are you waiting for, boys? Don’t tell me the years are catching up to you?”

Alan’s booming laugh chased after her, bringing a smile to her face. Together they marched through the gates of the first two walls, glancing up at the men stationed on each. All three were manned now, ensuring if one fell there would be enough to hold the others from a sudden rush by the enemy.

At last the outer wall loomed ahead. Inken’s eyes lingered on the ruined barracks as they moved past, remembering the stream of flames that had leapt from the building into the sky. Not even Enala and Eric’s best efforts had been able to save the barracks, but hundreds had been able to escape in the time they’d bought with their magic.

When the building had finally collapsed, the company had made their way into the ruin. The stench had been overwhelming, sending rescuers staggering back into the open air. But there was something they needed to retrieve, though Inken would rather have left the cursed things where they lay.

The *Soul Blades*.

She shuddered as she remembered uncovering them, finding them untouched amongst the wreckage. The blades still glowed with the eerie colours of the magic trapped inside, bathing her with their power. But she felt no desire to wield that power. It was a curse she was glad to avoid.

Gabriel had passed on Jurrien's words, that the Gods could not be returned to this world. Enala had paled then, stumbling away, open terror on her face. The rest of them stood in silence, unable to find an answer to the news. From this point on, the Three Nations stood alone against the might of Archon.

Shaking her head, Inken turned her thoughts back to the task at hand. There was no point stewing over matters beyond her control. She did not have the power to face the dark magic wielded by Archon, but she had her bow and her sword. War at least she excelled at, and she did not intend to lose that battle.

Silence carried down from overhead as they began their ascent to the ramparts. Inken breathed a sigh of relief, glad at least that the fighting had not yet started. Determined as she was, a few extra moments of rest would be welcome.

As they reached the top they moved quickly to their station and sank as one to the cold ground. Inken leaned back against the crenulations and looked up. The sky was an endless blue and the air was crisp and dry. A cool winter breeze blew across the wall, but in the shelter of the battlements they remained warm. Any other day and she would have called it beautiful. Today though she could think of little else but death. Blood stained the stones around them, reminding her all too vividly of the violence to come.

"Another lovely day at Fort Fall," she commented wryly.

Caelin laughed, stretching in the sun. "Almost makes me wish for a swim," he said, nodding towards the distant surf. "Although it looks a little rough."

"Little man," Alan chuckled. "You don't have the stones for that water."

Caelin grinned back. "That sounds like a challenge, big man."

"Oh the arrogance of youth," Alan shot Inken a wink and she smiled back. "You think the wolf worries when the puppy barks?"

"A challenge it is then," Caelin slapped his hand on his knee and pointed to the far off water. "When this business is done, we'll see who lasts the longest."

Alan raised an eyebrow. "Five silvers say you don't last five minutes."

"Deal!" Caelin held out his hand and they shook.

Inken grinned at them. They had spent most of their spare time over the last two days in similar debates and she had already lost count of their wagers. The contests between them would be something to look forward to after all this; if any of them survived. She had joined in more than a few bets herself, but today she could not find the energy. Weariness gripped her soul, and she yearned to return to the citadel and Eric.

She still hadn't told him; told anyone but the king for that matter. She was not sure why she hesitated, but the knowledge felt personal, a secret she was not yet ready to share. Perhaps because when the truth came out, it would become all too real.

And despite her trust in Eric and Enala, she struggled to find hope for their future. Even without his army, Archon was just too powerful. Antonia and Jurrien, with all their knowledge and power, had not been able to stop him last time. Archon had crushed them like insects beneath his boots.

Even with the Sword of Light, the Gods had only had the strength to banish him.

Horns sounded along the wall and with a long sigh Inken forced aside her doubt. There would be time for that later. For now, she had another battle to survive. Putting her hands beneath her, she pushed herself to her feet and hefted her bow.

From below came the familiar screams of the horde as they rushed forward to meet their deaths. Closing her eyes, Inken let the sound wash over her, trying to calm her racing thoughts. How she longed for the peace and quiet of the forest, to return to the glade in Dragon Country where she and Eric had first made love. If only they could leave all this behind.

But it was not to be. Biting her lip, Inken reached down and strung her bow. The familiar call went out along the line, ordering the archers to the fore. Below, the enemy dead covered the ground, marking the range of the defenders' arrows. Then the order to fire came and the first wave of arrows rose into the sky.

Inken could not have said how long the assault continued, only that her arms and legs were aching and that a dozen men or more had fallen to her sword by the time the enemy horns sounded their retreat. The whole time Alan and Caelin had stood strong beside her, their contrasting styles of brute force and subtle skill unstoppable. Together they held the centre of the line, their courage providing the backbone of the defenders.

As the last of the enemy fell Inken stepped back from the edge, her breath coming in heavy gasps. The blade was heavy in her hand and she knew she was close to the end of her strength. Turning away, her stomach lurched. Unable to hold the nausea down, she stumbled to the backside of the wall and hurled her breakfast over the edge. An acrid sting burned in her throat as another convulsion shook her. The strength fled her legs and she slid to the ground, gasping as she leaned against the cold stone.

"Inken!" Caelin was at her side in an instant. Alan was not far behind.

She waved a hand to show she was okay, but another wave of sickness swept through her and she found herself too preoccupied to reply. Tears stung her eyes as she struggled to breath between heaves.

"I'm okay," she croaked at last.

"What's wrong?" Caelin gripped her by the shoulder and forced her to look at him.

She saw the concern in his eyes and tried not to look away. "Not now," she whispered. Taking a hand from Alan, she struggled back to her feet. "Are they done?"

Caelin nodded. "For now," but even as he spoke, the horns began to sound again.

Around them, murmurs of fear came from the defenders.

"They're attacking again, already?" Inken groaned. She searched deep inside for some forgotten store of strength, but she had little left to give. Her energy was spent, stripped away by the endless days of combat.

"Ay," Alan stood at the edge of the ramparts, staring out at the enemy. "They're coming. But not men. Beasts."

Pain twisted in Inken's chest as her heart fell to the pit of her stomach. "The beasts?" she breathed.

She moved with Caelin to stand beside Alan, her eyes sweeping out to search the plains below. Far in the distance, but closing at a frightening speed, came a host of creatures born from the pits of their worst nightmares.

The Raptors led the charge, their razor sharp teeth glinting in jaws wide enough to swallow a man's head whole. Thick black tails stretched out behind them as their massive feet carried them across the open ground. Behind them

Inken glimpsed flashes of fur and scale, teeth and claw, but a cloud of dust obscured the details of the other creatures.

They carried no ropes or ladders – they did not need them. Tales from Archon's war told of how they'd scaled these walls, how their claws had dug deep into the mortar between the stones and carried them up to the defenders above.

"Where are the dragons?" Inken whispered.

Before the others could reply the horns sounded again, three long blasts echoing back to the citadel. Beyond the dragons had nested these last three days, lying in wait for when they were needed most.

Inken's heart soared as the first roar carried to her ears and the golden beasts rose into view, wings beating hard in the frigid air. She grinned, turning back to the oncoming horde. Let the beasts come; the dragons would burn them where they stood.

The crack of wings came from overhead and a shadow fell across the wall. Inken looked up in time to see the golden body of Enduran swoop past, the rest of his tribe following close behind.

Rest easy, little one. We will take care of these creatures. The great globe of the dragon's eye found her as he spoke in her mind. Then the dragons rose higher into the sky, sweeping out towards the oncoming beasts.

Inken grinned and a desperate longing rose in her chest. She wanted to be with them, soaring into the sky on the back of a dragon, ready to rain death down on those below.

The dragons soared past the first ranks of black creatures, then spun in the air, their wings folding as they dived towards the beasts below. They fell like darts, flames billowing out ahead of them as they unleashed death on Archon's creatures. An inferno ignited below them, roaring through the horde, consuming all in its path.

A cheer rose up from the defenders as Archon's beasts

disappeared into the firestorm. Along the wall, men and women embraced and raised their swords in salute. Inken watched with quiet joy as the dragons rose back into the sky and wheeled about, preparing for another attack.

Then she frowned as beasts started to leap from the inferno. From the distance she could not see what had happened, but it appeared as though the following ranks of creatures had already overtaken their fallen leaders.

The dragons dived again, catching the next wave in the white hot heat of their fire, and again the defenders cheered. But Inken watched closely now, a tingle of alarm racing down her spine. The beasts were closer now, and her stomach twisted as Raptors exploded from the columns of fire. Flames licked at their scales but they appeared unmarked.

Inken clenched her bow tight as the rest of the creatures followed, leaping through the inferno in an endless flood. Smoke clung to the plain below, obscuring the horde beyond. But the vanguard was in full view now, the Raptors leaping across the bodies of the enemy, their eyes locked on the defenders above.

The dragons' fire had done nothing. Somehow Archon had outmanoeuvred them, casting his dark magic over his creatures to protect them from the flames. And now they were closing on the wall, already within bowshot, and still the defenders stood frozen.

Inken looked up as the dragons roared and came again. But a flash from the enemy camp drew Inken's eyes. Beyond the columns of smoke, a ball of power gathered in the air. She opened her mouth to scream a warning, but it was already too late. The ball raced upwards, accelerating as the dragons whirled to avoid it. One lagged a second slower than the rest and the ball of energy caught it in the chest.

Darkness exploded outwards, enveloping the dragon in a shroud of black. Within the cloud the dragon stiffened, its wings locked in place, and without so much as a sound, it plummeted to the earth.

Along the wall, the defenders heard the sickening crunch as it struck the ground.

Howls of sorrow came from the sky and as one the dragons turned and retreated beyond the walls of the fortress.

I'm sorry, little one, Enduran's voice was heavy with despair. *His power is too great; we cannot stop them.*

Thank you for trying, Enduran, Inken thought back. *Join us on the wall. We will fight them together.*

A roar of agreement carried down and then the defenders were crowding backwards to make room for their allies to land. Only ten could fit atop the outer wall; the rest took up stations on the other battlements or the citadel itself.

Even with their support, Inken could sense the fear of the defenders, spreading like a sickness through their ranks.

Then May's voice carried over the whispers. "Archers, to the fore. Nock arrows!"

The calm in her voice cut through the panic and steadied their courage. Inken stepped up with the other archers, shaking off Caelin's arm.

"We have to stop them, Caelin. It will take everything we have to hold them back," she reached down and swung a fresh quiver of arrows onto her back.

Drawing an arrow, Inken nocked and sighted at the nearest Raptor. As May's cry to fire rang out she loosed, watching with satisfaction as her arrow found its mark. But the Raptor did not even stumble as the shaft embedded itself in its shoulder. It came on, black scales shining in the light of the flames behind it.

Inken nocked again but did not wait for May's command – volleys would not stop these creatures. Her next two arrows found the creature's neck and shoulder again, and finally the beast slowed. Its head swung around, the great jaws tearing the shaft from its neck.

Sighting, Inken put another arrow through its neck. This time as it struck, the Raptor tripped and went tumbling across the rocky ground. It took a long time to get back up and Inken prayed it would no longer have the strength to climb.

She emptied her quiver into two more Raptors before the first beasts reached the wall, and then tossed her bow aside. Drawing her sabre, she stepped back between Caelin and Alan, and waited.

"Up for this, missy?" Alan asked softly.

Inken nodded. "Ask me again after we see the damn things off."

"Just stay between us, Inken," Caelin grunted. "Eric will have our heads if we don't bring you back safely."

"You two concentrate on keeping yourselves alive," Inken replied, though fear flickered in her chest. "I can take care of myself."

She saw her own fear reflected in Caelin's eyes as he nodded back.

"Right then," Alan raised his voice so those around him could hear. "Let's show these beasts what we're made of!" Alan raised his war hammer and a ragged cheer went up from around them. Inken could see no fear in the big man's eyes, only the same steady determination she had seen in the last few days, and drew strength from his courage.

Silence fell then as they stood together, listening to the scrambling of claws on stone.

The Raptors appeared in a rush, surging over the crenulations to fall on the ranks of defenders. Along the wall the dragons roared their defiance and the defenders rushed forward to meet the beasts.

Inken dove backwards as a Raptor's claws slashed for her

throat. She stumbled on the bloody bricks but Caelin hurled himself into the fray, his sword slashing for the beast's head. It bounded out of reach, then the thick black tail swung round to catch Caelin in the chest. He staggered back, the breath wheezing from his lungs.

Recovering her balance, Inken lunged in. Her sabre lanced towards the creature's midriff, point poised to strike, but the Raptor leapt to the side and sparks flew as her blade struck stone. She flinched as the Raptor attacked then, the giant jaws stretched wide to tear off her head.

A strong hand grasped her by the collar and jerked her backwards, then Alan charged into the fray, his hammer crunching into the Raptor's jaws. It roared, staggering sideways and then leapt to avoid his next blow. The beaded eyes followed Alan as he turned. Charging in, the creature snapped at Alan's face, but his fist swung round to catch the creature's chin. To Inken's shock, the blow staggered the Raptor and Alan stepped clear.

Before it could recover, the big man turned back, hammer raised, and charged. The Raptor growled, swinging to meet him, but the slick stone slipped beneath its claws. Alan raised *kanker* high as the creature struggled for balance, and brought it down on the Raptor's skull with a crunch.

Black blood splattered the bricks as the beast collapsed beneath the blow and started to thrash. Alan retreated out of range as the wicked claws tore blindly at empty air.

Inken sucked in a breath and joined him as another Raptor hauled itself into view. Caelin was back on his feet too, standing on Alan's other side. Together they attacked, weapons slicing for the creature's stomach. It scrambled to face them, its claws flicking out to turn aside Inken's blade. Its other talon swept past Alan's guard and sliced through his jacket.

Alan staggered backwards but Caelin leapt in, dancing

past its claws to bring his sword down on its neck. The blade cut deep and the Raptor roared, turning to crush the foe that dared to harm it. As it turned, Inken darted in and drove her sword down into the same place Caelin had struck. It roared again and spun, but she was already retreating out of range.

A final blow from Caelin finished the creature.

As it collapsed, Alan stepped up and crushed its skull with his hammer. Looking around, he swore softly under his breath.

Inken followed his gaze and swallowed hard. The beasts swarmed across the wall, leaping from the crenulations to swamp the defenders. The climb did nothing to slow them, and only the pockets of men around the dragons were holding their own. But one of the golden creatures had already fallen, brought down by a mass of black-clawed beasts. The others fought on, their massive claws and teeth smashing the creatures from the wall.

Even so, the odds were quickly turning against the defenders as the flood of dark beasts continued unabated. In places their people were in open retreat. They fled down the staircases, their exposed backs easy pickings for the beasts above.

"The wall is lost," Caelin roared. "We have to retreat," a trumpet sounded with his words, the long, drawn out note of defeat. It was the first time Inken had heard the call, but she knew its meaning well enough. May had echoed Caelin's thoughts and sounded the retreat.

Inken looked at the wide open space between them and the next wall. It was a long way. How long would the gates stay open for them? Could they make it?

A growl came from behind her and she swung around. New creatures were pulling themselves onto the battlements, catching up with the vanguard of Raptors that had led the charge. Two crept towards them now. The first wore the black fur coat of a feline, its bright yellow eyes staring at them with hunger. The other was a lizard, its grey scales gleaming in the sun. It scrambled on all fours towards them, razor sharp rows of spines rippling along its back. The beasts growled, jaws opening to show rows of dagger-like teeth.

Inken raised her sabre, prepared to throw herself at the creatures, but Alan stepped between them.

"Go," he said calmly as he faced the beasts.

"*What?*" Inken yelled over the screams of the dying.

"Go, both of you," Alan spoke without turning, his eyes locked on the dark creatures. "I won't make the gates, but you two can," he risked a glance back. "Go, *live!* I never intended to leave this wall. I will not show these creatures my back. We part ways here, my friends."

Inken opened her mouth but could not find the words. Tears burned in her eyes as the weight of his decision fell on her shoulders. She could not let him do this, could not let him sacrifice himself for them.

"You don't have to do this!" a vice had closed around her chest but she managed to choke out the words.

Alan only smiled and turned away. "Go now, missy. *Kanker* and I have one last battle to fight, but you must live. I don't want to see you on the other side, not for a long time. *So go!*" he roared the last words as he charged, hammer raised high as the beasts leapt to meet him.

"Farewell, my friend," Caelin murmured.

"Farewell," tears streamed down Inken's face as Caelin grabbed her by the arm.

Together they turned and ran for the stairs.

CHAPTER 16

Caelin sat at the table, staring at his hands, his thoughts adrift on an ocean of sorrow. Another friend lost, another soul sacrificed so the rest of them might live. He could not stop the images from sweeping through his mind: Alastair lying on the beach, helpless beneath the sword of Balistor, Michael in Sitton, his eyes wide as the demon's *Soul Blade* took him in the chest. And now Alan, his life given to hold back the tide of Archon's creatures.

They had barely made it behind the second wall before the gates had swung closed. Inken and himself had been among the last of the defenders to reach safety, fending off a handful of creatures that had chased them across the killing field. The beasts had only turned back when they'd come within range of the defenders' arrows, allowing Inken and Caelin to turn and sprint the last fifty yards to safety.

There the men and women of Fort Fall had waited, breath held, and watched as the last pockets of defenders on the outer wall fell one by one. His heart twisted as he watched again the big man fighting alongside those others who had refused to retreat. Alan had mustered the last of the defenders around him, and together they had formed an island amidst the ocean of darkness.

They had fought longer than anyone could have imagined, dozens of the creatures falling beneath their blades. But there was no resisting the savagery of the beasts, and one by one the defenders had fallen. Alan had been the last, his hammer still raised in defiance as he was finally overwhelmed.

The council room was silent, empty but for May and the rest of their company. Their losses on the outer wall had been horrific and May's surviving officers were needed to command the defences in her absence. Their only relief had been the arrival of the Trolan forces yesterday evening. Their fresh soldiers had taken over the frontline defences, allowing the defenders a welcome respite.

Even so, morale was low. Yesterday Archon had shown them just how weak they truly were. In a single attack his beasts had swept them from the outer wall, and not dragon or sword or arrow had been able to halt their advance.

The silence stretched out, each of them sitting with heads bowed in respect for the ancient warrior and those others who had fallen. But Caelin knew they could not afford to brood long. The hopes of the living still rested on their shoulders. He did not intend to let them down.

"We need the *Soul Blades*," his voice cut through the silence, firm, desperate.

May nodded from beside him, lifting her chin from her hands. She had been unusually despondent, her sorrow clear for the men she had been forced to sacrifice, but she stood now and walked around the table.

"After Gabriel's discovery, I had the Magickers choose amongst themselves who would be best to wield Jurrien's blade," her eyes lingered on Gabriel, who had finally been freed after the battle. May had still argued against it, but there was no denying they needed every fighter they could get now.

"Have they chosen?" Eric spoke up.

"It seems so," May moved across to the door and leaned out.

A moment later a man appeared. He nodded as he entered, moving around the table to take an empty seat. He wore the blue robes of a Sky priest and his black hair was cropped short in the style of the army. Together they marked him as a battle Magicker, and the scars on his face suggested he was one of some experience.

His green eyes surveyed the table, lingering on each of them. "My name is Sylvander," he spoke in a soft, slippery voice. "I am a Sky Magicker, similar to yourself, Eric, but with only the power to control lightning. I hope I prove worthy of the challenge posed by the Storm God's magic."

Caelin's eyes slid to where the *Soul Blade* rested in the centre of the table. He had been trying to ignore its dark presence, but now the time had come to test its power. The dark blue glow shone across their faces, flickering in the eyes of his friends. Their fear hovered in the air, seeming to have a presence all of its own. The danger they faced was undeniable, but so was the fact they needed the power in that blade.

"Are you sure?" Enala asked. "You saw what happened to Gabriel. You know what happened to me. Are you sure you will be able to control it?"

A smile played across the man's face. "Reasonably confident. I grew up with this power. The Sky is a part of me, a part of my blood. It is as familiar to me as the back of my hand. The risk is low, for myself at least."

Caelin glanced at his hands and raised an eyebrow. "I hope you spend as much time practicing at magic as you apparently do studying your hands."

Sylvander chuckled and ran a hand through his hair. "A figure of speech, sergeant. Believe me when I say it was a unanimous decision amongst the Magickers to choose me."

"Very well then," May spoke with quiet authority, cutting through their hesitation. "Do it."

Sylvander nodded and reached across the table. His hand wrapped around the hilt of the *Soul Blade* and lifted it from the table. Light flashed from the black steel, glinting from the man's emerald eyes. Tension spread through the room. Caelin could almost taste the throb of power on the air.

The Magicker's eyes widened and his forehead wrinkled with concentration. Caelin gritted his teeth, holding his breath as he watched the battle playing out within the man. They needed this, needed all three God powers if they were to have a hope of victory.

Long minutes stretched out, the tension building within the council room as the lines on Sylvander's face deepened. He stood taut as wire, jaw clenched, veins bulging on his arm as the glow of the *Soul Blade* shone in his eyes.

Caelin jumped as the Magicker released his breath. Grinning, Sylvander looked around the room, and opened his mouth to speak.

But whatever he had been about to say never made it out of his mouth. A sudden crash shook the room and lightning exploded from the Magicker's chest. Blue light lit the room, blinding them all. The stench of smoke and burning flesh quickly followed, catching in Caelin's throat as he breathed.

Lightning danced around the room, narrowly missing them before dying to nothing, and Caelin silently gave thanks to Eric's magic, guessing the boy had protected them. Another boom shook the air, and then silence fell.

Ears ringing and half-blind, Caelin stumbled to his feet. He staggered across, desperate to see what had become of Sylvander.

He choked as he reached the spot where he'd last seen the Magicker. Acrid smoke clung to his nostrils and his stomach lurched. Where Sylvander had stood seconds before, only a pile of ash remained. The *Soul Blade* lay amidst the remains, its light dimmed back to a faint blue glow.

Gasping for breath, he turned away.

"What happened?" he croaked.

And then everything went black.

"What happened?" Eric heard Caelin speak over the ringing in his ears.

He blinked, trying to find Caelin through the stars dancing in his eyes. The room slowly came into focus, but something about it did not make sense. Eric closed his eyes again, willing his vision to clear, then looked around the table at his comrades.

Fear touched him as he realised why they had not replied. Caelin stood where Sylvander had disappeared, staring across the table, his mouth open as though to speak. But he did not move, did not so much as twitch.

Eric glanced across at Inken and May and found them still sitting in place, their faces twisted in fear, frozen in place by some dark spell.

Then Enala moved, turning to stare at Eric. Her face was pale and her hands clutched the oilskin wrapped around her own *Soul Blade* in a vice-like grip.

"What's happening?" she whispered.

Gabriel reached out and grasped her shoulder, shaking his head, his mouth wide with stark terror.

"I thought we should finally speak. In person," a voice spoke from behind them.

Eric spun, staring as a man stepped through the doorway.

He moved without sound, his black boots touching down without so much as a thud on the stone floor. A cloak of grey and orange feathers hung about his shoulders, the orange shimmering in the smoky air, so that it almost seemed the man were aflame. He wore a white doublet beneath the feathers, the pale skin of his hands appearing almost to fuse with the cloth.

His face was absent of any discernible wrinkle or imperfection, and there was an ageless way in which his eyes looked on them, as though he had lived a thousand years and more. He carried no weapon, but Eric could feel the power radiating through the room and knew this was no mortal man.

The man's dark blue eyes surveyed them each in turn, ignoring their frozen comrades. A warning screamed in Eric's head as the man's eyes reached him and he leapt to his feet, reaching for the Sword of Light. The man only waved, and Eric found his hand frozen, his fingers still an inch from the Sword's pommel. No matter how he strained, he could not reach the weapon.

"Come, come. Sit, let us talk!" he waved again and an invisible force pushed Eric back into his chair.

Looking around he saw the fear on Enala and Gabriel's faces as they strained against the same force. They looked up at the man, the devil that had strode unopposed into the depths of their fortress. Fear swamped Eric's every thought as he reached for his power and found nothing but a wall of darkness. With horror he realised they were helpless before this man's might, and knew beyond doubt who stood before them.

Archon had come.

The man laughed. "Such a quick mind, Eric," Archon's voice was soft but clear, without hint of emotion.

Eric opened his mouth, but only a low whine came out.

Fear had frozen his tongue, his wit, his magic. He could not find the courage to think.

"*You!*" Gabriel gave a strangled cry.

"Hello again, Gabriel," the man smiled. "I am pleased to see you here. You have done well, my son. Exceeded all my expectations."

"You are Archon," Enala interrupted and Eric felt a surge of pride for his sister. "You murdered my parents," hate twisted Enala's face and he could see her straining against whatever force constrained them.

Swallowing, Eric searched for his own courage, trying to reason away his fear. Surely Archon had not come to kill them – else they would already be dead. He shuddered at the man's power, to have walked alone through all their forces to come so casually to this room.

Archon moved to stand over Enala. He reached down and brushed the strand of copper hair from her face, a faint smile on his lips.

"Oh my dear, Enala, how the world has hurt you."

Enala flinched back from his touch, a shiver running through her. "*No!*" her shriek was pure desperation, a helpless cry against the dark creature standing in their midst.

"I am sorry," Archon moved away. "Sorry you have all had to suffer so," he approached Eric, his power overwhelming, though he was not a large man. "That you have had to run and flee amongst these weak minded fools," he cast a hand at their frozen companions.

"Why are you here?" Eric somehow found the strength to speak, grating the question through clenched teeth. "It was you who made us suffer."

Archon only smiled. "It was the Gods who made you suffer, sweet child. They are the source of all our suffering. They are the reason my people cower in the desert, their children dying at the breast for want of sustenance. Since the birth of the Gods, the so-called Three Nations have cowered beneath their yoke, bowing to the power they created. Only I dared rebel, to speak out against their tyranny."

"You slaughtered thousands of our people!" Enala cursed him.

Eric's heart raced as he strained to break the force holding him. He reached again for his magic but found only darkness, an all-consuming fog lying between himself and his power.

Archon bowed his head, but he wore a smile on his lips. "They left me no choice. I wanted only to see the Gods fall; to free us all from their power. But your people stood against me, time and time again."

"Why?" Eric looked up at the fire in Gabriel's voice. "Why have you haunted me? What do you *want?*"

Eric shivered at the truth behind the words, as he realised it had not been a demon haunting Gabriel, but Archon himself. He had been with them from the start, twisting the strings of their fates to his own desire.

Archon's eyes softened as they looked on the blacksmith. "Gabriel, my child. I have only ever tried to help you, to free you from the bounds of your mortality. It saddens me so, to watch my own blood waft through life without magic, without power."

The blood in Eric's veins froze at Archon's words. *His blood?*

"*I am not your child!*" Gabriel growled, the veins bulging on his forehead.

Archon laughed. "Do you not feel blessed? To know the blood of my family courses through your veins? How else could you have survived my *Soul Blade*?" he waved a hand at the pile of ash that had been Sylvander.

"Jurrien protected me," Gabriel snapped back, a snarl on his lips.

"Of course, of course," Archon waved a hand. "The Storm God saved you from his God magic. But *that*," he pointed. "That is what happens when one without my blood attempts to use my *Soul Blades*," Eric shuddered as the man's laughter swept the room.

Then his stomach twisted with nausea at another thought. "Enala used the *Soul Blade*," he whispered.

Archon grinned, leaning down to run a hand through her hair. "She did," he smiled, stroking her cheek as she struggled to free herself from his touch. "My sweet daughter, so strong, so beautiful."

A primal growl rose from the depths of Enala's throat. Archon chuckled as he straightened. "And Eric, my son, your strength has surpassed every challenge I placed before you."

"*Why?*" Eric hissed through bared teeth. "*How?*"

Archon sighed. "The Gods would not have told you; they have never been good at truth. They would not have wished for you to know it was my brother, Artemis, who first knelt before them. For his fealty, they named him as the Trolan king."

Eric shuddered as Archon continued. "For the longest time I hated them, those descendants of my blood who stood against me. When I rose to power I sent out my creatures to hunt them down and their line was all but destroyed. Only Thomas and his sister Aria survived."

"And they did all in their power to destroy you," Enala grated.

"Did they?" Archon's cold laughter filled the room. "It was not enough. Thomas' line fell to my magic or turned to my side."

"But Aria's children survived," Eric countered.

"Ay. She and her descendants were clever, always a step ahead of my hunters. Whenever I thought the line had been snuffed out, a new branch sprang up. Gabriel, for instance, is a rather distant cousin of a cousin to you," Archon sighed. "Eventually I was forced to settle on a new plan – to destroy the Gods and take their power, ensuring your line's survival no longer mattered when I rose again."

"Then why did you haunt me?" Gabriel growled.

"Because as my plan changed, I saw an opportunity. I have no wish to rule your Three Nations alone, children. With the Gods destroyed, I need faithful souls to rule in their stead. And who better than my own blood?"

Eric shook with anger, with fear; but as he looked up into the blue eyes of Archon, the same eyes he shared with his sister, he found his courage. "Why do you hate them so?" he hissed, refusing to cower before the man's icy stare. "What could they have done to you, what could have been so awful to feed your hate for so many centuries?"

Archon stared back and for a second Eric thought he saw a trace of humanity in those empty eyes. "They took everything from me."

At the words, Archon raised his hand and black light flashed across the room.

Before Eric could so much as cry out, the world turned to black.

CHAPTER 17

Enala blinked as her vision returned and she found herself standing atop a great canyon. Sheer granite walls stretched down to a winding river far below, while behind her the white peaks of snow-capped mountains stretched up into the sky. A cold wind blew across her neck and swept down into the ravine, bending the long grass on the plains beside the river. The rumble of tumbling water came from a nearby waterfall, the water racing over the edge to fall to the stones far below.

Then the first echo of thumping boots carried to her ears and she turned to look down. Men were marching around the bend in the canyon, heading upstream away from her. The blue of their cloaks marked them as Trolans, but there were far, far more here than the host that had joined them at Fort Fall.

Stumbling backwards, Enala searched the clifftops for her friends, but found herself alone. She bit back a scream as the world suddenly jolted and she was drawn backwards. For a second she watched the ground shift beneath her feet, and then with a thrill of fear she remembered the yawning drop behind her.

Diving to the ground, Enala threw herself at a nearby boulder, scrambling for purchase. But her hands sank through the rock as though it were empty air and then she was out over the edge, the five hundred foot drop stretching out beneath her.

Yet somehow she did not fall. Enala stared down at the canyon as she drifted in the open air. Picking up speed, she found herself racing towards the distant head of the army. Straining her eyes, Enala stared at the men as she soared over the never-ending mass of humanity. The canyon twisted and turned, the terrain below shifting from open grass, to swamp, to scattered fields of boulders and back. It made no difference to the soldiers. They marched on, eyes fixed on the distant peaks rising to the east.

Finally the canyon floor rose sharply towards a narrow pass between the cliffs. There, the green cloaked army of the Lonians waited, and she knew where she was.

And when.

Swallowing, Enala watched as the ancient army of Trola charged up the hill towards the Lonians. Somehow, she now found herself watching the Great Wars of a thousand years before, in the time just before the ancient priests of Lonia and Trola had joined their magic and given birth to the Gods.

The clash of steel carried up to her as the two ancient forces met, the roar of their voices drowning out the screams of the dying. The Lonians buckled before the ferocity of the Trolan charge, their line bending back into the narrow pass. Beyond, Enala saw thousands upon thousands of Lonian men waiting to join the battle.

Chaos enveloped the mountain pass as Magickers from both sides joined the fray. Enala shuddered as waves of fire tore through the helpless ranks of soldiers below. Caverns ripped through the earth, swallowing hundreds into the dark depths below, and lightning rained down from the blackened sky.

The destruction was beyond all imagining.

Yet Enala knew the worst was still to come. This could only be the final, catastrophic battle, when the best and brightest souls of the two nations had been lost to a great conflagration, to wild magic gone horribly wrong.

Slowly, inexorably, the Trolans pushed the Lonians back, until their blue cloaks filled the mountain pass. But even as they fell the Lonians refused to yield, stabbing out at their enemy's legs even as their lifeblood fled them. Enala could feel the hate radiating up from the soldiers, fed by the ancient enmity between the two nations.

Then she felt it, the pulse of a magic far stronger than anything she had sensed so far. She turned and saw the green cloaks of the Lonian Magickers on the ridge above the pass. Light shone out around them, blue and green hues mixing to form a sickly yellow light.

The Trolan Magickers saw it too, for she felt the throb of their magic rising in response. A brilliant white rose from their ranks, spreading out to envelop their army. A trickle of horror touched her as she saw darkness mixing with the light and realised the Trolan's had gone beyond the three elements. They were using dark magic now, such was their desperation to halt the Lonian attack.

The opposing magics stretched across the sky, tongues of power flicking out to clash with one another. Thunder roared within the canyon, echoing off the narrow walls, but this time there was no lightning. A grumbling groan came from all around, rising up from the pits of the earth itself.

Still the Magickers kept on, unrelenting. From her vantage point above, Enala watched as they began to collapse, blood gushing from their mouths and ears. Yet the magic continued unabated, thrashing in the sky overhead. Bolts of pure energy raced out, disintegrating rock and wood and flesh alike.

Then the groans coming from the earth rose to a shriek, and the sheer walls of the canyon tore loose of their bounds. The ground shook, sending the men of both armies to their knees. Terrified eyes looked upwards as they realised the doom approaching them. With another roar, the granite cliffs of the canyon began to close.

Panic spread through the armies below. Enala looked to the Magickers, unable to believe they would sacrifice their own army to defeat the other. But she saw then it was too late, that the Magickers had already fallen. Their broken bodies writhed on the ground, caught in the last throes of death.

This was not by design. This was wild magic, its uncontrollable intent on only one thing.

Death.

Enala wanted to look away, to close her ears to the screams below. But whatever spell Archon had cast would not allow it, and she watched the horror unfold below, her stomach twisting in knots as men raced to escape the death grinding towards them. Some leapt for the cliffs, but they stood no hope of scaling that five hundred foot climb. Even the most skilled of climbers would struggle to reach the top in an hour.

These men only had minutes.

Tears rushed down Enala's face as she watched on in terror. This was far worse than anything she had ever seen, had ever imagined.

Others were fleeing down the valley, down the ever narrowing gap between the canyon walls. They would never make it though. The valley had been some twenty miles long – only the rear guard stood a chance of escape.

The last of the men below simply sat, the blue and green of their cloaks mixing, a final show of peace before the inevitable. Anguish twisted their faces as they hugged men they had tried to slaughter moments before, the truth of their senseless war laid bare. Their hate had driven them to this, driven them to this doom.

A strangled moan rose in Enala's throat as she finally lost sight of the men below, as the ravine snapped shut.

Then there was only silence.

The image faded then, and Enala found herself instead in a tiny room. Three priests sat in the centre, their robes representing each of the three elements of Magic. The Light, the Earth, the Sky.

A tingle of recognition raced up Enala's spine. She had read of this fateful meeting long ago, the meeting where the head priests of the three orders had come together and resolved to end the slaughter between their nations. The cost of the wild magic had been beyond anything ever seen before. An entire generation had been wiped from the world, and they were determined to ensure their people never suffered such a fate again.

Leaning closer, Enala listened to their words.

"It has never been done," an old man in blue robes whispered. "Never been attempted. Even with all of our orders, would such a feat even be possible?"

"I am happy to listen to other suggestions," the man in white snapped back. He looked around at the other two but found only silence. Closing his eyes, he ran a hand across his face. Stress lined his skin, seeming to age him twenty years. "We must be reined in – there is no other way. Our people are not worthy of the gift of magic."

The woman in green nodded, the weariness showing on

her face. "We know; there is no argument of that. But how can we make the spirits a reality? There is no substance to them, no power. What can we do, trap them in an object? That would only serve to place even greater power in the hands of men."

The man in white rubbed his eyes. "Of course not," he shook his head. "The spirits possess thought, have purpose. We know that – our orders have studied their presence for centuries. They must have autonomy, the ability to use their power as they see fit. When we bring them forth, they must take human form. They will be our rulers, our Gods."

"They are already Gods," the old man in blue snapped. "Whether the people recognise them or not. They govern the rules of magic – their power is unlimited."

"And yet their influence is limited to the spirit realm," the woman replied. "That must change."

"How?" the old man growled.

"Sacrifice," the others replied in unison.

Enala's heart gave a painful lurch as the three priests faded away. Within seconds a great hall of people had replaced them, but questions still whirred through her mind.

Gods, what did they do?

She had never heard of the Gods' birth involving sacrifice. Was that how the priests had done the impossible? By slaughtering innocent people?

Enala floated through the throngs of people packing the hall, unable to control her path. Finally she came to a halt in the centre of the hall where a ring of priests stood in a circle. The blue, green and white of their robes told her all three orders were present, united in this great task. Each member held their hands raised and their eyes were closed. Magic throbbed through the room, stirring in Enala's chest as the priests sought their power.

"It is time," the voice of the woman from the secret

meeting rose above the whispers. “You who have volunteered, who have chosen, step into the circle.”

Enala’s gut churned as men and women threaded between the priests to enter the ring. There were dozens of them; people of all age and size and class. Men in the tattered rags of the poor stood alongside the rich garments of the nobility, and white bearded men held the hands of young women, offering their silent support. Enala’s heart went out for their quiet bravery – that these people were willing to give their lives to cease the wars that had torn their world apart.

As the last of the volunteers stepped into the circle, Enala sensed the ebb of magic begin to grow. The priests’ voices rose in a slow chant, their words curling through the crowd like a breath of smoke. The language was unrecognisable, but the power in each syllable was could not be mistaken. The hall rang with magic, its throb beating across Enala’s mind like a drum.

A glow emerged then from the hands of each priest, stretching up to engulf the volunteers in a dome of pure magic. The blue, green and white of the elements twisted and turned, absent of darkness, shining with the purity of natural magic. The light bathed the volunteers, illuminating their fear, their hope, their sacrifice.

Then the chanting of the priests ceased, and the glow of magic faded away.

A hush fell over the hall, as those who had gathered held their breaths and waited. Enala waited with them, eyes fixed on the circle. Had the priests’ magic failed? Each of the volunteers still stood, looking from one to another in confusion.

Whispers grew, spreading through the crowd like fire.

Then a man stepped forward from the volunteers, the others moving aside to let him pass. Silence fell instantly as every soul present turned to stare at the man.

Except he was no man. Enala would never mistake that face, those wild, electric blue eyes.

This was Jurrien, the Storm God of Lonia.

As one, the ring of priests fell to their knees. The crowd quickly followed, bowing in a wave beneath the eyes of the God. His gaze swept the room, the piercing blue eyes seeming to stare into the soul of every man and woman present.

"I am Jurrien, master of the Sky," he spoke at last. His tone was soft, yet his voice boomed across the hall.

The old man from the secret meeting rose, his blue robes rustling as he stood. "Greetings, Jurrien. Welcome to our world."

Jurrien gave a slow, sad smile, but said nothing. Instead, he turned to watch the other volunteers, and waited.

Enala swallowed, the breath catching in her throat. So this was how the Gods had been born, why they could not release Antonia or Jurrien from the *Soul Blades*. They had been freed from the spirit realm only by the courage of these volunteers – these brave souls who had sacrificed their bodies so that the Gods might be made flesh.

Stomach clenched, Enala turned to watch the remaining volunteers.

As she turned, a man stepped forth. His hair was long and grey, his eyes turning white as he walked – though it was clear he was not blind. Light shone from his skin, his eyes, his very being. His arms were thick with muscle, though he was clearly well into his fifties. His bare feet slapped on the smooth wooden floor as he joined Jurrien.

The hush embracing the room, if possible, gathered strength.

Enala stared at the man she did not recognise, though she knew his name long before he spoke.

"I am Darius, master of the Light," the God rumbled, his voice filled with power.

Enala stared at the man, at the God who had vanished long before her birth. She looked into the white glow of his eyes, searching there for some hint of the betrayal to come. She wanted desperately to scream, to demand the truth from him.

He will abandon you! She yelled to the silent crowd, but the words did not come out.

Smiling, Darius turned as well to the gathered volunteers, and waited.

Swallowing her anger, Enala turned from the God of Light and scanned the crowd of volunteers, seeking out the familiar face of Antonia. But she could see no children amongst them, no likeness to the young Goddess. The silence stretched out, the crowd waiting for the emergence of the third God.

"No, child, get back here!" a woman's sudden shout shattered the quiet.

Enala spun, staring as a young girl weaved through the crowd. Men and women turned to watch her, mouths open in astonishment. Her lime green dress fluttered as she ran, the silk slipping through her mother's fingers, the woman just a step behind her. Enala's heart went out to the woman as she recognised the desperation in her eyes.

As the girl reached the circle of priests she paused, turning back to her mother. "It's okay, Mum. Everything is going to be okay. She is with me, she will always be with me," she flashed a final smile, and then she was through the ring of priests, and her mother was screaming, fighting against the arms reaching out to stop her.

The girl strode two steps into the circle and froze. A ring of green light lit the air, drifting down to wrap around her fragile body. Sadness tightened in Enala's chest as she watched the transformation, watched as the girl's eyes changed, the innocent green giving way to the violet wisdom of the Goddess.

The mother's screams faded as the woman sank to her knees, face in her hands. Tears streamed from her eyes and she reached out one trembling arm for her daughter. But she was already gone.

As the light died away the girl turned back to the crowd. Her eyes glowed with violet power, the change unmistakable. Those eerie eyes surveyed the crowd, a bewildering contrast to the youthful body she had taken.

The youthful body she had stolen.

"I am Antonia, Goddess of the Earth."

The silence in the hall was palpable. The other volunteers retreated back into the crowd, leaving only the three Gods in the centre of the hall. Enala could only stare, breath held, sure there was more to come.

She did not have to wait long.

A creak came from the back of the hall as the outer doors opened. Two boys slipped inside, their eyes wide, desperately seeking out something or someone. They made their way closer, moving amidst the kneeling crowd, their eyes drawn inexorably towards the circle of priests.

As they reached the circle, the voice of one rang out in recognition.

"Father!" the boy pushed his way through the circle and ran to Darius. "Father, what have you *done?*"

The other boy joined him and the two of them stood alone amidst the priests, staring up at the man who had been their father. Yet whoever that man had been, it was not their father who looked back now.

Sadness swept across the face of Darius as he looked at the boys. "I am sorry, children. Your father… he loved you very much," he crouched then, staring into the eyes of each of them. "He has made a great sacrifice, but I swear to you, his sacrifice will not be in vain."

Tears appeared in the eyes of the boy who had not yet spoken. "Who are you? Where is Father?"

Darius reached out and gripped the child's arm. "He is still here, child. For a time at least. He wishes more than anything he could stay with you, but he says this was something he had to do. To make the world a better place for you."

The boy's head bowed and he started to sob. The sound rang loudly in the wooden hall, even as the crowd watched on in silence.

"*No!*" Enala turned as the other boy screamed. "*You are not him!*" he growled. "You will never be him!"

Darius tried to reach for the boy, but he flinched back out of reach. "You are no God," his words curled through the hall. "You are a demon, a darkness summoned here to destroy us!"

"No, child. I am the spirit of the Light. I am Darius," Darius offered his hand again, seeking peace.

"*No!*" before anyone could stop him, the child turned and fled the hall, his angry screams cut short as the doors slammed behind him.

Enala shuddered as the scene faded away, recognition screaming in her mind. She knew the boy, knew his voice, his face.

The boy was Archon.

ERIC SUCKED in a breath as he found himself back in the council room in Fort Fall. He stared around the room, his eyes wide, his heart still racing with the terrors of the vision.

He saw fear and shock in the eyes of Gabriel and his sister, and knew they had witnessed the same thing.

The Great War, the slaughter, the birth of the Gods.

And the boy.

Archon.

He turned to stare at the man. His presence cast a darkness across the room, but he recognised now the pain at its core, the pain of loss.

"It was you," he whispered.

Archon nodded. "Now you see why I hate them, why I have always hated them. They are nothing more than the demons you so despise."

"They saved us," Eric replied. "They pulled us from the wreckage our people had created, stopped the slaughter."

"And replaced it with *what?* With nations cowering beneath their thumb, ruled by puppet kings such as my brother to fool the people into thinking they still control their destiny?"

"What was the alternative?" Gabriel looked into Archon's dark eyes. "You? What have you ever done for the people?"

Archon stared back. "I have given *my* people hope, though they were rejected by your *wondrous* Gods," his arm swept out to the north. "They have united beneath me, for my promise of freedom from the wasteland. They gladly give their lives so that I might throw down the tyrannous Gods and kings who put them there."

Eric shook his head, straining to break free of Archon's bonds. "Do you not see your hypocrisy? That you let your people to die for your cause, but refuse to accept your father's own sacrifice?"

Archon looked down at him, disappointment in his eyes. "I had hoped you would see reason, my child," he waved a hand. "You cannot win, cannot hope to defeat me. Even should you somehow bring all three God powers against me, you do not have the knowledge to win. I have spent five hundred years mastering my craft – you are nothing to me."

He sighed then, shaking his head. "I will give you three days to consider. After that, I shall take my armies and my magic, and grind this fortress to the ground. One way or another, the time of the Three Nations is over. Farewell, kinsmen," with a final wave he swept from the room, vanishing into the shadow of the corridor.

Eric breathed out a long sigh as he felt the darkness release him. Reaching up he pulled the Sword of Light free of its sheath, drawing comfort from the surge of white fire that swept through him. Slowly his fear subsided and he looked around the room.

"What do we do now?"

CHAPTER 18

Eric reached for his mug of ale and took another long gulp of the bitter drink. He shuddered at the taste – he preferred the spiced wine Michael had served so long ago in Lon – but right now he needed the vigour. A shadow clung to his spirit, the knowledge of events five hundred years in the past weighing him down.

He was the ancestor of Archon, the ancient enemy of the Gods, the man whose darkness had hung over the Three Nations for more than a century. And the Gods, the very entities the Three Nations had worshiped for five hundred years, were usurpers, thieves who had taken the lives of innocents to come into this world.

And now Archon was offering them salvation, offering to spare the lives of every man and woman in Fort Fall, if only they joined him.

The weight of responsibility was more than he could bear.

"You are not alone, Eric," Inken's hand settled on his and he looked up, dragging himself back from his waking nightmare.

They sat alone in their room, in the chairs before the fire. The hour was late, but Eric knew he would not sleep tonight; not after Archon's appearance. Terror clung to his soul – that their enemy could walk so easily amongst them, could destroy them any time he wished. Even after all the time he had spent with the Sword, after the hours he had practiced each day with its power, Archon had overwhelmed him without effort.

They were mere puppets before the man's power.

Even more than the revelations, it was the screams of the dying which haunted him. How many men and women of the Three Nations had already fallen? Hundreds? Thousands? What was the point of it all now, knowing they could not win? That Archon's magic was beyond any defence they could muster?

Eric shuddered, unable to find a reply to Inken's words. He looked at her, trying to summon a spark of hope, of defiance. But he could not find it. For the first time since Alastair's death, he could not see any hope of victory.

"It is in the past, Eric," Inken whispered. "You are nothing like him; none of you are. Your ancestors were heroes, men and women who refused to give up, whatever the odds. You are no different – you will find a way to save us all, Eric. I believe in you."

Eric nodded, his eyes starting to water. "We cannot join him, we can't…" he trailed off. "And yet, I don't see how we can defeat him, Inken. He walked past all our armies, past our Magickers and dragons and guards, into the centre of the greatest fortress in the Three Nations. And there was nothing we could do to stop him," he took a deep breath. "What if it's all for nothing? How can I ask more to give away their lives for a lost cause?"

Inken stood and moved across, lowering herself onto his lap. She reached out, trailing a hand through his hair. "No one can make this decision for you, Eric. But I have faith in you, in all of you. So did Antonia, and Jurrien, and Michael and Alastair."

Eric stared into her hazel eyes. "I just wish I knew *why*," he replied. "Why did they believe in me, after all I have done?"

"Because you are *good*, Eric. Because you are strong. Because despite all that has happened, you have never hesitated to do the right thing. To stand against the darkness."

Eric released a long breath and looked down into the fire. Inken's words drifted through his conscious and the weight on his shoulders lightened, if only a little.

But even so, indecision still gripped him. "Are we even fighting for the right side?" he asked. "You did not see it, see the pain on the woman's face. She was only a *child*, Inken. Why would Antonia have chosen her?"

To his surprise he saw tears in Inken's eyes. "I don't know," she looked away, her hand drifting to her stomach. "I cannot…" her voice broke as she trailed off.

A twisting ache spread through Eric's chest as he watched her. Reaching out, he grasped her wrist. "Inken…"

Inken shook her head. "I cannot imagine her agony, to lose her child. I do not know what I would do if ours…" her eyes widened and she bit off her last words.

Eric gaped, staring into the depths of her hazel eyes. The twisting in his chest tightened as his heart started to race. He opened his mouth, then closed it again, struggling for the words.

Inken grasped his hand, clutching it tight to her throat. "I'm sorry," she murmured, her voice breaking. "I wanted to tell you, I don't know why I didn't. It never felt right, not with everything… not with death hanging over our heads."

"Inken…" Eric murmured. He stared at her, a warmth rising in his throat. "Inken…" he leaned in and kissed her.

She kissed him back, her tongue finding his as they came together. The warmth of her hands slid across his skin, slipping beneath his shirt and pulling him tight against her. Blood thumped hard in his ears as they entwined, her fingers twisting in his hair, reaching for him. And then they were falling, falling, falling.

And the fur rug before the fire rose up to greet them.

ENALA LAY on her bed and stared up at the blank stone ceiling. The chill air nipped at her skin despite the fire burning in the heath, and she yearned to crawl beneath the covers. But she could not bring herself to move, could not break free of her silent reverie.

Images flashed through her mind: the terrified faces of those ancient soldiers as they faced certain death, the terror and panic on the face of the woman as she chased after her daughter, the hatred on the face of the boy who had become Archon.

It was all too much.

And over everything loomed the dark Magicker's threat. His unstoppable armies and magic seemed to hover overhead, poised to strike their final blow to the fortress.

It was up to her and Eric to stop him.

How? Closing her eyes, Enala sent the question out into the void, praying for an answer.

But there was only silence. Opening her eyes, she rolled onto her side and stared at the *Soul Blade* where it lay propped against the wall. The very sight of it sent a shiver down to her stomach. She could almost taste the darkness lurking within the thing, waiting to strike. Her stomach churned, seeing again the fate of Sylvander, watching as the magic of the *Soul Blade* burned him to ash.

I can only wield it because of him, a creeping horror grew within her as she thought of Archon's blood running in her veins.

She heard the door squeak and looked up to see Gabriel enter. They now shared the room with two beds, though this was the first night since Gabriel had been freed.

Their eyes caught from across the room.

"I still cannot believe it," Gabriel whispered, moving to sit on his bed. "How many cousins of cousins of cousins do you think we are to each other?"

Enala laughed, the thought a welcome distraction. "Too many to count, probably. I guess Aria's secret adoption policy worked better than she could ever have imagined. My family is apparently not as endangered as we'd thought," she reached out and squeezed his hand, drawing comfort from his presence.

Gabriel shook his head, his smile slowly fading. "Do you think we have a chance?"

Enala swallowed. "I don't know. If I can summon the magic of the *Soul Blade*, we'll have the power of the Earth and Light behind us… With the power of the other war Magickers, we might just manage to match him."

Gabriel stared at her. "But we won't have Jurrien's power."

"No," Enala sighed. "Not his God magic at least. Eric's magic does come from the Sky though. And as I said, there are other Magickers to lend us their strength."

"You remember what happened when Eric used his magic against the demon in Sitton. It was not enough," he swallowed. "But maybe with the other Magickers…"

"We can beat him," Enala said again, her voice growing stronger.

"Okay," Gabriel breathed. "But what of his army?

Without the Magickers, what chance do the soldiers stand if the beasts come again?"

"If we can find a way to hold back Archon's magic, I have every confidence the men and women of the Three Nations will find a way to stop his beasts," she paused, staring at Gabriel. "They did before, the last time. They stood together and held the walls against man and beast alike. It was only Archon's magic that defeated them in the end. We won't let that happened again."

Gabriel smiled. "I believe you," he squeezed her hand and she found herself smiling back.

Without thinking she reached out and brushed a strand of hair from his face. As her fingers touched his cheek she almost gasped and her heart began to pound. She lingered, watching as Gabriel's face softened, his eyes drifting closed. Then, before thought or reason could stop her, she leaned across and pressed her lips to his.

His eyes widened and for half a second she thought he would pull away. But then he was kissing her back, his hands in her hair, his tongue hard against hers, and it was all she could do not to lose herself in the moment.

When they finally pulled apart, Enala found herself panting. She stared into Gabriel's eyes and saw the fear there had faded, replaced by desire. She knew that same desperate longing burned in her eyes, but as he leaned in again she placed a finger on his lips to stop him.

"What? Don't tell me you've finally found something to live for?" she teased.

Warmth spread through her stomach at the fire in Gabriel's eyes. "I have never met anyone like you, Enala."

Enala smiled, feeling suddenly hot in the cool room. But still she hesitated, doubt lingering in her mind.

Reaching up, she stroked his hair. "It was not so long ago, was it?" she breathed, remembering the tale Gabriel had told her back in Lon. "Not so long since you lost her. I'm sorry…"

She looked away, suddenly regretting the kiss. It had only been a few months since Gabriel had been engaged to another woman – a woman who had died in the wreckage of Oaksville. After all that had happened, had he ever been able to process that loss?

And hell, we're related! Enala swore at herself.

Enala looked up as Gabriel's hand brushed her chin. "Yes, I loved her," he murmured, and she saw his sadness. "I miss her, miss my family. But…" he paused, looking down. "But they are part of my past. Archon wiped that past from me, back in the desert. It no longer seems a part of me. I have changed too much, faced so many things since that time. I am not the same man who worked in my father's forge," he stared at her, and Enala could not look away.

This time when he made to kiss her, she did not stop him.

~

THE FIRE WAS long dead when Gabriel finally slid from the bed, though the freezing air almost drove him back beneath the thick covers and the warm body waiting there. The first light of the morning had just begun to shine through the window, but he had lain awake for hours, staring into the sleeping face of the woman beside him. Her peaceful presence brought joy to his soul, but deep within, he knew it could not last.

There was a darkness inside him, even without the lingering touch of Archon's magic. One born in the ruin of Oaksville, one that drove him to anger, to hate.

He shivered as he slipped out the door, the morning air outside even cooler than inside the room. Regret twisted in his stomach as he closed the door behind him, but there was no going back now. He could not stay. Despite what Enala had said, they did not stand a chance against Archon. Not unless he acted.

Jurrien had told him to pick up the *Soul Blade* when they ran out of other options. It seemed that time had come.

Slipping through the silent corridors of the fortress, he made his way toward the council room. They had left the *Soul Blade* there, locked and guarded by two soldiers who stood outside. No one wanted to go near the thing after what had happened to Sylvander, even if they wrapped it in cloth first.

Gabriel was not sure what he would do about the guards yet, but he knew what he had to do now. Archon's vision had shown him the truth behind Jurrien's words, the truth the God had done his best to hide. There was only one way to free the Storm God: to sacrifice himself, and allow Jurrien's spirit to possess him.

Just as his ancestor had done all that time ago.

It did not take long to pass through the empty hallways. He encountered only a handful of soldiers along the way, those few who preferred an early breakfast before taking up their stations for the coming day. Not that there had been any attacks in the last two days. Archon had given them three days, and so far, he had kept his word. An uneasy peace hung over the fortress, the men making the most of the rest. They all knew it would be over soon enough.

At last the door loomed, as nondescript as any other he had passed on the way. It stood unguarded and open, and Gabriel's stomach twisted as he realised May must have ordered the *Soul Blade* moved after all. Even so, he pushed the door wider and moved inside.

"Good morning, Gabriel," Gabriel jumped as Eric spoke from the corner.

He spun, searching out the young Magicker. "What are you doing here?" he hissed.

Eric shrugged. "I couldn't sleep," he stood, moving across the room to the table. "Apparently, I'm going to be a father. The thought has my mind spinning."

Gabriel joined him and together they looked down at the *Soul Blade*. It still lay beside the table where it had fallen, untouched. Its faint blue glow filled the little room. Gabriel shuddered, remembering the last time he had touched it. Would he have the strength this time to hold back the magic, at least long enough to free the Storm God?

"What happened to the guards?" Gabriel asked absently.

"I sent them away," Eric spoke softly. "I thought I would wait for you. I had a feeling you would come."

Gabriel looked across in surprise. "How?"

Eric shrugged. "Intuition? Reason? I'm not sure. But I've seen the look in your eyes, the fear there whenever Archon is mentioned over the last two days," Gabriel looked away from the knowledge in Eric's eyes. "You fear you are like him, don't you?"

"Why else would he have chosen *me* to haunt?"

"Because you don't have magic," Eric whispered. "It makes you vulnerable. But in truth…" he shuddered. "In truth he has come to me too, in my dreams. I did not remember them, not until he walked into this room. You are not the only one he has haunted. You are not the only one who has darkness within them."

Gabriel saw the ghost in Eric's eyes and reached across to grasp his shoulder. "I forgive you, Eric," he felt a tremble of relief as he spoke the words, as he felt the hate lift from his soul.

Eric's eyes watered as he stared back. A single tear spilt down his cheek. "Thank you, Gabriel," he choked.

They stood there in silence then, staring at the *Soul Blade.*

"Now is not the time," Eric said at last.

Gabriel looked across at him. "What do you mean?"

Eric met his gaze. "Now is not the time," he repeated. "If you truly wish to do this, you have to say goodbye, Gabriel. You owe the others that much. Enala, Caelin, Inken, they love you – they deserve better," he breathed out. "Besides, if Jurrien is freed, Archon will know. He will know we have rejected his offer, and we will lose our last day of peace. Better to wait, if that is what you mean to do."

"When?" Gabriel croaked, holding back tears of his own.

"You will know, Gabriel. You will know."

CHAPTER 19

Caelin stood atop the rampart of the second wall and looked out at the enemy. They had unblocked the gates of the outer wall, burning the rubble and wooden doors to clear a path for their army. Now they lined the ramparts and packed the grounds at the foot of the wall, waiting just beyond the range of the defenders' arrows. He knew more would be waiting outside the gates, eager to join the fray when the assault began.

He glanced across at May, reading the fear on her pursed lips as she stared out at the challenge facing them. This wall was higher, thicker, stronger, and the defenders had rested for three days. Even so, their morale was low, their courage crumbling beneath the memory of the beasts.

"We'll hold them, May," he growled.

The woman looked up and forced a smile. "I know, Caelin, I know. I just hope Eric and the others can do their job."

Laughing, Caelin shook his head. "Let's let them worry about their job, and us worry about ours, Commander."

"Easier said than done," May muttered and then shook

her head. "No, you're right. There's only so much one woman can do."

"I'm not sure about that," Caelin turned as Inken walked up. Her eyes were alight with fire and he was surprised by the hope there. "We can certainly do more than these blokes here," she waved at Caelin and Gabriel.

Caelin chuckled. "What's your tally again, Inken?" his chest tightened at the question. The competition between himself and Alan to slay the most enemy had been just one of their many bets. He bowed his head, sending up thanks again for the big man's bravery.

"I don't feel the need to count," Inken smiled and winked. "I know your numbers could never come close to mine."

"How much does a demon count for?" May grinned as she joined their banter.

"Oh, I don't know, I'd say at least a hundred," Inken offered.

It was Gabriel's turn to laugh then. "Good, that catches me up somewhat then."

Caelin grinned, glad to see the life in the young man's eyes. It was the first time he'd truly seemed himself since their imprisonment beneath the citadel of Ardath. A desire rose within him to reach out and draw Gabriel into a bear hug, but he resisted.

"So it's settled then," Caelin turned to look out at the enemy. "It's a draw between us men and you women."

"Pfff," Inken stepped up beside him. "In your dreams, little man," with her last words, Caelin knew she missed Alan's presence as much as he did.

He reached out and squeezed her shoulder. They stood together and waited then, the heat of the morning warming them. The crash of waves came from the distance and the tang of salt hung heavy on the air. Caelin breathed it in, relishing in the freedom of life.

His gaze drifted along the wall to the centre where Eric and Enala stood. There they would make their final stand, backed by the combined might of the Magickers of the Three Nations. He wished with all his heart he could stand beside them, but he would only be a liability in that fight. He and Gabriel and Inken alike, though he did not know how they had convinced the other two to stand aside. If it had been his love waiting to face Archon…

He shook his head as horns rang out from the enemy camp. Releasing a breath he had not realised he'd been holding, Caelin glanced at his companions. Inken nodded back, already stringing her bow. Steel rasped on leather as May and Gabriel drew their swords. Caelin reached down and did the same, his eyes drifting out to watch the enemy come.

May's cry rang out as the enemy came within range, carrying down the wall as her officers repeated the call. The twang of bowstrings followed as the first volley took to the air, then the screams of the dying as the enemy wilted beneath the deadly rain. A second volley followed, and a third, and then the enemy was at the wall and there was no more time to keep count.

Beside him, Inken tossed aside her bow and drew her blade. Caelin edged closer to her, determined to keep his friends safe. Gabriel stood on her other side, and May to his right, but he still felt the gap amongst them. Alan's presence had been enormous and they would miss his steely courage in the coming fight.

The thump of wood on stone heralded the arrival of the enemy. Staring at the ladders, Caelin gripped his sword tight and sucked in a breath.

"Ready?" Inken asked.

Caelin nodded. "Let them come."

Enala looked down at the enemy, watching as volley after volley decimated their ranks. Yet their numbers seemed without end and they came on, determined to wipe the defenders from the wall. As they closed in, the enemy archers began to fire back, and black shafted bolts flashed up towards them.

Ducking beneath the crenulations, Enala glanced at Eric. He stood resolute beside her, a host of Magickers at his back. They came from every nation and discipline: The Sky Magickers of Lonia, the Earth Magickers of Plorsea, and the Light Magickers of Trola. They stood together atop the walls of Fort Fall, ready to give their lives to keep the darkness from their hearths.

Eric glanced at her. "Ready?"

Enala swallowed, looking down at the *Soul Blade* sheathed at her side. Dread curled up in her stomach and she had to will herself not to vomit. Her knees shook as raw terror robbed away her strength, but she nodded. "As ready as I'll ever be."

Closing her eyes, she reached down and drew the *Soul Blade* from its scabbard.

As her hands closed around the leather hilt a flash of green light lit her mind, burning its way up from the cold steel. Energy surged through her as a harsh glow threaded its way along her veins, twisting ever deeper. She gasped as pain burned her wrist, tearing at her concentration. Her eyes watered as the pressure within her built, but she bit back a second cry.

From deep within a flame rose, her power responding to the threat of the foreign power. Its red light flickered, and then a tower of fire rose, beating back the twisting vines spreading from the *Soul Blade.* The two powers twisted in her mind, thrashing against one another for supremacy.

Somehow, Enala sensed it was a battle her magic could not win, not without direction. Swallowing her fear, she reached out and grasped the flickering red flames and drew them to her. The magic fought against her touch, the flames turning to fangs that bit and tore at her soul, but still she held on, determined.

At last the red flames calmed, and with a rush of elation she twisted her power into lines of red and sent it out to wrap about the God magic.

The green light flashed again, igniting the deepest corners of her mind, but she did not flinch now. She held on as the God magic fought against its bindings and tore at her, desperate for freedom.

You can do it, Enala, from somewhere came her brother's voice, and biting her tongue, Enala drew her magic tighter. With one final jerk, the column of green collapsed in on itself, succumbing to the binds of her power.

Enala breathed out and opened her eyes, finding Eric's concerned face not three inches from her own.

She smiled. "I have it."

Eric nodded back. "Well done. Then let's go to work," he turned to face the ranks of enemy below.

Soldiers stood ahead of them, fending off those attackers who had already reached the battlements, but they parted now as Eric and Enala walked to the fore. The Magickers followed, flashes of their magic sizzling outward as they cleared the enemy from the ramparts.

As Eric reached the edge of the wall he reached up and drew the Sword of Light. White light washed over the wall as flames leapt along the length of the blade. Enala glanced down at her *Soul Blade*, staring with hate at its brilliant green. It felt corrupted, *wrong*. Even so, they needed it.

But even with the two God powers and all the Magickers aligned behind them, Enala doubted it would be enough. They still lacked the Storm God's magic, and Eric and herself could not come close to mastering the God powers they possessed. The Earth magic of the Goddess might be pumping through her body, but she had yet to truly wield it. She would need to rely on instinct and guess work in the coming battle. The thought did not fill her with confidence.

But still, they had to try. She glanced at the other Magickers, seeing the fear on their grim faces, and knew she could not back down. The odds they faced in the coming fight were far worse than hers. They had only their mortal magic to protect them.

Enala drew in a long breath of salty air, struggling to calm her racing mind. Together they were about to draw the wrath of Archon down upon them. God powers or no, it would be a miracle if any of them survived.

Below the enemy flooded across the killing ground between the walls, an endless black tide, fearless, unstoppable. Except they were about to stop it, to burn them all where they stood. Their angry voices rose up to wash over the defenders like thunder, but that would soon change.

Moving to stand close to Eric, Enala reached deep within and unshackled the power of the Earth. Light spread from the *Soul Blade*, its green washing out to mingle with the white of the Sword. The glow slowly brightened, flashing out to cast the soldiers below in eerie shadows. For the first time that day, the enemy hesitated, their charge faltering as they paused to look up.

But they were not without protection either. As with the beasts before, they were clothed in Archon's magic. She could sense it now, a darkness rising from them like a foul scent, shielding them from fire and magic alike. It rose up above them, mingling with the power of the Sword and the *Soul Blade*.

Thunder rolled across the Gap as the two forces came together, though the sky above remained clear. Enala gritted her teeth as she felt the force of darkness pushing back, driving off their power.

It's too strong, but even as Enala formed the thought, she sensed the building of power behind her as the other Magickers stepped up to join the fray. Light spread from their hands, red and white and blue and green shooting up to join the fray. Less than the God powers, but joined they still created a formidable force.

Flame flashed across the sky, followed by the rumble of thunder as lightning crackled. Enala gritted her teeth, driving the magic of the *Soul Blade* outwards, straining to unleash its power on the enemy below. Bit by bit, the darkness started to give way to the elemental power streaming from the wall.

A sudden *snap* reverberated through the air, followed by a whoosh as the dark magic flickered and went out. The combined magic of the Three Nations poured through into the void, streaming down towards the enemy below.

The roar of Archon's forces turned suddenly to screams as their magic erupted into life and chaos spread through their ranks. The flames came first, the white fire burning down to strike the massed ranks on the killing grounds, followed by the flash and crackle of lightning. Together they scorched all they touched.

Green light flashed again from the *Soul Blade* as its power rushed from Enala to join the fray. Hate curled around her soul as she watched the slaughter. These men had come here to kill them, to destroy her people and murder her friends. They had allied themselves to darkness – this was what they deserved. Their souls were not worthy of pity, of mercy.

The massacre spread through the enemy ranks, sweeping

them back from the wall. As one they turned and fled, desperate to retreat back to the protection of their master.

Enala would not allow it.

Raising the *Soul Blade*, Enala drew on its magic, rejoicing in the surge of power flooding her weary body. Its green light flashed out over the enemy, chasing them across the killing field.

A smile twisted Enala's lips as her spirit soared with the magic. Reaching out, she gripped the ground beneath their feet, the green light of the Earth seeping deep into the soil. Then, with casual ease, she hauled it back.

As one the enemy crumpled like leaves as the ground shifted beneath them, driving them to their knees. Terrified faces looked up at the wall, desperate for mercy, but they would find none there. The earth groaned and tore apart, swallowing pockets of men before they could so much as scream.

Looking down at the enemy, Enala began to laugh, taking joy from their terror. Magickers turned to stare at her, but she waved aside their concern. She breathed out, releasing her grip on the earth. As the shaking slowed the enemy climbed to their feet and fled towards the far off gate, desperate to escape her deadly power.

With a shake of her head, Enala waved the *Soul Blade* again.

A groan rose up from below as the ground before the outer gates exploded, hurling chunks of dirt and stone across the killing field. Vines twisted their way up into view, a great thicket of impassable thorns taking form in the instant between blinks. The snakelike vines whipped upwards, tearing into the enemy who still stood atop the ramparts of the outer wall. On the killing field the enemy drew to a halt, staring at the impassable barrier now blocking their path.

Then the thicket moved again, turning from the now

empty wall to the enemy below. Snakelike threads of green flashed out, snatching men from their feet and dragging them screaming into the impenetrable depths of the copse. Hundreds fell, torn to shreds before the might of the Earth, before the power in Enala's hands.

Turning away, Enala nodded to the other Magickers. "They're all yours," she smirked.

She moved away down the ramparts, thrilling in the pull of the power within her. Before she could take three steps a hand grabbed her by the shoulder and spun her. Growling, Enala swung the *Soul Blade*, the razor sharp steel striking for Eric's head. The Sword of Light rose up to block the blow and sparks of green and white scattered across the bricks.

Eric stepped back, his eyes wide with shock, his mouth agape. "Enala, what the *hell* was that?"

Enala stared back, the *Soul Blade* slipping from her fingers. It clattered to the stones, the green glow dying to a whisper. As she released it, the hate curling its way around her soul fell away and she gasped. The blood fled her face and she swayed, feeling suddenly faint. She wavered, and would have fallen had Eric not caught her.

"What… What have I done?" she whispered.

Eric shook his head. "It was necessary," he shook her, forcing her to look at him. "We said before this started we could show them no mercy, that we had to break their spirit. I'd say we've done that," he paused. "Except it was not you, was it?"

Enala shuddered. "No… yes… I'm not *sure!*" she closed her eyes. "I… I don't think I've ever felt hate like that, so intense, so powerful."

Eric's eyes flashed and he drew her into his arms. "You did well, Enala. It was the *Soul Blade*; it was whatever black magic Archon left embedded in it."

She nodded, feeling tears in her eyes and burying her

head in Eric's shoulder to hide them. "I don't know how much longer I can do this, Eric," she gasped, her words half-muffled. "How long I can keep fighting. It's too hard, too awful."

His arms squeezed her tight. "I know. Even the Sword has its own darkness. Each time I use it, it feels as though I lose a bit more of myself, like a bit more of me is burnt away. But we have to keep going, just a little bit longer."

Enala bit her tongue to keep herself from crying. Before she could find a reply, a scream from behind interrupted her thoughts. They spun together and saw the group of Magickers staggering backwards, their faces pale. One stumbled a step too far and tripped through the gap in the crenulations. He disappeared without so much as a scream.

"Pick up the *Soul Blade*," Eric hissed, moving past her, the Sword of Light crackling in his hands.

Enala swallowed. Steeling herself, she reached down and lifted the *Soul Blade*. Its power swept through her once more and the bitter bite of hatred returned. She struggled to push it down, holding the love for her brother and her friends close to her heart.

Taking a breath, she followed after Eric.

Below, the killing ground lay piled with the enemy dead, with the thousands who had fallen to their magic. Now the few survivors no longer fled, but were turning back to face them, their faces twisted with a wicked joy. Enala squinted her eyes, straining to see what was happening.

A dark light seeped through the thicket by the gate, spreading out to cover the last of the enemy force. Where it touched her vines they withered and died, whilst the ranks of enemy straightened, their burns and injuries fading to nothing.

The darkness spread across the plain and through it came Archon, his stride calm and measured, as though he did not walk through a field of his dead. The feathered cloak fluttered out around him, caught on the ocean winds, but he did not slow. His face registered no emotion, no hint of compassion for his fallen soldiers. His eyes stared straight ahead, fixed on the ramparts where Eric and Enala stood.

"What now?" Enala whispered.

"Now it ends," Eric growled, the veins of his wrist straining as he gripped the Sword of Light tighter.

Wind whipped around them and then Enala felt the familiar lifting sensation beneath her feet. She flashed Eric a grim smile and nodded. Together they lifted off the wall and dropped to the killing field below. Behind them the Magickers hesitated, looking from one to the other. But after a moment they followed, the Sky Magickers amongst them lifting the others and carrying them down.

Enala caught the eyes of the leaders and nodded, then returned her attention to Archon. A wave of relief swept through her; at least they would not be alone in this fight. The other Magickers had already helped to break Archon's magic once today. Perhaps they might stand a chance after all.

They came together in the centre of the field: Archon standing alone amidst the legion of his dead, Eric and Enala with all the might of the Three Nations behind them.

Archon wore a grim smile as his cold blue eyes surveyed them. "So, Enala," he rasped. "You have finally tasted the magic of the *Soul Blade*. How does it feel, to wield such power, to cast such destruction upon your enemies? Does it call to you?"

Enala swallowed and scowled back. She gripped the *Soul Blade* tighter, the truth of Archon's words clear on her face. "It doesn't matter – we have made our decision. We will never serve you."

Archon laughed. "If only life were so simple, my child.

My offer was only meant to lessen your suffering, to spare you the pain of what is to come," he spread his arms and Enala sensed the dark power crackling around them. "But make no mistake; you *will* serve me. Your refusal will not stop that," he took a step towards them and Enala could not help but shrink back.

But Eric stood strong. "You are wrong, Archon."

"Ah, young Eric, ever the optimist. But you do not see," Archon waved a hand and the very air around them darkened. "You never stood a chance in this fight, my child. You have only ever been able to delay the inevitable. But the end was never in question," his cold eyes locked them in his gaze. "I will break those feeble bodies of yours, shatter your souls. And then I will unleash the untamed God powers on each of you."

A chill swept through Enala's heart as Archon's words seeped in. Could that truly be his plan – to crush their resistance and then allow the God magic to take them? She shivered, remembering the helpless terror as the God power had taken control of her body. To suffer that fate for eternity…

Archon laughed. He waved at the dead around him. "In truth, I am impressed by your strength, your ruthlessness. You have made me proud," he smiled. "But no more. This ends today. I will see this fortress torn down, stone by stone, and the last resistance of your Three Nations ground to dust," with that Archon raised his fist.

Shadows swirled around his clenched hand, spreading outwards in a ball of all-consuming darkness.

Enala swallowed and gripped the *Soul Blade* hard in her fist. She glanced at Eric and nodded.

Eric nodded back. "Now or never?"

CHAPTER 20

Eric swallowed his fear and roared. The white-hot flames of the Sword of Light bathed his face as he pointed the blade. Light flashed and a rush of energy swept through him, leaving his every muscle quivering and his magic flickering with renewed strength.

Archon still stood in place with his arm raised, concentration etched across his ageless features. Eric stared at the gathering darkness, the very sight sending a shiver of fear right to his soul. They had to stop him, before he could unleash that power. A rush of magic came from beside him as Enala drew on the power of her *Soul Blade,* then from behind as the other Magickers gathered their strength.

Now or never, Eric repeated the words, and pointed the Sword.

White fire rushed from the blade and raced towards the dark Magicker. Enala's cry echoed his own, followed by the rush of Earth magic, and then there was only Archon, and the battle for survival.

Archon threw down his fist as the inferno reached him. With a *whoosh* the flames vanished into the gathered darkness. A second later the earth beneath him tore open, revealing a crevice leading down to the depths of hell itself.

Archon only smiled as he hung in the air, his head rolling on his shoulders as though to remove a crick in his neck. He drifted over the gap and dropped back to the earth.

Fear gripped Eric, but there was no time to retreat now. He reached again for the magic of the Sword, drawing on the power of the world around him, and hurled it at Archon. The lines connecting the world bent inwards before the white energy of the Sword and then its invisible force struck the dark Magicker, hurling him out over the gaping canyon.

For a second Archon's eyes widened, but he still did not fall. Instead he twisted in the air, a dark grin on his face, and threw out his hand. Eric's heart fell into his stomach as a wave of darkness swept towards him. Backing away, Eric summoned the white magic within and hurled it outwards. Pure energy crackled around him as the power of the Light rose up to meet the darkness.

A boom came as the two forces met, but within seconds the light was overwhelmed. The dark surged forwards and Eric barely managed to throw himself clear. He rolled across the hard ground, coming to a rest alongside a fallen body. Looking away from the burnt ruin of a man, Eric pulled himself to his feet, the Sword still clenched tight in his hand.

Archon stood calmly ten feet away, arms folded and a thin smile on his lips. Gritting his teeth, Eric fed his anger to the magic of the Sword, and charged. Flames crackled along the blade as he swung it at the dark Magicker, its white light casting them all in shadow.

With an almost sadistic slowness, Archon reached up and caught the Sword of Light with his empty hand. Eric cursed as the blade shuddered in his fist and his arm went numb, but he refused to drop his only weapon against the darkness. Straining his arms, he released the power of the Sword from his grasp, allowing it free reign. The magic crackled and roared, the heat of its white fire sweeping out to bathe them both.

Archon cursed and thrust the Sword aside. His fist swept out and caught Eric in the face. As it connected a dark energy coursed through him and suddenly he was airborne, hurtling backwards toward the group of Magickers. Raising his arms, he braced himself for impact and prayed the Sword would not injure him.

Before he could hit the hard ground a gust of wind rushed up to catch him. He gasped in a breath of cold air as the winds lowered him gently to the ground, and nodded his thanks to a woman in blue robes. The other Magickers gathered around him then, and together they turned towards the dark Magicker.

Enala beat them to it. The green flash of her *Soul Blade* swept out across the field, followed by a rumble from deep within the earth. Dirt flew through the air as vines erupted from the ground, the thick tendrils thrashing out to trap Archon in their iron grasp.

Archon smiled and raised a hand. A dark glow seeped from his skin, and as the thorny vines reached him they suddenly stiffened and turned black. Then they were turning back on themselves, leaving the dark Magicker untouched and rushing for Eric's sister.

Eric raised the Sword of Light and swung it, unleashing its white inferno on the thicket. The flames swept through the black and green, turning all they touched to ash. Smoke spread across the open ground, hiding Archon from view as Enala stumbled back to join them.

Straining his eyes, Eric searched the smoke for sign of Archon. He could sense his dark magic building again. The power made his head throb, more powerful than anything he'd ever felt before.

Then suddenly Archon was there, arms raised, and a wave of darkness swept towards them. Eric flinched back, the Sword raised before his face, its magic rising to meet the oncoming force. But this time the black magic did not so much as slow. It came on, death incarnate, ready to claim them all.

A brilliant flash of light lit the air, and then a rush of energy swept past him. Fire and lightning crackled in its midst, the very earth itself spitting open at its passage. He staggered as the combined magic of their allies warped the world around them. With a boom it struck Archon's dark magic and shattered it. Gathering force, it swept on.

Archon roared as the magic found him and ignited. The air shook and the ground splintered, cracks racing out as a shock wave knocked them from their feet. Flames soared into the sky and crashed down towards them, but before Eric could reach for the Sword's magic, Enala was there. She raised her empty fist and hurled the fire back on itself, protecting them all from its wrath.

Eric spared her a nod as he climbed back to his feet. Behind them, he could feel the energy gathering as the Magickers prepared another attack. Taking a firmer grip of the Sword, he added its strength to theirs. Power warped the air between them, the skies overhead darkening as lightning rippled across the underbellies of the clouds.

A low growl echoed across the barren field. Eric turned back to the pillar of smoke rising from where Archon had stood. A boom shook the air and a gust of wind rushed outwards, tearing the smoke from the ground and snuffing out the last of the flames.

Archon stood amidst the scorched earth, his face twisted now with rage, his shoulders hunched as he summoned his power. Darkness collected in his fists, swirling out like storm clouds – though Eric could sense nothing of the Sky in that magic. Only evil, only death.

Throwing out his fist, Archon unleashed the chaos gathered there.

Fear swept across the faces of the Magickers as Archon's power surged towards them, but they did not waver. They stood as one, arms raised, and unleashed their gathered magic. The forces surged towards each other, meeting again with a boom and a roar. This time though it was the black magic that won, swallowing up the swirling colours of their attack. Ripples of energy raced outwards as the magic scattered, forcing Eric and Enala to retreat.

The other Magickers were not so lucky. They staggered as their magic shattered, some crumpling to the ground with the shock of their magic's loss. Blood gushed from the eyes and noses of others as they stumbled blindly amidst their comrades.

Either way, it did not matter. The wave of shadow magic came on, unrelenting.

And together, the Magickers of the Three Nations fell screaming before the power of Archon.

Gabriel stared as the Magickers aiding Eric and Enala disappeared beneath the wave of dark magic. A dread silence fell across the wall, the defenders on the battlements reduced now to silent spectators in their own war. They stood helpless before the powers aligned beneath them, their fates in the hands of those below.

And they were losing.

Swallowing, Gabriel turned away. The time had come. He felt a pang of regret as he looked down at Enala one last time. Despite Eric's words, he had said nothing of his decision to the girl. And now it was too late.

Tears burned in his eyes but he wiped them away, pushing down his fear. This was a sacrifice he had to make. There was no other choice; they would not survive without aid, and there was only one being powerful enough to shift the balance.

"Gabriel, where are you going?" Inken's voice stopped him at the top of the stairs.

He turned back, the lies catching in his throat as her eyes caught his. He bowed his head. "I am going to free Jurrien. It's the only way we stand a chance."

Inken stared, mouth open. Emotion swept across her face and for a moment Gabriel thought she would try to stop him. She shook her head, glanced at Caelin, and closed her eyes. A tear ran down her cheek, then she was stepping up to him, pulling him into her embrace. He hugged her back, drawing strength from her presence.

He felt a strong hand on his shoulder and looked up at Caelin. "Good luck, Gabriel," the sergeant's voice was soft, almost breaking. "You're a brave soul."

Gabriel nodded back as he disengaged himself from Inken. She wore a small smile on her face now, but she did not look away. "Thank you, Gabriel. Good luck."

Gabriel sucked in a shaky breath and turned away before they saw his tears. He forced himself not to look back, knowing that if he did, he would lose his nerve. The pull of life was strong now, the call of the shadows a dim reflection of what the world could offer him.

Friends, love, life.

But he had to leave that behind, say goodbye to the promise of a new future.

If only so the others could have what he longed for.

The race to the citadel seemed to pass in an instant, his

feet treading the familiar path by intuition alone. His mind was far away, joying in the three days he had spent with Enala. They had passed far too quickly.

At last he found himself back in the council room, staring down at the blue glow of the *Soul Blade*. The guards on duty only nodded as Gabriel swept past – he was expected. Eric and May had made sure of that.

Gabriel blew out a long sigh, his chest constricting not with exertion but fear.

I can do this! He whispered in the silence of his mind.

You can, a voice answered back, and whether it was his own, or some last vestige of the dark magic, or Jurrien, or someone else, he could not have guessed.

Either way, it was enough.

Reaching down, Gabriel wrapped his hand around the hilt of the *Soul Blade*.

ENALA SWORE as she flung herself backwards, a dark shadow tearing through her jacket. The metallic scent of blood bit the air, sending her back another step. Pain stabbed at her arm. She spared it a glance and then looked away. Blood soaked her sleeve, but already the Earth magic was rising from the *Soul Blade*, driven by instinct, restoring the strength in her arm.

She had already repeated the feat several times for both herself and Eric. She moved by instinct alone now, at one with the green glow of the earth magic, sending it out to heal the cuts and bruises before they could slow them.

Yet despite their best efforts, Archon remained untouched, with barely a mark on his clothes or skin. With the other Magickers dead, they were hopelessly outmatched. But then, even with their aid it had never been a fair fight.

Still they would not surrender. A chill ran through Enala's blood at the thought of the fate Archon planned for them. She would rather die than allow the God magic to make a puppet of her again, than to watch on, helpless, as it destroyed her friends. To suffer beneath the yoke of her magic as a thousand years passed, unable to have even the final relief of death.

Fear fed Enala's anger and she brought about the *Soul Blade*, drawing on its power to attack again. The earth shook beneath her feet, a crack tearing open and racing towards their foe. Archon watched it come, an amused smile on his lips.

Drawing on her own magic, Enala shot her brother a glance. Eric nodded back, and as the gulf opened up beneath Archon, they unleashed their attack. Lightning leapt from Eric's hands as Enala hurled her flames.

Their combined energies lashed out, striking Archon squarely in the chest. The dark Magicker only raised his arms and laughed, but they were not done. Pointing the Sword of Light, Eric unleashed its magic. White fire joined the conflagration, and then an invisible force gripped Archon and drove him down into the crevice.

A boom came from below as lightning and fire burst up from the crack, but Enala did not hesitate. Elation stirred in her chest as she screamed, the green light of the *Soul Blade* flashing in the morning sun, and the earth snapped closed.

Cheers erupted from the wall behind them and Enala's heart pounded hard in her chest. She glanced at Eric, seeing her own disbelief reflected on his face.

"Did we do it?" she whispered.

A dark, booming laughter cut off his reply. Silence fell across the wall as the sound echoed across the killing field. Eric and Enala edged closer to one another, eyes scanning the empty ground, waiting.

With a long, grating groan the earth broke back open. Archon rose up from the fissure, his feathered cloak torn and shredded, but a smile on his lips. He drifted across and alighted on solid ground. Reaching up, he unclipped his cloak and tossed it away. It struck with a heavy thud, loud in the silence.

"Are you done?" Archon gave a dark chuckle.

Enala shuddered, despair rising up within her.

You cannot defeat me, Enala staggered as Archon's words rang in her mind. She spun to stare at Eric and saw his terror, and knew he had heard the words too. *You cannot even keep me from your minds, you poor, frail mortals.*

Archon stepped closer, his grin widening, his teeth glinting in the light of their swords. Magic swept out from him, stretching up like great wings of darkness. Tendrils of black magic wove through the air, reaching for them, calling to them.

Enala shrank away, a voice answering deep inside her, stirring the shadows of her soul. Beside her, the colour fled Eric's face as the magic caught them both. In her chest, Enala felt her hate stirring, her rage and desire rising up to claim her.

Gasping, Enala doubled over, desperate to fight the forces wrapping about her soul. The flames of her magic rose to defend her. It burned at the darkness, tearing at its edges, but the black was like a flood, overwhelming. Bit by bit the spirit of her magic died away, snuffed out, suffocated.

A groan rose in Enala's throat as she sank to her knees. She stared down at the *Soul Blade*, willing herself to hurl it away. But her hand refused to move. It remained fixed around the sword's pommel, and with creeping dread she sensed the first prods of the God power as it seeped into the void left by her magic.

"No," Enala sobbed, her body frozen now, helpless before the power of the *Soul Blade*. "No, please, not again."

Fear rose within her, stronger than belief. Never before had she experienced such terror as on Witchcliffe Island, when the God magic swept her away. Her will and soul had been nothing to it, mere play-things to torment and torture. She had never wanted to touch the damn thing again. It had only been for her friends that she had taken up the *Soul Blade*, to defend them against Archon's power.

And now… now they would die by her own hand.

Enala sucked in a breath as the first surge of power tore through her body. The God magic had discovered her weakness, that her magic was lost beneath the darkness of Archon's power. Enala fled into the depths of her subconscious, searching desperately for a hint of the flame, for some small ember with which to fight. But she found only darkness.

And the burning touch of God magic.

Throwing back her head, a scream rose from her throat.

Then, all at once, the dark magic surged back from her, fleeing her mind as though sucked out through a vortex. The red of her magic flickered back into existence and with a rush of joy she caught it and hurled it at the God magic. The green flames gave way before its heat, retreating back into the *Soul Blade.*

Enala opened her eyes to the boom of thunder, the crackling of lightning. The air rippled with power, the taste of it like ice on the wind. A column of lightning as thick as the towers of Fort Fall fell from the sky, enveloping Archon in its electric blue. The crack as it struck deafened her.

A blast of wind rushed across the killing field, sending Enala rolling backwards over the barren ground. She clutched desperately at the *Soul Blade* as she rolled, suddenly desperate to keep its magic.

In her heart, she knew who had arrived, what had happened.

Grief twisted in her soul as a figure fell from the sky. He landed with a thud on the ground between them and Archon, a sly smile on his familiar lips, power shining from his eyes. It was Gabriel, Gabriel as she had never seen him before.

But it was not the man she had grown to love. She could see it in his eyes, in the ancient wisdom there, in the once brown irises now changed to crystal blue.

It was Jurrien who stood before her now, not Gabriel.

Jurrien, wearing the body of the man she loved.

"Jurrien," Archon's voice boomed across the field. Darkness flashed and the lightning vanished, the wind dying away.

Archon strode from the cloud of smoke where the lightning had fallen, his chest heaving, darkness curling all around him. The earth crunched beneath his feet, scorched black and crystallised by the heat of the lightning.

And his face… Enala had never seen such rage on a human's face.

"In the flesh," Jurrien smiled back. "Did you miss me?"

"Oh, I will enjoy this," Archon growled. "I will enjoy sending your spirit screaming back to the void. The time of the Gods is *over!*"

Archon's last word came out as a scream. Darkness grew from every inch of the man now, curling about him like a living thing. He faded into the magic as it spread from him, as though he were a part of it, as though he were more shadow than real man.

Ice seeped into Enala's veins as she watched the shadows grow. She could sense the power thumping through the air. The sickly twist of dark magic was so thick she could taste it. There was no denying it now; the man within the magic was no longer mortal, no longer even human. No human could withstand the transformation now twisting the dark Magicker's body.

The magic swept out, swirling and changing. Great wings of fire took shape first, stretching up to the sky as black embers scattered on the wind. Feathers of darkness formed, fire lighting from their tips. A hooked beak reached out for them, burning teeth lining the twisted keratin. Within seconds nothing remained of the man who had been Archon.

In his place stood a Phoenix, its burning wings casting them in shadow, the heat of its flames driving them backwards. It towered over the three of them, its bulk filling the killing field, far larger than any dragon, taller even than the walls behind them.

Enala staggered backwards. Slipping in the mud, she fell to the ground, unable to look away from the colossus towering over them.

The great beak opened and a scream tore the air. If she hadn't already been on the ground, the sound would have sent Enala to her knees. As it was, she clapped her hands over her ears and waited for the world to end.

When the scream finally ceased, she heard Archon's whisper in her mind.

Time for this game to end.

A fiery wind buffeted them as the flaming wings beat down, lifting the beast into the sky. Turning in the air, it swept towards the fortress.

CHAPTER 21

Eric staggered to his feet as the Phoenix lifted off, its burning wings carrying it skyward. In his mind he heard Archon's words, but they were dim compared to the memory screaming in his ears.

"Then Archon took his place on the battlefield. He flew overhead, morphed beyond all recognition, darkening the heavens with his magic," Antonia's words from so long ago rang in his head, her warning now clear with the beast before them.

Archon had surrendered his humanity long ago, had become one with his own power. Dark magic was the antithesis of everything natural and good, flaunting the laws of magic and the physical world.

With it, nothing was beyond his power.

Eric watched as clouds gathered around Archon. Flames leapt from the Phoenix's wings to spread across the sky, and he remembered how Antonia's tale had ended. Archon had unleashed his power and an inferno had fallen from the sky, burning the ranks of their army to ash.

They could not let that happen now, not again.

A roar sounded from overhead and Eric spun, his heart

surging as the gold dragons dropped from the sky. The sun glittered off their scales, turning the sky into a gold-speckled tapestry. As one they alighted around them, growls rumbling up from their chests.

It is time, Enduran's voice echoed in his mind. *We must stop him here, or all will fall.*

The dragon stepped forward as the others ringed them and offered his leg. Eric nodded, but turned back to Gabriel – or Jurrien, he guessed now.

"Do you have a plan?" he shouted over the howling wind.

Jurrien laughed. "The plan is yours, Eric. Gabriel seemed to think you had one. All I know is, alone, we cannot match his power. Last time I tried, he snuffed my magic out like a candle."

Eric sheathed the Sword of Light as he climbed up onto Enduran's back. He nodded as Enala slid past him and took her seat in front of him. She flashed him a weary grin.

"Mind if I steer?" she laughed.

"You're the dragon rider," he turned back to Jurrien. "Well, we have all three God powers now," he pointed to the sky. "So we stop him, whatever the cost."

Jurrien nodded, the hint of a smile on his lips. "Lead on then, young Eric."

Eric felt the muscles of the dragon bunch beneath him, and quickly wrapped his hands around Enala's waist. Then Enduran leapt for the sky and Eric's stomach fell into his boots. The dragon's wings swept down as his roar echoed off the walls around them and then they were surging upwards, driving ahead to where the dark Phoenix waited.

The gathered roar of the other dragons came from behind as Enduran's tribe joined them, followed by a boom as Jurrien took to the sky. Glancing across, he saw lightning flickering in the God's fists as he flew past them.

Swallowing, Eric reached up and redrew the Sword of Light. Its energy surged through him but he kept its flames extinguished, ensuring they would not do any harm to Enala. She still held the *Soul Blade* clenched in her fist, its green glow glittering on the scales of Enduran's back. He held her tight as they raced upwards, closing fast on the beast Archon had become.

Enala glanced back as they flew and he saw a wild joy on her face, a sharpness to her eyes that had been missing before. She swung the *Soul Blade* and pointed it skyward, her wild scream carrying to him over the thump of wings.

Eric smiled as he remembered the first time he had laid eyes on this girl, his sister. He had been dying on the black sands of Malevolent Cove, but even so the image remained crystal clear: Enala astride the dragon Nerissa, her golden hair billowing in the wind, her brow creased with righteous anger.

He saw that girl again now and the sight warmed his heart. They would need her courage in the battle to come.

Hoisting the Sword of Light, he drew on its energy. His mind tingled with its power, but he was still searching for a plan, for a way to halt the inferno Archon was about to unleash.

"We have to stop his attack," Eric shouted over the wind. "Jurrien, you and I will fight fire with fire. Hopefully we have enough to match what he throws at us. Enala, do what you can to protect the fortress from whatever gets through!"

Enala nodded but she did not look back. Instead she hoisted the *Soul Blade* and stood, a wicked grin on her face as she balanced on Enduran's back. Then she turned and slid back down so that she faced the ground, the *Soul Blade* already flashing as she worked its magic.

Thunder crackled in the storm clouds above them, but Eric could sense no rain or wind within them. These were no natural clouds, but dark things, born of Archon's black magic. They held only one thing – death.

Then a roar shook the air and the sky opened up.

And the flames began to fall.

~

FEAR CLUTCHED Inken's chest as the dragons took flight, chasing after the black beast that had risen from the mud.

Archon.

The name sent a shiver down to her soul. The man's shadow had hung over their lives for so long now, leaving a dark taint on even the most joyous of memories. Always there, waiting in the distant future, waiting to destroy them.

But now that future had finally arrived. Archon had come, his legend made flesh. They had watched together from the wall as he slaughtered their most powerful Magickers, as he brought Enala and Eric to their knees. Only Caelin's strong arms had stopped Inken from racing to their aid then, and a wave of relief had swept through the defenders as Jurrien arrived.

But now they stood helpless, unable to aid their friends in the desperate fight in the skies above the fortress. There atop the battlements of Fort Fall they waited, tame sheep for the slaughter.

A rumble carried down from overhead and Inken sucked in a breath of fear.

The clouds gathering around the Phoenix had vanished, washed away by a firestorm now falling towards them from high above. Flames licked across the sky and Inken flinched as she felt the first kiss of their heat on her face. Around her the men and women of the Three Nations started to scream and run, but she could only stand and stare, knowing there was nothing they could do to escape the doom rushing towards them.

Above, the dragons still flew towards the firestorm. A surge of hope flickered in Inken's chest as light leapt from the leading dragon. The blue flash of lightning joined it and she knew Eric and Jurrien were fighting back. She just prayed they had the strength to halt the inferno.

Lightning collected around the dark figure of Jurrien, spreading out to coat the sky. White fire joined it, rushing from the Sword of Light to swirl around the dragons, its strength building with each second.

Inken's ears popped as a sudden energy surged in the air, and then the forces of the Light and Sky were rushing up to meet the oncoming inferno.

A deafening crash fell across the wall as the two forces met. Light flashed, blinding the defenders, and it seemed the forces would tear the sky itself asunder. Tears streaming from her eyes, Inken forced herself to look away as white spots swept across her vision.

Please, please, please, she chanted the silent prayer in her mind.

A gust of air struck her then, knocking her from her feet. She tumbled across the cold stone and only the crenulations stopped her from toppling from the wall. Groaning, she blinked her eyes to clear them and looked up, desperate to see her fate.

Overhead the sky had cleared, the waves of black fire all but destroyed.

Not quite, she realised with a trickle of despair. Spots of flame still marked the sky, tumbling down towards them, too close to stop now. Closing her eyes, Inken waited for the end to come.

Then she gasped as the wall beneath her shook and the earth rumbled. Struggling to stand, Inken stared across at

Caelin, mouth wide, unable to speak. The rumbling grew around them, turning to a roar, and then the ground behind the wall split open and a cliff-face of rock rose into the air. Groaning and crackling, the rock grew upwards, surpassing the wall and the pale faced defenders, and spread out overhead to form a shield against the flames.

Inken shivered as dull booms came from above, the flames crashing onto the rock with impotent fury. She hugged herself, tears stinging her eyes, and sent her silent thanks to Enala.

Slowly their rocky shelter receded back into the ground, disappearing into the field behind them until it seemed it had never been. Breathing out a long sigh, Inken searched the sky for sign of the dragons.

Before she could find them, the horns of the defenders began to sound.

Climbing to her feet, Inken stumbled to the edge of the ramparts and looked out across the killing field.

Through the smoke below came the black cloaks of the enemy, emerging like the ghosts of the past. Beasts ran amidst them, Raptors and felines and lizards alike, the whole host of Archon's army come to claim their revenge.

Atop the wall, the defenders watched them come. Not a single man or woman wavered. Pride for her people swelled in Inken's chest. Each of them had witnessed the battle below, the bravery of their Magickers as they went to their death. They had watched as Eric and Enala refused to give an inch to Archon, as they refused to surrender.

Now they faced the tooth and claw and steel of the enemy, and they would live by that example.

Smiling, Inken reached down and drew her blade. It was almost a relief now to see the enemy return, to feel her helplessness swept aside. This was a threat she could face, an enemy she could defeat.

Caelin stepped up beside her, a smile on his face.

"Let's go to war."

ENALA LET out a long breath as Archon's firestorm died on the rocky shield she had torn from the earth. Then she turned her attention back to the sky, and the black creature Archon had become. Reaching into the *Soul Blade*, she sent a pulse of magic into Eric and Enduran, and allowed its healing warmth to flow through her own body.

Thank you, child, the dragon rumbled in her mind.

"Thanks, Enala," Eric echoed the dragon's words, his voice raised over the crack of the wind.

"Do you have a plan?" she shouted back.

Eric laughed, nodding to the smoke drifting around them. "That was about the extent of it."

Enala's heart pounded hard in her chest, but she grinned back. Joy swept through her soul at being a-dragon-back again, to soar through the sky with nothing but the strength of the dragon holding her aloft. It was freedom to her, a final connection to her parents and the gifts they'd given her. If she was to die today, she was glad to have had this last ride.

You are welcome, little one, she heard Enduran's voice and smiled.

It is good to be with you, Enduran. But let us hope this is not *our last ride,* she thought back.

A tremor shook the dragon and she smiled at Enduran's laughter. Ahead the phoenix loomed, its black wings beating the sky. Flames curled out around it, tainted by its dark magic, but there were no clouds now.

"Enduran!" Eric shouted over the howling wind. "Send the others back. There is no point in them risking their lives in this fight."

No, the roar of the other dragons tore the air. *This is the final battle. We shall not flee.*

Enala smiled, warmed by their presence. Beneath her Enduran roared his own response, and then the world erupted in flames, and there was no going back for any of them.

Archon folded his wings and dropped towards them. Around them the jaws of the dragons opened and they unleashed their fire. The dark flames of the Phoenix threaded down to meet them, mingling with the red of the dragon fire and then exploding outwards. Heat washed across them, forcing Enala to draw on her own magic to protect herself from its burning touch.

Behind her she heard Eric shout and then sensed the surge of the Sword's power. White flames leapt past her as Eric pointed the blade, racing up to join the conflagration overhead. Then a boom rocked her in her seat and she looked across to see lightning rushing from the hands of the Storm God.

She stared up, watching the blue and black, the red and white flickering across the sky, and knew she could not hold back. Raising the *Soul Blade,* she threw herself into the green of its magic, seeking out some way to attack the Phoenix up here in the sky, so far from the powers of the Earth.

But this was God magic she held, and with a thrill she remembered what that meant. While normal magic could manipulate the world around it, God magic could *create,* could pull power from the air itself.

Gritting her teeth, Enala released herself to the draw of the God magic, willing it to aid her. In her mind's eye, she imagined the sky filling with stone.

Enala's ears popped and a shudder went through her as energy poured from the *Soul Blade*. She looked around to see great boulders appearing in the air around them, and with a scream she turned back to Eric. *"Catch them!"*

Eric smiled and spared her a nod. White flashed from the Sword of Light and then the boulders were racing upwards, slicing through the inferno overhead without resistance. A scream came from beyond the flames, echoing across the sky, and Enala threw back her head and laughed.

Around them the wind shrieked, rushing past to gather in Jurrien's hands. Enala glanced across at the Storm God, her eyes widening as she saw the forces swirling around Gabriel's body. Wind roared in from every direction, tearing through the flames licking the sky. Lightning thundered, flickering amidst the winds as a tornado of electricity swept around Jurrien.

With a scream of rage, Jurrien threw out his hands, directing the hurricane upwards. Wind howled and then the tempest of wind and lightning was racing into the depths of the firestorm overhead, hurling it back at the Phoenix.

The black scream came again, more beast than human, and then the Phoenix was falling, twisting in the air to sweep past the host of dragons. For a second a rush of elation swept through Enala, but terror still clung to her soul and she knew they had not won yet.

Her fears were confirmed as the wings of the Phoenix swept out, halting its fall. Spinning, the black wings swung towards them and a wave of flame raced out to catch the nearest dragon.

The gold dragon's neck arched backwards as it screamed, the dark flames eating through flesh and scale and wing. With a final roar, its wings crumpled and it began to fall.

Panic gripped Enala as she threw out her arm. A ray of green streamed from the *Soul Blade*, racing down to catch the injured dragon in its warmth. Within the span of seconds, she watched its flesh knit back together and golden scales reform like feathers from its skin. The dragon yelped, the reversal catching it by surprise. Then the wind caught in its restored wings and it surged back up towards them.

Lightning crackled and Enala looked across to see the clouds regathering around Jurrien.

The Phoenix drew to a halt in mid-air, its head twisting, almost in curiosity.

Have we not fought this battle before, Storm God? Archon's words hissed through Enala's mind.

"Yes," Jurrien roared. "But this time we have the Light. Eric, now!"

Enala twisted around to look at Eric, expecting fire or raw energy to rush from the Sword. But her brother's eyes were closed, the light of the Sword washing over his face.

"Eric, what are you doing!" she shrieked.

Then the Phoenix screamed, convulsing in the air as chunks of darkness tore from its wings. The sound stabbed at Enala's ears and sent a tremor through Enduran. Closing her eyes, Enala strove to force the noise from her mind, to focus against its darkness.

She heard Jurrien shout his hatred and sensed the rushing throb as the Storm God unleashed another attack. Forcing open her eyes, she watched through tears as the reformed twister rushed down to engulf the Phoenix.

The beast screeched again, flames tearing from its body as it shook, wings beating hard to escape. But the winds had already caught it, trapping the creature within the power of the twister.

Thunder shook the sky as the first bolt of blue fire struck, tearing fresh chunks of darkness from the cruel body. The wind roared, catching in the Phoenix's wings and whirling it around. Another crash and another screech followed as the lightning crackled, burning at the foul creature.

Enduran's great head shook and his wing beats faltered,

the awful sound tearing at his strength. Enala struggled to cover her ears, unable to release the *Soul Blade* for fear of losing its power. At any moment she might need it.

Glancing back again at Eric, she saw blood trickling from his ears. A sudden shudder swept through him and he started to convulse. His hand slipped from the dragon's back, and he would have fallen if she had not reached out to steady him. Still the white flashed from the Sword of Light, and with a rush of realisation, Enala knew what he was doing.

Eric had delved into the arsenal within the Sword, and finally unleashed its greatest power. He was using the magic of the Light to fight Archon's magic, to render him defenceless against their attacks. And watching the Phoenix writhing within the twister, the winds and lightning tearing it to pieces, she knew it was working.

But how long could he last?

Enala shuddered as she twisted on the dragon's back to face her brother. Blood ran from his eyes and nose, streaming down his throat, and she knew he was giving everything he had to hold back Archon's magic.

Gripping tight to the *Soul Blade*, Enala reached for its magic and sent it pouring into her brother.

A cough came from Eric and she breathed out in relief as the flow of blood slowed. Smiling, she held him close, offering her silent comfort. The darkness within the *Soul Blade* seemed less now, a small thing beside the love she felt for her brother and those below. She held that feeling tight, and gathered her strength.

Then Eric gave an awful groan and coughed. Blood splattered her shirt as his head lolled and his eyes rolled into the back of his head. His hand remained clamped around the Sword of Light, an iron grip that would not release until death, but the rest of his body went limp.

Enala pulled him close as the howling wind ceased with a

sudden tearing sound. The lightning flashed blue one final time and went out. The air cleared, the storm clouds sucked away in a rush of noiseless movement.

The dragons hovered in place, their wings beating hard as they turned to face where Archon had been. As the last of the clouds faded away, a single word hissed through their minds.

Die!

Enala raised the *Soul Blade* as the Phoenix reappeared, coalescing from a ball of darkness back to the flaming bird of before. But before she could reach for the *Soul Blade's* power, darkness exploded from its flaming wings and rushed outwards in all directions.

The dragons roared, their wings beating hard in desperate retreat as they tried to escape the flames. But there was nowhere to go, no place to hide in the empty sky. Enala screamed, an icy hand clutching her heart as she stared at the unstoppable tide closing on them.

Around her the dragons roared again as the flames found them, a terrible, gut-wrenching noise, their agony made sound. Gripping Eric tight, Enala squeezed her eyes shut and waited for the end to come.

She did not have to wait long. Tongues of flames licked at her flesh, igniting waves of pain that rippled through her body. Agony filled her, robbing her of the breath to even scream. Her voice caught in her throat, her mind exploding, her sanity washed away on a river of pain.

The magic of the *Soul Blade* poured into her, into Eric and Enduran, but it could not hold back the burning agony, could not stop the torturous fire. It was not enough to save them.

Enala's stomach rose into her chest as they began to fall, Enduran still beneath them, but his strength gone. Wind whipped at Enala's hair, her clothes, its icy touch agony on her blackened flesh. She screamed then, finally finding her voice. But now she could not stop, could not cut it off.

Opening her eyes, Enala watched the earth race up to meet them.

And then everything went black.

CHAPTER 22

Inken ducked beneath a wild swing and plunged her blade into the chest of the man facing her. Stepping back, she felt the breath of an axe sweep past her face. Then Caelin was there, his short sword smashing into the head of the hulking giant who had just made the wall.

As the man toppled backwards, Inken heard a growl from behind and spun. A Raptor stalked across the ramparts, a hungry longing in its sickly yellow eyes. She screamed a warning to Caelin as it leapt, throwing herself to the side as it swept past. Its claws tore through the fabric of her sleeve and a burning sting lanced from her arm as they found flesh.

Then she was up, already spinning to drive her blade into its side. She had lost her sabre what seemed like hours ago and she now wielded a short sword. Its razor sharp blade bit deep into the beast's stomach and lodged between its ribs. She released the hilt as it swung to bite her and threw herself backwards.

Caelin raced in from its other side and drove his own short sword into the Raptor's neck. The beast screeched, staggering on the slippery stones, turning from one to another.

But the blades had made their presence felt, and as it tried to charge them the strength went from its limbs. It toppled to the ground and lay still.

Recovering his blade, Caelin stabbed it through the creature's eye to ensure it was dead. Inken stepped up and retrieved her blade before anything else came at them.

They stood together for a moment in a pocket of calm, back to back as they surveyed the battle. Along the wall the enemy streamed up their ladders to throw themselves at the defenders. The roar of the beasts chilled her, the clack of their claws on the stone wall mixing with the clanging of steel.

But despite the odds, the defenders were holding their ground. They fought with grim faces, stretched with exhaustion, their clothes and armour torn and broken, but they *stood*. Comrades in arms, they refused to give an inch to the dark creatures and men fighting beneath Archon's flag. Hundreds of them had fallen, but for every man that fell another defender would step up to take his place in the line.

Inken unleashed a wild laugh, adrenaline surging through her veins as another black-garbed man rushed at her. He fell within seconds, another victim to add to her countless tally. Pride filled her as she watched the defenders fight around her. Nearby she glimpsed May, moving through the men and beasts like a dancer, a sword in one hand and a dagger in the other. Even the dark creatures of the wasteland gave her dance of death a wide berth, and behind her the defenders mustered.

All along the wall, the brave souls of the Three Nations held strong, fighting back to back in places, determined to make the enemy pay dearly for their lives. Defenders streamed up the staircases, reinforcements rushing from the third wall to join them. It seemed an unspoken command had gone out – that this was the final battle, that they would hold them at the second wall or fall in a glorious final stand.

Then a boom rang out from overhead, crashing over the wall like the tolling of a bell. Inken stole a glance up as the enemy closed again, and choked back a cry of despair.

The dragons were falling, tumbling from the sky as black fire licked at their golden scales. The flames were eating them alive, burning away the flesh and bone of all but one of the wondrous beasts. Inken stared as that last golden body plummeted towards the earth. A green glow covered the dragon, shaking off the last of the black flames, and she knew it was Enduran, and that Eric and Enala still clung to his back.

The falling dragon disappeared behind the spires of the citadel, followed the distant echo of a thud. A groan rippled through the defenders as their eyes went to the sky, watching for the Phoenix, waiting for the firestorm to fall.

Inken watched as Archon streaked through the sky, but for now he seemed to have forgotten the fortress. The Phoenix chased after the fallen dragon, a trail of flame licking out behind it, and vanished behind the walls of Fort Fall.

Tears stung Inken's eyes and she bit back a groan.

"Eric!" she roared as the enemy came at them again.

Every fibre of Inken's being screamed for her to go to him, but instead she threw herself at the enemy. She blinked through her tears, swinging her sword with a wild rage she could not control. She refused to give in, refused to accept defeat now, not after they had all sacrificed so much. The enemy flinched back before her fury and fell beneath her blade. Caelin joined her, his own blade a blur, a rage burning in his eyes that almost matched her own.

Yet their ferocity was not matched by their fellow defenders. The sight of the dragons falling had stolen something from them – their courage, their hope. She could sense it in the air, in the hesitation of the men around her. Despair hung across the wall like a cloud, stealing away their strength.

They all knew the truth. With the last of their Magickers gone, it would not be long before Archon came now. And when he did, there was no one left to protect them from his wrath. They would be helpless before his magic.

In contrast, the enemy had drawn strength from the sight, and attacked now with renewed fury.

Bit by bit, the defenders gave ground before the enemy. Inken struggled against the pull, surging forward again and again, drawing the boldest of the defenders with her. But one by one they fell around her, and others no longer stepped up to replace them.

The enemy numbers swelled, the weight of their bodies forcing her back. Her sword flashed like a living thing, an extension of her own body that lanced out to slay the black tide before her. But now she hardly had space to move, and one step at a time she retreated with Caelin towards the stairs.

She glanced at her friend and caught the desperation in his eyes. A blade lanced for his throat and she threw up her sword to deflect it. Caelin shook himself and took another step back, nodding his thanks.

Then they were at the stairs and there was no choice left but to turn and flee. Her sword heavy in her hand, Inken grabbed Caelin's hand and spun, leaping for the first step. The bigger man came after her, and together they raced after their retreating comrades.

Ahead of them defenders streamed across the field between the walls, churning the ground to mud beneath their boots. Inken gasped as beasts jumped down from the ramparts overhead, landing without trouble despite the height. Raptors raced after the defenders, leaping high to land on the backs of fleeing men. Their weight drove them to the ground as the razor sharp teeth flashed out to tear chunks from their helpless victims.

Inken's heart lurched with fear as they reached the ground and joined the fray.

"It's a rout!" Caelin's voice carried over the screams of the dying.

All around them their people were being slaughtered as they ran, falling to the claws of the beasts and arrows from the enemy atop the wall they had just lost. And every second more of the enemy reached the ramparts above, adding their weight to the slaughter. A crash came from nearby as a battering ram slammed into the gates.

Inken could hardly find the will to run. Her eyes scanned the scene, staring at the slaughter as though she were apart from it, as if this were happening to someone else. Another crack came from the gates as the wooden beam holding them shattered. Then a fresh wave of enemies poured into the fight, rushing through the gateway to join the slaughter.

She looked at the third wall and the scant defenders atop its ramparts – those few who had obeyed their orders and remained at their posts. The gates stood open, just a hundred yards away.

So close, but so far.

Even so, they had to try. Steeling herself, Inken charged into the fray, dragging Caelin with her. Her sword licked out, catching the enemy fighters as they stood and hacked at the fallen defenders. Guilt clawed at her soul as they ran past their injured comrades, their desperate screams chasing after them. But there was no time to save them – it was everyone for themselves now.

Staring ahead, Inken fixed her eyes on the open gates and prayed they could reach them in time. But even as the thought came the wooden doors began to close, swinging in towards them. A cry of despair came from the men around her as others picked up speed, desperate to reach the relative safety of the third wall.

The strength fled Inken's legs as she staggered to a stop. The gap between the gates quickly closed, shrinking to a thin sliver through which a few stragglers managed to slip. She stared at the wall, her gaze catching on the eyes of the men above. Caelin drew to a stop beside her, his shoulders slumped, despair carving deep shadows beneath his eyes.

Side by side, they turned to face the oncoming enemy, swords raised in defiance. The other defenders gathered around them, forming a thin wall in the middle of the field. Shoulder to shoulder, they watched the black tide sweep towards them. Claws shone and fangs flashed in the mouths of the massive felines as the enemy charged.

Then a boom came from the wall behind them and Inken spun. The gates were opening again and those nearest the gates were throwing themselves to the side. From beyond came the rhythmic thump of hooves on the hard ground.

Inken's breath caught in her throat as the first of the horsemen appeared. They rushed through the gateway like a river from a narrow gorge, the red horses of the Plorsean cavalry. At their head rode King Fraser and Elton, a wicked joy on their faces as they charged at the enemy. Lances pointed, they raced past the survivors of the second wall and plunged into the unsuspecting enemy. Caught in the open, beast and man alike fell to their steel-tipped lances.

A cheer rose up from the men atop the third wall as the Plorsean cavalry turned and charged again, crushing the enemy as they tried to reform beneath the shelter of the second wall. Pressed in on themselves with the stone to their back, they died by the hundreds.

Beside her Caelin gave a whoop of joy, raising a fist in triumph. "They made it!" he turned and lifted Inken off her feet. Swinging her around, he shouted again. "They made it!"

Inken joined his laughter, but reason quickly returned as he lowered her back to the ground. They had lost the second wall, and the Plorsean cavalry could not change that. Their turn of fortunes would not last long. Already the enemy was forming up again, gathering atop the wall. Arrows rose up from the ramparts to fall on the Plorseans and several horses crumpled in the deadly rain.

"Come on," she shouted back. "Let's go."

Together they stumbled towards the open gates.

ARCHON STRODE across the burning ground, the flames dying at his touch. The body of the dragon lay nearby, its last pitiful gasps echoing from the walls of the fortress behind him. He ignored it; its death was of little concern. He had eyes only for his ancestors now. Jurrien had vanished, but he would deal with the wily God soon enough. For now, he was preoccupied with his magic, with the dark threads of power he had wrapped around the two Magickers, binding their souls to their broken bodies.

They lay beside each other on the icy ground, their arms outstretched, almost touching. Their legs and arms lay at awful angles, their bones shattered by the impact. In normal circumstances their hearts would have already given out, but Archon refused to give them the satisfaction of death. His magic washed over them, holding them to life.

The Sword of Light lay nearby. Smiling, he reached down and lifted it from the ground. Light flashed from the blade and then died away. Shaking his head, he moved to Eric's side.

"Such a curse," he whispered, staring at the blade. "If only I had known."

Leaning down, he placed it in the boy's hand. The light flashed again and a groan rattled up from Eric's broken chest.

Archon smiled, sensing the flow of God magic streaming

from the Sword into Eric's undefended body. It would not take long to take hold, to crush the feeble resistance of his soul and gain dominion over his body.

Moving away again, he recovered the *Soul Blade* Enala had wielded.

"My sweet daughter, please, accept my gift," his voice was hard as he reached down and placed the blade in Enala's hand.

"*No*," the groan came from the girl's torn lips, but his magic kept her unconscious.

Her back arched as green light flooded from the *Soul Blade.* He grinned, watching as it took hold, burning through her veins to cast off the feeble remains of her magic.

Turning away, he walked to the dragon and sat on its broken head.

Smiling, he waited for his Gods to be born.

CHAPTER 23

Enala groaned as sensation came rushing back. To her surprise she felt no pain, but even so the sudden return to reality was overwhelming, her whole body throbbing with the shock of her return. Biting her lips, she forced herself to open her eyes.

"*What?*" she whispered, unable to comprehend the sight that greeted her.

There was nothing. No burning sky or broken dragons, no Fort Fall, no Archon. Only empty white, stretching out to eternity without so much as a shadow to break the nothingness. She lay amidst that emptiness, alone in oblivion.

Standing, Enala looked around, mouth wide as she struggled to come to terms with her surroundings. She shuddered, knowing she could only be dead, that her soul had been sent to the otherworld. Her breath caught in her throat as she thought of spending eternity in this place, alone but for the memories of the world she'd left behind. She would surely go mad.

"Where am I?" she breathed, tears burning in her eyes. This could not be happening, could not be the end.

Her words echoed out across the void and returned to mock her. She groaned, reaching up to cover her ears, her eyes, anything to deny the reality around her.

"You are in the spirit realm," Enala jumped as a girl's voice spoke.

Heart pounding hard in her chest, Enala spun, the hackles on her neck rising in warning. She gasped as her eyes found the girl behind her, and if anything, her heart beat faster.

Antonia stood before her, her violet eyes pinched with sadness. She wore the same lime green dress as in the vision Archon had shown, and her auburn hair hung limp about her shoulders. A pale glow seeped out around her, staining the whiteness of the void an emerald green. Enala stared into the ancient wisdom hiding in the depths of her eyes, unable to find the words to speak.

"Hello, Enala," Antonia gave a sad smile. "It's nice to finally meet you."

"I... I... How are you here?"

Antonia reached out, drawing Enala into her arms. "You put up a brave fight, Enala."

Enala shuddered and sank to her knees, the comfort of the Goddess doing little to warm her despair. "We lost," she whispered.

"You did better than any of us could have ever imagined," she squeezed Enala tight and drew back. "I'm sorry..."

Enala looked away. "I thought we had him there, at the end."

"You almost did. I wish I could have given you the strength to finish him, but Eric's soul was not strong enough to cope with the God magic pouring into his body. It burned him, body and mind, until he could hold on no longer. Our magic was never meant to be used by mortals."

"What will happen now?" Enala could not keep the

despair from her voice. "To the others, to Inken and Caelin and May, all those soldiers in Fort Fall?"

"You will kill them all," Antonia murmured.

A shiver ran down Enala's spine. "*What?*"

"Archon has done as he promised. He is holding your body to life and has put the *Soul Blade* in your hands. That is why I am able to come to you. But even as we speak, my power is flooding your body, taking it for its own. This time you will not have the strength to take it back, Enala."

"No, no, no," Enala wrapped her arms around her chest. "I have to wake up."

Reaching up, she twined her fingers through her hair and pulled. The fragile strands tore from her scalp, sending pain shooting through her head, but it did nothing to change the void around them.

"There is no fighting it, Enala," tears watered in Antonia's eyes. "Your body is broken. Were you to wake, even for a second, the pain would drive you insane and the God magic would take you anyway."

"Then what?" Enala leapt to her feet. "Do we just sit here and watch? Watch as I slaughter every man and woman in that fortress? Watch as the light fades from the eyes of my friends?"

Enala stalked across to the tiny Goddess, rage burning away her despair. She wanted to kick and scream and *fight*, anything but sit here as helpless witness. She could not bear it, could not sit back as the God power destroyed everything she had fought for. There had to be *something* they could do.

Antonia bowed her head, refusing to look her in the eye. "There is something," she murmured.

"*What?*" Desperation made Enala bold. Reaching out, she grabbed the Goddess by her dress, dragging her close, forcing Antonia to meet her gaze. "*What can we do?*"

Tears spilt from Antonia's eyes. "I promised I would

never ask again," she tore herself loose of Enala's grasp and turned to stare out into the empty whiteness. "Not after last time. I cannot do it."

Enala hesitated, shocked by Antonia's grief. She approached slowly, placing a hand on her shoulder. "What is it, Antonia?"

Antonia turned, misery in her violet eyes. "To ask someone to make the ultimate sacrifice. To ask you to give me your body and allow me to be reborn."

Enala staggered back as the dreadful truth of Antonia's words rang in her ears.

"No," she breathed, staring at the Goddess. "You can't ask that; you can't make me."

Antonia shook her head. "I would never. It is your choice, Enala, yours alone."

Groaning, Enala spun, searching the void for some escape. But there was only the emptiness, the relentless nothing of the spirit plain. Despair clung to her soul, and she wrapped her arms around herself again, desperate for comfort. She longed for one last moment in reality, to breathe in the scents of the forest, to ride on a dragon's back one final time, to find comfort in the arms of the man she loved.

Gabriel.

Enala closed her eyes, feeling again the pain as she realised his sacrifice. Now Antonia had asked her to make the same choice, to give away her life so the rest of the Three Nations might survive.

"What will it be like?" she asked at last, her voice no more than a whisper.

"You will feel no pain," Antonia's words were laced with grief. "For a time… your soul would remain, bound with mine. But eventually…" her voice broke, "eventually it would succumb. Your being would be enveloped by me, become a part of me, and you would be no more."

Enala took a deep, shuddering breath, summoning the last dredges of her courage. Looking up, she found the violet glow of the Goddess' eyes.

"Do it."

~

LIGHT. Brilliant, shining light, everywhere Eric looked. He spun, searching for a break, a single flaw or contrast to offer some hint of reality. But there was nothing – only the never-ending nothingness.

Finally, he abandoned the search. Releasing his breath, he sank to the ground, still struggling to come to terms with the reality around him.

"What is this place?" he breathed.

What had happened, there at the end? They had been so close, so close to destroying Archon's darkness. If only he could have held on a few moments more, if only he'd had the strength. But the white fire had swept through his body, flooding every crevice of his mind. It burned at his soul, tearing at his every thought, his every memory. Even now he struggled to put the pieces of the battle together.

Jurrien's voice had been whispering in his mind, images flashing through his thoughts, leading him into the depths of the Sword of Light's power. He had seen then what he had to do, how to use the magic of the Light to bind Archon's power.

And it had almost worked. Deprived of his dark magic, the Phoenix had lost its form and been trapped within the tempest of Jurrien's magic.

But the power of the Sword had been too much, and Eric's soul had finally given way before its all-consuming flame. He'd found himself falling, his magic crumbling to dust as the Light overwhelmed him.

Perhaps that was why he found himself here in this empty domain.

Eric looked up as a distant thud echoed through the void, the sound like a rock dropped on a tiled floor.

Or the thud of heavy boots.

Another thud followed, and another, coming close. A tingle spread down his spine as he spun to search the void anew. Heart pounding in his chest, Eric pulled himself back to his feet. He stared into the white, searching for the first hint of danger, half-expecting Archon to appear from some hidden crevice.

Instead he was met by the image of an old man. Lines of age streaked his face and his skin hung from his cheeks in paled bags. Thin white hair grew down to his knees, its wiry lengths fading into the emptiness around them. He wore grey robes of rough fabric, but came unarmed, his empty hands trembling as he walked. A faint glow came from the man and his white eyes were filled with sadness.

"Eric," the man rasped, his voice as soft as falling snow. "It is nice to finally meet the man beyond the veil."

A tingle of recognition ran through Eric and for a second he thought of his mentor, Alastair. Sadness filled him, but he knew this was not his tutor. This man was far older, his age beyond counting.

"Who are you?" he asked, a creeping suspicion rising in his throat.

The old man sighed, sadness sweeping across his face. "I am Darius."

The name tolled in Eric's mind, ringing like a bell through his memories as he looked on the face of the God of Light. He recognised him now, though the man seemed to have aged far faster than his siblings.

A sickness curled through Eric, a violent anger at the spirit standing before him now. The God of Light had abandoned the Three Nations centuries ago, and in his absence the power of Archon had grown to fill the vacuum.

"Where have you been?" Eric hissed, unable to control his rage. "What are you doing here, now, after a thousand lives have been lost, when the war is all but done? *Why?*" he all but shouted the last word.

Darius closed his eyes, the wrinkles on his forehead knotting with pain. "You do not understand," his eyes opened again, catching Eric in their ancient depths. "I have been *here*, Eric. I have been here all along."

Eric found himself frozen in the God's gaze. "What do you mean?" he growled. "Where are we?"

"We are in the spirit realm, in a portion of it twisted by Archon and trapped within his *Soul Blade*," Darius paused. "His very first *Soul Blade*. I believe you call it the Sword of Light."

"*No,*" Eric staggered back, his heart freezing in his chest, unable to believe the words. He shook his head. "No…"

Ice spread through his veins as he stared at the wasted figure of the God of Light, at the ancient spirit standing amidst the nothingness of the void.

No, it can't be.

But Eric could not deny the truth standing before him. He felt his world turning on end, the story of Darius and his absence cracking the very fabric of his reality.

The God of Light had not abandoned them. He had been trapped, locked away for eternity.

"All this time?" Eric breathed, a sharp pain burning in his chest. "*How?*"

Darius moved past him, his movements slow, weighed down by his centuries of imprisonment.

"We never expected him to return," emotion laced his

voice, sad and filled with regret. "Five hundred years ago there was a boy who hated us, who hated me because I took his father from him," he shook his head. "It has been our everlasting shame, that three mortals gave up their lives for us to be born. But we did not expect the hate it would nurture in the boy, the path it would send him down."

"His name was Archon, son to Nickolas, brother to Artemis – your ancestor. While his brother ultimately accepted his father's sacrifice, the boy Archon could not do the same. Both wielded powerful magic, but my birth sent them down separate paths. Artemis welcomed the new world, joining us in our efforts to rebuild his nation and bring peace to the Three Nations. But Archon, he spurned us and the future his father had sacrificed himself to build. Instead he turned to the darkness, embracing the power offered by black magic, and used it to slay the priests who had brought us into the world."

"But you did not kill him," Eric whispered.

"No," Darius met his eyes. "We have never used our power to kill. When we caught him, he was banished to the wasteland in the north. And that was the end of it."

"Except it wasn't, was it?" Eric's anger bubbled up again but he pressed it down now. Who was he to judge the mistakes of the Gods?

"We thought we had done the right thing, showing mercy, even to one so steeped in dark magic. We did not expect his hatred to fester, for him to surrender so completely to that darkness. He spent decades in that wasteland, brooding, preparing his revenge. And we forgot," he paused. "But when he stabbed me in the back, somehow, I knew it was him."

"How did it happen?"

Darius shook his head, the pain on his face evident. "I took another criminal north, leaving him where he could do no more harm to our people. I did not expect an ambush, certainly not by such a powerful magic. Somehow Archon had discovered where I usually appeared to release the banished, and there he waited for me, concealed by his dark magic. Before I sensed his presence, he drove his foul blade through my back."

"Then how did we get the Sword?" Eric frowned.

Darius gave a wry smile. "I am the God of Light. Even with my magic pouring into the *Soul Blade* and the life fleeing my mortal body, I was not going to allow my magic to fall into his hands. I broke free of his dark magic, and we fought – the Light against the darkness. But Archon had grown more powerful than I could possibly have imagined, and I quickly realised it was a battle I could not win."

"Archon knew it too. He hammered at me with his magic, determined to see me fall. But when I felt his final attack building, I reached back and tore his *Soul Blade* from my flesh. I held it high, feeling its pull tugging at my spirit. But I had enough strength left for one final effort, and with the last of my power I hurled it into the void, back to Trola and the host of Magickers waiting in the Temple of Light."

"And they thought you had abandoned them," Eric croaked.

Darius waved a hand. "I have spent a century listening to the thoughts of the Trolan royalty. I know what they thought, Eric. But I never had the strength to reach them," his words were filled with sorrow. "So many died, thinking I did not care."

Eric stared at the God of Light, imagining his desolation as centuries of Sword wielders passed by while he lay trapped within the blade. He could not begin to envision the pain, the despair of such a fate. It would have driven Eric mad. Yet here Darius stood, withered by his entrapment, but *alive*.

One question still remained though: was it too late to turn the tide of the battle?

"We need your help, Darius. Archon, he's winning."

Darius shook his head. "No, Eric. He has *won*. Even now the Sword's magic is burning through your body, giving it life, taking control. Soon you and your sister will become the very demons you fought to stop. The Three Nations will fall before your power."

"I won't let that happen," Eric stepped towards the God and grabbed his wrist. Before Darius could free himself, Eric pulled him close. "I know what I have to do. Gabriel has already done the same, sacrificed himself to allow Jurrien to be reborn. I can do the same for you."

Darius tore his arm free. "You do not know what you ask," he looked around the void, the white nothingness. "I cannot return to the world now, not after all this time. Here… it is peaceful. I can feel the pain, the sorrow coming from beyond the veil. I cannot face that world again."

"You must!" Eric grabbed the old man by the shoulders and shook him. "The Three Nations need you, they need the God of Light to return to our world. Whether you meant to or not, without your power the world outside has withered, and evil has crept into the void left by the Light. Dark magic has wiped entire lands clean of life, and not even Antonia can restore them. If Archon wins, there will be no more light, no more life. Only darkness."

Anger flashed in Darius' eyes. "That is not my fault. I fought this fight, gave my magic to your world. I tried to help you foolish creatures. *And how did you repay me?"*

Eric refused to retreat before the God's fury. "And do you not want revenge for that? Don't you want to show Archon your true power? To cast him down as he did to you?"

"Do not try to bait me, boy. I do not need revenge,"

Darius growled. He turned away, then back again. "You won't stop, will you? You won't give up?"

"Never."

Darius sighed, a weary resignation crossing his face. "I guess one way or another, my peace has come to an end then," he drew in a deep breath and stared down at Eric. "You are sure?"

Eric swallowed, thinking of all he was about to give up. Inken's face drifted through his thoughts and pain twisted in his chest. She would be alone now, their child left without a father. But he could see no other way to save them, to save them all.

Closing his eyes, he summoned his courage and nodded. "Do it."

CHAPTER 24

Inken stood atop the ramparts of the last wall and stared down at the endless ranks of the enemy. It had not taken them long to reform on the killing ground below. They looked up at the defenders now without fear, knowing the end was within sight, that victory would soon be theirs. They filled the space below, knowing the defenders had nothing left to hurl at them. The dragons were dead, their Magickers destroyed – even their stocks of arrows had run dry.

Her stomach clenched with regret. *If only we had run, Eric, all that time ago in Lon. We could have been free.*

But it was too late now for regrets, for second thoughts. The time had come for the Three Nations to make their last stand, to take their final breaths of freedom. With the arrival of the Plorsean army, the combined might of the Three Nations now stood atop the wall, ready to defy the forces below one final time. The weight of responsibility weighed on all their shoulders. Behind them the land stood open, their friends and families defenceless.

Caelin and May stood to her left while Elton and King Fraser waited on her right. The king had driven his army hard, leaving the stragglers behind in his desperation to reach the fortress. His forced marches had caught them up with Elton's vanguard, and the bulk of the Plorsean army had arrived together.

Their reunion had been quick, stolen hugs and tears turning quickly to the matter at hand. Inken's heart soared to see the king again. They had conquered the darkness together, the three of them, and had emerged stronger for it. Now they had one final battle to face together and she was proud to stand alongside them.

Behind them there had been no sign of the Phoenix or dragons or Eric and Enala. Inken drew strength from that, from the thought there might still be hope. It flickered in her chest, its tiny flame keeping her alive.

If Archon had not returned, it could only mean their friends continued to fight.

"Here they come," Fraser spoke. His voice rose to a boom. "Here they come, boys and girls. Let's show them what we're made of!" he drew his sword, the steel flashing in the afternoon sun.

Inken smiled, reaching down to unsheathe her own blade. If she had to die, she was glad to do so with the company around her.

Below the enemy surged forward, their hateful voices rising up to wash across the battlements.

Together the men and women of the Three Nations watched them come.

THE SENSATION BEGAN as a tingle in Eric's arms, a warmth

that quickly spread through the rest of him. But the feeling felt strangely detached from him, as though he were perceiving someone else's body. Then his arms moved, shifting as though by a will of their own, reaching down to push him from the mud. Pain shot through his elbow as something went *crack* and he made to scream, but his mouth did not respond.

A groan rattled up from his chest, but he felt curiously disconnected from the movement, as though it had been someone else's groan.

Relax, Eric. This is no longer your fight. Sit back and watch, Darius' voice whispered through his mind.

Eric's eyelids fluttered and opened, revealing a world torn by chaos. Dark clouds raced across the sky, the sun streaming through gaps to light the world below. The earth beneath him was blacked and broken, while a few yards away the body of a dragon lay dead.

Sadness clenched his chest as his eyes lingered on Enduran, then drifted up to the man sitting atop the dragon's head.

Archon looked back, his eyes shining with hate.

A hand settled on his shoulder. He looked up and warmth blossomed in his chest, a love far stronger than any mortal emotion.

"Antonia," the word slipped from his mouth.

The face of Enala stared back, but changed, her eyes now a brilliant violet and filled with the ancient wisdom of the Goddess. A tear spilt from her eyes as she reached out to touch his cheek.

"Darius, brother, how is this possible?"

"A long story, my dear sister," Darius sighed as heat spread from her fingers.

He nodded his thanks as the warmth spread and the

broken parts within him knitted themselves back together. Within seconds he found himself whole, and stood. Together they turned to face Archon. A boom of thunder shook the sky, followed by the crackling of lightning. Then Jurrien stood on his other side, his face dark with anger.

"Brother," he nodded at Darius. "Glad to see you again. I'm about ready to be done with this pitiful excuse of a mortal."

Archon laughed as he climbed to his feet, but Darius saw the hesitation on his face. He could not have expected this. The man had no empathy; he had never been able to understand how his father could have given his life to create a better world for his children. For Gabriel, Enala and Eric all to have made the same decision was beyond Archon's comprehension.

"I am hardly mortal," Archon hissed, his breath misting on the cold air. He dropped from the dragon, landing lightly on the blackened ground.

Darius closed his eyes, joying in the breath of wind running across his skin, in the scent of mud and the feel of the earth beneath his feet. Memory of such sensations had long since faded in the void of his imprisonment, and he experienced them now with renewed wonder. Truly, Eric had given him a gift beyond measure.

"You were born of my Earth, Archon. Now we shall return you to it," his sister's voice was laced with anger.

Reaching across, Darius grasped her hand. "Careful, little sis," she scowled at him for using his nickname for her. "Even with the three of us, he is still dangerous."

Pain flashed across Antonia's face. "Believe me, Darius, we know that all too well."

Darius nodded, regret at his absence eating into him.

"Let's end this," Jurrien growled.

CAELIN SCREAMED as a blade swept past his guard and slashed across his ribs. He staggered backwards, an awkward swing of his sword knocking aside a second attack. Inken stepped past him, her blade flashing out to crush the helmet of his attacker. Then Elton was at his side, steadying him, and he nodded his thanks.

Swallowing his pain, Caelin hurled himself back into the fray. Blood ran from his arm but it did not slow him. An axeman charged him and the wicked blade came around in a wild swing. Ducking back, he charged in as the axe swept past. The man's eyes widened as he buried his sword in his chest.

Stepping sideways, Caelin spun as footsteps crunched behind him. Elton shouted and flung himself backwards, and Caelin managed to pull back the blow before it landed.

Elton nodded at him and raised an eyebrow. "A little jumpy there, Caelin. Try not to do the enemy any favours would you?"

Caelin laughed, the blood surging in his veins. Grinning, he shoved Elton aside as another man charged them, parrying a blow and then slamming his elbow into the man's face. As he prepared to finish him, Elton swept past and stabbed the man in the chest.

Panting, Caelin shook his head. "Thief."

Elton only laughed, already moving on to his next opponent.

A low growl came from behind and Caelin spun to see Inken engaging with a feline. Elton stepped up beside him and together they charged to their friend's aid.

"Nasty looking one," Elton commented as Inken retreated from the beast.

Inken laughed. "How can you tell?"

Caelin stared at the approaching beast, its long fur bristling as it crouched low. The golden eyes studied them with a frightening intelligence. Though fewer in number, the felines had proved just as deadly as the Raptors, and he had no wish to underestimate this one.

As it slunk towards them they spread out, splitting the cat's attention as much as they could on the narrow ramparts. Blood ran from the beast's jaws, matting in the fur beneath its chin. Its claws were extended, scraping on the stones beneath it.

"Now!" Caelin screamed as the thick muscles of the cat's back bunched.

The beast sprang towards them, its paws raised to smash them from their feet. Inken threw herself sideways, her sword sweeping up to deflect its blow. Caelin leapt forwards, the jagged claws coming within an inch of his face, and lashed out with his sword. A judder ran up his arm as the blow struck bone and was turned aside.

Then the momentum of the beast's charge carried it past. They turned and watched it come again, waiting for an opportunity to strike. The cat moved with unbelievable speed, giving them only a second to react before it charged.

This time Caelin was not fast enough. The air exploded from his lungs as the massive paws smashed into his chest, sending him bouncing back to the stone. He heard a scream from somewhere overhead and a cry, then he rolled. The scrape of claw on stone grated in his ears as the beast's paws smashed the ground where he had fallen.

Wheezing hard, Caelin climbed to his knees, watching as Elton and Inken drew the feline's attention. It stalked towards them, the sergeant forgotten behind it, and he smiled. Lifting his sword, he finally caught his winded breath and stood.

Before he could strike, the beast charged the others, its

wild roar echoing across the wall. Inken stumbled back, slipping on the slick stone, and the feline leapt. Caelin cried out as it smashed Inken from her feet and sent her crashing to the stone. Its jaws opened, revealing the massive fangs.

Caelin acted without thought, hurling himself forward to land on the back of the feline. Driving his sword deep into the beast's back, he held on for dear life. Beneath him, the cat threw back its head and screeched. It twisted and leapt, desperate to throw him off.

With a final shake, Caelin's fingers slipped from its fur and he bounced across the stone, his blade still embedded in the beast's back. Before he could move, it bounded forward and sank its jaws into the flesh of his leg.

A scream slipped from Caelin's throat as its fangs tore into his flesh. He scrambled backwards but found himself trapped, the iron jaws refusing to release him. He looked into the yellow eyes of the creature, almost imagining it smiling. With a shake of its massive head, it hurled him across the ramparts.

Then Inken was there, charging at the beast with a short sword in each hand. Before it could turn to face her, she drove the twin blades deep into the feline's chest.

Inken danced back out of range as its claws swiped at her. But this time the blades had found their mark. The strength went from it in a rush and the beast collapsed to the ground.

Caelin groaned, pulling himself to a sitting position and leaning his head back against the ramparts. Pain washed through his body and without looking he knew he was done. His last stand was over. Blood gushed from his leg, spreading across the stone with frightening speed.

Inken strode across and crouched beside him, tearing the jerkin from her shoulders. Caelin sucked in a breath, biting back a scream as Inken wrapped the jacket around his wound. Tying it off, she looked around, and he saw the desperate fear in her eyes.

"It's okay, Inken," he coughed. "Leave me."

Inken shook her head. "Why did you do that, Caelin?"

Caelin shrugged, fighting back the pain. "Couldn't let the future mother go off and get herself killed."

"Fraser told you?" Inken swore. "That man needs to learn how to keep his mouth shut."

Smiling, Caelin shook his head. "Eric, actually. He asked me to look out for you. I didn't want to let him down."

"In that case, I'll be giving him a piece of my mind when he gets back."

"I'm sure that will terrify him," Caelin gave a weak laugh. He stared at the blood now soaking Inken's jerkin. "There's too much, Inken. I don't think I'm going to survive this one."

Inken swore again and shook her head. "I'll be damned if you're going to die on me, Caelin. Elton!" the young commander stood over them, his back turned and his sword raised to fend off any enemy that came near.

He glanced back at them, concern written across his face. "How is he?"

Inken shook her head. "Not good, we need to get him to the healers."

Elton nodded and, with a final glance to ensure there was no one close, crouched down and took Caelin under his shoulder. Caelin groaned as the young commander took his weight, his leg pulsing with the beat of his heart.

"Quit your complaining," Inken whispered in his ear. "It's your own fault you got half your leg bitten off."

Caelin gritted his teeth, unable to respond through the pain.

Together, Inken and Elton carried him towards the stairs and the citadel below. Men streamed past them in the opposite direction, rushing to reinforce the defenders on the wall.

They joined the steady stream of injured stumbling down towards the distant infirmary.

Not that Caelin had much hope of making it that far.

As they reached the ground men and women rushed towards them, but his friends shook them off. Despite his protests they would not leave him in the hands of strangers.

They would not let him die alone.

Even so, a man joined them, leaning down to inspect Caelin's leg as they continued in the direction of the citadel. The purple diamond on his chest marked him as a doctor from the Earth temple. A rush of sadness swept through Caelin as he remembered Michael, and the diamond his friend had worn proudly to the end.

"What happened?" the man asked.

"Feline," Inken grunted.

"Got the bugger," Caelin managed to croak.

Inken smiled. "Pretty sure I had to finish him off for you," he didn't miss the wink she flashed at the young doctor.

Before any of them could continue, a boom shook the ground beneath them. Caelin groaned as his friends staggered and almost fell. He looked up to see the earth rippling like a wave, throwing men and women from their feet as it rushed across the open field.

A second before it struck Inken and Elton dropped to the ground, pulling him down with them.

Then the world erupted in chaos.

A DEEP EXHAUSTION wrapped around Enala as she stared across at Archon, a desperate weariness that stretched down to her very soul. Magic coursed through her veins, its touch soft yet all-consuming. Her legs moved, her eyes sweeping out to meet those of Gabriel and Eric, but the movements were beyond her comprehension now.

Brothers, the Goddess' thoughts whispered in her mind.

Are you ready? Darius replied.

Hatred unlike anything Enala had experienced swept through her, followed by the surge of God magic. It swirled in her chest, but the power no longer seemed alien or threatening. It was a part of her, its green tendrils embedded with her very being. The *Soul Blade* was no more; it had crumbled to dust as she stood, its remnants catching in the wind and scattering across the ocean.

There was only *her* now.

Antonia smiled. "Let's put an end to this, brothers."

The dark laughter of the false God shook the air, but Antonia was not afraid. For the first time in centuries, the three of them stood together once more, their mastery of the elemental world complete. No force on earth could stand against them.

"Come now, my old nemeses, you cannot think that shrivelled excuse for a God can help you?" Archon grinned. "There is nothing left of his spirit. *I can see it!*"

At his final words Archon threw out his arms. The air crackled as darkness gathered in his palms and surged towards Darius. Her brother stumbled backwards, a thin, pale light rising to meet the attack. But the darkness smashed through it and caught Darius in its awful power.

And the God of Light crumpled like leaves before an autumn breeze.

"*Darius!*" Antonia screamed, reaching out for the soul of her brother.

Fear not, sweet sister, Darius' words echoed in her mind, even as Archon's laughter gathered force.

"So much for the God of Light," Antonia shivered in disgust as the dark Magicker's words hissed in her ear.

Antonia spun, but she was not fast enough. Pale fingers whipped out and grasped her by the throat. She choked as the icy fingers began to squeeze and a dark shadow clawed its way inside her. She kicked feebly in Archon's grasp as he lifted her into the air.

"So much for your sacrifice, children. You could have ruled the world, could have conquered these puny people. But instead you chose death," Archon growled, holding her high.

Fighting against the darkness burning at her spirit, Antonia reached out and hurled her magic at their foe. The ground erupted beneath them and a fist of earth smashed Archon from his feet. Antonia spun through the air as his iron grasp released her, twisting to land gracefully on a rocky column that reached up to catch her.

She smiled as Archon regained his feet, glad at least for her new body's agility. Then the joy faded, sadness rising to replace it. She could feel Enala's soul within her, already shrivelling, overcome by Antonia's being.

I will not let your sacrifice be in vain, she whispered in her thoughts.

"They did not choose death," Jurrien dropped from the sky to land beside her.

"They chose life for everyone they loved," Darius appeared from thin air on her other side.

Archon growled, brushing dust from his clothes. "I see you are still a master in the fine art of running away, Darius."

Darius grinned. "You have grown used to battling the limited powers of mortals, Archon. Yes, we are masters. Together, there is nothing we cannot do."

"*You know nothing of my power!*" Archon roared.

Archon raised his arms and darkness congealed around him, swelling outwards to engulf his body. A tingle of warning came from deep within Antonia and the image of a Phoenix rose from Enala's memories.

But she could sense Darius' magic rising in response, the Light bubbling in his raised fist. He gave a wild howl, the sound filled with the pain of centuries, and threw out his arm. Light erupted across the plain, casting the world in a brilliant white. A beam of power shot towards Archon, smashing through his darkness, pressing it down, driving it back to whence it came.

Archon's face twisted with rage as the darkness retreated. For a moment his magic faltered and his features warped, revealing the horror beneath. Time had ravaged his mortal body, boiling his skin into waxy lines, eating away his teeth and turning his ice blue eyes to white. His hair had died away, leaving only a few tangled wafts that fluttered on the breeze.

With a scream, Archon threw out his hand and the image vanished, replaced again by the ageless face of the dark Magicker. He pointed a finger and a spear of darkness tore through Darius' light, shearing its way towards her. Antonia shook her head, her magic racing out to defend her, and a shield of stone erupted from the ground to block the darkness.

Lightning crackled from Jurrien as the Storm God joined the fray. The electricity dancing along his body raised the hairs on Antonia's arms, but she was too preoccupied to notice. Magic swelled in her chest as she tore her shield aside, allowing her brothers to attack. Blue and white fire rippled through the gap as they unleashed their power.

Antonia drew more power from within, determined to add her strength to the fray. It would take all of them to end this, and though she drew no pleasure from the destructive might of the Earth, she would make an exception for Archon.

Vines split the ground beneath the dark Magicker, whipping up to bind him tight. Black flames rippled from his body, burning the shoots to ash, but they were everywhere now, the thicket re-growing in the instants between blinks. Drawing a breath, Antonia pulled at the vines, trapping Archon tighter as they tore at his mortal body.

Archon thrashed amidst the green of her creation, but she sensed his power weakening now, and knew Darius was working his own magic. The Light throbbed around them, driving back the darkness. She smiled, relief pouring through her. Before Archon had overwhelmed her magic without effort, but now he was suffocating, his power cut off at its very source.

Another pulse of darkness swept from Archon, eating at her power, but Antonia gritted her teeth and poured more of herself into the fray. Beside her, Jurrien took to the sky, raising his fists to summon the storm. Wind swirled around him, hail and lightning rushing in to join his hurricane. Darius throbbed with power, light flashing from the body he wore, so bright even Antonia had to look away.

The darkness around Archon shrank further, the black fire dying with each boom of light. With a final flicker, the shadows around Archon went out, disappearing to nothing. Beneath the glow of Darius' power, the ancient face of Archon reappeared amidst the thicket of vines.

"*No!*" Archon screeched. The word rang with his mortal fear, his sudden terror, and Antonia knew Darius had trapped his power.

Without it, Archon was helpless.

"It's time," Darius' voice was quiet, filled with sorrow.

Antonia nodded, feeling the same emotion sweep through her. In all their time in the mortal realm, they had never killed, never used their powers to take a human life. Yet Archon left them no choice now, no other alternative.

He could not be allowed to live.

"*Please*," Archon had ceased to struggle now. He hung limp amidst her vines, his body shrunken with age, the fear in his eye a pitiful sight.

But Antonia would not be fooled. Given one second, a single opening, and Archon would turn them all to ash.

Releasing a long breath, Antonia summoned her power and dove deep into the earth. A rumble came from far below as the ground shook. Then with a shriek of shattered rock a fissure opened beneath their feet, tearing apart the fabric of the earth itself. A soft red light came from far below, the fires of the earth themselves, their unquenchable heat awaiting their sacrifice.

Above Jurrien nodded, and as one the three Gods drew on their magic.

Lightning boomed as Jurrien unleashed the storm. The dark clouds rushed down into the bramble of vines, tearing the last remnants of darkness from Archon. He screamed, limbs thrashing amidst her entrapments as lightning burned and the vines pulled him down beneath the crust of the earth.

Darius rose into the air, drifting across until he hovered over the crevice. Below Jurrien's storm still raged, the flicker of lightning catching amidst the red glow of the earth's core. Flames roared as white fire took form around the God of Light, burning with the heat of the sun. Closing his eyes, Darius pointed at the conflagration far below.

White fire rushed down into the crevice. A roar carried up to them as the inferno joined the hurricane.

Pain tore at Antonia's spirit as she sensed the life fleeing the body below, but she knew the job was not done yet. Regret clawed at her soul, but she did not hesitate. The air popped as she sent a last wave of magic down into the earth.

A column of light burst from the fissure: white, blue and

red mingling in the sky overhead. A final shriek came from far below, desperate and filled with fear. But there was no stopping her magic now, no mercy left to save Archon. The red glow of molten rock crept up to meet the storm, its power inexorable.

With a final roar, the insatiable fires of the earth claimed their ancient enemy.

When the shaking finally ceased, not a soul moved. The enemy stood silent amongst the soldiers of the Three Nations, staring at the sky in silent expectation. A note of finality hung in the air, a sense that the battle was over, the outcome decided. They had only to wait and see whose side had emerged victorious.

Inken held her breath, her eyes with those of her comrades, praying for a glimpse of her friends in the skies above Fort Fall. Caelin sat beside her, his face twisted with pain but his eyes still on the sky, Elton on his other side. Together they waited.

Eric and Enala came first, soaring over the fortress as the clouds cleared before them. Gabriel followed behind them, his arms folded as the wind tossed his auburn hair. Inken felt a twist of pain as she looked at him, knowing he was no longer the man she knew. It was Jurrien, wearing the body of her friend.

Even so, Inken could not keep the elation from her spirit. They had survived, had won the final battle and cast down the dark powers of Archon. Tears ran down her face as she watched them come, her hands covering her mouth as she struggled to contain her joy.

Cheers rang out across the fortress as men and women threw up their hands in victory. Blades clattered to the ground as the enemy dropped their weapons, the despair of defeat sucking away their strength. Without Archon they knew they could not stand against the magic of the Gods. Their cause was lost; there was no point in throwing away their lives as well.

As one the beasts turned and fled, tails flashing as they raced from the battlefield, eager to put as much distance as they could between themselves and the power that had defeated their master.

Inken watched the three drift down, coming to rest in the field on which they stood. Swallowing, she glanced at Caelin.

"Go," he waved a hand, obviously fighting back pain but still managing a smile.

Inken surprised herself with a yelp of delight. She sprang to her feet, leaving Caelin behind with Elton, and raced across the barren field, her boots slipping in the torn up mud.

Ahead Eric turned to watch her come, but as their eyes met he did not move. Instead, sadness swept across his face and his shoulders slumped. Inken slowed as she stared into the eyes of the man she loved, her heart thudding hard in her chest.

Something was different. Something was wrong.

Step by step, she drew closer, the terror rising in her stomach.

At last she stood before the three of them.

And she knew.

Eric's gaze enveloped her, filled with love and sadness, but the difference now was unmistakable. She could see it in his eyes. They were no longer the blue of lightning, but a pale white, filled with an infinite depth. An ageless knowledge stared back from those eyes, soft and caring.

But Eric was not there.

Inken turned to Enala, opening her mouth to scream, to ask why, to demand an answer, but the words caught in her throat. Enala's eyes had turned to violet and glowed with power, but there was no sign of her friend there.

Sinking to her knees, Inken felt her hope crumble to dust.

Amongst them the enemy still stood, their eyes wide with fear. They stared at the Gods, their faces filled with dread.

Somehow, the eyes of Darius found each of them. "As for you who have fought against us…" his eyes hardened. "You may return to your homes in the north. When we are done healing the damage you have caused to the Three Nations, we will come to you. Those of you who have committed no crime will have the chance to return. *Now go!*"

Darius' final words shook the air itself, and as one the enemy turned and fled.

After that, the three Gods had bid their farewell, fading away until there was nothing left of them but empty air.

And Inken sitting alone in the mud, staring at the space where Eric had stood.

Back in the council room, the dagger in Inken's chest twisted again at the memory, driving deeper. The pain was too much and she could not hold back her groan.

Caelin's eyes found hers from across the table. "Are you okay, Inken?"

Inken blinked back tears. "How could this happen?"

"Our hearts go out to you, Inken," she hated the kindness in Fraser's eyes. "The Three Nations will never forget their sacrifice."

"Ay," May bowed her head. "They were brave souls, each of them. They saved us."

Within, Inken railed against the unfairness, the cruelty of this awful world. A rage burned in her, and no matter how she tried, she could not put it out.

"I don't care!" the words tore from her. The others jumped as she slammed her fist into the table and stood. "I don't care," she grated again. "They took him from me. Took them from us all!"

"They had no choice, Inken," Caelin murmured. "You know that. It was the only way to stop him."

"Who? Archon?" she snapped back. "They *created* him, planted the seed of hatred in a boy too young to know better. It was never our fight, it was *their's*. So why do they still live, while everyone and everything I have ever loved is dead?" the last words came out as a sob, her voice breaking before her sorrow.

Caelin stood and moved to her side. She shuddered as his arms pulled her to him. His fingers stroked her hair as he offered his meagre comfort, but she could not stand it. She struggled in his grasp, her breath coming in sobs, her vision blurred by tears.

Memories of Eric flashed through her mind: the day they had met in the desert of Chole, how he had fed her and comforted her. The time in the forests of Dragon Country, their night in the thermal stream, their desperate fight against the red dragon. The quiet escape of the temple in Sitton, and the tears as she had forced Eric to leave her.

And their reunion here in Fort Fall, and Eric's joy as she told him of their child.

She tore herself loose from Caelin as the last thought taunted her. Her hand drifted to her stomach as she whispered. "How could they have done this?"

Caelin squeezed her shoulder. "It was their choice, Inken. Gabriel's and Enala's and Eric's. You know that," he released a long breath. "He did it for you, for all of us. To give us all our freedom, to give your child a future."

"*Our* child," Inken hissed, pulling away again. She hugged herself, looking around the room in search of an ally. "It's our child," her voice broke. "How can I do this without him? *Alone*."

A tremor went through her, the familiar despair rising up to steal away her strength. Her knees trembled as she sank into the chair and buried her head in her arms.

"You will never be alone, Inken," May's voice was firm.

"So long as we live, we will be here for you. You only have to ask."

Inken shook her head. "I just want him back," she breathed. "I want them *all back*."

"We all do," Fraser replied. "But we can't. They're gone, Inken, and there is nothing we can do to bring them back. We can only respect the sacrifice they made for us by living our lives. Together we can rebuild the Three Nations. Without Archon's shadow hovering over our lands, we can finally prosper again."

May nodded. "There are three Gods again," Inken could not miss the wonder in the commander's voice and she hated it, hated her for it. "Together they will rid our lands of the last of Archon's beasts. They can restore the Badlands around Chole. Our nations will prosper once more, and we will have peace."

"But at what cost?" Inken demanded. "We will build our dreams on the souls of the innocent."

"What else would you have us do, Inken?" there was sadness in Fraser's voice. "We cannot bring them back."

"I would have you *fight*," Inken snapped, not really believing the words but knowing she hated them, hated the Gods for everything they had done. For saving her, for forcing her to live in a world without hope. "I will hate them until the day I die," she said into the long silence that followed her outburst.

Standing, Inken turned and walked away. The silence followed her, suffocating, but she could not stand the pity in their eyes any longer. She strode out into the long corridors of the fortress and took the first doorway outside. She found herself in an open courtyard, the sun streaming down from the bright blue sky.

For a moment the world seemed a brighter place, free of the darkness of just a day before. The yellow rays of the sun warmed her skin, digging their way deep inside, until even the hate gave way before it, if only a little.

Her legs carried her to a stone bench. She sat and closed her eyes, feeling the heat of the sun mixing with the cold breath of winter, and knew it was all a lie. Winter was approaching, and with it the last of her hope would curdle and die.

Staring up into the empty sky, Inken wept for the future that might have been.

EPILOGUE

"This doesn't sit right with me," Antonia sat on a rock, staring across at her brothers.

Two months had passed now since the events at Fort Fall, and peace had finally settled over the Three Nations. Together they had worked with the new leaders of Plorsea, Lonia and Trola to put the pieces back together. Each nation had suffered horrible losses and without her help many would have starved in the harsh winter snows.

But spring was now approaching and the Three Nations were safe. They had hunted down the last of the dark creatures Archon had unleashed on the Three Nations and a fragile peace had finally settled, breathing life back into the land.

Archon was finally gone, his army defeated, his magic finished.

Antonia could hardly believe it.

Days ago the Three Nations had begun to send their emissaries into the wastelands of the north, to talk with the people there and offer the hand of peace. It would take time, but King Fraser and the councils of Lonia and Trola were eager to welcome the innocent back into their lands. In truth, they needed them now, after all they had lost.

"I agree," Darius interrupted her musings. "There is peace, but in my heart I feel a wrongness. Our rebirth has sown the same seeds of hate that led to our fall the last time," he closed his eyes. "And I'm tired."

"But they need us," Jurrien answered, his blue eyes looking from Antonia to Darius. "Look what happened in your absence, Darius. The world was torn apart again, and a darkness far worse than we could ever have imagined almost took our place. Now they finally have peace."

"Ay," Darius met their brother's gaze. "But for how long? How long before another rises up to strike at us, to stab us in the back when we least expect it? How long before the hatred we have sowed bears fruit?"

"And how many will die without us?" Jurrien argued. "How long before the wars begin again?"

"That is up to them," Antonia whispered. She closed her eyes, feeling the soul dying within her. "It has been five hundred years since the priests called on us to save their lands. The people have changed, grown. They *want* peace, they *want* freedom. Two of the Three Nations are now ruled by councils. What is our place now? To rule over those elected by their own people?"

"We will become tyrants to them, Jurrien," Darius added.

Jurrien scowled. "At least we'd be benevolent ones."

Antonia laughed, enjoying the warmth of her brother's humour. It was good to see the weight lifted from his shoulders. In Darius' absence, Jurrien had shouldered the burden of his brother's responsibilities. They had not sat well with him, and he had grown unbearably grim.

She took a breath, sensing the soul stirring in her chest.

"I cannot bear the guilt again," she looked at her feet. "To feel another's soul die within me."

Jurrien sighed. "You're right, of course, little sis."

Antonia scowled and flicked a hand. Jurrien yelped as the rock beneath him shifted, sending him tumbling backwards. He came back up with his hands raised in surrender.

"All right, all right," he grinned. "You win."

Antonia sighed. "So it is time?"

Darius nodded. "They don't have long, I think. If we don't act now, there would be little point."

"You truly think they can be trusted?" Jurrien asked. "If we return ourselves to the spirit realm, there will be no one to save them should the darkness come again."

"You're wrong," Antonia smiled. "They will stand together; they will find a way to win, whatever the odds. It's what they do."

Letting out a long breath, Darius nodded. "It's decided then?"

One by one, each of them nodded.

Antonia smiled, reaching out to grasp the hands of her brothers. Their skin felt soft beneath her fingers, and she took joy in the touch. Soon they would feel no more, see no more, hear no more. They would be spirits once more, watching over the land, but never able to touch it.

In a way, it was a relief.

Looking from Darius to Jurrien, Antonia smiled.

"See you on the other side, brothers."

ERIC BLINKED as sunlight pierced the canopy of trees stretching out overhead. Rubbing his eyes, he looked up at the leafless limbs, glimpsing hints of blue between the branches. The trees swayed to a gentle breeze, but beneath the canopy the air was still, at peace. He yawned then, struggling to find the strength to sit up. A dull ache throbbed in his chest, stretching down to his very soul.

A surge of elation took him as realisation finally struck.

He was alive, free, his body his own again.

Looking around, he found his own amazement reflected on the faces of Gabriel and Enala. They blinked back at him, their eyes wide, their mouths open with astonishment. The rustling of nearby animals carried to their ears, but the peace in Eric's soul did not relent. In his heart he knew they were safe, that it was only the gentle creatures of the forest. The chirp of birds and buzz of insects rose around them, mingling together to form the sweetest song he had ever heard.

Farewell, children, the words whispered on the air itself, and Eric had to fight back tears.

Thank you, Eric thought back, wonder at his sudden freedom replacing the grief of the God's departure.

Eric stood with a groan and stumbled across to his sister. Offering his hand, he drew Enala to her feet and embraced her. Gabriel joined them, the tears streaming down his face matching their own. They stood together, overwhelmed by the raw emotion of the world, of life.

Finally they drew apart and looked at the wilderness surrounding them.

"What now?" Enala asked, a smile on her face.

"Now, we live."

~

ENJOYED THIS BOOK?

Then follow Aaron for a free short story:

www.aaronhodges.co.nz/newsletter-signup/

AFTERWORD

Wow, what a journey. It still amazes me that the concept for this story came to me in a first year English class for high school. It took another ten years for those first stumbling words of Eric's journey to be introduced to the big wide world. But anyway, thank you to everyone who has joined me on this journey. I hope you enjoyed the Sword of Light Trilogy! And fear not, I will be returning to the Three Nations in the future.

As always, reader feedback is a huge part of its continued success, and all reviews on your vender of choice would be appreciated.

FOLLOW AARON HODGES:

And receive a free short story…

Newsletter:

http://www.aaronhodges.co.nz/newsletter-signup/

Facebook:

www.facebook.com/Aaron-Hodges-669480156486208/

Bookbub:

www.bookbub.com/authors/aaron-hodges

ALSO BY AARON HODGES

If you've enjoyed this book, you might also like a **free copy** of the first book in my all new series:

The Praegressus Project

For centuries our evolution has stagnated. Surrounded by technology, we ceased to adapt. Until now...

When eighteen year old Chris is accused of treason, his world is changed forever. Abducted in the night, he wakes in a facility hidden deep in the Californian mountains. There he is subjected to the depraved experiments of the Praegressus Project – a government led initiative to enhance the human race. Unfortunately for Chris, the chances of survival are slim. But only the lucky get to die.

Read on below for a free preview...

REBIRTH: CHAPTER 1

Chris let out a long sigh as he settled into the worn-out sofa and then cursed as a broken spring stabbed at his backside. Wriggling sideways to avoid it, he leaned back and reached for the remote, only to realise it had been left beside the television. Muttering under his breath, he climbed back to his feet, retrieved the remote and flicked on the television, then collapsed back into the chair. This time he was careful to avoid the broken springs.

He closed his eyes as the blue glow of the television lit the room. The shriek of the adverts quickly followed, but he barely had the energy to be annoyed. He was still studying full-time, but now his afternoons were taken up by long hours at the construction site. Even then, they were struggling. His only hope was winning a place at the California State University. Otherwise, he would have little choice but to accept the apprenticeship his supervisor was offering.

"Another attack was reported today from the rural town of Julian," a reporter's voice broke through the stream of adverts, announcing the start of the six o'clock news.

Chris's ears perked up and he opened his eyes to look at the television. Images flashed across the screen of an old mining town, its dusty dirt roads and rundown buildings looking like they had not been touched since the 1900s. A row of horse-drawn carriages lined the street, their owners standing beside them.

The sight was a common one in the rural counties of the Western Allied States. In the thirty years since the states of California, Oregon and Washington had declared their independence, the divide between urban and rural communities had grown exponentially. Today there were few citizens in the countryside who could afford luxuries such as cars and televisions.

"We're just receiving word the police have arrived on the scene," the reporter continued.

On the television, a black van with the letters SWAT painted on the side had just pulled up. The rear doors swung open, and a squad of black-garbed riot-police leapt out. They gathered around the van and then moved on past the carriages. Dust swirled around them, but they moved without hesitation, the camera following them at a distance.

The image changed as the police moved around a corner into an empty street. The new camera angle looked down at the police from the rooftop of a nearby building. It followed the SWAT unit as they split into two groups and spread out along the street, moving quickly, their rifles at the ready.

Then the camera panned down the street and refocused on the broken window of a grocery store. The image grew as the camera zoomed, revealing the nightmare inside the store.

Chris swallowed as images straight from a horror movie flashed across the screen. The remnants of the store lay scattered across the linoleum floor, the contents of broken cans and bottles staining the ground red. Amongst the wreckage, a dozen people lay motionless, face down in the dark red liquid.

The camera tilted and zoomed again, bringing the figures into sharper focus. Chris's stomach twisted and he forced himself to look away. But even the brief glimpse had been enough to see the people in the store were dead. Their pale faces stared blankly into space, the blood drained away, their skin marked by jagged streaks of red and patches of purple. Few, if any of the victims were whole. Pieces of humanity lay scattered across the floor, the broken limbs still dripping blood.

Finally turning back to the television, Chris swallowed as the camera panned in on the sole survivor of the carnage. The man stood amidst the wreckage of the store, blood streaking his face and arms, stained his shirt red. His head was bowed, and the only sign of life was the rhythmic rise and fall of his shoulders. As the camera zoomed on his face, his cold grey eyes were revealed. They stared at the ground, blank and lifeless.

Standing, Chris looked away, struggling to contain the meagre contents of his stomach.

"The *Chead* is thought to have awakened around sixteen hundred hours," the reporter started to speak again, drawing Chris back to the screen. "Special forces have cleared the immediate area and are now preparing to engage with the creature."

"Two hours." Chris jumped as a woman's voice came from behind him.

Spinning on his heel, he let out a long breath as his mother walked in from the kitchen. "I thought you had a night class!" he gasped, his heart racing.

His mother shook her head, a slight smile touching her face. "We finished early." She shrugged, then waved at the television. "They've been standing around for two hours. Watching that thing. Some of those people were still alive when it all started. They could have been saved. Would have, if they'd been somebody important."

Chris pulled himself off the couch and moved across to embrace his mother. Wrapping his arms around her, he kissed her cheek. She returned the gesture, and then they both turned to watch the SWAT team approach the grocery store. The men in black moved with military precision, jogging down the dirt road, sticking close to the buildings. If the *Chead* came out of its trance, no one wanted to be caught in the open. While the creatures looked human, they possessed a terrifying speed, and had the strength to tear full-grown men limb from limb.

As the scene inside the grocery store demonstrated.

Absently, Chris clutched his mother's arm tighter. The *Chead* were almost legend throughout the Western Allied States, a dark shadow left over from the days of the American War. The first whispers of the creatures were believed to have started in 2030, not long after the United States had fallen.

At first they had been dismissed as rumour by a country eager to move on from the decade-long conflict of the American War. The attacks had been blamed on resistance fighters in rural communities, who had never fully supported their severance from the United States. So the government had imposed curfews over rural communities and sent in the military to quell the problem.

Meanwhile, the rest of the young nation had moved forward, and prospered. The pacific coast had boomed as migrants arrived from the allied nations of Mexico and Canada, replacing the thousands of lives lost in the American War.

But through the years, reports of attacks continued, and accounts by survivors eventually filtered through to the media. Each claimed the slaughter had been carried out by one or two individuals – often someone well known in the community. One day, they would be an ordinary neighbour, mother, father, child. The next, they would become the monster now standing in the grocery store.

It was not until one of the creatures was captured, that the government had admitted its mistake. By then, rural communities had suffered almost a decade of terror at the hands of the monstrosities. Newsrooms and government agencies had been beside themselves with the discovery, with blame pointed in every direction from poor rural police-reporting, to secret operations by the Texans to destabilise the Western Allied States.

The government had extended curfews across the entire country and increased military patrols, but the measures had done little to slow the spread of attacks. Last year, in 2050, the first *Chead* sighting had been reported in Los Angeles, and was quickly followed by attacks in Portland and Seattle. Fortunately, they had yet to reach the streets of San Francisco. Even so, a perpetual State of Emergency had been put into effect.

On the television, the SWAT team had reached the grocery store and were now gathering outside, their rifles trained on the entrance. One lowered his rifle and stepped towards it, the others covering him from behind. Reaching the door, he stretched out an arm and began to pull it open.

The *Chead* did not make a sound as it tore through fthe store windows and barrelled into the man. A screech came through the old television speakers as the men scattered before the *Chead's* ferocity. With one hand, it grabbed its victim by the throat and hurled him across the street. The thud as he struck the ground was audible over the reporter's microphone.

The crunch of their companion's untimely demise seemed to snap the other members of the squadron into action. The first bangs of gunfire echoed over the television speakers, but the *Chead* was already moving. It tore across the dirt road as bullets raised dust-clouds around it, and smashed into another squad member. A scream echoed up from the street as man and *Chead* went down, disappearing into a cloud of dust.

Despite the risk of hitting their comrade, the rest of the SWAT team did not stop firing. The chance of survival once a *Chead* had its hands on you was zero to none, and no one wanted to take the chance it might escape.

With a roar, the *Chead* reared up from the dust, then spun as a bullet struck it in the shoulder. Blood blossomed from the wound as it staggered backwards, its grey eyes wide, flickering with surprise. It reached up and touched a finger to the hole left by the bullet, its brow creasing with confusion.

Then the rest of the men opened fire, and the battle was over.

REBIRTH: CHAPTER 2

The screen of the old CRT television flickered to black as Chris's mother moved across and switched it off. Her face was pale when she turned towards him, and a shiver ran through her as she closed her eyes.

"Your Grandfather would be ashamed, Chris," she said, shaking her head. "He went to war against the United States because he believed in our freedom. He fought to keep us free, not to spend decades haunted by the ghosts of the past."

Chris shivered. He'd never met his grandfather, but his mother and grandmother talked of him enough that Chris felt he knew him. When the United States had refused to accept the independence of the Western Allied States, his grandfather had accepted the call to defend their young nation. He had enlisted in the WAS Marines and had shipped off to war. The conflict had quickly expanded to engulf the whole of North America. Only the aid of Canada and Mexico had given the WAS the strength to survive, and eventually prevail against the aggression of the United States.

Unfortunately, his grandfather had not survived to see the world change. He had learned of Chris's birth while stationed in New Mexico, but had never returned to see his grandson grow. So Chris knew him only from photos, and the stories of his mother and grandmother.

"Things will change soon." Chris shook his head. "Surely?"

His mother crinkled her nose. "I've been saying that for ten years," she said as she moved towards the kitchen, ruffling Chris's hair as she passed him, "but things only ever seem to get worse."

Chris moved after her and pulled out a chair at the wooden table. The kitchen was small, barely big enough for the two of them, but it was all they needed. His mother was already standing at the stove, stirring a pot of stew he recognised as leftovers from the beef shanks of the night before.

"Most don't seem to care, as long as the attacks are confined to the countryside," Chris commented.

"Exactly." His mother turned, emphatically waving the wooden spoon. "They think it doesn't matter, that our wealth will protect us. Well, it won't stay that way forever."

"No." Chris shook his head. "That one in Seattle..." he shuddered. Over fifty people had been killed by a single *Chead* in a shopping mall. Police had arrived within ten minutes, but that was all the time it had needed.

Impulsively, he reached up and felt the pocket watch he wore around his neck. His mother had given it to him ten years ago, at his father's funeral. It held a picture of his parents, smiling on the shore of Lake Washington in Seattle, where they had met. His heart gave a painful throb as he thought of the terror engulfing the city.

Noticing the gesture, his mother abandoned the pot and pulled him into a hug. "It's okay, Chris. We'll survive this. We're a strong people. They'll come up with a solution, even if we have to march up to parliament's gates and demand it."

Chris nodded and was about to speak when a crash came from somewhere in the house. They pushed apart and spun towards the kitchen doorway. Though they lived in the city, when Chris's father had passed away they had been forced to move closer to the city's edge. It was not the safest neighbourhood, and it was well past the seven o'clock curfew now. Whoever, or whatever, had made the noise was not likely to be friendly.

Sucking in a breath, Chris moved into the doorway and risked a glance into the lounge. The single incandescent bulb cast shadows across the room, leaving dark patches behind the couch and television. He stared hard into the darkness, searching for signs of movement, and then retreated to the kitchen.

Silently, his mother handed him a kitchen knife. He took it after only a second's hesitation. She held a second blade in a practiced grip. Looking at her face, Chris swallowed hard. Her eyes were hard, her brow creased in a scowl, but he did not miss the fear there. Together they faced the door, and waited.

The squeak of the loose floorboard in the hall sounded as loud as a gunshot in the silent house. Chris glanced at his mother, and she nodded back. There was no doubt now.

A crash came from the lounge, then the thud of heavy boots as the intruder gave up all pretence of stealth. Chris tensed, his knuckles turning white as he gripped the knife handle. He spread his feet into a forward stance, readying himself.

The crack of breaking glass came from their right as the kitchen window exploded inwards, and a black-suited figure tumbled into the room. The man bowled into his mother, sending her tumbling to the ground before she could swing the knife. Chris sprang to the side as another man charged through the doorway to the lounge, then drew back and hurled the knife.

Without pausing to see whether the knife struck home, Chris twisted and leapt, driving his shoulder into the midriff of the intruder standing over his mother. But the man was ready for him, and with his greater bulk brushed Chris off with little effort. Stumbling sideways, Chris clenched his fists and charged again.

The man grinned, raising his arms to catch him. With his attention diverted, Chris's mother rose up behind him, knife still in hand, and drove the blade deep into the attacker's hamstring.

Their black-garbed attacker barely had time to scream before Chris's fist slammed into his windpipe His face paled and his hands went to his neck. He staggered backwards, strangled noises gurgling from his throat, and toppled over the kitchen table.

Chris offered his mother a hand, but before she could take it a creak came from the floorboards behind him. The man from the lounge loomed up, grabbing Chris by the shoulder before he could leap to safety. Still on the ground, his mother rolled away as Chris twisted around, fighting to break the man's hold. Cursing, he aimed an elbow at the man's gut, but his arm struck solid body armour and bounced off.

That explains the knife, the thought raced through his mind, before another crash from the window chased it away.

Beside him, his mother surged to her feet as a third man came through the window. Still holding the bloodied knife, she screamed and charged the man. Straining his arms, Chris bucked against his captor's grip, but there was no breaking the man's iron hold.

Stomach clenched, he watched his mother attack the heavily-armed assailant.

The fresh intruder carried a long steel baton in one hand, and as she swung her knife it flashed out and caught her wrist. His mother screamed and dropped the knife, then retreated across the room cradling her arm. A fourth man appeared through the door to the lounge. Before Chris could shout a warning, he grabbed her from behind.

His mother shrieked and threw back her head, trying to catch the man in the chin, but her blows bounced off his body armour. Her eyes widened as his arm went around her neck, cutting off her breath. Heart hammering in his chest, Chris twisted and kicked at his opponent's shins, desperate to aid his mother, but the man showed no sign of relenting.

"*Mum!*" He screamed as her eyes drooped closed.

"Fallow, situation under control. You're up." The man from the window spoke into his cuff. He moved across to his fallen comrade, whose face was turning purple. "Hold on, soldier. Medical's on its way."

"Who are you?" Chris gasped.

The man ignored him. Instead, he went to work on the fallen man. Removing his belt, he bound it around the man's leg. The injured man groaned as the speaker worked, his eyes closed and his teeth clenched. A pang of guilt touched Chris, but he crushed it down.

"What the hell happened?" Chris looked up as a woman appeared in the doorway.

The woman was dark-skinned, but the colour rapidly fled her face as her gaze swept over the kitchen. She raised a hand to her mouth, her eyes lingering on the blood, then flicking between the men and their captives. Shock showed in their amber depths, but already it was fading as she reasserted control. Lowering her hand to her side, she pursed her red lips. Her gaze settled on Chris.

A chill went through Chris as he noticed the red emblazoned bear on the front of her black jacket. The symbol marked her as a government employee. These were not random thugs in the night – they were police, and they were here for Chris and his mother.

Taking a breath, the woman nodded to herself, then reached inside her jacket and drew something into the light. The breath went from Chris's chest as he glimpsed the steel contraption in her hand. For a second he thought it was a pistol, but as she drew closer he realised his mistake. It was some sort of hypodermic gun, some medical contraption he had seen in movies, though in real life it looked far more threatening, more deadly.

"Who are you?" Chris croaked as she paused in front of him.

Her eyes drifted to Chris's face, but she only shook her head and looked away. She studied the liquid in the vial attached to the gun's barrel, then at Chris, as though weighing him up.

"Hold him," she said at last.

"What?" Chris gasped as his captor's hands pulled his arms behind his back. "What are you doing? Please, you're making some mistake, we haven't done anything wrong!"

The woman did not answer as she raised the gun to his neck. Chris struggled to move, but the man only pulled his arms harder, sending a bolt of pain through his shoulders. Biting back a scream, Chris looked up at the woman. Their eyes met, and he thought he saw a flicker of regret in the woman's eyes.

Then the cold steel of the hypodermic gun touched his neck, followed by a hiss of gas as she pressed the trigger. Metal pinched at Chris's neck for a second, before the woman stepped back. Holding his breath, Chris stared at the woman, his eyes never leaving hers.

Within seconds the first touch of weariness began to seep through Chris's body. He blinked as shadows spread around the edges of his vision. Idly, he struggled to free his arms, so he might chase the shadows away. But the man still held him fast. Sucking in a mouthful of air, Chris fought against the exhaustion. Blinking hard, he stared at the woman, willing himself to resist the pull of sleep.

But there was no stopping the warmth spreading through his limbs. His head bobbed and his arms went limp, until the only thing keeping him upright was the strength of his captor.

The woman's face was the last thing Chris saw as he slipped into the darkness.

REBIRTH: CHAPTER 3

Liz shivered as the air conditioner whirred, sending a blast of icy air in her direction. Wrapping her arms around herself, she closed her eyes and waited for it to pass. The scent of chlorine drifted on the air, its chemical reek setting her head to pounding. Her teeth chattered and she shuddered as the whir of fans died away. Groaning, Liz opened her eyes and returned to studying her surroundings.

Ten minutes ago, she had woke in this thirty-foot room, enclosed by the plain, unadorned concrete walls and floor. A door stood on the opposite wall, a small glass panel revealing a bright hallway beyond. It offered the only escape from the little room, but it might as well have been half a world away. Between Liz and the door stood the wire mesh of her little steel cage.

Shaking, she gripped the wire tight in her fingers and placed her head against it. Silently, she searched the vaults of her memories, struggling to find a cause for her current predicament. But she had no memory of how she had come to be there, lying shivering on the concrete floor of a cage.

She cursed as the blast of the air conditioner returned. Her thin clothes were little better than rags, fine in the warm Californian climate, but completely inadequate for the freezing temperatures the central heating system had apparently been set too. To make matters worse, her boots were gone, along with the blade she kept tucked inside them. Without it she felt naked, exposed inside the tiny cage.

At least I'm not alone, she thought wryly, looking through the wire into the cage beside her.

A young man somewhere around her own eighteen years lay there, still dozing on the concrete floor. His clothes were better kept than her own, though there was a bloodstain on one sleeve. From the quality of the shirt he wore, she guessed he was from the city. His short-cropped brown hair and white skin only served to confirm her suspicions.

With a low groan, the boy began to stir. Idly, she wondered what he would make of the nightmare he was about to awake too.

Liz shivered, not from the cold now, but dread. She cast her eyes around the room one last time, desperate for something, *anything*, that might offer escape. As a child, her parents had often warned her of what happened to those who drew the government's ire. Though they were never reported, disappearances had been common in her village. Adults, children, even entire families were known to simply disappear overnight. Though few were brave enough to voice their suspicions out loud, everyone knew who had taken them.

It seemed that after two years on the run, those same people had finally caught up with Liz.

The clang of the door as it opened tore Liz from her musings. Looking up, she saw two men push their way past the heavy steel door. They wore matching uniforms of black pants and green shirts, along with the gold-and-red embossed badges of bears that marked them as soldiers. Both carried a rifle slung over one shoulder, and moved with the casual ease of professional killers.

Liz straightened as the men's eyes drifted over to her cage, refusing to show her fear. Even so, she had to suppress a shudder as wide grins split their faces. Scowling, she crossed her arms and stared them down.

"Feisty one, ain't she?" the first said in a strong Californian accent. Shaking his head, he moved past the cages to a panel in the wall.

"Looks like the boy's still asleep," the other commented as he joined the first. "Gonna be a nasty wake-up call."

Together, they pulled open the panel and retrieved a hose. Thick nylon strings encased the outer layer of the hose, and a large steel nozzle was fitted to its end. Dragging it across the room, they pointed it at the sleeping boy and flipped a lever on the nozzle.

Water gushed from the hose and through the wire of the cage to engulf the unconscious young man. A blood-curdling scream echoed off the walls as he seemed to levitate off the floor, and began to thrash against the torrent of water.

Liz bit back laughter as another scream came, half gurgled by the water. The men with the hose showed no such restraint, and their laughter rang through the room. They ignored the young man's strangled cries, holding the water steady until it seemed he could not help but drown in the torrent.

When they finally shut off the water, the boy collapsed to the floor of his cage, gasping for breath. He shuddered, spitting up water, but the men were already moving towards Liz, and she had no more time to consider his predicament.

She raised her hands as the men stopped in front of her cage. "No need for that, boys. I'm already clean, see?" She did a little turn, her cheeks warming as she sensed their eyes on her again.

The men chuckled, but shook their heads. "Sorry girl, boss's orders."

They pulled the lever before Liz could offer any further argument.

Liz gave a strangled shriek as the ice-cold water drove her back against the wire of the cage. She lifted her hands in front of her face, fighting to hold back the water, but it made little difference against the rush. Gasping, she choked as water flooded her throat, and sank to her knees. An icy hand gripped her chest as she inhaled again, turning her back to protect her face. The power of the water forced her up against the wire, and she gripped it hard with her fingers, struggling to hold herself upright.

When the torrent finally ceased, Liz found herself crouched on the ground with her back to the men. She did not turn as a coughing fit shook her body. An awful cold seeped through her bones as she struggled for breath. Water filled her ears and nose, muffling the words of the men until she shook her head to clear it.

Tightened her hold on the wire, Liz used it to pull herself to her feet. Head down, she gave a final cough and faced the room.

The men were already returning the hose to its panel in the wall. They spoke quietly to themselves, but fell silent as the hinges of the door squeaked again. Liz looked up as a group of men and woman entered the room. There were five in total, three men and two women, and each wore a white lab coat with black pants. Four of them carried electronic tablets, their heads bent over the little screens, while the fifth approached the guards. They straightened as he drew up in front of them, their grins fading.

"Are our latest subjects ready for processing?" the man asked, his voice cool.

One of the guards nodded. "Yes, Doctor Halt. We've just finished hosing them down."

A smile twitched at Halt's lips. "Very good," he dismissed the men with a flick of his hand and turned to face the cages.

Pursing his thin lips, Halt moved closer, pacing around Liz's cage in a slow circle. His eyes did not leave her as he moved, and eventually she was forced to look away. He moved like a predator, his grey eyes studying her like prey, eyeing up which piece of flesh to taste first. Wrapping her arms around herself, Liz fixed her eyes to the concrete and tried to ignore him.

When Liz looked up again, Halt had moved on to studying the young man in the other cage. But her fellow captive was ignoring him. Instead, he stared at the group of doctors, his brow creased with confusion, as though struggling to recall a distant memory.

"*You!*" the boy shouted suddenly, slamming his hands against the wire. "You were at my house! What am I doing here? *What have you done with my mother?*" His last words came out as a shriek.

Halt glanced back at the group of doctors. "Doctor Fallow, would you care to explain why the subject knows your face?"

The woman at the head of the group turned beet red. Biting her lip, she replied. "There were complications during his extraction, Halt," her voice came out soft, but Liz sensed her defiance behind them. "I had to enter before the subject was unconscious, or we risked casualties amongst the extraction team."

Halt eyed her for a moment, apparently weighing up her words before he nodded. "Very well." He turned back to the cages. "No matter. Elizabeth Flores, Christopher Sanders, welcome to the Praegressus Facility."

Cold fingers gripped Liz by the throat, silencing her voice. They knew her last name. That meant they knew who she was, where she came from. The last trickle of hope slipped from her heart. It was no mistake she had found herself here.

Christopher was not so easily quelled. "What am I doing here? You can't hold us like his, I know my rights–"

Halt raised a hand and her neighbour fell silent. Moving across, Halt stood outside Christopher's cage and stared through the wire. "Your mother has been charged with treason."

Colour fled the boy's face, turning his white skin a sickly yellow. He swallowed and opened his mouth, but no words came out. Tears crystallised at the corner of his eyes, but he blinked them back before they could fall.

Biting her tongue, Liz watched the two stare at one another. She was impressed by Christopher's resilience. He might speak with an urban accent, but it seemed he possessed more courage than half the boys she'd once known in her boarding school. If his mother had been convicted of treason, it meant death for her and her immediate family. A pass was given for the elderly, but there was no such exception for children…

Swallowing, Liz eyed the group still lingering behind Halt. If that was the reason Christopher was here, she didn't like her chances. She had always guessed the authorities might come after her and had done her best to avoid detection. With cameras on every street corner, she had been forced to keep to the countryside she knew so well. Even then, she had always known it would only be a matter of time before someone found her.

Even so, she wanted to find out how much they really knew about her.

INTERESTED?